A SMALL SACRIFICE

A SMALL SACRIFICE

A JANE LAWLESS MYSTERY

ELLEN HART

SEAL PRESS

This book is a work of fiction. Any resemblence of the characters, events or locales in the book to actual persons, events or locales is unintentional and entirely coincidental.

Cover art by Debbie Hanley
Text and cover design by Clare Conrad

Library of Congress Cataloging-in-Publication Data
Hart, Ellen
A Small Sacrifice : A Jane Lawless Mystery
1. Lawless, Jane (fictitious character)—Fiction.   2. Women detectives—Wisconsin—fiction.   3. Lesbians—Wisconsin—Fiction.   I. Title.
PS3558.A6775S6   1994   813'.54—dc20   94-9481
ISBN 1-878067-55-9

Printed in the United States of America
First printing, October 1994
10 9 8 7 6 5 4 3 2 1

Distributed to the trade by Publishers Group West
Foreign Distribution:
In Canada: Publishers Group West Canada, Toronto, Ontario
In the U.K. and Europe: Airlift Book Company, London, England

*For R.D. Zimmerman and Lars Peterssen.
Here's to the wonderful candlelight dinners we've
had together, to drive-by signings and Lars'
fabulous chocolate pecan cookies.
May we always be friends.*

CAST OF CHARACTERS

CORDELIA THORN: Artistic Director for the Allen Grimby Repertory Theatre in St. Paul. Member of the Shevlin Underground.

JANE LAWLESS: Owner of the Lyme House Restaurant in Minneapolis. Old friend of Cordelia Thorn's.

ORSON ALBERN: Owner of the Blackburn Playhouse in Shoreview. Member of the Shevlin Underground.

THEODORE (THEO) DONATI: Member of the Shevlin Underground.

DIANA STANWOOD: Actress. Owner of the Summer Green Playhouse in Summer Green, Wisconsin. Member of the Shevlin Underground.

ANNIE WHITTIG: Professor of Theatre Arts at Northwestern. Married to Curt. Member of Shevlin Underground.

CURT WHITTIG: Stage Manager for a community theatre in Chicago. Married to Annie. Member of Shevlin Underground.

HILDA BARNES: Caretaker/Gardener at the home of Diana Stanwood.

AMITY SCARBOUROUGH: Fourteen-year-old daughter of Diana's deceased lover.

CHICKIE JOHNSON: Junior-high-school friend of Amity's.

JOHN HUBBLE: Director of the Summer Green Playhouse.

O, For a Muse of fire, that would ascend
The brightest heaven of invention . . .

King Henry V
Shakespeare

A SMALL SACRIFICE

PROLOGUE

University of Minnesota
Spring 1972

Orson bent over the morning paper, sipping from a tepid cup of coffee. Halfway down the front page he read the headline, "Body of Minnesota Business Legend Stolen from Eastwood Cemetery." The article went on to say that the granddaughter of Edgar Davis Collingwell, the founder of the Collingwell Baking Company, had posted a ten-thousand-dollar reward for information leading to the arrest of the individual or individuals responsible. The gravesite, near the entrance to the cemetery, had been tampered with two nights ago, sometime after midnight. Since the body had been buried prior to 1930, no cement vault was used. The grave was an easy target. Nothing like this had ever happened at Eastwood before, and officials were baffled as to a motive.

God, thought Orson, as he glanced around the dining room of his cramped campus slum, could he use that kind of money. In the wake of last night's party, stacks of dirty dishes, filled ashtrays and empty bags of chips were scattered around the room. Neither of his two roommates had bothered to clear away any of the mess. Then again, neither had he.

Drumming his fingers impatiently on the table top, his thoughts returned to what the reward money could buy. Ten thousand dollars. Lord! As a third-year theatre major, he was as penniless as the proverbial church mouse. By the time he got his M.F.A., he'd be buried in unpaid loans. He didn't have a rich family picking up the tab, unlike his Gatsbyesque roommate, the golden Curt Whittig. Thankfully, Curt liked the student slums. He even paid most of the rent. And on weekends, he threw parties for the other theatre majors. Curt was majoring in theatre himself, though he was more interested in the high-tech aspects of lighting and stage design. Orson and Theo Donati, the other roommate, had only one agenda in mind. Acting. More specifically, the legitimate stage. Their rivalry had become a source of contention—as well as amusement. But one way or another, however long it took, Orson was going to prove that his was the greater talent. Unfortunately, Theo had the exact same goal. Only time would tell.

Orson looked up as Theo entered the room. He didn't try to hide his surprise as his eyes took in the suit and tie. And briefcase! Something was up. "Should I salute?" he asked, finishing the bitter coffee in one gulp.

"Stuff it," said Theo, stopping in front of a mirror to adjust his tie. His shaggy hair had been clipped short and combed away from his forehead, making him look a bit like Al Pacino. "And quit staring," he ordered, kicking an empty bag of corn chips out of his way. "Christ, this place is a freaking pit. Who the hell are those two people out there in the living room watching cartoons?"

Orson shrugged. "Leftovers from last night's prom. I think they passed out on the living room floor."

Theo grunted, sitting down at the table and pulling the newspaper in front of him.

"Aren't you coming this morning?" asked Orson. He,

Curt and Theo, and three others, Cordelia, Annie and Diana were known humorously in the theatre department as the Shevlin Underground because they nearly lived in the cafeteria in the basement of Shevlin Hall. They were also fast friends. Every Monday morning they had a standing date for breakfast. "I'm driving. Cordelia and Annie should be here any minute."

"I've got an appointment," muttered Theo. "I'll have to pass." His eyes fell to the article Orson had been reading. "Jesus. Did you see this? A body was stolen. Gives you the creeps, doesn't it?"

Before Orson could respond, the doorbell rang. "That must be our other half," he said, rising from the table and charging down the long narrow hall to the front door. Instead of being greeted by two young faces, he was met by the sight of mounds of deep purple and white lilacs. One of the mounds had Cordelia's voice.

"Your hovel needs a bit of sprucing up, Orson. Find us some vases. Chop chop."

He put his hand on his hip and grinned. "Sorry. Fresh out of *vases*. But I might find you an ice-cream bucket or two."

"I suppose that will have to do." One of Cordelia's eyes peeked through the purple, narrowing in disgust at the two people sitting on the couch. "You need a bouncer."

"You applying for the job?" asked Theo, breezing into the room followed closely by Curt. He squinted into the second mound. "Is that Diana behind there or Annie?"

"Annie," came a rather husky voice.

"Hum. Then where's Diana?"

Orson moved over to the closet door and opened it. There, among the sneakers and the tennis rackets, wrapped in a quilt and snoring like a truck driver, was the sixth member of the group, Diana Stanwood.

Curt took the flowers from Annie's arms. "She got pretty ripped last night. Last I looked, all the bedrooms were occupied, so I'd say she found the next best spot."

Everyone stood silently, gazing down at her.

"I don't think she'll be coming to breakfast," announced Annie. "That's too bad."

"Why?" asked Theo. "She won't die if she doesn't get her soft-boiled egg. Neither will I."

Annie tweaked him under the chin. "We're going to study for Hanson's mid-term this morning. Remember? Orson knows the stuff backwards and forwards. He's going to coach us."

Cordelia nudged the sleeping form with her foot. Diana let out an angry snort and turned over. "No sweet rolls for this princess." She unloaded her flowers on Orson and then raised an eyebrow at Theo's strange clothing. "Willy Loman. *Death of a Salesman,*" she pronounced.

"I'm not auditioning for a part," said Theo, "if that's what you're suggesting. I have an appointment."

"Where?"

"None of your business." He pulled on his cuffs. "Did anyone ever tell you you're entirely too nosey?"

"Frequently." Cordelia was a large—some might say shiplike—young woman, nearly six feet tall. She had mounds of flowing auburn curls and an expansive manner. In other words, Cordelia was a *presence*. Everyone watched in amused silence as she swept into the room, snapped off the TV set with great distaste and then waved her arms at the couple sitting on the couch. "Shoo!" she scowled. "Show's over. Rocky & Bullwinkle have just been canceled."

The couple didn't move.

"Did you hear me?" She tapped her foot, waiting until she was confident of their full attention. "Your life is hanging by a thread unless you depart! Evaporate. Set sail. Sally forth. Take wing!"

They blinked.

She lowered her voice to a more ominous tone. "And if you aren't gone by the time I count to five, I'll break your knees. Got it?"

In an instant they had scrambled to their feet and were out the door.

Cordelia brushed her hands together with a satisfied smirk and then returned her gaze to Theo. "You don't think I'm going to accept that brush off as some kind of answer to why you're dressed so strangely. I've never seen you in a suit. I didn't even know you *owned* one."

Theo gave her a secretive grin but said nothing more.

Nuts, thought Orson as he sprinted back down the hall to the kitchen. If Cordelia couldn't get Theo's destination out of him, no one could. He found several plastic buckets under the sink and began stuffing the lilacs into them. "Curt, bring the rest of those flowers back here. And everybody—that is, everyone who's headed over to Shevlin—my VW is leaving in five...no, make it ten minutes. You can buy your tickets after you're seated." He began filling one of the buckets with water. What the hell was Theo up to?

Orson was the first one out to the car. Cramming six people into a Beetle was a trick, but one they'd mastered over the years. Today, without Theo and Diana, there would be only four. Piece of cake. Unfortunately, the doors no longer locked. Not that it mattered. The car was so rusted and dented it was invisible.

"What's that plastic sack in the back seat?" asked Cordelia, twirling her finger languidly. "We better put it in the trunk. That is, if you have *room*." On the last word, she bugged out her eyes. It was common knowledge Orson was a pack rat. He collected everything that wasn't nailed down.

"Looks like a garbage sack," said Curt. He brushed a blond lock of hair away from his eyes.

Annie gazed at him with barely concealed lust. It was also common knowledge Annie had a thing for Curt.

Cordelia had a sneaking suspicion Curt and Theo were sleeping together. If it was true, she felt sorry for Annie. Theo and Cordelia had made no secret of their sexuality. They referred to themselves lovingly as The Inverts. Orson and Annie were clearly hetero. But Curt and Diana —who knew? After all, it was 1972. Other than your priest, your pastor or your parents, who cared?

Orson grabbed the sack and started for the trunk.

"Yesterday's lunch?" asked Cordelia smiling snidely.

Annie moved closer to Curt, slipping her arm through his.

"Actually, I don't know what it is," replied Orson. "I suppose I should take a look." He opened it, peering at the contents for several seconds before looking up.

"What is it?" asked Curt, seeing Orson's face pucker with disgust.

"This must be some kind of joke."

Cordelia inched closer and glanced into the sack. "Yuck!" she exclaimed, patting herself on the chest.

Orson reached inside and drew out a skull.

"Been doing some late night work over at the biology lab?" asked Curt.

Ignoring the question, Orson knelt down and dumped the contents onto the sidewalk. Bones, bits of wood and shreds of cloth all tumbled out together.

Cordelia watched a look of recognition dawn on

Orson's face. "What's going on?" she asked. "You act like you know what it is."

He closed his eyes for a moment. "I'm probably way off base, but did you read that article in the morning paper? The one about that body stolen from Eastwood cemetery?" He didn't look up. His gaze was transfixed by the sight of the bones.

"No," said Cordelia. "I don't read right-wing rags."

He wiped a hand across his mouth. "One of you needs to go call the police."

"Why?" asked Curt.

"You're probably going to think I'm crazy, but this may be . . . the body."

Annie pulled Curt closer. "How awful!"

"What's it doing in your car?" asked Cordelia, raising a skeptical eyebrow.

Orson shook his head. "Beats me." He stood slowly, his mind working something through. Finally, after looking each person square in the eye, he said "I want you all to understand one thing. This is *my* car. And I'm the one who opened the sack and made the connection. If I'm right, you all have to admit this to the police."

"So," said Annie. "What's the big deal?"

"The big deal," repeated Orson, a slow smile pulling at the corners of his mouth, "is . . . right now, you may just be speaking to a very rich man."

Cordelia bounced joyfully around the kitchen as she put the finishing touches on the meal she was preparing for tonight's celebration. The new Stones album was playing loudly in the dining room. The smell of lasagna filled the apartment, spilling out the back door into the alley and no doubt making the rest of the student tenants drool. Cheap red wine was chilling in the refrigerator—she knew that was tacky, but everybody liked it better cold. The salad was made. And the garlic bread—*lots* of garlic bread—was just about to go into the oven. All of this in honor of the evening's special guest. Orson.

After a morning of questioning, tests and more questioning, it appeared that he would be receiving some kind of reward for finding the remains of the filched dead body. Cordelia was thrilled. However that sack got into his back seat, the family of Edgar Davis Collingwell was relieved to have it back. She couldn't wait for Orson to arrive and elaborate on his day. He was driving over with Curt and Theo. Annie was still at the costume shop, but would make it for dinner. And Diana was asleep in her bedroom. Her hangover was huge.

The East Bank slum Cordelia shared with Annie and Diana was almost a mirror image of the guys' apartment. She figured it was a popular floor plan during the westward expansion. On one end was a tiny living room. No fireplace. Decoratively cracked plaster and unwaxed hardwood floors—scuffed by students and marred by heavy furniture since the dawn of time—completed the ambiance. A long hallway led to the dining room and kitchen. Both of these rooms had wonderful views of brick walls, initially terribly arty, but ultimately confining and depressing. Off the hallway were three bedrooms. The only real difference between the two apartments was the decorating—or lack thereof. Cordelia was heavily into her purple phase. The wall color and *objets d'art* scattered here and there confirmed her influence. Annie liked posters of handsome blond men. A Robert Redford shrine had been set up in her bedroom. Cordelia, whose room contained only one star photo—Bette Davis—told Annie she was fixated on *blond,* but Annie just shrugged it off. Diana liked clothes. Her room was a jungle of outrageous costumes hung on hangers dangling from strings she'd affixed to the walls in a crisscross pattern. As far as anyone could tell, Diana fixated on only one person. Herself. No photo of any kind had found its way to her walls.

"Smells good in here," said a voice from the doorway.

Cordelia turned to find Diana limping into the room, her long brown hair a tangle, her clothing crumpled. She must have just gotten up. Ultimately, Cordelia had confidence that Mick Jagger *could* wake the dead. "You feeling better?"

"Yeah. We got any tomato juice?"

"Sorry."

She ran a hand through her matted brown tresses and shambled over to the counter, picking a cucumber slice out of the salad and crunching it. "What's the occasion?"

Cordelia dropped her minimal effort at concern and brightened. "It's Orson. He found some human bones in a plastic bag in the back seat of his car."

"Doesn't surprise me. You never know what you're going to sit on in that heap of his." She pretended a shiver. "Still, I suppose any old reason for a party."

"Just listen, will you? See, there was a grave robbery at Eastwood cemetery two nights ago. Someone stole the remains of some wealthy cookie maker."

Diana did a double take. "Is this a joke?"

"No joke. You know the one—Collingwell Mills? They make Chocolate Bombs, Minty Marvels."

Diana held up her hand. "I would never have made it through high school without them."

"Exactly! Anyway, somebody dumped the remains in Orson's car. He found them this morning when we were on our way over to Shevlin. And the best part is, there's a reward!"

"How much?"

"I'm not sure. I think it depends on whether the

information leads the police to the grave robbers."

Diana selected another cucumber slice and nibbled the edge. "And I missed all this?"

"You were snoring so belligerently in the closet, we didn't want to wake you."

"Really. How flattering." She moved to the screen door and stared out at the trash cans in the alley. "Lucky bastard."

"Yeah. I hope so. That's why we're throwing the party tonight. The guys should be here any minute." Cordelia watched Diana's back. Something was wrong. She hated playing Mom, but since she looked like an earth mother—or Mama Cass, take your pick—she was often cast unwillingly in the role. "What's up, dearheart? You seem kind of depressed." Then it dawned on her. Sure. Diana was up for the lead in an experimental play over at Scott Hall. She must have blown it. "Is it that Carver piece? Didn't you get the part?"

Diana turned around, a smug look on her face. "Oh ye of little faith." She fluttered her eyes.

"Don't toy with me."

She sauntered back to the counter and leaned against it, dramatically closing her eyes. "I was so emotionally and technically brilliant during the audition, how could they even *think* of giving the part to Rowena Todd? My timing was impeccable. My movements...delectable." She opened one eye. "Of course I got it."

Cordelia threw her arms around her and together they giggled, dancing around the kitchen floor. "Then we'll have even more to celebrate tonight. But one word of caution. I hope your acting loses a bit of its...broadness before opening night. I doubt they want Theda Bara playing a drug addict."

She laughed at the allusion. "Spoken like a true director. You know, buddy of mine, one day, you're going to be the best. The top of the heap. And I'm going to be there, cheering."

Cordelia blushed.

"It'll happen," continued Diana. "For all of us." She seemed to have regained her zip. "So, where's the wine?"

Cordelia shook her head. She wished Diana could party occasionally without all the booze. "Why don't we wait till the boys get here?"

"You have no sense of timing," said Diana, her head already inside the refrigerator. "Here it is." She withdrew the jug and held it up, a mischievous grin on her face.

The doorbell sounded.

"I'll get it," said Cordelia, stuffing the garlic bread into the oven. She raced down the hall to the front door. Orson was the first to enter, followed by Theo, no longer in his suit and tie. Curt and Annie brought up the rear.

"We found Annie lurching over the Tenth Avenue Bridge," said Orson, handing Cordelia a bunch of daisies. "We decided to offer her a ride. Otherwise, there wouldn't be any food left when she got home." He put his arm around her and gave her a squeeze.

"Good point," said Theo, flopping on the couch and lifting his feet up on the coffee table. He spread his arms wide over the back and gave everyone his most beatific grin.

Too beatific, thought Cordelia. She was determined to get his little secret out of him before the night was over. Why had he cut his hair? He looked so . . . establishment. She shivered inwardly as she thought of the draft lottery. It might not be long before he was forced to cut it anyway.

Diana appeared in the doorway with the jug of wine and six plastic wine glasses. Plastic was a student necessity when dealing with the various cattle that mooed in and out of their apartment on a daily basis. Glass wouldn't last a day. "So," she said, handing the jug to Annie and passing out the glasses. "Do we really have something to celebrate?"

Cordelia smiled exuberantly. Except for one other person, a high-school buddy by the name of Jane Lawless, the people she loved most in the world were all in this room.

"Come on," said Curt, grabbing Orson by the shoulders and shaking him. "Out with it."

Orson couldn't contain his emotion any longer. He burst out laughing as he sat down on the couch next to Theo. "You're talking to a new man. Money, although not everything, does give one a certain... renewed outlook. Yes. I'm going to get the reward."

Everyone cheered. Cordelia bent down and gave him a kiss on his cheek, mussing up his shaggy black hair. Diana began dancing around the room, pouring a glass of wine here and there.

"The granddaughter of Edgar Collingwell was so beside herself with joy to have the old guy's bones back, she called her bank right away. It seems, even though they can't positively ID the remains just yet, they found a ring in the sack. It belonged to him. They're doing lots of tests on the contents—even the sack itself. And my car was gone over with a fine-tooth comb. They especially liked the assortment of lamp shades in the trunk."

"God, I remember the day we found those," said Theo, stretching his arms high over his head. "We were in Dinkytown eating a leisurely breakfast when you saw that guy's U-Haul pull to a stop right outside the restaurant. You would have thought it was a Brinks truck passing out cash the way you bolted out of there."

"Say," said Curt, scratching his chin, "come to think of it, I lent you twenty bucks that day. You never paid me back."

"He's good for it now," winked Cordelia.

"And besides," offered Annie, "you never know when

you're going to need a battered lamp shade." She leaned back in her chair as Diana filled her wine glass. Evening sunlight streamed in through the front window, striking her red hair and turning it into a soft flame.

Curt glanced at it briefly before returning his gaze to Theo. Annie might look lustfully at Curt, thought Cordelia with a kind of detached amusement, but at least for now, Curt reserved his lustful eyes for another. Cordelia had already formed some rather cynical opinions on the course of true love.

"Anyway," said Orson, nudging Theo in the ribs, "I should get the money sometime next week. But there is one other issue."

"What's that?" asked Diana, filling his glass and then stepping back. She set the jug on top of the TV set.

"Oh, it's nothing much. Just...well, I think I've found the girl I'm going to marry."

"*Woman,*" roared Cordelia, ignoring his cow-eyed expression. Would these boys never learn!

"Right. Woman."

"Not the granddaughter of old Collingwell," said Curt. "She must be well into her forties."

Orson sipped his wine. "Nope. The *great-*granddaughter."

"How do you know she'll marry you?" asked Theo. He smirked at Curt.

"I don't. But I'll bet I'm right."

"How much will you bet?" asked Theo, still smirking.

"I don't know. I hadn't thought about it."

"Fifty thousand dollars?"

"Come on," said Annie. "Where would you get that kind of money?"

Theo shrugged. "I'm not always going to be a student."

"Actors don't make shit," offered Curt pleasantly.

Again, Theo shrugged. "Maybe. Or maybe they just don't take the right parts."

"There you go again," snapped Diana, her wine glass already empty. "You may have a talent for acting, Theo, but you have no sense when it comes to money. Now me—"

Everyone hooted and jeered.

"Queen of the bounced check," shouted Annie.

"You mean queen of the borrowed buck," laughed Cordelia, turning at the sound of a knock. "Who the hell is that?" she muttered as she crossed to the door and opened it. She could smell the garlic bread. It was time to take it out of the oven. "Yes?" she said, peering impatiently at two men in business suits.

The taller of the two said, "We're looking for Theodore Donati. Is he here?"

She cocked her head. "Who wants to know?"

The man took out his wallet and showed her his ID.

"Christ. FBI? What do you want with him?"

"Is he here?" The man didn't look particularly friendly.

Theo stood and walked toward them. "I'm Theo Donati."

"We'd like to talk to you," said the taller man.

"What about?"

He hesitated, then said, "Impersonating an IRS agent."

The room became silent.

"Who the hell told you that?" demanded Theo, his back stiffening.

"This is ridiculous," said Curt, moving up behind him. Diana and Annie followed. "I know this guy. He'd never do something like that."

Cordelia was aghast, yet as she watched them talk, she couldn't help but wonder. Of all her friends, Theo had the greatest tendency to do dumb things—to live on the edge. Could it be?

Slowly, Orson stood. Even though he said nothing, Cordelia could see the frightening intensity in his stare.

"Do you deny it?" asked the agent.

"Of course he denies it," shouted Diana. "This is harassment! It must be that anti-war march you were in last month."

"Don't say anything," said Curt, putting a hand on Theo's shoulder. "You need a lawyer."

The FBI agent motioned to the man standing behind him. In an instant, Theo's hands were cuffed and he was being led out to a waiting car.

Curt followed, his voice trembling as he tried to talk them out of it. Everyone else seemed paralyzed.

The scene progressed as if in slow motion. Diana poured herself more wine. She stood in the corner, dazed, massaging her right temple. Annie watched Curt out the window, wringing her hands together as she saw him try to get into the back seat of the car with Theo. Orson just stood in the center of the room. His eyes were wide open, but he seemed someplace else.

And lastly... Cordelia. She felt the daisies slip from her hand, falling to the floor with a small thud. The garlic bread was burning. It was as if she had just witnessed an explosion. Her ears tingled. Her body was numb. And worse. An inner sense told her that the ramifications of Theo's actions would touch all their lives. The world, as she'd known it, might never be the same again.

17

1

Late Summer 1994

"What are you staring at?" asked Jane. She and Cordelia were sitting in Jane's living room, drinking a relaxing cup of after dinner coffee and discussing the events of the day.

Cordelia blinked. "Was I staring?"

"Unless you're having problems with catatonia, yes. You were. Is something wrong with my hair?" Jane touched the back of her French braid. Normally, she thought her hair was one of her best features. Deep chestnut brown. Graying at the temples. Maybe it was her new glasses. Not that she thought moving from silver wire rims to gold was a big deal. She did find that she was wearing them more lately.

"No. It's just . . . I was wondering. I suppose we look a lot different than we did back in college."

So that was it, thought Jane. "You're thinking about your friends from—"

"The Shevlin Underground."

"Right." Jane smiled. "Are you worried about your meeting tonight with Orson?" Jane knew Cordelia had received a rather cryptic phone call from him two days ago asking that she come to his house at eight on Friday evening. Tonight. From the way Cordelia kept drumming her fingers on the rocking chair and staring at the clock, she was as nervous as a cat. Or a poodle. Jane had known more nervous poodles in her day. All of Cordelia's cats appeared to be lumps of perfect serenity. It was a poor metaphor. Then again, nervous as a poodle somehow didn't cut it.

"Not worried, exactly," said Cordelia. "More apprehensive. Orson refused to be specific about why he wanted to see me, but from the tone of his voice, I'd say it's serious. I can't for the life of me figure out what's going on. He just got back from Summer Green."

"What's Summer Green?"

"It's a small town in Wisconsin. He grew up there. I thought I told you all this."

Jane sipped her coffee. "Must have been your *other* best friend."

Cordelia mimicked a smile. "Well, you remember Diana Stanwood?"

"Sure. Of all the people in your group, she's become the most famous."

"You wound me when you say things like that, Janey. My star is rising."

Jane cleared her throat. "I used to catch her occasionally on that soap opera. What's the name? *The Sordid and The Shallow?*"

"For your information, she's also done a lot of work in the legitimate theatre. Mostly New York. Before she left last year, she had the lead in a new production of *A Doll's House.*" Cordelia shook her head sadly and looked away. "But something happened. I don't know. Orson said she wasn't getting along with the director. Diana told me she left the production because of exhaustion. I'm not sure who to believe."

"So, you're wondering if this meeting tonight has something to do with his trip to Summer Green?"

Cordelia set her empty cup on the coffee table and began to rock. "Diana's living there now. A little over a year ago, Orson told her about this old country church on the edge of town. A fire destroyed the rear of it. The congregation decided not to rebuild. Instead, they erected a new church on the other end of town. Near The Mall." She rolled her eyes. "They've been trying to sell the partially burned one, but with no luck. That is, until Diana came along. Orson convinced her it would make a perfect space for a playhouse. He knew Diana was having trouble figuring out what to do with her life. As much as possible, we all still try to take care of each other. Keep in touch. Since she's had good financial management all these years, she's not hurting for money. And I guess it turns out he was right. When she saw it, she got really excited. She spent all last winter having it rebuilt. Most of the summer was spent finding a permanent company. On Labor Day, The Summer Green Playhouse will officially open."

"I assume you're invited."

"But of course." Cordelia waved the question away. "Since the town is midway between Appleton and Green Bay, it will draw from both cities. A perfect spot. Last time I called, she'd decided to do a fall, spring and summer season. No winter."

"Good thinking."

"Summer Green is a beautiful little town. Orson and I drove there once about ten years ago. He doesn't go back very often. All of his family is gone, but he still knows a lot of people. He went to school with just about everyone."

"I suppose being president of Collingwell Mills doesn't give him much free time."

"Between that, his family and running the Blackburn Playhouse in Shoreview, he doesn't have a minute."

One of Jane's dogs hopped up on the couch and nestled

his head in her lap. She stroked his soft fur as she asked, "Have you seen Curt and Annie recently? I remember they stayed at your house several years ago. You brought them over to my restaurant for dinner."

Cordelia shook her head. "With Annie's teaching schedule at Northwestern, she doesn't get much time off. Curt is another story. After graduation, he just never seemed to settle down. It's hard to believe he and Annie have been married for thirteen years. She's been his rock. Other women might have given him the heave ho, but not her. He's tried his hand at so many projects, but nothing ever sticks. I guess he's stage manager at a community theatre in Chicago right now. Every time I see him, he seems so . . . listless. I don't think he's really been himself since—" Her voice trailed off.

"Since what?"

"Well, he never really got over what happened to Theo."

Jane remembered the time well. She and Cordelia had both attended the University of Minnesota, but Jane had never been part of Cordelia's inner circle of theatre friends. Even so, she'd known Theo slightly, and admired his talent. The night he was arrested, Cordelia had come over to the sorority where Jane was living. She was beside herself with worry. She couldn't fathom what had happened to make him do something so bizarre. She didn't necessarily believe the FBI, but she couldn't ignore Theo's reaction. He'd left her apartment with little protest. Almost like a lamb to the slaughter. After his conviction for impersonating an IRS agent—made worse by the accusation that he'd stolen over fifteen thousand dollars from the office safe—he'd simply disappeared inside himself. Cordelia said everyone in the group had visited him in prison at one point or another, but he wouldn't open up. To this day, his reasons for committing such an act remained a mystery.

Even though Jane had known Cordelia's friends only peripherally, she remembered that back in the early seventies, Orson, Theo and Diana had cut highly romantic figures. All penniless aspiring actors. On stage, their styles were very different. Orson's skills were more cerebral. He came across as quick, intelligent, wry. Comedy came naturally. His voice was powerful, deep and resonant. He could play the part of a much older man because of his size and bearing.

Theo, on the other hand, was all passion. The audience felt his intelligence as well, but only as it was filtered through his emotions. Consequently, he seemed more vulnerable. Less sure of himself. People identified with Theo. The viewer experienced the play through him. Jane often heard Cordelia refer to him as the heart and soul of their group. And even though the Shevlin Underground wasn't a formal title, it had been a tight circle. Others in the theatre department envied the six of them, not just for their talent, but for their friendship and loyalty.

And Diana? On stage she was like a slow explosion. Sometimes Jane didn't even notice her presence at first. But by the end of the performance, she had taken the audience captive. Her range was much broader than either Theo or Orson's. Unfortunately, Jane had always been a bit put off by Diana. When she wasn't in front of an audience, she seemed . . . deflated. Oh, she could be charming, but she could also be nasty. Cordelia had never minded *nasty*. She found it amusing. Jane, on the other hand, didn't find the quality—or Diana Stanwood—particularly appealing. Fourteen years ago, right after Theo had been let out of prison, Diana had visited Jane's restaurant in south Minneapolis for Sunday brunch. The usual celebrity commotion had ensued, with people forming a line to get an autograph. Jane found it tedious. Diana had drunk too many Bloody Marys and talked too loudly. Mostly about herself. Cordelia finally had to help her out.

Jane noticed Cordelia looking at the clock again. "Is it about time to leave?"

"It appears so."

"Maybe Orson wants you to direct something at his playhouse."

"We've discussed my schedule at the Allen Grimby. I'm directing four plays this season. I don't even have time to brush my teeth."

Jane gave her a sympathetic nod. "I suppose that means our ten-mile run is off for tomorrow morning."

Cordelia gave an indignant snort. "I'll have you know that Mugs, I mean, Mary Katherine—I have to remember to use her real name. When I do, she blushes. And *I* just *melt*. Janey, it's better than chocolate truffles from the St. Paul Hotel! Anyway, Mary Katherine's put me on an exercise regimen. I go to the gym now every... well, every *other* day."

Jane grinned. She liked Cordelia's newest love. "Good for you."

"Not that I want to be thin. Heaven forbid. I do *not* want to take up *less* space in the world. I should like to take up more. My cosmic context is large—always will be. But I want to be healthy." She sighed. "So I beat the crap out of myself on those torture machines several times a week."

Jane laughed. The clock on the mantle struck the half hour.

"I'd better hit the bricks," said Cordelia, rising from the rocking chair and striding into the front hall, "and get this meeting over with."

Jane helped her on with her coat. "Good luck."

"Thanks. By the way, dinner was wonderful. As usual. I will say, the risotto could have used a bit more parmesan."

"I'll make a note of it."

"And a little less spinach."

"Spinach is good for you. Ask Mugs."

"And the salmon. Where did you buy it?"

"Good night, Cordelia."

"Don't get huffy."

"Give my regards to Orson."

2

Cordelia expected Orson's wife, Ingrid, to greet her at the front door when she arrived, but instead, Orson himself appeared—dressed all in black—and led her into his study. Other than a quick hi, he said nothing. The entire house was silent, unusual for this time of night. Normally, his teenage kids were pole-vaulting through the kitchen on their way to the evening's entertainment—partial destruction of the family room. Ingrid must have taken them out tonight. That knowledge made Cordelia even more ill-at-ease.

Stepping hesitantly into the room, she came to a sudden stop. There, seated on the couch, a golden lock of hair falling casually over one eye, was Curt. He smiled up at her, his expression pleasant but subdued. As he stood to give her a hug, she blurted, "What are you doing here?"

"I asked him to come," said Orson, sitting down behind his desk.

"Why?" She looked from face to face. "Did Annie come too?"

Curt shook his head. "She wanted to, but her class load wouldn't allow it." He gave Cordelia the hug and then stepped back. "But she'll be in Summer Green next weekend for the intervention."

"Excuse me? The what?" Cordelia put a hand on her hip. What the hell was he talking about?

"Just sit down, will you?" said Orson. "I'll explain everything."

Out of the corner of her eye, Cordelia caught sight of another figure emerging from a rear door. She turned, expecting to see one of the kids after all, but instead, found herself staring into the eyes of a man she hadn't seen in over fourteen years. Not since her last visit to the prison. "Theo!"

He grinned, and then looked a bit annoyed. "You recognized me."

She was so stunned, she forgot to close her mouth. He looked much the same as he had in college, though older with a few more wrinkles. His hair remained dark and longish, no traces of gray anywhere, but now professionally styled, not combed by the wind as it had been so many years ago. And he had grown a beard. Jeans, boots and some gold jewelry finished the picture. He'd put on weight, and it looked good. He still could have doubled for Al Pacino. "Did you think I *wouldn't* recognize you?"

He shrugged, touching the beard. "It's new. I'm not used to it yet."

They held each other's eyes for a second longer and then both burst out laughing, throwing their arms around each other and holding on for dear life.

"How come you've never made it up here before?" she demanded, a pout forming. From the look Theo gave Orson, she knew the truth instantly. He had been here. He simply hadn't contacted her. She took a second to let that sink in.

"This place has some bad memories," he smiled. "You understand."

She didn't. She also didn't understand why his whole

27

life had been so damn secretive, but for now, she decided to let it drop. She didn't know what was going on, so it was best to tread lightly.

After getting out of prison, Theo had lived for a short time—just a couple of months—in Chicago. Cordelia had made plans to visit him there, but before it could happen, he'd disappeared. No one knew where. About a year later he resurfaced in Florida. He'd been living in Miami ever since, refusing to let anyone come see him. No one even knew his address, or what he did for a living. Once, two years ago, he'd stayed with Diana in New York. But he'd never returned to Chicago to see Curt and Annie. Annie had made that clear on more than one occasion. Cordelia knew there was still a certain friction between Annie and Theo. Annie had won her man, but Curt and Theo *had* been lovers in college. From comments Annie had made over the years, it still rankled.

Orson visited Diana frequently in New York. Cordelia had also stayed several times at Diana's apartment near Central Park, but never for more than a couple of nights. And never when anyone else was there. So, however you looked at it, this was the first time in many years that so many members of the old group had been in the same room together at the same time. She knew it wasn't an accident. She returned her scrutinizing gaze to Orson.

"Just sit down," he said impatiently. "Dr. Bernson should be here any minute."

Cordelia's frustration was rising. "And who, pray tell, is Dr. Bernson?"

Orson's expression grew pained. "All right. I've already explained some of this to Theo and Curt. It's not a pleasant subject. That's why I thought I'd wait and let the doctor handle it. But since you're obviously about to explode, I'll fill you in on everything I know."

Cordelia plunked herself down in front of the desk.

She tried not to glare, but her face wouldn't cooperate.

"On my last trip to Summer Green," Orson began, making an arch of his fingers, "I became increasingly frightened by the extent of Diana's drinking. I know it's been bad for years, but this felt different. Maybe it was because we were spending so much concentrated time together, I don't know, but when I mentioned it to her, she wouldn't even discuss it. She said it was none of my business. One afternoon I was talking to a friend of hers and I discovered that Diana's new doctor in Appleton said if she didn't quit drinking and fast, her liver wouldn't last a year."

Cordelia was stunned. "Did the doctor tell that to Diana?"

"Of course he did. But apparently Diana has chosen to ignore the warning. She's so wrapped up in this new playhouse, she told me she doesn't have time to deal with anything else."

"But if she doesn't . . . I mean, she might—" Cordelia couldn't finish the sentence. It was too awful to even contemplate.

"Exactly," said Curt from his position on the couch.

"Have you ever heard of something called an intervention?" asked Orson.

"Vaguely," answered Cordelia.

"It's when friends and family—in this case, the five of us—get together and, with the help of a therapist, try to hold up a kind of life mirror to the person who's drinking too much. Our experiences with their drinking become that mirror."

The doorbell sounded.

"At last," said Orson, breathing a sigh of relief. "That should be Dr. Bernson. She can explain this a lot better than I can." He rose and headed quickly out of the room.

While he was gone, Cordelia looked at Curt and then

Theo. So that's why they were here. "You mean, Orson wants us all to go to Summer Green and tackle Diana? Tie her up and force her to listen to reason?"

"That's not what it's like," said Theo. "Besides, if we took that approach, it would never work."

Cordelia knew one thing. Someone was going to have to explain this to her more fully. But she did agree. If what Orson said was true, Diana needed help.

Orson returned to the room a few seconds later, followed closely by a small dark-haired woman in a navy blue linen suit and heels. She carried several packets of paper in her arms and smiled at everyone before taking a seat next to Curt. After introductions were made, she set the papers down and leaned forward, ready to take charge of the meeting. Orson resumed his chair behind his desk, and Theo sat down next to Cordelia. "Is this everybody who's coming tonight?" she asked, directing the question to Orson.

"Yes. There will be one more person at the intervention. Annie Whittig."

"My wife," said Curt, not looking at Theo.

"Fine. Well, remind me to give you an extra packet of information to take home for her. I'd like you all to fill out these forms before next weekend." She passed them around.

Cordelia studied the first page. It asked her to list the ways in which she had seen alcohol negatively affect Diana's life. And, interestingly, the next page asked her to list the ways in which Diana's addiction had affected *her* life negatively. She could think of dozens of answers to both.

"I'd like to begin tonight by talking about the disease of alcoholism in general terms," continued the doctor, folding her hands together loosely. "Alcoholism is, by definition, a disease of denial. The last person to know how sick he or she is, is the person with the disease. Normal perception becomes altered. The individual is not only out of focus while drinking, but also when sober. It's my personal opinion that people drink over feelings. Though many other tangential issues may be involved, the core issue is self-esteem. This often sounds strange when you realize how many interventions are done on doctors, lawyers, professionals of all kinds. We resist the notion that someone so obviously successful could also feel rotten about themselves. But self-image problems aren't confined to any single stratum of society." She paused to allow the meaning of her words to sink in. After a moment she added, "To most people, alcohol is a beverage. To the alcoholic, it's medication."

"What happens during the intervention?" asked Theo.

"Well, first of all, before the intervention ever takes place, I see to it that all the pre-admission work is done. In this case, we're going to ask Diana to fly with me that same day to a clinic in Minnesota."

"Is that the way it's usually done?" asked Cordelia, surprised it would happen so fast.

"It is. We need to create a sense of urgency in your friend. Since her doctor has said the liver is severely damaged, it's even more urgent. Her life is literally hanging in the balance. Near the end of the intervention, I'm going to ask each of you to explain how your relationship with her will change if she doesn't get on that plane. She has to know you all mean business."

Curt nodded. "But how do we get started? How do you explain *your* presence?"

"Well, when I arrive at the house, I'll tell Diana that I'm a family therapist who has been asked to be part of a meeting called by all of you because you're worried about her. The element of surprise is crucial. I can't stress that strongly enough. Then we begin immediately. I believe

Orson said he would go first. You'll all use the sheets you've filled out. There's no shaming. No attacking. But we do use tough love. In specific terms, you all tell her how you've seen her abuse of alcohol affect her life. Each of you gets a turn. Then we move on to how her drinking has negatively affected *your* life."

"And these... interventions? Are you usually success-ful?" asked Curt.

"In nine out of ten cases, we are. For me that means we'll be able to move your friend from her head to her heart."

"What about her chances in treatment?" asked Theo.

"That's harder to predict. But at least she has a chance if she can break through the denial. Otherwise, I'm told her doctor has given her a year to live."

Everyone's eyes fell to the carpet.

Finally, Orson said, "How long does it take?"

"A normal intervention takes a couple of hours. Some-times it can go longer. I did one last week that lasted over five. It all depends on Diana."

"Why us?" asked Cordelia.

Dr. Bernson's smile was gentle. "Because you love her. I understand most of her family is gone. Orson tells me you've all known each other since college. That's good. It gives you a vantage point from which to view her life. I'm most interested in the quality of your individual relationships. Blood ties, in and of themselves, mean noth-ing."

"I'm just curious," said Cordelia. "I know this isn't common knowledge, but did Orson happen to mention to you that Diana is... a lesbian?" Cordelia knew Diana wasn't out to most people. She'd been married briefly many years ago and had used that as a cover. But since the early eighties, she'd been living with her personal secre-tary, Jill Scarbourough. Still, it wasn't an obvious living

32

arrangement. Until Jill's death, two years ago, they'd kept separate bedrooms.

"He did. As a matter of fact, I work primarily through a gay and lesbian institute in St. Paul. The fundamental issues are the same—medicating the pain, self-esteem problems—but the reasons for those issues are often different. It's hard to be a member of an oppressed and stigmatized group and not show the effects. Society dumps a lot of shame on anyone who deviates from the norm. Hiding and denial are often used as defense mechanisms against a hostile atmosphere, but hiding and denial intensify an alcoholic's problems. There are many dynamics associated with gay and lesbian alcoholism that are unique. We'll work with her on all of that."

"So," said Cordelia, leaning back in her chair. "When is this all going to happen? Did I hear Curt say something about next weekend?"

Orson nodded. "I hope you're free. Annie was having some difficulty getting five days off—"

"Five days!" Cordelia swallowed hard.

"Right. Diana is expecting all of us to be in Summer Green for the opening performance at her new playhouse on Saturday night. But we're supposed to arrive on Friday. She's planned a party. And then on Monday, she's throwing a Labor Day picnic. I told her I'd arrange everything. She's like a little kid, she's so excited. And besides, I think it would be a good opportunity for all of us to spend some time together again. We'll need that before . . . well, before Dr. Bernson arrives on Tuesday."

"It's the first day I have free," said the doctor.

"But I'm in rehearsals right now for two different plays," protested Cordelia. "I don't suppose it could wait until—" She knew it was pointless to ask. Of course it couldn't wait.

"It's a small sacrifice," said Theo, his face betraying

the intensity of his feelings, "when you compare it with what we might lose."

Cordelia nodded, lowering her eyes. Of course he was right.

"Besides," added Orson, "it might be fun."

"Sure. A relaxing, stress-free vacation," agreed Cordelia.

Orson narrowed one eye. "Look, we haven't been together in years. I, for one, think that should change."

"Right-on," said Curt, knowing he'd just said something not only dated, but obtuse. "And far-out," he declared. His grin told everyone he didn't care.

Cordelia wondered if she recalled the past a little more clearly than everyone else. She not only remembered the caring, she also remembered the rivalry and the volatility. "Well, I agree we should do it. No question about that. But all I can say is, I hope we keep from killing each other." She arched an eyebrow at Theo. Like her, he wasn't smiling.

3

"So," said Jane, watching Cordelia shamble into the downstairs pub of the Lyme House, the restaurant Jane had owned for many years, "Are you all packed and ready to head for Wisconsin?" She motioned to Johnny, one of the early afternoon bartenders, for another cappucino. Cordelia looked like she could use some caffeine.

Easing herself onto a bar seat, Cordelia heaved a deep sigh. "I guess I'm ready. I've cleared everything with the powers that be at the Allen Grimby. Jeff Kelling is going to take over my directorial duties until I get back. He's competent, but uninspired."

"Then they'll miss you all the more. And besides, you won't be gone that long."

Cordelia fluffed her auburn curls. "It may turn out to be the longest five days of my life."

Jane knew Cordelia felt strongly about the intervention. It had to be done. She also knew Cordelia wasn't looking forward to this *reunion,* as Diana was now calling it. Diana had phoned her two nights ago and talked for several hours about her hopes and plans for the visit. She'd even gone so far as to suggest that everyone in the old group consider leaving their current jobs and homes to relocate in Summer Green. The playhouse would finally have a permanent staff. It would be like old times. Together, they'd make it the biggest and best regional theatre in the nation!

So much for Diana's grip on reality.

"Well," said Jane, pushing a bowl of fresh popcorn toward Cordelia as the cappucino arrived, "At least you know you're doing the right thing."

"That's what I've been telling myself all week. The needle seems to be stuck."

"Come on. It won't be that bad."

"Easy for you to say." She took a sip of the frothy drink, appearing to relax just a bit. "You'll be here, in the bosom of your family. Promoting your new cookbook. Being interviewed by the press and adored by the culinary public. Eating your beef Wellingtons and salivating over your plum puddings."

Jane held up her hand, knowing when Cordelia was on a roll, she could go on like this forever. "Plum pudding doesn't appear on the menu until November."

Cordelia tapped her fingers impatiently on the counter. "Raspberry trifle then. Pretty soon you're going to be right up there with Julia Child and the Frugal Gourmet."

Jane smiled at the exaggeration, but didn't correct her.

"And don't forget your promise," continued Cordelia without so much as a pause. "My cats need to be fed and cuddled once a day. I would have asked Mugs, but she's going to be in Cleveland."

"Cleveland?"

"It's one of her home security conventions. I know it's her job, but she's almost incommunicado when she's there. It drives me crazy."

"Don't worry. Your cats will be fine."

"Lucifer likes to hide next to the spaghetti noodles in the pantry. If you can't find him, that's where he'll be."

"I know."

"And Melville—"

"—likes to pretend he's a book. He sleeps on top of an old copy of *Moby Dick*. I know, Cordelia. I've been taking care of your cats for years. I'm aware of all their idiosyncrasies."

Cordelia raised an eyebrow, tossing several popcorn kernels into her mouth. "All right. But remember, these are my *children*."

"Put your mind at rest. Beryl may even go over and babysit. Bounce them around the bathtub a few times."

"Oh, they'd love that!" Cordelia's expression brightened. "Your aunt is a peach, Janey."

"I know. But she may not get to be a peach much longer if the INS has anything to say about it."

"What do you mean?"

"Unless Dad can pull some more strings and get her another extension, by March, she'll be back in England."

"What a dreary thought."

Jane nodded. "But listen, kiddo. You've got enough on your plate right now. We'll worry about that later."

Cordelia squared her shoulders and climbed down off the stool. She finished her cappucino is three quick gulps. "I'll call you sometime during the weekend."

"Fine."

"Wish me luck?"

"All the luck in the world," said Jane, putting her arm around Cordelia's shoulders and walking her out.

After many hours of driving through some of the richest farmland in America, Cordelia saw a sign that said, "Summer Green, 4 miles." She felt her hands tense around the steering wheel. She'd never been afraid of confrontation before—she'd even prided herself on her forthright handling of sensitive issues in both her work and personal life. But somehow, this was different. So much was riding on the outcome of the next few days. She'd dutifully filled out the forms Dr. Bernson had given her. It provided a good perspective from which to view Diana's life as it touched her own. What she'd once seen as merely high spirits mixed with bad judgement, now formed a more ominous picture. Diana had been having problems with alcohol ever since college. Cordelia felt more than a little guilty that she'd turned such a blind eye, allowing her friend to drown quietly.

Then again, the apprehension she was experiencing wasn't limited to Diana and the intervention. All week she'd been wondering what it would be like to spend time again with the Shevlin Underground. Even the name now caused her acute embarrassment. It was so...so silly. So dated. So hopelessly *young*. And, if nothing else, no one was young any longer. Even though she was excited to see her friends again, she knew the old tensions were just under the surface. They would all be walking through a mine field until they got to the final day. If they got that far.

Stop it! she ordered herself. Her melodramatic nature was running amok. The visit would go just fine. Oh, there might be the unavoidable glitch or two, but what the hell. They were all human. She had to think positively. For one thing, they loved each other. That was never in question. Each person, in his or her own way, was making a certain sacrifice to be at the reunion. They'd each be on their best behavior because nobody was an idiot. They all knew, like Cordelia, what the potential problems were. Everyone would put Diana first. No, it would be just fine.

Just fine.

As she slowed the car to forty, she began to see more houses and lawns instead of cows and corn fields. Another sign at the edge of town proclaimed, Welcome to Summer

Green, Radish Capital of the Upper Midwest. Cordelia laughed out loud at that bit of hype. God, what people couldn't get excited over. At the bottom was the population—3,487. Over three thousand avid radish-lovers. Each, no doubt, with a recipe for creamed radishes on toast or radish preserves handed down directly from Grandma. She'd have to alert Jane. Perhaps a new cookbook should be considered.

Another half mile and she spotted a billboard. This one advertised the new Radish Hill Mall. Cordelia bit her lower lip. It was clear what had just happened. Sure. Rod Serling owned the hardware store. She'd finally entered The Twilight Zone. She'd always had a sneaking suspicion it was somewhere in the Midwest.

Orson had given her a rather crude map before she left. Now, if she could just find Main Street. She looked up at the street signs whizzing past and realized that the highway had ceased to exist and she was already on Main. Up ahead, she could see stores on either side of the street. The town was probably deserted, except for a small child, a dog and an old man. The townspeople had mysteriously vanished. A metallic object had been sighted falling from the sky into a ditch just south of The Mall. Two men, dressed in leopard skins and Robin Hood hats, had walked into town and entered the cafe. Fade to morning.

Cordelia knew she needed to eat something before she actually started to hallucinate. The tuna sandwich, corn chips and Ho Hos she'd packed for the trip had been devoured before she'd left the Twin Cities city limits. She was just like a kid. She could never wait. Passing through the business district—such as it was—she turned left onto Oak Avenue and picked up speed. Once again the houses began to dwindle as the road turned into a highway. By the time she spotted the church, now turned playhouse, she was back to fields and cows.

Diana lived next door to the church in what had once been the parsonage. It was a lovely sight, the evening hues subtle, like a Wyeth watercolor. Driving up to the white wood-framed buildings she couldn't help but notice how the simplicity of their design fit perfectly into the rustic surroundings. Clean, sharp lines. Cordelia pulled her car off the road and sat looking at the restful, yet slightly smarmy scene. Give me downtown St. Paul any day, she mumbled, listening to the disconcerting silence. The fading summer sunlight had imbued the buildings with a kind of angelic glow, casting deep shadows along the east side of the parsonage. The church steeple, which once housed a bell tower, now served as the anchor for a large wooden sign: The Summer Green Playhouse. Diana had mentioned that the fire which destroyed the back of the church had spared the carved wooden pews. She'd left them untouched, knowing they lent a kind of reverent formality to the interior. To her, theatres were intensely spiritual places. People sitting in the dark, listening to other people in the light talk about the experience of being human.

Cordelia crooked her neck and saw that, though most of the tall pointed windows on the side were clear glass, some of the old stained-glass panels still remained. Two of them flanked the arched double doors in the front. She couldn't wait to get inside and see what Diana had dreamt up for the stage. She'd hired an architect from New York City. A personal friend.

As Cordelia sat and contemplated the deepening sunset, its reds and golds settling into the grassy fields, a white Cadillac rolled over the distant rise. It came to a stop in front of the parsonage. The windows were dark, preventing her from seeing inside. Whoever was behind the wheel was probably just satisfying his curiosity because, after a moment, he drove on. Maybe it was a resident of the town, though by now, everyone must have had their fill of this new construction. It was probably the biggest event to hit Summer Green since the radish blight of '05.

She returned her attention to the church and the gloomy graveyard which stretched behind it. Not a particularly welcoming sight for visitors to the new theatre. Nevertheless, unlike Brigadoon, it wasn't going to disappear. Diana had made the best of it by keeping the lawn manicured. Here and there, flowers sprouted in thick clumps. She might even be able to use it to her advantage by offering prospective repertory players their own plot should anything untoward happen during a performance. Cordelia snickered at the thought. After all, perks *were* perks.

Out of the corner of her eye, she caught sight of a figure skulking in the shadows near the back of the parsonage. She squinted to get a better look, thinking it might be one of her group. They were great skulkers, all of them. But this person appeared to be elderly. Gray haired. She also seemed to be peeking in one of the side windows! Jesus, was this the town Peeping Tom? The idea that she was actually witnessing *a peeping* gave Cordelia the willies. She honked her horn, but her reaction had been too slow. The woman had already disappeared around the rear of the house.

Yuck. As she was about to pull back onto the road and head for the parking lot, the same white car she'd seen a minute ago rumbled by once again. Just as before, it stopped in front of the house, but closer to the front windows this time. Was someone casing the joint? The happenings inside the parsonage seemed to be of interest to one and all. As the sky grew darker, the lights inside grew brighter. It was possible now to see into the front room. She checked her watch. Nearly eight. Lights were also glowing inside the playhouse. She decided to take the direct approach. She rolled down the window of her car and leaned her head out calling, "Hi! Great house, huh! My name's Cordelia! What's yours?" The chill night air smacked her square in the face.

No sooner had she called her greeting than the Cadillac revved its motor and sped off. But before it did, she fixed on the license plate. She couldn't get the number, but she caught the state. Illinois. Interesting. An out-of-towner. From the same state as Curt and Annie.

Good riddance she thought to herself as she pulled her car into a parking space right next to Orson's Lincoln. She turned off the motor and got out, her nose twitching as she sniffed the itchy summer air. The scent which assaulted her was very different from what she'd grown accustomed to in south Minneapolis—car exhaust mixed with just that right hint of ozone. Not that she had anything against city life. God *made* her for concrete and late night bistros. But this smell was decidedly pleasant. Earthy and sweet, with a slight whiff of cow. She could do without the cow—unless it gave chocolate milk.

"Bellboy!" she shouted, hearing no response except the buzz of mosquitos. All itching for blood.

"Ahhhhhh," she sighed, heaving her heavy bags out of the trunk and letting them thump to the ground. "Ain't country living grand?"

4

Cordelia approached the screened porch, her ears pricking at the sound of Janis Joplin being played somewhere inside at the correct, ear-splitting decibel level. She smiled as she recalled Annie's record collection. Lots of Janis, Elton and Jethro Tull. Music had been such an important part of their lives. It had been the backdrop, the atmosphere against which they laughed and loved. Climbing the steps, Cordelia rang the bell knowing no one would hear. But, surprise, surprise, as she peeked through the window, she saw Orson dash into the hall and come barrelling toward the door.

"We wondered when you were going to get here," he declared, out of breath.

Cordelia swatted a mosquito away from her face and handed him her bags, realizing with a sense of relief that she didn't have to tip. Then, sweeping into the small foyer, she took a moment to look around. Well, well. Straight out of St. Mary Mead. Diana had done nothing to modernize. Instead, even the furniture furthered the image of small town life—*tasteful* small town life, circa 1920. Except, here and there, her personality did leak out. A dramatic arrangement of red gladiolus in a tall Lalique vase dominated the central hall. Signed photos from famous friends dotted the walls. A huge teddy bear from F.A.O. Schwartz sat in a rocking chair under the stairway, monitoring comings and goings. Cordelia knew the bear was from F.A.O. Schwartz because she'd been looking at one just like it in Minneapolis. She also knew the price.

"Everyone's in the parlor," said Orson, straining under the weight of five days worth of Cordelia's clothing. He had to shout to be heard over the music.

Cordelia nodded, noticing a floor to ceiling poster of Diana which served as the focal point in the dining room. So much for humility, not that Cordelia had ever been much into humility herself. At least Diana didn't have candles burning at the shrine. In the poster she was dressed as her character in "The Bald and the Snooty"—or whatever the name of that soap opera was. Cordelia never watched daytime TV, yet she was painfully aware that Diana had become famous playing the highly seductive mega-bitch, Morgana Richmond. Such stereotypes. It made her feel slightly nauseous. Nevertheless, actors had to be pragmatists. The part had made Diana a rich woman.

"I'll take these up to your room," said Orson, puffing up the stairs.

"Thanks." She followed the music into the first room on her right. The parlor was another period piece, with one sop to the modern. A comfortable leather couch. The rest of the furnishings were antique. The small room had an almost stark quality to it, though the smell of food and the soft glow from a wood fire made the scene inviting. Theo was standing with his back to her, leaning over a table filled with chafing dishes. He seemed to be unable to make up his mind. Curt was stretched out on the couch, paging through a soap opera magazine. He looked bored and tired. The trip from Chicago had no doubt been a long one. And Annie, her red hair done up in frizzy bun, was sitting cross-legged on the floor in front of the stereo, poking intently through Diana's old records and new CDs. Cordelia saw that the speakers were mounted on the wall above the fireplace. Another sop to modernization.

Diana, however, was nowhere in sight.

Attempting to restrain herself from sprinting over to the food table and diving head-first into the bean dip, Cordelia crossed regally to the hearth and rested her arm on the mantel. She waited for Janis to stop yelling and then cleared her throat.

Everyone turned to look.

"Cordelia!" shouted Annie, turning down the volume and jumping up. She threw her arms around her. "I didn't hear you come in."

"I'm a master of stealth," she grinned, hugging her back.

Theo also came forward, giving her a welcoming kiss. "We thought you might have had car trouble."

"Nope. I was simply mesmerized by my bucolic surroundings."

Curt snorted. He remained on the couch, but offered a deep, heartfelt, "Moo."

"Hello to you too," replied Cordelia. "Did anyone think to bring the insect repellent?"

"The house is completely stocked," said Orson, returning to the room and dumping himself into a chair. His face had reddened from his brief stint as hotel staff.

Cordelia put a hand on her hip. No one would cast a man who looked like Raymond Burr as a bellboy, she thought to herself. When it came time to leave, she must remember to choose someone else to carry her bags back down. "Where's our host?"

"The company's doing a full dress rehearsal tonight," said Orson. "All very hush hush. Diana didn't want us anywhere near the church. She wants the production to-morrow night to be a complete surprise."

Cordelia nodded, spying a keg of beer sitting on a table in the far corner of the room.

Annie followed her gaze. "Diana said we should all help ourselves. I guess she thought a keg was pretty funny. Sort of for old-times sake."

No one laughed.

Janis droned on about Bobby McGee.

"Christ, put another record on," said Curt. "I'm sick of hearing that woman scream."

Cordelia noticed Annie stiffen. She wondered how things had been between the two of them recently. By the tone of this interaction, not so friendly.

Annie walked back to the turntable and switched everything off. "There. Is that better?"

He glared at her. "I hope we're not going to spend the entire weekend wallowing in nostalgia. My stomach can't take it." He stood, tossing the magazine on the couch, defying anyone to challenge him on the subject.

The first skirmish, thought Cordelia. There would be more.

"This reminds me of the night we realized we all had the flu," Theo piped up, ignoring Curt's angry look. "Remember? We were all in incredibly rotten moods."

"Wasn't that the same time we all took turns making chicken soup?" asked Annie.

Theo nodded. "Whoever felt the least rotten would go to the store and buy more chicken and vegetables."

"And garlic. Don't forget the garlic," insisted Cordelia.

"God, we were sick for weeks," groaned Curt, thawing just a bit.

"I'm sure we kept re-infecting each other with the food," offered Orson.

Everyone laughed.

"Remember that time we decided to go sledding," said Annie, warming to the conversation. "I borrowed those sleds from my cousin."

"Right," agreed Orson. "Cordelia had just finished that paper, and we wanted to do something to help her celebrate."

Theo draped his arm over Cordelia's shoulder. "All I remember is Diana barrelling down the hill heading for the river."

"She must have closed her eyes," said Annie, shaking her head. "I was so scared. Remember how cold it was that day? If she'd gotten wet—"

"If it hadn't been for that snow fence," scowled Orson, "she would have gone straight into the water."

Curt hooted. "And then you, Theo old boy, wouldn't even use your sled. You said it was too dangerous."

"Oh, that wasn't it. He wanted to try out his newly memorized soliloquy," grinned Cordelia.

"Of course," agreed Orson. "You stood on top of that hill and gave a rare performance."

The room grew still as everyone remembered the magical moment. Theo, surrounded by mounds of freshly fallen snow and a cobalt blue sky, had spoken words from Hamlet.

"Act two," smiled Orson. "Do you remember any of it?"

"Of course." Theo gave a small bow.

"No you don't," said Curt. "That was twenty years ago. You couldn't possibly."

Theo cleared his throat. After a pause he began,

Now I am alone.
O, what a rogue and peasant slave am I!
Is it not monstrous, that this player here,

47

But in a fiction, in a dream of passion,
Could force his soul so to his own conceit.

The words seemed to stop him.

"Go on," prodded Annie.

Theo looked over at Curt.

"Someone feed him the next line," said Orson.

Again, Theo held up his hand. Very soberly he continued,

Yet I,
A dull and muddy-mettled rascal, peak,
Like John-a-dreams, unpregnant of my cause,
And can say . . . nothing.

"What's this?" asked a forceful voice from behind them.

Everyone turned to find Diana framed in the doorway. Her hair, her skin, her clothing, everything was the color gray. She was wearing a gauzy, fringed flapper outfit and a thin band around her twenties' haircut. The make-up she wore emphasized the gauntness of her now aging face. She was a mannequin—a ghost with a mischievous smile.

"What happened to the party?" She moved into the room like she owned it. Which she did. "Annie, put on some music. Hamlet is much too dreary for a celebration. I feel like . . . how about some vintage Elton John? What do you say?" Her grin was irresistible.

"Fine," said Annie. She found a new CD and the music once again resumed.

"Much better," said Diana. She grabbed Cordelia's arm and gave it a hearty welcoming squeeze as she waltzed her over to the keg.

Conversations resumed.

"This should stay cold for several hours," said Diana. "Hey, you don't have anything to drink yet. Who the hell

is the host around here?" She filled two mugs, and handed
one to Cordelia. "Bottom's up," she smiled, finishing hers
in one try. "Acting always makes me thirsty."

Cordelia took a small sip. Normally, she liked tap
beer, but tonight it tasted bitter.

"You look fabulous," said Diana.

"Thanks. And you look . . . like a corpse."

She gave Cordelia an impish smile.

"How's the play going?"

"Good. Really good. I don't have the best talent to
work with yet, but the company as a whole is solid. You'll
see tomorrow night." She refilled her mug and eased over
to the food table.

The doorbell chimed. Cordelia saw Orson disappear
into the foyer. He certainly took his role as butler seriously. A moment later he came back and motioned Theo
over to the door. Odd. Was the visitor for Theo? Who
would come calling at a parsonage in the middle of nowhere? After a short conversation, they both left the
room. Cordelia's curiosity moved instantly into high gear.
She was itching to get over to the window to see what was
going on, but she couldn't just dump Diana.

"Have a radish," said Diana, picking one up and taking
a tiny bite. "They're an obsession around here."

Cordelia attempted an understanding smile, the one
she reserved for people on the brink of insanity. "I noticed." She also noticed Diana's figure. She'd lost a great
deal of weight since the last time they'd seen each other.
Not that Diana had ever had a weight problem. In fact,
the radish she was holding was probably tonight's dinner.
Cordelia eyed the Swedish meatballs in the tallest chafing
dish.

"What's on the agenda for tomorrow?" asked Annie,
walking up and slipping her arm through Diana's. Curt
had resumed his position on the couch, arms crossed over

his chest, eyes closed.

"Well," said Diana, finishing beer number two. "I thought we'd stick around here in the morning. If I recall correctly, we all have different opinions as to what constitutes breakfast time."

"Not a moment before ten," said Cordelia. "I refuse to be up before the birds."

Diana took a deep breath. "Right. And then in the afternoon, everyone can explore the town at their leisure. I've written up some of the sights to see."

"That should take about ten minutes." Cordelia set the beer down.

"Still the big city girl?"

"What do you think?"

"You may not believe this," said Diana, "but I thought of myself that way too. Once. I was wrong. There's something about the American character that makes me believe we're all from a small town. Deep inside, we all grew up in a place like Summer Green."

"Hopeless romanticism," remarked Cordelia, trying not to be disagreeable, even though she disagreed.

"Just listen to us," laughed Annie. "We haven't changed a bit since college."

"Right. I still tie-dye my underwear." Cordelia gave them a pained smile. "Helps me maintain a youthful outlook."

"No. Really. Think about it."

"You mean Diana still *knows* everything," said Cordelia.

"And Cordelia still has to *control* everything," smirked Diana.

"I beg your pardon?" Cordelia's hand rose indignantly to her chest.

"And Annie quietly gets everything she wants. She never lets anything stand in her way." Annie said the

50

words without a trace of humor.

"Well, whatever." Diana gazed into her empty mug of beer. "Just remember, give the town a chance. It might grow on you. And then in the evening, you'll all put on your finest big city duds and take your place in the front pew of the new Summer Green Playhouse. I'm going to knock your socks off!" She glanced around. "You know, this celebration calls for something stronger than beer. Wait here." She dashed out of the room.

Cordelia seized her opportunity. "I'll be right back, Annie. I have to...freshen up." Didn't people always need to freshen up?

"Ah...sure."

"Don't eat all the food before I get back."

"I wouldn't dream of it." She selected a radish.

Christ, what was *wrong* with these women! Bean dip and meatballs and they grab the freaking radish? She didn't have time to dwell on it. Striding into the foyer, she crossed to the front door and peeked out the window. Orson was standing on the porch, deep in the shadows. Theo had moved out to the end of the walk. He was talking to a bald man who was leaning on—oh my god, there it was again! The Cadillac. So they *had* been watching the house. The conversation seemed to be calm enough. No shouting. But it made her uneasy. Why didn't the guy come inside? Why all the secrecy? After a few moments, the man got into the car and Theo headed back up the walk. When he got to the steps, Orson stepped out of the shadows. Cordelia opened the door just a crack to hear their conversation.

"How did he find you?" asked Orson.

"No idea."

"I don't understand. It can't be a coincidence. The odds against it have to be astronomical."

"Apparently not."

"What are you going to do?"

"That depends on you."

Orson didn't move.

"You still my banker?"

"Jesus. When is this ever going to end?"

Theo smiled. "You owe me your life, buddy."

"I know."

"What are you looking at?" asked Diana, poking Cordelia in the ribs. She was holding a bottle of vodka.

Cordelia jumped. She turned around and tried to look innocent. She'd never been very good at that. Not even when she was a baby. "Why...nothing." She smiled. "Just...appreciating the sunset."

"The sun goes down in the west, Cordelia."

"Oh. Right." Some people were such a store of useless information. "Is that for me?" She glanced at the booze.

"For all of us." Diana turned and breezed back into the parlor.

Reluctantly, Cordelia followed.

"Can I have everyone's attention?" called Diana, waving her hand like the prom queen she wasn't. She looked around the room. "Where's Orson and Theo?"

"Right here," said Theo. They both moved in behind her.

"Good. I want to propose a toast," said Diana. "Does everyone have something to drink?"

Curt handed Theo, Orson, and Cordelia a mug of beer.

"Great," said Diana. "Before the toast, I want to say one thing. Thanks to brother Orson's big mouth, I'm sure you've all heard the news that I'm at death's door. Well, buckos, we're all dying. Everyone of us. I just may have a better idea of the date. I don't want to make that little tidbit the focus of this gathering, is that clear? Doctors have been wrong before." She held up the bottle. "All right then, to us. To the best bunch of friends anyone's ever had. And to our reunion after far too many years. We all came for our own reasons. Whatever they are, may we each find what we're looking for."

They clinked their mugs together, Diana using the bottle as her glass. She unscrewed the top and took a swig.

Except for Elton John, the room grew quiet. No boisterous *here here's* accompanied the toast. Cordelia could see each person silently retreat into himself or herself. Thoughts grew louder than words.

And, for the second time that night, Cordelia looked up and saw Theo staring at Curt.

5

Around one in the morning, after everyone had gone up to bed, Cordelia crept quietly into the kitchen and picked up the phone. She punched in some numbers and then waited. After a few seconds a woman's voice answered, "Hello?"

"I missed you. I simply *had* to hear your voice."

"Excuse me?" came the confused reply.

"This is not a crank call, dearheart. This is a plaintive cry from a faraway land."

Jane let out a deep growl. "Cordelia."

"C'est moi. Were you asleep?"

"No. I always sound like my head is under a pillow."

Cordelia sat down behind the counter. The room was dark except for a hood light on the stove. She could hear a soft buzzing.

"Couldn't you have missed me a few hours ago?" asked Jane. "Before it became the middle of the night?"

"I wasn't even thinking about you a few hours ago. I was having too much fun."

"Oh, I get it. And now you're bored."

"Well...not exactly." Her eyes searched the darkness for the source of the buzz. "Something isn't right here."

"You mean in Summer Green? I take it you made it without mishap."

"The drive was straight out of a Norman Rockwell painting, Janey. You know Wisconsin. Cheese flowing down the hillsides like lava. Cows, chickens and bratwurst all grazing together in the open fields." She swatted away a mosquito as it dive-bombed her face. Ah ha!

"Then what's the problem? Can't find an espresso bar when you need one?"

"Cute. No, actually something happened tonight. I need to run it past a disinterested party."

"Is that what I am?" She snorted. "You make me feel so special."

"Well, I mean, you know everyone here. You simply don't know them as well as I do. But just listen, okay? You tell me what you think. When I first got here, I noticed this Cadillac casing the parsonage where Diana lives. It stopped in front of the house for a few seconds and then just sped off."

"Curiosity seekers?"

"That's what I thought. But later, the doorbell rings and Orson says it's for Theo. So, Theo goes outside. I happened to glance out the front door a few minutes later and there's the Cadillac again. Only this time, Theo and a bald man are standing next to it, talking."

"Could you hear what they were saying?"

"Nope. Too far away."

"Did they seem angry or upset?"

Cordelia played the scene over again in her mind. "Not really. But finally the bald guy gets back in the car and drives off. That's when Theo comes back up to the porch and starts talking to Orson."

"Where was Orson when all this was happening?"

"Standing in the shadows on the porch. I'm sure the bald guy never saw him. Anyway, Orson says something to Theo about wondering how the man found him. Then Theo tells Orson he needs money. Calls Orson his banker."

"How did Orson take *that?*"

"Before he could say much, Theo reminded him that he—Orson—owed Theo his life."

Jane whistled. "Do you know what he was referring to?"

"I haven't the vaguest idea." Cordelia could hear the faint buzzing again. The mosquito was back for round two. "I can't help but wonder if it has something to do with the time Theo spent in prison." She flailed at the air in front of her as the speck flitted past. "And something else strikes me as odd."

"What's that?"

"Diana seems to be angry at Theo. She barely spoke to him all evening. I wasn't the only one who noticed it."

"Did someone comment on it?"

"Yeah. Annie. She got me aside before everyone went up to bed and asked if I knew what was going on."

"Sounds like you're having a great time."

"Actually," said Cordelia, smacking the counter but missing the intended victim, "tonight was wonderful. We all sat around the fire and reminisced. I laughed so hard my fingernails hurt."

"Well, I'm sorry I can't help you more," said Jane, trying to stifle a yawn. "You'll work it out."

"Yeah," said Cordelia, slamming her fist down hard on a plate. She could just *feel* the mosquito's smug smile as it whizzed past her face. "I'll keep you posted."

"You do that."

"Nighty night, dearheart." Cordelia set the phone back in its cradle. Climbing down off her stool, she spotted an aerosol can of RAID on the far counter. "Say your prayers," she whispered, her eyes gleaming wickedly.

6

Before going to sleep, Cordelia made the mistake of leaving the window open in her bedroom. She awoke on Saturday morning to the sound of a DC-10 attempting to make a crash landing on her pillow. Knowing she had mere moments to react, she shot out from under her quilt and hit the floor, covering her head with her hands. Seconds ticked by. When nothing happened, she cracked open one eye. Hmm. No dust balls under the bed. How hygienic. Next, she hoisted herself up on a chair. It took a moment before her mind completely focused. When it did, she realized the sound she'd heard wasn't a jet engine, it was a lawn mower. By the roar it made, a damn big one! Anybody could make the same mistake, she thought to herself as she yanked her pink satin pajamas into place. She found her fake zebra-skin robe in a heap on the floor and trudged out the door, heading for the stairs. She might as well see who else was up.

As she passed the parlor on her way to the kitchen, she saw someone had already cleaned away the mess from last night. Gremlins, no doubt. She knew Diana had passed out on the couch and had to be carried up to bed. A bad beginning to their stay.

"Who are *you?*" asked a young voice.

Cordelia turned to find a girl standing at the bottom of the stairs. She had brown hair, cut very short—almost a crew-cut—and very green eyes. And, she was chewing gum. Loudly. She couldn't be more than fourteen. The army fatigues she wore looked like they came straight off the rack at Bloomingdales. Combed cotton. Nicely tailored. Cordelia raised a highly approving eyebrow. She wanted to touch the collar, but knew it would be gauche.

"You must be one of Diana's friends," said the girl, realizing she was being scrutinized. She bumped past Cordelia and flopped down on the couch. She had a magazine under one arm and quickly took it out, covering her face.

Cordelia noticed the title. *The New Republic.* A bit different from the other reading material scattered on the end tables. With the exception of *The Independent Film & Video Monthly,* and *Interview,* Diana appeared to read mostly soap opera gossip. But then she knew the *gossipees* personally. Cordelia had great faith that one day, gossip would be recognized as the primal need it so obviously was. For pete's sake, that's why we *had* celebrities. So we could talk about them.

She cleared her throat. "My name is Cordelia Thorn."

The magazine didn't move.

"What's yours?"

A page turned. "Amity. Amity Scarbourough."

The last name was familiar. Cordelia thought for a moment. Of course. Jill Scarbourough had been Diana's personal secretary and lover for many years. She'd recently died. This must be her daughter. "It's nice to meet you. I knew your mother, though only slightly."

"Me too," came the quick response. Another page was turned.

The kid was fast. Cordelia sat down. She didn't mind talking to a magazine. It gave her an opportunity to stare at the fatigues with total abandon. Perhaps she could have her dressmaker sew one in a larger size. She knew Bloomingdale's failed miserably at large sizes. No doubt, fat women weren't supposed to look like they'd served in the Gulf War.

Amity lowered the magazine to see where Cordelia had gone.

She gave a little wave. "I'm right here."

"You're weird."

"Thanks."

"What'd you say your name was?"

"Cordelia."

The magazine lowered even further. "I like that name."

"Me too. What are you doing in Summer Green?"

"Hiding."

"From whom?"

"My grandparents. After Mom died, I went to live with them. We didn't get along."

"Umm. So you came here."

"Yup. Two days ago."

Really. No wonder Diana hadn't mentioned anything about her the other night on the phone. "Have you checked out the town yet?"

"What town?"

Smart kid. They were going to get along. "Have you had any breakfast?"

"Yeah. I had a bagel. It was awful. Totally gummy. I don't know how Diana can eat that crap."

"Thanks for the warning. I think I'm going to head into the kitchen. Being up before dawn has made me ravenous."

"It's after ten, but I know what you mean." The magazine rose. "Later."

"Later," repeated Cordelia.

The kitchen which greeted her weary morning eyes was cleaned and polished. A far cry from last night. It was the one room in the house which didn't look as if it had come straight out of an antique Sears catalogue. The cabinets and counters were all new white laminate. A center island served as both a work space and an eating area. Six stools fit comfortably along one side. She turned to the window as she shuffled to the refrigerator, noticing an elderly gray-haired woman outside on a riding mower. Cordelia narrowed her gaze to get a better look. Damn if she wasn't the same person Cordelia had seen last night looking in the side window.

"Top of the morning," chirped Annie, entering the kitchen with a newspaper tucked under one arm. She was already dressed.

Cordelia glared. She'd forgotten Annie was one of those tediously cheerful morning people. "Right" she grunted.

Annie gave her an amused smile. "There's orange juice in the fridge. And fresh blueberry muffins on the counter."

Come to think of it, Cordelia did smell something wonderful. "Who made them?"

"Hilda Barnes. She's outside cutting the grass. She's sort of a jack of all trades. Gardener. Cook. I think the minister who used to live here hired her as a housekeeper. When Diana moved in, Hilda knocked on the front door and offered her services. She lives about a mile up the road. Her husband died many years ago. She just likes to keep busy, I guess. If you'd been up a couple of hours ago, you would have met her. We had a nice talk."

Cordelia raised a skeptical eyebrow. She got out the juice and poured herself a hefty glass. Then she sidled over to the muffins and selected the largest. "Where is everyone?"

"Diana and Theo are still upstairs sleeping. And since it's such a lovely morning, Curt went for a walk after breakfast."

"You didn't go with him?"

Her mouth tightened. "No. I didn't. And Orson drove into town. He has a lot of friends around here."

"I know," said Cordelia between bites. The muffin was delicious. Real blueberries. "Local boy makes good."

"That he has."

Cordelia pulled up a stool and sat down across from Annie. She might be perky as hell, but she didn't look happy. "So, what's new with you?"

"Not much. My teaching schedule is pretty full this term."

"You still like it? Teaching, I mean?"

She nodded. "It's the only thing I've ever really wanted to do. I can't act. I'm not good at the tech stuff, like Curt is, and I've no interest in directing. But I love the theatre."

Cordelia finished her muffin and washed it down with the juice. Then, reaching for a mug, she poured herself a cup of coffee. Nice touch, having the coffee maker on the center island. "You want some?" she asked, still holding the pot.

"Why not," said Annie. She grabbed a mug. "You know, fresh squeezed orange juice always reminds me of that winter I came down with pneumonia. Remember?"

"I brought juice to the hospital every day," said Cordelia, smiling at the thought. "Along with an assortment of Robert Redford photos."

"You were all wonderful. Orson and Theo did those

silly drawings and then plastered them all over the hospital room. And Diana stayed with me at night. I'll never forget that. She'd leave in the morning and go to class and to work, but every night she'd be back. She must have been exhausted, but she kept it up until I got well. The doctors terrified me. I don't think I ever said that to anyone. But I felt so warm and safe with all of you. So...loved. It was the first time I think I realized how special you'd become to me. I've had lots of friends since, but I've never felt that same intensity. Maybe it only happens once in a lifetime."

Cordelia had wondered about that too.

"And Curt." Annie's eyes grew wistful. "He came in the evenings with his guitar and sang to me. That's when I first realized my feelings for him went beyond friendship. He was so gentle. And so beautiful. He read me poetry and silly limericks. Tried to get me to smile. Seeing you all again has made me miss that time in my life terribly. I wonder if we can ever get it back."

Cordelia squeezed her hand. "We can try, dearheart. We can give it our best shot." She poured Annie's coffee. "I hear Curt is stage-managing for a community theatre in Chicago."

She nodded, taking a sip. "It's not full time, but it's something."

"You aren't hurting for money are you?"

"No. My salary's pretty good now. And Curt's parents give him anything wants. We're fine. But as far as I'm concerned, they've crippled him. He's never been very self-motivated, and since he doesn't need a regular job to survive, he just drifts."

Cordelia already knew about Curt's inability to settle on a career. She'd been surprised that he'd settled on a marriage partner.

"He's a good man, but we've had our problems. Especially lately."

"Want to talk about it?"

Annie shook her head. "I don't know. Maybe. We've started arguing over small things. Nothing that has any importance. But our home has begun to feel like an armed camp. I know he's unhappy, but he never does anything about it. I suggested a marriage counselor, but he drags his feet. Won't make a decision. One minute he thinks it's a good idea, the next he's not so sure. I know he loves me, but—"

Cordelia turned the mug around in her hand. "How do you feel about spending the weekend with Theo?"

She looked away. "Okay, I guess. What can happen? And besides, I couldn't turn my back on Diana, no matter what the cost. Actually, the more I've thought about it, the more I see that this visit might be a good move. Maybe we can finally get our problems out in the open. I've always known Curt's feelings for Theo were never resolved. After Theo was put in prison, Curt just crumbled. That's when we first really talked. He knew I liked him when we were in college, so he purposefully kept our relationship light. But later, he needed a confidant—especially after graduation when we all scattered to the four winds. He followed me to Chicago. And then we got married. Maybe that was a mistake, I don't know anymore. It's what I wanted. I thought it was what he wanted too."

"Does Curt think he's gay?" Cordelia had often wanted to ask the question, but she and Annie had rarely talked this intimately in the years since college.

She shook her head. "Curt considers himself bisexual. We've never had any sexual problems, if that's what you mean. For him, it's more the person than it is the gender."

Cordelia nodded. It was what she had suspected. "Didn't Theo spend some time in Chicago right after he got out of prison?"

"Yes, though we didn't see him very much. And then

one day he was just gone."

Cordelia had always wondered why he'd left so abruptly. To be honest, she'd never really understood why he'd gone to Chicago in the first place. Her gut feeling told her it had to do with Curt, though she could be wrong. "Well, I'm sure Theo and Curt will have ample time to talk while we're waiting for the other shoe to drop."

"I know what you mean. That's exactly how it feels. Everyone's so jumpy."

"Maybe I'm a coward, but I'm not looking forward to Tuesday's little meeting."

"I'm not looking forward to any of this."

Cordelia knew the subject had once again returned to Curt and Theo.

"I'll just say one thing," said Annie, pushing her mug away. "If Theo hurts Curt any more than he already has, this time, he'll have me to answer to."

It was obvious Annie's emotions were stretched as taut as a drum. Even though her voice was calm, Cordelia could read the tension in her eyes. And it worried her.

7

Diana stood in the bathroom and splashed water into her face. Mornings were always a shock. An entire bottle of aspirin couldn't help this hangover. Maybe a sledge hammer—right between the eyes. Or an entirely new head. She looked up, catching sight of herself in the mirror. "Oh crap," she scowled, seeing the damage much more clearly than any camera. It had been quite a party last night. Terrific to see her friends again—the four she could still call friends. But it was hell to watch them watching her. She hadn't counted on that. She felt like a zoo animal. Damn that Orson! He had no right! Maybe she did drink too much, but so what? Her life was completely fucked. It was the only thing that helped.

"Make-up," she called, turning around too quickly and losing her balance. "Oops." She caught herself on the edge of the sink. God, she felt awful. She was still dizzy. That was often the worst part. What she really needed was another drink. Walking very carefully back into her bedroom, she opened her lingerie drawer and felt around for the bottle. Her heart sank when she realized it was empty. She should have remembered to grab a fresh one from the liquor cabinet before coming up to bed last night. Not that she actually knew *how* she'd gotten upstairs. She didn't remember a lot of things these days.

In a depressed funk, she slid to the floor in front of her closet and began to cry. What was the use? Everything she touched turned to ashes.

Everything except...Jill. Her lover. Her companion. Her lifeline. They'd been happy for so many years, making plans for the future. Not that life together had been perfect, but it was good. But then—.

Diana pulled her legs up close to her body and began to rock. It wasn't fair. The one part of her life that made sense—God should have looked out for Jill. The doctors should have been able to prevent her death. But then, everyone knew you couldn't prevent a New York truck driver's stupidity.

Her head fell back against the wall. And now, what the hell was she supposed to do with a fourteen-year-old? She knew nothing about kids. School would be starting in a matter of days. Army fatigues and ripped tank tops wouldn't go over well in Summer Green. It was too much. She couldn't deal with any more right now. "Jill, what do I do?" she whispered, covering her face with her hands.

Jill's death had been the worst. Nothing could even touch the pain. But, crazy as it sounded, what happened the morning of the funeral was almost as bad. Since that day, nothing had been the same. Looking up, Diana saw the picture she'd attached to the inside of her closet door. It was stapled about three feet off the floor. A photo of her nemesis, minus two small body parts which no one would miss. The button she'd affixed to the chest was nothing short of genius. Cordelia had mailed several of these buttons to her after Diana had made a hefty contribution to the Minnesota Abortion Rights Council. No, it was the perfect touch. Just the right statement. Why didn't anyone ever get the parallel?

She stared at the photo, her eyes starting to burn. "Notice the rat-like expression," she said out loud, as if to a crowd of onlookers. She swept her hand to the picture. "The sly, pinched smile. The oily condescension of someone who always knows best." No doubt about it, this rodent had never been a friend, though the disguise had been masterful. The name Judas came to mind.

Her eyes fell to a kitchen knife just inside the door. A moldy chunk of cheese and a box of crackers rested next to it. Must have been a late night snack. She couldn't remember when. Picking up the knife, she felt its weight, running her hand appreciatively along the razor sharp edge. Suddenly, in one lightning swift movement, Diana slammed the blade into the picture. The knife sank deep into the door.

"Have a nice day," she whispered, easing herself into a standing position. "You never know when it's going to be your last."

8

After lunch, Curt decided to check out the graveyard in back of the parsonage. He'd spent the morning walking south along the highway. He hadn't run into much, except a couple of farms and three friendly horses. Everything was so lush and green, yet the air felt heavy with a kind of end-of-summer sadness. Even though autumn didn't officially arrive for almost a month, it wouldn't be long before the fields were covered in snow. Curt hated winter. Hated the cold and the damp and the bitter winds. Yet the root of his melancholy had nothing to do with the seasons. He simply couldn't stay around the house today, trying to ignore Diana's drinking. She'd started early. If she didn't get a grip, tonight's performance would be a disaster. Orson had taken her aside and tried to talk to her about it. He wished him luck. The others all seemed to have so much to catch up on. Curt just felt tired. All he wanted was silence.

He knew Annie was upset with him. She'd tried to get him to open up last night before turning in, but he couldn't. She wanted to know if it was hard to be around Theo again. What could he say when he didn't know himself. One thing he did know: Theo had taken on the force of a symbol in his life. Curt's reaction to him was completely out of proportion to what had actually happened. He'd become a symbol of a kind of confused longing. But hadn't Curt always sensed an emptiness inside himself—even before he'd met Theo? He crouched next to a gravestone and looked around. Sometimes he felt like an archaeologist attempting to dig up a lost life. His own. Annie could never understand that. She wanted him to live in the present because that's where she was. She didn't understand limbo. She didn't even believe it existed.

He squeezed his eyes shut, trying to focus. His mind was slippery today. He couldn't hold it still. Getting up, he began to run. The cool wind felt good against his face. His senses took over, the exertion making his body feel strong. He stretched his arms high over his head and tried to relax. The graveyard was bigger than he'd first thought. As he came to a massive elm, he put out his hand and leaned against it, catching his breath. The tree was old, its leaves already yellow. Not because of the season. It was dying. Close to its enormous roots was a row of headstones, all from the late 1800s. Curt moved toward them, fascinated by how the years had erased the names and images. He bent down and touched the surface of the first. The date was unreadable. Glancing to his right, he jumped at the sight of a hand lying motionless in the grass. It was holding a can of cola. Curt shot to his feet, nearly losing his balance. "Christ! You nearly scared me to death."

Theo's eyes were open and he was staring up at the cloudless summer sky. "Thought I'd get the lay of the land. See the real *coffin's* eye view." He propped himself up against a gravestone. "You out for a run?"

"Yeah."

"It's too nice to stay inside." Theo paused, chewing on a blade of grass. "So, why don't you pull up a rock and have a seat."

"I don't know. I'm feeling kind of anti-social today."

"Oh, come on." When Curt continued to hesitate, Theo added, "I'd like to talk to you."

It seemed a reasonable enough request. Not that they'd made any attempt to talk so far during the visit. They just threw words at each other. He moved around a carved pillar and sat down, keeping a good distance between them. "All right. What's up?"

Theo scratched his beard. He took a sip of cola.

Curt could tell he was nervous. That was interesting.

"Annie looks great."

"Yeah. I agree."

"You two still pretty happy there in Chicago?" Theo's eyes rose to the sky.

"Get to your point."

"No point. Just curious."

"We have our ups and downs. Just like everyone else. How about you? You like it in Florida?"

"I'm living in Texas right now."

"Really? I didn't know. Why the move?"

"Oh, the climate I suppose. Among other things."

"You always have reasons, Theo. You just don't share them."

Theo's gaze dropped to the horizon. "You sound angry."

"I don't know what I am. Maybe you're right. I mean, Jesus, I don't even understand why you went to prison. You never answered my letters. You won't give anyone your phone number so I can't call. If you really want to talk, maybe that's a good place to start."

He shook his head. "Why get into all that now."

Curt just stared at him. Why did he think this conversation would be any different? "Right. Sorry. I just thought that since we loved each other once, I deserved more than your standard brush off. But I was wrong. Forget it."

Theo looked down. He was quiet for a long time. Finally, he said, "We wouldn't have stayed together. It never would have worked."

"Why?" Curt felt his stomach lurch.

"I wasn't ready to settle down back then. I'm not sure I'll ever be ready."

Curt laughed out loud. "A word of advice, Theo. Get some new lines. You're starting to sound like one of Diana's soap operas."

"You never saw yourself the way I did. You were such a lost kid back then. Your mom and dad were the original ice king and queen. You deserved more—from them *and* from me. But I couldn't give you what you wanted. I still can't."

Curt was suddenly furious. "That piece of psychobabble is supposed to explain my life? What happened to *us?*"

Theo's face grew very sad.

"It's not enough. Where have you been, Theo? Why did you leave Chicago so abruptly—you never even said good-bye!"

"You didn't need me. You had Annie. Besides, you needed a clear shot. I was only in your way."

"A clear shot at what?"

"Happiness."

Curt snorted. He got up and began to pace. "I know you've always prided yourself on what a great actor you are, but I can tell when you're lying, Theo. And you're lying now. Why?" He stopped, waiting for an answer.

"I'm not lying about us. You wanted a life like Ozzie and Harriet. I couldn't give you that."

"That's a crock of shit."

71

"Is it? You wanted a stable relationship. Someone to come home to. Someone who would listen to you and love you, eat dinner with you and soothe your world-weary soul. I couldn't be that person."

"Why not?"

"Because it's not what *I* wanted." He took a deep breath, giving himself a moment to regroup. "Curt, listen to me. If what you need to be happy is another man, then go find him. It may take some time, but Annie will understand. Some things work and some things don't. She knows that. She's a realist."

And she hates your guts, thought Curt, though he had the sense not to say it.

"Trust me, there are plenty of guys who want to nest, build a home, live monogamously. I just don't happen to be one of them."

Curt was silent. This conversation felt like shadow boxing. Nothing of substance. Theo kept talking in circles, never really answering a direct question. But he couldn't hide forever. Curt had seen the way he'd looked at him the night they arrived. Theo had thought he was being cool, standing in the shadows while everyone's attention was elsewhere. Curt was talking to Diana, waiting for Annie to come up from the car. He was wearing his mirrored sunglasses so Theo couldn't see his eyes. But Curt could see Theo's. The pain in them was undeniable. And the longing. It was all there. The love. The passion. The sadness. It wasn't as simple as he was suggesting.

"What's wrong?" asked Theo. "What are you thinking?"

Curt shrugged.

"Damn it Curt, what did you expect from this reunion? Did you think we'd get back together?"

He couldn't believe his ears. What arrogance. "No, Theo. I'm not a kid any longer. I refuse to let you make

72

this sound like we're back in college. You're the captain of the football team and I'm some pimply-faced ex-lover who can't let go. Don't flatter yourself. I expect nothing from you."

"Yes you do!"

"Go to hell!"

Theo reached out his hand, but Curt backed up.

"I don't need you to fulfill my life, Theo. But I do need to understand what happened so my life can go *on*. Is that so incomprehensible? Do you even understand what I'm saying?"

Theo slammed his fist on the ground. "You're missing my point!"

"Am I?"

"What do you want from me, Curt?"

"The truth."

He looked away. After a moment he said very softly, "I don't love you. I did once, but not now."

Curt stood very still. "I don't believe you."

"What?"

"I said, *I don't believe you*." He shoved his hands deep into his pockets and waited.

Theo was stunned. But he recovered quickly. With a slightly crumpled smile he said, "It would be easier if you did."

"Easier for whom? You?" Brushing the grass off his jeans, Curt started back toward the parsonage.

"Wait," said Theo, grabbing his hand as he walked past.

Curt shook it off. "You've said what you wanted to say."

"But you haven't."

"What's the difference? You're not interested."

"Don't be angry with me, Curt. I know I've hurt you."

73

As Curt stared down at him, he was overwhelmed by a feeling of disgust. He had to get away. Striding toward the parsonage, he heard Theo call, "Look at your life, man. You may already have what you need. You just can't see it because I'm in the way."

Curt ignored the words, breaking into a dead run.

9

Cordelia stood in front of the full-length mirror in her room, zipping up the formal gown she'd brought for the opening performance of the new Summer Green Playhouse, now just two hours away. She knew she was overdressing but didn't care. Any old chance to wear something gorgeous was a chance taken. She'd considered bringing along her tux but had been in a flowing mauve and silver beaded-silk mood when she'd packed. So, alas, that was to be tonight's costume. Not that she was unhappy with the way she looked. She might be large, but she was still a knockout.

Outside her door she heard the sound of footsteps. Then a hard rap. "It's open," she called as she adjusted her earrings. After a second, another knock.

"Just a minute," she said impatiently, as she scurried around the bed. Flinging open the door, she beheld the same tall gray-haired woman she had seen earlier in the day cutting the grass. Tonight, she'd shed her overalls for a rather baggy cotton dress. Pink and blue flowers on a cream background. Cordelia approved of the look. Sort of a 1950s grandmother. The woman had very sharp features and an expression like a chicken hawk. Her shoulders were square and quite strong for a woman of her advanced years. "Yes?" said Cordelia, her hands rising to her hips.

"Ms. Stanwood wanted me to tell all her guests that she's over at the playhouse and won't be seeing any of you until after the show. She asked me to prepare a light supper. Just some cold chicken, potato salad, homemade biscuits and a radish tray. It's downstairs in the dining room. I've laid everything on the sideboard so you can help yourself." She said the words as if they were a prepared speech.

Cordelia nodded. "That's kind of you."

"Kindness has nothing to do with it. It's my job."

"I see. Well, thanks anyway."

"Just leave your dishes on the dining room table. I'll get them later."

"Fine." She waited. The woman didn't move. Instead, she seemed to be trying to get a better look inside the room. Blatant nosiness! Cordelia was intrigued. "Is there something else?"

"No. Just looking. It's a free country last I heard."

"Would you like to examine my suitcases? I could show you photos of my cats."

"What are you implying?"

"Why nothing." She glanced down the hall. All the other doors were closed. Everyone else was, no doubt, busily getting ready. Her gaze returned to the woman. "I don't believe we've been formally introduced. My name is Cordelia Thorn."

"I know."

"I don't doubt it."

"Hey!"

"And *you* are?" Cordelia's tones had become entirely too rounded.

"Hilda Barnes." She stuck out her hand.

Cordelia shook it limply. "I enjoyed your blueberry muffins this morning."

"Yeah. I'm a good cook. Some people are artists, and some aren't." She eyed Cordelia's dress.

"I beg your pardon?" Her eyebrow arched slowly upward as she straightened her plunging neckline. Was this criticism from the same woman who had planted the entire front yard full of marigolds? Definitely Park Board taste. Cordelia sniffed. "Well, this has been delightful, but I have to finish dressing."

"You known Ms. Stanwood long?"

"Since college."

"All of you people staying here are old college friends?"

"Last I heard."

"Old friends are the best kind."

"I'm glad you think so."

"It's about time someone came to help."

"What do you mean?"

She tipped her head back and mimicked drinking from a glass. Then she winked.

Cordelia got the point. "Who told you we came to help?"

"I got eyes. Ms. Stanwood's all right by me. I know she's a little weird. Got some unusual... inclinations, if you know what I mean. But then she's artistic. I understand the artistic nature. I got one myself." She lowered her voice. "Don't let that bearded man ruin things."

"Excuse me?"

"I clean Ms. Stanwood's room. I'm not blind."

"To what?"

A door opened and Orson's head popped out. He whistled when he saw what Cordelia was wearing.

Hilda moved quickly down the hall. "Mr. Albern, Ms. Stanwood wanted me to tell all her guests that she's over at the playhouse and won't be seeing any of you until after the show. She asked me to prepare a light supper. Just some cold chicken, potato salad, homemade biscuits—"

When Hilda got to the part about the radish tray, Cordelia could see Orson flinch, but, stalwart man that he was, his attention remained rapt. Strange woman, thought Cordelia. What the hell had she been talking about?

10

As the final curtain came down on the first performance of *Blithe Spirit,* Cordelia found herself leaping to her feet with the rest of the crowd. The performance had been nothing short of brilliant. Diana's comic timing was impeccable, and the rest of the cast had risen to the occasion. Even Diana's periodic slurred words only added to the hilarity. If the audience had only known the truth, they might not have laughed so easily.

Diana had broken her word to Orson. She hadn't stopped drinking after lunch. But even so, she'd made it through the performance and, to her, that was probably all that mattered. The reviews—from as far away as New York and L.A.—would be fabulous. She would receive national attention because she was a national celebrity. She had a hit on her hands and was riding a career high. Her own playhouse. The star. Even though it was a small production, her name gave it clout. No, this would be a night to celebrate. Cordelia glanced at Orson who had been seated in the pew next to her. As their eyes met, she knew he was thinking the same thing. How dreadful was the party going to be which Diana had planned for later?

Right now, it was time to go backstage and hope the

congratulations wouldn't be fueled by too much champagne. Cordelia spotted a *Minneapolis Star Tribune* reporter near the rear exit and gave her a wave. Theo was already making his way to the stage door. And Curt and Annie had resumed their seats, waiting for the crowd to clear. As Cordelia turned to watch the audience make its noisy exit, she gazed up at the stained glass windows above the front entrance, silently saying a prayer. Tuesday was a long way off. A lot of things could happen before the intervention. If they ever needed some cosmic help, it was now.

"Where are we?" asked Cordelia, as Theo pulled his Acura into a dirt parking lot and stopped. Orson was in the back seat, stuffing his pipe with tobacco.

"This is Al's Roadhouse."

"Figures." Cordelia gazed out the window at a reasonably attractive wood-framed building. At least it looked clean. Other cars had already arrived. From what Diana had said, she'd rented the place for the night. Everything was on her. "Probably the hottest spot in the entire county."

"Actually, I think it is," said Orson.

"We're about three miles from the playhouse," Theo added, turning off the motor. "Diana tells me she comes here often."

Orson opened the rear door and got out. He lit the pipe and then stood leaning against the fender, looking up at the stars.

"Let's get inside before the mosquitos smell blood," said Cordelia, poking him in the stomach.

They waited for Theo to lock the doors and then, arm in arm, they climbed the steps to the entrance. They were comrades, bound together by a shared history and now a common goal. Cordelia felt contented in their presence, momentarily overcome by a feeling of gratitude. The second she stepped inside the roadhouse, her thoughts returned to earth. Cigarette smoke enfolded them in an acrid haze. She spotted Diana sitting at a table in the back talking to Annie and Curt.

"You want a pitcher of beer?" asked Theo.

Cordelia lowered her eyes and gave him her best *you've got to be kidding* stare.

"Right. One pitcher of cherry Coke coming right up."

"I'll help you with the glasses," said Orson, following him to the bar.

Cordelia weaved through the crowd, extending congratulations here and there. As she got to the table, she saw that Diana's eyes weren't particularly focused. Her head was propped on one hand, a cigarette dangling from the other.

"I thought you gave up Virginia Slims," said Cordelia, pulling up a chair and sitting down.

"I've come a long way, baby—but not that far," snorted Diana. "And don't be such a party pooper. Have a drink and relax." She blew smoke out of the corner of her mouth.

With a valiant effort, Cordelia did not roll her eyes.

The champagne at the playhouse had taken its toll. Diana was already pretty high. She was sipping now from a glass in front of her. It looked like pure vodka.

Like everyone else, Cordelia knew tonight was going to be a big blowout, and she wasn't looking forward to it. Still, it was better to keep a close eye on Diana than let her trip over a cow and fall down a ravine. At least until the intervention. After that, the ball was in her court.

"Did you see the article in the Chicago paper about us?" asked Curt. He fidgeted with a napkin.

Cordelia's head popped up. "About *us?*"

"I have a friend who works for the *Sun Times*,"

explained Diana. "I gave him the information about the opening tonight, and I also told him about my five best friends from college who were coming for the weekend. He thought it made a great story, so he printed it."

"All our names and occupations," muttered Curt, his expression growing sour. "There are a bunch of copies back at the parsonage if you want one for your personal scrapbook." He glanced over at Theo who appeared to be talking intimately with a handsome young man at the far end of the bar. Curt's face sank even deeper into a funk.

"It was the least I could do," said Diana, entirely missing the dejection in his voice. Curt's *occupation* had always been a sore point. "I'm so proud of you all."

"I'm amazed by what your architect friend did with the stage," said Annie, attempting to change the subject. "I like the idea of making it a modified thrust. The audience feels more a part of the action."

"Yeah," agreed Diana, "Donald's a magician." She giggled into her glass. "I sort of *groove* on the idea—how's that for a good seventies word?—that I'm performing in a church. The stage is the altar. And I, dear children, am the sacrificial lamb." She saluted the air and downed the vodka in one gulp.

"Is there some cosmic meaning to that, Diana?" asked Cordelia. She eyed Curt who was still looking at Theo. His expression had turned angry.

"Why, don't you know? My life has become a sacrifice on the altar of human progress. The good of the group at the expense of the individual. Thanks to Theo, my life now has greater meaning. The world is a better place, the air sweeter. Only problem is, my career's in the toilet. But then, who needs to eat when the fucking group needs *spiritual* sustenance."

"Don't be so cryptic," growled Curt.

"Why honey, that's no way to talk to a role model. I'm

82

deeply...wounded." She flapped her eyelashes seductively.

"You've been acting cool to Theo ever since we got here," he continued. "Maybe you better explain yourself so we can all understand."

Suddenly, the sound of breaking glass drew everyone's attention to the front. Through the smokey haze, Cordelia could see Orson and Theo shoving each other. The pitcher of Coke next to them had shattered. Liquid was pouring over the side of the counter, spilling onto the stools.

The room became silent as the crowd tried to hear their words.

"You're making some awfully quick assumptions," said Orson. He was inches from Theo's face. "If I were you, I'd back off."

"God, you're full of hot air," snapped Theo. "You haven't changed a bit."

"And you're still a fool. I never should have listened to you."

"You owe me, you overweight weasel. You owe me big!"

Orson lunged at him. "Who owes who is a matter of definition!"

Theo pushed him away, knocking the pipe out of his hand. "Still Mr. Erudite. Always in control. Well, I happen to have principles too, and unlike you, I'm not afraid to fight for what I believe."

"That's your trouble. You don't know when to *stop* fighting!"

Theo took a swing at him, left hand to the stomach, right to the jaw. He was an experienced brawler. Orson folded like a paper doll. He crashed back against the bar and slid to the floor.

In an instant, Curt, Annie and Cordelia were all on their feet, shouting for the two of them to stop. But before they could reach the front, a burly, middle-aged man stepped out of the crowd and grabbed Theo by the arm, twisting it roughly behind his back. "Just calm down," he ordered.

Theo winced with pain.

"Orson? You all right?" asked the man.

Orson felt a lump on the side of his jaw. After examining the inside of his mouth with his tongue, he took the hand being offered him and got up. "I think I'll live."

The man let Theo go. "You wanna press charges?"

Theo rubbed his knuckles. "Yeah. I do."

"Not you," said the man. He glanced at Orson. "Say the word and this guy spends the night on us."

Orson's smile was smug. "I'd like you all to meet Matt Hesslund. Our local sheriff. He also happens to be an old friend."

Theo grunted. "Lucky me." He began brushing off his tux.

"Of course he doesn't want to press charges," said Diana, lurching to a stop in front of the bar. She held the empty glass in her hand. "There's been a mistake. Just go away now. Let us handle it."

"I think there has been a mistake," said Orson, his voice thick with anger. "And Theo's the one who made it." He turned to the sheriff. "Matt, after deep reflection, I think I'll take you up on your offer. This man assaulted me." Turning to Theo, he added, "Do you get the point *now?*"

Theo looked from face to face, but said nothing.

Diana yanked Orson's arm. "Just stop it, will you? This is a party. We're all supposed to be having a good time!"

"It's all right," said Theo, straightening his tie. He was attempting to regain some of his damaged dignity. "I'm no stranger to jail. Besides, I'll be out in a flash."

"Don't count on it," said Orson.

As the sheriff handcuffed him and then led him through the crowd and out the front door, Cordelia sank down into a chair. The smoke that circled her head felt like a toxic cloud. This reunion was getting worse by the minute. She wondered, with a growing sense of dread, just what else could go wrong.

11

"Me again."

Jane let out a deep groan.

"Here with your nightly update." Cordelia held the phone in one hand, a cold chicken leg in the other.

"This is a plot, right? You're trying to deprive me of sleep so you can get me to admit to a crime."

"A minor change in your will would suffice."

As soon as Theo had been carted off by the police, the party began to disintegrate. A simple brawl wouldn't faze a big city crowd, but in Summer Green, the locals quickly said their goodbyes and drove off into the cricket-infested night. After another hour, Diana had to admit the obvious. The party was over.

Once back at the parsonage, everyone had gone directly up to bed. No one wanted to dissect the evening over a nightcap. Not even Diana.

"Do you know what time it is?" asked Jane.

"No, dearheart, but I'm sure you're going to tell me."

"You know, Cordelia. My aunt doesn't even ask anymore when the doorbell or the phone rings in the middle of the night. She *knows* who it is."

"I'm glad I can bring some constancy—one might

even call it a sense of ritual—into your days, Janey. It helps give life meaning." Cordelia could hear Jane's bed squeaking.

"Where are you?"

"Sitting on the front porch with the cordless phone. Do you want to know what I'm wearing?"

"I want to be allowed to sleep!"

Cordelia put her feet up on a wicker footstool. "I don't know how you can sleep when I'm so upset."

A small shriek.

"You'll never guess what happened tonight." When Jane didn't respond immediately, Cordelia sat up very straight. "Well, don't you have any curiosity?"

"Of course, Cordelia. Tell me, what happened tonight?"

Cordelia knew she was being *handled*. She didn't care. "Orson and Theo got into a fight at a local bar. It was at the party after the performance."

"And?"

"Orson had Theo arrested."

"Seriously?"

"He's in the slammer even as we speak."

"That's awful."

"Damn straight."

"What was the fight about?"

"No idea. I heard one of them say something about principles. They argued briefly over who owed the other. But on the way home, Orson wouldn't say a word."

"Do you think it has anything to do with that business last night? The bald guy? Theo asking Orson for money?"

Cordelia had wondered the same thing. "Maybe."

"So what's going to happen to the intervention? If Theo's in jail, will that change things?"

"I don't know." Cordelia took a bite of the chicken leg and chewed thoughtfully. "Diana is furious. She can't believe Orson would try to ruin the reunion over something so petty."

"I doubt it's a plot. Besides, maybe it isn't petty."

"God, I wish I knew more."

"I wish you did too. What's on the agenda for tomorrow?"

"Just a day to relax, I guess. Diana's planned a Labor Day picnic for Monday."

"Cordelia?"

"Hum?"

"What are you eating?"

"A chicken leg."

"Do you think I could go back to bed now?"

"I suppose."

"Goodnight, Cordelia."

"Goodnight, Jane."

"Oh, and one more thing?"

"Yes?"

"Let me sleep tomorrow night. Please!"

12

Early Sunday morning, Diana phoned her lawyer in Green Bay and demanded that she find a way to get Theo released from jail. Orson remained adamant. He wouldn't say what the argument had been about, and he refused to drop the assault charges. He seemed perfectly happy to see Theo cool his heels behind bars for a few days. To eliminate any further conversation on the matter, he'd driven into town after lunch.

By four in the afternoon, Diana was fuming. Cordelia found her pacing the floor in the kitchen, waiting for a phone call. Curt was having a cup of coffee, keeping her company. No one had seen Diana take a drink all day. Her attention was completely focused on freeing Theo.

"Any word yet?" asked Cordelia, scrambling to get out of Diana's path—more like her war path. She sat down next to Curt.

"Nothing. I thought we'd hear something before this."

Without being asked, Curt poured Cordelia some coffee and pushed the mug toward her. His eyes warned her it might be a long wait.

"I just can't understand why Orson is being so

hardheaded," continued Diana. "It's not like him. He won't listen to reason." She stopped and glared at Curt, then at Cordelia. When they said nothing, she turned around and kicked the refrigerator. "You two act like you agree with him!"

Cordelia could see what was happening. Diana needed a punching bag for her growing frustrations. Since the refrigerator didn't exactly work, and Orson was nowhere to be found, Curt and Cordelia were elected. Cordelia had seen her do this many times. She found it childish. But before she could say anything, the phone interrupted them.

Diana leapt to the counter. "Yes," she said, her voice almost breathless as she held the receiver to her ear. "Oh. Annie." She slumped onto a stool. "Right. I'm glad you called. How's it going? Did you find some decent school clothes for Amity?" She tapped her nails on the table and looked out the window. "Well, tell the kid she can't wear that sort of thing here. This isn't New York." A pause. "Then find her size, buy it and we'll discuss it later. Right. Thanks again. I just couldn't deal with shopping today. I'll see you when you get back. Oh, and tell Amity somebody named Chickie called. Right. See you tonight. Bye." She got up and dropped the receiver back on the hook.

"I take it Annie took Amity to buy some new school clothes," said Cordelia.

Diana grabbed her hair, pretending to pull it out by the roots. "What am I supposed to do with a teenager? She's used to Manhattan. How the hell is she going to deal with the Radish Hill Mall?"

And what was she going to do while Diana was in treatment, thought Cordelia? Another complication. One that would have to be worked out in a way that didn't make Amity feel like a yo-yo. "Amity said she wasn't getting along with her grandparents."

Diana sighed. "She ran away. After Jill died, her

90

grandmother insisted Amity come to live with them in Montana. It's what Jill would have wanted. You know me. I've never been much of a kid person, but even I could see that taking her away from the only home she'd ever known was a bad move. We got along okay. She was really close to Jill. I thought about fighting it in court, but my life was crumbling in New York, and I had no idea where I'd end up. So, I just let her go. We wrote. Talked on the phone. She came out to see me here during spring vacation. Stayed for a week. I knew she was unhappy— she hates Billings—but I thought she was going to stick it out. Last Thursday, she simply appeared. I came back from rehearsals, and she was sitting on the couch. One suitcase. Hardly a dime left in her pocket. I called her grandmother right away so she wouldn't worry, and do you know what that old bat had the gall to say? *Good riddance!* She washed her hands of her. So, I guess I'm back in the kid business. Unfortunately, this time, it's without Jill. I don't know what the hell I'm going to do." She began pacing again.

"Where's her father?" asked Curt.

"The original deadass dad."

"Don't you mean dead*beat*?"

"That too. He runs a greenhouse out of his basement. Occasionally does some general contracting. But basically, he just screws around. Goes to a lot of movies. Doesn't make much money, or if he does, he's learned how to hide it. He hasn't wanted to see her since she was five. He doesn't like strong women. Five years old is about his limit."

Cordelia shook her head.

Again, the phone rang.

Diana jumped at it. "Yes," she said, her voice hopeful. She listened. "Great! When?" Another pause. "No problem. We'll be there to pick him up. Thanks. You're a lifesaver, Donna." She hung up and turned around. Her expression was intense, though distracted. Even more strange, she didn't look the least bit happy. But she did seem vindicated. "I knew we'd get him out."

"When will he be released?" asked Cordelia.

"Around six." She looked at her watch. "I've got to make one more phone call, and then we can all take a glass of lemonade, or whatever, and go sit out on the porch. I've hardly had time to talk to you two since yesterday. Too much going on." She dialed the number. Several seconds later she said, "Hello, Hilda? This is Diana. I need you to do me a favor. I know it's your day off, and this is kind of short notice, but I was wondering if you could pick up some food at the grocery store and cook us one of your fabulous dinners? You can! Wonderful! Let's see. How about your pan-fried Walleye with that lime butter sauce? I'll leave the rest to you. Great. See you in an hour." She hung up and turned around. This time, her smile lit up the room. "What do you say we go find those drinks?"

Diana sat at one end of the formal dining room table, Theo on her right, Cordelia on her left. At the other end sat Orson. Annie and Curt faced Amity. The conversation was subdued during the first course—a cold yoghurt and cucumber soup (which Cordelia thought contained entirely too many minced radishes)—but picked up slightly over the salad. Since no one was able to settle on a wine, Diana had scattered several bottles around the table. She knew, even with fish as the main course, Orson preferred Italian reds. Theo liked the sweeter German wines, so she'd given him his own bottle of Riesling. Cordelia and Curt sipped from their glasses of white Zinfandel. Only Annie refused the bottle of California Chardonnay set in front of her. Cordelia could tell she didn't have the stomach for it tonight.

Thankfully, neither Orson nor Theo had made any mention of last night's fight. Perhaps they'd called a truce. Instead, the dinner conversation centered around the next production Diana was going to mount, once *Blithe Spirit*'s run was ended. She had several plays in mind, but hadn't yet decided.

"You know Diana," said Orson, giving Amity a confidential wink, "you built this playhouse just so you could get some decent parts."

Everyone laughed.

Everyone except Diana. Her voice defensive, she said, "You're right. There are some women I'd like to play."

"Like who?" asked Theo, pouring himself another glass of Riesling.

Diana laid down her fork and folded her hands over her plate. With her eyes fixed on Theo she said,

Naught's had, all's spent,
Where our desire is got without content:
'Tis safer to be that which we destroy,
Than, by destruction, dwell in doubtful joy.

She held his eyes for a long moment and then resumed eating her salad.

"Lady Macbeth," said Cordelia, intrigued by the brief performance.

Theo seemed shaken by Diana's choice of quotes. He downed his glass of wine and then poured another.

"Kind of morbid," said Amity, playing with a tomato slice.

Curt smiled. "Yeah, and besides, it's bad luck."

"What do you mean?" she asked.

"To actors," replied Orson, wiping his mouth with a

napkin, "even the mention of the name Macbeth is considered very bad luck. It goes way back. I'm not even sure of the origin."

"Haven't a lot of people died while acting in the play?" asked Annie.

Theo put his hand on his chest and coughed several times.

"You okay?" asked Curt.

"Fine. Just fine."

"I don't know," said Orson, considering the question. "That could be."

"What's wrong?" asked Cordelia. She saw a frightened look pass over Theo's face. He seemed to be having trouble breathing.

Diana patted him on the back.

"God," said Theo, doubling up in pain. He started to gasp.

"What is it?" demanded Diana.

Theo slipped off his chair and fell to the floor.

"Help him, somebody!" cried Annie.

Orson got up and knelt down next to him. "Are you choking?" he asked.

Curt's face had gone white. "Do something!"

"Try the Heimlich maneuver," blurted Cordelia.

Theo shook his head.

"I'll call 911," said Orson. He jumped up and raced out of the room.

"Give him some air," called Cordelia. In a flash she was by his side. His breathing was rapid and shallow. His color still looked normal. Perhaps a good sign.

As if in a trance, Diana inched to the liquor cabinet and removed a bottle of vodka.

Indignantly, Annie grabbed it out of her hand. "Not now! For god's sake, get a hold of yourself."

"They'll be here any minute," said Orson, returning to

the room. "How is he?" He rushed to Theo's side.

Theo's eyes were shut. His body seemed to have relaxed. Cordelia bent down close and listened. "Theo, can you hear me?" she asked. Looking up she said, "He's still breathing, but I think he may be unconscious."

Backing into the table, Amity knocked over Theo's wine glass. "Sorry," she said, her eyes pleading for forgiveness.

Annie put her arm around the girl. "It's all right."

Curt stood looking down at him, unable to move.

"I think he said something once about a heart condition," said Orson. "It was just a couple of days ago. He'd come over to the Blackburn Playhouse in Shoreview, and I'd asked him to help me lift an old trunk off the stage. I thought he was kidding—that he simply didn't want to get his clothes dirty."

"He was in Minnesota?" repeated Diana. "He never said anything to me about that."

Orson realized he'd put his foot in it. He had to cover. "Yeah. He stopped on his way here."

"Here's the ambulance!" cried Curt, nodding to the window. He bolted into the hall to open the front door.

Cordelia got to her feet and waited for the two men to make their entrance. They carried a stretcher, two boxes resting on top of it.

"Hello Orson," said one of the men. He was dressed in a shirt and tie. The other man had on bib overalls. They were obviously volunteers.

Orson nodded. "Ted."

The man named Ted asked everyone to get back. He immediately checked Theo to see if he was breathing. He was. He popped his jaw forward to make sure there was a good airway. Next he felt for a pulse. "Slow and irregular," he said to the man in overalls, the one who looked like a farmer. He then checked his eyes with a small stick

95

of light. "Reactive. Good. Let's get him on oxygen."

Cordelia watched the men work. They seemed to know what they were doing. Hilda slipped into the room just as they lifted Theo onto the stretcher. She stood flush against the wall, her chicken-hawk eyes missing nothing.

After they covered Theo with a blanket, Ted walked over to Orson. "He's stable. What happened?"

Orson explained that they were having dinner when Theo clutched his chest and fell to the floor.

"Any history of heart problems?"

"I'm not sure. We haven't seen him recently. He did say something jokingly a few days ago, but I thought he was just trying to get out of doing some work."

"Is he on any medication?"

Orson looked around the room. "Not that I'm aware of."

"Any history of drug abuse?"

He shook his head.

"What about allergies?"

"Sulfa drugs," said Curt, his voice wooden.

"Anything else?"

No one responded.

"His blood pressure's low," called the other man.

"We've got to get him to a hospital right away. I need a phone," said Ted.

"Right down the hall," replied Diana, weaving to the door and pointing.

"Thanks." He left the room.

"Is he going to be all right?" asked Cordelia. She stood next to the stretcher now, holding Theo's limp hand.

"He's stabilized," said the farmer. "That's all I can say. We'll take him over to the hospital in Binghamton. Summer Green's only got a clinic. He needs an emergency room."

Ted returned to the room. "I got space in the cab for

one rider. You want to come along, Orson?"

Orson seemed to hesitate. "All right. Sure." He turned to the others. "I'll call you as soon as I get any news."

"But—" Annie clearly wanted to come too.

"Really, there's nothing you can do right now," said Ted, quickly folding his stethoscope into a small bundle. He glanced at the wine bottles littering the table. "Besides, I don't want any other emergencies tonight if I can help it."

They all got the point.

As Theo was wheeled out, Diana grabbed the bottle of vodka back from Annie. "This is my house and I'll do what I damn well please."

Cordelia could see a look of shock mixed with disgust pass over Annie's face. "Just terrific. One of your best friends is on his way to the hospital, and all you can think to do is drink yourself into a stupor."

"You don't understand *anything*."

"No? I understand more than you think."

Diana narrowed her eyes. "What do you mean by that?"

"Put that bottle of vodka away and I'll tell you."

She seemed to consider the request. She knew everyone was watching. "Screw it," she said finally. "I'm not interested in any of your moral superiority."

Annie stared at her for a moment and then tossed her napkin on the table and stomped out.

"Bye Annie," said Amity to her retreating back. The words were mumbled.

Cordelia felt terribly sorry for the kid.

"Hilda," continued Diana, her voice taking on an imperial quality, "you can clear the table. We're done." She swept the room with her eyes. "I'm going up to my room. Please call me when you know anything more." Swaying slightly, she made a stab at a dignified exit.

13

Cordelia was the first to grab the phone in the front hall when it finally rang.

"He didn't make it," whispered Orson's voice. He was crying, almost choking. "I don't know what happened. He was doing fine. Even Ted said so."

Cordelia felt her mind disconnect from her body.

The others gathered around.

"We were on our way out of town when he seemed to have another attack. They did everything they could, but it didn't help. Ted called the local coroner, and he just got here. He pronounced Theo dead." Orson could hardly speak through his sobs. "God, what am I supposed to do?"

"It's all right," said Cordelia, trying to comfort him. Though she knew nothing was all right. "You did everything you could. Were you . . . with him when it happened?"

"Yeah." His voice cracked.

"I'm sure he knew that."

"I don't know. He kept trying to say something. I have to believe it was important, but he never actually looked at me. I couldn't understand a word of it."

Cordelia looked up at her friends' faces. By their stunned expressions, she knew they understood.

Orson broke down again. Cordelia could hear him put his hand over the phone.

A few moments later he returned. "Are you still there?"

"Right here," said Cordelia.

"Arnie—the coroner—owns the funeral home in town. He said we could bring the body over there. What do you think? I can't make this decision all by myself!"

What the hell did Cordelia know about funeral homes? Very gently she said, "That's a good idea. Are you going to ride over in the ambulance?"

"I guess so. I'll have to talk to someone about the . . . arrangements. He doesn't have any family to speak of. Just a brother he hasn't seen in years."

Of course. There would have to be a funeral. A lot of decisions would have to be made.

"What happened?" said a thick voice from the stairway. Diana, looking like a crumpled bed and clutching the railing for dear life, eased herself down the steps to the first-floor landing. "Is that Orson?" Her head wobbled from side to side, and her pronunciation was too precise for normal speech.

"Yes," said Cordelia, holding her hand over the phone. She motioned for Annie and Curt to help. Diana could barely stand up.

"Is Theo all right?" she demanded.

"He's dead," said Cordelia. She knew her voice was cold, but she couldn't help herself. She was furious with Diana and her drinking, and she wasn't going to hide it.

"Dead," she whispered, as if examining the word for its exact meaning.

Cordelia resumed her conversation. "Listen Orson, we've got kind of a . . . situation here."

"You mean Diana?" he asked.

"Yes. I think Curt and I should stay here and help her up to bed. Give me the directions, and Annie can drive over and pick you up."

"Fine."

Cordelia found a pen and note pad next to the phone. She wrote as legibly as she could under the circumstances. Her hand was shaking. She knew the catastrophe hadn't sunk in yet. She'd never see Theo again. Never. It was too much. "I've got it," she said into the receiver. "Orson?"

"What?"

"Are you okay?"

Silence. "No. Are you?"

"No," she said softly. She was starting to cry. "I'll see you soon."

After hanging up, she took several deep breaths. Then, turning resolutely, she entered the parlor. Diana was propped up on the sofa, Annie and Curt on either side of her. Amity was in a chair all the way across the room. Her back was to them, but Cordelia could see she was staring out the front window. What a horrible time for her to arrive.

Diana held her head in her hands and was sobbing and babbling at the same time. Her words came out in fits and starts, none of it making much sense.

"Annie, Orson would like you to pick him up at the funeral home. I've got directions."

"Okay," she said, wiping the tears from her eyes.

Curt's eyes were dry. "I'll stay with Cordelia and make sure Diana gets up to bed. Are you all right to drive?"

"I'll be fine," said Annie. "Don't worry." She flicked her eyes to Amity, giving Cordelia a *what should we do?* look.

Cordelia shook her head.

As if sensing that the lull in the conversation had to do with her, Amity said, "I've seen her drunk lots of times." She didn't turn around; she merely sat in her chair and looked straight ahead. "Once in a while Mom and I would have to go get her from a restaurant or something. We'd take a cab. Only, it didn't happen so often back then. She's really . . . sick now."

Cordelia bit her lip. God, what she must have seen in her young life.

"But I did love him," said Diana, her voice projecting as if she were on stage. "You all know . . . that. I didn't . . . mean . . . he was a good . . . and I never meant—"

"Let's take her upstairs," said Cordelia, motioning for Curt to lift her up.

Annie stood with them, her eyes still on Amity. "Are you going to be all right while we're gone, Amity?" Her voice was kind.

"Fine. No problem."

Nobody was fine, thought Cordelia. But she couldn't handle any more right now. She grabbed Diana's other arm and helped Curt carry her out.

"Just put her on the bed," said Cordelia, looking around the messy room. Diana hadn't changed much since college. She still liked clothes.

"Do you think she's going to get cold?" asked Curt, trying to disentangle a sheet and pull it over her.

"Yeah, maybe. I'll see if there's a blanket." Cordelia kicked a pair of shoes out of her way as she moved across the room.

"God, she's really plastered," said Curt.

"I know. She didn't have time to drink that much. Her liver must not be processing well at all any more. That's a very scary sign." She moved to the closet and lifted down a quilt from the top shelf. Turning back to the bed, her calf brushed against something hard. She bent down to take a closer look and saw that a knife had been thrust through a Minnesotans for Choice button. Cordelia had sent it to Diana last spring. Behind it was a picture. "Holy shit," she muttered, her eyes opening wide as she realized it was an old college photo of Theo.

"Need some help?" asked Curt. He was closing a window Diana had left wide open.

"No," said Cordelia. "It's nothing." She felt bad for lying, but how could she tell him Diana had stuck a knife into Theo's chest—even if it was only pretend? After all, a picture wasn't a human being. But it was such an angry, violent thing to do. Almost as if she wanted to see him— "*Dead,*" she whispered.

14

"How are my cats?" sniffed Cordelia. She was sitting up in bed, a heavy quilt pulled over her head, a flashlight held in one hand, the cordless phone in the other. The house was dark and silent.

"I waited up for you tonight."

"Did you? What a dear human being."

"You're late."

"Am I?"

"And you sound strange."

"I have to be quiet."

"Why?"

"It's a long story." Again, she sniffed.

"Why don't you ever call Mugs at three A.M.? She's the love of your life. Destroy her sleep patterns for a change."

Cordelia felt warmed by the reference to her newest tootsie. Lately, she had begun to use the term *consort*. Not only did she like the word—with its smutty Elizabethan connotations—but she liked every modern definition. *A harmony of sounds. One ship traveling with another.* Cordelia had no difficulty seeing herself as a ship.

"So?" said Jane. "You've got thirty seconds. After that I'm hanging up and going to sleep."

"Fine. As long as you set an alarm."

"Why should I set an alarm?"

"You have to be down to the Greyhound depot by five. I've already called to check out the times. Your aunt Beryl can drive you. The bus leaves at five-fifteen. Gets in here around one. The picnic starts at three, so don't worry about missing a thing."

A long pause. "Cordelia... what are you talking about?"

"At first I thought you should just drive up, but I don't think that car of yours would make it past the city limits."

"I'm dreaming. This is just a bad dream."

"I suppose you could rent one, but if you take the bus, you can use my car while you're here. We can drive home together."

"Cordelia!"

"Shhhh!"

"Will you tell me why I should take a bus to Summer Green? If that's what you're actually suggesting."

Cordelia lowered her voice even further. "It's Theo. Janey, I don't even know where to begin." She grabbed a fresh Kleenex. "He's... dead."

"Dead!"

"Just listen. Tonight at dinner, he sort of clutched his chest. Before we knew what was happening, he'd fallen to the floor. I tried to get him to talk to me, but he couldn't. That's when Orson called 911. These two volunteer paramedics came and took him away in an ambulance. About half an hour later, Orson called and said he was dead. The first attack didn't kill him, but the second one did."

"This just happened tonight? Out of the blue?"

"Yes." She could feel the panic rising in her chest again. She had to stay calm. Get through this. "He was drinking some wine, eating his salad, and he just... keeled over. I guess he had a heart condition, though he never told anyone." She blew her nose. "Then again, he was so ridiculously private about his life, it doesn't surprise me."

"I'm really sorry, Cordelia."

"Thanks. The funeral will be Tuesday or Wednesday. The actual date hasn't been set yet."

"And . . . you want me to come?"

"I do. But not just for that."

"What about the intervention?"

"Orson is going to call the doctor in the morning. See what she thinks. We talked about it some when he and Annie got back from the funeral home tonight. I think we were all in agreement that it should be postponed until after the funeral."

"But why should *I* come?"

Again, Cordelia took a deep breath. "Janey, I'm not sure Theo's death was . . . natural."

A long silence. "You think Orson had something to do with it?"

"No—I don't know. It's too awful to contemplate. But see what you think. After the paramedics took Theo away, Diana went up to her room and proceeded to get totally plastered. When we got the news of Theo's death, she came down the stairs and started babbling and crying. Meanwhile, Annie drove over to the funeral home to pick Orson up while Curt and I stayed behind to help put Diana to bed. While I was getting a blanket out of her bedroom closet so she wouldn't freeze to death, I noticed a knife sticking out of the door. Jane, the knife had been thrust through a Choice button—"

"Abortion rights?"

"Yes, but behind it was an old college publicity photo of Theo. The knife went straight through his heart!"

Again, Jane was silent. After a long moment she said, "And you think this means Diana murdered him?"

"I don't know! I realize it's not proof of anything, but

what the hell was it doing there?"

"Good point."

"It got me to thinking. I decided to go downstairs. You know how my mind works. I started wondering if someone had put something into Theo's food—or his wine."

"Who had access to it?"

"Any one of us, really."

"You know, Cordelia, there are poisons that react in the body like a heart attack. I was just reading something about that recently."

"For your next cookbook?"

"Don't be snide."

"Anyway, I waited until no one else was around and then I ducked into the kitchen. Hilda—she's Diana's part-time cook and bottle washer—was still doing dishes. I asked her for the bottle of Riesling—that's what Theo was drinking tonight, and I hasten to point out, he was the only one who liked such sweet wine. Everybody knew it. Anyway, Hilda said she'd left all the bottles on the buffet in the dining room. I thought that was a good place to start, so I checked." Her voice grew low and thrilling. "It wasn't there."

"Really?"

"And I know he hadn't finished it. There was at least a third of a bottle left."

"That is odd. But I'm not sure any of this constitutes foul play."

"I know, but Janey, you have to understand. I have this awful *feeling*. I just *know* something isn't right."

"You have a feeling."

"Right. You've got to come and help me figure all this out. Theo's body is being cremated in the morning."

"Cremated? Did they already perform the autopsy?"

"Nothing was said about an autopsy. Annie remembered that Theo had said once he wanted to be cremated when he died. Curt thought he remembered something about it too. So, since directory assistance couldn't find Theo's brother in the Los Angeles phone book—that is, if he's still living there—and there was no one else left to contact, Orson just said to go ahead with it."

"That's kind of fast. Normally, they have to wait forty-eight hours. But back up a minute. I don't understand why the coroner didn't order an autopsy. I think it's pretty standard in cases of sudden death. If Theo's body is cremated, there's no hope of further testing."

"Are you saying someone might be trying to cover up . . . a murder?"

"Maybe."

"Should I try and stop it?"

"I'm not sure you could. Since neither of us knows all the facts, we're in no position to suggest anything. The coroner makes those decisions. He should know what he's doing."

"He also runs the funeral home."

"You're kidding."

"That's what Orson said. It happens in small towns."

"Seems rather—"

"Inbred?"

"I was thinking of the word *convenient,* Cordelia."

"Whatever."

"But you're right. This is a strange situation."

"Then come to Summer Green! You liked Theo. If someone murdered him, we have to find out who did it and why."

"Even if it's one of your friends?"

Cordelia knew it came down to that. Unless it was Hilda or Amity, and what would their motives be? Come to think of it, what was anybody's motive? None of this made sense. "All I know is, if I leave here and this isn't settled in my mind, I'll never have another night's rest."

"I know what that feels like."

"You have to come, Janey. I realize I'm asking a lot. But who better than you to figure this out. After all, you're the Jane Marple of the Midwest. The Sherlock Holmes of the wild prairie."

"And you're full of crap."

"Can I take that as a yes?"

More silence.

"Janey, I'll never . . . make fun of your car again."

"How kind of you."

"And I'll never call you cheap."

"Because I'm not."

"Right. And I promise to . . . get you front-row seats— all comps—to this season's new plays at the Allen Grimby."

"And?"

"What else do you want!"

"Just seeing how far you'd go."

"Bring something other than jeans and high-top tennies. The funeral will be rural, but tasteful."

"Cordelia!"

"You won't change your mind, will you?"

"No . . . I'll come. If for nothing else, than for your peace of mind. And also for Theo. I liked him a lot."

Cordelia could feel herself beginning to crumble. She knew it would be a long, sleepless night. "You can stay here at the parsonage. There's lots of room. I'll talk to Diana about it in the morning."

"What time did you say that bus left?"

"Five-fifteen."

Jane let out a muffled shriek.

"I think it stops at the Sunburst Motel just south of town. I'll be there to pick you up."

"You'd better be."

"You're a lifesaver, Janey. See you anon." Cordelia clicked off the phone, switched off the flashlight, and uncovered her head. Sitting now in the chilly blackness of her bedroom, her eyes readjusting to the dark, she contemplated a trek to the medicine cabinet in search of an antacid. As she was about to get up, she heard a soft knock on the door. "Come in," she whispered.

A dark form entered and moved quietly to the foot of the bed. It hovered there, not saying a word.

Cordelia felt her skin prickle with a cold anticipation. Remembering the flashlight in her hand, she switched it back on.

"Turn that goddamn thing off!" ordered Diana, covering her eyes with her arm.

Even in that brief second, Cordelia could see enough to know Diana looked terrible, her eyes red and swollen. "What do you want?" she asked, knowing her tone wasn't exactly friendly.

Diana eased herself onto the edge of the bed. She was trembling. "No one came and told me. How's Theo doing?"

Cordelia was momentarily lost. "But we—"

"I must have fallen asleep. Jesus, Cordelia, I'm not a princess. Why didn't someone wake me?"

"Don't you remember coming downstairs?"

"I . . . what?"

"While I was talking to Orson on the phone. You came down the stairs. We explained everything."

"Oh . . . uh, sure." She ran a hand through her hair. "I must have . . . you know. I just woke up." She attempted a smile. "Everyone's a little fuzzy when they wake from a sound sleep. Just . . . tell me again." The smile faded.

She was obviously lying. And there was only one logical explanation for her behavior. Diana had had a blackout. Cordelia wondered if she would even remember this conversation. "He had another heart attack in the ambulance on the way to the hospital. He was pronounced dead by one of the paramedics."

"Dead?"

Cordelia could feel her draw away. "His body was taken to the DeLappe funeral home."

Diana sat very still, her head tilted up toward the open window. The weak moonlight filtering in through the sheers made her face look bleached. Drained of all blood.

"Are you all right?"

Without a word, Diana got up and left the room.

Humph, thought Cordelia. Just charming. She could at least have said *something*. *I'm sorry,* would have been nice. *Gee that's too bad.* Or, *tough luck.* Anything. Cordelia could hear a door shut farther down the hall. She wondered if she should go to her. Make sure everything was okay. But something prevented her normal empathy. Too much was unknown. Too much unsaid. Instead, she got up and moved to the window, looking out at the playhouse.

It was a windy night, the trees rustling in the distance. As her eyes fell to the parking lot, she heard a motor start. A second later, a car backed out of a parking space and drove to the edge of the highway. With its lights still off, it turned left and began its climb over the rise and out of sight. Cordelia froze as she realized it was the same car she'd seen the other night. The white Cadillac.

15

By ten the next morning, Cordelia had already done her morning exercises—five sit-ups and a minute and a half of running in place—and dressed in a comfortable cotton caftan. She trudged down the stairs to the first-floor parlor feeling like a zombie.

Orson was already up. Since the morning was cloudy and cool, he'd built a fire in the fireplace and was sitting in front of it, reading the paper and sipping from a mug of coffee.

"Morning," she mumbled, dumping herself onto the sofa. "Where is everyone?"

Orson looked up from the paper, his eyes blinking rapidly as he gazed into the fire.

Cordelia could see he'd been crying.

"Diana's still in bed," he said, wiping a hand across his mouth. "Curt went out for a walk a few minutes ago, and I'm not sure about Annie. She's probably in the kitchen making herself some breakfast."

"And Amity?"

"Still in bed. She had kind of a late night."

"What do you mean?"

"Some kid came over here about eleven. Chickie

Johnson. Apparently, they'd met last spring during Easter vacation. He and Amity left together. She didn't get back until after one."

Cordelia wondered what Diana's rules were. Surely she and Jill had enforced many while they lived in New York. Amity was older now, but she couldn't be allowed to run wild. Someone had to keep track of her for her own safety.

"I didn't say anything to her about a curfew," continued Orson. "I'd never allow my fourteen-year-old to stay out that late, but last night I just let it pass. I couldn't deal with it anymore. What I'm really worried about is what's going to happen to that kid after the . . . you know." He didn't want to say the word *intervention*.

Cordelia had already registered the same thought. She hadn't come up with a solution.

Just then, Annie walked into the room, a half-eaten English muffin held in one hand, a glass of orange juice in the other. Theo's death had obviously not affected her appetite. "Did you ever get hold of Theo's brother?" she asked Orson, sitting down next to Cordelia.

Annie's thick red hair was loose around her shoulders today. For years, she'd never worn it any other way than pulled back tightly into a bun. It gave her an air of professionalism. Competence. Something she no doubt needed in her job. But this morning, she looked ten years younger. More relaxed. Even the way she moved her body seemed different. Cordelia had forgotten what a strikingly lovely woman she could be. Giving the air a surreptitious sniff, Cordelia also noticed that Annie was wearing a light scent of roses. In some strange way, she felt as if she were witnessing a transformation.

Orson seemed to notice it to. He stared at her for a long moment before speaking. "I talked to James about half an hour ago."

"James?" repeated Cordelia.

"Theo's brother."

"Right. But I thought you weren't able to locate him in the L.A. phone directory."

"I wasn't." Orson looked a little sheepish as he explained, "I was in Theo's room earlier this morning and I noticed an address book on the nightstand next to his bed. So I checked to see if his brother was listed. He was. He's living in Sacramento now."

"Is he coming?" asked Annie.

"Yes. But he asked if we could hold the funeral off until Wednesday. It's just two days. I didn't think it would be a problem."

"What about Dr. Bernson?" asked Cordelia. "The... *you know what* was supposed to happen tomorrow morning."

"I talked to her too," replied Orson, taking a sip of his coffee. "She agreed with us. It should happen after the funeral. So we've rescheduled for Thursday."

"Rescheduled what?" asked Diana. She slunk into the room, a bathrobe pulled haphazardly around her satin nightgown. She looked awful, her hair a stringy mess.

"The...ah...our final breakfast together," smiled Orson, standing as Diana entered.

Under the circumstances, Cordelia felt Orson's genteel formality was ludicrous. The day was starting out in cartoon-land once again.

"Oh. Right," said Diana, lurching a bit further into the parlor. "Well, I've got a solution for that. You must simply all stay in Summer Green. Orson, you can run the playhouse. Cordelia, you can direct. Curt can do the lighting and the stage managing, and Annie—" She hesitated. "Well, Annie can do what Annie does best." An eyebrow rose slowly as she eyed Annie's hair. "What the hell happened to you?"

"I beg your pardon?"

Diana waved the matter away. "Then it's settled."

Cordelia wondered if she'd already been drinking. Her behavior had that unmistakable alcohol-induced imperiousness.

"Hilda!" barked Diana. "Breakfast."

"She's not here," replied Orson. "She's over at the playhouse helping prepare for the picnic this afternoon."

"God." She flopped down on a chair. "I'd forgotten about that. Horrible timing."

Cordelia assumed this was finally a reference to Theo's death. Not that she'd even so much as mentioned his name.

"Yeah," said Orson, looking deep into the fire. "The worst. A woman called this morning while you were sleeping. She wanted to know if the plans were still on."

"What did you say?"

"I told her yes, unless they heard from you directly."

"Good. I've invited the entire goddamn town. Also some big shots from Appleton and Green Bay. It's a good way to publicize the theatre. All my actors will be there. I can't cancel."

"Everyone will understand," said Annie.

"Yeah." Diana rubbed her eyes.

Still, thought Cordelia, no one spoke Theo's name.

"Well, I'd better get back upstairs," muttered Diana. "Take a shower and slip into some clothes." She stood to leave. Before she got all the way to the door she stopped. "Oh," she said, not turning around, "What about the . . . funeral?"

"Wednesday afternoon. At three," said Orson.

Diana nodded.

"One other thing," said Cordelia. She watched Diana's back grow rigid.

"What?"

"You remember Jane Lawless?"

"Sure. Why?"

"She'd like to come for the funeral. Can she stay here?"

"Fine." Diana dismissed the question with a wave of her hand and proceeded out the door.

After she'd gone, Orson turned to Cordelia and asked, "When is she arriving?"

"This afternoon. The bus gets in around one."

"Why's she coming so early?" asked Annie.

"Jesus," said Orson. "That bus leaves Minneapolis at five A.M!"

"Five-fifteen," Cordelia corrected him.

"You must have called her in the middle of the night."

"I needed to talk."

"About Theo?"

Cordelia nodded. "It's a lot to deal with."

"I know." His eyes fell to the floor. "I called my wife before I turned in. She won't be able to come, but she sends her love to all of us."

"She never knew him," said Cordelia, trying to be comforting.

He turned his head away. "How are we ever going to get through this?"

"Together," said Cordelia, reaching for his hand.

Annie just sat and sipped her orange juice.

16

Jane glanced at her watch, realizing the bus was already half an hour late. Cordelia was probably sputtering around the Sunburst Motel's parking lot, contemplating a long, scathing letter to the bus company. She was a stickler for punctuality.

For the last two hours, the deep green fields whizzing past Jane's window had been bathed in a delicate mist. Trees looked indistinct, the landscape permitting no sharp lines of any kind. It was a perfect day to reflect on the subtleties of life. Perhaps even the subtleties of death. All morning, Jane had thought of little other than Cordelia's phone calls. Even though she hadn't known Theo well, his loss seemed to touch a place deep inside her. He was a figure from her past. Since she hadn't seen him since college, in her mind's eye he would forever remain that passionate young actor, handsome, living on the edge, doing the inexplicable. What kind of man had he grown up to be? And would the questions surrounding his death shed any light on his very private life?

Over the past few years, Jane had lent a hand in solving several unexplained deaths. Some silly people were even starting to think of her as a sleuth. Even though Jane considered these incidents as completely out of the ordinary, one-time occurrences, she did have to admit she had a certain facility when it came to ferreting out the truth. Because she had recently hired a new day manager for her restaurant, initially so that she would have more time to publicize her new cookbook, taking a few days off to visit Summer Green presented no problem to the Lyme House. Jane's Aunt Beryl, who had come from England two years ago to live with her, could take care of their home—and Cordelia's cats. So, if this trip would help ease Cordelia's mind, it was certainly worth the trouble.

Up ahead, Jane could see a sign which said, Welcome to Summer Green. The bus began to slow. Stuffing the paperback she'd brought with her—but never looked at—into her backpack, she readied herself for the end of her journey. She slipped on her leather jacket and touched her hair, making sure everything was in place. Jane was a handsome woman in her late thirties, with deep blue-violet eyes and a great smile. She'd always felt the smile was one of her best features—and her nose, one of her worst. It was too large. Then again, perhaps it was a cosmic message. With a nose like hers, what else could she be other than a snoop? Might even make a good logo if she ever had business cards printed up. If you need the police, call them. If you're looking for a good PI, try the Yellow Pages. But if you want a trained Nose, call Jane Lawless. Yes. It had a certain ring to it.

When the bus came to a full stop and the driver announced the name of the town, Jane grabbed her suitcase and swung into the aisle.

Cordelia was waiting for her, leaning against the hood of her car. Even from a distance, Jane could see she looked tired. A little more make-up had been used to give her cheeks some color. Jane had never worn make-up herself. She couldn't be bothered. But Cordelia had never met a lotion or a cream, a blush or an eyeliner, or even a lipstick she didn't like. All her life, she'd been experimenting with different looks. It was part of the fun of being alive she always said. Jane had to hand it to her. Cordelia never tried to squelch a natural inclination for a political reason. All during the seventies and eighties, she'd steadfastly worn her make-up, even though she got some nasty looks from women who felt she was a sellout to the patriarchy. Now, as time and luck would have it, Cordelia was probably considered on the cutting edge of the new dyke-chic. But whatever, Cordelia just kept on doing what came naturally. No matter who it annoyed.

"Not a great day for a picnic," said Jane, striding up to the car and letting her suitcase hit the dirt with a thunk. "Don't I get a hug?"

"Of course you do," said Cordelia, her eyes brimming with tears. "I'm so glad you're here."

Jane felt the breath being squeezed out of her. "Are you all right?"

Cordelia stepped back. "I've been better. But I think I'll live." She opened the trunk. "One suitcase. A small one at that. You amaze me, Janey. You truly do." Even her attempt at humor seemed strained.

Jane could feel a light drizzle begin to fall.

"Get in," said Cordelia. "They've decided to hold the picnic in the church basement—I mean, the playhouse basement—because of the weather. No one wanted rain-soaked radish casserole."

"I beg your pardon?"

Cordelia patted Jane's hand. "I shall explain everything on the way."

"So this is what Diana's been working on for the last year," murmured Jane, admiring the arched double-doors as they entered. The vestibule was small, a rose-and-emerald Oriental covering the floor. At one end, a stairway led to the basement. Moving into the main part of the building, Jane took in the stage. It was built in the shape of a wide V. The set was still in place from the opening performance. She looked up and saw a huge metal grid filled with spotlights. What this church had undergone was nothing short of a transformation. Then again, since only the rear of the structure had been rebuilt, it felt like she was standing in some strange hybrid. Half sanctuary, half theatre. An interesting marriage. "How was the opening performance?" she asked, following Cordelia down the center aisle.

"It was fabulous. Except, Diana had been drinking. She muffed some of her lines, but the audience ate it up. Thought it was all part of the show."

Descending the concrete steps at the right of the stage, they entered an underground hall. The basement, once the domain of church suppers and wedding receptions, had now been turned into the costume shop and prop area. Today, everything had been pushed to the side and covered. It was already filled with people. Bright pink and blue balloons were affixed to the walls. One long table in the rear was loaded with fried chicken, steaming corn-on-the-cob, beans—the standard picnic fare.

On the ride over in the car, Cordelia had warned Jane to stay away from the locally grown radishes, explaining that they contained an hallucinogenic substance which reduced the townspeople to incoherent puddings. In response, Jane suggested that perhaps she should drive. Cordelia gave her a nasty look. The subject was dropped.

"There's Orson," said Cordelia. She waved at him, unable to get his attention. "And Annie and Curt are over by the coffee urn, talking to John Hubble—he's the director. Let's go join them." She grabbed Jane's hand and dragged her though the crowd.

"Jane!" said Annie, turning as they approached. She gave her a small peck on the cheek. "It's good to see you again."

Curt smiled his hello.

They were still a handsome couple, thought Jane. Annie looked particularly wonderful. "Good to see you, too."

"Did your bus just get in?" asked Curt.

"It was late," grumped Cordelia. She turned to a lanky, sandy-haired man with a blond beard and said, "John, I'd like you to meet my old friend, Jane Lawless. She's also from the Twin Cities."

He held out his hand. "It's a pleasure. Do you work at the Allen Grimby with Cordelia?"

"No," said Jane, "I own a restaurant on Lake Harriet."

"Ah." He nodded and then smiled. "I've never been to Minnesota. I'm originally from New York. Spent the last ten years in L.A."

"A long way from either coast here in Summer Green," said Jane.

"Yeah." The smile faded. "I thought this was going to be my big break. A chance to work with the great Diana Stanwood. I even signed a two-year contract. Now I wish I hadn't."

"Why?" Jane wondered if his tone held anger, or merely disappointment.

"No one told me Diana was a drunk." He glared defiantly at Cordelia, and then at Curt and Annie. "I know she's your friend, but she's going to single-handedly sink the next two years of my life."

"Do others in the company feel the same way?" asked Jane.

"Most everyone," he said, "though I'm the only one who was asked to sign such a lengthy contract. I've done some sitcoms. A *Matlock* episode. Several *Knot's Landing*'s. So I have more of a name than anyone other than Diana. That also means I have more at stake. And I'm also the only one with enough guts to say out loud what we're all thinking. The rest of the sheep feel matters will improve now that the stress of opening night is past. That's crap, if you ask me."

"I'm sorry to hear that," said Jane. Though, she wasn't surprised.

"You do have *understudies,* don't you?" asked Cordelia. "I mean, in case someone gets . . . sick?"

Jane assumed this was a veiled reference to the intervention.

"Of course we do. That might be what saves the season." He folded his arms over his chest. "If Diana would just come down with a small but potent case of the flu—let's say, for the next two months?—we'd probably do okay."

"That's unlikely to happen," said Curt, cutting him off. He had apparently taken a dislike to the director and wasn't interested in hiding it.

"You never know," said John.

"Who's that with Orson?" asked Cordelia. She stretched her neck to get a better view.

"Beats me," said Curt. He didn't even bother to look. Turning to Annie he said, "I have to go back to the parsonage. I can't handle this today."

She nodded. "I'll come with you."

"No, really. I'll be fine by myself."

"Don't be silly." She turned to Jane. "Will we see you this evening?"

"You bet."

"Good. We can talk more later."

Jane could tell Curt wanted to be alone. She found it curious that Annie didn't take his hint. Or, maybe she felt it best that he not be by himself today. Whatever the case, it wasn't much of a day for celebration.

"I better shove off too," said John.

"Do you live in town?" asked Jane, curious where the people in the company were staying.

"For the time being. I made a deal with the guy who owns the Sunburst Motel. I got a pretty good monthly rate. Unfortunately, there aren't many choices around here."

Jane didn't have trouble believing that. "Well, nice meeting you."

"Yeah." He hesitated. "I don't suppose—"

God, he wasn't going to ask her for a date.

"There's a roadhouse just south of town. Would you like to have a drink with me later tonight? It would be nice to have some female company." He moved a bit closer. "It gets pretty lonely around here."

"I don't think so," said Jane.

He looked at Cordelia, who was still straining to see who Orson was talking to. "Oh, sure. I get it. You two—"

She shook her head. "Not exactly, but you got part of it right."

"You're gay."

She nodded.

"No problem. But that doesn't change things. I'd still enjoy the company."

"Maybe another time."

"Suit yourself." He turned and walked away.

After he was gone, Jane continued her perusal of the room. She could see Diana working the crowd, talking to people, shaking hands, patting some on the back. She looked older than she had the last time they'd met, but her charisma hadn't dimmed with age. She was holding a beer in her left hand, but she didn't seem high or unsteady.

Jane turned to Cordelia. "What *are* you staring at?"

"That guy talking to Orson. I've seen him before."

"So?"

"Remember I told you about the white Cadillac?" Cordelia closed her eyes for a moment to review the scene in her mind. "Well, I'm almost positive that's the bald man. The one I saw talking to Theo."

"Why would he be at the picnic?"

"Good question." She crooked her neck again, trying to get a better view. "Damn. They're gone." She bolted for the stairs. "They must have gone outside," she shouted over her shoulder.

Jane followed. She raced up the steps and out the back-stage door. "Jesus, is this a cemetery or a movie set?" she asked, coming to a dead stop.

Cordelia stood a few feet in front of her, her eyes sweeping over the misty countryside. "There they are," she whispered, pointing to a weeping willow about a hundred feet in the distance.

Jane could barely make them out. The weather lent a sinister quality to their conversation. "What are you going to do?"

"I don't know. I'd sure like to hear what they're saying. Come to think of it, why should I give a rip? Come on, Janey." She strided off toward the tree.

Jane shrugged. At this point, Cordelia knew more about what was going on than she did. She quickly picked up the rear.

As they approached, Jane saw that Orson was doing most of the talking. Cordelia's advancing form must have caught his eye because almost immediately he stepped away from the tree and called, "Cordelia. And Jane." He sounded entirely too pleased.

"Orson!" replied Cordelia, matching his tone. "Haven't seen you in, gosh, it must be two hours."

His smile disappeared. "What do you want?"

She flicked her eyes to the man by the tree.

"Not now," he growled.

"Why not?"

"It's personal."

"Don't be trite."

"Cordelia, this is none of your business. Why don't you take Jane back to the parsonage and fix some fresh coffee. I'll join you there in a few minutes."

"I am *not* your secretary! I do not make coffee."

"I wasn't suggesting you were."

Cordelia lowered her voice to a whisper. "I demand a full explanation."

"No explanations. This is none of your business."

"I beg to differ. Anything that has to do with Theo's death *is* my business."

Orson's eyes opened wide, but he recovered quickly. "Get out of here," he said, his teeth clenched. "This is not your concern."

"It's a free graveyard. I can stay if I want."

Jane watched the face-off with interest. Orson and Cordelia were standing nose to nose, neither blinking. Two huge bears on the verge of a roar.

"I'm going, Orson," called the man, moving from behind the willow. Dressed in an expensive dark suit, he looked well past middle age. His face was lean and intelligent. "If I need to, I'll find you later."

Orson's body seemed to deflate. "Fine."

Cordelia waited until he was out of earshot and then said, "I demand to know who he is!"

"Drop it." Orson started to walk away.

Cordelia blocked his path.

Pinching the bridge of his nose, he said, "I'm going to say this one more time. Who that man is, is none of your goddamn business. You can scream your bloody head off, but that's all you're going to get on the subject." With that, he marched off toward the playhouse. He'd only gotten a few yards when he stopped, swiveling around. "Where are my manners?" he muttered. "Welcome to Summer Green, Jane. I'm sure we'll be seeing more of you."

"You will."

"Wonderful." His voice held no warmth. Again, he turned, this time, heading for the parsonage.

17

Cordelia knocked softly on Jane's door and then poked her head inside. "You ready?"

"All set," said Jane. She was sitting on the bed, paging through a copy of the *Summer Green Gazette*. Theo's death had made the front page. So had a picture of Orson.

"Just be quiet. Diana's downstairs in the parlor with everyone else. Dinner will be served in fifteen minutes, so I doubt she'll be back up before that. But we can't take any chances."

Jane followed Cordelia out into the hall. As they walked to Diana's room, Jane eyed some of the framed awards Diana had won. They were hanging in a row on the long wall. She stopped in front of the largest.

"Come on!" urged Cordelia in a barely whispered voice.

"I didn't know about—"

"Diana has won three Emmys and a Tony. Plus everything you see there. Now get over here!"

Jane took one last look and then crossed to the closed door. She waited for Cordelia to enter.

"You've got to see this for yourself," insisted Cordelia, leaving the door slightly ajar. "If you do, you'll understand what I meant last night. It's really bizarre. But remember, we have to listen for footsteps."

Jane nodded. She didn't like any of this. They should have waited until everyone was out of the house.

Diana's room was neat. The bed was made and fresh flowers brightened her bureau. The windows were wide open, letting in the scent of rain. A rumble of distant thunder made Jane wonder if Summer Green wasn't in for an evening storm.

Cordelia swept to the closet and opened the door. "Oh shit!"

"What is it?"

"It's gone!"

Jane moved closer.

"It was right here." Cordelia bent down and ran her hand across the painted wood. "A knife that big would leave a mark. I don't get it. I don't feel a thing."

Jane touched the wood herself. "You're sure it was here?"

"Positive!"

She got down on her knees and examined the surface more closely. In the dimly lit room, the new paint wasn't all that apparent, but she found it. "Look, Cordelia. Someone touched up this spot. They probably filled it with wood putty first. If you get real close, you can smell it."

Cordelia put a hand on her hip. "Diana must have done it."

"Probably."

"That means she was scared someone would see it."

"A good guess. But didn't she notice you looking at it last night?"

Cordelia shook her head. "She was too out of it."

"You're sure?"

"She didn't even remember Theo had died!"

"Right. Good point. Describe it to me again."

"Well, it was an old college photo of Theo. Publicity for some play, I don't remember which one. A kitchen knife was stuck through a button right into Theo's chest."

"Weird."

"I know."

"Describe the button again?"

"It said 'Minnesotans for choice.' Diana made a sizable contribution to the Minnesota Abortion Rights Council so I sent her a couple of them."

"Interesting. You mentioned she was cool to Theo the first couple of days. Did she ever say why?"

Cordelia shook her head. "When she's been drinking, she becomes rather cryptic. Sometimes I don't have a clue what she's talking about. I'm not even sure she does."

"I think we should get out of here," said Jane.

"Say, come to think of it, she did do one odd thing."

"What?"

"The night Theo died, we were all sitting around the dinner table. She quoted from Macbeth. She was staring straight at him when she said it. It seemed to make him uncomfortable."

"What was the quote?"

Cordelia closed her eyes, holding up her hand for silence.

Naught's had, all's spent,
Where our desire is got without content:
'Tis safer to be that which we destroy,
Than, by destruction, dwell in doubtful joy.

"Lady Macbeth. I don't remember the act or the scene. Sorry."

Jane considered it for a moment. "Sounds like maybe she thought Theo had hurt her in some way. Is that possible?"

"Jesus. I don't know how."

In her mind's eye, Jane saw the abortion rights button with a knife thrust through it. "You know, Cordelia, this doesn't make any sense."

"I know."

Suddenly, from down the hall came the sound of a door creaking open.

"I thought you said everyone was downstairs," rasped Jane, scrambling to her feet.

"I thought they were!"

Before they could make a move to hide, a hand knocked softly.

"Diana?" came Curt's voice. He stepped into the room. "Hi," he said, glancing around. "Where's Diana?"

"That's . . . uh, what we were wondering," said Cordelia, attempting a smile.

"Come on, let's go find her," he said. "I think it's about time for dinner."

"Right," agreed Cordelia. "Good plan."

As Jane walked past him, she couldn't help but feel he knew they were lying. They had no business alone in Diana's room. She wondered why he hadn't called them on it.

18

"So," said Diana, passing Jane a basket of homemade rolls, "How was the bus trip?"

"Uneventful," answered Jane. She took a bite of her Caesar salad. This cook, whoever she was, was excellent.

"And what did you think of our playhouse?" Diana lifted a glass of weak looking orange juice to her lips. Jane assumed it was mostly vodka.

"I was very impressed."

"We'll be having Wednesday, Thursday, Friday and Saturday night performances until Thanksgiving."

"Except for this Wednesday," Orson corrected her.

She looked at her drink, setting it down next to her plate. "Of course. You don't have to remind me." A shaky hand moved briefly across her eyes. "Have you made all the . . . arrangements yet?"

He nodded. "Theo's body is being cremated, but the remains will be buried. We thought it was best to do it in the church cemetery out back. He never really stayed in one place long enough to call it home. I think he'd like to be here—with you."

Diana's face flushed.

"Have you picked out a spot?" asked Curt.

Again, Orson nodded. "It's all been handled."

"I'm . . . glad you've taken the initiative, Orson," said Diana, her words slurring slightly. She'd been drinking all day, but this was the first time she sounded high. "I've been . . . unable to deal with some of this. You all understand how hard this has hit me. I'm not one to talk about my feelings openly." Another drink of vodka. This time a gulp.

"We understand," said Annie.

Diana's head wobbled backwards as she attempted to straighten her sweater. "I just think it would be good if we all . . . spent some time talking about it."

"We have been, Diana," said Cordelia. The irritation in her voice was apparent to everyone. Except Diana.

"Don't get me wrong, Theo and I had our differences." Another sip. "I don't know why he felt he could—" She stopped.

"Could what?" asked Jane.

Suddenly, Diana burst out crying.

Everyone was momentarily stunned.

Annie shot Jane a cautionary look. "Diana, I think perhaps you need to rest."

"Everybody always knows what's best for me!" she shrieked. "Theo thought that too. I'll never forgive him."

"Calm down," said Curt. His voice was impatient.

"Why should I?"

"Because he's dead, that's why. There's nothing more you can do."

She folded her arms over her chest and began to rock. "I know," she sniffed. "I never wanted it to end like this."

Jane and Cordelia exchanged glances.

Hilda came to the door. "Are you all finished with your salads?" she asked.

No one responded.

"Would you like me to take the plates away?"

As if aroused from a deep sleep, Diana's body jerked. An unconvincing smile replaced her tears. "I'm being a terrible hostess. Yes, all done, Hilda. Bring on the . . . beef, or whatever."

"Roast duckling," replied Hilda, moving into the room and removing the plates to a stand near the buffet. Every so often, she would steal a glance at Diana.

Diana's head tilted confidentially toward Jane. "Quack," she muttered soulfully.

Jane raised an eyebrow.

"Seems like we should have a toast," said Diana, rousing herself from the vestiges of her melancholy.

"To what?" asked Orson.

"To . . . our memories of Theo. Does everyone have some wine?"

No one did.

Diana didn't notice. She raised her vodka high, and the rest raised their water goblets. "To Theo."

"To Theo," everyone responded.

"May he rot in hell."

"Diana!" exclaimed Orson, his face frozen in surprise. "Jesus, get a goddamn grip on yourself!"

Ignoring him, Diana finished her drink. "I think Annie's right. I need to rest." Lurching out of her chair, she muttered, "Catch you all later. Maybe we can build a bonfire and sing camp songs. You all make me sick."

Everyone was silent as Diana shambled out of the room. A few moments later she began singing "Kumbaya" as she climbed the stairs.

"Lord," said Curt, pushing back from the table. "I can't take much more of this."

Annie laid her hand gently on his arm.

"We've got to hold together until Thursday," said Orson. "We have to remember the Diana we all love.

Keep that in our minds. I know it's not easy, but we *have* to try."

Curt tossed his napkin on top of his silverware. "Of course. You're right."

"Let's talk about something else," said Cordelia.

"Like what?" asked Annie.

"Oh, I don't know. Politics. Religion. Let's keep it light."

Jane shook her head. "Where's Amity tonight? I haven't met her yet."

"She had dinner up in her room," answered Annie. "She said she had a headache."

"Who doesn't?" grumped Curt.

Hilda entered the room with the main course. "What happened to Miss Stanwood?"

"She wanted to find her guitar. Practice some old John Denver songs," answered Cordelia.

Hilda humphed. She set the plates down in front of everyone and then said, "When are you people going to do something to help her!"

"We're trying," said Orson.

"Not very hard if you ask me." With a nasty backward glance, she left the room.

"Charming woman," said Curt.

Annie picked a piece of parsley off her potatoes. No one was very hungry. "Cordelia tells me that Jane was instrumental in solving a murder last year. Something about a women's club in Minneapolis."

"Right," said Orson. "I read about that in the Minneapolis paper. You're getting a reputation for being quite the detective."

Jane smiled. She was glad for the change of subject; she just wished it was another topic.

"Maybe you can figure out why Diana was so pissed

at Theo," said Curt. He wasn't even making an attempt to eat.

"I am curious about one thing," said Jane "The night Theo died, Cordelia tells me the coroner never ordered an autopsy. Do you know why?"

"Why would they need an autopsy?" asked Annie. "We all know how he died. A heart attack."

"But normally," explained Jane, "in cases of sudden death—especially when the person is considered healthy— an autopsy is ordered."

"But he told me he had a heart condition," said Orson.

"That's not enough. He could have been kidding."

"What are you suggesting?" asked Annie. "That someone was trying to cover up. . . what? A murder?"

"Of course not," said Orson, patting his mouth with the edge of his napkin. "How could he have been murdered? We were all in the same room with him. We saw what happened. I even rode in the ambulance. The paramedics didn't see anything unusual. Neither did I."

Annie wasn't convinced. She glared at Jane. "You actually think one of us killed him, don't you!"

"I didn't say that," said Jane.

"No, but it seems pretty clear to me."

Curt put his hand on the back of her neck. "Don't get so excited, honey."

Annie looked as if he'd just slapped her across the face.

"I was simply wondering about the autopsy," said Jane, trying to keep her voice neutral. "I wasn't accusing anyone." Boy, were these people jumpy. She'd have to be more careful.

"See," said Orson. "The question was entirely innocent. Besides, Jane's father is a defense attorney. She would know about these things."

"Well, not really," said Jane.

"You don't have to be modest," continued Orson.

"But, in this case, even though your curiosity is understandable, I think your concern is unnecessary."

Jane nodded. She was suddenly very tired herself. She'd been up since four.

"I've got to get some air," said Curt. "I feel like I'm suffocating."

"It's pouring rain outside," said Annie.

"I don't care." He pushed away from the table. "Sorry. See you all later."

"Later," said Cordelia. She and Orson were the only ones who had eaten any of their duck. Cordelia elbowed Jane in the ribs. "Come on. You need your strength."

To be honest, Diana's little *quack* had really gotten to her. She knew she needed a long night's rest. But Cordelia was right. She also needed food.

"So," said Orson attempting to pick up the pieces of an otherwise ruined evening, "What aspect of religion would you all like to argue about?"

19

Shortly after Annie and Cordelia had left for an evening of fun and frolic at the new Radish Hill Mall—they insisted they couldn't stick around the parsonage one moment longer and maintain their tenuous grip on sanity—Jane came down the stairs in search of cup of tea before bed. It was only eight-thirty, but she was exhausted. As she was about to enter the kitchen, Orson came barreling out, nearly knocking her down. He was wearing a raincoat and a tweed hat, and carrying an umbrella.

"Going somewhere?" she asked.

"I'm meeting a friend in town for coffee. I grew up here, you know. I've still got some buddies. I figured I might as well see them while I'm visiting. There's nothing else to do."

"Sure. Have a nice time."

"Right." He touched his hat and steamed off down the hall.

After making herself a mug of Earl Grey, Jane strolled back into the foyer. The house felt pleasantly quiet after such a stressful dinner. Before heading upstairs, she noticed Curt stretched out on a rug in front of the fire. The scene looked so inviting, she walked into the room. He didn't hear her so she cleared her throat, hoping she wasn't ruining a private moment.

He turned his head. "Jane. Hi. I thought you'd gone to bed."

"I'm on my way," she said, holding up her mug, "but I just can't pass up such an inviting scene. Do you mind if I join you for a few minutes?"

"Not at all," he smiled. He got up and moved two chairs closer to the hearth. "I'd enjoy the company. I thought I'd wait up until Amity got home. She starts school tomorrow. I don't know how she's going to like it. She didn't sound too thrilled when she found out she had to be bussed to another town. Summer Green has a grade school, but the high school is over in Pine Creek."

"From what Cordelia's told me, she's really been bounced around since her mother's death."

"Yeah," he said, shaking his head. "It's a rotten shame. She's a nice kid."

Jane made herself comfortable, enjoying the added warmth. It was a cool night. Autumn was definitely on the way. As they sat in companionable silence, Jane took a moment to study Curt. At dinner, and earlier at the picnic, his blond hair had been combed straight back, flat against his head. But tonight, after his walk in the rain, he'd towel-dried it and simply left it natural. He now looked more like the Curt she remembered from college. He was a good-looking man—tall, well-built, prominent nose, strong chin, full lips. Yet he'd always struck her as somewhat distracted, as if he continually had something on his mind which kept him from living fully in the present. She wondered if he was happy.

Out of the blue, Curt said, "You didn't come for Theo's funeral, did you? You came because Cordelia asked you to." It was less a question than a statement.

"I don't—"

"It's all right. You don't have to explain. But it surprised me. She must feel pretty strongly that Theo's death wasn't... natural. I suppose she has a right to her opinion."

Since he'd brought it up, Jane decided to run with the ball. "What do *you* think?"

He rubbed his chin, giving himself a moment. "Who of us does Cordelia suspect?"

Not an answer, thought Jane. Even so, she had to respond. "You have to understand. She's not accusing anybody."

"So, what you're saying is she suspects nobody. And everybody."

"Well—" he had a point.

"Why were you in Diana's room earlier this evening?" Before she could say anything in her defense, he said, "Let me guess. Cordelia wanted you to see the photo of Theo that Diana had hung inside her closet door."

Jane was aghast. "How did you know?"

"Cordelia took a little too much time getting that quilt last night. I saw her looking at the door. Since she was so secretive about it, I came back later and took a look myself."

Jane sipped her tea. "And what did you make of it?"

"Diana was upset with Theo. I knew that from the moment we walked in the door."

"Do you know why?"

He shrugged. "With Diana, it could be anything. Big or small, you never know. She's got a terrible temper, but I hardly think she wanted to murder him." When Jane didn't say anything, he added, "She's not an easy person to figure, I'll grant you that. But when she accepts you as a friend, she's your friend for life. She writes Annie and me faithfully. We used to get a letter a month, no matter what she was doing. She's been a real encouragement to me over the years. Helped me with jobs. And she's an incredibly generous person. Ask anyone here. They all have stories. She came to speak to Annie's university class several times. Once she took the entire theatre department to a play in downtown Chicago. Made quite a splash. When Annie's mother died four years ago, she flew out and spent a week with us. Even though it was a sad time for Annie, having Diana there meant the world. The thing is, when it comes to alcohol, it's like she's been on a greased slide all her life. And now she's fallen off the edge."

Jane had never known Diana the way the rest of them had, but for five people to drop everything in their lives and come to a small town in Wisconsin, well, she had to be someone very special. There was a lot of love here. Jane knew how much it hurt Cordelia to even think one of her friends had harmed Theo. Perhaps, in the end, they would find nothing amiss. But for Cordelia's peace of mind, Jane felt compelled to search a bit deeper. "The night Theo and Orson got into that fight, were you at the roadhouse?"

"Ah, now we're moving on to Orson. It was just a fight, Jane. They've had many."

"But had Orson ever pressed charges before? Had they ever come to blows?"

Curt shook his head. "That was a fluke. An old friend of Orson's just happened to be at the bar. After Theo decked him, Orson couldn't pass up the chance to teach Theo a lesson. There was always a rivalry between them. If you ask me, someone should have ended the competition long ago."

"But what actually happened that night?" asked Jane. "What were they arguing about?"

"Don't know. I was across the room. Didn't hear the argument until the very end. I don't even remember what they said."

"All right." She took another sip of tea. "So Theo hits

Orson, he goes down. The officer comes over, and Orson has Theo arrested."

"That's about it. They pull Theo's arms behind his back, slap on the handcuffs and haul him out to the squad car."

"That's everything you remember?"

"Well, yeah. Everything until...later."

"Meaning?"

He hesitated. "It's kind of personal. But I suppose it doesn't matter if you know. Theo sent me a note."

"How?"

"Through Orson."

"What kind of note?"

Curt raked a hand through his hair. "Theo and I had had a conversation the day before. It ended with me getting pretty hot under the collar. I suppose he wanted to clear the air. While he was in the squad car, he wrote down a message and asked Orson if he'd give it to me."

"What did it say?"

Curt felt in the pocket of his jeans. "You might as well read it for yourself." He handed it to her.

Jane opened the piece of yellow stationery. In pencil, Theo had written:

> *Curt—Sorry about yesterday. It was all my fault. I think we need to talk. I don't know how long I'm going to be in jail, and I don't want to put this off. Could you come down tomorrow morning? I'm sure they'd let me have a visitor—I'm not an ax murderer. Please come. I'll be waiting.*
>
> *Theo*

Jane looked up. "Did you go?"

Curt turned his head away.

Jane could tell he was struggling with his emotions. "Are you all right?" she asked gently.

After a long moment, his chin began to quiver. He put

a hand to his forehead, covering his eyes. This was a fresh wound. "God, I was so mad at him. I thought he was jerking me around again. Same story, different chapter. He'd never give me a straight answer to anything."

"So you didn't go?"

"Annie saw me reading the note. She demanded to see it. Needless to say, she was furious. She thought he wanted to... did you know Theo and I were... lovers in college?"

Jane nodded.

"Annie felt terribly threatened by him. We've had a few problems in our marriage. But I love her. I told her that. I want things to work between us. It's just... I needed to have Theo tell me the truth just once!"

"So, did you go?"

"No," he said, his voice barely audible. "I promised Annie I wouldn't. And to be truthful, I thought it would hurt Theo if I didn't come. And I *wanted* to hurt him."

Jane could see the pain in his eyes. "Did you talk when he got back on Sunday night?"

He shook his head, biting a trembling lower lip. "There wasn't time."

"Listen Curt," she said, turning the mug around in her hand, "you couldn't have known he was going to die. You probably thought you had all the time in the world."

He squeezed his eyes shut.

Jane wanted to touch him, to reassure him, but Curt wasn't the kind of man you could approach easily. Even though they were talking intimately, he seemed to have a wall around him.

"Do you realize," he whispered, "that I don't even know why Theo went to prison."

"I thought he'd impersonated an IRS agent."

"Oh, I know that part, but *why* did he do something so stupid? He wasn't that reckless. When I asked him, he always made a joke of it."

"I'd heard he'd stolen fifteen thousand dollars. Maybe he needed the money."

Curt eased back into his chair. "On that point, Theo was adamant. From the very first, he insisted he hadn't taken a penny. He maintained that the head honcho at that widget company, or wherever it was he went, was probably embezzling funds and that Theo's arrest gave him an opportunity to blame it on someone else."

"Do you believe him?"

"I do." His gaze dropped to his hands.

Jane could tell that he was moving away from her. Perhaps it was time for bed. She quickly finished her tea.

Wearily, Curt stood and tossed a couple more logs on the fire. As he moved them around with the poker he said, "You're going to have a hard time coming up with a murderer from this group."

Jane wasn't so sure. He may not have realized it, but he'd revealed some rather intense emotions during their brief conversation. People had been killed over far less.

"Besides, what was the murder weapon?" He turned and stared at her.

"I don't know."

"No. That's because there wasn't one." He resumed his seat.

Jane's eyes felt like gravel. Her mind was shutting down. "Well, I think I'll turn in," she said, getting up. "I'm pretty bushed."

"Right," said Curt, his attention fixed on the fire. "Hope you sleep well."

"Thanks." As she walked up the stairs, she had the vague sense that something he'd said hadn't rung true. Unfortunately, she was too tired tonight to do any more thinking. It would have to wait until morning.

20

Jane didn't wake the next morning until after ten. She quickly showered and dressed, knowing the day was going to be a busy one. She had only forty-eight hours before the intervention. She hadn't slept well. Instead, she'd spent the night going over everything she'd learned. Cordelia had been right to think something was amiss. Jane's conversation with Curt last night had confirmed it. What she must do now was simply follow the threads to see where they led.

As she moved silently down the upstairs hall, she noticed that most of the doors were still closed. Only Orson's was open and empty. She didn't knock on Cordelia's door, she merely entered, lifting the shade slightly to allow some light into the room before sitting down on the edge of the bed.

"You don't need to get up," she said softly.

The covers rustled. Cordelia was completely buried in them.

"Just tell me where your car keys are."

"Why?" came the muffled response.

"I want to drive over to the funeral home. Check it out."

"Without *me?*"

"I didn't think you'd want to get up. I know you had a late night at The Mall."

An eye appeared. "Cute."

"So where are they?"

"When are you leaving?"

"Fifteen minutes, maybe. I thought I'd run downstairs and grab a bite to eat first."

"Make it twenty and I'll meet you out in the parking lot."

"Don't you want any breakfast?"

"I went a little berserk last night at the frozen yoghurt stand."

"I got it." She stood. "See you in twenty minutes."

As Jane passed the parlor, Hilda was running the vacuum cleaner over the carpet. The fireplace had already been cleaned. Newly picked daisies adorned the coffee table, and the smell of freshly baked bread told Jane that Diana's one person staff didn't let her mornings get away from her.

She entered the kitchen. Orson was sitting at the center island, having a cup of coffee. He was bent over a newspaper.

"Good morning," she said, getting down her own mug.

He didn't look up. "Morning."

"Something interesting in the paper?"

He nodded. "Theo's obituary."

"Oh . . . sorry."

He took a sip of coffee and then leaned back, scratching his unshaven chin. "*The Summer Green Gazette.* All the news that's fit to swat deer flies with."

Jane slid onto a stool.

"If you're up for it, Hilda made some rhubarb coffee cake. It's quite good. Heavy on the nutmeg and brown sugar."

"Thanks," said Jane. "This is fine." She poured herself some coffee. "How was your evening?"

"My evening?"

"You were meeting a friend in town."

"Oh. Yeah." He folded the paper and pushed it away. "It was okay. I suppose you went to bed early."

He'd changed the subject rather quickly. She wondered why. "Around nine. Where is everyone this morning?"

"Diana's still in bed. She never gets up before noon. And I assume Curt and Cordelia are still asleep too. Annie was up pretty early. She wanted to help Amity get ready for school. When I came down, they were leaving for the bus."

"That was nice of her."

"Annie's a great person."

"Where is she now?"

"Well, after Amity was safely on her way, she got in her car and drove off."

"Did she say where she was going?"

He shook his head, refilling his cup.

Jane's attention was drawn to the window as Hilda marched past it, a shovel over one shoulder. "You know, she's like a one woman army."

Orson turned to look. "Good description. She has the same energy level as my twelve-year-old. And the same annoying curiosity." He sighed, touching his graying temples.

Unlike yesterday, the sun was beating down on the cemetery in the distance. It was going to be a hot day. Jane was glad she'd brought some cool clothes along. "How long did you live in Summer Green before you left?" she asked.

"Nineteen years. Until I went to college."

"I suppose your family's happy to see you."

He shook his head. "They're all gone."

"I'm sorry. I always thought it would be great growing up in a small town."

"It was. My dad ran the local hardware store. Only problem was, I had a lot of interests I couldn't share with anyone. That's why I had to get out."

"But you probably come back often to see friends."

"Not really."

"I'm curious. How did you know about the church next door?"

He stood and walked to the refrigerator, lifting out a pitcher of orange juice. "It was kind of the town mystery. Friends mentioned it in letters."

"Really?"

"No one ever figured out why it burned. There were no electrical problems. Nothing wrong with the furnace. The insurance company wasn't going to pay off because they thought the fire was set."

"By whom?"

"The pastor, or someone in the congregation. They'd been trying to sell the building for years. They wanted to erect a new church on the other end of town—closer to the mall. This one was getting too small. Problem was, no one wanted to buy it."

"But couldn't the authorities prove something, one way or the other?"

He shook his head, grabbing two glasses and returning to his seat. "Want some?" he asked, nodding to the juice.

"Sure."

He poured Jane's first. "The pastor vehemently denied

that he or any member of his church had anything to do with the fire. He told the insurance company to either prove their contention that it was arson, or pay up."

"And?"

"They paid up. Eventually. The church sat idle for almost a year."

Interesting, thought Jane.

"It was a stroke of luck for Diana. She got it for next to nothing. I've always thought that church would make a perfect theatre. Except—" His expression sank. "It didn't help. I hoped beyond hope it might. I thought Diana could get it together if she just had some focus to her life."

"It was a good try. It might be just the thing to help pull her through—after the intervention I meant."

He put a finger to his lips.

"Sorry." She tried the juice. It was fresh squeezed. "I wanted to tell you how sorry I am about Theo."

"Thanks."

"Funny how things work out."

"Yeah." He looked up. "What do you mean?"

"Well, that you'd be unfortunate enough to get into a fight with him one day before his death." She knew the comment was insensitive, but she wanted to see how Orson would react.

"Are you trying to draw some conclusion from that?"

"No. I just think it's sad."

"It's more than sad. It's tragic."

Maybe it was her mood, but she didn't believe him. "What was the fight about?"

"It was personal."

"Oh. I see."

"No you don't. You couldn't possibly. But I can't explain it to you."

"You mean you won't."

"Quite frankly, Jane, I don't care what you think of

me. But you should understand one thing. I loved Theo like a brother. I would never hurt him."

"But you had him arrested."

"I mean hurt as in *murder*. That's what we're talking about, isn't it?"

She shrugged. "Maybe."

"I hardly think being knocked down in a bar is a reason to kill someone."

"I never said it was."

He studied her openly. With his growing anger held carefully in check he said, "Back off, Jane. Your insinuations are the last thing we need around here right now."

She finished her juice. She wasn't going to let him intimidate her. Besides, she was in Wisconsin. Her *Minnesota Nice* internal programming wasn't functional this far from home. "I'm not insinuating anything, Orson. I'm merely asking some questions."

He glared at her.

Cordelia chose that exact moment to breeze into the room. "I'm ready," she said, her eyes drawn like a magnet to the coffee cake. "I thought I smelled nutmeg."

Jane stood, glad for the interruption.

"What's wrong?" asked Cordelia, noticing Orson's scowl.

"Nothing. Jane and I were just . . . clearing the air."

"I didn't realize it was cloudy."

"Don't forget the unveiling this afternoon at three," said Orson.

"What unveiling?" asked Cordelia. She inched over to the counter.

"Oh. I forgot. You two weren't in the parlor last night before dinner. Diana got a call from an artist she commissioned in Chicago. Seems she's been sitting for a portrait. It's going to be hung in the vestibule as you come into the playhouse. The official unveiling is this afternoon." He added, rather ominously, "It's a command performance. Everyone is to be there."

Cordelia broke off a piece of the cake. "Black tie, or can we wear our grungies?"

"Something in between," he said, his scowl mellowing a bit.

"It's a date." She turned to Jane. "Ready?"

"Where are you off to?" he asked, trying not to sound too interested.

Before Cordelia could respond, Jane said, "Just some exploring."

"Think of us as local prospectors," grinned Cordelia. "Tapping away at the cow-infested hillsides, searching for gold, precious jewels. Lost farm machinery."

"Don't dig too deeply," he said, his scowl returning. "You may not like what you find."

21

The DeLappe Funeral Home was on Myrtle Street, just south of the library. It was an old two-story brownstone that had once been the home of the town's mayor. A tasteful black and gray sign hung high over the front door announcing its current occupants.

Jane led the way into the grand foyer, now turned reception area. No one was behind the desk. In fact, no one seemed to be around at all.

"Come here," whispered Cordelia, motioning Jane over to what appeared to be a chapel. Two fake marble pillars stood on either side of the archway. "Look at all the plastic flowers. I feel like I've died and gone to K-Mart."

Jane had to agree. The decorations were ghastly.

"And look at that podium," said Cordelia, trotting over to take a closer look. "Decals!" she gushed. "Little blue and white angels."

"Can I help you?"

Jane turned to find a short middle-aged woman with a blue smock and orange hair—very heavy on the make-up—staring at her. "Yes," she smiled, backing up several steps. "I'd like to talk to the coroner. I understand he owns the funeral home."

The woman eyed Jane's hair, touching an errant wisp that had slipped out of her French braid. "Great texture. I could do you up nicely."

"Excuse me?"

"Sorry, I should introduce myself. I'm Cora DeLappe—Arnie's sister. I do the corpses."

"You do the—" Out of the corner of her eye, Jane saw Cordelia's head ooze from behind one of the pillars. "Corpses?"

"Right," said Cora, her voice matter-of-fact. She moved behind the desk and sat down. "You know. The hair. Make-up. Nails." She took out an emery board from the top drawer. "I do it all. Used to be a hairdresser in Chicago, but I couldn't stand the pace. This is better."

Jane didn't doubt it.

"Except, I always say, the tips aren't as good." She laughed, catching sight of Cordelia. She gave a little wave. "I suppose you want to see my brother."

"Is he the coroner?" asked Jane.

"For the last eight years."

"Is he also a physician?"

She shook her head. "Coroners are elected officials here. He appoints a real doctor to work with him as his assistant, but Arnie's just...a regular guy. I'll go get him. He's in the back, arranging a cremation."

"You do cremations?" asked Jane.

"Nah. We send the bodies over to Appleton. I'll be right back." She crossed to a door at the rear of a short hall and disappeared.

Cordelia inched a little further into the room. "I'll bet she decorated the chapel."

"Good guess," said Jane. She took another moment to look around. "No Smoking" signs were plastered everywhere, so much so that she had the urge to light up, even though she loathed cigarettes.

A few seconds later, Cora came out of the back room, followed closely by a stocky man of approximately the same height. They could have been twins, except the man's hair was brown. "Good morning," he said, his voice low and calm. "Arnold DeLappe."

Jane could see a mixture of curiosity and sadness pass across his solid face. He obviously wasn't sure why they were there and he didn't want to seem too chipper in case Uncle Bob had just bought the farm. At least he wasn't rubbing his hands together. "I'm a friend of Theo Donati's," said Jane. Was it her imagination, or did the man's expression tighten.

"Yes. Your name is—"

"Jane Lawless. And this is my friend, Cordelia Thorn."

"Nice to meet you both." He shook their hands. "Mr. Donati's . . . remains are just being taken to the crematorium as we speak. We generally hold them for forty-eight hours, but in this case, we had to rush a little. The service is set for three tomorrow afternoon. "

"I know."

"Are you familiar with cremations?" He looked at Cordelia for an answer.

"Familiar?"

"No. Most people aren't. Fire has been used to dispose of our dear departed since prehistoric times. The Greeks started using it around 1000 B.C. Even the Bible talks about the cremation of King Saul. I know the Jewish religion forbids it, but the Catholic church—are you Catholic?"

Cordelia blinked. "No."

"Neither am I. But as I was about to say, even the Catholic church has removed its ban. Did you know that in Great Britain fewer than one third of all bodies are buried?"

Cordelia was becoming annoyed. "Fascinating."

"It is, isn't it. You learn something new every day."

"Actually," said Jane, "I was hoping you could answer a couple of questions for us."

"Why certainly," he smiled, again sadly. "Would you like to sit down?" He swept his hand to the folding chairs in the chapel.

She shook her head. "This shouldn't take long."

"All right." He waited, a pleasant look on his face.

"Did you sign the death certificate?"

"I did. One of our volunteer paramedics called me from the ambulance right after your friend—Theo—had passed away. I was on the scene in a matter of minutes."

"Do you have a copy of it here?"

"The death certificate? No. Sorry. You'll have to go over to the courthouse for that."

"I'm just curious. Why didn't you order an autopsy?"

Arnie DeLappe jutted out his somewhat weak chin. "But there was no need. It wasn't an unattended death. Three people witnessed the trauma. The body was pronounced dead by a police officer who was called to the scene shortly before I arrived. One of the witnesses suggested the man had a history of heart problems—confirmed, I might add, by a bottle of prescription heart medication I found in his pocket. I did order a blood test. The findings are in the case file with the death certificate and police report. Nothing was amiss. Orson Albern, an old friend, was also present. You can ask him if you have any lingering doubts about the manner of Mr. Donati's death."

"He's not a physician."

Arnie blinked several times. "I don't quite understand your concern, Ms. Lawless. Are you suggesting Mr. Donati's death wasn't . . . entirely natural?"

"I'm not suggesting anything. However, the fact that no autopsy was performed does give me pause."

He squared his shoulders. "I have been the coroner in

this county for many years, Jane. May I call you Jane? And never *once* has one of my death certifications been called into question!"

"I'm not attacking your honesty."

"I should hope not."

She knew she had to give him the benefit of the doubt. Besides, small towns did things differently than big cities. "Did the blood test reveal anything unusual?"

"Absolutely nothing out of the ordinary. He'd apparently been drinking, so that was recorded. You can look at the findings yourself if you go over to the courthouse." He puffed out his chest, such as it was.

"What about this heart medication?"

"Aldomet. Yes. Apparently he hadn't been taking it. No traces were found in the blood. That could be why he had the problem that night."

"What about his personal effects?"

"I have them in the back room. Since you're staying at the parsonage, you might want to take them with you." He stepped to a door off the chapel and returned a moment later with a small plastic suitcase, handing it to Cordelia. "It's all included in the cost of the cremation."

Cordelia held it up, pointing to the words DeLappe Funeral Home written in black gothic script across the front of the case. She gave Jane a sickly smile.

"By the way, who's paying for all this?" asked Jane.

"Orson Albern and Annie Whittig. At least they signed the forms. You just missed Mrs. Whittig."

"She was here?"

He nodded.

"Do you know why?"

Cora DeLappe, who had been sitting quietly behind the reception desk filing her nails, answered, "Oh, she brought by a map. She wanted to give us the exact location of the cemetery plot—where the cremains will be buried."

"I see." Jane didn't feel entirely satisfied. Still, she couldn't think of anything else to ask. "Well, I guess you've answered my questions."

"I sincerely hope so," said Arnie, his official tone tinged with a certain reproof. "You mustn't worry, Ms. Lawless—Jane. Everything is being handled properly."

"Thanks. I suppose we'll see you tomorrow."

"You will," he said, his voice once again sad.

As they got out to the car, Cordelia put a hand on the door handle and then stopped.

"What is it?" asked Jane.

"Just answer me one thing."

"What?"

"How did he know we were staying at the parsonage?"

Jane cocked her head. "Did he say that?"

"He most certainly did. All we told him was that we were friends of Theo's."

Odd. "Maybe he assumed."

"Quite a leap of faith."

Or maybe he was warned, thought Jane. "Who could have told him we were coming?"

Cordelia held up her hand and ticked the names off one by one. "Orson, Annie, Curt or Diana. They all know you came to Summer Green for one reason, and one reason only. To find out if Theo was murdered."

"You think this DeLappe guy was lying to us?"

"How should I know! It makes me sick to think one of my friends might be involved in Theo's death. All I've got to go on are feelings—impressions. A knife in a door. A guy driving a white Cadillac. A fight in a bar. What the hell am I supposed to think?" She turned her back to Jane and took several deep breaths. "Maybe I'm just neurotic. Don't answer that."

Jane gave her a moment to calm down. "I'm sorry this is so hard on you."

"Last night I thought maybe we should just give it up. Leave well enough alone."

"Is that what you really want?"

Cordelia held Jane's eyes. "No," she whispered. "I want to know the truth."

Jane's heart went out to her. "I can't lie to you, Cordelia. I think your impressions are accurate. Something isn't right here. I just need more time."

"We haven't got much."

"I know."

"The problem is—" She kicked a rock across the lot. "—I always tell people that . . . well, that I've had a large part in helping you solve some of these mysteries."

"Is that right," said Jane. "I was under the impression you told everyone *I helped you*. Minimally, of course."

"Well . . . I suppose I might have said that. I will admit to a certain penchant for hyperbole."

"That's good of you."

"But I'm desperate here! The truth is, when it comes to solving crimes, I'm a dud."

"No you're not."

"I am. You're my only hope."

"Don't say that. Besides, you've helped me a great deal."

"I have?"

"Sure. For instance, let me ask you this. What part of our conversation with Arnold DeLappe do you think was a fraud?"

Cordelia closed her eyes and shook her head, leaning

back against the car door. "I don't know. It all sounded plausible to me. I mean, what the hell do I know about autopsies? You're the real sleuth, for chrissake. You tell me."

Jane could feel her teeth clench. "Don't wimp out on me now, Cordelia. We've *both* got to use our heads."

"Right."

"Get in." She opened the driver's door.

"Why?"

"You'll see."

22

Jane and Cordelia drove to a small park directly across the street from the First Bank of Summer Green. Since it was now nearly noon, and Cordelia needed a dose of saturated animal fat to keep her going until dinner, they'd stopped at a hamburger stand on the way and bought some lunch.

"Nice spot," said Jane, setting the DeLappe Funeral Home suitcase on one of two picnic tables. She was anxious to examine the contents, but first things first. Swings and an old-fashioned teeter-totter nestled against a stand of pine. Since school had now officially started for the year, the park was empty of children. One lone dog trotted across the grass, heading for the woods which bordered the property.

"Very bucolic," replied Cordelia, dumping the white food bag on the table and sitting down. She unwrapped one of the burgers. "This is yours. I ordered extra mustard, no pickle."

"Thanks." Jane sat down on the other side. "These look pretty good."

"Try the cole slaw. The sign said they're famous for it."

"Are they also famous for onion rings?" She fingered the hefty sack.

"Janey, you *know* I've been searching for the perfect onion ring all my life. Of course, it would be just my luck to find them at Mannie's Hamburger Heaven—since I come here so often."

Jane tried one. "Not bad." She took a bite of her hamburger while Cordelia did the same. "Tell me something. Has Diana been drinking pretty steadily ever since you got here?"

"She's usually got something in her hand, though most of the time she doesn't seem all that high. It's generally in the evenings when she starts showing the effects."

"Like last night at dinner."

"Exactly. Her attitude changes. She becomes more confrontational. More—"

"Obnoxious."

"Well, sort of."

"Refresh my memory. Does she have any brothers or sisters? Are her parents still alive?"

Cordelia took a sip of Coke. "She's an only child. Her mom and dad live in St. Paul. They've never gotten along very well. I don't think Diana has kept in contact with them."

"That's too bad. Do they know she's a lesbian?"

"God, no. I forget you don't know Diana very well. She's a very closeted person. She's always maintained she needed to be because of her career."

"Is that true?"

Cordelia took another bite of her burger, thinking the question over. "Yeah, I suppose in some ways it is. Not so much with the theatre, but certainly on TV and in film. There are lots of gay and lesbian actors who are very secretive about their sexuality. Things leak out, but you never know for sure. Maybe the nineties will change some of that. Still, up until now, specific knowledge could easily hurt or even ruin somebody's career. For some reason, when you think about a woman doing a love scene with a man, you realize the audience wants to believe they really are watching a piece of reality. Even if the two people in question can't stand each other, even if the guy's got halitosis from hell, or she's a rabid racist or he's a hopeless sexist, the fact that this interaction *could* be true carries the audience along. When one of the actors is gay, it removes that possibility. Of course, we also see lesbians and gay men kissing and mauling each other all over the place in movies and on TV—and, I might add, very realistically— we just don't *know* that's what we're seeing."

Jane shook her head. "What crap."

"It is. In many ways, by keeping our identities in the dark, we're perpetuating the notion that gays or lesbians can't act any role that's given them. After all, that's the bottom line, isn't it? It *is* acting."

"What about Theo? Was he pretty out in college?"

"He and I both were—unlike you, my dear, who never told a single soul in that godawful sorority you belonged to."

Jane wiped her hands on a napkin. "Coming out is a process, Cordelia. Everyone does it at their own pace and in their own way."

"And some people never do it at all."

"Meaning what? You think people should be *outed*? Forced out of the closet by some sleazy exposé in a magazine or a newspaper?"

Cordelia shrugged, popping an onion ring into her mouth. "Theo thought that."

"Seriously?"

"Orson told me he and Diana had a big argument about it once. Diana said people had a right to their privacy. Theo agreed—in principle—but in today's world, he insisted we all needed to do our part, no matter what the cost. Claim our identities and our rights. We can't do that hidden in a closet...and other stuff like that." She took another bite of burger.

Jane had heard the arguments before. "I always love it when other people make decisions for my life."

Cordelia raised an eyebrow.

"What does Curt think about it?"

"Curt's about as private as they come. If I had to guess, I'd say he'd agree with Diana. He's spent the last twenty years with his hand on the mute button."

"He is a quiet man."

"That's an understatement."

"But is it possible he's the kind of person who keeps everything bottled up deep inside until one day it explodes?"

Cordelia finished her burger. "Sounds a little too slick to me."

"What do you mean?"

"We all keep stuff bottled up inside. They're called memories."

Jane smiled. "Thank you Dr. Bradshaw."

"You're welcome."

"Come on," said Jane, stuffing the remnants of her lunch back into the paper sack, "Let's look at that suitcase."

Cordelia grabbed the last onion ring before Jane whisked everything away. She sipped her Coke as Jane removed Theo's clothes. Jeans. A shirt. A sweater. "Are you looking for something specific?"

"His wallet. And that heart medication DeLappe said he'd found." Jane felt a certain revulsion, pawing through a dead man's effects. Still, it had to be done. "Here it is," she said, finding the wallet at the very bottom. She opened it, slipping out his driver's license. "Hey, will you look at this."

"What?"

"It's Theo's picture, but the name on it says Rob Wilson."

Cordelia scrunched up her nose. "Come again?"

"And didn't you tell me he was living somewhere in Florida."

"He is. Was. At least, that's what Orson told me."

"This is a Texas license."

"Let me see that." Cordelia grabbed it and read out loud: "Rob Wilson, 4837 Freemont Way, Houston, Texas. It expires in January." She looked up. "I don't get it."

"He was using an alias."

"Obviously. But why?"

Jane shook her head. "Did any of you know?"

"Not to my knowledge."

"What did Theo do for a living?"

Cordelia looked a bit startled by the question. "You know, I've got no idea."

"You never asked him?"

"Janey, I haven't seen Theo since he was in prison. He never came back to Minnesota—at least, not that I knew of—and according to Orson, he never gave away his address."

"But I thought he visited Diana in New York."

"He did. Orson saw him there once. And he visited Curt and Annie right after he got out of the slammer. Spent a couple of months in Chicago, but then he disappeared."

"And during the first two days of his stay here, no one ever asked him about a job?"

"I didn't. I guess maybe I thought it might embarrass him. Just in case times were tight."

"Isn't that his new Acura in the parking lot?"

Cordelia nodded.

"Times weren't too tight."

"Well, whatever. Maybe someone else talked to him about his work life. But I wasn't in on it."

Jane shook her head. "It doesn't matter. I doubt he would have told the truth anyway." She retrieved the wallet from Cordelia and continued her search. "Everything's in the name of Rob Wilson. Credit cards. A library card."

"Let's see the picture of the Shevlin Underground."

"What picture?"

"The one Theo showed us the other night. He said he always kept it in his wallet. In the money flap. It was taken of the six of us in the fall of our sophomore year. He was arrested the next spring."

Jane emptied the pouch of cash and then looked behind the flap. "Nothing." She held it out for Cordelia to see.

"I don't understand."

Jane searched the rest of the wallet, but found nothing other than a paper clip, two stamps and a folded newspaper article.

"Do you suppose someone stole it?"

Jane shook her head. "Why?" Then again, her gut feeling told her it was gone for a reason. "You're *sure* he kept it in his wallet?"

"Positive. I saw him put it away." Cordelia tossed a piece of hamburger bun to a squirrel. "What's that newspaper clipping about?"

Jane opened it up. "It's from the *Chicago Sun Times*. A small piece about the opening of the Summer Green Playhouse. Someone must have interviewed Diana." Jane read down the column. "She mentions all of you by name. Talks about your directorship of the Allen Grimby. Mentions Orson's ownership of the Blackburn Playhouse.

Talks a little about Annie and Curt. And then it just mentions Theo's name. Says you'll be attending the first performance."

"That was nice of her," said Cordelia absently. "Oh yeah, it was a press release."

"Hum." Jane finished reading it. "I wonder why he saved it?"

"Sentimental reasons, I suppose."

"And here's the heart medication," said Jane, finding a small orange plastic bottle in one of the suitcase's side compartments. She read the printed matter on the front. "RX 498205—Dr. Smith. Rob Wilson. Take one tablet daily. Aldomet. 0.625 MG. Net—34 tablets. No refills. 08/15/94."

"Sounds legitimate enough."

Jane turned it over, trying to picture what her own prescriptions looked like. "Something isn't right."

"Be more specific."

"There's no pharmacy name or address. No phone number." She removed the cover, shaking one of the pills into her hand. It was small, round and white. She showed it to Cordelia.

"Looks like an aspirin."

Jane held it closer. "It says APAP on the front."

"Oh, sure. I take APAP all the time for heartburn."

"Be serious."

"How the hell should I know what APAP is?"

"One way to find out."

"And that is?"

"See that drug store over there—next to the bank."

"I have eyes."

"I'll lay you odds they have a pharmacy. All we have to do is walk over and ask."

"I'll bet it's Aldomet."

"Put your money where your mouth is."

Cordelia stood up and started putting Theo's belongings back into the case. "An ice-cream cone. You buy if I'm right."

"You're on." Jane scrambled to her feet.

"God, I feel... guilty."

"Why?" Jane knew, even before Cordelia said the words. She watched her zip up the suitcase and then cradle it lovingly in her arms.

"We're here talking about ice-cream cones, and Theo's—"

"I know," said Jane. "It's not fair."

"Maybe he's having an ice-cream cone wherever he is."

"Maybe."

"I hope so. With a cup of coffee. He loved coffee." She sighed. "Come on. This day doesn't have enough hours in it. We still have to get over to the courthouse."

Jane was glad for the show of enthusiasm. If they kept up the pretense of movement, maybe she wouldn't be depressed by the realization that she didn't know what the hell she was doing.

23

Jane walked directly back to the pharmacy at the rear of the store and waited while a clerk standing in front of the cash register broke open a new roll of nickels. The building was long and narrow, with scuffed wood floors and a high, neon pink ceiling. Jane spied a row of condoms *behind* the counter. Great place for them, she thought as she examined a bottle of mouthwash. When the woman was done and had closed the register, Jane asked, "Could you help me?"

"Certainly." She moved closer. "Do you have a prescription?"

"No," said Jane. She handed over one of the pills. "Can you tell me what that is? I was told it was Aldomet—a heart medication."

The clerk put on her glasses which had been hanging by a black cord around her neck. "Offhand, I'd say you were misinformed. But, wait a minute. I'll show it to the pharmacist." She stepped behind a door.

Jane could hear a muffled conversation. A minute later the woman returned.

"I was right," she announced. "It's not Aldomet. It's acetaminophen."

"What's that?"

"It's like Tylenol. This is just a generic form." She handed the pill back and readjusted her glasses, eyeing Jane a bit more critically.

Jane nodded her thanks. So, she'd been right.

"If someone thinks this is a heart medication," continued the woman, "they need to be warned." Her face was full of concern.

"It's nothing like that," said Jane. "But thanks for the information." She turned and headed back to the front of the store. Cordelia was standing near the soda fountain, reading a list of ice-cream flavors posted on the wall.

"You owe me a double dip," said Jane, moving up beside her.

"What was it?" asked Cordelia.

"A generic form of Tylenol."

She whistled. "No kidding. Somebody was trying to pull a fast one." She sat down on a stool. "I wonder why?"

Jane had already formed a couple of theories. For now, she decided to keep them to herself. She glanced up at the wall. "Let's see. I'll have a scoop of the praline cream and one of the chocolate brownie."

"You took the words right out of my mouth," smiled Cordelia. She placed the order.

A few minutes later as they were about to exchange the cool interior of the drug store for the sweltering interior of Cordelia's car, Jane pulled her to a stop.

"What's wrong?" Cordelia licked a major drip off the side of her cone.

"Look over there," said Jane, pointing to a silver Honda which had just parked across the street next to a red truck. "Isn't that Curt and Annie's?"

Cordelia squinted. "Since Curt and Annie are getting out of it, I'd say that's a good guess." She took another lick. "Doesn't Annie look nice with her hair down like that? I'd never tell her this to her face, but she looks ten years younger."

Jane watched them stroll casually into a restaurant several doors down. She read the name on the dark green awning. "Johnson's Bar and Deli." On the side of the building she saw another sign which said, "On Sale/Off Sale Liquors. Biggest selection in the county."

"I don't blame them for wanting to get away from the parsonage for a while," said Cordelia, biting into a caramelized nut. "It's beginning to feel like a prison."

Jane glanced to her left and was surprised to see Orson come out of the bank building right next to them. His eyes darted furtively both ways down the street as he stuffed an envelope inside the pocket of his sport coat. "And look there," she said, dragging Cordelia further into the shadows. "Brother Orson. I wonder what business he has at a bank."

"Probably something monetary," offered Cordelia.

Jane closed her eyes and shook her head.

Orson gave the street one last perusal and then trotted across to the same restaurant Curt and Annie had just entered.

"A meeting in town?"

"I'd say it's a conspiracy to have lunch," replied Cordelia, elbowing Jane in the ribs. "Just a little joke."

Jane's eyes rose to the sky.

"And pay attention to your ice cream, dearheart, or it's going to turn into a disgusting puddle."

She licked off the biggest drips.

"Come on. Let's go. We've still got to hit the courthouse. And remember, we promised to be back at the playhouse before three."

"You go get the car. I'll wait here," announced Jane.

"Why?"

"Just get it, will you? Let me watch for another min-ute."

Cordelia gave an exasperated snort. "I think we're about to cross the border into paranoid-land, Janey."

Jane glared at her.

"Sorry. Just an observation."

Jane returned her gaze to the restaurant.

"Right. Well. I'm off. Miss me." She sauntered slowly across the street. Her Le Sabre was parked in a lot on the other side of the park. At her current pace, it would be a ten-minute stroll.

As Jane continued to watch, licking her ice-cream cone somewhat absently, the minutes ticked by. Just as she was about to give up her post, Orson appeared in the restaurant's doorway. Again, he looked both ways down the street. It was clear to even the most amateur observer that he was being very careful. Since he hadn't been inside long enough to have a meal, Jane wondered what his purpose was for meeting Curt and Annie. Maybe it was a chance encounter. Or maybe it wasn't. She watched him get into his car. Just at that moment, Cordelia roared up. She might walk with the casual insouciance of a bored tourist, but she drove like a maniac.

Jane hopped in. "You're not going to believe this next request."

It was Cordelia's turn to glare. "Which is?"

"See that light blue Lincoln over there?"

"That's Orson's car."

"Right. Follow it."

Cordelia crunched the last bit of her cone. "Why?"

"And don't be too obvious. I don't want him to know he's being followed."

"I am not a New York City cab driver."

"Good. Then perhaps we'll survive the ordeal."

"I despise chase scenes."

"This isn't a chase scene. I just want to know where he's going."

Orson's car pulled out into the street and turned west on the highway which led out of town.

Cordelia eased in behind him, keeping a safe distance.

"Now," continued Jane, "if he stops somewhere, just keep going. We can double back after a couple blocks."

"There are no blocks in the country."

"Fine. Then turn around at the second cow."

"You're mocking me."

"How could you think that?"

Orson's car was beginning to slow.

"You have to admit, there *are* a lot of cows around here," sniffed Cordelia.

"Wisconsin is the dairy state."

"Thank you for that civics lesson. Perhaps we'll have time to visit a creamery while we're here."

"Say, there's that motel," said Jane. "The one where the bus dropped me off." She couldn't miss the horrid turquoise siding even from a distance.

"Ah yes. The Sunburst Motel. I remember it fondly. Probably Summer Green's version of the No-Tell Motel."

"Isn't that where that director is staying? You know, John Hubble?"

"I empty my mind of such trivia as soon as I hear it."

The blue Lincoln turned into the dirt lot in front of the motel and kicked up a cloud of dust before pulling to a stop.

"Keep going," said Jane.

"I know what I'm supposed to do!" Cordelia pressed the accelerator and sped down the highway. About a quarter of a mile up the road she spied a fruit stand. "Want a watermelon?"

"Just turn around. When we get back to those trees just this side of the motel, pull off."

"You're sure you don't want a . . . cantaloupe?" She wiggled her eyebrows.

"Cordelia!"

"Just checking." She turned the car around.

"I wonder what business he could have at a motel?"

Cordelia shrugged. "Is that our hiding place?" she asked, nodding to a thickly wooded spot on her right.

"It's perfect. He won't be able to see us, but we can see him."

Cordelia drove slowly in between two huge elm trees. She slipped the car into neutral and let it idle. "Now what?" she asked, tapping an impatient finger on the steering wheel.

"We wait."

"For how long?"

"Until he comes out." Jane swept her eyes down the long row of rooms. Only two other cars were in the lot. Summer Green wasn't a particularly busy spot for adultery, or anything else. As they sat and waited, one lone truck passed them on the highway.

"Can I turn on the radio?" asked Cordelia.

"You won't find anything other than polka music."

"My, aren't we into stereotypes."

"All right. See what you can get." Jane had already tried the radio back at the parsonage. This far from a large town, the selection was pretty slim.

Cordelia switched it on, adjusting the controls until she found a station. Polka music blared from her four, perfectly balanced speakers. Gasping, she lunged for the off button. "Okay," she growled, "be smug. See if I care." She turned her head away and started humming.

Thankfully, their wait didn't turn out to be long. Less

than ten minutes later, a tall dark-haired woman came out of the last room on the right. She got into her car and sped off without a backward glance. A few moments later, Orson reappeared. Once again, he surveyed the country-side, looking both ways down the highway. Apparently satisfied that he wasn't being watched, he got back into his car and started the engine.

"Looks like he's renting a room," said Jane.

"If he's cheating on his wife again!" erupted Cordelia, "I'll strangle him with my bare hands."

"I didn't know Orson—"

"He and Ingrid were having some problems a while back. He said it was just a brief encounter. It didn't mean a thing. But this!"

"I don't think you have anything to worry about."

"How can you be so sure?"

Jane was beginning to put a few of the pieces together. It looked like one of her theories might just hold water. "Quick," she barked, "or we'll lose him."

Cordelia pulled back onto the highway. "He's heading out of town. Where the hell is he going?"

"Don't let him get away!"

Orson's car picked up speed. In fact, as Cordelia's Le Sabre barreled around a steep bend about half a mile down the road, the Lincoln seemed to have disappeared.

"Keep driving," said Jane. "He's trying to ditch any tail he might have picked up. I'm sure he's moving as fast as he can."

"He's going to kill himself on one of these curves," she said, trying to keep her own car in the proper lane.

"Just drive!"

About five miles out of town, the road straightened and the land became flat. They could now see for miles.

"He lost us," said Jane, banging her hand on the dash-board. "Damn it!"

"Where do you suppose he is?"

"He could be anywhere. He could even be at that god-damn fruit stand eating a peach."

Cordelia slowed the car to fifty-five. "What are we going to do?"

Jane had to think. "Listen, Cordelia. I want to go back to that motel. I have to know for sure if Orson's rented a room."

"So what if he has? What does it tell us?"

Jane rolled her window down all the way and let the fresh country air rush over her. "It tells us, Cordelia, that Orson is up to something. And I'll bet the farm it has to do with Theo's untimely demise."

24

"Pull up over there by that last room," said Jane, pointing to the spot where Orson's Lincoln had just been parked. The motel's office was all the way at the other end of the building. She wondered if Orson had chosen this room with privacy in mind.

"What do you expect to find?" asked Cordelia.

"I'm not sure." Jane slid out of her seat, glad that so few people were around. It would make this a lot easier. Stepping up on the sidewalk that ran in front of the units, she crossed to number twelve's picture window and peeked through a crack in the heavy drapes. Inside, the room was dark. She could make out a bed, a TV set, two chairs, a nightstand and a dresser. Nothing very fancy.

"Is anyone in there?" asked Cordelia, coming up behind her.

Jane shook her head. "It's quiet." She turned around, her eyes readjusting to the brilliant afternoon sunlight.

"So? Do we break in?"

Jane smiled at her enthusiasm. "No. Now we go talk to the manager."

"Oh goody."

Halfway to the office, a door opened and out stepped John Hubble. "Afternoon ladies," he said, a look of mild surprise on his face.

Jane took in the cashmere jacket, brown tam and dark glasses. He wasn't even pretending to look like one of the locals. "Hi," she smiled.

"To what do I owe such an unexpected visit?"

So, he thought they'd come to see him. Jane decided to play along. "Did you know about the portrait of Diana that's going to be unveiled this afternoon at the play-house?"

"I certainly did. I'm on my way right now to pick up a couple of the actors."

"Now?" said Jane.

He checked his watch. "It's nearly two-thirty."

"My, how time flies when you're eating ice cream," chirped Cordelia. She shielded her eyes from the sun.

He fished inside his pocket for his car keys. "That was nice of you two to drive all the way over here."

"We were in the neighborhood," said Cordelia, breaking an awkward pause. "Searching for watermelon."

"Watermelon?"

"Say," said Jane, "as I think of it, perhaps you could answer a question for me."

"Anything," he smiled.

"Do you know the man who's renting the end room here?"

"You mean your friend, Orson Albern?"

It was Jane's turn to be surprised.

"I think people have a right to their privacy. He doesn't bother me, and I don't bother him. As far as I can tell, we're the only two people here."

"Do you see him come and go a lot?"

He shrugged. "Only once. The first and last time was

yesterday evening. He drove in just after dark."

So Orson hadn't gone for coffee with a friend as he'd said. Jane wondered what he'd been doing here.

"I'd better get moving," said John, feeling in his back pocket for his wallet. "If we're late, Diana's going to have our hides—and perhaps other, more essential parts of our anatomy. Come to think of it, if I don't show up, maybe she'll fire me!"

"You want out of that production pretty badly, don't you," said Jane.

"That's an understatement." He seemed to grow uneasy. "Alas, duty calls. I gotta run." He dashed to his car. "See you two at the playhouse."

Jane waited until he'd driven off before continuing on to the office.

"Seems like a nice enough guy," said Cordelia, puffing to catch up.

Jane didn't respond. She was already thinking about what she would say to the manager. Before they got to the door, she stopped. "Have you got a twenty?"

"Dollar bill?"

"We may need to bribe her... or him."

"This is Summer Green, Janey. Wouldn't a five do?"

"And you call me cheap?"

Glumly, Cordelia reached into her front pocket and drew out a money clip. She pulled off a twenty, handing it over.

"Let me do the talking."

"While I do the paying."

"Shhh." As she opened the door, a wave of musty, rancid smelling air rolled over her.

Cordelia began to choke.

"Get a grip," whispered Jane. She approached the counter. No one was around. The furnishings were about what she'd expected. A study in 60s grotesque—right down to the dark blue shag. The only thing missing was a lava lamp. She rang the buzzer.

Out from the back room came a middle-aged man. He was wearing shorts and a T-shirt. "Yeah?" he said, a cigarette dangling from the side of his mouth.

"I've got a couple of questions."

"So?"

Jane put the twenty down on the counter top.

"What about?"

"The man in number twelve."

He looked her up and down. Then he eyed Cordelia. "What do you wanna know?"

"When did he check in?"

The man's eyes flicked to the twenty. "I'm not allowed to give out that kind of information."

"Fine," said Jane. She picked up the money and turned, starting for the door.

"Just hold your horses," he said, removing the cigarette from his lips and tapping the ash into an ashtray. "Bring that back here." He pointed to the bill in her hand.

She slid it onto the counter.

He quickly slipped it into his pocket. Then, opening a plastic file sitting on the counter next to him, he removed a small card. "The guy's name is Able. Martin Able. Said he's from Duluth. He checked in on the fourth. That would be Saturday afternoon."

"How long is he staying for?"

The man put the cigarette back in his mouth. "He left that open."

Jane looked at Cordelia, dropping her eyes to the pocket where Cordelia kept her money clip. She rubbed her fingers together.

Cordelia got the message. Reluctantly, she removed it again and handed it to Jane.

"I want to see inside the room."

"Impossible."

She pulled off another twenty.

"If you get caught, it's my butt that's in the sling."

Another twenty went down on the counter.

"Nobody will catch us," said Jane. "This is how we're going to do it. Is the room next to number twelve connected by an inside door?"

"Yeah." He scratched his shoulder.

"Let us in that one like you're showing it to us. Then unlock the connecting door. I'll go in and look around—it'll only take a minute. Then we're out and gone. And you're sixty bucks richer. What do you say?"

He continued to scratch his shoulder. "Yeah, well . . . I guess so. That sounds okay."

"Great." Jane swept to the door and held it open.

The man grabbed a set of keys off a hook and followed her out and down to the next to the last room. Cordelia brought up the rear. She'd completely lost her enthusiasm.

As they entered unit number eleven, Jane was once again struck by the awful smell. Centuries of cigarette smoke. She waited while he unlocked the connecting door.

"Make it fast," he mumbled, moving over to the drapes and looking outside. "If I see anyone pull up, I'll holler—quietly, that is. I expect the two of you to get out of here pronto. You got it?"

Jane nodded. She let Cordelia go first.

Once inside, Jane found a light switch that turned on a dim lamp on the nightstand next to the bed. She couldn't believe people would actually spend time in a place this filthy. The rug looked like it hadn't been washed since the Crusades. Cigarette burns were everywhere.

"What are we looking for?" whispered Cordelia.

"Anything," said Jane. "And everything." She crossed

to a closet and opened the door. It was empty. One crooked hanger dangled from a hook. Same with all the dresser drawers. All empty. "He's using this place for something."

"Like what? Cheap sex? I'd rather do it in a feed bin in central Iowa."

"You read too many romance novels," said Jane.

"So what if I do?"

Standing in the center of the room and searching it with her eyes, Jane saw an answering machine next to the phone. "That's it."

"What's it?"

"He's getting private calls here." She moved over to the bed and sat down. "This isn't the kind of place that offers amenities like an answering machine."

"You got that right." Cordelia backed away from the dresser. She didn't seem to want to touch anything.

Jane pushed the playback button. After a few clicks, a woman began speaking. "The train arrives at one thirty. I can't *wait* to see you!" The voice was breathy. Seductive. "Bye."

"I was right!" roared Cordelia.

"Shhh." Jane was confused. She waited for another message, but that was it.

"Time's up," called the manager. He sounded like he meant business.

"We better hit the bricks," said Cordelia, checking her watch. "We've got exactly ten minutes to make it back to the playhouse."

"What about the courthouse?"

"It's going to have to wait." Cordelia made a swift but dignified exit.

As Jane got up from the bed, she realized she was more confused now than she'd been before. Maybe what she needed was a break. If she gave her mind some time to work this all though, she was sure she would come up with an answer. Well, pretty sure, she thought as she switched off the light.

25

"Step on it," said Jane, glancing at her watch as they sped out of town. "We're going to be late."

"No, we aren't," Cordelia assured her. "If Diana said three, she meant in the vicinity of three. She's not known for her punctuality." She slowed for a truck driving erratically along the dirt shoulder.

"Watch it!" cried Jane. The truck veered suddenly into their lane. As Cordelia slammed on the brakes, a hard object hit Jane's foot.

"Fucking moron!" shouted Cordelia as the rusted heap lumbered in front of them and then turned onto a country road.

Jane bent down and picked up an empty wine bottle. "A little late night party?" she asked, waving the evidence in front of Cordelia's nose.

"Where did you get that?"

"When you braked, it rolled out from under the seat."

Cordelia grabbed it from Jane's hand, her eyes growing wide. "This is the wine bottle I told you about! The one I couldn't find. See? It's a German Riesling. The very same one Theo was drinking from the night he died."

Jane held it at arms length. "How'd it get in your car?"

"Good question." Their eyes met briefly.

Jane removed the cork and sniffed the contents. A tiny bit remained in the bottom. "Smells like regular old wine to me. Nothing out of the ordinary." She dipped her finger into the top.

"Don't taste it!"

"Why not? A little won't hurt me."

"You don't know that, Janey! Just leave it alone."

Jane gave an exasperated sigh. "Do you realize how toxic it would have to be to—"

Cordelia gripped the steering wheel. "Don't argue! Just do as I say." Her lips pressed together tightly. "Look, I'm sorry, but I've really had it with this entire situation. I'm...on overload, okay? You're just going to have to put up with me." She relaxed her grip a bit. "Maybe we should have it tested."

"I doubt they have the facilities to do that sort of thing in Summer Green. We'd have to drive to Green Bay. It would take a while to get the results back. We'd never have them before it was time to leave."

Cordelia shook her head. "This is all happening too fast."

"I know." Jane turned the bottle over and read the back. "Look at this. It was bought at Johnson's Liquors. Remember that place we saw Orson, Annie and Curt go into at lunch time? It was a restaurant, bar and off-sale liquor store. I wonder if Diana buys all her liquor there?"

Cordelia shook her head, braking as she saw the playhouse's spire come into view. "I'm pretty sure Diana has everything sent from a store in Appleton. Summer Green is a little too provincial for her tastes."

"Then why was this bought at Johnson's?"

She shrugged. "Maybe Diana didn't buy it."

They both realized the importance of Cordelia's words at exactly the same instant.

"Let's not leap to any conclusions until we know for sure," said Jane.

"Right. I never leap. I have weak ankles."

Jane could see Orson's car already parked in the lot. Curt and Annie's Honda was next to it. Where had Orson disappeared to? Wherever it was, it wasn't far away. She knew it wouldn't be smart to grill him on the subject, but maybe she could think of some low key way to bring it up.

Once inside the playhouse, Jane and Cordelia found others milling about, waiting for Diana to arrive. The canvas had been placed on an easel in the center of the stage, a white sheet tossed over it, covering it from public view.

Curt strolled up, holding a glass of champagne. "Kind of a lot of folderol if you ask me. But then Diana loves the dramatic moment."

"Where'd you get the booze?" asked Cordelia.

"On a table behind the stage. A bunch of the actors are already back there. That's where the party's going to be after the unveiling." He drained the glass. "So, what have you two been up to all day?"

"Just seeing the sights," smiled Jane.

"I'll bet."

"We noticed you and Annie go into Johnson's restaurant in town."

"Really? Spying on us?"

"No," snapped Cordelia. "For your information, we were just coming out of the drug store across the street. We felt an irresistible urge for a double dip. Praline Cream and Fudge Brownie. Very hush-hush stuff," she added with more than a hint of sarcasm.

"Were you meeting Orson there for lunch?" asked Jane, trying to sound casual.

"No. Annie and I saw him come in, but we were sitting towards the back. The place was full so he didn't see us. I think he walked up to the bar and ordered a beer. He drank it pretty fast and left." Curt ran a hand through his hair. "Actually, Annie and I wanted some privacy. We needed . . . to talk."

Jane would have liked to ask what about, but didn't want to seem too nosey.

"What about?" asked Cordelia.

Jane turned and glared at her.

"Oh, you know. Everything that's been going on. Theo's death. Diana's . . . drinking. This waiting around is really getting to me. Even though I know it's important, I was never really looking forward to the intervention—but several days ago I felt more prepared. Almost psyched. Now, I'm sort of losing my nerve. I hate confrontation."

"I know how you feel," said Cordelia.

"Hey, here's Amity," said Curt, his scowl changing to a smile. She had just come through the front entrance. He waved her over. "So, how was your first day at school?" he asked.

She gave an indifferent shrug.

"Not much of an answer."

"Not much of a school."

Another teenager accompanied her. He looked about the same age and was as thin as the proverbial reed. Amity introduced him to everyone as Chickie Johnson.

"Johnson," said Jane, smiling pleasantly. "Any relation to the Johnsons who own the restaurant in town?"

"Yeah," he said, his voice unusually deep for someone his age. "That's my parents." He took a look around the theatre. "Seems kind of strange to be back in here again. This used to be our church."

"Really," said Curt. "What denomination was it?"

"First Church of Christ."

"Sounds like a bank," muttered Cordelia.

Jane stuck a discreet elbow into her ribs.

"Yeah, my dad's a deacon. He was one of the leaders who wanted to build a new church. A bigger one. Over on the other side of town. God, they were having one hell of a time getting rid of this turkey." He put his hand over his mouth. "Sorry."

"And there was a fire?" said Jane.

He nodded, then looked away.

"I was told the police never found out why it burned," said Curt.

"Yup. That's right." Again, his eyes darted away.

"Chickie's got a band," said Amity, obviously bored with the subject.

"Is that right," said Cordelia. "Marching?"

"What?" He bit his thumb nail. "No. Heavy metal. A little reggae sometimes."

Jane saw Orson waving at them from one of the front pews. He shook hands with the person he was talking to and then dashed to the back of the hall where they were standing. "Where's Diana?" he asked, a bit breathless.

Jane glanced at her watch. It was nearly three-thirty.

"Maybe someone should go back to the parsonage and see what the trouble is?" he suggested, his gaze coming to rest on Cordelia.

"I suppose that means I'm elected," she grumped.

"Do you want me to go?" asked Amity. "I don't mind."

"No, that's all right. I'm sure Diana's just...just lost track of time," offered Cordelia.

"Right." Orson nodded his agreement.

"I'll be back in a flash."

Famous last words, thought Jane.

Cordelia entered the parsonage and looked first into the parlor. She was in luck. Diana was standing in front of the fireplace, both arms resting on the mantle, staring at herself in the mirror.

"So, you've finally sent out a search party, have you?" she said, seeing Cordelia's reflection enter the room. A large vodka and tonic rested on the coffee table behind her.

Cordelia's eyes fell to the drink. "Consider me the cavalry."

"Well, I'm *coming,*" she declared, smoothing an eyebrow with her little finger. "By the way—" She hesitated. "Tell me the truth. Do you think . . . I'm still attractive?"

This was hardly the time for a discussion of physical disintegration. Then again, maybe it was the perfect time. Cordelia sensed a reticence in Diana, as if she didn't really want to go over to the playhouse at all. "Are you apprehensive about seeing the painting for the first time?"

She whirled around. "Don't be silly. It was just a simple question—requiring a yes or no answer."

Cordelia didn't care for the acid in her voice. Yet, by saying nothing, she knew she'd made a big mistake.

"Never mind. I know what I see when I look at myself. A beautiful . . . woman."

Cordelia was sure it killed Diana not to be able to put the word *young* in the sentence. Youth meant so much on TV and in the movies. Except for that rare exception, women didn't get leading roles without it. Just thinking about such inequity made Cordelia furious. But Diana had had to live in that make-believe world. She'd simply caught the same disease which afflicted so many others. Cordelia felt sorry for her, knowing at the same time that it was the last emotion Diana wanted to elicit.

"Have you ever considered . . . a little cosmetic surgery?" asked Diana, picking up her drink.

"You mean like a face lift? No. I haven't."

"Ah, always the good little feminist."

"Don't patronize me, Diana. If you want to have one, you don't need my permission."

She sat down. "You're right, I don't."

"Don't you think we should get over to the playhouse? Everyone's waiting."

"There's plenty of champagne. The troops won't mind if I'm late." She sipped her drink. "I suppose you think age looks good on people. Gloria Steinem is a role model."

"What's the point, Diana?"

"We all go to pot in the end."

"Yeah. And I'm as vain as the next person."

"I'm glad you admit that about yourself." She closed her eyes and leaned back against the couch. "It's true. We all crumble. Unless something gets us first—in our prime, so to speak."

"You mean like self-pity?"

Diana leveled her gaze. "I don't want to grow old, Cordelia. And, unlike all you sober folk with your sensible opinions and your appropriate behavior, I've got the guts to say it out loud." She stood once again and moved a little unsteadily back to the mirror. "I want an answer. Do you think I'm still in my prime?"

"Yes," said Cordelia, knowing not to hesitate this time. Besides, it was true. She was in her prime—or, at least she should be.

"I think so too." Diana leaned closer and examined one eye. "Do I look dissipated to you?"

"A bit."

Her entire body stiffened. She turned. "Thank you for that vote of confidence."

"Do you want lies?"

"Yes!" she roared. "I want all my mirrors to lie."

"I'm not a mirror."

"Of course you are!"

They stared at each other. "Diana, we've got to go. We can't make those people wait all day."

"Why not?" She finished her drink. "And you know what? I had a plan. I was going to put that portrait in my attic and have *it* age—not me."

"That's a story, Diana. It's not real."

"Did it ever occur to you that I don't want reality?"

Many times, thought Cordelia. "All right then. Let me take back what I said and start over. What I meant to say was that the gallons of booze you've guzzled over the last twenty years have left your skin, your hair, your eyes, your voice, *and* your mind completely untouched. Not to mention your liver."

Diana charged past her. "Get out of my way," she growled, stumbling into the foyer and out the front door.

Cordelia felt rooted to the floor. In the silence of the empty house, she couldn't seem to move. She knew she'd handled this badly. Her patience was just about gone. All in all, it had been a miserable day.

Lurching ever so slightly, Diana entered the playhouse near the stage and clapped her hands for attention. "Let's all gather in the main theatre," she shouted, her eyes searching the crowd. "There you are," she called to a man seated in the front pew. "Ethan, I'd like you to introduce yourself and then present the portrait."

Jane sat down next to Annie and Amity and waited while the tall lanky artist in jeans and a Cal State sweatshirt took the stage. He waited for everyone to be seated. Diana had hopped up next to him and was standing on the other side of the easel.

"My name is Ethan Burgess," the man began, "and I live and work in St. Charles, Illinois, just outside of

Chicago. Diana contacted me last spring and asked if I'd be interested in doing her portrait. We got together several times over the summer, and what you see here today is the result of those meetings." He swept his hand to the covered canvas.

Everyone clapped.

"Shall I uncover it, or would you like to?" he asked Diana.

"Please," she said, deferring to him.

Carefully, he slid the sheet off the portrait and dumped it behind him on the floor.

Jane kept her gaze fixed on Diana, not realizing for a moment why the audience was silent.

Diana stood back from the easel. "Is this some kind of joke?"

The audience began murmuring.

Jane's eyes moved to the painting. "Jesus," she found herself whispering. There was nothing there—nothing except a large piece of heavy cardboard.

The artist moved around to the front. "What the—?"

"Explain this!" demanded Diana.

"I . . . can't!"

"This is fraud. I paid you nearly twenty thousand dollars for that portrait!"

"It was right here! I put it here myself this morning. I don't understand."

Diana took in the assembled crowd. She seemed disgusted, accusing, as if it was their fault. Her eyes rose to Cordelia's face as she came through the back door. "Somebody's playing games with me," she whispered.

Orson rushed up on stage. "I'm sure it's just a mix-up," he said, taking her by the arm. "Why don't we just go back to the house and—"

She broke free of his grip. "I'm not a child. I don't

need a keeper." With one last angry glance around the room, she bolted to the back curtain and disappeared stage left.

Orson held up his hands for silence. "I'm sorry about all this," he said, waiting while everyone quieted down. "I don't know what happened, but I'm sure we'll locate the portrait very soon and you'll all be able to enjoy it hanging in the front entrance. In the meantime, there's lots of food and drink. Please. Enjoy yourselves." He took out a handkerchief and wiped his damp forehead. Then, ignoring the artist and everyone else's confused stares, he turned and ducked behind the curtain in search of Diana.

26

Half an hour later, Jane was on her way back into town. She had just enough time to make it to the courthouse before it closed for the day. She wanted to take a look at Theo's case file. She wasn't sure what she was looking for, but for Cordelia's peace of mind, and for her own, it had to be checked.

Cordelia wanted to remain at the parsonage. After the unveiling—such as it was—Diana had stomped out of the playhouse and returned to her bedroom where she had not only slammed, but locked the door behind her. Annie had tried to talk to her, but Diana insisted she wanted to be alone. Cordelia felt confident Diana had stolen the portrait herself, and what they'd witnessed on stage was just another one of Diana's little dramatic moments—as well as some rather unconvincing acting. Jane, on the other hand, wasn't so sure. She'd been watching Diana's face when the sheet was removed. From what she could tell, Diana had been genuinely shocked. Then again, if Diana hadn't taken the canvas, who had? And for what reason?

Since Jane didn't have any immediate answers, she shook the questions out of her mind as she pulled into a parking space just down the street from the courthouse.

Walking up to the two-story building, she could see the fa-
cade was constructed of brown bricks and white painted
wood. Two thick pillars on either side of the front entrance gave the structure a kind of historic formality,
though it was obviously a new building.

Once inside, she crossed to the front desk and waited
while the man behind the counter finished a phone conversation. He appeared to be in his late sixties and was
wearing a dark business suit, complete with red silk handkerchief in the vest pocket and a white carnation in the
buttonhole.

After hanging up, the man asked somewhat supercil-
iously, "May I help you?"

Jane nodded. "I'd like to see the case file on Theodore
Donati."

He looked her up and down. "May I ask why?"

"It's a public record, isn't it?"

"Yes."

"Then I'd like to see it."

He studied her for a moment longer and then stepped
to the end of a long row of filing cabinets and pulled out a
white folder. "Would you care to use a conference room to
look at this?"

Good idea. She didn't want him in her face while she
examined the documents. "Yes. That would be great."

He led the way down a side hall to the third room on
the right. Switching on the light, he said, "I'll be at the
desk if you need any further assistance."

"Thank you," she replied, matching his preciseness.
She shut the door, knowing he was still standing on the
other side. Perhaps she should make some odd noises,
hum the theme from *Twin Peaks*. Give him some small co-
nundrum on which to dwell while she was out of sight,
but not out of mind.

Hearing his footsteps finally recede, she turned to the

table and sat down in the nearest chair. She placed the folder in front of her and stared at it for a second before pulling out the contents. On the top of the pile was a series of black-and-white photographs taken of Theo the night he died. They were all from different angles. He was lying on a stretcher, his eyes closed, his body limp. He appeared to be inside the ambulance. In one, she could make out Orson's face in the background. He looked devastated, the palm of one hand held flat against his forehead. Jane was glad Cordelia hadn't come with her. These would have been hard to take.

Laying the pictures aside, she found a small card with Theo's fingerprints on it. She studied it briefly. Next was a property receipt for his wallet and clothing, as well as the contents of his pockets. Since she'd already seen this first hand, and nothing on the list seemed to be missing, she went on to the police report. It had been filed by a Sergeant Steve Bossing. Jane found his comments clear and to the point. He had arrived on the scene shortly after Theo's death. He'd made a note that the volunteer paramedics had done everything they could to save his life. He pronounced Theo dead at exactly 8:47 P.M., Sunday, September fifth. Jane was surprised to find a copy of Theo's prison record included in the documents. Something like that probably followed a person everywhere. No wonder he'd used an alias, also noted by the sergeant in his comments. Lastly, the coroner's report. Sure enough, it was signed by Arnold DeLappe. She pushed everything else aside and studied the report more closely.

She read through all the information on the decedent. Name. Date of birth. Place of death. Marital status. Race. Educational Background. Religion. When she came to decedent's occupation, she saw that someone had written Contractor in the space provided. Next to it were the words, Blandin Builders, Houston, Texas.

Jane took out a small note pad from her pocket and wrote it down. It might be important. Evidently, Orson had not only known where Theo lived, but what he did for a living. Odd that Orson should be privy to such a wealth of information about Theo when everyone else was almost totally in the dark. Under the heading, Parents, each space was blank. Under Informant, Orson had signed his name. She read through to the bottom. The report seemed to be in order. As she looked up from the pile of papers, she felt an empty feeling deep in her stomach. It was such a cold act, this picking over the legal remains of a man's life.

Stuffing everything back into the file, Jane opened the door, switched off the light and walked back to the front desk.

"All finished?" asked the man.

"Yes." She handed him the file.

"Did you know Mr. Donati?"

"I did."

He took the folder back to the cabinet. "It's a sorry business," he muttered, shaking his head. "Well, have a good day."

She nodded her thanks and tried to walk as calmly as she could to the door. She realized with a sinking sensation, that seeing the photos and reading the coroner's report had made Theo's death all too real—much more so than she'd ever wanted it to be. All she could think of now was breathing some fresh air.

After a short walk to clear her head, Jane remembered she had one more stop to make before she returned to the parsonage. She needed to check out Johnson's Bar and Restaurant. It might not prove anything, but she had a couple of questions she wanted to ask.

Walking two blocks south along the business district, she caught sight of the building half a block down on the other side of the road. Since it was a little early for dinner, very few cars were parked in front of the restaurant. Jane waited for a stoplight to turn green and then sprinted across the street, removing her sun glasses as she entered the dark interior. Instead of going into the bar, she made a hard left and walked straight into the liquor store. A middle-aged woman in a bright pink sun dress stood behind the counter, paging through a magazine. She looked up as Jane entered.

"Can I help you?" she asked.

"I hope so. I'm . . . staying at the old parsonage out on County Road C, and—"

The woman took off her bifocals and gave Jane a hard once-over. "You one of Diana Stanwood's friends?"

Jane smiled. "I guess you could say that."

"My son's a friend of Amity Scarbourough."

"Oh. Sure. You must be Mrs. Johnson. I met Chickie earlier this afternoon."

"That right?" She closed the magazine. "We had Amity over to dinner the other night and I don't mind telling you, I'm worried about that child's welfare."

"Really? Why?"

"We had that Stanwood woman checked out before she moved into town."

"We?"

"My husband's a deacon at the First Church of Christ. People around here like to know who's moving into the area."

"I see."

"You probably know all about it, since you're a friend of hers."

"Well, really, I'm just here for a funeral. I can't say I know Diana all that well."

The woman hunched her shoulders and bent closer. "She's one of them *gays*."

Jane backed up a step. "Really?"

"It's true."

She was surprised by the woman's knowledge. From what Cordelia had said, Diana was very closeted about her sexuality. She was sure nothing had ever been printed on the subject. "Who'd you hear that from?"

The woman gave a knowing nod. "Jack—he's my husband—drove over to that big library in Appleton. Got everything he could on the woman. There was an article in the Greenwich Village Sentinel about her relationship with some personal secretary. I assume it was Amity's mother since they had the same last name. Anyway, ever since we found out I guess you could say we haven't been too thrilled with the idea of her living out there. We never would have sold her the building if we'd known."

The woman acted like the church was her personal property. "But I'd heard you were desperate to get rid of it. You needed the sale to finance the new church you were building over by the mall."

Mrs. Johnson squared her shoulders. "Well, not that desperate."

Jane picked up a bottle of Merlot and examined the label. "The scuttlebutt around town is that someone in your church set the fire." There. She decided to chuck that little pebble into the pool of their somewhat one-sided discussion. See what the ripples looked like.

"Who told you that?"

"Lots of people."

"It's a lie! Nobody in our congregation would do something so... wrong."

Jane shrugged. She wasn't going to let the woman off the hook that easily. "Maybe."

"You tell those people *from me* to mind their own

business. That's always the best policy. People should keep their noses in their own nests."

Jane was pretty sure the woman didn't find any irony in her statement. "I'm curious. Does Ms. Stanwood order much wine or spirits from your store?"

The woman shook her head. "When she first arrived, we sent out a few cases, but I suppose she found another supplier." Pulling up a stool, she added, "She did order a bottle of German Riesling from us about a week ago. I took the order. She said she had a guest coming who liked sweet wine."

So the bottle had been purchased by Diana. So much for jumping to conclusions.

"How come you want to know?"

Jane set the bottle of Merlot down. "No reason, really. Just making conversation."

"You're not from around here."

"No, I'm from Minneapolis. I own a restaurant on Lake Harriet."

The woman scrunched up her face in thought. "The Lyme House?"

"That's the one."

"We've been there! Jack and I loved it."

Jane grinned. "That's kind of you to say."

"No, I really mean it. The food was great. I loved the way you could sit out on the balcony and hear music playing from the bandstand way across the lake."

Another customer entered the store.

"I wish we could have sold that church to someone like you," she continued. "Maybe one day you'll decide to expand. Summer Green is a growing metropolis, you know."

"I'll remember that."

"It was nice meeting you, Miss—?"

"Lawless. Jane Lawless."

The woman stuck out her hand. "A real pleasure."

Jane shook it and then leaned closer. In a confidential whisper she added, "By the way, Mrs. Johnson, just for your information, I'm one of them *gays* too."

27

Except for Diana and Amity, Jane found everyone gathered in the parlor when she got back to the parsonage. Wonderful aromas filled the house. Jane could see Hilda dashing about in the kitchen, preparing dinner. Across the hall in the dining room, the table was already set with Diana's favorite bone china.

"What smells so good?" she asked, sitting down on the sofa next to Cordelia.

"It's Cornish game hen," said Orson. He was sprawled in an easy chair reading the paper, his feet up on a footstool. "I was just in the kitchen getting the particulars. Seems Hilda marinates it in orange juice, garlic, capers, brown sugar and cinnamon. She serves it as a hot salad— sort of Niçoise—over fresh sautéed green beans and slivers of red potato. Oh, and just a tad of chopped tomatoes and shallots."

Jane looked to her right and saw Cordelia trying not to drool.

"Where did Diana *find* that woman?" asked Curt. He was lying on his stomach next to the cold fireplace, a couch pillow propped under his chin. "She should be the executive chef at an exclusive restaurant."

"I second that," said Annie who was sitting on the floor next to him, paging through one of Diana's many scrapbooks.

"Where's—" Jane's eyes rose to the ceiling. She didn't want to say Diana's name out loud.

"In her boudoir," answered Cordelia, twisting an auburn curl around her finger.

"Is she okay?"

"She hasn't sent out for another case of vodka, so at least she's content."

Jane grimaced. "Has anyone seen her since . . . this afternoon?"

Orson shook his head. "She's probably just asleep. We'll wake her before dinner."

"Hey, remember the summer we took that stage craft practicum?" asked Annie, turning a page in the scrapbook.

"I'll never forget it," muttered Cordelia, covering her face with her hand.

Jane was intrigued. "What happened?"

"It was just the six of us," said Orson, putting down the paper. "We were the only ones taking the class. The professor, what was his name?"

"Pelty," snickered Curt. "Lambert Pelty."

"Right. He really had it in for us right from the start."

"Why?" asked Jane.

"I'm not really sure," said Orson. "He knew we were all good friends."

"He also knew we thought pretty highly of ourselves," replied Curt, "and he was going to take us down a notch or two."

"He wouldn't have had the chance if it hadn't been for me," said Cordelia, lowering her head. "It was so incredibly stupid."

"It was funny," said Curt. "He simply overreacted."

"What'd you do?" asked Jane.

"Well, it was during a break. Pelty had gone upstairs to get a cup of coffee, and so I took the opportunity to hop up on stage and continue teaching the class from his notes on the blackboard. With a few of my own additions, of course."

"Of course," nodded Jane.

"She could really mimic him," grinned Annie. "It was hysterical."

"Did he catch you?" asked Jane.

Cordelia shook her head.

"Then what happened?"

"It was what she wrote," said Curt, a slow grin forming. "During one of her digressions—Pelty liked to digress—she wrote *and blah blah blah* after every one of his points."

Orson started to laugh. "I know it was childish, but we were just doubled up it was so funny."

"When Pelty got back," continued Cordelia, "he went berserk. He demanded to know who'd done it."

"And did you tell?"

"God no," exclaimed Cordelia. "I thought he'd have my hide."

"That's when he said that if we didn't offer up the guilty party, he'd flunk us all," said Orson.

"Could he do that?" asked Jane.

"He was the professor," said Annie. "I think we all thought he could."

"But no one ever told?"

"Well," said Curt, "after he threatened us, Diana raised her hand. She got up and very meekly replied, 'Mr. Pelty, I cannot tell a lie. It was me.' Then she just stood there, in utter contrition, her head bowed. Needless to say, Pelty didn't know what to think. He just glared."

"Then," said Orson, "I stood. I couldn't let Diana have all the best lines. I said that in good conscience, I mustn't allow a friend to take the heat for something I'd done. I promised to write *I shall never annoy Lambert Pelty again* five hundred times on his blackboard."

Jane began to laugh.

"Then Theo stood," said Annie. "He started to cry. He squeezed his baseball cap in his hands and said that his parents had never paid any attention to him when he was a child. That's why he'd done it. He thanked Orson and Diana for attempting to shield him, but he was ready to pay the price. He suggested that he crawl from Scott Hall to Northrup on his hands and knees at midnight during a rainstorm. By this time, Pelty's expression had turned sort of glassy-eyed."

"That's when I got up," said Curt. "I said my friends were just being noble. I'd written the heinous *blah blah blah* on the board and I was ready to take my punishment. Of course, I also mentioned that my father was a close friend of the president of the University. And I pointed out that he played handball every Wednesday afternoon with several of the regents, but what the heck, punish away."

"We all got up eventually," said Annie. She cast an amused eye at Cordelia. "Even the real culprit."

"So what did he finally do?" asked Jane.

Orson put a finger to his cheek. "I think we confused the poor man. He simply got up, picked up his pointer, and continued on with the day's lesson."

"Thanks to Diana's quick thinking, my college G.P.A. was saved from total ruin," said Cordelia.

"And with a little help from your friends," winked Orson.

Jane could tell they needed this story tonight. It reminded them of who they had once been, and what they still wanted to be to each other.

After a few seconds Jane asked, "Where's Amity?"

As if roused from a sleep, Annie looked up and said,

"She's out with that boy." She pushed the scrapbook aside and drew her legs up to her chest, her back resting against Orson's chair. "Chickie. But she'll be back for dinner. I told her seven."

"What kind of name is Chickie?" asked Orson.

"He wants to be a rock star," said Annie, as if that explained everything.

"I'd say the name's inspired more by his *rural* background," offered Cordelia with a smirk.

Curt glowered. "Cut the kid some slack, will you?" He got up and crossed to a table where Hilda had set out a pitcher of lemonade and some glasses. She'd also fixed a plate of cheese and fruit, but no one had eaten any. "Is everything all set for the funeral tomorrow?"

"As far as I know," said Annie. "I drove over to the funeral home this morning and dropped off the exact location for the grave site. Just so there wouldn't be any confusion."

An awkward silence followed. No one knew quite how to pick up the conversation.

"Well," said Curt finally, taking a chair by the fireplace. "How's the murder investigation coming, Jane?"

Annie and Orson turned and glared at him.

"Just making conversation."

"Drop it," said Orson.

"Why? I have a right to know." He stared at Jane. "Do you still think one of us murdered Theo?"

The doorbell sounded.

"I'll get it," said Orson, looking like he had just been released from prison.

Jane was about to answer when she heard Orson exclaim, "We're so glad you're here! Please, come in." A moment later he appeared in the doorway accompanied by a man who looked a great deal like Theo, only taller, beardless and much younger.

"This is James Donati," announced Orson. "Theo's brother."

Everyone stood.

James looked curiously from face to face. "I've never met any of you, but I know you all." His smile was warm.

"Come in and sit down," said Orson.

"Okay. Sure, for a few minutes." He made himself comfortable in a chair opposite the couch.

"Can I get you anything?" asked Orson.

"A brandy would be great. This has been kind of a long day."

"I'll only be a second." He left the room.

"So," said Annie, picking up the conversational threads, "How was your trip?"

"Fine. Too long." His eyes took in the parlor. "This is a nice house. Kind of old fashioned."

Orson returned with his drink.

James took a sip. It seemed to relax him. "You know, while Theo was in jail, he wrote me so many letters. I still have most of them. I was pretty young when he left for college, so we didn't know each other all that well." His eyes stopped at Curt. "You must be Curt Whittig." He took another sip. "Theo thought the world of you, though I'm not sure I'm telling you anything you don't already know. He wrote about you so . . . affectionately."

Curt was stunned. "He wrote to you about *me?*"

"Many letters. At first, they were almost *all* about you. How talented you were. How much fun you'd had together."

"I . . . didn't know."

"But you certainly were aware of how much he cared about you."

Curt shook his head. "I wasn't . . . sure." He looked at Annie. Strangely, her eyes were full of tears.

"And you must be Cordelia," smiled James, moving

on. "Theo wrote lots about your midnight conversations. You used to sit on the counter in your apartment with your feet in the kitchen sink."

"He wrote you that?"

"Theo thought you had a totally weird mind. He was sure someday you'd be recognized as a theatrical genius."

Cordelia raised her chin. "The boy had taste."

Again, James moved on. "And, of course, you're Annie. The woman with the fiery red hair. Theo said you were the kindest person he'd ever met."

Annie put a trembling hand over her mouth.

"We all loved him," said Cordelia.

"I know," said James. "But sometimes I just wish I could have . . . understood him better. After he got out of prison, he simply evaporated. He was going to come and visit my wife and me in Sacramento, but he never did. He wrote every now and then, and occasionally he'd call, but he'd never tell me where he was living."

"Join the crowd," said Curt.

James glanced at Jane. "I'm sorry. I don't—"

"Jane Lawless. I'm not part of the Shevlin Underground. Just a friend."

"Sure. Nice to meet you." He turned to Orson. "You know, Theo told me you were like a brother to him. I don't mind telling you I used to be pretty jealous of that. But when I got older, I guess I was just happy he'd found such good friends."

"Can you stay for dinner?" asked Annie. "I'm sure we've got plenty of food."

James shook his head, finishing his drink. "Sorry. My wife's back at the motel. We're pretty beat. We got up this morning at the crack of dawn and drove the kids to her sister's in Bakersfield. Then we hopped a plane to Chicago and drove up here. I think we're going to pull the shades and hit the sack."

"The funeral is at three tomorrow afternoon," said Orson.

James nodded. "We'll be there." As he got up to go he asked, "I do have one question."

"Anything," replied Orson.

"Well, I was just curious. Who made the decision to have my brother's body cremated?"

Annie slipped her arms around her stomach. "I remembered Theo saying once that when he died, that's what he wanted."

"Really?" James scratched the back of his neck. "That's so weird. When he was a kid, he was almost phobic about fire. It just seemed odd to me that he would say something like that."

Annie looked up at Curt.

"Well, it's done now. No use worrying about it." James turned and crossed into the foyer. He stopped when he saw Diana coming down the stairs.

"You must be Theo's brother," she said, extending her hand as she got to the bottom.

"I am," he smiled, shaking it warmly. "And you're Diana Stanwood. It's great to finally meet you. I just wish it could have been under . . . you know. Other circumstances."

"So do I," she said, still holding his hand.

Everyone moved in closer to watch.

"I'm sorry, I haven't packed Theo's things yet," said Diana, her voice a bit too regal for normal speech. She took hold of the banister to steady herself.

If James had caught the fact that she'd been drinking, he didn't let on. "That's all right. I can get everything tomorrow."

"And he has a car out in the parking lot," she continued. "I'm sure he'd want you to have it."

James turned to Orson.

"Absolutely," Orson replied. "Diana's right. Theo didn't have much, but I know the car is paid for. It should go to you."

James passed a hand across his eyes. "Thanks. But... what I'd like most is to be able to talk to you all. Maybe tomorrow... after the service. I need to... know more about him. Hear your stories. See him through your eyes."

"Of course," said Diana, putting her arm around his shoulder. "There isn't a person here who wouldn't be happy to sit down with you and reminisce. As far as I'm concerned, it's a date."

He beamed his thanks. "Theo was a lucky man."

Diana nodded. "The sad thing is, we often don't realize how lucky we are until it's too late." Her eyes flicked to Orson, and then away.

"Well," said James, clearing his throat, "I'd better shove off." He moved to the door. "Will there be a lot of people from Summer Green at the funeral tomorrow?"

"I don't think so," said Orson. "Theo didn't know anyone here other than the six of us."

"That's what I thought," said James, shoving his hands into his pockets. "But as I was coming up the front walk, a guy stopped me. He asked if I was Theo's brother. Asked if I was coming for the funeral."

"What did he look like?" asked Orson.

"Bald. Well dressed. After we were done talking, he got back into his Cadillac and drove off."

Diana shook her head. "I haven't the faintest idea who that could be."

"Me either," said Annie.

"Well, maybe we can ask him tomorrow," said James.

"What a good idea," replied Cordelia, her eyes locking on Orson. "I think I will."

28

After dinner, Jane spent several hours walking in the graveyard. She had a great deal to think about and needed some privacy. After a sweltering day, the evening had turned deliciously cool, a light breeze ruffling her hair as she passed aimlessly among the gravestones. This visit to Summer Green wasn't in any sense a vacation, yet she was enjoying the change of pace. She was glad Cordelia had called her. Glad most of all that she could bring a perspective Cordelia entirely lacked.

Returning to the parsonage around nine, Jane found Cordelia and Orson in the dining room, engaged in a subdued game of cribbage, while Annie, Curt and Amity were sitting over Cokes in the kitchen, talking in hushed tones about a subject which looked quite serious. Jane was curious, but felt it best not to disturb them. Diana had gone to her room directly after the peach cobbler saying she had a splitting headache. No one had any trouble believing *that*.

After reading for a couple hours in the chair next to her bed, Jane switched off the light and slipped under the covers. She closed her eyes and tried to empty her mind, knowing she was still suffering from lack of sleep. But, as she suspected, the events surrounding Theo's death were too much in her thoughts to allow her any rest. Every half hour or so, she could hear someone trudge up the stairs, use one of the two bathrooms and then retreat into their bedroom. Finally, around one, Jane decided to give up and go downstairs in search of a cup of tea. She grabbed her bathrobe and started down the darkened hall. As she passed the end room, she noticed a light on and the door ajar.

She knew Theo had used this room during his visit. She'd planned on exploring it early tomorrow morning before anyone was up. Getting caught once in someone else's bedroom was enough. She'd never seen anyone in this room before, but tonight, Diana was sitting on the bed, a suitcase open in front of her.

Jane hesitated for a moment, watching her fold a pair of pants.

"Oh, it's you," said Diana, looking up. "I thought everyone had gone to bed."

Jane opened the door a bit further. "I couldn't sleep."

"A common malady. Come in and keep me company." She fingered a button on one of Theo's shirts. "I promised James I'd have all this packed by tomorrow afternoon. Theo didn't bring much. I started going through his things yesterday, but I just couldn't handle it."

A large drink sat next to her on the night stand. It had no ice in it. Diana's speech was considerably more slurred than it had been earlier in the evening. Even so, she seemed to be reasonably coherent, though Jane knew that with someone under the influence, appearances could be deceiving.

"It's hard to believe I'm never going to see him again," said Diana, taking a deep sip from her glass.

"It takes a long time for a death to feel real."

She picked up his wallet and pulled out the driver's license. "Did you see this? He was using an alias. What the hell was going on, that's what I'd like to know."

Jane knew Diana wasn't interested in her opinion. Instead, she decided to ask a question. "Cordelia said he visited you once in New York."

She nodded. "For Jill's funeral. It was an awful time. But . . . life goes on." She stared at the license photograph for a moment. "He has a bad haircut in this photo. That's not like him."

"What did Theo do for a living?"

Diana shrugged. "He was always evasive about that. It's hard getting a good job after you've been in prison." She picked up a piece of notebook paper and unfolded it.

"What's that?" asked Jane.

"It's . . . well." She paused, but only for a second before plunging ahead. "Listen to this. *Dear Curt.*"

Jane was a surprised and a bit aghast. "Where did you get that?"

"It was in his suitcase." She looked over at the closet. "Funny. When I was going through his stuff before, I never noticed it."

Jane wondered what condition she'd been in. Depending on how much vodka she'd consumed, it wouldn't have surprised her if Diana had failed to notice a rhinoceros next to the shoe rack.

Diana continued:

I've always written letters when I'm upset—most of the time I've had the sense not to mail them. I guess I've never written to anyone very much, with the possible exception of Orson and my brother, James. But rest assured, Curt, you have been in my thoughts more than you know. I didn't like the way our conversation ended this afternoon, and I don't know what to do about it.

"Do you think you should be reading that?" interrupted Jane, not sure she wanted to be hearing it.

Diana waved the question away and continued as if she had every right in the world to be reading another man's letter. "I'll skip part of this. Here—this is where it gets good.

Do you remember the book I made both you and Orson read in college—Beau Geste? For some reason, it's been on my mind a lot lately. It was my favorite story when I was growing up. I suppose that says more about me than it does about anything else, but still, odd as it sounds, my life has paralleled that tale. It's funny. Life moves in a certain way and it becomes hard—sometimes impossible—to change directions even if you want to. That's what life did to Michael Geste—perhaps to me too.

Diana took several sips of her drink.

The thing is, Curt, I couldn't be anything to you other than what I've been—someone who loved you once—someone who went away, and for all practical purposes, never came back. You've always had trouble letting go. I saw it years ago in the way you nursed your anger against your parents. They were crummy to you, I realize that. What they produced was a very lonely boy. Perhaps some part of you will always be lonely because, deep down, that's who you are. But for God's sake, Curt, take a long look at your life now. Annie loves you very much, and I know you love her. I'm sorry if it seems I never answer your questions as completely as you'd like. All I can say is, if we meet some day on the other side, I'll happily fill you in on every detail. I've made a mess of many things, Curt, but I hope to God you're not part

*of that. I'm sad to think ours wasn't the love story you
wanted. If it's any consolation, it's not the story I wanted for
us either. But we play the hand we're dealt. It's strange.
When we all agreed to come to Summer Green, I thought it
was going to be a real downer. I've never been a big fan of
psychologists or the psychological cure—*

"What do you suppose he means by that?" asked
Diana.

Jane shook her head. "I haven't the foggiest."

Diana considered it for a moment and then continued:

*but I've really enjoyed getting away. It's given me a perspec-
tive I didn't have before. Maybe you'll leave too, a more
grateful man. I doubt I'll send you this. Maybe I will. Who
knows? I think, for now, perhaps we should just try to enjoy
the country air. I know how much you like to be outside.
Maybe the sun and the somber mists, and most of all, the
friendships that have sustained each one of us over many
rough moments will continue to sustain you now. When I
think of you all, and especially you, Curt, I know my life
has been very rich indeed. My love to you always.*

Theo

She let the paper fall face up on the bed. "Wasn't that
beautiful?"

It was. "Are you going to give it to Curt?"

Diana acted as if she hadn't expected the question.
"Well, sure. After all, it's addressed to him, isn't it?" She
emptied half her drink.

Jane could see Diana's eyes lose focus as she set the
glass back on the table next to the bed. Once again, she began pawing through the suitcase. Unlike a few minutes
ago, she was now making more of a mess than anything
else.

"Cordelia tells me you picked up his belongings from

the funeral home this morning." Diana held up an argyle sock, studying it with great intensity.

"We did," said Jane.

She gave her head a small shake. "Uh. Felt kind of dizzy there for a moment, but it passed." She dropped the sock. "Anyway, what was I saying? Oh yeah. Cordelia was pretty vague about your reason for going over there. I hate it when people are vague."

"Me too."

Diana cracked a smile. "Why did you go?"

Jane shrugged. "I had a couple of questions I wanted to ask the funeral director. I was told he was also the county coroner."

"What questions?"

"Well, I wanted to know why an autopsy was never ordered."

Diana's head wobbled back ever so slightly. She regarded Jane with undisguised suspicion. "Why would they perform an autopsy?"

"As I understand it, it's generally standard in cases like this. If one had been done, any question of... foul play could have been ruled out."

"Foul play? You mean like—"

"Like murder," said Jane.

"Ridiculous!" Diana dismissed the question and returned to the sock, holding it up again as if she'd never seen it before. "Who would want to hurt Theo? Dear Theo. Saintly Theo. Noble Theo. The little rodent."

Jane wondered if Diana was capable of a real conversation—or if she'd crossed the line into drug-induced la la land. She decided to take a chance. "Why did you have a photo of him hanging on your closet door?"

Diana's face twitched. "What?"

"You'd hung a Choice button on his chest and then stuck a knife through it."

She broke into a smile. "I did that, yes."

"Why?"

"Because it was the perfect statement."

"What does abortion rights have to do with you and Theo?"

"Abortion? No, no, Jane. Choice. That's the crux of the matter. Choice, don't you see? We rant and rave about it all the time when it comes to abortion. Choice is sacred. It's hallowed ground. We shout it from the rooftops. Why can't we see it's the same issue when it comes to other aspects of our lives? We *must* have a choice. No one should take that away from us. Not some anti-abortion group, or . . . some sleazeball with a pencil and a column in a newspaper who can, in the name of some larger purpose, ruin a person's career!"

"What larger purpose?"

"The advancement of gays and lesbians, of course! Just ask Theo. He said that we all have to come out of the closet. If we're invisible, then society will never realize we're just human beings like everyone else. Some of us are good, and some bad. Some rich, some poor. You've heard the arguments. But try telling that to a producer. Sometimes I think half the people in Hollywood are hiding. I suppose I could have done that too—stayed married, had a kid, denied the reports, insisted they were slander. But I couldn't. God, I was so naive. I thought I could just keep my private life *private*. Is that so much to ask? But it wasn't enough for Theo. If I didn't announce my identity on cue, if I didn't sacrifice my life on the altar of the greater good, then the rumor press starts pumping. Sooner or later, unless you live in a dark hole, they get you."

Of course, thought Jane—the light was beginning to dawn. It was that article the woman in the liquor store had mentioned. "Someone outed you?"

Diana ran a hand over her face. "Two nights after Jill

died, Theo and Orson came to New York for the funeral. We were sitting in a bar, talking to this guy. I knew he was asking a lot of questions, I just never thought Theo would be so stupid as to bring up my real relationship with Jill. I'll never forgive him! Do you think I could get a part after that article appeared? I'd already left the soap. I couldn't stand the grind any more. I was up for a great role in a movie, but interestingly, it fell through. Then another, and another. Then I was offered a leading role in a Broadway show. But that went sour too. And all because of Theo. He deserved to pay for what he did! He took my life as surely as if he'd put a gun to my head."

"Bullshit!" said a voice from behind them.

Both women turned to find Orson standing in the doorway. He was fully clothed and he was furious.

"Theo never told that man anything!"

"Of course he did," sputtered Diana. "How else did the guy know what to print?"

"You told him."

"I what?" She blinked.

"Just like always, you got drunk. But that night, you got really drunk. I knew you didn't know what you were saying. Both Theo and I hustled you out of there as fast as we could, but the die had already been cast. If you want to blame someone for the way your life has turned out, blame yourself!"

She swallowed hard, picking up her drink. Her hand was shaking so badly, she nearly dropped it. "I—"

"And that play you're always whining about? It went sour because of your boozing. I talked to the director. I know."

"I beg your pardon?"

"You lost the part because you couldn't cut it. You kept forgetting your lines. Showing up late for rehearsals."

"That's not true!"

"It is." He moved further into the room. "I can't listen to your self-pity any more, Diana. I've tried to be patient, but I'm just about out. I know why you were so cool to Theo the first couple of days. I'd heard your argument in New York—the one about being in or out of the closet. I knew where you both stood. And I also knew you blamed Theo for the article when it finally appeared. You couldn't find him, or you would have slit his throat. You didn't see him again until last Friday. He didn't deserve your abuse, Diana. He didn't agree with you, but he respected your privacy. That's more than I can say for you." His eyes fell to the note. "Is that Theo's handwriting?"

"Maybe. So what if it is?"

"Give it to me."

"Why? You want to read it too?" She climbed off the bed but lost her balance and crumpled to the floor.

"Christ," said Orson, bending down, "I think she's passed out." He slapped her face lightly. "She probably won't remember a word I said."

"Don't be too sure," said Jane.

Orson had already lifted her into his arms. "I better get her to bed. I'm sorry you had to see this. Don't take what she said too seriously. She'd never hurt Theo—not in the way you're thinking. She was trying to make him pay by withdrawing her love."

"Are you so sure of that?"

He looked her squarely in the eye. "I'd stake my life on it."

Curious, thought Jane. All these people were so protective of one another. Theo was dead, and even Cordelia couldn't imagine that anyone of her friends could have done it. "Do you need some help?"

"No," he muttered as he swung her out the door. "I think we all just need to get some sleep."

After they were gone, Jane stood and looked at the mess on the bed. There would be time in the morning to clean it up. Before she turned off the light, she folded Theo's letter and stuffed it into her pocket. Tomorrow, she'd give it to Curt. In the meantime, no one else should be reading it.

She felt more awake now than she had half an hour ago. Diana's revelation had been nothing less than a clear and highly charged motive for murder. But had she actually done it? In the cold light of day, had Diana wanted to get back at Theo so badly for a perceived injustice that she'd plotted his murder? Or, even more tragically, had her drinking emboldened her? Had it altered her perceptions enough so that she could give vent to a violent emotion without fully comprehending the results?

Jane mulled over these and other questions as she tiptoed down the stairs. A cup of tea was the best company when she needed to think. As she passed the parlor, she saw someone had built a fire. The room was softly aglow.

"Who's there?" said Curt, standing as he saw a shadow fall across the floor. He'd been sitting in one of the wing chairs.

"I just came down for a cup of tea."

"Couldn't sleep, huh?"

"Don't let me disturb you." She remembered the note in her pocket. "Actually, I have something that belongs to you."

He slipped his hands into the pockets of his bathrobe. "What?"

"Diana found this in Theo's suitcase." She handed it to him. "It's a letter to you. I thought you . . . might want to have it."

He took it and unfolded the paper, holding it close to the firelight.

Jane watched as he read the first few lines. His face betrayed no emotion. "So...I guess that's it," she said, backing out of the room. "See you in the morning."

His eyes remained fixed on the note. Slowly, he sat back down. "Goodnight, Jane. Thanks."

29

Around four in the morning, Jane was awakened from a fitful sleep by the hum of a car motor. Rising from her bed, she stood at the window and looked down on the parking lot between the parsonage and the playhouse. No one was stirring. She counted six cars, all parked in their usual spots, all empty and dark. Perhaps the one she'd heard had been driving by on the highway, and in her sleep she'd misinterpreted the nearness of the sound. But it had seemed too loud to be such a distance away. As she looked again, searching the grounds for any sign of life, she saw a pinpoint of light wash over one of the windows in the playhouse. She held her breath. There it was again! She could feel the hairs prickle on the back of her neck. It was undoubtedly a flashlight. Someone was inside.

Jane dressed and then crept down the hall to Cordelia's room. Even though she couldn't ignore the potential danger, she had to know what was going on.

She leaned over Cordelia and gently shook her shoulder.

Cordelia groaned and turned over.

"Come on!" whispered Jane, as loudly as she dared. "Wake up. You've got to help me."

Cordelia's nose twitched. "Hmm?" she said pleasantly.

Jane shook her again. "Roast goose and blueberry pie."

"What?" An eye opened. "Repeat that."

"I said you've got to get up. Someone's broken into the playhouse. We've got to get over there—see what's going on."

Cordelia rubbed the sleep out of her eyes and then took a better look. "I don't like this dream. Go away."

"Get dressed and meet me downstairs in five minutes. I'll find a flashlight."

"Are you serious? It's the middle of the night!"

"Shhh." Jane held a finger to her lips. "What's the difference? You think ten A.M. is the middle of the night."

"True. Why don't you call the police? Let them handle . . . whatever it is."

"Two reasons. First, I'm not sure I trust the police in this town."

"Excuse me?"

"And two, if it's one of your friends over there, do you want the police to find them or do you want us to handle it?"

Cordelia pulled herself back against her pillows. "Good point. I'll be down in a jiff."

"Great. Just make sure you're quiet."

Jane and Cordelia stood in front of the playhouse, wondering what the best plan of attack was.

"First things first," said Jane, handing Cordelia the flashlight. She tried the lock. "It's open," she whispered, a note of triumph in her voice. She examined the door for signs of damage. "They had a key. I knew it."

"Kind of narrows down the number of people who could be inside, doesn't it?" muttered Cordelia, glancing up at the tall bell tower directly above their heads. In the weak moonlight, it was a forbidding sight, an image straight out of the mind of Alfred Hitchcock.

They moved quietly into the vestibule.

"Where to now?" asked Cordelia.

"Just follow me." Jane led the way up the center aisle, remembering the path the light had taken as she'd watched it from her window. The stage was dark. As they stepped around to the back, she saw the light leading down to the basement had been turned on. She pointed to the stairs and then put a finger to her lips.

They both stood very still and listened. Sure enough, someone was moving around deep in the bowels of the building.

Cordelia mouthed, "What are they doing?"

Jane gave her a perplexed shrug, motioning her away from the stairs. "Listen," she whispered, drawing her close, "is there another way to get out of the basement?"

"There are two stairways. This one, and one that leads up to the vestibule."

"Right. Okay," said Jane, thinking the situation over. "Here's what we do. I'll stay here. You take the flashlight and go back to where we entered. Find a spot to hide and just wait. All I want to know is who's down there. We can figure out the why later."

"Gotcha." Cordelia turned to go but instead tripped on an electrical wire taped to the floor and caught her sleeve on the edge of a pew. The flashlight hit the ground with a crack, shattering the glass face. The light went out instantly. "Damn," she groaned.

Downstairs, the movement stopped.

"Oh, Jesus!" said Cordelia. "We've got to get out of here."

Jane could hear running footsteps. "No time."

The light coming from the stairway was minimal, but

it was enough for them to find their way up on stage. "This way," whispered Jane. "We can hide behind a curtain."

Cordelia brought up the rear. "I don't think so, Janey. They're pretty sheer."

"Where then?"

"Dive!" Cordelia grabbed Jane's hand and dragged her behind a sofa just as the downstairs light went off.

The playhouse was plunged into total blackness.

"Our intruder probably thinks they heard a noise," whispered Jane. "They can't be sure it meant anything."

"God, I can't see a thing."

"Shhhh!" Jane heard a loud creak—it sounded like it was above them, but far away, towards the back of the theatre.

Suddenly, the amber stage lights were switched on. Jane felt a searing pain in her eyes. She was momentarily blinded by the intense brightness. "Stay down," she whispered to Cordelia.

More lights were switched on. Red. Blue. It was like a Christmas light show, only orchestrated by a madman.

"How is this happening?" she asked, shielding her eyes as they tried to adjust.

"Someone's in the light booth," said Cordelia. She was lying flat on the floor, her legs sticking out at least two feet from the end of the couch. Clearly, they'd picked a lousy place to hide. "You enter the light booth from the basement. I forgot about that."

More creaking.

"What are we going to do?" asked Cordelia. "I feel confident we've been noticed."

Jane glared at her. "How the hell should I know?" She peaked up over the cushions. All she could see beyond the stage lights was blackness. Summoning all her courage, she called, "We know you're out there."

"Oh, great," shrieked Cordelia, covering her head with a couch pillow. "If you can't intimidate them, kill them with comedy."

"Stick a sock in it." Jane was at a loss. "If they were going to hurt us," she whispered, "they would have done it by now."

"You mean, if they have a gun."

Jane could feel the adrenaline pumping. "Can we talk?" she called, inching away from the non-safety of the sofa. She didn't know what else to say.

The theatre remained silent.

"Try, *let's do lunch,*" whispered Cordelia.

"Shut up," barked Jane. She walked to the edge of the stage. "I know you're there. You obviously know we're here. What do you want? What are you doing here in the middle of the night?"

Cordelia's head popped up. She scrambled to her feet. "If it's insomnia, we totally understand. We wouldn't blame you in the least."

Just as quickly as the lights had gone on, they were turned off. Jane could hear a door open. Then, movement in the darkness. Footsteps.

Cordelia found Jane's arm. She held on for dear life. "Let's get out of here," she pleaded.

"You got it." Together, they inched their way to the side stairs and climbed down. Jane knew the pews started a few yards to their left. The basement stairs were farther around the back of the stage to their right. Perhaps they'd lost their pursuer in the darkness.

Suddenly, every light in the theatre went on. Bells began ringing out the hymn, "Blest Be the Tie that Binds." It was so loud, Jane covered her ears.

Cordelia pointed to the ceiling. "It's a recording," she shouted. "It's hooked up to a loudspeaker in the bell tower. Diana showed me the first day I was here."

Remembering the danger they were in, Jane crept a few paces farther into the main hall, her eyes searching the room. Seeing no one, she walked slowly down the aisle, glancing both left and right, making sure no one was hiding in the seats. As she got to the back, she bumped smack into Annie who was just coming through the door.

"What's going on?" she shouted above the pealing bells.

They were now well into the second stanza of the hymn.

Cordelia rushed up behind them and threw herself into a pew. "I just checked out the basement. As I suspected, it's empty. And," she bellowed, in as confidential a tone as the noise would allow, "I didn't see anything unusual."

Annie looked confused.

"Out for a late night walk?" hollered Cordelia.

"No," she replied, a bit indignantly. "I was downstairs in the kitchen getting a glass of milk when I saw the stage lights come on over here. I wondered what the hell was going on."

"Kind of a dangerous thing to do on your own," shouted Jane.

"Why?"

"We could have been burglars."

"Doing what? Reciting Hamlet? If you were stealing something, why turn on all the stage lights?"

After a rather grand yet flat Amen, the bells stopped, the last note lingering in the air like an electrical buzz.

Orson and Curt burst through the front door. Both men were in their pajamas, each wearing a plaid bathrobe.

"It's the MacPhersons!" cried Cordelia.

"What's going on?" demanded Orson.

Jane slumped into the pew. What a night. "It's a long story."

"I don't doubt that." He put his hands on his hips. "Well?"

"Don't you appreciate religious music?" asked Cordelia, standing and putting her arm around his shoulder. "A tinkling canticle. A reverent little *pastorale*. Pity. I felt, under the circumstances, that our intruder's musical choice was quite...interesting. 'Blest Be the Tie that Binds.'" The arch of her eyebrow was pregnant with meaning.

Orson glared. "What intruder?"

Jane knew she had to explain. "It's very simple," she began. "The sound of a car motor woke me about four, so I got up and looked outside. I didn't see anyone, but I noticed a light in the theatre. Cordelia and I came over to check it out."

"And what did you find?" asked Curt.

"Someone was in the basement. We could hear movement."

Curt and Orson exchanged glances.

"But then Cordelia dropped our flashlight and the culprit must have heard."

"That's right. Blame me." She gave an indignant sniff.

"We tried to hide on stage, but the stage lights came on. After a minute or two, they went back off. I didn't know what to do. Cordelia and I were trying to get out when those bells started playing."

"And what about you, Annie?" asked Curt.

"Well, I saw the stage lights go on and came over to see what was going on. I guess I thought it might be Diana, giving an unscheduled performance."

He gave her a hard stare.

Orson looked carefully around the playhouse. "I think it's fair to conclude that whoever was in here is long gone by now. I suggest we all get back to the parsonage and try to salvage what's left of our night's sleep."

"Maybe I should look around the basement first," offered Curt.

"I already did," said Cordelia. "Nothing was out of place."

Everyone seemed a bit uneasy, but resigned to the situation.

Following Annie and Curt, Jane and Cordelia trudged wearily across the damp lawn. "I wonder who would know how to run those stage lights," she whispered.

"It's not hard," replied Cordelia. "Everything's labeled."

Not the answer she wanted. "What about the bells?"

"Those are controlled by a panel in the basement. Anyone with some electrical knowledge could do it. You can even put them on a time switch. Diana showed me. She wanted to keep the system intact—she thought she might be able to put it to some use."

Someone sure did a few minutes ago, thought Jane. It was a memorable way to begin a day. The sun would be up in less than an hour. Unless she was sadly mistaken, the bell incident had a distinctly theatrical smell about it. Unfortunately, that realization narrowed her list of possible suspects by exactly zero.

30

Curt crouched next to the rear wall of the parsonage, smoking a joint. The funeral was at three—several hours away. If he ever needed a mellow buzz, it was this morning. He took another toke, watching the huge, puffy clouds float across the sky. A crow sat on one of the tallest gravestones, surveying the graveyard with a wary eye. All in all, it was another beautiful day.

Receiving that note from Theo late last night had really thrown him. It was like reading a letter from a ghost, not that Theo hadn't already felt like a ghost more than once. Curt hadn't said anything to Annie about it, knowing it would only upset her. On the subject of Theo, she had long ago ceased to be rational. Curt couldn't blame her. She'd put up with a lot.

Yet, in Theo's own convoluted and cryptic way, Curt felt he'd finally said something real. That letter was his first genuinely honest attempt at addressing the past and assessing the present. Great timing, now that there was no chance of continuing the conversation. Still, even though what he'd said was incomplete, interestingly, by mentioning the story of Beau Geste, Theo may have given away more than he'd intended. That intriguing aside had occupied all Curt's thoughts since he'd read it. He hadn't come to any conclusions yet, but he was working on it.

"I thought I smelled weed," declared Amity, breezing around the end of the house. She had a small CD player hooked to her belt. A pair of earphones hung around her neck.

For an instant, Curt considered dropping the joint between his legs, but knew it was useless. "You caught me." He gave a weak smile.

"Yeah, well. I guess that makes you a bad influence."

"I guess."

"Just like every other adult."

"I'm . . . not perfect."

"I know. Neither am I." She sat down cross-legged on the grass in front of him. "So what's up?"

"Not much."

She picked up a rock and flipped it from one hand to the other.

"No school today?"

"Annie got me a reprieve because of the funeral."

He nodded. "What are you listening to?" He nodded to the CD.

"Soul Asylum."

"Umm."

"You a fan?"

"Not really." He took another toke. "You know, it's funny. Sometimes I get really down on myself because I think I'm stuck in the past. But, in some ways, all adults are stuck there. Take music. I thought I'd always be up on what was new. I love rock, or at least I used to. But after I turned thirty-five, it was like I fell off a cliff. All I ever listen to now are oldies. The Stones, The Who, Fleetwood Mac, Jethro Tull, The Doors, all the old bands. I wouldn't know Soul Asylum if they walked up and bit me in the ass. Uh . . . sorry."

"Don't patronize me, Curt. I know what an ass is."

He let some ash drop to the ground.

"Maybe you need someone to help you," she said.

"Help me how?"

"Get unstuck."

He smiled. God, she was a great kid. He was sick to think what would happen to her if she stayed with Diana. Not that she *could* stay here. He knew Diana loved Amity, but right now, she wasn't capable of being a parent. If Diana did consent to go into treatment, then Amity would have to find a temporary home. She couldn't go back to her grandparents house. They didn't want her. That left what? A foster family? The streets?

"Sure," replied Amity. "I could give you a list. Let you borrow some of my CDs. I'm sure in, say, a month or two, I could bring you up to speed."

He smiled. "That's a tall order."

"Nah. No problem. You just need to loosen up a little. Relax. Try something new. You and Annie'd get along a lot better if you did." She tossed the rock over her shoulder. "She's a neat lady."

"You think so?"

"Absolutely."

"She likes you too."

"Really?"

"We both do."

Amity's face flushed. "How come you never had any kids?"

"I don't have a good answer for that." He stared at the burning tip of his joint, thinking back to the times he and Annie had talked about having children. "I guess we just never got around to it. We both like kids."

"You think you're too old now?"

"Yeah. Well . . . I don't know, maybe."

"For a baby, you mean."

He glanced at her.

She stretched out on her back. "Do you ever just like to sit and watch clouds?"

"That's what I was doing before you came."

"Funny. You looked more like you were worrying."

"I did?"

"Something on your mind?"

"Well . . . sort of."

"Wanna talk about it?" She brushed a fly away from her face.

Curt looked at his watch. They still had plenty of time before the funeral. "You want to hear a story?"

"What kind of story?"

"It's about three young men."

"I prefer stories about young women."

He laughed. "Try to cope." Sitting down on the ground, he fished a roach clip out of his pocket. He carefully pinched the end of the joint and took another toke. "Okay, here's the story. These three young men were brothers. They lived in England back in the late eighteen hundreds. Michael was the oldest. People called him Beau because he was beautiful and had a noble heart. He had a twin brother named Digby and a younger brother named John. They lived with a very kind woman who had befriended them as children. She was quite rich, though unhappily married. One day, Beau learns something about this woman. Something he keeps a secret for many years. When he and his brothers are fully grown, a priceless jewel is stolen from the woman's house. No one knows who's done it—or why. But Beau disappears late one night, leaving a note behind that says he's guilty. He's taken the jewel and gone off to join the French Foreign Legion. The next morning, Digby is found missing. Another note is discovered. In it, Digby says he can't let his brother take the blame for something he did. He took the jewel, and he's

230

also left to join the Foreign Legion. That evening, John doesn't show up for dinner."

"Another letter's found."

"Right. From John saying he can't let his brothers take the blame for what he's done. He took the jewel and he's off to—"

"Join the Foreign Legion."

"Exactly."

"So who stole the jewel?"

"We don't find that out until the very end. But the point is, Beau is the only one who knows for sure what really happened. And he willingly sacrifices his life to protect someone he loves."

"He dies?"

"Yes," said Curt, his voice soft. "He does."

"That's very sad. And kind of romanticized."

"I agree."

"But it sounds like a great story. So tell me what happened."

He shook his head. "No, I think you should read the book yourself."

"Do you have a copy?"

"At home in Chicago. It was Theo's favorite."

She closed her eyes. "It's sort of like you and Orson and Theo. You were like brothers."

"We were."

"And one of you died."

He nodded.

"Did he die to protect someone he loved?"

"I don't know," said Curt, his eyes returning to the clouds. "But I intend to find out."

31

Jane stood with the rest of the group crowding silently around Theo's grave. As the minister intoned a final prayer, a small casket containing Theo's cremated remains was lowered into the ground. Everyone's head was bowed. Diana was leaning on Cordelia's arm. Curt, Annie and Amity stood next to her. Peppered among the assemblage were the members of the Summer Green Playhouse. Hilda stood with James Donati and his wife. And Orson stood alone, off to the side, his eyes wet with tears.

Jane carefully watched the faces of those who had come. In each she saw a reflection of the pain of human loss—each, that is, except for one. Strange that no one else seemed to notice. Perhaps she was misreading the situation, but she didn't think so. She had to be careful. She didn't want to be caught staring.

"Into the depths," lamented the minister. He must like that phrase, thought Jane. It was the fourth time he'd used it. She tuned him out, thinking instead about the last few hours. It had been a trying morning. Orson had awakened Diana at ten, insisted she shower and dress, and then he'd stood over her while she ate some lunch. No alcohol had been allowed. He'd blustered around the house saying he knew he was being controlling, but he didn't care. He wasn't going to allow anyone to ruin Theo's funeral. Diana did look a bit better than she had yesterday, but only slightly.

"Holy Father," said the minister, raising his voice as he looked up, his eyes still closed, "we commend our loved one's spirit into your hands." He paused dramatically. "Amen."

"Amen," repeated the crowd.

Jane breathed a sigh of relief. The service was finally over. Without being directed, Diana bent down and picked up some dirt. Leaning over the hole, she let it slip from her fingers, watching as the wind carried some of it away while the rest drifted onto the beautifully polished wood. Then, standing back, she allowed others to take their turn, ending with Curt.

Finally, Annie stepped out of the crowd and invited everyone back to the parsonage for coffee and cake. "I'm told it's a custom around here," she said, smiling sadly. "And we mustn't break tradition."

The crowd began to drift toward the house.

"Well," said John Hubble, emerging out of the group and walking up to Jane, "Another beautiful day in Summer Green. Too bad it had to be such a sad one."

She was about to answer when a thought occurred to her. "Say that again."

"Pardon me?"

"About the weather."

He cocked his head. "I said it was another beautiful day."

She gave a slow nod. "Right. It was, wasn't it." She looked away, trying to pull it all together in her mind.

"Actually, except for the day of the picnic, the weather around here's been nearly perfect for several weeks."

"Is that right?"

He watched her. "Why all the interest?"

"Oh . . . just making conversation." She smiled. Of course. Why hadn't she seen it before. Then again, this wasn't the kind of clue on which to base an entire theory, but it was something.

"Well, if I may be so bold as to change the subject— that is, unless you want to discuss corn prices. Or radish futures."

Again, she smiled.

"That was too bad about Diana's portrait yesterday. Have they found it yet?" He adjusted his tie.

"No. Orson called the police and they're checking on it. So far, nothing." Jane still wasn't sure how the theft fit into the larger picture.

"Pity." His eyes swept over the graveyard. "I was looking forward to seeing it. Well, perhaps later. Say, who's that guy talking to Orson? The one in the dark shades." He pointed to an oak about thirty yards away. "I've seen him before, I just can't place the face."

Jane held her breath. It was the bald man. "I don't know."

John shrugged. "Well, it's probably none of my business. Unless he's a theatre critic, that is." He gave a small wink.

"I don't think so."

"Are you coming over to the parsonage for cake?"

"In a few minutes."

"Okay. I'll leave you to your private thoughts. By the way, I'm very sorry about your friend, Theo."

"Thanks."

He set off toward the house.

Jane wished she could hear the conversation Orson was having with the bald man. Then again, she knew it might be dangerous to intrude. Before she could formulate a plan, she saw Cordelia trudging across the lawn, heading straight for her.

"Diana's finally settled in the living room," she announced, slightly out of breath. "Annie and I saw to it that she got the chair that was most thronelike. She's having a pretty awful time of it."

"I'm sorry," said Jane, her voice distracted. Every now and then she would sneak a peak at the distant conversation.

"I've never seen her take something this hard. I wish I understood why she had that picture of Theo in her room. It might explain some of this."

Jane cleared her throat. "Well, actually, she was angry at him because she thought he'd given some personal information to the guy who then outed her in a New York magazine."

Cordelia's eyes grew large. "What? You're kidding!"

"Afraid not."

She placed an indignant hand on her hip. "Excuse me, but did I miss something here? How did you find *that* out?"

"Diana told me."

"Is that right. She just tapped you on the shoulder and said, by the way Jane dear, Theo's a snitch."

"Not exactly. I found her going through Theo's things late last night. She was packing them for James. She was pretty drunk, and she just started talking about it."

"Really. How fortuitous."

"Except, Theo didn't do it."

In a very teacherly voice Cordelia asked, "And how do we know that, Jane dear?"

"Orson said so. He was there the night it supposedly happened. Theo never said a thing to the guy. Diana did."

"I beg your pardon? Diana outed herself?"

"She'd had so much to drink, she didn't realize what she was saying—or, more importantly, who she was saying it to."

"How did Orson get into this discussion last night?"

"He must have heard us talking. When we got to the part about Theo and the outing incident, he walked into the room and informed Diana that she was wrong. He was furious."

"This all happened while I was asleep?"

Jane nodded.

"That should teach me to go to bed with the farm animals—figuratively speaking, of course. Janey, what *are* you looking at?" Cordelia turned to see Orson walking the bald man back to his car. "Hey, there's that guy!"

"I think we should leave it alone."

"Not on your life," she growled, stomping away without so much as a backward glance.

"Wait," called Jane, but it was too late. She'd already caught up with them. Jane rushed to her side, hoping that she could temper any angry outburst.

"What the hell are you doing at this funeral?" demanded Cordelia, raising herself up to her nearly six foot height.

Orson took hold of her arm. "This is a private conversation, Cordelia. Please leave us alone."

She ignored him. "Who are you?"

Very calmly the man answered, "A friend of Theo's. Just like you."

"I doubt that."

"I knew him many years ago, Ms. Thorn."

"Hey! How come you know my name? I don't know yours."

He turned to Orson. "I need to be going. Once again, thank you for your time, Mr. Albern. Please extend my heartfelt sympathies to the Donati family."

"I will," said Orson, still holding Cordelia's arm.

As he walked away, Cordelia wrenched it free. "Who is he?" she demanded.

Orson waited. When he saw the man get into his car he heaved a deep sigh. "He's a judge."

"A judge! From where?"

"Chicago."

"How does he know Theo?"

"I don't know."

"I don't believe you."

Orson drew a heavy hand across his eyes. "That's your privilege."

"Did he have something to do with Theo's death?"

He gave her a hard look.

"Answer me!"

Orson started to speak, but then stopped himself.

"Well?"

"Just leave it alone, Cordelia."

"How can you ask that?"

"I can't tell you anything else."

"You mean you won't."

Again, he sighed. "I've got to get back to the parsonage. See how Diana's doing."

"She's fine."

"I doubt that."

They stared at each other. "All right," said Cordelia, folding her arms over her chest, "Just tell me this much. He wasn't Theo's friend, was he?" She waited.

Orson looked at Jane and then at the hearse which had brought the casket over from the mortuary. "No," he said finally. "He wasn't." In the bright afternoon light, his face looked ashen, his body drained of all energy. "I'm sorry. That's all I can say." Unbuttoning the top button of his shirt and loosening his tie, he walked off toward the parsonage.

"He's exhausted," said Jane.

Cordelia nodded, then exploded. "God, I wish I knew what was going on around here!" She flung her arms in the air. "What the hell do you make of that bald guy?"

"He's dangerous."

"Is that a theory or a fact?"

"Both, I suppose."

Cordelia stood for a moment, looking toward Theo's grave. Men were already at work shoveling dirt into the hole. "Am I crazy for thinking someone might have murdered him?"

"We'll know before we leave."

"How can you be so sure?"

"Just trust me," said Jane.

She shook her head. "Somebody's lying."

"No, Cordelia." She lowered her voice. "Somebody's acting."

32

Jane sat in one of the four white wicker rockers on the porch and watched two cars pull out of the parking lot. The sun was finally setting on a very long and sad day. After the funeral, James had mentioned again how much he wanted to talk to Theo's friends—reminisce about old times. Diana suggested they do it over a pitcher of beer at Al's Roadhouse. Since no one wanted to make a scene, everyone had agreed. Jane had begged off, saying she wanted to get to bed early. The truth was, since she hadn't known Theo all that well, she felt like a fifth wheel. And also, she had some matters she wanted to check on while there was still time.

After the intervention tomorrow morning, if all went as planned, Cordelia was going to fly back to Minnesota with Diana and the psychologist. Jane was to drive Cordelia's car back to Minneapolis. Orson was staying on in Summer Green for a while to make sure everything ran smoothly at the playhouse. Diana's understudy would have to be ready to go on starting Thursday night. A press release would need to be issued about the reason for Diana's untimely absence from the production. With the exception of Cordelia, no one was more qualified than

Orson to take care of such matters. And Annie and Curt were heading back to Chicago. Whatever Jane determined was necessary to finally get to the truth behind Theo's death, it would have to happen before tomorrow afternoon. There wasn't much time left to decide on a course of action.

The first order of business was a long distance call to Houston, Texas. If she was lucky, she had just enough time before the end of the business day to call Theo's place of employment. There were a couple of questions she wanted to ask.

As she entered the house, she could see Hilda bustling about in the kitchen, cleaning up the coffee and cake dishes. Jane grabbed the cordless phone from the foyer and sat down in the parlor. She retrieved a slip of paper from her pocket—the one on which she'd written some notes about Theo. She got the number of Blandin Builders from Texas directory assistance. After dialing, a woman's voice answered, "Blandin Builders. How may I direct your call?"

"Hello. My name is Jane Lawless. First of all, are you a construction company?"

"Yes ma'am."

"Great. Okay, I'm calling for Mr. Rob Wilson." That had been Theo's alias.

"Just a minute."

Jane was put on hold. She drummed her fingers on the arm of the chair and waited.

After several seconds the woman returned. "I'm sorry, Mr. . . . Wilson no longer works here."

"Really? As of when?"

"I can't say."

"Is there anyone there who can say?"

"Just a minute."

She was put on hold again.

Finally, a male voice answered. "This is Fred. Can I help you?"

"I hope so. My name is Jane Lawless. I'm a friend of Rob Wilson's. I was told he no longer works for you."

"That's right."

"Was there some problem?"

"No."

"Do you know why he quit?"

"I'm sorry. I don't."

"Can I ask what he did at Blandin Builders?"

"Sure. He was an estimator. Went out and gave bids on various jobs."

"How long had he worked there?"

"Sorry, but that's all I can tell you. If you need further information, I suggest you write to our personnel office."

"Thanks," said Jane. She knew this was all she was going to get. "I appreciate your time."

"No problem." He hung up.

When Jane had seen the name Blandin Builders on the death certificate, her immediate reaction was that a job in construction was a poor choice for a man with a heart condition. But if he'd been an estimator, major physical exertion probably wasn't part of it. So, it fit. He could have been ill and still employed there. Yet she knew she'd been lied to. What wasn't she being told?

Returning the phone to the foyer, Jane decided it was time to have a chat with Hilda. She walked back to the kitchen. As she came through the door she saw a bowl of radishes sitting on the counter next to a salt shaker. In between wiping plates, Hilda would select one, salt it and pop it into her mouth. So much for local idiosyncrasies.

"Can I help you with anything?" asked Jane, moving to the center island and pouring herself a cup of coffee.

Hilda turned, surveying her visitor. "Nope. I'm almost done." As she returned her attention to the sink, the phone rang. "I'll get it," she said, wiping her hands on a kitchen towel. She picked up the receiver. "Stanwood residence." She leaned against the counter. "No, sorry Mrs. Albern. Orson isn't here right now. Would you like to leave a message?" A pause. "Fine. I'll tell him you called. Goodbye." She dropped it back on the hook. "That woman calls here every day. You'd think she doesn't trust the man."

Jane let that pass. "I don't know if you remember my name. I'm Jane Lawless."

"I know who you are." She began wiping off the large coffee urn that had been used in the dining room. "All you people say you're Diana's friends. Well, if you ask me, you're pretty miserable excuses."

Jane sipped her coffee. "I understand your feelings. You like Diana, don't you?"

An eyebrow raised over an eagle eye. "And why not? She's a fine woman. Has a good heart. And talk about talent? Why she could act circles around any of you."

"I don't doubt it."

"I've been here ever since she came, and let me tell you that woman's in trouble. I've tried to help. I've even hid the booze. Watered it down whenever I could. But nothing works. You people've got to do something! But all you've brought is your own kind of trouble."

"What do you mean?"

"I see what's going on around here."

"Can you be more specific?"

"No." She walked back to the sink.

Jane decided to try another approach. "The night Theo died, did you notice anything unusual?"

"Like what?"

"I don't know. What about the wine he was drinking. Do you know what happened to it?"

She shrugged. "Your friend Cordelia asked me the

same question. Maybe Diana took it upstairs with her, although I know she hates sweet wine. She ordered it especially for Mr. Donati."

"You didn't see anyone with the bottle before dinner?"

She shook her head. "That night was a blur. Diana was angry about something. She wouldn't say what. Before dinner, she'd called down for another bottle of vodka. A bad sign. Then, at dinner, your friend Theo had his heart attack." She put a thoughtful finger to her chin. "Come to think of it, I did notice something kind of strange."

"What?"

"Well, as they were leaving in the ambulance, I walked out on the porch. No sooner had they headed up the highway than this car pulled over the rise and proceeded to follow them. Not too close, you understand, but close enough."

"What kind of car?"

"It was a Cadillac. White. I'd seen it a couple of nights before just sitting across the road."

The judge, thought Jane. He was obviously keeping a very close watch on the house. "One more question. Does Diana get the local newspaper?"

"Sure does."

"I suppose you've thrown all the recent ones out."

"No. I save them. Everything that hasn't been burned is in a kindling box next to the fireplace."

"Great," said Jane. "Thanks."

"What do you want them for?"

"Oh, I just thought it might be interesting to read up on the local news."

Hilda gave her an appraising look and then turned back to the sink. "You people kill me, you really do."

33

After searching out the newspapers and confirming what she had already suspected, Jane stepped onto the porch once again for a breath of fresh air. She was close to the truth now. For the first time since coming to Summer Green, she could allow herself a moment to relax. She loved being in the country. Except for the hum of crickets, she couldn't hear a sound. No airplanes or freeway noise interrupted her thoughts. Perhaps someday she'd retire to her parents' cabin on Blackberry Lake. Spend her later years surrounded by a comfortable solitude. But that was a long way off. And even then, she knew another part of her would miss the familiarity of the Twin Cities—the bustle of Uptown, the popcorn stand at Lake Harriet, the Como Park Conservatory, her favorite bookstore and coffee house. So many conflicting feelings were at war inside her. She wondered if it had been like that for Theo. From what she'd found out, he'd been a man of many faces. But only one of them could be real.

At the sound of giggling, Jane turned. Inside Cordelia's car she could see movement—two heads bobbing up and down and laughing. She climbed down off the porch and crossed to the parking lot. Sure enough, Amity and Chickie Johnson were in the front seat. They were having such a good time, they didn't even see her walk up—until it was too late. An open wine bottle sat in the seat between them. Jane recognized it as one of Diana's. She rapped on the window.

Both kids froze.

"Uh...Jane," said Amity, rolling down the window. Her smile was something less than confident.

Jane could smell cigarettes. Cordelia would be hysterical. "Good evening."

"Hi." She swallowed hard. "See...Chickie and I were just—"

"Can I talk to you for a minute?" asked Jane. She motioned for her to get out.

"Uhm...sure." She didn't look particularly thrilled. Slamming the door behind her, she squared her shoulders, bracing herself for the worst. "What can I do for you?"

"First, I think you and Chickie should find someplace else to smoke."

"I don't smoke," said Amity, a bit indignantly. "And, you're right. I'll tell him to beat it."

"Second, where did you get the wine?"

"Well, I, ah...borrowed it."

"Borrowed?"

"You're probably not going to believe this, but I don't drink either."

"But Chickie does."

"Right."

"Kind of a mass of bad habits, isn't he?"

"Yeah. Kind of."

"He do drugs too?"

"Well—"

"Do you do drugs?"

"Certainly not!"

"Kind of hard not to when your friends do them."

She nodded weakly. "But he quit."

"Really? Why?"

"Well . . . something happened. Something bad."

"Like what?"

She drew Jane further away from the car. "He's trying to go straight. You understand." She gave Jane a knowing nod.

"You make him sound like he's done hard time. Amity, he's only fourteen."

"So?"

Jane realized she was far too removed from teenage life to approach this rationally. It was best to let Amity do the talking. "What happened?"

"Do you promise not to tell?"

Jane sighed. "All right." What could the kid have done? It couldn't be that big of a deal.

"Did you hear about the church fire?" Her eyes flicked furtively to the playhouse.

Jane raised an eyebrow. "I did."

"Well, Chickie and some of his friends accidentally set it."

Jane blinked. "Are you serious?"

"Absolutely."

"Were they doing drugs?"

"Well . . . sort of. It's a long story. See, before the mall was finished, there weren't many places to go at night. And in the winter, if you wanted to keep warm, and you didn't have a car, and you didn't want to stay home—"

"They broke into the church."

"Well, not exactly. Chickie had keys. His father's a deacon. Anyway, they were inside one night . . . and they all fell asleep. Chickie said a velvet pew pad caught fire. But see, they couldn't tell their parents. Chickie's been to-tally freaked ever since it happened. He's sure someone's going to send him to reform school."

"Reform school."

"Sure. Anyway, he stopped doing the drugs. Now he just smokes . . . and, well, drinks a little wine every now and then. He's going to stop smoking next week."

"Do tell."

"Look, I know he's kind of a mess, but he's my friend. I don't see that there's any difference between him and Diana. They both got problems, but that doesn't mean we should push them away—refuse to love them."

She had a point. "Let me ask you something. The night Theo died, did you take a bottle of wine off the dining room table?"

She lowered her eyes. "Yeah. I did. For Chickie, though, not for me. He gets super stressed sometimes."

"And you sat in Cordelia's car that night, just like tonight."

"Yup."

"Did he drink it all?"

She nodded.

"Did he feel sick afterwards?"

"Come on, Jane. There was less than a third of the bottle left. That's why I chose it."

"And he never felt sick?"

"Not that I know of. He's sort of the original chronic whiner, if you know what I mean. If he'd started to feel crummy, I would have heard about it."

Jane gave her a serious look. "All right. But you two've got to leave Cordelia's car alone. And the rest in the lot as well."

"No problem. We're history." She ducked back inside the car and yanked Chickie out. "I'll be back in a few minutes."

"All right," said Jane, taking the bottle from Chickie's hand. She watched them as they ran around to the other side of the parsonage. Well, she thought, shaking her head, so no one had tampered with the wine. It was just as she'd suspected. Tomorrow, if everything went as planned, she would be able to put the last pieces in place. And then she'd have to explain everything to Cordelia.

That, in the end, might be the hardest part.

34

The day of the intervention had finally come. Jane headed downstairs, knowing she had less than fifteen minutes before the psychologist arrived. The tension in the house was as thick as a Lake Superior fog. She wondered if Diana could feel it.

As she walked into the foyer, she saw that Annie was in the kitchen, sitting at the center island with a cup of coffee. She was going over some notes. Curt was doing the same, only he was in the parlor with a glass of orange juice. Orson was reading the newspaper in the dining room, and Cordelia was pacing on the front porch, waiting to intercept the doctor. Lastly, Diana was in her room, upstairs, preparing herself for what she thought was the final breakfast before everyone left for home.

As Jane stood alone in the quiet house, she knew one of four people held the answer she'd come all the way from Minneapolis to find. It was now or never. Glancing again in each direction, she squared her shoulders and walked resolutely into the dining room. Orson looked up as she took a seat next to him.

"Morning," he mumbled.

"Good morning," she said, keeping her voice low.

"We need to talk."

He put down the paper. "About what?"

"Theo."

He gave an exasperated sigh. "Do you realize what's happening this morning?"

"I know the psychologist will be here any minute. I'm willing to wait until after the intervention. But as soon as it's over, we have to talk."

"I have nothing to say to you." He started to rise.

"All right. That's your privilege. But if I don't speak to you, I'm going to speak to the police—and I don't mean the police in Summer Green. I'm talking about the police in Green Bay, Orson. I think they'll be very interested in what I have to tell them."

Slowly, he sat back down. "Why are you doing this?" His expression was a strange mixture of anger and caution.

"You know why. Cordelia asked me here to see if I could shed some light on Theo's death. And that's what I've done."

He ran a shaky hand over his forehead. "How much... do you think you know?"

"Enough to make your friend the judge very upset."

"He's not my friend."

"I know."

He tapped his fingers nervously on the table. "What do you want?"

"The entire story."

"You don't know what you're asking."

She looked him square in the eye. "I'm asking for the truth, Orson."

He stared at her a moment and then looked down, laughing bitterly. "I haven't told the truth in so many years, I'm not even sure I'd know where to start."

"Start with the body that was stolen from the cemetery when you were a college student."

His head snapped up. "What do you know about that?"

"I know it's where this all started. But I don't know why."

He held her eyes. "You think you're pretty smart."

"Yes," she said. "Smart enough."

The sound of voices broke their concentration. Cordelia and the psychologist had just entered the parlor.

Orson rose quickly.

"So," said Jane. "Do I talk to you or do I talk to the police?"

He hesitated. "All right. After this is all done, I'll meet you out on the porch."

"Fine."

Diana appeared in the foyer, all decked out in a cashmere sweater and gray wool slacks. "Who's that?" she asked, seeing the stranger. She turned to Orson for an explanation.

In an instant, Orson was by her side, his arm around her shoulders giving them a protective squeeze. "Diana," he said, his manner sober and yet very gentle, "I'd like you to meet Dr. Bernson."

"*Doctor?*" She scowled.

Orson maneuvered her into the parlor and saw to it that she got a comfortable chair.

"My name is Lynn Bernson," said the doctor. "I'm a family therapist from Minneapolis, and I work with families all over the country. Your friends asked me here today to facilitate a family meeting. They're concerned about you, Diana, and they didn't know how to handle it. That's why I'm here."

Diana froze. "Is it about my—" She looked from face to face, her manner growing tentative. "—drinking? Because if it is, I suppose . . . I owe all of you an apology. I've behaved badly these last couple of days. But it was because of Theo. You all know that. A drink calms me down. It's going to change now, I promise. And besides, I don't always drink this much. It's just . . . the stress."

The room was silent.

"Diana," said Orson, sitting down next to her, "since we've been here, we've all done a lot of reminiscing. It struck me last night when we were talking to Theo's brother, how many of our stories are colored by your drinking."

"That's not true!"

"It is," said Orson, his voice firm. "The first night we were here, Annie brought up that time in college when we all went sledding. Do you remember?"

Hesitantly, she nodded.

"You nearly landed in the river. The day could easily have ended in tragedy."

"But I didn't know how to steer my sled, Orson. That's all. Why are you making such a big deal out of it?"

"It was a big deal, Diana. And it had nothing to do with steering the sled. You'd brought a flask with you. Everyone saw it, but like always, we ignored it. Or maybe we thought it was cool—dangerous. We were young and we took chances. Some of us did it one way—" He paused. "You did it with booze."

"So?" Her body grew rigid.

"You don't get that many chances in life, Diana. And you've just about used yours up."

"We all have stories we want to tell you," said Annie. "Please, if our friendship means anything to you, you've got to listen."

"This is a trap," said Diana indignantly.

As Curt shut the double front doors, Jane could hear Cordelia say, "I suppose, in a way, it is. But we just can't leave you here, knowing that—" Her voice grew very gentle. "You're drowning, dearheart. We've got to try to get you to see that. And also . . . that there's hope."

Jane stuffed both hands deep into the pockets of her jeans and walked out onto the porch. She stood for a moment looking at the marigolds which lined the sidewalk all the way to the house. She'd heard enough about Dr. Bernson's style to know the intervention wouldn't include angry confrontation. This meeting, even though painfully honest, would be full of love. Jane hoped it could work. Yet even if Diana consented to go into treatment, that was only the beginning. Jane felt that, deep down, Diana knew her life was hanging by a thread. She wanted help, she just didn't know how to get it. What her friends were asking of her now was to take a hard road, but one that, in the end, would give her back her life.

Jane turned as Hilda came around the side of the house. She had a shovel over one shoulder and was carrying a basket of freshly dug potatoes. As she stepped up on the porch, Jane nodded a good morning.

"Well," said Hilda, setting down the basket, "you people finally did something. It sure took you long enough."

"It was all planned from the beginning."

"That right." She took off her gardening gloves and shoved them into the back pocket of her overalls. "Well, let's just pray this doctor of yours knows what she's doing. Annie seemed pretty high on her."

"You talked to Annie about the intervention?"

"This morning. Just after dawn. I was making muffins."

Jane nodded.

"Well, anyway, I got to change my clothes. I promised I'd help Amity pack."

"Where's she going?"

"Back to Chicago with Curt and Annie. They're taking care of her until Diana gets on her feet. Then they can all have a powwow about her future. If you ask me, I think the Whittigs would like to keep her permanently."

Jane smiled at the thought.

"Oh," said Hilda, her hand on the screen door. "And one more thing. If you're looking for that oil portrait of Diana, I've got it."

"You what?"

"I took one look at it and decided that artist was just plain mean. It was the last thing Diana needed. She already thinks she's over the hill—a lot of crap, if you ask me."

"How did you do it?"

"I took it Monday morning. When I was setting up the buffet table. I hid it in the basement. I know that old church like the back of my hand, I even used to run the bells for our pastor. I came back to get it that night—I thought I'd store it in my garage and hope some water dripped on it. That's when I ran into you and Cordelia. Sorry about the light show, but I had to remove the evidence without being caught. I mean, I didn't want to get arrested or anything, I just wanted to keep Diana from being hurt."

"You're a good friend." Jane was touched by the woman's gruff kindness.

"So, if you want it, it's over at my place."

"Thanks."

"Don't mention it. If it was up to me, I'd sell it at a garage sale."

Jane grinned. "I'll pass along your suggestion."

"You do that." She disappeared inside the house, leaving Jane alone with her thoughts.

35

Cordelia was the first to emerge from the parlor a little less than three hours later. She saw Jane sitting on the porch and immediately came outside. "She's agreed to go." Her tone was a mixture of exhaustion and elation.

"Great! What happens next?"

"She has to pack a small suitcase and then Hilda will drive the three of us to the airport in Green Bay. I've decided to accompany Diana and the doctor. Diana asked if I would, and I couldn't say no. Anyway, we'll fly directly to Twin Cities International." She rubbed her hands together. "Mission accomplished, Janey."

"Congratulations."

"Thanks. So, what are your plans?"

"Well, I'm leaving pretty soon too. I've already got your car packed."

"What about—" She glanced back into the house.

"Theo?"

She gave a confidential nod. "You said you'd know the truth about his death before you left."

"I will."

Cordelia gave her a skeptical look. "And?"

"I haven't left yet."

"Very funny." She put a finger to her lips. "Here come the hordes. Act natural."

The door opened and out flowed Curt, Annie and Amity, each carrying a suitcase, and each with a big smile on their face. If not a happy day in the Stanwood household, this was at least a hopeful one. Cordelia gave them all a huge goodbye hug and made them promise to visit her soon. Then she begged off, saying she had to find Diana and help her pack. They had to leave for the plane in less than an hour.

Jane took Amity's suitcase and walked them to their car.

"Well," said Curt, after stuffing the cases into the trunk and shutting it with a thud, "it was good seeing you again, Jane."

Annie was helping Amity get situated in the back seat.

"Thanks. It was good seeing you too."

"Tell me something." He reached into his pocket and drew out his keys. "Do you still think one of us murdered Theo?"

Her eyes moved to the graveyard just over his shoulder. "No. I don't."

"I'm glad. None of us would ever hurt him."

"I know that now."

"Well, I guess we'd better shove off." He took one last look at the parsonage. "This has been quite a visit."

Jane could only guess at the full meaning of his words.

"You know, Theo was trying to tell me something important in the note you found in his belongings. He made a comment about the book, *Beau Geste*. It's really got me stumped. Are you familiar with the story?"

She nodded.

"I'm convinced he took some sort of secret to the grave with him. I've always felt there was something important he wasn't telling me. Truthfully, it's driven me nuts. Now, I may never know what it is."

"He probably had his reasons."

"That's just it. By mentioning that story in his note, he was telling me he had a *good* reason for not taking me into his confidence. Not that it makes it any easier." He looked off in the distance. "But, I guess learning to live with incomplete answers is all part of life."

"You may be right."

"I think I am. For now, it's enough to know that he really cared. I feel like my life has been stuck in the past far too long. I want to get on with it now."

"I envy all of you," said Jane.

"Why?"

"I think your love for each other is remarkable."

"Yeah. We're still friends after all these years, and that's a lot." He walked to the car door and opened it. "Everyone all set?"

"All ready," came Amity's eager voice from the back seat.

Curt gave Jane a wink. "She's going to help me get unstuck."

"You couldn't have picked a better person."

"I know." He grinned. Then, slipping behind the wheel, he started the motor and backed up. Everyone waved excitedly as the car sped out onto the highway and disappeared over the rise.

"Good luck," called Jane, knowing they couldn't hear. She felt a very real sadness, watching them leave.

Half an hour later, after the rest of the group had left, Jane found Orson sitting in the parlor, his body bent forward, his head resting in his hands.

"I think we're finally alone," she said, sitting down opposite him.

He didn't look up.

Jane could see he'd been crying.

"God, for a minute there, I thought Diana was going to change her mind." He took out a handkerchief and wiped his eyes.

"But she didn't."

"No." He patted his brow. "You'll have to forgive me. This has been an emotional morning."

The phone interrupted them.

"I better get that," he said. "It's probably my wife." He rose and crossed into the foyer, picking up the receiver. "Orson Albern," he said, his voice once again completely controlled. "Yes, hi." He glanced back at Jane. "Sure, no, I'm glad you called. How's everything?" A pause. "Good. Good. What? No, not right now." Another pause. "I'll do that. Let me write it down." He found a note pad and pencil on the phone table. "Okay. Repeat that again." He scribbled quickly. "Fine. Right. I love you too, honey. Bye." He carefully folded the paper and stuffed it into his pocket. Then, returning to the parlor, he sat back down on the couch.

"How is he?" asked Jane.

His hand froze halfway to his face. "What?"

"I said, how is he?"

"How's who?"

"Theo."

"What do you mean?"

"Maybe I should ask, where is he?"

Orson remained motionless.

"I told you I knew the truth. Theo's not dead. That was him on the phone, wasn't it?"

"I—" He ran a hand through his hair.

"It's time for the truth."

"This is preposterous!"

"No more than this charade, Orson. I told you, either

258

you talk to me, or I talk to the police. It's your call."

He shot to his feet and crossed to the mantel. Keeping his back to her he asked, "How . . . I mean . . . how did you find out?"

"From the moment I got here, I knew things weren't what they seemed. Someone was lying. It took me a bit longer to figure out it was an act. I just wasn't sure who was doing the acting until yesterday."

"What do you mean? What happened yesterday?"

"Your performance at the grave site, Orson. The tears. They weren't real."

He turned around, a slow smile pulling at the corners of his mouth. "You're accusing me of being a lousy actor?"

She wondered why he would find that so amusing. "I'm accusing you of feeling relieved. You thought you'd pulled it off. You were simply allowing yourself a momentary character break. That is, until the judge showed up."

The smile evaporated.

"I want the whole story, Orson. But first, I want you to say it. Theo's alive, isn't he."

He stood with his face in profile, considering his options. Finally he said, "What I tell you has to be kept in the strictest confidence. Your life would be in danger if . . . certain people found out what you know."

"I have to tell Cordelia. That's part of the deal."

He rested an arm on the mantel. "All right. But you *must* understand the danger."

"Believe me, I do. And so will Cordelia. Whatever you tell me today will go no farther than the two of us."

He gave a slow nod.

"I know this is hard for you."

"You have no idea." He sat down wearily on the couch and took several deep breaths. Then, very slowly, he began, "Once upon a time, there were two very silly young men. One was named Orson. The other, Theo. Each thought he was the best actor the world had ever seen. To prove who was the greatest talent, a competition was devised. And thereby, Jane . . . hangs the tale."

36

The Blackburn Playhouse in Shoreview was an old log building built shortly after the end of World War II. Orson had purchased it from the Blackburn family in the early eighties, and had turned it into a thriving business. The next play on the theatre's agenda was *The Mousetrap,* by Agatha Christie.

Late the following evening, Jane drove to the deserted parking lot in back of the building and got out. The moon rose low over the wood-shingled roof. Cordelia had handled the rehearsals tonight. She'd gotten a ride out with one of the actors. Jane was supposed to pick her up afterwards and drive her back to Minneapolis.

As she entered the front door, she carefully locked it behind her. What she had to tell Cordelia must be done in absolute privacy. Cordelia had called around noon wanting to be filled in on all the details, but Jane had put her off. What she had to say had to be done in person.

She found Cordelia up on the stage, rearranging some of the props on the mantelpiece. The setting was a cozy English drawing room, complete with antique furnishings and a large, floor-to-ceiling window. On the other side of the glass, the machine that dropped the fluffy plastic snow was still on, giving the set a sense of protected warmth, even in the dead of winter. An electric fire in the fireplace cast shadows against the far wall. Above the hearth was a portrait of Agatha Christie.

Even though none of it was real, Jane was pulled in by the atmosphere. Just as she had been in Summer Green.

"Ah, you're finally here," said Cordelia, throwing herself into one of the two wing chairs on either side of the fireplace. "Just give me a minute and I'll turn everything off. Then we can leave."

"No. Leave the snow on. It's beautiful."

"I forget that you're a winter freak."

Jane smiled. "Are we alone?" She hopped up on the stage and sat down opposite Cordelia.

"That we are. Everyone took off an hour ago. It was a good run through. Orson will be pleased."

Jane made herself a bit more comfortable. "I have some things I need to tell you."

Cordelia seemed to come to life. "I should hope so!" She sat up straight.

"Before we start, how's Diana doing?"

"Fine. Dr. Bernson and I got her all checked into the Institute. She'll be staying there for at least a month. On the plane ride back to Minnesota, she was pretty quiet. I started to get worried. But when we left her, she thanked us. I think she really wants to change her life. She's got a lot of work to do, but I feel the motivation is there. I promised to visit sometime next week. Orson will too, once he gets back from Summer Green."

Jane looked up at the fake snow. It was *so* convincing.

"So, give, Janey! Is it time to call the police? What happened to Theo? Did someone . . . god, I can't even say it. Did someone murder him?" Her voice was eager, yet she looked as if she was steeling herself for a blow.

On the drive home from Wisconsin, Jane had thought

over what Orson had explained to her. They'd sat and talked in Diana's parlor for almost three hours. It was an incredible story. And just like Orson, she wasn't quite sure where to begin. "No, Cordelia," she said, her tone serious, "none of your friends tried to hurt him."

Cordelia let out a deep sigh. "I'm so glad. Then his death . . . it was natural."

"Well, not exactly."

She gave Jane a blank look. "Was it that judge? I could tell right off he was trouble."

"It wasn't the judge, Cordelia."

"Then who!"

Jane reached for her hand. "I'm glad you're sitting down."

"Why?"

"Well, because . . . the truth is, Cordelia, there was no death. Theo's alive."

Cordelia blinked. Then she blinked again. "Repeat that?"

"It's true. He didn't die."

"That's . . . incredible." Her amazement slowly turned to joy.

"It was all an act. He faked the heart attack. The two men you saw come in the ambulance really were volunteer paramedics, but they were also Orson's friends. It was all staged."

"Staged," she repeated, still smiling. Then, "*Staged?*" Her smile gradually became clenched teeth. "This is . . . monstrous! What possible reason could they have for doing something so . . . so cruel? We've been mourning that little turd all week! And now you tell me it was just a bit of theatre! A joke?"

"Calm down, Cordelia. It was no joke. Theo's life was in danger. He didn't think he'd get out of Summer Green alive unless—"

Cordelia ignored the explanation. "All I can say is, if he thought his life was in danger before, wait until I get my hands on him!"

"But he's alive. Aren't you glad?"

"What? Of course."

"Then just relax and let me tell you the whole story."

She yanked her sweater into place. "I'm completely calm."

"Good. It all began when you were in college. You remember the day Orson found that sack of bones in the back seat of his car? The remains of a body stolen from Eastwood Cemetery?"

"Of course I remember. It was the same day Theo was arrested for impersonating an IRS agent."

"Right. But, the fact of the matter is, Orson was the grave robber. He'd dug up the grave two nights before and planted the remains in his car. It was all part of a . . . competition of sorts—an acting contest between Orson and Theo. They wanted to prove once and for all who was the greatest actor. Each was to choose a situation within the larger community in which to test his skills. It had to be *real*—for real stakes. And it had to have an element of danger associated with it. If they were caught, there would be repercussions. That would only serve to heighten the tension—make it even more imperative that they give the performance of a lifetime. They were both in love with the idea. Couldn't wait to test their mettle."

"They were idiots!"

"Of course they were. But they were young and—"

"Full of testosterone."

"I suppose. And as Orson was quick to point out, terribly arrogant. The rules stated that neither was to know what the other was planning. Orson acted first. And, much to his delight, he got away with it. Not only did he receive a reward for finding Edgar Collingwell's remains, but he ended up marrying his granddaughter and inheriting the man's company. But if the truth had come out early on, he would have gone to jail. And if it had come out years later, not only would he have been ruined personally, but financially."

"The only one who knew was Theo?"

"Exactly. Unfortunately, Theo hadn't made out so well. The same day Orson turned the remains over to the police, Theo decided to try his luck impersonating an IRS agent. Everything went well at first. He'd done some studying. Thought he knew the best approach. He picked a small company in Bloomington. And he actually succeeded in intimidating the head of the firm into letting him see his books. While he was there, he called in the bookkeeper and made him explain various parts of their most recent tax statements. He was having a ball watching them sweat. He even brought along a small tape recorder which he'd concealed in his briefcase. He wanted Orson to be able to hear how well he was handling the whole affair. But he hadn't counted on one of the secretaries recognizing him. He'd been in far too many theatre productions over at the university to remain totally anonymous. After he left, the police were called. Then the FBI. You know the rest. He was arrested at your apartment that night. He was assigned a lawyer, but the woman's hands were tied because Theo refused to say why he'd done it. He knew if he revealed anything, the authorities would put two and two together and Orson would be arrested as well. He couldn't let that happen. As much as he feared going to jail, he refused to drag Orson along with him. So, in essence, he took the rap for both of them. After all, they'd both known and supposedly accepted the risks. He cared deeply about Orson. They were like brothers. And so, unable to form a credible defense, he went to jail."

"Did he take that money he was accused of stealing?"

"No. He never touched it. Probably someone in the company saw an opportunity to help himself to a nice vacation or a new car."

"Good. That always bothered me. You know, I was there the day he was sentenced. The judge seemed to really have it in for him. No one could understand why he received so much time. After all, it was his first offense."

"I think his very vocal stand on the Vietnam war may have had something to do with it. Orson told me that he found out years later that the judge's son had died in combat only months before Theo's sentencing. He thought guys like Theo were scum. He had the chance to throw the book at him and he took it."

"So, Theo went to jail. Seven years of his life down the drain." She made a sour face.

"And when he got out," continued Jane, "he headed straight for Chicago to see Curt. He knew Curt felt shut out—all of you did. He couldn't talk about why he'd been put in jail, so he just withdrew. Orson was the only one who knew, and therefore the only one he kept in contact with. But he really had loved Curt. He'd always hoped that some day they would have a life together. Still, he refused to ask him to wait until he got out of prison. He thought that kind of request was not only melodramatic, but pointless. By the time he was finally released, Curt and Annie were living together in Winnetka. They hadn't married yet, so Theo made a beeline for Chicago to feel out the situation. See if he still had a chance. In the meantime, a man he'd met in prison had arranged a job for him. Theo knew it might not be totally on the up and up, but he didn't have a dime, and he knew getting a regular job would be difficult. So he took it. He became the chauffeur for a judge."

"Not the one who sentenced him to prison?"

"No, the bald guy in Summer Green. All Theo had to

do was drive the guy from Chicago to the Twin Cities two or three times a month. The judge had a girlfriend he kept secret from his wife. He'd installed her in a house in south St. Paul, and Theo would drop him off, drive the car to a specific parking lot in downtown Minneapolis, and spend the rest of the day roaming around. He would stay the night in the hotel of his choice, and then the next day pick up the judge and head back to Chicago. He did this exactly twice before he realized what was really happening."

"Some kind of drug deal."

Jane nodded. "On his third trip to Minneapolis, he waited in the parking lot. Sure enough, two guys appeared and removed several packages from the underside of the car. Before they took off, they deposited a suitcase in the trunk. When Theo got to the judge's girlfriend's house the next morning, he saw that the place was surrounded by cops. He knew there was probably a bust in progress, so he just split. He dumped the car at a grocery store in west St. Paul, but not before checking out the suitcase. Sure enough, it was full of money. Over a million dollars. So, not knowing what else to do, he bought a used Toyota, stuffed the suitcase in the back, and headed south. No one ever caught up with him. But he found out several months later that there was a contract out on his life. Apparently the judge thought Theo had blown the whistle on him. Since the police found no money or evidence of drugs at the house, they just let the judge go. But he was highly connected. Theo was on the run for years. He couldn't contact any of you because he was sure all his friends were being watched. The only good thing to come of it was that he didn't have to worry about money any more. He sent most of it to Orson, and Orson invested it for him. Whenever he needed anything, he'd just send a note. Theo became a very rich man. He also learned how to buy himself different identities as he needed them. Remember the name on his Texas driver's licence? Rob Wilson?"

Cordelia nodded.

"He used that name when he traveled in the South. You never saw the coroner's report, but it said his place of employment was Blandin Builders in Houston. That was only partially true. He didn't work there, he owned it. Another man ran it for him. His involvement was totally anonymous. It was the same all over the country. He owned a number of businesses. Then, about five years ago, he heard through a Chicago contact that the contract on his life had been withdrawn. He still didn't feel safe enough to come out of hiding, but he did take a few more chances. That's why he felt he could go to New York for Jill's funeral."

"But he never dared return to Chicago?"

"No. That was too dangerous. The contract might have been withdrawn, but that judge was still alive and well, and no doubt pissed as hell."

"And he never got to explain to Curt why he disappeared so abruptly."

Jane shook her head. "That was the saddest part. He couldn't expect Curt to drop everything and risk his life to go underground with him. So he didn't do anything. A year later Curt married Annie. For Theo, that was the end of the story. He would never have tried to interfere with that kind of commitment. But I know from talking to Curt that he felt the situation with Theo was never resolved. It drove him nuts. Theo felt the same way, of course, but his hands were tied. And even if he had made contact, what would he say? He couldn't tell the truth. It would just be more non-answers. There were already too many secrets. It was best to simply leave Curt and Annie alone."

"Which he did. Until the intervention."

"That's right. Coming back to the Midwest so openly

was taking a real chance. Yet, he felt he had no choice. Diana needed him. He couldn't turn his back on her just because there was some risk involved. He never dreamed she would include his name in that interview she did with the *Chicago Sun Times*. When he got to Summer Green, he was already a sitting duck. That's who you saw the first night. The judge was already there, staking out the house. That same night he met with Theo, and Theo denied any involvement in the drug bust. But he couldn't exactly deny that he'd taken the money and run. The judge wanted it back. Theo promised he'd get it if he could just have a couple of days. He knew the minute he handed it over, he was dead meat. So he and Orson cooked up another little plot."

"Another bit of theatre."

Jane gave a grave nod. "Theo's life depended on pulling it off. Which, for all practical purposes, they did. They were lucky. Orson knew just about everyone in the town since he'd grown up there. The chief of police was an old high-school buddy. So were a lot of other guys on the police force. And so were the paramedics and the coroner. Everyone who was essential to making it work was in his pocket, so to speak. He convinced them all that this was a grand mission. Saving a good man from the clutches of evil. You should have heard him yesterday, Cordelia. He was so persuasive. He could have talked the devil himself into giving heaven another try."

"That's Orson," said Cordelia with more than a hint of pride.

"So they faked the heart attack. Theo was taken to the funeral home where he spent the night. The next day, he was driven to a farm just outside of town. Orson immediately went to work on getting him a new fake passport, credit cards and other necessary papers. Because of Theo's connections, it took less than two days. But Orson couldn't make phone calls from the parsonage. That's why he rented the room at the Sunburst Motel. He hooked up an answering machine so that he could receive messages when he wasn't there. That woman we saw meet him on Tuesday afternoon—she came to see him several times. He tried to make it look like a sexual liaison, just in case the judge was watching. But she was actually the one who messengered the papers. As soon as Orson got everything together—including having his bank in Minneapolis wire cash to the First Bank of Summer Green, Theo was off. He rode a milk truck to Madison where he bought a car and drove to Cleveland. He made a couple of plane connections, and right now I believe he's in London. I think he's planning on settling in Paris. Orson will fill you in on the details later. But remember, Cordelia, this can't go any farther than this room."

Cordelia gave Jane a freezing stare. "You mean, Diana, Curt and Annie are never to know?"

"The fewer people who are privy to this information, the better. You have to promise."

She tapped her fingers impatiently on the arm of the chair.

"Just say you understand."

"Of course I understand. But I think it's awful."

Jane had to agree.

"What about the fight Theo and Orson got into at the Roadhouse? Was that real?"

"No. Also a fake. Remember, Theo's life was in danger. Who knew if the judge was going to wait until Theo handed back the money before he made a move on him. I mean, they had no guarantees of anything. The safest place for him until he could die of that heart attack was jail. So, they staged the fight. Very simple. Theo was whisked away for his own protection."

Cordelia shook her head. "This is too incredible."

"I know."

"If I didn't know better, I'd think those radishes in Summer Green *were* hallucinogenic."

Jane gave a weak smile. "Only if you smoke them."

"So what tipped you off?"

"Several things. The night I arrived, Curt showed me a note he'd received from Theo. Orson had given it to him two nights before, explaining that Theo had written it while he was in the squad car before the police hauled him off to jail. In it, Theo asked Curt if he'd come down to the police station in the morning to talk. They'd apparently had a conversation earlier in the day, and Theo didn't like the way it ended."

"So?" said Cordelia. "Theo wrote him a note. What's strange about that?"

"Well, first of all, the police chief put handcuffs on Theo before taking him outside. Remember, Theo did have a record, and he'd just assaulted Orson. He might be dangerous. It seemed unlikely that the the handcuffs would be taken off just so he could write a note."

"Good point."

"But the real tip off was the fact that the note was written on a piece of colored stationary. I don't think small towns stock their police cars with writing paper. That was a major flaw in their plan. Theo had obviously written the note earlier, when he'd had more time and could give it more thought. If that was true, then he knew he was going to be arrested, and that meant the fight had been staged. Orson and Theo were both in on it. And if *that* was a setup, what else was? If the police chief was also in on it—and he had to be, otherwise it might not have gone as planned—then who else in the town was in cahoots with Theo and Orson—and for what reason? It still didn't offer a complete answer, but it did point me in the right direction. What I saw was not necessarily what was real."

"Amazing," said Cordelia. "What else did you see that I missed?"

"Well, I was immediately suspicious when I found out the coroner hadn't ordered an autopsy. His explanation didn't satisfy me at all. Then we found the fake heart pills. I found out from Orson that he'd slipped them into Theo's things after I came. He knew my reputation for—"

"Being a busybody," replied Cordelia, with a small smirk.

"*Sleuthing,*" said Jane. "So, he thought he'd better be as thorough as possible. Unfortunately, the druggist in Summer Green *wasn't* an old buddy, so he was forced to make something up on his own. Faking prescriptions is not one of his strong suits."

Cordelia gave another nod. She was totally mesmerized.

"The next thing to catch my eye was something Diana found in Theo's belongings. She was packing them for James when she found a piece of notebook paper. It was another note Theo had written to Curt. I remember her saying she'd started going through his suitcase the day before and hadn't seen it, but she said she'd probably been preoccupied. She simply dismissed it."

"But you didn't."

"No. And fortunately or unfortunately—however you want to look at it—Diana read the whole thing to me. I felt it was completely inappropriate for us to be reading another person's correspondence, but I just sat there."

"How utterly unethical."

Jane resisted rolling her eyes. "In it, Theo mentioned the weather. He'd been in town since Friday. He died Sunday night. With the exception of Monday—after he was dead I should point out—the weather in Summer Green had been perfect. But in the letter, he mentioned something about dark mists—or some such thing. Curt should just enjoy the summer sun and the dark mists. But he hadn't seen any dark mists—there weren't any until after he died. It just seemed odd to include that in what he'd written."

"And he couldn't do that from the grave."

"Exactly. Diana found the note Tuesday night. I asked Orson about it yesterday, and what I'd suspected was accurate. Orson planted it in Theo's things Tuesday afternoon. Theo was heartsick that he hadn't had a chance to talk to Curt privately just one last time. He knew he'd hurt him and was terribly upset that he hadn't made a better attempt to put things right."

"But Theo is never going to let Curt know he's alive."

"No. Never. He feels it's better to let things simply be. It would just cause Curt and Annie more pain if they ever found out the truth. Theo has taken all his secrets to the grave with him, and frankly, I think that's where they belong."

"His love for Curt," said Cordelia. "The truth behind Orson's wonderful good luck."

"All buried in that cemetery in Wisconsin."

"Just like *Beau Geste*. That was his favorite book in college, Janey. He talked about it all the time. In a very real sense, by going to prison, he sacrificed part of his life for a friend. By coming to Summer Green, he made another sacrifice. And by dying, he's made the most important sacrifice of all. He's finally set Curt free."

"Not without pain and not without confusion," said Jane. "But I think, under the circumstances, he made the only decision he could." She stared into the fake fire. "If only he and Orson had never made that bet."

"Crazy idiots," said Cordelia, her eyes welling with tears. She wiped a heavy hand across her face. "But I can't be angry with them."

"I know."

"The Shevlin Underground," she repeated, her voice wistful. "Who would have thought." A small sniff. "Diana, a beautiful and internationally loved actress, in treatment because she couldn't love herself. And Curt, the Jay Gatsby of the bisexual crowd, finally married and settled down with Annie—who has just given birth to a bouncing fourteen-year-old girl. And Orson, a famous Midwest cookie maggot—I mean, magnate. Such talent we all have."

"And Theo?"

She smirked, placing a finger against her cheek. "How about, *Dead, and living in Paris.*"

Jane laughed out loud. "That's quite an epitaph."

"Yes," said Cordelia, stretching her arms high over her head. She lifted her feet up on the footstool in front of her and gazed up at the oil portrait of Agatha Christie. "Under the circumstances, he could have done a lot worse."

Mysteries from Seal Press

The Jane Lawless Mysteries by Ellen Hart
The Twin Cities are turned upside down in these compelling whodunits featuring restaurateur cum sleuth Jane Lawless and her eccentric sidekick Cordelia Thorn.
Hallowed Murder. $8.95, 0-931188-83-0.
Vital Lies. $9.95, 1-878067-02-8.
Stage Fright. $9.95, 1-878067-21-4.
A Killing Cure. $19.95, cloth, 1-878067-36-2.

The Meg Lacey Mysteries by Elisabeth Bowers
From the quiet houses of suburbia to the back alleys and nightclubs of Vancouver, B.C., divorced mother and savvy private eye Meg Lacey finds herself entangled in baffling and dangerous murder cases in these two gripping novels.
Ladies' Night. $8.95, 0-931188-65-2.
No Forwarding Address. $10.95, 1-878067-46-X; $18.95, cloth, 1-878067-13-3.

The Cassandra Reilly Mysteries by Barbara Wilson
Globetrotting sleuth Cassandra Reilly gets herself into intriguing situations whether she's on a gender-bending romp through Barcelona, Spain or hitch hiking to a crumbling health spa in the Carpathian mountains of Transylvania.
Gaudí Afternoon. $9.95, 0-931188-89-X.
Trouble in Transylvania. $10.95, 1-878067-49-4; $18.95, cloth, 1-878067-34-6.

The Pam Nilsen Mysteries by Barbara Wilson
Three riveting mysteries, featuring Seattle sleuth Pam Nilsen, take us into the worlds of teen prostitution and runaways, political intrigue, and the controversial pornography debates.
Murder in the Collective. $9.95, 1-878067-23-0.
Sisters of the Road. $9.95, 1-878067-24-9.
The Dog Collar Murders. $9.95, 1-878067-25-7.

Seal Press has many other feminist titles in stock: fiction, self-help, health and psychology, women's studies, sports and outdoors and international literature. Any of the books above may be ordered from us at 3131 Western Avenue, Suite 410, Seattle, WA 98121. Please include 15% of the total book order for shipping and handling. Write to us for a free catalog.

P9-AGA-671

Eudora: A Writer's Life

Ann Waldron

Doubleday

New York London Toronto Sydney Auckland

Eudora

❧ A Writer's Life ❧

PUBLISHED BY DOUBLEDAY
a division of Bantam Doubleday Dell Publishing Group, Inc.
1540 Broadway, New York, New York 10036

DOUBLEDAY and the portrayal of an anchor with a dolphin are trademarks of
Doubleday, a division of Bantam Doubleday Dell Publishing Group, Inc.

Book design by Maria Carella
Photo insert design by Bonni Leon-Berman

Library of Congress Cataloging-in-Publication Data
Waldron, Ann.
   Eudora Welty : a writer's life / Ann Waldron. — 1st ed.
     p.   cm.
   Includes bibliographical references.
   1. Welty, Eudora, 1909–   —Biography. 2. Women authors,
American—20th century—Biography. I. Title.
PS3545.E6Z934   1998
813'.52—dc21
[B]   98-5708
                                        CIP

ISBN 0-385-47647-7

Printed in the United States of America

November 1998

First Edition

10 9 8 7 6 5 4 3 2 1

To the Tuesday Club

"Your private life should be kept private. My own I don't think would particularly interest anybody, for that matter. But I'd guard it; I feel strongly about that. They'd have a hard time trying to find something about me."
EUDORA WELTY, 1972

Contents

ᴖ Finding Her Feet ᴄ

ᴚ Stretching Her Wings ℮

ᴚ The Last Years ℮

Eudora: A Writer's Life

A Point of View

On Thursday, January 25, 1996, a cold, wet day, I drove from New Orleans to Jackson, Mississippi, dumped my luggage in the apartment I had arranged to rent for a short term, and then went straight to the Old Capitol building in downtown Jackson, next door to the Mississippi Department of Archives and History, where Eudora Welty's papers are kept. I had worked with her papers before and would work there again, but on that day I wanted to go to the Old Capitol first.

Eudora Welty was to receive the Légion d'honneur from the government of France, and I wanted to see it. "Is the ceremony open to the public?" I asked a well-dressed, white-haired woman at a table in the rotunda of the Old Capitol.

"The public has to sit in the gallery," she told me. "The House chamber is reserved for invited guests." I headed upstairs to the gallery and found a seat in the second row. Below me, I could see the reserved seats on the main floor of the House chamber. We would be watching, I saw from the printed program, the award ceremony at three o'clock, when the Honorable Gérard Blanchot, consul general of France, would present the Légion d'honneur to Eudora Welty. It was only two twenty-five, and the gallery was almost completely filled.

The House chamber was well cared for and imposing, like all the well-coifed, white-haired ladies it held. This was the room where Andrew Jackson once spoke and where the members of the Mississippi Legislature voted to secede from the Union in 1861. Tall windows were hung with red draperies adorned with gold fringe. Two Ionic columns, their scrolls covered with gold leaf, flanked the back wall on each side of the Speaker's rostrum. Brass vases of magnolia leaves—the magnolia is Mississippi's state flower—stood on the rostrum. An American flag and a Mississippi flag hung on staffs.

The floodlights set up for the television cameras were so bright that people sitting near the rostrum had to shade their eyes. Besides the white-haired ladies, there was a critical mass of younger women, equally well turned out, and a few men.

I recognized one of Eudora Welty's sisters-in-law, who came with her nurse and sat near the front. Eudora, escorted by the writer Richard Ford, a native of Jackson and her literary executor, entered and sat down. She was eighty-six years old, and her body was bent with osteoporosis, but her white hair was beautifully done. She wore a dress boldly printed in black and white, with a long matching scarf that hung from one shoulder. Eudora is truly admired and loved in Jackson, the town where she was born and grew up and has lived all her adult life. She has been a good citizen, happy to help with many worthy causes, leading an apparently blameless life. She has written four collections of short stories and five novels, but her most recent novel, the Pulitzer Prize–winning *The Optimist's Daughter,* appeared in 1972, and she has not published a new short story since 1966. Her memoir, glowing with remembered happiness, was a best-seller in 1984. She had been honored in this room before—in 1973 on Eudora Welty Day, and again in 1987 when she was named a Chevalier de l'Ordre des Arts et des Lettres by the French government. Her friends had turned out in amazing, heartwarming numbers for these events, just as they had this time.

This afternoon, when things got under way, former governor William Winter, possibly Mississippi's most liberal governor (which of course does not mean that he was very liberal), presided. He introduced all the state officials who were present—the secretary of state, the state treasurer, the chief justice of the state supreme court, members of the legislature—and then other notables, including the president of the Alliance Française, Richard Ford and his wife, Eudora's two sisters-in-law, her two nieces, her cousin from West Virginia, and her close friend Charlotte Capers.

Sitting up in the gallery, looking down at the invited guests, I realized that there before my eyes were a great many of the people I wanted so badly to interview for this biography. That is the fate of the unauthorized biographer: to be the uninvited guest.

I had been working on a biography of Eudora Welty for two and a half years and had had to deal with the refusal of her closest friends to talk to me. They all knew that she did not want a biography written. I like to think she did not want a biography written by *anybody,* and I refused to take her feelings about the matter personally. But when I used great ingenuity and persistence in tracking down one of her friends from another era who lived in a faraway place, the old friend would usually call Eudora. "I'd rather you didn't talk to her," Eudora always said.

"I'd rather you didn't talk to her." These were the only words she had to say, for Eudora Welty is genuinely loved—no, adored, in Jackson and in fact everywhere. She has proved herself a loyal and generous friend and relative. No wonder she has inspired unstinting devotion.

Why, then, did I go against her wishes and pursue an unauthorized biography? Because I had to. I had written about another southern woman writer, Caroline Gordon, and about a Mississippi newspaper publisher, Hodding Carter, and next I wanted to write about Eudora Welty. I wrote to her and asked her if I could do a book about her, and she never answered. When I was in Mississippi working on the Hodding Carter book, I stopped by her house in Jackson. She could not have been more pleasant. She invited me in, we chatted, and I told her that I would like to write about her, and she said she did not want a biography written. "I want my work to stand on its own," she said.

After that, whenever I was in the vicinity, I stopped by her house and repeated my request. She was always hospitable, but always opposed to a biography. After the book on Carter was published, I took her a copy and asked her again. It seemed to me that her negative answer was not as adamant as it had been. I went home and thought about it a long time. I talked to several people who had contemplated writing a Welty biography but had abandoned the idea in the face of her stony opposition. With amazing fool-hardiness, I figured that they were Yankees, that they didn't have a chance. After all, I was a southerner; I had grown up in Alabama, right next door, and I had worked for southern newspapers and written books about south-erners. I knew the dialect, the code. I wrote a proposal and got a contract and warm encouragement from Jacqueline Onassis, my first editor at Doubleday, who understood thoroughly that the biography would be unauthorized.

I persevered. Welty's biography needs to be done, and certainly would be done, either by me or by another biographer who could no longer resist exploring the life of this towering literary figure. And as a loyal friend of mine said, "Her opinion on the matter is irrelevant." I do not feel that a biography is an invasion of privacy, especially when it is a biography of a woman who has been on innumerable television talk shows and given count-less print interviews to newspapers all over the country. For thirty years, Eudora Welty appeared a thousand times on college campuses to read her work and to lecture, drawing enormous crowds and on one campus, Stan-ford, almost causing a riot. She is no J. D. Salinger, living a life of pure seclusion, never giving interviews to the press or on television. She has been very much in the public eye, but she has—with great charm and invariable courtesy—managed to control the interviews so that few personal questions are asked, and when asked, they are not answered.

This may be the first Welty biography, but it certainly will not be the last. Perhaps later biographers will be able to use some sources that I could not, but here is a full account of the life of Eudora Welty. I have drawn on Welty's own extensive collection of papers in the Mississippi Department of Archives and History, many of which are available to the public; on letters she wrote, sold by their recipients to various research libraries all over the United States, and on letters her friends wrote to other friends; on the hundreds of interviews with her that have been published in newspapers and magazines; and on interviews with people who were willing to talk to me. An incredible amount of information was out there to be picked up, and I have gathered it before it was too late. But let me say that it would have been much easier and more pleasant to do an unauthorized biography of a person who was less beloved than "Miss Welty," since absolutely no one wants to hurt or displease her by talking to her biographer.

. . .

It was time for Eudora Welty to come to the front to receive the Légion d'honneur; the audience, upstairs and downstairs, rose as one and applauded ferociously. As Richard Ford led her forward, she walked slowly and carefully.

In his presentation speech, the consul mentioned that Miss Welty's first short story, one that begins "Monsieur Boule inserted a delicate dagger in Mademoiselle's left side and departed with a poised immediacy," is set in Paris. "Monsieur Boule was a vicious murderer, but we forgive him," said M. Blanchot. As he began to pin the medal on Miss Welty, he said, "I have to speak in French now, because we want it to *be* French. *Au nom du président de la république, et en vertu des pouvoirs qui me sont conférés, je vous fais chevalier de la Légion d'honneur.*" After he had pinned the badge on the shoulder of her black-and-white dress, he kissed Eudora Welty on each cheek.

Tearful, she turned to the audience and said, "I'm so happy and honored and proud to be here among a group of people who love the written word as I do. I feel grateful to everyone."

Once more the audience rose to its feet and delivered a standing ovation. I slipped out, avoiding the reception in the rotunda, and went over to the archives to finish my research.

Part One

The
Early Years

Chapter 1

The Teenager

"As you have seen, I am a writer who came of a sheltered life. A sheltered life can be a daring life as well. For all serious daring starts from within."
EUDORA WELTY, One Writer's Beginnings

By all rights, Eudora Welty should have been miserable every minute of the day when she was growing up.

"The thing you have to understand about Eudora is that she was not a belle," said a man a few years younger than Eudora who grew up in Jackson. "She was not pretty, and that is very important." He talked about this a little more. "Oh, she had friends who were boys—not boyfriends—but one of them, Frank Lyell, was such a sissy that even his own brother made fun of him."[1]

"It wasn't that Eudora was plain," said a woman who had grown up in Jackson and now lives in Boston. "She was ugly to the point of being grotesque. In the South, that was tantamount to being an old maid. You could either teach school, be a librarian, or teach music, or, if you were far out, teach dancing. That's the way life was then." She added, not especially warmly, "At least Eudora found her feet."[2]

"I was pretty," said one former Jackson belle, now in her eighties, "so our paths didn't cross much. She didn't go to dances or up to the Delta." (The Mississippi Delta had a reputation for raciness. Dances there started at eleven o'clock at night and lasted until breakfast.) "Oh, Eudora had beautiful blue eyes, and beautiful hands," she added. "But she never stood up straight, and she hunched over to hide her height."

A man a few years older than Eudora who was still living in Jackson said he had known who Eudora was, although she had been several classes behind him in high school. "She was not good-looking," he said. He was a nice southern gentleman, uncomfortable with saying something that was not strictly complimentary about a woman, and he shifted in his chair before he blurted out, "That's the only reason I knew who she was—because she was . . . well, different-looking."[3]

"They would be checking off the girls' names who had escorts for a class party or something, and Eudora's name would not be checked off," recalled Sarah Gordon Hicks, a high school classmate. "They would say to my husband, Graham Hicks, 'Would you go pick up Eudora?' And he'd be glad to. He and Bill Wells looked after her. Everybody was glad to. She was not pretty, but everybody loved her. They thought the world of her."[4]

Eudora's personality triumphed over her looks even when she was a teenager. As another woman classmate of Eudora's in high school said, "I wouldn't call her pretty, but Eudora was fun. We were all crazy about her. Everybody liked her. I don't remember her having dates with anyone, but a lot of us were just going out with a crowd."[5]

Eudora was elected "Best All Round Girl" by the members of her senior class in high school—a title not given to an unpopular girl. In fact, all her life most people who met her would say something like this: "The first time I saw her, I thought she was the ugliest person I'd ever seen. Five minutes after I started talking to her, I thought she was the most wonderful person I'd ever known." Her looks mattered to people who were not close to her. People who knew her, even in high school, liked her and forgot her looks.

Jackson was a small town on the verge of growth in the early 1920s. Its population of 22,817 was about to double during the decade, and it would soon surpass Meridian as the largest city in the state. About 13,000 of its residents were white, the rest black, and this small white society was in a sense closed. Almost everybody in town was a native southerner. Therefore, if Eudora's looks made her remarkable when she was growing up in Jackson, her origins also almost made her an outsider. Both her parents had grown up outside the South, her father in Ohio, her mother in West Virginia, which had separated from Virginia because its citizens objected to secession.

"I could never talk about the old family home that was burned during the Civil War," Eudora once said. But then she said another time that because her mother was from West Virginia and her father from Ohio and they held views about the world that sometimes differed from those of the parents of her friends, she learned early on that there wasn't just one side that was right.[6]

There's an old way of telling news in the South, rather like a folk version of "I have good news and bad news for you": "It's a pity that . . . , but it's a blessing . . ." The pity for Eudora Welty the teenager was that she was not pretty, that she was tall, and that her parents were not from the South. The blessing was that she was smart, that she was nice, and that her father was a prominent, well-liked citizen in town. Christian Welty had joined the Lamar Life Insurance Company soon after he and his wife, Chestina, arrived in Jackson in 1904. He rose steadily in its ranks until, when Eudora was in high school, he was vice president and general manager.

Eudora entered Central High School in 1921, when she was thirteen years old, after spending seven years at Davis School (named, of course, for Jefferson Davis, the president of the Confederacy). She and her classmates had stayed in the same classroom for seven grades—nobody moved around—and they knew each other quite well by the time they all went to Central High. (All her life Eudora could remember all the new people who had come to Davis School while she was there. The class's first Yankee arrived from Indiana when she was in the fourth grade and said "cor-dju-roy," while Mississippi children said "cor-du-roy."[7]

Jackson had always provided only eleven grades of school, with freshmen entering high school in the eighth grade. The powers that be decided to add a twelfth grade in 1925, the year that Eudora would finish the eleventh grade, so her class would have to remain an extra year. That meant there would be no graduation, no valedictorian, no senior pictures in the yearbook in 1925. To prevent this, the administration selected some of the seventh-graders from all the grammar schools to take a little extra work each year at Central and accomplish four years' work in three. Eudora, who had been an outstanding student at Davis School, was of course selected.

By all accounts, Eudora seems to have enjoyed high school. She had plenty of friends who were boys, if not boyfriends. "They were all devoted to her," said a girl in her class. "They were all intellectual. She could talk to them."[8]

These young men were brainy and funny and astonishingly literary, considering the time and the place; they liked her and remained her friends for life. One was Nash Burger, a classmate who became an editor at the *New York Times Book Review,* and another was Ralph Hilton, whom she admired because he wrote sports news from Central High for the *Jackson Daily News.* She gave Hilton two chapters of an untitled work and seven thousand words of notes and asked his opinion. He found the material years later, after he had retired from a diplomatic career and was running a newspaper at Hilton Head, South Carolina, and sent it to the Mississippi State Archives, where her other papers were stored.[9]

Nash had trouble with Latin, especially Virgil. Eudora, who loved Latin, often helped him before class with his translations. She was often so good in Latin that she could read something else during class. Half a century after she finished high school, she confessed that she fell in love with the work of the humorist S. J. Perelman in Cicero class, while the other students were translating "How long, O Catiline, must we endure your orations?" An entire issue of *Judge* magazine was filled with Perelman's drawings and writings, and she hid it in her lap.

Eudora was a member of the Girgil Club, which was featured in the *Quadruplane,* the high school annual. Obviously a creation of someone's imagination (probably Eudora's), the Girgil Club had for a motto "Listen, cram and be careful,/For the eighth period you may read," and its colors were black and blue. The club book was the *Aeneid.*

When Eudora had to write a book report for English class, she always chose one of the "better books"—something by Jane Austen or Walter Scott, recalled Nash Burger, while he tended to report on Zane Grey and Edgar Rice Burroughs. Once he gave an oral report on a nonexistent book by an imaginary author, Milton C. Milton (the class had just read "L'Allegro" and

"Il Penseroso"), complete with plot summary, characters, and setting, all fabricated. Eudora, who knew what he was doing, raised her hand and said that she would like to read that book. Would Nash bring it to school? Nash promised he would. Every day for several days Eudora repeated her public request, to no avail.[10]

Eudora, Nash, and Ralph Hilton all wanted to be writers and haunted the local library, waiting for the appearance of the annual volumes of *Best Short Stories* so they could see which authors had won and why. When they had to write their own stories in English class, Eudora's were "invariably smooth, beautifully and painstakingly written."[11] Eudora also wrote for *Tiger Talk,* the school paper (Bill Wells, her occasional escort, was the editor), and in her senior year was art editor of the yearbook, the *Quadruplane,* for which she did a drawing of an Olympian athlete.

When construction crews began work on enlarging the Central High building, Eudora wrote an editorial for the school newspaper wondering what would happen to the wisteria vines and noting that the pupils studied while bricks and timbers crashed about them. "Very sentimental," she later said.[12] She also wrote an essay for the *Quadruplane,* "Youth and Age," in which the New Building talks to the Old Building, saying, "It may be pleasant to be old, but I *love* being New and Young. I adore it."

The theme for the *Quadruplane* in 1925 was the Greek myths, and those elected to the Olympic Council (of outstanding seniors) were given Greek names. Eudora was called not only Irene, "Best All Round Girl," but Demeter, "Most Dependable." Under her picture was the legend "Of talents and good things she owns such a store,/You think where they come from there'd never be more."

Graduation brought a flurry of parties for every girl in the senior class—"bridge parties, seated teas (where a plate was served with frozen salad or chicken salad), luncheons, teas (olive and pecan sandwiches, cheese straws, beaten biscuits and ham, salted almonds, fudge cake, and mints), buffet suppers, and dinner parties."[13] Many of these parties took place at Shadow Lawn, Anita Perkins Pate's home on the Terry Road, where she provided catered meals that were the height of fashion in Jackson. A feature of the garden at Shadow Lawn was the Cofrana rosebush, planted in 1874 and fifteen feet tall by 1926.

Eudora was a guest at what the local newspaper called in its cozy, hometown voice "a merry party of high school girls" who "enjoyed a 'Slumber Party' in the home of Miss Doris Comly." After a "delicious" supper, the girls played games and sang until midnight, when they had a "feast" and told ghost stories. "On Saturday morning before returning to their homes, the party had pictures taken so that they all might keep a souvenir of the happy party."[14]

Chapter 2

Richard Wright

1923–1925

*"Though I had long known that there were people called
'white people,' it had never meant anything to me
emotionally . . . They were . . . somehow strangely
different because I had never come in close touch with any
of them."*
RICHARD WRIGHT, Black Boy

In the fall of 1923, when Eudora and her classmates were beginning
their junior year at Central High, another young Jackson writer was starting
out at Smith-Robertson, the town's black high school. He worked for a white
family named Wall to earn money to pay for his books. His name was
Richard Wright, and he was six months older than Eudora Welty. Compared to Central High, Smith-Robertson was a shack. As an African American, Richard could not use the public library, where Eudora and her friends
eagerly read each year's volume of *Best Short Stories;* he looked for magazines, comic books, and newspapers in garbage cans in white neighborhoods.
Like Eudora and her friends, though, he wanted to write, and he did write a
three-thousand-word story about a villain trying to take the home of a poor

widow, "The Voodoo of Hell's Half-Acre," in three days. It was accepted for publication in the Negro newspaper *Southern Register* in 1924 and ran in three installments.

Although African Americans accounted for 43 percent of the population, each white person in Jackson knew no more than two or three black people—usually their servants. Nothing could illuminate the horror and stupidity of the segregated South more vividly than the fact that Richard Wright and Eudora Welty never met, although they were the same age, had similar interests, and lived in the same town for several years. The picture that Eudora paints in her memoir of Jackson as a safe, comfortable town where families walked to the park for band concerts on summer evenings becomes a mockery when it is compared with Wright's hand-to-mouth existence in the rundown, poorly lit, unsanitary black section of town.

Lehman Engel, a contemporary of Eudora Welty's who became a Broadway composer and musical director, however, noticed the black people who lived in shacks, for which they paid fifty cents in rent a week. He once saw two white men get out of a car, grab a black girl on the sidewalk, and force her into their car. White men who were watching from their front porches, including Engel's father, did nothing.[1] Eudora, in her safe enclave, was unaware of this kind of thing.

Eudora has spoken of how when she was a child, she listened to grown people talking and to the way they dramatized their lives. (She would sit between two people in the car as they set off for a Sunday afternoon ride and say, *"Now talk."*)[2] An interviewer asked her if she heard the stories of black people, and she replied that she never saw black people except as servants in white households. She did hear bits of superstitions or remarks she remembered, but she never heard black people talking among themselves.[3]

Richard Wright spent less than one year in school before he was twelve years old; a coal-delivery man taught him to count, and he learned to read from schoolbooks he found on the sidewalk, discarded by more fortunate children, and from a thrown-away Sunday newspaper that had an account of the sinking of the *Titanic.* He saw plenty of white brutality toward blacks: the father of one of his friends was taken out in the countryside and lynched, and once Wright accepted a ride from some white men, who threw him out of the moving car when he neglected to say "sir."[4] He caddied at the Municipal Golf Links, the golf course where Eudora's little brothers later distinguished themselves.

Wright was valedictorian when he graduated from Smith-Robinson in May 1925, at the same time that Eudora, Nash Burger, and Ralph Hilton were graduating from Central High. The assistant principal wrote his speech for him, but he refused to give it and wrote his own speech, which concerned the South's educational system and how it deprived the black population of intellectual life and human qualities.[5]

After graduating, Wright worked in Jackson at various jobs, trying to accumulate enough money to get out of town. Finally he stole money from the Alamo, the black movie theater where he worked, and took the train to Memphis. (The Alamo was owned by the family of Eudora's friend Lehman Engel.) He published his first book, a short story collection called *Uncle Tom's Children,* in 1938 (three years before Eudora's first book, also a short story collection). Then came *Native Son,* in 1940; *Twelve Million Black Voices,* in 1941; *Black Boy,* in 1945; and nine other books.

"It's awful that people my age didn't even really know the conditions of the black schools," Eudora said later.[6] When Eudora found out that Richard Wright had been growing up in Jackson at the same time she was, someone asked her, "Did you all play together?" "That would have been like playing with somebody from the moon," she replied. "It's just so sad and worrying to think of that."[7]

Eudora was like her contemporaries in being unconscious of Wright's presence in her home town, but unlike most white women from that time and place, she was never very involved with black servants and seldom mentioned them in letters or interviews. She was not like other white people in Jackson, who blocked out awareness of black people unless they were faithful domestic servants. The astonishing thing is that she was able to break out of that atmosphere of apartheid to take wonderful, sensitive photographs of Jackson's African Americans in the late 1930s.

Chapter 3

Role Models

*"This was the decade when Jackson's first 'skyscrapers' were
built or planned—the Edwards Hotel, Lamar Life
Building, Standard Life Building, Lampton Building."*
JACKSON: A Special Kind of Place

While Eudora was in high school, her parents became prominent residents of Jackson. A farm boy from southern Ohio, Christian Welty had taught in a country school before he went to West Virginia to work in a lumber mill. There he met Chestina Andrews, who also taught school. She lived on top of a mountain near Clay, or Clay Courthouse, as the little county seat of Clay County was sometimes called, with her widowed mother and five younger brothers, all left-handed and all banjo players.

Christian was a go-getter. He wanted to move to a place that was booming, and he investigated several areas of the United States. After he and Chestina became engaged, he gave her the choice of living in the Finger Lakes region of New York or in Jackson, Mississippi. She chose Jackson.

They married on October 13, 1904, at Chestina's home and went to the World's Fair and Louisiana Purchase Centennial Exposition in St. Louis on their way to a new life in a new place. As Eudora Welty told a French interviewer in the 1980s, for her parents to settle down in Jackson "was an adventure as exalting as today exile in Africa would be for a Parisian. My grandmother thought she would never see her daughter again."[1]

When the couple arrived in 1904, Jackson was indeed a boom town, its population in the process of tripling, from 7,816 in 1900 to more than 21,000 in 1910. In 1906 Christian went to work as a cashier for the Lamar Life Insurance Company, which had been founded not long before by five hustling young businessmen, two of whom possessed invaluable resources for a new insurance company: mailing lists, one from the election campaign of Governor J. K. Vardaman and one from a fraternal organization, the Knights of Pythias. Governor Vardaman bought the company's first policy, and Lamar Life was soon one of the thriving new businessess in Jackson.

Christian built a new home in 1908, just north of the new state capitol, at 741 North Congress Street, with two and a half stories, a big front porch, a bay window on one side, and a Palladian window on the other. Chestina and Christian were living in this house on April 13, 1909, when Eudora Alice Welty was born. (The Weltys' first child, a boy, had died soon after he was born. Chestina never mentioned this baby until Eudora found a small box with two shiny buffalo nickels in her mother's bottom bureau drawer and asked if she could have them. Chestina cried "No!" and explained that they had lain on the little boy's eyelids after his death. He died because she herself had almost died, she explained to her daughter, and "they too nearly forgot about the little baby.")[2]

Eudora hated her name until her mother told her it meant "good gifts."[3] In 1912 her brother Edward was born, and three years after that, in 1915, Walter, the last child, came along. The three children grew up playing jump rope, hopscotch, and jacks and riding their tricycles on the sidewalk in front of the house. As they grew older, they rode bicycles down the terraced steps of the capitol and rollerskated on the marble floors inside, circling the rotunda and the Hall of Fame.[4] Christian Welty built elaborate kites for them, and Eudora and her brothers flew these on the lawns of the capitol, where they also played ball.

But North Congress Street—the neighborhood Eudora used in her 1941 short story "The Winds"—was declining by the early 1920s, and many houses were being converted to multifamily homes. While Eudora was in high school, Christian Welty built a fine new house befitting his prominence in the business world. This was on Pinehurst Street across from Belhaven College, a small Presbyterian school for girls. Pinehurst was then a gravel road, and Belhaven had only one building, built of wood.

Christian did not choose what was almost Jackson's vernacular architectural style—the big house with white columns and wide veranda that the well-to-do native families, whose ancestors' homes had been burned in the Civil War, picked when they built new houses on North State Street. Christian, the Yankee from Ohio, chose the newly popular Tudor or Old English style, of dark brick, stucco, half timbering, and tall gables. With six rooms and a sleeping porch, this was the house that would be Eudora's home for the rest of her life, the base to which she would always return after trips to college, New York, Europe, or San Francisco.

Christian built the house on what he called a hill, but Eudora's mother, always homesick for the West Virginia mountains, never quite saw it as a hill. The lot had seven big pine trees and one oak tree, which Chestina refused to cut down. "Now the pines are gone and the oak tree is majestic," Eudora said in 1977. "She said, 'Never cut an oak tree.' And that's the fact."[5]

During Eudora's high school years, Christian Welty was in charge of a much larger construction project, a new headquarters for Lamar Life. "Jackson's first skyscraper" was begun in 1923, across the street from the state capitol. After he visited insurance buildings all around the country, Welty asked the architects Sanguinet-Staats & Hedrick of Fort Worth, with N. W. Overstreet (who also designed the Pinehurst Street house) as the Jackson associate, for a building that would be at home with the gothic St. Andrew's Episcopal Church next door (he discussed the matter with the rector, Dr. W. B. Capers) and with the white-columned governor's mansion across the street. The new building was thirteen stories tall and topped with a clock tower, for which Seth Thomas designed the clock. The building was white gothic, with gargoyles carved in the form of alligators. In 1977, Eudora Welty expressed public regret that they blasted off the gargoyles when the building was remodeled.[6]

Christian took his family to see the building often during its construction. The five of them would climb to the top by the fire escape and look at all Jackson spread below them.

On the night of January 17, 1925, when the building was formally opened, it was lit from top to bottom. Christian announced that not a dollar had been borrowed to build it. Jackson's *Clarion-Ledger* called it "the Pride of the South" and reported that at a reception for "the whole public of the city and state and south," five thousand men, women, and children "went up to the top floor and worked their way down, looking at everything and gathering souvenirs." A banquet at the Edwards Hotel formally celebrated the opening. Speeches lasted until midnight. "Mr. Welty, vice president-manager . . . is the man upon whose shoulders the responsibility for putting over this big task had rested," said the *Clarion-Ledger*.[7]

Christian always referred to the building as "the House That the Agents Built," and on that gala night the agents saluted him. Since February was his birthday month, they had worked "to present Mr. Welty with applications for insurance aggregating $1,000,000."[8]

As a teenager, Eudora often drove downtown at five o'clock to pick up her father from work. She made a U-turn in front of the governor's mansion, pulled up in front of the Lamar Life Building, and blew the horn: one long and two shorts. Her father would appear at the window of his office on the tenth floor and signal that he would soon be downstairs.

While Eudora's father climbed the ladder of business success, her mother was increasingly active in civic work. She was president of the PTA at Central High School in 1924 and was a member of the Research Club, a "study club" whose members had to prepare programs. A charter member of the Woman's Club, she served for two years as its chairman of service, helping to apply pressure for local enforcement of the child labor laws and campaigning to increase the minimum school requirements. She was appointed to the Mississippi branch of the National Child Labor Committee. She conceived the idea of a Garden Lovers Club and launched this group in her second year as the Woman's Club's chairman of service. "Her imagination stretches beyond the limits of our own town and sees a vision of glorious highways, planted on either side with colorful Crepe Myrtles, the club flower," the *Clarion-Ledger* noted.[9] The new Welty house on Pinehurst won the ten-dollar prize from the Garden Lovers Club for the best landscape and garden in town at least one year.

Chestina worked backstage at the Little Theater, going all over town to gather up the right furniture, lamps, and pictures for a play. The Little Theater put on its plays in the auditorium of the Blind Institute, where actors had to dress downstairs in the schoolrooms and walk outside, around the building, and climb the fire escape into a little space close to the stage. When it rained, someone with an umbrella went up the fire escape with each actor to keep him dry. Thus, for a long time the Little Theater could do only one-act plays, since costume changes were so difficult.[10] As a child, Eudora followed her mother up the winding iron fire escape and got her first taste of the theater. She became permanently stagestruck.

Although Chestina often read the Bible at home and belonged to Galloway Methodist Church, neither she nor her husband went to church or said grace at meals. Demonstrating her independent turn of mind and lack of conformity to the mores of Mississippi, she refused to give money to the Methodist Church's Missionary Society, saying that she did not believe in telling other people what to believe.[11] Flannery O'Connor once said that everybody in the South is "Christ-haunted," but the Weltys—the northerners—were not. They did send their children to Sunday school, though, Eudora in starched dresses and white gloves, clutching coins for the offering. All her life she liked the cheerful tunes of Methodist hymns like "Throw Out the Lifeline" and "I was Sinking Deep in Sin," despite their despairing words.

Finished with high school, settled into the house that would be her base for the rest of her life, Eudora was ready to make her first excursion into a larger world.

Chapter 4

The W

1925–1927

"I defy anyone . . . to be more alive or more in evidence
on this particular stamping ground of the flowers of
Mississippi than Eudora Welty. I stand back in amazement
at the things that woman does."
The *Spectator*, Nov. 14, 1925

When Eudora graduated from Central High School in 1925, she wanted to go away to college. Since she was only sixteen, however, Christian and Chestina thought she should stay in Jackson and go to Millsaps, the local liberal arts college. They finally consented to her going not out of state, but a hundred and fifty miles away to the Mississippi State College for Women in Columbus.

MSCW had been founded in 1884 as the Industrial Institute and College for the Education of White Girls of the State of Mississippi in the Arts and Sciences, to teach everything from art and science to telegraphy, stenography, and needlework. It was the first state college for women in the country and was the model for similar colleges in other southern states. William Faulkner's mother, Maud Butler, had attended the Industrial Institute and

College not long after it was established, and Tennessee Williams's mother, Edwina Dakin, had walked to the campus to study voice when her father was the rector of the Episcopal church in Columbus. (Eudora had heard of none of these people. Faulkner's first novel, *Soldier's Pay,* would not be published until the next year, and Tennessee Williams was in high school in St. Louis.)

Gradually the curriculum became more academic, and in 1920 the name was changed to Mississippi State College for Women. Every resident of the state called MSCW "the W"; it is now Mississippi University for Women, but everybody still calls it the W.

Although the W was a state school, its catalogue announced firmly that its "principles and influence are distinctively Christian." Compulsory chapel was held twice a week; in addition, each student was required to attend some church, "and no change will be permitted."

All students had to wear navy blue uniforms. In winter, the dress uniform, which was worn to church, to town, and to public functions on campus, was "a plain coat suit, cut on conservative lines, or a one-piece woolen dress with which a long separate coat may be worn." Fur was not allowed. In fall and spring, the dress uniform was a crepe-de-chine blouse and a woolen skirt or a one-piece silk dress. Short skirts and shingled hair were all the rage in other parts of the United States, but there were to be no flappers at MSCW: skirts could be no shorter than ten inches from the floor and sleeves no shorter than nine inches from the armhole. Seniors could wear a white collar, maximum width three and one-half inches. Students could not go off campus without a hat. For classes, students were to wear cotton or woolen dresses or blouses and skirts, with all trimmings in navy blue or black. "Every student must provide herself with a pair of shoes with low heels . . . either brown or black. French heels are discouraged."

"We made a great to-do about hating [the navy blue]," said one contemporary of Eudora's, "but most of us were grateful for it. All you had to do before coming to the W was to toss everything possible into a pot of navy blue dye." A great many girls had only "one good dress for church, trips to town, and, if we were lucky, dates."[1]

Rules were strict. After the night whistle blew, the campus gates were locked. Bridge was forbidden, but Rook was allowed, so girls learned to play bridge with Rook cards. (Rook, a patented Charles Parker game popular with children and young people, was played with cards in four suits, each with fourteen cards in one color. To play bridge with Rook cards, the girls pulled out the fourteens.)

Each dormitory at the W had six registers in which students signed in and out: one if they were leaving the campus, but staying in Columbus, one for leaving town, one for going to the college hospital, one for dates, one for guests, and one for spending the night out. A student from the 1930s recalled the shock a chaperone received when she entered a dormitory date parlor to give a girl a message. She had never thought, she said, to see a young man visiting a girl behave that way—he had pulled his coat off and folded it up on the couch and then *propped his feet up.* On-campus dances with boys were not allowed until long after Eudora's day.

The W charged no tuition, but room, board, and laundry came to about $155 a year. This was steep for some of the students, who sometimes arrived with boxes of home-grown and home-canned vegetables to help defray their board bills. (Annual per capita income in Mississippi was the lowest in the nation—$396.) It was a small school—enrollment in 1925 was 1,201—but its facilities were inadequate for even those few. The library, which occupied two rooms, contained only 17,340 bound volumes. (The University of Texas and Duke University were the only two southern colleges that had as many as half a million books in their libraries at that time.) Gloria Renfro, a character in Eudora's 1970 novel, *Losing Battles,* attended a school like the W, called "Normal" in the book. Here's how she remembered it: "Not enough of anything to go round, not enough room, not enough teachers, not enough money, not enough beds, not enough electric light bulbs, not enough books." Not too different, muses Gloria, from the orphanage where she grew up.[2] As many as six girls shared one dormitory room; no room had fewer than three occupants.

Gloria's description of Normal follows Welty's sketch of MSCW in her memoir: girls fighting to get their mail in the basement post office, where the gym teacher tried to teach modern dance when she had to bring her classes inside on rainy days. Some girls would be dancing "The Three Graces" while others screamed over their letters or sampled food in boxes from home. "It was life in a crowd," Welty wrote.[3]

In her freshman year, Eudora lived high up in Old Main in a room with three other girls. When the chapel bell rang, it shook the floor under their beds—"shook us all like a poker in a grate," as Gloria Renfro says in *Losing Battles.*[4] Each freshman was assigned a member of the junior class for a "big sister." Eudora's big sister was Lillian McLaughlin, known as "Lily Mack," who was an editor of the school paper, the *Spectator.* On the day the freshman arrived, Lily Mack went up to Old Main to see if she could help her little sister get settled. She found the room bare, luggage unopened, and Eudora sitting on the uncovered mattress, looking lost. "We talked a long time, and she showed me some things she had been writing for her own satisfaction," recalled Lily Mack, who saw that Eudora was "obviously gifted" and soon had her writing for the *Spectator.*[5] In fact, Eudora was one of only three freshmen named to the newspaper staff that year. (After graduation, Lillian McLaughlin went to work for Hodding Carter's *Delta Democrat-Times* in Greenville and later for the Des Moines *Register and Tribune.*)

The administration did everything it could to foster a close relationship between the freshmen and the juniors, including staging a mock wedding between the junior class and the freshman class, which was designed to teach loyalty and friendship. The freshman class furnished the bride and her attendants, while a group of juniors dressed as men played the roles of groom and groomsmen. The biggest excitement on campus in September 1925 was the election of the dozen young women (out of the 250 freshmen) who would participate in the wedding. The election took five hours. Two months later, when the wedding took place in the gym, the bride and groom and their attendants were elaborately clad in white, with the groom and groomsmen in satin knee breeches. Eudora was not included.

Physical education was mandatory, and Miss Emma Ody Pohl was the department chair. She developed dance classes, May Day ceremonies, and in 1912 started the famous Zouave drill, which was based on French military drill routines. This activity grew until it involved the entire student body. In *Losing Battles,* Judge Moody's wife confesses that she majored in gym at the Normal: " 'Led the school-wide wand drill. I still have my Zouave cap.' Judge Moody bent a surprised look on her. *'Ta-ta ta da!'* She gave him a bar of the *Hungarian Rhapsody.* 'Then I had to go forth and teach Beginning Physics.' "[6]

It was great fun for Eudora to be more or less on her own. She immediately bought a book, a copy of *In April Once,* by William Alexander Percy, a banker, planter, lawyer, civic leader, and poet in Greenville, Mississippi.

The W also gave Eudora her first chance to meet people from other parts of the state, and she stored in her memory the different accents, manners, and turns of speech of girls from the rich Delta, the poor hill country, and the coastal area.

At MSCW, Eudora was immediately popular and busy with extracurricular activities. Students provided much of their own entertainment. Not only did they present published plays, they wrote their own skits and produced pageants, talent shows, and minstrel shows. Eudora appeared in almost every production, wrote poetry and prose and drew cartoons for the *Spectator,* and worked on the yearbook, *Meh Lady,* in various functions, most often as a photographer.

Everyone knew her and later remembered her height ("I was tall, but she made me feel short," said one classmate), and several spoke of her wonderful, expressive blue eyes. Years later they would recall the way she "loped" across campus and greeted everyone with "that great big smile."[7] Helen Michel, who was involved with the publications at MSCW, remembered years later that Eudora was "a joy" to work with—"always punctual, always cooperative."[8]

In October, reporting on the results of the freshman class elections, the *Spectator* noted that Eudora Welty, "a very talented and original" member of the class, had been elected annual representative, which meant she had to collect the price of the yearbook from each of her classmates.[9] In November she played Miss Trimbull in *The Rector,* a one-act comedy about a congregation interested in its minister's activities. The next semester she was stage manager for a play called *The Goose Hangs High* and appeared, dressed as a man, in the spring minstrel show.

The columnist who wrote "Peeps at People" for the *Spectator* paid tribute to Eudora during her first year. "I defy anyone . . . to be more alive or more in evidence on this particular stamping ground of the flowers of Mississippi than Eudora Welty," this person wrote. "I stand back in amazement at the things that woman does. Anybody want posters drawn? Page Eudora—she'll dash you off an exceedingly effective one in no time at all. Somebody to collect annual money? Eudora will do it. Something clever and funny for the 'Spec'? That's the best thing she does. Someone for the Dramatic Club play? Why, faith and begorra, here's Eudora again—absolutely perfect as wheezing, sneezing, pleasing (?) Miss Trimble in 'The Rector.' But wonder of wonders—the honor that pleases this freshman the most is none of these—it is that she has the greatest chest expansion in school."[10] (Chest expansion, or "vital capacity," had nothing to do with bra size. In physical education classes at that time, chests were measured before and then after inhaling. A big expansion was considered very healthy.)

During her sophomore year Eudora played another spinster in *Icebound,* which was produced at the W in January and moved to the all-male Mississippi A & M College at Starkville for a performance in February. "Eudora Welty was splendid—pathetic, stubborn, self-centered Emma—a true Jordan," said the story in the *Spectator.*[11] She was secretary of the Dramatic Club and appeared in a *Meh Lady*–sponsored skit that burlesqued the faculty. She played the part of Ignorance in a pageant presented at vespers in the chapel one Sunday night. She was chosen, on the basis of "scholarship, personality, and student government record," as one of thirty-five sophomores to teach the rules and regulations to freshmen. She and her good friend Dana Davis were named to the art staff of *Meh Lady* and charged with taking photographs. She was also again the annual representative for her class.

Eudora was writing short stories at college, as was her high school classmate Nash Burger, a freshman at Millsaps. He sent her a story about a black fireman on a Mississippi River steamboat furiously stoking a fire beneath the ship's boiler while flames leaped ever higher in "plutonic glee." Ever polite, she told him that the story had merit but he really should be careful about phrases like "plutonic glee."[12]

Eudora wrote short stories about Paris when she was a freshman. This was when she wrote, "Monsieur Boule," which cannot be found in the *Spectator*'s microfilms. But soon after she arrived the paper carried an 1,800-word short story called " 'The Great Pinnington Solves the Mystery' (By a Mear Freshman)," embellished with three cartoons signed "W." and the credit line "Illustrated by the Arthur."[13] Its form is interesting, since Eudora Welty doted on detective stories throughout her life. Of her writing in college, she recalled, "I became a wit and humorist of the parochial kind, and the amount I was able to show off in print must have been a great comfort to me."[14]

"The Great Pinnington" begins: "I am going to write a book. All my friends say that they are confident I can write something big and different, and this is it." It wanders on to announce that the author is going to write it in the first person "so that I can be the hero," and that the hero will be "a detective with a magnetic eye and a long front name." The story is full of unexplained events. When the narrator can't open the door to the room where he heard a shot because it's locked on the inside, he says, "I did not know what to do for a minute, but suddenly I remembered. So I did what I thought of, and it opened the door." Pinnington goes on to solve the murder but never lets the reader in on the solution. "The heroine's name is Josephine," the story goes. "I have named her Josephine so that you can remember that she is the heroine on account of both words ending in 'ine.' . . . A suggestion for a hero is Nero." "The Great Pinnington" has comic lines, but its structure leaves much to be desired.

That same month, Eudora's poem "Autumn's Here" also appeared in the *Spectator,* with lines such as "There's a dusky, husky, musky, smoky smelling in the air!" and "And the yellow, mellow pumpkins slowly ripen in the sun."[15] In the same issue, she had three cartoons, "Suggested Illustrations for the Classics." One, titled "George Eliot: Eppie in de Toad-Hole," was a totally black rectangle. Her best cartoon for the *Spectator* appeared on the front page on February 20, 1926, with the caption, ". . . and will the poor dog have none?" Mother Hubbard is opening an empty cupboard labeled LEGISLATURE, while a small dog, labeled NEW STUDENTS, sits forlornly dreaming of a large bone labeled NEW BUILDINGS.

"The Gnat," a playlet, appeared in the *Spectator* in Eudora's sophomore year, on November 6, 1926. "I saw *The Bat* and wrote 'The Gnat,' laid in MSCW," she explained.[16] *The Bat* was a wildly successful mystery play by Mary Roberts Rinehart that opened on Broadway in 1920, and Eudora had seen it when her father took her to New York for the first time. "The Gnat" is set in the MSCW library, where Miss Culbertson [Beulah Culbertson was head librarian] is counting up the money taken in that day. The Gnat enters. "He is right scary looking, especially around the feelers," say the stage directions.

"Beulah Culbertson, I have come for that jake," says the Gnat. He wiggles his feelers and shows his fangs.

"Take the money if you must, you insect, but leave me my reading cards," says Miss Culbertson.

"I leave nothing!" replies the Gnat.

The second and final scene is full of inside jokes about faculty and staff members. The president of MSCW, Dr. John Clayton Fant, seeks the identity of the Gnat by counting out among them, "Acka Backa Soda Cracker . . ."

Eudora continued to contribute cartoons and poetry to the *Spectator,* as well as a short essay about her Ohio relatives, who, while she was visiting them, urged her to go to see I. Smith, an artist and a newcomer to the neighborhood. "It is generally believed among my relatives that I have an artistic temperament," she wrote.[17]

In the spring of 1927, the Mississippi River flooded catastrophically, leaving parts of the Delta under water for months. On the other side of the state, the Tombigbee rose dramatically too, leading Eudora to write a society item in the *Spectator* for April Fool's Day. "Misses Frances Davis, Lois Prophet, Katie Davidson, Frances Motlow, Thomasine Josephine Burnadetta Kathleen Cady, Dana Davis, Eudora Welty, May Risher, and Earline Agatha Robinson were drowned Thursday evening while boating on the Tombigbee," the story read. "Everyone expresses regret that these promising young women should meet so untimely a death. Miss Frances Davis had been editor of *The Spectator* and Miss Lois Prophet had been editor of *Meh Lady,* while the remaining girls were all very popular with faculty and students." But then there was more room for the other students in the dormitories, she added.[18] Many years later, she wryly noted that "H. L. Mencken read my story . . . And he wrote in *his* newspaper that things were in such a terrible shape down in Mississippi that students were just being allowed to float away."[19] Eudora used the 1927 Mississippi flood in the story "At the Landing," just as her contemporary from Jackson, Richard Wright, wrote about it in a story called "Down by the Riverside," in *Uncle Tom's Children.*

In her sophomore year, Eudora was named a fire marshal for the fourth floor of the dormitory called Hastings, a job that entailed giving each girl a push as she got into the silo-like fire escape to send her down a spiral chute. Gloria describes the fire escape at Normal in *Losing Battles*: "A black iron round thing four stories tall, like a tunnel standing on end, and a tin chute going round and round down through it. You have to jump in, stick your legs around the one in front of you, and sit on her skirt, and the next one jumps on yours, and you all go whirling like marbles on a string, spinning on your drawers—they grease it with soap—round and round and round—it's everybody holding on for dear life."[20]

Many girls were genuinely frightened of the fire escape; Marjorie Magruder, a classmate, said that she was sure Eudora had to push hard to start her down it.[21] But it held no terrors for Eudora. She slid down it to go to class and to go outside at night for a few minutes before she went to bed.

A favorite excursion for students at the W was the fifteen-mile hike to Waverly, an antebellum mansion outside Columbus that had been empty since 1913, when the last son of the builder, Colonel George Hampton Young, had died. Katie Davidson Guion, who went on one such trip with Eudora, recalled it years later. It was "a sweater-weather day in December," and the girls intended to cook their meal out and to cut a Christmas tree for the dormitory lobby. Lois Prophet, Eudora, and Katie Davidson, all wearing drab blue dresses, carried the food. Frances Davis had the coffeepot swung over her shoulder, and Dana Davis carried the hatchet secured to her belt. (Those two were town girls and could wear knickers, boys' shirts, and caps.) Also along were Earline Robinson, May Risher, and Anna Lou White. Forbidden packs of cigarettes were tucked in the pockets of their navy blue sweaters.

When they got to the Tombigbee, they had to take a ferry operated by a man who raised bees or walk across a railroad trestle. Eudora was always fearless on the trestle, while other girls trembled and had to be led across. (Waverly, the bee man, and the trestle turned up years later in *Delta Wedding*.)

As they neared Waverly, they could smell the tall, hundred-year-old boxwood bushes that lined the approach to the old mansion. On the front porch, they could hear rats and mice scurrying inside. The house was ghostly and yet seemed curiously lived-in. Fishing poles hung on the walls of the octagonal entrance hall, from which magnificent twin circular staircases led up to the cupola on the roof. The staircases appeared to have no support, since they were built on cantilevered cypress timbers. A piano with mother-of-pearl keys stood beside one wall, and three tall pier glasses remained. On each side of the entrance hall was a bedroom, with curtains still at the windows and bedclothes on the canopy beds. In the library, the shelves were still full of books, including a complete set of Sir Walter Scott's Waverly novels, for which the house had been named. A well-known print, *The Prophet,* hung on one of the walls. A large sideboard and table were in the dining room. The upstairs bedrooms were locked.[22] (It tells a good bit about the stability of society in rural Mississippi that this magnificent mansion stood empty for fifty years without being vandalized or robbed. When the new owner took over, the only damage to the house was three missing spindles in the stairway banisters.)

On the trip Mrs. Guion described, the girls went outside and explored the icehouse and the cemetery before they built a fire and cooked. At dusk they flagged down the Columbus and Greenville train, known as the C & G, or the "Creep and Grunt," and returned to Columbus.

Jane McLaurin recalled late-night storytelling sessions at MSCW in which Eudora held the whole dormitory floor spellbound. When somebody mentioned these years later to Eudora, she brushed aside the compliment to talk about how hungry the students got late at night. They all loved Hershey bars, and someone said that if the chairman of the board of the Hershey company in Pennsylvania only knew how they loved his chocolate and how hungry they were, he'd do something about it. So Eudora wrote to him and told him the girls at MSCW were starving. Not too long afterward, a case of Hershey bars arrived. "We ate every crumb, and the experience was delightful," recalled a fellow student. Mrs. Welty, however, was *not* delighted to find out that her daughter had proclaimed to a prominent stranger that she was hungry.[23]

In March 1927, Eudora, always hospitable, invited five girls—Lois Prophet, Katie Davidson, Thomasine Cady, Dana Davis, and Lucy Platt—home to hear the Chicago Civic Opera, which the newly organized Jackson Grand Opera brought to town. They sat in the top of the old Municipal Auditorium at Congress and Pearl streets and gloried in *Pagliacci.*

During her two years at MSCW, Eudora took classes in English, French, Latin, history, and art. A most important teacher for her was Lawrence G. Painter, who taught English, supervised the *Spectator,* and sponsored the Dramatic Club. The only male professor on campus, Painter was wildly popular, handsome, and an excellent teacher who read aloud beautifully, and he was known to generations of W students as "Dear Teacher." Eudora had him for a sophomore survey course that covered English literature from Chaucer to Alan Seeger, the young American poet who wrote "I have a rendezvous with death" and died on the Somme in 1918. Like all Professor Painter's students, Eudora was impressed. One of her contemporaries remembered that the two of them "vied for A's and A+'s" in Mr. Painter's class: "Both of us got them more often than not and more often than others."[24]

Eudora's most interesting enterprise at MSCW was her participation in the founding of the humor magazine *Oh, Lady!* in the spring semester of her sophomore year. "We had fun with that magazine," Ruth McCoy Harris, the editor, remembered years later. "May Risher got us a lot of local advertisements so we were self-supporting."[25] Eudora did many cartoons for *Oh, Lady!* and appeared in another burlesque of the faculty to raise money for it. But at the end of the school year 1926–1927, after only three issues had appeared, President Fant called the editor to his office. He wanted her advice. Didn't she think *Oh, Lady!* was a little undignified for young ladies to put out? Perhaps there was a reason why it was, as they boasted, "the only women's college humor magazine." Harris tried to argue that the magazine was harmless, if not brilliant. In the end she "meekly agreed to discontinue the magazine, since I would not be there after graduation. This made the underclassmen very angry with me."[26]

Eudora also did the cover for a short-lived statewide college literary magazine, *Hoi-Polloi,* started by a group that included Nash Burger. Nash and his fellow founders hoped to include writers from what they called Mississippi's Negro colleges, and Burger went to see officials at the all-black Jackson State College. The officials were "cautious but pleased," Burger recalled forty years later. "In our youthful innocence and enthusiasm, we didn't realize what an innovation we were attempting."[27] Only one issue appeared.

Chapter 5

On, Wisconsin

1927–1929

*"I was sent to the Middle West to School. I was very timid
and shy, younger than the rest, and those people there
seemed to me like sticks of flint, that live in the icy world."*
EUDORA WELTY, 1941[1]

After two years at the W, Eudora had grown up enough, her parents
felt, for her to go out of state to college. She was accepted as a transfer
student at Randolph-Macon Woman's College, in Lynchburg, Virginia, as
well as at the University of Wisconsin, which her father admired for its
leadership in progressive education.

In September 1927, she took the train to Randolph-Macon, which had
been founded as a kind of eighth sister, not a finishing school but a college
for women in the South with the same high standards as Wellesley, Smith,
and Bryn Mawr. When Eudora got there, however, college officials said she
would have to repeat her sophomore year. "Is that because these credits come
from a little college in Mississippi that you never heard of?" she asked.
"Even if they came from Harvard, we wouldn't verify them," she was told.
Eudora, reluctant to have her parents pay for a fifth year of college, sadly

decided to go on to the University of Wisconsin. She took the train and, as she said years later, left Lynchburg and "crossed the James River, weeping."[2]

Although she may have preferred Randolph-Macon, she found at Madison, Wisconsin, one of the most exciting educational environments of the day and one of the world's most dramatic physical settings for a university. A mile to the west of the state capitol, the main building of the University of Wisconsin stood on top of a tall hill overlooking Lake Mendota. From Bascom Hall, a broad grassy plaza swept down in the direction of the capitol. (State law forbids the erection of any building that would block the view from campus to capitol.) Academic buildings bordered this sloping plaza. On the lower campus, near the lake, stood the gymnasium, boathouses, and the gray-columned library with its marble stairs. Under construction right on the lakeshore when Eudora arrived was the new Memorial Union building, which would house dining halls and social centers. The lake provided year-round recreation—swimming and boating in the summer, ice-skating in the winter.

Glenn Frank, a former editor of *Century* magazine and the president of the university, was young, brilliant, and a great orator, which led H. L. Mencken to call him "the great gliberal."[3] Frank persuaded Alexander Meiklejohn, the president of Amherst College, to come to Wisconsin and implement his ideas on curriculum with an Experimental College within the College of Letters and Science. This college, which began the semester Eudora arrived, had 125 students, all male, who lived together in a dormitory and studied a uniform curriculum that emphasized the glories of Athenian civilization. They were taught by the tutorial method. The Experimental College was expected to do nothing less than bring about a "renaissance in American education," according to the *Daily Cardinal,* the student newspaper.[4]

By conventional standards, Wisconsin got high marks. When the American Council of Education ranked eighteen departments in colleges around the country in 1925, Wisconsin was among the top fifteen in all of them, and first in German.[5] The intellectual temperature of the campus was high. The literary magazine, the daily student newspaper, and the humor magazine all ran serious book reviews. Since 1893, every student in Letters and Science had been required to write a senior thesis, a scholarly paper on a subject in his or her major field.

Since dormitories were reserved for students from Wisconsin, Eudora and her MSCW friend Dana Davis lived in a rooming house approved by the university's administration at 625 North Frances. (Davis did not stay at Wisconsin long.) The rules of the Women's Self Government Association applied to these rooming houses just as strictly as they did to dormitories: girls had to be in by ten o'clock on weeknights and twelve-thirty on weekends. The house, a tall, narrow, three-story building with a stained-glass transom above the big double front doors, was separated from the lakeshore by only two houses. In fact, the YMCA pier began at the end of Frances Street. The landlady, Mrs. Lenzer, and her family lived on the first floor, girls on the second and third floors. There was a telephone and one bathroom on each floor. Eudora lived in a single room at the end of the hall on the third floor for two years. "She had a bookcase," recalled Mary F. Garstang, who also lived in the house. "She was the only one who bought books besides textbooks."[6]

Although fraternities and sororities completely dominated the social life of the university, Eudora did not join a sorority, as most of the girls in her rooming house did. Since the house did not serve meals, she had to eat at the Union cafeteria, which was right across from the library on campus, or in restaurants, probably around the corner at Miss Brown's Cafeteria or the Chocolate Shop. She had to walk a couple of blocks to reach the edge of the campus, a little farther to the library, and then make quite a steep hike up to the English Department in Bascom Hall. They all got used to that walk, said Marion Gallinger Reel, one of Eudora's housemates. "Wisconsin was wonderful, and for the rest of your life you don't mind winter," she said. "All the girls had fur coats, and you put them on in October and kept them on until April."[7] (Eudora's fur coat was possum.)

It rained every day during the first weeks of school in 1927. It rained on students while they registered for classes and bought their textbooks ($1.33 for *Wooley's Written English* and $.51 for a copy of Shakespeare's *Hamlet*). It rained as they went downtown to buy fabric for curtains for their rooms ($.19 a yard for cretonnes and $.50 for damask). It rained as new registrants went for compulsory physical exams, where doctors reported that the "chief complaint of coeds" was foot trouble caused by wearing high heels on the hill. Enrollment that fall was 8,702, a record (and eight times that of

MSCW); the unprecedented increase, said the *Cardinal,* was a result of national publicity generated by the Experimental College.

After Christmas vacation, Eudora, coming back from warm Mississippi, must have been amazed at the winter sports carnival on Lake Mendota, where competition for the western intercollegiate skating and skiing championships, iceboat races, curling matches, and fancy skating exhibitions were all under way. Next came the prom, scheduled for February 3 at the state capitol; it dominated the columns of the campus newspaper all during January. The day after the prom, a special *Cardinal* issue reported it all. The orchestra swung into "On, Wisconsin" as the prom chairman and his queen led the grand march into the rotunda of the capitol. Eudora had not gone. "I don't think she ever had a date," said Marion Reel. "But she always helped the rest of us get ready for dates."[8]

"She was a lovely girl, but so plain," said another. "She had straight hair while the rest of us had croquignole permanent waves. We set our hair with combs to make waves."[9]

Elinor Hegland Spring remembered that Eudora was reserved and shy and initiated no friendships, while the other girls were always clustered together to "bubble" over everyone's clothes and dates.[10] Other housemates remember her as "brilliant," "charming," "quiet," but "no Emily Dickinson." Eudora described herself at Wisconsin as frightened, timid, shy, and younger than the rest of the students, who seemed to her like "sticks of flint . . . in an icy world."[11] She said fifty years later that she was "too naive and inexperienced and shy" and "missed out on the Jazz Age campus excitement."[12]

But some of the Jazz Age revolutionary fervor spilled onto everyone. According to the *Cardinal,* a psychology professor "created a sensation throughout the middle west" when he said in a speech that "the flapper is the hope of the race" and advised female students to smoke cigarettes and wear short skirts and find intellectual freedom for themselves "if we are to strike a death blow at established sex institutions."[13]

Visiting lecturers, most of them celebrities such as the adventurer Richard Halliburton and the South Pole explorer Admiral Richard E. Byrd, made frequent appearances at Wisconsin. In March 1928, George Russell, whose pen name was A.E., lectured on W. B. Yeats, George Moore, Lord

Dunsany, and James Joyce. Eudora fell in love with the work of Irish writers while she was at Wisconsin, and perhaps Russell's lecture sparked her interest. Wandering in the stacks of the library, she said later, she came across a book by Irish writers, and it was "a little like first waiting on a shore and then being enveloped in a sea . . . a tender and firm and passionate experience."[14] She told a friend that she had discovered Yeats one morning right after the library opened and was still there reading his poetry when the library closed.[15] The poem that struck her so that she had to memorize it was "The Song of Wandering Aengus," and it furnished a key motif for her stories in *The Golden Apples*. She used this experience sixty years later, she said in a lecture, when she worked on a short story in which the main character puts himself through Wisconsin and muses about discovering Yeats in the library stacks. He read Yeats's poems all one afternoon, "standing up, by the window . . . by the light of falling snow." It seemed to him if he could make himself move, he could go into a poem as he could into the snow.

Years later, she told her literary agent, Diarmuid Russell, George Russell's son, that at Wisconsin she had moved from Yeats to A.E.'s autobiography *The Candle of Vision*, reading A.E. during "the first crisis of a certain kind in my life."[16] That crisis may have been homesickness or profound depression.

At Wisconsin, campus dramatic groups were active, producing serious drama such as Karel Čapek's *R.U.R.,* but Eudora, in spite of her theatrical work at Mississippi State College for Women, did not take part. She did not belong to either of the two literary societies for women, Castalia and Pythia. She did make one contribution to the *Wisconsin Literary Magazine,* a poem, "Shadows," in her junior year. It was a gloomy poem from its opening line, "Even candle-snuffers rust—(snared in candle-smoke)," through the last three lines, "Dreams are smothered in their sleep,/And beauty goes out with the wind/Through the cracks in the night."[17]

That Eudora left such a small footprint at Wisconsin is remarkable, and is perhaps another indication of deep depression. *The Badger,* the yearbook, lists no activities under her name. None of the surviving contributors and staff members of the *Wisconsin Literary Magazine* remember her. "I did not know Eudora Welty, nor did I hear of her while she was at Wisconsin," said Naomi Rabe Graham, a classmate and fellow English major who won writing prizes and lived in another boarding house on North Frances Street. "I never met her at Arden House, the English majors' retreat," Graham said.[18] As a matter of fact, Eudora went once to Arden House and never went back. The students there "poured tea, burned candles, and read Sara Teasdale," she explained.[19] After Eudora became famous, Graham and her friends from college marveled that she had been among them for two years and they had never heard of her.

It is hard to account for this invisibility, when Eudora had been so active and popular at MSCW. Contributing factors were undoubtedly the fact that she was a transfer student, her shyness in the strange environment, and her southernness. Her feeling that she was among "sticks of flint" was probably not unwarranted. Nancy Schmitter, a year behind Eudora at Wisconsin and one of the few other southerners on campus, was quoted in the *Cardinal* as saying that she was "sincerely astonished at the indifference and self-absorption of the people I met . . . They were polite but entirely uninterested in me."[20]

Those two cold, lonely years almost certainly, though, provided two enormous dividends. The awful sense of icy separateness Eudora felt there would make any feelings of being an outsider in Jackson seem ridiculous. Compared to Wisconsin's, Jackson's society was warm and welcoming. She had had a healthy youthful ambition to get out of Jackson, but now she must have seen that provincial Jackson had given her the kind of acceptance and love—along with drama and conflict—that neighborhood and family ties and southern connections can bring.

Distance also gave her a clearer view of her home state. The two years on the shores of Lake Mendota must have made her conscious of how different Mississippi was from the rest of the world. It wasn't just the climate. The way of life, the people, the conversation—in other words, all the components of fiction—were different in Mississippi. They were worth reexamining. Perhaps it took two years away for Eudora to recognize the possibilities in the people where she had spent all her life and would spend much of the rest of it.

At the same time, she reaped intellectual benefits from those two years. At Wisconsin, she discovered, as she put it, "the profundity and scope of great literature."[21] She was reading a wide range of English literature for classes; she also read every contemporary book she could. "I was coming along when you could read Proust and Thomas Mann, all those people were publishing. And Chekhov."[22] She made up her own reading list, dictated by her own taste.

Eudora intended to major in art when she went to Wisconsin. In *One Writer's Beginnings,* she describes the surprise she got when she walked into her first art class and saw, instead of a still life, as she had drawn at MSCW, a young woman model who dropped her robe and stood before the class naked. She said it was like the shock she got at MSCW from the "immediacy of poetry." Her art teacher told her that she did not know enough about anatomy to draw the human figure and suggested that she go over to the library and practice drawing the statues, "to learn how people were made instead of drawing these people in their clothes without knowing how a foot was made or where a shoulder went into its socket or anything."[23] Eudora drew the statues and made a good grade but realized that fine art was not for her.

She majored in English and minored in art history. "You couldn't take anything I did in painting seriously," she told an interviewer. "I loved it, and I studied it, but I had no serious ambition about it . . . I just loved painting. I minored in art history because they had such marvelous professors . . . And I could go into Chicago and see the real thing. That was just wonderful."[24]

Eudora went into Chicago as often as she could, to wander about the department stores and spend hours in the galleries of the Art Institute, which by 1927 had a fine collection of outstanding pictures, thanks to astute purchases and the generosity of many patrons. She could see El Greco's *Assumption of the Virgin,* Georges Seurat's monumental *Sunday Afternoon on the Island of the Grand Jatte,* and Picasso's *The Old Guitarist,* as well as works by Cassatt, Monet, Manet, Renoir, Van Gogh, Toulouse-Lautrec, Gauguin, Cézanne, Reynolds, Rembrandt, and Delacroix.

But it was the English classes that stirred her. Eudora has often mentioned one of her teachers at Wisconsin, Assistant Professor Ricardo Quintana, who arrived with a brand-new Ph.D. from Harvard the same year she did. She told an interviewer fifty years after she left the university that she had been heavily influenced by Quintana's course in eighteenth-century literature. The class, she said, began with the seventeenth-century, of which Quintana said Swift was a child. "So we had almost a course on John Donne and all of those other people and then on through Swift . . . He really made us realize the strength and truth of poetic feeling. I saw what a vast force literature was and the seriousness of the whole thing. It was exhilarating. It really opened the door to me . . . It was a revelation."[25]

"I had never heard a teacher use the word 'passion' before," she said another time when speaking of Quintana, "and it really taught me what was meant by that word, and the whole meaning of the poetic imagination."[26] Quintana went on to become a world-class authority on Swift. Eudora gave his name as a reference when she applied for jobs, as well as that of Professor R. E. N. Dodge, the chair of the English Department. Wisconsin offered courses in creative writing, but Eudora has said that she never took one. She did take what she described as the most advanced composition course from Professor Dodge.

Most English majors wrote scholarly and critical theses, but three seniors wrote creative theses in 1929. Naomi Rabe Graham wrote a collection of short stories, *Gather Ye Rosebuds.* Mark Schorer, who went on to become a critic, a novelist, and a biographer of Sinclair Lewis, also wrote short stories, *Please God.* Eudora wrote a novel, first called *All Available Brocade* and then retitled *Katie.* (Most senior theses, including Eudora's, have disappeared.)

At commencement in 1929, 1,500 people were to receive diplomas. Eudora's parents came up for the ceremonies, which began with baccalaureate services on Sunday at the Stock Pavilion. On Monday, graduates gathered in cap and gown on the upper campus at 3:15 to march over Observatory Hill and across the agricultural campus to the pavilion. After the procession, graduates sat on the field of the pavilion, guests in the bleachers. The program began with the university hymn, "Light for All," followed by an invocation. When the governor came forward to present greetings from the state, the graduates rose and sang "On, Wisconsin" as a salutation. When President Frank rose to give the charge to the class, members stood up and sang the varsity toast and then gave a locomotive cheer. After each honorary degree was conferred—two went to novelists that year: Zona Gale Breese, who was also a trustee of the university, and Ole Edvart Rölvaag, of Northfield, Minnesota—the class gave a "Skyrocket" cheer. Prizes were awarded, including prizes for theses and essays. Eudora Welty did not win one.

Chapter 6

Columbia

1929—1931

*"Miss Eudora Welty, charming daughter of Mr. and Mrs.
C. W. Welty, has returned from Madison, Wis., where she
has just received her bachelor of arts degree from the
University of Wisconsin."*
Jackson Daily News, JUNE 27, 1929

By the summer of 1929, Eudora knew she wanted to be a writer. On
August 26 she wrote an awkward application letter to Charles Scribner's, for
some reason writing to the Chicago office instead of the main office in New
York. She said that she was "desirous of getting a position in a publishing
house which will serve toward stimulating and finding a field for my own
writing." She said that she had elected the highest courses in composition at
Wisconsin under Professor R. E. Neil Dodge, and she enclosed a letter from
him. Professor R. B. Quintana, she said, would answer any questions they
might have about her critical ability.

The letter was forwarded to Maxwell Perkins in New York, who wrote
that he regretted extremely to have to say that the staff was completely filled
and "we cannot avail ourselves of the opportunity offered."[1]

A few days later she wrote an almost identical letter to the *Bookman,* a New York magazine about books and publishing, and received another polite rejection.

Eudora has said that both her parents backed her in her wish to become a writer, but in very different ways. Her mother was generally supportive, because she was a great reader and revered the written word. For some time, however, Eudora thought her father opposed her ambitions to write because he mistrusted fiction. "He said, 'It's not the truth about life.' And he thought I might be wasting my time, because he thought I was going to write the sort of things that came out in the *Saturday Evening Post,* and if I didn't write those things I couldn't earn a living. We never really talked about the kind of things I did want to write. I couldn't have done that with either one of my parents, with anybody. And how did I know what I *could* do? But he did support me. All he wanted to do was to make sure I could survive, make my living. And that was good advice. I was rather scornful at the time— 'Live for art,' you know."[2]

But Christian really believed that Eudora should be able to support herself. Eudora refused to consider teaching school. Eventually she and three other young women in Jackson agreed that they wanted to spend a year in New York. To go to graduate school at Columbia University seemed to be the most feasible way to persuade their families to finance this scheme. Aimee Shands would study psychology and Mary Frances Horne would be in classics. Leona Shotwell was the fourth. With her father's full approval, Eudora decided to take courses in advertising and typing at Columbia's business school. Both her parents "believed in the value of new experiences."

Before she left Jackson, Eudora wrote an occasional story for the *Daily News.* One story, on May 25, 1930, described the Junior Auxiliary League's weekly clinics for babies. "Imagine twelve babies, none of whom knows any of the other babies, gathered in the basement of the Lampton Building and you get the appeal of the Baby Clinic which the Junior Auxiliary has established for the aid of underprivileged or undernourished babies in the city of Jackson," wrote Eudora. The doctor, she went on, was trying to see the tongue of "one happy infant," who would rather "gurgle at the nurse." It would take A. A. Milne, she said, "to fully give the force of this scene in the clinic."[3]

At some point Eudora joined the Junior Auxiliary, which later became a full-fledged Junior League, and it is possible that she was doing her stint of community service in the clinic. (It is a telling commentary on the racial situation in Jackson in 1930 that on the same day Eudora's story on the clinic appeared, a much bigger story about minor flooding had the headline "Pearl River Flood Hits Capital City. Pickaninnies Are Swimming in Amite Street.")

Another Welty story, an essay on family vacations, appeared in the *Daily News* on June 15. "Vacation time officially begins when Junior receives his report card," she wrote in the first paragraph, "and officially ends the day before the fish are going to start biting, the day after Sister has at last met a Notre Dame man, and the very day Mamma runs out of stamps. . . . [The vacation] is variously known as 'a big lie, that's what,' 'just a nice rest,' 'the real McCoy, dearie,' and 'a hallucination.' "[4] The story rambles on as though it were in a high school humor magazine.

On Thursday afternoon, June 19, 1930, reported the *Clarion-Ledger,* Chestina Welty gave a bridge party with eight tables in honor of Eudora. "The reception suite was a bower of loveliness with gorgeous roses, gladioli, larkspur, and other blossoms in which the purple tones predominated," ran the newspaper account. High-score prize was Coty perfume and second prize was a French compact. "Miss Welty was lovely in pink chiffon and Mrs. Welty was very attractive in blue georgette."[5]

In the fall of 1930 the four Jackson girls went to New York. All female graduate students at Columbia who were under twenty-one had to live in Johnson Hall, a women's dormitory on 116th Street. The Jackson girls "were all segregated in the same hall in the women's dormitory so we wouldn't annoy other people with our accents, our terrible accents."[6] Eliza Reese Butler, the sister of the president of Columbia and a chaperone at Johnson Hall, warned the girls quite seriously to beware of white slavers, who might kidnap them.[7]

The Columbia School of Business, which had opened its doors in 1916, had a distinguished faculty and an enrollment of almost five hundred students in 1930. Howard Kenneth Nixon taught the practical aspects of advertising, and E. C. Norris taught advertising research. Special courses in typing were offered. Fees, including tuition and room and board, averaged $1,288 for the year. In 1994, none of the surviving alumni of the business school in 1930–1931 remembered Eudora. Several of them pointed out that this was not surprising—the school was large and diverse, with many of the students commuting and some of them working at full-time jobs while they were in school. There was little sense of collegiality.

Other young people from Jackson joined the girls in exploring New York. Frank Lyell was also in graduate school at Columbia. Lehman Engel, Jackson's twenty-year-old musical prodigy, who had written music for Central High School's alma mater, an opera, and a cantata, had a fellowship to Juilliard. Herschel Brickell, from Yazoo City, and his wife, the former Norma Long of Jackson, invited the Jackson girls for dinner several times. Brickell had edited the *Jackson Daily News* from 1916 to 1919 and then had gone to New York, where he became an important figure in the literary world. As a book reviewer for the *New York Post,* he was the first to call attention to the southern writers Julia Peterkin and T. S. Stribling and the first journalist to interview Margaret Mitchell. In 1930 he was an editor at Henry Holt and Company, but he later returned to work as a book reviewer and columnist for the *Post* and then edited the O. Henry short story collection each year. He was to be a loyal and useful friend to Eudora.

That was a time when southern girls "were just thought to be the most attractive, cutest things in the world," and the Jackson group made the most of it.[8] Eudora's studies were not onerous, to say the least, and she used the year to soak up everything New York had to offer. It was the first chance she had ever had to attend the theater with any frequency, the first time she had lived in a city with an art museum. She went to the Metropolitan Museum of Art every Sunday and went out every night with a group, to the theater, down to Greenwich Village, or up to a Harlem nightclub to dance to the music of Cab Calloway. They went to foreign films at the Thalia or to Romany Marie's, or just wandered around Minetta Lane.

With the lightest load of anybody in the group, Eudora was the one who went every day to the drugstore in Times Square to pick up theater tickets for $1.10 each. The New York theater was enjoying its finest hour. Among the shows on Broadway were Marc Connelly's *Green Pastures; Elizabeth the Queen,* with Alfred Lunt and Lynn Fontanne; Moss Hart and George S. Kaufman's *Once in a Lifetime;* Ira and George Gershwin's *Girl Crazy* and *Strike Up the Band;* Richard Rodgers and Lorenz Hart's *Simple Simon;* Eugene O'Neill's *Mourning Becomes Electra,* with Nazimova (much admired by Eudora); *Private Lives,* with Noel Coward and Gertrude Lawrence; and Katherine Cornell in *The Barretts of Wimpole Street.* "Martha Graham was dancing solo in some little cubbyhole somewhere, and I would go and watch her dance," Eudora said later.[9]

Her mother sent her boxes of camellias from the garden in Jackson. In those days, Mrs. Welty could take a package to the train station, send it by express, and it would be in New York the next day. As Eudora remembered, "It was lovely to be up there in the ice and snow and these lovely tropical flowers would arrive."[10]

Chapter 7

Home Again
1931

In the fall of 1931, Eudora received ominous news from Jackson: her father was dying. She left New York and hurried home. Christian Welty had leukemia, the first case she had ever heard of. "The doctor told us about it, and said, 'Hide the encyclopedia so he won't look it up.' Of course, he already had," she said.[1]

Christian was in the hospital, the Jackson Infirmary. In a last-ditch attempt to save his life, the doctor decided to try a blood transfusion. It was Wednesday, September 23, 1931. Doctors did not understand at the time that unless blood types are carefully matched, the procedure can be lethal. Eudora was in the hospital room when her mother, determined to give the blood herself, lay on a cot with a tube running from her arm to Christian's. "All at once his face turned dusky red all over," Eudora wrote in *One Writer's Beginnings*. He was dead, at fifty-two.

Funeral services were held at the house on Pinehurst, with the pastor of Galloway Memorial Methodist Church and Dr. W. B. Capers, rector of St. Andrew's Episcopal Church, officiating. The offices of Lamar Life were closed, and the flag flew at half-mast on the day of the funeral. WJDX, the company-owned radio station, which he had founded, was mute. (He had worked on his speech for the opening of the station in 1929 in the same way that his daughter revised fiction; he had cut it up and rearranged the pieces with pins.)[2]

"Mr. Welty came to Jackson as a man who started from scratch and stepped out in front of his competitors in highly spirited fashion," said an editorial in the *Clarion-Ledger*. "He ran the race of life in a constant sprint, achieving thereby heights few of his fellows ever scale. This sudden blow of death finished a career as truly inspirational as any Jackson has seen at first hand."[3]

In a will made less than a month before he died, Christian left an insurance policy and one hundred shares of stock in Lamar Life to each of his children and everything else, including insurance, to Chestina. Edward Welty was a sophomore at Georgia Tech at the time, and Walter was still in high school. Eudora was twenty-two years old and unemployed.

Eudora has written that her mother never recovered emotionally from Christian's death and ever after blamed herself for failing to save his life. She said that her mother put no pressure on her to stay in Jackson, "but there weren't any jobs in New York, and I decided to stay in Jackson."[4]

"I quit advertising," she told an interviewer. "It was too much like sticking pins into people to make them buy things that they didn't need or really much want. And then, too, advertising is so filled with taboos—you are scared to say this thing and that thing; scared to use this page and that kind of type, and so on. What's the use of learning fears?"[5]

In 1929, Christian Welty had hired his friend Wiley Harris to manage Lamar Life's WJDX, which opened in December, and it was Wiley Harris who gave Eudora her first paying job, in 1931. WJDX had offices in a "little birdcage" of a space on the roof of the Lamar Life building, right next to the clock, and the job was "part-time and vague," the "nicest job I ever had."[6]

The rooftop office, "about as big as a chicken coop," was just big enough for Harris and Eudora. Harris was also the announcer, and he sometimes went in the clock tower to clean out the canary's cage and, absentmindedly as he was, forgot the time. Someone in the office across from his would yell, "Mr. Harris! Mr. Harris!" and make frantic signals to him that it was time to announce the station on the air. When this person finally got his attention, he would go in the studio and say, "This is station . . . uh, this, this is station . . ." At last the employees would hold up a piece of paper with "WJDX" written on it, and Harris would say it. Eudora sometimes rode out to the transmitter with him and reported later that he was so absent-minded he would forget to shift gears.[7]

At the station, Eudora's duties were various. She edited the *Lamar Radio News,* a four-page mimeographed newsletter that included the program schedule, which the station had to print because the *Daily News* would not carry it. (Fred Sullens, the editor, called the station personnel "traitors" and accused them of taking away the newspaper's advertising and news.) She also wrote feature articles on the local talent that appeared on the air: the Leake County Revelers, the Venetian Trio, which played "elegant" string music, and Lois McCormick and her accordion. She wrote scripts for programs, dramas, commercials for mule feed, Santa Claus talks, life insurance playlets, and letters to the station purporting to be from listeners, saying things like "We love the opera on Saturday afternoon. Don't ever take it away."

Her column, "The Editor's Mike," was ironic and funny. "There we went, promising you a shakeup on the schedule this week and we've still got Daylight Saving Time on our hands," she wrote in the issue of September 18–24, 1932. "We don't mind, of course, but we were expecting to do away with it this week and we feel cheated. Daylight Saving Time is like someone else's baby. You don't want to hold it forever—when you didn't even ask for it in the first place. However next week will see the big upheaval, so set your ears up an hour by next Sunday."

A story in the same issue reported that the "xylophone-banjo-saxophone-piano alliance that broadcasts at 8:45 every Wednesday night is looking for a two-word name for their program." There would be a prize for the winning name, the story went on, "so collect your wits and send in your choice . . . something short and snappy, because that's the kind of music the 8:45 boys play and it looks better on the schedule than a title like 'Royal Rhythm Hotsy Totsy Vagabonds.' "

In that same issue, Eudora interviewed Miss WJDX, three-year-old Gloria Chapman, who won the Majestic Theater's Tiny Tot Parade. Miss WJDX revealed to her interviewer that "I'm going to school when I get old" and that Clark Gable was her favorite movie actor. "In character as Miss WJDX, Gloria blows you a kiss, but she wants it understood that in real life she is a great home girl."[8]

A script Eudora wrote for the special twenty-sixth anniversary program for the Lamar Life Insurance Company survives. It calls for music and provides three skits on Mississippi history and Lucius Quintus Cincinnatus Lamar, for whom the company was named. Lamar was a Mississippi congressman who wrote the state's Ordinance of Secession in 1861. After the Civil War was over, he went back to Congress and demonstrated the remarkable statesmanship that made John F. Kennedy include him in *Profiles in Courage*. This script may have been Eudora Welty's first chance to mine Mississippi history for material to use in her writing.

Still not quite ready to settle down in Jackson for good, she returned to New York in early 1933 and spent six weeks looking for a job. She sent the editors of *The New Yorker* a very funny letter of application. She supposed they would be "more interested in even a sleight-o'hand trick than you'd be in an application for a position with your magazine, but as usual you can't have the thing you want most," she said. She told them she had been a New Yorker for a year while attending the Columbia School of Business but admitted, "I am a Southerner, from Mississippi, the nation's most backward state." She offered to review movies and art exhibitions and said she had coined a word for Matisse's pictures after she saw his show: concubineapple. As for book reviews, she read voraciously and could drum up an opinion later. She continued her lighthearted letter by confiding that she would like to have an apartment, not to mention a small portable phonograph. "How I would like to work for you! a little paragraph each morning—a little paragraph in the evening." If *The New Yorker* turned her down, she said, her alternative would be the University of North Carolina, which had offered to let her dance in Vachel Lindsay's *Congo* for twelve dollars. "I congo on. I rest my case," she concluded.[9]

The New Yorker thanked her for her "interesting letter" but said it had no openings. It added that any contributions, whether art, fiction, or Talk of the Town material, would receive careful consideration.

Eudora tried to stay in New York, subsisting "mostly on party snacks, spending her occasional earnings on the theater and finding no one willing to cash her mother's perfectly good checks."[10] "Eudora did not want to come home from New York, but her mother wanted her," said an old friend from Jackson.[11]

Eudora was, as always, ambivalent about her mother's possessiveness, confessing guilt every time she left but insisting that she *wanted* to be in Jackson. "I came on home finally. I had to," she told a friend. "And it was the best thing I ever did, to come home and get a job, so I could write at home. The angels were looking after me."[12]

Part Two

Finding
Her Feet

Chapter 8

Local Literati
1931–1935

"Founded and platted as the seat of government, and for
116 years the funnel through which all the turbulent events
of the State's history have poured, Jackson has a background
which is, in turn, murky with political intrigues and bright
with historic associations."
Mississippi: A Guide to the Magnolia State, 1938

Jackson was not much like New York. Although its population had leaped from 22,817 in 1920 to 48,282 in 1930, it was still a small town. Country people, including dignified women sitting on rush-bottom chairs in mule-drawn wagons, flocked into Jackson on Saturday nights, crossing the bridge over the Pearl River. People had vegetable gardens in their back yards and went blackberry-picking in the summer. Peddlers still cried their wares from wagons creaking up the streets—watermelons, fresh snap beans, butterbeans, okra, and turnip greens.[1]

The Great Depression had the country by the throat, but as Eudora often said, Mississippi had always been so poor you could hardly tell the Depression from the normal way of life. Actually, Jackson was better off than most other places in Mississippi. The state government continued to function and provided jobs with regular pay to most of the city's white population. Natural gas had been discovered on the outskirts of town, and its production provided some jobs and money.

The Depression caused many young people to go back home to Jackson and live with their parents for a few years, and Eudora quickly became part of a remarkable group of talented people with literary interests who temporarily perched in town.

Hubert Creekmore, a couple of years older than Eudora, had graduated from the University of Mississippi in 1927 and spent a year studying drama at Yale. He was back in Jackson, living with his parents on Pinehurst Street (his father was a lawyer), working for the Mississippi Highway Department, and appearing in Little Theater plays. Ambitious and tireless, he wrote constantly. He began his first novel in 1926, when he was only nineteen, and finished it in 1928, although it was never published. From 1930 to 1932 he worked on another never-published novel, and his papers include fragments of other handwritten manuscripts dating from the early 1930s, one of which was called "The Natchez Trace: A Romantic Novel." He submitted his work indefatigably and in the early 1930s was placing short stories and poetry in little magazines. He was at first a mentor to Eudora.

Eudora stopped by the Burger family's house one afternoon and happily renewed her friendship with Nash. He had attended Millsaps and Sewanee and wanted to be a writer, but he returned to Jackson in 1932 to teach English at Central High School. William B. Hamilton, a year older than Nash and Eudora, was teaching history at Central High. He later got his Ph.D. at Duke and went on to write books and edit the *South Atlantic Quarterly*. George Stephenson, another high school classmate, was working for the bank so he could put himself through college and Episcopal seminary.

Frank Lyell, who had graduated from the University of Virginia, earned his master's at Columbia, and later taken a Ph.D. at Princeton, was home every summer, even after he began teaching at North Carolina State and then the University of Texas. Lyell, his friends recall, was the most sociable, most amusing member of Eudora's crowd. Even people who called him "sissy," a polite term for the unspeakable "homosexual," admitted that he was funny, charming, and extraordinarily bright.

Lehman Engel was home from Juilliard that summer. Already composing music, Engel later became a top Broadway composer and conductor and the author of several books.

Bill Hamilton's good friend and fraternity brother at Ole Miss, John F. Robinson, joined the group when he came home from a year of graduate school at Louisiana State in 1933. Robinson was inclined to be a perpetual student. A tall, handsome man with literary interests, he had been born in the little Delta town of Sidon, where his father, Douglas Robinson, had inherited large landholdings from his mother and stepfather, Governor James K. Vardaman, the Mississippi politician who was called the "white chief" for his noisy abhorrence of racial equality. (Vardaman, a racist demagogue, became the most popular politician in Mississippi history.) Douglas Robinson moved his family to Jackson, where they lived in a spacious old house with a huge front veranda at 8 Park Avenue, across from Millsaps College. Eudora and John Robinson became the best of friends, and some people expected Eudora to marry him, although "the family never did," according to Robinson's sister-in-law. Robinson was viewed with mixed emotions by other young Jacksonians. Like Lyell, he was a little bit "sissy," said one, and always got drunk at parties. (Eventually, everyone knew that Lyell, Creekmore, Engel, and Robinson were all homosexual.)

Young women who floated in and out of the circle included Helen Lotterhos, an artist who had studied at the Art Institute of Chicago, Seta Alexander, and Charlotte Capers, who later became head of the Mississippi Department of Archives. But Eudora was the circle's center.

Nobody in Eudora's crowd had any money, so they concocted their own entertainment. (Eudora said she made her own clothes, and added, "I must have looked like the end of the world.")[2] Homemade entertainment was simple but fun, and a drive to Alabama in a rented car was a great adventure. Their own cars were unreliable. Eudora recalled the time she and Bill Hamilton and two other people drove out to a place called Brown's Wells and drank home brew while someone named Swayze Neyland played "Shine On, Harvest Moon" on the piano. Coming home singing, they ran out of gas in Terry, a little town that was "pitch black dark" at night in those days, and there was nobody to pump gas.[3]

Picnics were cheap, and they had favorite spots for alfresco meals. They liked Port Gibson, the town "too pretty for the Yankees to burn," which had a hand on top of its church steeple with the index finger pointing to heaven. They went to the site of Grand Gulf, the town that the river had sucked away; to Bruinsburg Landing, where Aaron Burr's "flotilla" had tied up; to Vicksburg, where they climbed around on the fortifications left from the siege during the Civil War. A favorite place was the romantic ruin of Windsor Castle, a mansion built in 1861 by the planter S. C. Daniel. It had originally had five stories and a tower, which Mark Twain used as a landmark when he was a pilot on the Mississippi. Confederate soldiers had occupied the tower to keep watch on river traffic; Federal forces had turned the house into a hospital. Windsor burned in 1890, but still standing were twenty-two stone Corinthian columns linked by the wrought iron railings of what had once been an upper gallery. These ruins had a powerful effect on Eudora's imagination; she drew on Windsor when describing the mansion for which Salome Musgrove longs in *The Robber Bridegroom*: "at least five stories high, with an observatory of the river on top of that, with twenty-two Corinthian columns to hold up the roof." It also sparked the short story "Asphodel," in which a modern satyr appears to three genteel southern ladies who are picnicking at a mansion like Windsor.

The crowd explored the ghost town Rodney, established as Rodney's Landing in 1828, which had once been a busy port on the Mississippi River where steamers from Liverpool, England, docked. By 1930 the river had moved away, leaving the ghost town at the foot of a bluff, with a few houses and more churches than people. Every house wore a black belt—the high-water mark of the latest river flood. Eudora used Rodney as the place where Clement Musgrove of *The Robber Bridegroom* lived, and as the setting for the story "At the Landing."

Everyone in the group was intensely interested in Mississippi history. Creekmore wrote articles for the WPA Mississippi Writers Project on state place names (Petal, on the Leaf River; Shellmound; Panther Burr; Duck Hill), crafts (quilt patterns and bottle borders for flowerbeds), hunting stories, outlaws and criminals (the Harpe Brothers, John Murrell).[4] Whereas he listed and described methodically, Eudora picked up the same information, stored it, and infused it with life and romance in her fiction. Hamilton introduced them to Robert M. Coates's *The Outlaw Years: The History of the*

Land Pirates of the Natchez Trace, which came out in 1930. That book piqued Eudora's curiosity about the Natchez Trace and the outlaws who used it.

Eudora's house was the group's social center. Her brothers were away at school, and she and her mother were hospitable. A contemporary who was not a close friend recalled that Eudora and her mother "often clashed head-on. I think they clashed about her lifestyle. Eudora played jazz all the time, and Mrs. Welty disapproved of drinking."[5] But Nash Burger and Seta Alexander do not remember tensions between mother and daughter; they recall Mrs. Welty as "jolly," and "in and out, helping to fix snacks." Eudora was a good cook. "Eudora would disappear into the kitchen and come back with something like an onion pie," Seta recalled.[6]

There were the homely pleasures of southern summers—turning the ice cream freezer to produce gallons of homemade ice cream or frozen custard, slicing cold watermelons and eating them out of hand, and taking hay rides that wound down country roads at night, in trucks lined with hay and filled with singing young people.

Sometimes the group played charades or other games, and once Eudora rented a jukebox, but games and jukeboxes interfered with their constant talk, mostly about the current fiction that they were all reading. They were wildly interested in the Fugitives, a group of Vanderbilt University writers including Robert Penn Warren, Allen Tate, and John Crowe Ransom, who had published a magazine for a while and then a symposium on the future of the South called *I'll Take My Stand.* They were therefore delighted when Hubert Creekmore introduced George Marion O'Donnell to the group. O'Donnell was fond of saying he grew up on Blue Ruin Plantation, between Midnight and Louise. (In the first sentence of Eudora's story "The Hitch-Hikers," Tom Harris, the traveling salesman hero, "got out of Victory a little after noon and saw people in Midnight and Louise, but went on toward Memphis.") Actually, O'Donnell's family lived in Belzoni. O'Donnell had met the Fugitives when he was at Vanderbilt and had even contributed to their second book, the Agrarian symposium *Who Owns America?* He briefly produced a small literary magazine in Memphis, the *Observer,* which published some of Creekmore's poems, before he went on to an academic career.

"O'Donnell was one of the legends in this part of the country," Eudora said. "He died young. He would come through here on the train and come out to my house and regale us with anecdotes about all the great southern writers. He knew them all, we didn't know any. We'd all drink whiskey and then go and help him onto the Pullman as best we could, and he'd go on his way."[7]

Sometimes they dressed up at night, the girls wearing long dresses even if they had only four or six people for dinner. Once Eudora gave a "garret party," to which each guest came as an artist with a work of art; for it she produced a painting called "A Horse of Another Color."[8] They took pictures of each other in costumes; a notable one shows Frank Lyell kneeling to serenade Eudora, who is swathed in a shawl and sitting in a tree. "Eudora invented camp," Lehman Engel said of this picture in his autobiography.[9] Another photograph shows Eudora making fun of advertising; she is Helena Arden using Campbell's Pea Soup, Sunbrite Cleanser, and NuShine for cosmetics. There are time exposures of Eudora, Helen Lotterhos, Margaret Harmon, and Anne Long dressed as fashion figures among jars of pampas grass. "These were all fun, you see," Eudora said. "We all had jobs, most of us, by day, and thought up our own entertainment in the evenings. We were all young, just out of college. We had a good time in the Depression."[10]

They longed for the smart world and read *The New Yorker* and *Vanity Fair* religiously. Edited by Frank Crowninshield, the *Vanity Fair* of the twenties and thirties printed fiction by Kay Boyle, Clare Boothe, Frank Sullivan, William Saroyan, and Gertrude Stein as well as humorous pieces and news and photographs of celebrities. Eudora's group managed to keep up with theater, art, and music in the outside world.

Sometimes they had parties in "the Hut," a small structure Eudora's brothers had built out of scrap lumber in their back yard. After Edward and Walter outgrew it, the crowd took it over and renamed it the Penthouse. They plastered the walls with the covers of old copies of *Vanity Fair* and pictures of people they admired—Alfred Lunt and Lynn Fontanne, Fred and Adele Astaire, and Noel Coward.

They did not drink a great deal, and when they did it was usually bourbon, although Hubert Creekmore occasionally turned up with a bottle of rare brandy.[11] They cheerfully patronized a bootlegger on the other side of the Pearl River, from whom they bought bourbon, not moonshine.

To avoid arrest, the bootlegger kept moving his place of business. Once when Eudora went over to buy bourbon, she saw a little black boy sitting on the bridge reading *Time* magazine. Left there to guide people to the new headquarters, he did not look up from the page when her car approached, but raised his arm and pointed her in the right direction.[12] Going to the bootlegger was exciting; nobody really wanted things to change. As the saying went, "Mississippi will vote dry as long as the drunks can get to the ballot boxes."

Each October the group visited the Mississippi State Fair every night it was open ("Sawdust, side-shows, fireworks, and foolishness," said Nash Burger, who was particularly addicted to riding the Ferris wheel).[13] Once they went to hear Bessie Smith at the Alamo, the black theater from which Richard Wright had stolen money to get out of town. Eudora and her friends, the only white people there, sat in the balcony, and she physically restrained one of the young men when he wanted to call out a request for a song. "It would have spoiled everything if they knew white people were there," she said.[14]

When someone in the group had a guest from outside Jackson, they all entertained him. An Englishman, Shaun Wylie, who came to visit Frank Lyell, wore a feather in his hat, and said he had "stopped on his way to Frank's house to bathe in a stream," which turned out to be the Pearl River. To introduce him to the flavor of the South, the group took him to a mint julep party and to a Holy Roller meeting.

Occasionally they went to New Orleans, taking the train out of Jackson very early in the morning, spending the day in the French Quarter, having one good meal at, say, Galatoire's, and one drink at Pat O'Brien's, and taking the train back home that night. They were generally too poor to spend a night in a hotel, but once or twice they splurged and stayed at the Monteleone Hotel so they could go out to listen to jazz at Preservation Hall. That's where Eudora later heard Sweet Emma play the piano. "She would come in wearing a house dress and her hat, and she'd put her purse and a bag of groceries to take home afterwards on top of the piano, an old upright, and sit down and start in . . . She was just like a good housewife coming to give it a good cleaning down where she played."[15] Jackson people tended to choose either New Orleans or Memphis for their big-city activities; Eudora always went to New Orleans. It must have been on these trips that she found copies of William Faulkner's novels, which were not for sale in Jackson and not in the libraries.

One summer Eudora, Lehman Engel, Frank Lyell, and Hubert Creekmore became fascinated with the night-blooming cereus, an exotic houseplant that was all the rage during the Depression in the South. A form of cactus that supposedly bloomed only once in a decade, the cereus, would sport one marvelous white bloom late at night and then almost immediately turn brown and droop pathetically. Residents of Jackson would put a notice in the paper when their night-blooming cereus was due to blossom and invite everyone to come by and watch it. The four young people organized what they called the Night-Blooming Cereus Club—its motto was "Don't take it cereus, life's too mysterious"—and went to someone's house where they sat up all night to watch the flower open. "And tomorrow it'll look like a wrung chicken's neck," one plant's owner said.[16] The night-blooming cereus became a part of their vocabulary, and Eudora sometimes saluted a friend in letters as "You night-blooming cereus, you." The plant also found its way into her fiction. In *Losing Battles,* Judge Moody's wife says, "You've produced a night-blooming cereus. I haven't seen one of those in years." Even more dramatically, in "The Wanderers," one of the stories in *The Golden Apples,* a neighbor woman brings Virgie Rainey her night-blooming cereus, a "naked, luminous, complicated flower," late at night after Virgie's mother's funeral. "Tomorrow it'll look like a wrung chicken's neck," the woman tells Virgie.

Soon after Eudora came back to town, she, Seta, and Jimmy Wooldridge, another friend, appeared in *Gold in the Hills* at the Little Theater. The curtain rose on Eudora, wearing a gingham dress and hightop shoes, as the housekeeper, dusting a vase of artificial flowers with a feather duster. "It brought down the house," said Seta Alexander.[17] Every night after rehearsal the friends went either to Dan McGrew's, a little café on South State Street, or to the Rotisserie, a favorite restaurant north of town.

Hubert Creekmore also took an active part in the Little Theater, which was a very social group. People came to the plays to see their friends, on the stage or in the audience. A receiving line of ladies wearing corsages greeted audience members as they arrived. Coffee girls served refreshments during the lengthy intermissions while the sets were being changed. The richest young ladies in town always seemed to play the parts of maids, tripping out and smiling across the footlights as they said, "Tea is served, madame," to wild applause.[18] Newspapers reported every detail of every performance, even the dresses of the ladies in the receiving line, although one story neglected to mention the name of the play.

Chapter 9

The Journalist

1933–1935

꩜ All of Eudora's literary friends worked on a newspaper, the *Jackson State Tribune,* that Ralph Hilton started in the summer of 1933. Hilton found office space over a store in a building that had a flat tin roof, and "it was like working inside a popcorn popper," Eudora recalled.[1]

No copies of the *State Tribune* can be found in the Mississippi State Archives, but the Welty collection includes a clipping from June 19, 1933, of a feature story by Eudora about Lehman Engel, who was back in New York. Hubert Creekmore reviewed books for the paper, but an editor for Macmillan to whom he sent a request for review copies complained that she could not find it listed in *Ayer's Guide.*[2] The paper did not last long, and Hilton went on to a job with the Associated Press and a career in the Foreign Service. When he retired from diplomacy, he started a much more successful newspaper in Hilton Head, South Carolina.

A little later Eudora went to work as a part-time correspondent for the *Memphis Commercial Appeal,* which was trying to build up its coverage of society news in the towns and cities of Mississippi but had not been able to find a society correspondent from Jackson. For a few weeks in 1933 the *Commercial Appeal* took the unusual step of using its Jackson bureau chief and capitol reporter, Ken Toler, to write social notes for the Sunday paper.

(Toler put his wife's name on some of them.)[3] On August 27, 1933, the society news from Jackson, which ran without a byline, was very dull: "Honoring Mr. James Butler and Mr. Gordon Fowler, both students of the United States Naval Academy, who are their house guests, Mr. and Mrs. Paul Chambers entertained Tuesday evening with a buffet supper . . . ."

Things were very different the next week, on September 3, when Eudora took over with great éclat. Like Cassie, the experienced dancer who tries out for the chorus in *A Chorus Line,* she was *too* good; she gave it her all, and her all was almost too much. The newspaper played her first contribution under a two-column headline, "Jackson Society Revels in Splendor Attached to Natchez Garden Ball":

> JACKSON, Miss., Sept. 2—You must consider, you must admit, that it has taken time to produce a complete magnolia tree in bloom, a row of accurately colored azalea bushes, a line of iris, eternally fresh, and a flock of hollyhocks, all snipped, stitched, cut and contrived out of cotton stuffs; not to mention 55 very beautiful girls in the flesh; and transport all, leaf and baggage, 125 miles.
>
> Yet that is what the Natchez Garden people have done; and the tableaux they brought to Jackson at the Natchez Garden Ball on Friday evening . . .

This lively, ironic column, fully two newspaper columns long, included news of local people (many of them Eudora's close friends) on their way to the World's Fair in Chicago.

> Jackson, looking her raggediest in a girdle of faded dahlias and summer loves, spends her time waving good-byes from a garden deck chair where she remains prone generally through July and August. . . . [In Chicago] this week are Mrs. Clifford Pullen and Miss Ann, who coincidentally won a trip apiece to the World's Fair. . . .
>
> They will be among the smartest to rickshaw beneath the Avenue of Flags. Judge H. H. Creekmore, Mrs. Creekmore, Mr. Hubert Creekmore, and Miss Mittie Creekmore are up too, along with Miss Creekmore's young friend, Miss Mary Jane Eager; they will see

everything with Mr. Creekmore to snapshot it and the young girls to act as daisy exclamation points. Mr. A. Lehman Engel, New York composer, who spends his summers with his family here, is going back via Chicago too. . . .

One of our other celebrities departed not long ago in a colorful flurry—Mrs. Herschel Brickell. . . . She had an eventful summer in Jackson just talking—she knows simply everybody marvelously, and so does her mother, Mrs. Sallie E. Long, who is going back with her. Mrs. Long, by the way, let it out that she has the manuscript copy of "Heaven Trees" by Mr. Stark Young from up in the Delta, but it annoys her very much by being written out in handwriting. . . .

They are driving up in a clever Ford with red wheels, by Chicago and Niagara Falls; not having seen Niagara Falls is a naiveté they feel they must remedy! We happened to see the departure, and Mrs. Brickell's hat was either a bird of Paradise's or Gloria Swanson's— nothing as gay for arriving at the World's Fair had yet left Jackson. It was of cosmopolitan feathers, an inspiration.

Eighty Boy Scouts left Friday too—that made quite a vacant place at our table. They will see the Fair in their five days and buy all the souvenirs up—m.p.t.t. (more power to them).

Readers had never seen anything quite like this *Vanity Fair* style in the society pages of the *Commercial Appeal*. In these first columns we can see flashes of the wit and the eye for detail, even the feeling for family, that would distinguish Eudora's fiction in years to come.

"All they let a woman do in those days was society—for *any* paper," Eudora said in 1992. "I was trying to make a living. You got paid space rates, that is, by the time they pasted all your columns together . . . you got something like $3.65. But it was worth doing for me."[4]

On September 10, 1933, she reported:

The I.C. Terminal is the social spot of the week. Our young are leaving us. They are going to college. Our hands, black with ink, wave them down the track, even though all our tired brains can think of, at this point, is their initials. We sigh. When we see them

next they'll be fudge-makers and scamps of the campus (we know—
we were a girl once). They'll come home with high hopes and
esoteric raincoats. We sell them a quantity of postage stamps but
nothing ever happens, and they all grow up to be president of their
classes. . . .

Mr. and Mrs. L. M. Adams and brown-as-a-berry L. M. Jr. are in
Jackson to stay now, to everyone's high approval. The two-year-old
with his mother in the bookshop the other day was casting the glad
brown eye on the new schoolbooks, a globe of the world, and "The
Photographic History of the World War," which he wanted. His
uncle John Sharp Donald is a freshman at Mississippi State this year
and all Major Donald's family drove Uncle Johnny up to enter.
L. M. Jr. wanted Mississippi State.

Perhaps the biggest social news Eudora covered was Jackson's first
experience with its own debutantes. Here is the lead of her dispatch for
October 1, 1933: "Jackson society is going to get what it has wanted for a
long long time—debutantes! The first will be introduced to a waiting society
the first week in November under the wing of the University Club. A
reception will be the first event when several will make their first bows."

Eudora Welty enjoyed her society reporting—at least for a while—but
when she got bored by the repetitiveness and triviality of society news, she let
quality slide. She wrote about the Matrons' Luncheon Club, the Girls' Cotil-
lion, the Girls' Dinner Club, the Colonial Dames of America, the Poetry
Society of Mississippi, Ladies' Day at the Country Club, the University
Club's duplicate bridge parties, where players were learning "P. Hal Sims's
one-over-one bidding system," and the celebration of Constitution Day by
the Magnolia Chapter of the Daughters of the American Revolution. She
wrote about endless debutante parties, the costume ball at the University
Club, the New Year's open house at the governor's mansion, and the Junior
Auxiliary Style Show. ("Before 300 persons passed the cream of society in the
cream of fashion. And certainly the old fashioned wedding dresses were the
loveliest things ever seen.")

Although none of this journalism is included in bibliographies of her
work, Eudora continued to write the Sunday society column for the *Commercial Appeal* until "someone took it away from me," she said. "Somebody

went to the *Commercial Appeal* and said, 'That Eudora doesn't need the money. She's a rich girl.' " At least, she said that's what an editor at the *Commercial Appeal* told her years later. Her last column, after almost two years, appeared on May 12, 1935.[5]

One of the most interesting things about this foray into society journalism is what Eudora did *not* do with it. She did not become the Edith Wharton of Jackson. Balls and fashion shows, bridge tournaments and dinner dances, do not appear in her short stories and novels. Instead of recording in her fiction the manners and social activities of the gentry, she turned her gaze outward, to people who were invisible to most of her friends. She chose to photograph, to listen to, and to write about black people, the retarded, the deaf, freaks, and the lonely small-town people who, out of sheer boredom, dramatized events in their own lives for diversion. It would be many years before she wrote about middle-class people at all, and the upper crust seldom provided her with her dominant themes.

Hubert Creekmore started his own literary magazine, *Southern Review,* in 1934, and Eudora worked on the business end, sold advertisements, and typed. Nobody asked her to write anything. Nash Burger wrote an article on Sherwood Bonner, whom he identified as "Mississippi's only successful woman of letters and a pioneer in the rise of a regional Southern literature after 1870," and George Marion O'Donnell contributed poems. Two other Jackson writers were listed as contributors: the poet Anne Elise Roane Winter and the short story writer Robert White.

Creekmore's magazine was not a success, and Eudora and the others went with him the night he decided to throw the leftover copies of the first and only issue into the Pearl River. "If it's not a success, it will be *rare,"* said Creekmore.

Eudora, like all the members of the group, was a faithful reader of *The New Yorker,* and in early 1935 she wrote to the magazine, commenting on an article by Robert M. Coates that appeared under the rubric "Onward and Upward with the Arts: Life of the Party." Coates lovingly described products of Johnson Smith & Company of Racine, which sold "puzzles, tricks and joke goods."[6] She and Coates both loved tricks, Eudora said in her letter, but whereas he ordered explosives, she craved the beautiful. She ordered the

Remarkable Fire Fly Plant (nineteen cents), which could grow more than twenty-five feet in a single week. The most amazing of her choices was the ten-cent Sex Indicator, which you could hold over somebody to tell whether he or she was a man or a woman. "We children held it over our mother one night and found out she was a man," she wrote. "There was nothing we could say, or mother either. We just rose and filed out."[7]

Her letter, held in the magazine's archives, has been heavily edited, as though the editors considered running it in the magazine. Wolcott Gibbs wrote to her that they had enjoyed it but did not feel they could run any more comments about the parlor trick situation. Her letter was so good, Gibbs said, that he was sure she could contribute successfully to *The New Yorker,* "and I hope you'll try."[8]

Chapter 10

The WPA

1935–1936

After the *Commercial Appeal* fired Eudora, she went to work as a junior publicist on the five-member local staff of the Works Progress Administration, one of President Franklin Roosevelt's programs designed to provide employment during the Depression. As junior publicity agent, she wrote the features, while Louis Johnson, the senior publicity agent, wrote the news stories.

Their job was to publicize WPA projects, which included everything from building new juvenile courts to teaching the blind to read Braille, from graveling or paving roads for farmers to making a new landing field for airplanes in a farmer's field, and from running bookmobiles to setting up booths at county fairs. Thus, she might interview anyone from a juvenile judge to farmers who lived along a new road.

In her young life, she had not traveled in Mississippi, except to Columbus for college and with her family by car to the Gulf coast. Working for the WPA took her to all parts of the state—she visited every one of the eighty-two county seats—and she called the experience an education. The poverty shocked her, and the state's diversity fascinated her.

She was independent, traveling on her own, driving her mother's car for one-day trips or riding the bus to small towns, where she spent the night in small hotels. She didn't need a reservation; nothing was ever crowded. The Dulcie Hotel in her story "The Hitchhikers" is a "perfect portrait" of the kind of tacky place she stayed in.[1] Those hotels were "hot as flusions, as we used to say. Flusions, you know, the ultimate."[2] They had poor lights, and the good ones had electric fans in summer, the only thing that would help in the heat before air conditioning. The phone was out in the hall or downstairs, but that didn't seem to matter. Running them were "nice people" like, presumably, "Mr. Gene," the Dulcie's proprietor.

As Eudora learned about the lives of all kinds of people, she realized what a protected life she had led. "You know I had been so sophisticated in New York, and I didn't know a thing. I didn't know what people were really like."[3] People's kindness struck her. Nobody was suspicious of her. Inhabitants of the little courthouse towns did not have many visitors and were glad to see somebody from somewhere else. She sensed their loneliness when they came up to speak to her and asked her where she was from. When they found out she was interested in local things, they delighted in showing her around and were even more pleased if she asked to take pictures. "It never occurred to me that people might be upset or suspicious," she said.[4]

She also began seriously writing short stories, many of which grew from the sights and sounds she was absorbing as she traveled around the state for the WPA. She wrote as the ideas came to her, the stories pouring out spontaneously, almost compulsively. The whole state of Mississippi was like a stockroom from which she could draw bright and shining materials for her craft. Around Crystal Springs, in Copiah County, she met tomato farmers and learned about their living conditions that undergirded that disturbing story of blacker-than-Dickens social conditions in rural Mississippi, "The Whistle." In another hamlet she saw an ironing board open in a country post office, and that glimpse germinated and bloomed into "Why I Live at the P.O.," one of her most enduring and popular stories, a wildly funny soliloquy in which Sister recounts the quarrel with her family that made her move to the post office.

One day, putting up a booth at a fair, Eudora had coffee with some of the people who worked on the midway. They talked about a sideshow act that featured a little Negro man, a geek, who was made to eat live chickens.

"I didn't see such a thing, thank God," she said. "Nothing on earth would have induced me to go and look at the show." But she wrote the story "Keela, the Outcast Indian Maid," about a similar geek. It was "the only actual story I've used . . . it was too horrible to make up," she said.[5]

She worked for the WPA until the state publicity office was disbanded, right after the presidential election in November 1936.

Chapter 11

Photography
1935–1937

꧁ Eudora became a photographer almost by accident. Her father had taken pictures with an Eastman camera with a bellows, and he and Chestina had developed and printed family snapshots at night when Eudora was a little girl. Eudora started with a similar camera that used 116mm film. It had a good lens and a shutter that allowed for a time exposure and faster exposures up to one one-hundredth of a second. "I could really see the negatives before I printed them or made enlargements," Eudora said. "I could learn from the mistakes I made."[1]

Without training, she began taking pictures for her own pleasure, with no particular purpose in mind. "I just took them because I wanted to. Just impulse," she said. "I had no position I was trying to illustrate. They were pictures because I would see something I thought was self-explanatory of the life I saw."[2]

The WPA used some of her photographs, but she was not a WPA photographer. She sent some of her photographs along with the releases she wrote to weekly newspapers, which might or might not use them. She photographed political rallies, country fairs, revival meetings, people coming to town on Saturday, people carrying ice, and people on their front porches. As she traveled through Mississippi, she walked around town squares and down

side streets and country roads to lonely places. And when she wasn't traveling for the WPA, she would drive out to towns near Jackson—Raymond or
Port Gibson—for the day and take pictures.[3]

She photographed everyone—family, friends, white people, and then
black people. Nobody got angry, or questioned what she was doing, or tried
to avoid her. Even when she, a young, white woman, wandered into black
neighborhoods, she was treated politely. "And I was polite too," she said.[4]
She first ventured onto Farish Street in the black neighborhood of Jackson
looking for jazz recordings, which white people then called "race records."
When she saw possibilities for photographs, she asked people on the street,
"Do you mind if I take this picture?" They never did. (A black woman
bootlegger in Utica, Mississippi, said, "I'm gone kill you," but she was teas-
ing.) Some of the people had never had a picture of themselves before in
their lives and wanted one, so she tried to get a print back to them. She did
not intend to mock or exploit but to show the life around her. She had no
sense that she was engaged in preservation. If she had, she said, it would
have ruined everything.[5]

"There was no sense of violation of anything on either side," Eudora
said more than fifty years later. Such a relationship would be impossible
today, she noted.[6] To upper-class white women like Eudora, black people
were then virtually invisible, except when they were servants. Her independent perception of them as worthy of her time and attention in the 1930s is
one of the most astonishing and admirable facets of Eudora Welty's character.

Three of her pictures were used in *Mississippi: A Guide to the Magnolia
State,* published by the WPA: a shot of people gathered for a political rally, a
group of shanty boats on the Pearl River, and a mule-powered cane-syrup
mill.[7] Before the WPA guide came out, she contributed a photograph in 1935
to *Eyes on the World: A Photographic Record of History-in-the-Making,* one of
the first books of photographs to be published. Eudora's picture, "Pickup—
Deep South," showed a black man and woman on a downtown street.[8] She
was in good company; other contributors included Margaret Bourke-White,
Ansel Adams, and Charles F. Jacobs, Jr.

In New York she bought a Recomar, which used a film pack. It was
large and expensive and so unhandy that she took it back and sold it to the
store where she had bought it. Later, in 1936, she bought a Rolliflex with a

good ground glass viewfinder the same size and shape as the picture she would take. "I got a sense of composing a precise picture, and the negatives were lovely to work with," she said.[9]

The proprietors of Jackson's Standard Photo, the Schleuter brothers, who developed Eudora's film, became her friends. When they went to Jackson, Christian Welty had encouraged the Schleuters to investigate the possibilities of opening a camera shop next door to Lamar Life. Eudora made contact prints in an exposure frame her brother Edward built for her until she acquired an enlarger discarded by the Mississippi Highway Department. She set up a darkroom in the kitchen at night, with the enlarger clamped onto the kitchen table. The enlarger had only one shutter opening—wide—and the only way she could modulate the exposure was by timing, which took trial and error.

Even with the Rolliflex, she had only one camera lens until she bought a portrait attachment, which she didn't use very often, since she liked to show people in the context of their surroundings. She sometimes used a cloud filter, but she never used artificial light.

It was much later that Eudora saw the work of Walker Evans and Dorothea Lange, the Resettlement Administration photographers who toured the South documenting the poverty of southern tenant farmers. "In the case of Evans, I didn't like what I saw," she told an interviewer. "In *Let Us Now Praise Famous Men* he posed people to tell what their situation was. I shot what I saw."[10] Evans was a professional, she said, and she was not. Her pictures were unposed on principle. "I let my subjects go on with what they were doing, and by framing or cutting and by selection found what composition rose from that. So I think there's a quality that makes them different from those of professionals who were purposefully photographing for an agency or a cause."[11]

When a reporter asked Eudora what she thought of the photographers who went back and rephotographed some of the people who had been subjects for Evans and Lange during the Depression, she replied that it would seem to her that going back was exploiting them—"for a second time."[12] She voiced an equal disdain for the "freak" photographs of Diane Arbus, feeling that they violated human privacy "and by intention." She took photographs, she said, of posters of freaks, not the human beings, because they were naive folk art.

Although Eudora never had any lessons in photography, she always felt that her artistic training, especially the painting lessons she had had from Marie Hull in Jackson, were helpful. (Mrs. Hull taught her students to put their hands around their eyes to frame a scene before they drew it.) Eudora was certainly not as technically proficient as Walker Evans, the master of printing a negative, but her soft-focus, low-contrast work shows a compassion for the people she photographed that is often missing in Evans's work. She may be amused by her subjects, but she is not ridiculing them, nor is she using them to make a point. The people in her pictures always seem relaxed and sometimes downright joyful. They may be poor, but life has not wiped them out. An indomitable spirit prevails, and the young photographer seems to have a kindred *joie de vivre*. She and her subjects—poor whites, poor blacks—are living and glad of it; they enjoy each other.

Those years of making photographs were important to Eudora's writing, although she herself points to a profound difference in photography and writing. "Writing fiction, I am interpreting every minute, but always by way of the characters' own words and acts," she said.[13] "Writing has everything to do with interior feelings and apprehensions," she said elsewhere. "Photographs are exterior, capturing the look of things, the quality of light at a certain time of day. For me the two activities have always run on parallel lines."[14] She has conceded that photographer and writer both try to portray life truthfully; a camera can catch a fleeting moment, and so can a short story. Still, taking photographs made her look more closely at images that she used in her fiction.

She took a great many photographs in New Orleans in the winter of 1936, including pictures of Mardi Gras celebrants and their costumes. When she was writing *The Optimist's Daughter,* she went back to these photographs for details of costumes she wanted to describe. She also took pictures of New York during the Depression: "lines of people waiting at soup kitchens, people selling apples and sitting there in Union Square . . . It was a different homelessness from what we see today in New York. These people of the Great Depression kept alive on the determination to get back to work and to make a living again."[15]

Photography helped her to understand that Mississippi was worth writing about. She had traveled enough in the North to see how different rural Mississippi was from New York or Wisconsin. She was struck by the tombstones she photographed in a graveyard: immigrants had died in duels and of yellow fever. "All these lives began to take on meaning for me, and soon the settings of my stories changed," she said. "They stopped being in an imaginary world and began to appear in a real place."[16]

At first Eudora simply passed her pictures around to friends as though they were snapshots from a trip. Then she started trying to market them in various ways, seeing photography as a possible source of income. She even tried fashion photography for a while and took one picture every Sunday for a Jackson shop called Oppenheimer's, and, later, the Emporium. The shop picked out the clothes; she persuaded her friends and her brothers' girlfriends to pose. Aping *Vanity Fair,* she photographed them in different places—in front of the New Capitol, in the park, and around town. Those pictures "were not very good," she said.[17]

In June 1936 Eudora applied for a job as photographer with the Historical Section of the Resettlement Administration, headed by Roy Stryker, for whom Evans, Lange, and Carl Mydans worked. She sent a portfolio of photographs along with her letter of application and letters of recommendation. Stryker did not hire her, but his failure to do so is no judgment on her ability as a photographer, as Stuart Kidd has pointed out, for Stryker also rejected Lewis Hine, America's foremost documentary photographer, whose pictures of child labor changed the country.[18]

Once a year she went to New York for at least two weeks, carrying a bundle of photographs so she could show them to publishers. And she carried them home again. With her father, she had traveled in luxury, in Pullman cars. On these trips she sat up on the train for three days and two nights, changing trains several times, the first time in Meridian, only ninety miles away. (She wrote about changing trains in Meridian in *One Writer's Beginnings,* sketching in a black woman who carried a big black iron coffeepot and shouted out the train's destinations—"Birmingham, Chattanooga, Bristol, Lynchburg, Washington, Baltimore, Philadelphia, New York"—before carrying passengers' luggage down the platform to the day coach. The woman also appeared in "The Demonstrators.") The trip was cheap. Round-trip railroad fare to New York was something like seventeen dollars, and Eudora stayed with friends or took a room at the Barbizon, which cost nine dollars a week. She was able to do the two-week trip for a hundred dollars and still go to the theater. She was present for the opening of the Mercury

Theater and saw the black *Macbeth* in Harlem directed by Orson Welles, with voodoo priestesses playing the witches and a black man wearing nothing at all dancing on a drum as Hecate.

She soon began taking manuscripts as well as photographs on her annual trips to New York. In those easy-going days, she would leave her material on editors' desks, hoping to hear from them the next day. She never did. She varied her methods of presentation. She tried a ring notebook with little contact prints pasted in sequence to tell a story, which she called "Black Saturday," because that was the day when there was the most variety in what black and white people did at work, in town, and at home. Along with the pictures she submitted a set of stories she had written, not related specifically to the pictures, except that they were all set in the South. Many of these stories later appeared in her first collection, *A Curtain of Green.*

All publishers rejected her work. Whit Burnett of *Story* turned down "Black Saturday" because the price of a book of photographs would be prohibitive—at least $3.50, and "the text would not support such a high price."[19] In 1935, Harrison Smith of Smith and Haas, which published William Faulkner's work in the 1930s, regretfully returned the project, saying that the photos were excellent and engaging, but that Julia Peterkin's book *Roll, Jordan, Roll,* essays on black plantation life in South Carolina illustrated with photos by Doris Ulmann, made it impossible to publish another book like it.[20] This is an interesting point. Eudora's photographs are much more akin to Ulmann's photographs of the black people on Lang Syne Plantation in central South Carolina than they are to pictures by Walker Evans and the other Farm Security Administration photographers. Ulmann had no political agenda; she came out of the soft-focus, pictorial, nineteenth-century tradition. Ulmann, like Eudora, tried to get copies of her pictures to her subjects, and she photographed them in their churches, at work on the plantation, in chain gangs, and in the river at baptism services. *Roll, Jordan, Roll,* which came out in 1933, was endorsed by the National Association for the Advancement of Colored People for its sympathetic and understanding portrayal of rural black people.

Eudora also began circulating a book of contact prints, with notes to explain what she would do with the pictures, to a list of magazines in alphabetical order, from the *Atlantic Monthly* to *Yard and Garden.*[21] No luck there, either.

In 1935, through the influence of Frank Lyell, who was teaching at Raleigh, North Carolina, her photographs were exhibited in Chapel Hill and in Raleigh. At Chapel Hill, she said, she gave a speech about the photographs, "after which everybody got drunk—the cart before the horse."[22]

Once when Eudora was in New York she wandered into Lugene Optics on Madison Avenue, which sold photography supplies, and saw on display some photographs by an amateur photographer. She turned to the man in charge, whose name was Samuel A. Robbins, and told him about her own pictures, "three hundred unposed studies of Mississippi Negroes."[23] Robbins arranged an exhibition of forty-five of her photographs, all taken with the Kodak or the Recomar. The show was up from March 31 to April 15, 1936. Apparently the program stated that the pictures were printed in Mississippi under "primitive conditions." She said in a lecture many years later at the Museum of Modern Art that it described the pictures as "an example of what can be done with the crudest of materials by the most ignorant of photographers, which was perfectly true."[24]

When Robbins left Lugene and opened his own store, the Camera House, on East 60th Street, he asked Eudora about photographs for another show. This time he wanted some of the "poor white photos." About this time Eudora acquired her Rolliflex, and Robbins was sure she would be able to take even better photographs with it.[25] He gave her invaluable advice on paper, chemicals, and other things she had known nothing about, writing on each of her prints what was wrong, "like not enough contrast, too much, and so on."[26] Some negatives she sent him in December 1936 were overexposed, but he thought it was because of the "wrong choice of paper." These negatives required a soft paper, he said. If she was already using #11 Velour Black, then they would have to look for something else. (When she printed them again on higher-quality paper, the prints were much better, with more contrast.)[27] And when she was taking pictures of tombstones, Robbins told her, she had to realize that there was a great deal of reflection from the white masses and she must take that into consideration. "A higher shutter speed, or even better, a smaller stop opening would do the trick," he said.[28]

Tombstones were a consuming interest. Somehow Eudora had made a connection with *Life,* the new magazine that was filled with photographs, and she sent the editors some tombstone prints in 1937. Frank Hall Fraysur, an editorial associate in charge of developing photographic correspondents, thanked her for her trouble but said the accompanying story had been put off indefinitely and he would hold on to them a while. He regretfully returned her "Valentine collection," which he called a "true vintage bit of Americana"; the magazine had not been able to use them because of other color pages planned. He thought her Negro Holiness Church story sounded interesting. "I hope you can get it without the communists getting you first!" he wrote.[29]

Life praised her and paid her seventy-five dollars for the research she did and the photographs she took for a "Mount Olive elixir" story. "Elixir" was a cruel joke. Dr. Archie Shepherd Calhoun of Mount Olive, Mississippi, had prescribed a new liquid form of sulfanilamide, made by a Tennessee drug firm, for his patients, and had been horrified to find that "some mysterious quality" in the bottled compound caused six of his patients to "turn blue, writhe in agony, die." *Life* used six of Eudora's photographs, including portraits of Dr. Calhoun, his nurse, and a patient who survived the medicine, and pictures of the graves of three patients who had died (more tombstones).[30]

Chapter 12

The First Stories

1931–1936

ᐁ No matter how interesting Eudora might find photography, she never forgot that her real goal was to become a writer. All this time she was writing fiction. Writing, she said, was her "secret life," since she was too shy to show her stories to anybody.[1]

Of course, she had always been a writer. Like most children who read widely, Eudora began to write early. Her first efforts were little books she made up to give to her mother. She illustrated one of these, called "Why We Have Easter," with a picture of a rabbit using the telephone.

Her very first publication was a drawing of two children on a beach with sailboats in the distance. It won a silver badge in a readers' competition in *St. Nicholas* magazine and was published in the August 1920 issue, when Eudora was eleven. Three years later, her quite dreadful poem "Once Upon a Time" also appeared in *St. Nicholas;* it began, "Once upon a time—that sounds/A great long distance back from now,/But that is when our dear ST. NICK/To our grandparents made its bow."[2] She also sent contributions to the children's page of the *Memphis Commercial Appeal.* In 1921, when she was twelve, she won twenty-five dollars—an enormous sum for a child at that time—for first prize in the Jackie Mackie Jingles Contest, sponsored by the Mackie Pine Oil Specialty Company in Covington, Louisiana. The company congratulated her and said that it hoped "as you go through life, that you will improve in poetry to such an extent to win fame."³

Eudora wrote humorous pieces at the W, and in the 1930s she turned once more to satire. One summer she and Robert Daniel, Frank Lyell's young friend from Sewanee, produced (with some contribution from Lyell) a truly marvelous fake anthology of poetry called "Lilies That Fester." Robert Daniel, who had a fine sense of the absurd, thought up the title. They fabricated the poems, made up the names of the poets, and composed the poets' biographies. They typed one copy of the anthology and pasted in photographs of the poets. Eudora said when she saw "Lilies That Fester" almost fifty years later that it was "still absolutely wonderful."⁴

The first poet represented was "Undine Hecht," pictured leaning on a guitar. The editors said regretfully that Undine Hecht "has never received her heritage." One of the earliest prophets of Orphism in poetry, she had made brief excursions into Infanticism and Drollerism. She was fluent in twelve languages and had lost her husband on a camera expedition to the Paps of Jura. She was now living in Florence, Mississippi, near a large plantation where she was "learning Negro." Hecht's poem, "Night Watch," begins, "Peep, peep/Snivel-my-forefinger . . ."

Other poets were Dawn Jacobstein ("D.J."), whose poem, "Vassar Side View," was composed in Small's Paradise in Harlem and was the only one not burned in a Liberty League demonstration on Park Avenue; Bruce Fairlie, the Escapist; Stanley Groupz, who composed the octaves for his sonnets during the preliminary "aura" of Saint Vitus's dance attacks and added the sestets later; Samuel Smithovitch, whose father owned a cattle ranch that included all of Montana lying southeast of a line draw diagonally from the southwest to the northeast corner of the state and who became revolted by his father's business methods and fled to Moscow, where he Russianized his name and joined the Communist party; Wanda Lohegan Aimee, who did not secure recognition for her work until she obtained a position as a typesetter on the *Frantic Fringe Annual* and printed one of her own poems while the editor's back was turned; and Erdine Praed, who was only two years old but was the author of *Ballads in a Bassinette, Pease Porridge Hot,* and a long prose tract in German, "Kunst, Knaben, und Kinderschmerz" before she was three months old.⁵

Photography, poetic spoofs, and an active social life did not keep Eudora from writing serious fiction, and many of her very earliest stories reflect her ambivalent feelings toward her strong-minded mother. Her relationship with her mother was complicated and conflicted, often rewarding and blissful but also tortured and painful. The long, close interaction went on for fifty-seven years of Eudora's life.

Snapshots of the family show Chestina invariably frowning. When someone called her a pessimist, she replied, "I certainly *am*." But she "expected nothing but perfection," even in appearance, from Eudora when she was growing up. Chestina rolled up Eudora's hair on rags and tied enormous bows on top of the sausage curls, and Eudora was still not a pretty little girl. Like all the women of her class in Jackson, Chestina did embroidery, and she made her daughter dozens of hand-embroidered dresses. Eudora always remembered one dress that had wreaths and hoops embroidered on it, which she wore to a party at a friend's house. She was hiding outside near a woodpile during a game when another girl spotted her and "brought a whole pile of kindling down all over me. My dress was dirty and torn," she said. "When I got home, I saw Mother outside, and I prayed and prayed to Jesus to mend my dress before Mother came in from milking the cow. She had worked so hard on that dress."[6] She did not say what happened.

When the Welty children got mad at one another and fought, Chestina would say, "I don't understand where you children *get* it. I never lose my temper. I just get hurt." When she recounts this in her memoir, Eudora comments, "But that was it. A child has no greater burden to bear than a mother who 'just gets hurt.' "[7]

Chestina often wanted Eudora to have things she had never had, and when she told her this, Eudora "wanted, or partly wanted, to give it back." Eudora felt that her own happiness was bought with her mother's sacrifices. Still, she knew that this attitude was unfair to her mother.[8] It took her a long time, she wrote, to manage to become independent, "for I loved those who protected me . . . I have never managed to handle the guilt."

At one point Chestina decided that Eudora must have piano lessons, and to pay for them she bought a little Jersey cow, churned its milk, and sold part of the butter. (A little Jersey cow turns up in the back yard in the early story "The Winds.") Eudora never enjoyed the piano lessons very much, but she sensed that she and her mother "were in this together." At one of Eudora's recitals, Mrs. Welty sat through the evening, although she faced breast surgery the next morning and (rightly, as it turned out) feared a malignancy. She did not tell Eudora, for fear that "she wouldn't do herself justice."[9]

Chestina's "overprotectiveness and 'morbid streak' taught Eudora that the world was a dangerous place," wrote a reporter who interviewed Eudora when she was old. Eudora added that whenever she left home, she went in an "iron cage" of guilt.[10] She even wrote in *One Writer's Beginnings,* that paean to childhood bliss, about the "torment and guilt" she felt at leaving home. Before she got to New York, her mother wrote a letter telling her how much she missed her but insisting that she "only wanted what was best" for Eudora. Chestina stayed in the house until she got a telegram from her daughter with the news that she had reached New York safely.

"I had an awful guilt feeling all my life about going away," Eudora said. "Whenever I was . . . leaving town, we would ride, as the train pulled out of the station, past that sign up there: 'Where will you spend eternity?' I used to think, 'Oh, God! that's reproaching me.' I don't mean I took it literally and seriously, but it was just my last view of Jackson. My family was always willing and anxious for me to go away and be things. They never opposed it . . . That was early on. After I grew up a little, I saw that they could do quite well without me and I without them, for periods of time."[11]

Elizabeth Evans's essay "Eudora Welty and the Dutiful Daughter" demonstrates how in so many published stories, Eudora pictured the dutiful daughter who pays a price for her devotion to duty.[12] In Eudora's earliest stories, mostly unpublished, a mother was often the enemy, feared and hated. In at least three of her earliest tales, a young man or a young woman seeks in various metaphorical and literal ways to escape the interference or domination of a mother. "Beautiful Ohio," written around 1936 and never published, is filled with the way the mind of an imaginative child works. Celia comes home from a musical evening at the chautauqua with her parents. In bed on the sleeping porch, she calls out to a vision of one of the lady musicians, and her mother comes out to ask her if she is lonely there in the dark by herself. " 'Oh—no—,' she said. Celia turned her face to the wall. It was as though she wanted to be lonely and could not. Something had come to stay." In "The Children," written around 1934 and also never published, a young woman named Nora tells a young man she loves him. He rejects her. Nora thinks of throwing herself in the well. "But my mother, she thought, even while she sank into sudden release—will call me back. I will have to go back. She holds a blade of grass. There was that for all the shame in the world."[13] In "Retreat," which was published in *River* in 1937, a man is going through a breakdown; the last line of the story is "Even his mother could not get in"— could not reach him in the dark place to which he was going.

Although Eudora's mother was a powerful, terrifying woman who could be very critical, she was also energetic, generous, and devoted. She was in many ways a very positive influence, introducing Eudora to books and reading early on and later supporting her when she wanted to be a writer. She was at least partly responsible for Eudora's assurance of her own worth, as a person and as a woman. In 1970, only four years after Chestina's death, Eudora gave wonderful, down-to-earth answers to a questionnaire sent to her by Barbara Diamonstein for a book, *Open Secrets: Ninety-four Women in Touch with Our Times*. She dismissed the women's movement as "noisiness" and replied, "Not at all" to the question "Mother oppressed?" when asked, "Brought up to believe woman's place was in home?" she replied, "I don't think I was ever told where it was."[14]

Chapter 13

Getting Published

1936–1940

ᴥ Οne day in 1936, Eudora asked Hubert Creekmore how she could sell her short stories. He suggested that she send something to *Manuscript,* a little magazine published by John Rood and his wife, Mary Lawhead, who also ran a print shop in Athens, Ohio. She sent two stories, "Death of a Traveling Salesman" and "Magic." They were the first stories she had ever submitted to a magazine, and John Rood accepted them both.

When Rood wrote to her, he got the title of one of the stories slightly wrong, but his message was so cheerful that it didn't matter. "DEATH OF A SALESMAN is one of the best stories that has ever come to our attention—and one of the best stories we have ever read. It is superbly done," he said. "And MAGIC is only slightly short of it in quality."[1]

Eudora was astonished. "Is this the way it happens?" she wondered. "You just put something in the mail and they say okay?" She didn't care that they couldn't pay her anything. "If they had paid me a million dollars, it wouldn't have made any difference. I wanted acceptance and publication," she said.[2]

She always remembered why she wrote "Death of a Traveling Salesman." A friend of her family's, Archie Johnson, traveled around the state for the Mississippi Highway Department, buying up land for the rights of way for new highways. Mississippi had fewer miles of paved roads than any state in the union. Often gravel roads would simply disappear beneath a traveler's wheels and Johnson would have to get out and walk to find the landowner's house. When he came home on the weekends, he always had stories to tell. Once he quoted the wife of a man he had gone to see on business. "He's gone to borry some fire," the woman said.

"Well, those words just hit me," Eudora said later. "They were electrical. It was just so far back in time, and so remote. It made me think of something . . . elemental . . . The story grew from that." As she would often do, she automatically drew on the myths and legends she had absorbed as a child. "Prometheus was in my mind almost at the instant I heard Mr. Johnson tell about borrowing the fire," she explained.[3]

Eudora used myths in her stories as she would any common and natural resource. She found that her Mississippi characters quite naturally went through the steps of myths as they acted out their own dreams and obsessions.

R. J. Bowman, the traveling salesman in that first published story, has been ill and is still feverish. He loses his way when the road runs out and goes in search of help. He hears a stream running. "Clearly I was trying to suggest that he'd come near, now, to the stream of life," Eudora wrote.[4] (She regretted later that she had used the word "stream" instead of the colloquial "creek." Streams were in West Virginia, not Mississippi, she said, and "stream" sounded pretentious.) The lonely, unmarried Bowman finds, in an unpainted cabin, the pregnant wife of Sonny, the farmer who has "gone to borry some fire."

Eudora realized later how daring she had been, as inexperienced as she was, to try "to convey a middle-aged traveling salesman deprived of the fulfillment of self-knowledge, of the ability to love; a hill-country farmer and moonshiner; a woman in the prime of a fruitful marriage; . . . to show a man as he is dying and show it as the explosive revelation of what it was he wanted all his life . . . I drove my imagination to put me inside these characters on a premise I accepted, then as now, that the emotions, in which all of us are alike involved for life, differ more in degree than in kind."[5] This helps to answer the question that many people ask about Eudora Welty and her work: how can a woman who has never been married or had children write about love and marriage and families? It also may be a clue to the meaning of the puzzling last sentence in *One Writer's Beginnings:* "As you have seen, I am a writer who came of a sheltered life. A sheltered life can be a daring life as well. For all serious daring starts from within."

"Death of a Traveling Salesman" appeared in the June 1936 issue of *Manuscript.* Under the heading "The Contributors," Eudora wrote that she was twenty-six years old and living with her family in Jackson. "It would be interesting if I had been in jail or trodden grapes like other young people," she wrote. "I didn't even suffer early in life, except for my father's being from Ohio—a Yankee! . . . In Mississippi there is still a lot to be written . . . I [have] lost interest in writing stories that took place in Paris . . . In this one year I seem to have got my bearings."

"Death of a Traveling Salesman" has been the focus of many articles by academic critics. When someone mentioned to Eudora that a scholarly article discussed what the mule's face looking in the window meant, she replied tartly, "It means a mule was looking in the window."[6] She also said that the story was not a hallucination—that she wanted all her work to be taken as an event, wanted it to "stand on solid ground all the way through."[7] "Death of a Traveling Salesman" has also won great acclaim, with one critic, Eleanor Clark, comparing Arthur Miller's play *Death of a Salesman* invidiously to the Welty story.

Eudora's second publication was a story called "The Doll," which was published in the *Tanager,* a little magazine at Grinnell College in Iowa, in June 1936. It has never been collected, nor has "Magic," the second story to appear in *Manuscript.* "Magic" is about a working-class couple, Myrtle and Ralph, who make love in a cemetery. Myrtle has smeared on a perfumed love potion, but when she, a child of the Bible Belt, sees a statue of a lamb in front of her and one of an angel behind her, she screams, runs home, and throws out the potion.

The third magazine to buy a story was *River,* which was published briefly in Oxford, Mississippi. While she was working for the WPA, Eudora came to love the *Oxford Eagle,* a newspaper in which correspondents reported the news from all the little settlements around Oxford. One day in 1936 she wrote to the editor of the *Eagle,* enclosing a dollar for a six-month subscription and promising to find the dollar for the rest of the year before the six months were up. She told him that she had been reading his paper in the WPA Publicity Department and that she saved the country news in her scrapbook of Mississippiana.[8] She also said that she relished a letter from a man who moved from Corinth to Oma, in which he told the *Eagle* that he liked it down South but he had not seen a hill yet.[9] Eudora read a great many small Mississippi papers in addition to the *Oxford Eagle,* and they all carried letters from correspondents in even smaller towns. Her attachment to country newspapers led to her story "A Piece of News." "What Ruby Fisher [in "A Piece of News"] reads in the newspaper was the kind of thing that would be in those columns," she said. " 'So and So became shot,' or 'The Sunday visitors in town were . . .' That gave me a picture of what life was like, much as I think it did for Faulkner. I did know people like that. They are the material of Southern gothic."[10]

Dale Mullen, son of the *Eagle*'s owner, had ambitions to edit something more literary than a country newspaper. In 1934 he started the *Oxford* magazine, which survived for several issues and had published a poem and a short story by Eudora's friend and neighbor Hubert Creekmore, poetry by George Marion O'Donnell, and four poems by Shelby Foote, then a high school student at Greenville, Mississippi. In 1937 Mullen decided to start another magazine, *River,* even though he feared it would have "more subscribers in Montana than it did in Mississippi."[11] The first issue had notable contributions: Eudora's story "Retreat"; short stories by Peter Taylor of Memphis, who was then a student at Vanderbilt; fiction by Nash Burger and Hubert Creekmore, both living in Jackson; work by James K. Feibleman, the author of a book of poetry and three books of philosophy; and a critical article on the poet Merle Hoyleman by George Marion O'Donnell, at the time the best known of these Mississippi writers.

Mullen liked "Retreat" and wrote to ask Eudora if she had anything longer. They did not meet, though, until Eudora went to Oxford in June 1937, when they spent a long boozy afternoon drinking beer upstairs at the College Inn, a place run by two men whom Oxford people called "the Greeks." Kafka's *Metamorphosis* had run in two installments in *Transition,* and Eudora had read one installment and Mullen the other. They agreed to swap magazines.

Chapter 14

More Stories

1936–1940

In September 1936, Robert Penn Warren, the editor of the newly founded *Southern Review* at Louisiana State University in Baton Rouge, rejected a poem Eudora submitted.[1] He also turned down two of Eudora's stories, "The Petrified Man" and "Flowers for Marjorie," writing her that the comic effects in "The Petrified Man" were "absolutely first-rate" but he wasn't satisfied with the way it held together as a story. "About many aspects of your work we are enthusiastic, and we are absolutely confident that if you are good enough to submit other work to us, we can publish your things in THE SOUTHERN REVIEW," he wrote.[2]

A month later Warren wrote again to say he was beginning to regret that they had rejected "The Petrified Man" and they "might like to reopen the question of publication some time in the near future. But if you have anything else on hand, will you please let us see it."[3]

"The Petrified Man," a howlingly funny story told mostly by the appalling beauty shop operator Leota, zipped around to every magazine in America—and zipped back to Jackson. Some readers have regarded it as horrifying, but Eudora has said, "I thought it was funny."[4] It seems shocking now, but *Esquire* rejected the story because its author was a woman. "Wonderful beauty parlor atmosphere," an editor noted in an interoffice memo to the editor-in-chief, Arnold Gingrich. "Maybe we should make an exception." "Sorry," said Gingrich, "the atmosphere is fine, but on occasion the plot-details strain credulity."[5]

Warren finally bought a story from Eudora—"A Piece of News"—on May 17, 1937. He ran it quickly, in the summer 1937 issue, and paid real money. (Tradition has it that Albert Erskine, the business manager and later the husband of Katherine Anne Porter, "discovered" Eudora's stories at the *Southern Review*.)[6] It was the first money Eudora had earned from fiction, and she used it to screen the side porch, a repair that cost a little more than forty-two dollars. Years later, winds from Hurricane Camille took off the screening, and "they wanted something like $400 to rescreen it, so I just had the old screen carried away," she said.[7]

Although they did not meet face to face for twenty years, Red Warren and Eudora became friends by mail, and remained good friends until Warren died. Warren had gone to Vanderbilt, where he was one of the Fugitive poets. Back from Oxford and a Rhodes scholarship, he was teaching English at Louisiana State University in 1935 when the flamboyant Louisiana governor Huey Long decided he wanted "his" university to have a literary magazine. Warren, then thirty, and Cleanth Brooks, another young professor, Vanderbilt alumnus, and Rhodes Scholar, were chosen to run it. They announced the founding of the *Southern Review* at a writers' conference in Baton Rouge.

Around the same time, *Prairie Schooner* took "Flowers for Marjorie." One of Eudora's few stories set outside Mississippi, it is a tale of the Depression, recounting the despair of an unemployed man who kills his wife. Eudora later dismissed it as "a poor story" and "too literary" and said she had no business writing "an artificial story" about a city. The only thing about it she could remember in a 1979 interview was how the murderer "walked up from the subway between those heavy, fat, warm ladies."[8]

Eudora's good friend John Robinson was now working in New Orleans as a claims adjuster for New York Life Insurance. He and Eudora stayed in touch, even though his work took him all over Mississippi and Louisiana. In New Orleans he lived with Bob Farley, a friend of William Faulkner's from Oxford, and Farley's wife, Alice.

Robinson was wildly interested in the old houses and cemeteries in Louisiana and Mississippi and spent his time on weekends exploring. He crawled under brambles in the old cemetery at Woodville, Mississippi, to look at tombstones. He found the house of his great-great-grandfather, Nicholas MacDougall, in Port Gibson, two houses down from the Presbyterian church, which had a hand with a finger pointing heavenward on top of its steeple. He visited the Stanton sisters, three "crack-brained old relics," in their old home, Windy Hill Manor, in Natchez; they had nothing left but "faded ancestral glory" and a family portrait by Gilbert Stuart.[9] It was also about this time that Robinson was urging his cousin Nan to have his great-great-grandmother's diary, which she owned, copied. He threatened to run up and hire a stenographer and get it copied himself. This was the diary that stoked the fires of Eudora's imagination when she started on *Delta Wedding*. He relayed all his findings to Eudora and to Bill Hamilton.

In the summer of 1937, Eudora drove to Mexico with Robinson, his sister Anna Belle, and another young man. The trip was a real adventure, from which Eudora brought back drawings. They wandered off the beaten track and stayed in a little house "with tiles and tiger skins," in the mountains where people hunted big game. The people who lived there had made the furniture, carved the doors, and woven the rugs. At one point they were flooded in and had to be pulled out by two teams of oxen.

When they were on the way home, a little Mexican girl ran out in front of their car on the highway north of Mexico City, and they hit her. When they stopped, a handsome man at a filling station/souvenir shop offered to take the little girl to Mexico City to get the best treatment. They gave him money and he departed with the child. There was supposed to be some sort of legal action, so the four young Americans waited. The little hotel where they stayed was so hot that they had to sit outside during the daytime. They could not drink the water, and Eudora said they even had to brush their teeth with Coca-Cola.[10] Robinson was threatened with jail, Eudora told George Marion O'Donnell.[11] Bob Farley wrote to Bill Hamilton that he heard Robinson talk about "his imprisonment," but whether Robinson was actually imprisoned or not is not clear.[12] When the young people finally called the American consul in Mexico City to ask for advice, the consul told them to leave town. Wait until late in the day, he said, get in the car, and go—and don't stop until you cross the border.

Back home, Eudora continued to write. "I sent off stuff in the mail to magazines, and it all came back," she said. "That didn't bother me. I just sent it somewhere else. Because I was writing something new."[13] Her little literary group was still active. Eudora urged O'Donnell to come to Jackson to see them. She had some African dance and song records—drums—and the Brandenburg Concertos, and Frank Lyell had some Johnnie Walker.[14]

On September 23, 1937, Red Warren bought "A Memory," a story of a young girl who lies on a lakeside beach like the one at Livingston Park in Jackson and makes a frame of her hands through which she looks at the world around her, just as Mrs. Hull had taught her art students to do. Eudora has said that "the tableau discovered through the young girl's framing hands is unwelcome realism."[15] The girl thinks about the boy with whom she fell in love during the school year just past. She loves him silently and from a distance, and apparently they do not speak. A group of vulgar bathers settles down near this innocent, fastidious dreamer. Is she the young Eudora? In love with a mediocre youth to whom she doesn't speak? Repelled by those inferior to her in sensibility?

A few months later, Warren bought "Old Mr. Grenada," which he said was "very brilliantly done."[16] Old Mr. Grenada of the fictional town of Brewster later became Old Mr. Marblehall of Natchez, who lives a double life, maintaining two families—two wives, two sons—unknown to each other. Asked if this story was a fantasy, Eudora replied that it was not, it was an expression of the fantastic life of Natchez.[17] One critic has speculated that one of Mr. Marblehall's families was black.

Eudora sent Warren "The Key," which is about a deaf-mute couple waiting for a train. Thirty years later, when she was visiting a student seminar at the University of Kentucky, one student tried to find symbols in the many insects she had mentioned in "The Key." When he finished, Eudora said, "There sure are a lot of bugs in Mississippi," adding that the bugs were her first conscious use of symbolism in a story.

Warren returned "The Key." "I remember the day 'The Key' came back, there was no letter at all attached, just the naked story—it may have been a mistake, but that was a blank feeling," she wrote a few years later. "Even with the good luck I had in finding [the *Southern Review*] at the start, I wonder that I kept on writing."[18]

.   .   .

"My friend Eudora Welty is in New York," John Robinson wrote to Nancy Farley, Bob Farley's sister, in January 1938. "I think she is trying to sell some negro pictures and a story. They are marvelous. Get her to show them to you. She is staying at the Barbizon and I told her to get in touch with you all. Make her tell what has been happening to her. She's marvelous. Everything happens to her and she feels it all and conveys it all. See if you don't think so."[19]

Eudora was now turning out a torrent of first-class short stories. She wrote every minute and revised nothing, and she pretty much ignored publishers who wanted her to write a novel instead of stories.[20] Rood had told her that New York publishers noticed *Manuscript,* and he was right. Harold Strauss of Covici Friede, a left-wing publisher, wrote immediately after the publication of "Death of a Traveling Salesman," talking about Eudora's "broad social perspective." He thought she "owed it to herself to undertake a novel," and he refused to consider a volume of short stories by an unknown author.[21] Nevertheless, Eudora sent him "Black Saturday."

Strauss wrote to Eudora that she had "the dubious honor of having occasioned the most protracted discussion in this office of any author I can remember." After they had looked at her book of photographs and stories, they had no doubt that she had great talent, both as a short story writer and as a photographer, he said. But their research indicated that booksellers would not like the book—they would not know how to classify it. It was essential, Strauss said, if she was to make progress in the world of letters, to devote herself to a novel.[22]

Harriet Colby of Reynal and Hitchcock admired "Lily Daw," Eudora's study of three busybody matrons who send a young girl off to the state insane asylum, and wondered if Eudora was working on a novel. When Eudora did not answer, Colby wrote again.[23] Eudora offered her "Black Saturday," and Colby wrote declining it, but suggested that she save the stories until she became an established novelist.[24] Whit Burnett turned down "Keela, the Outcast Indian Maid" and asked her to submit a novel for Story Press, and Harriet Colby wrote for the fourth time asking about the novel. "We don't want to lose track of you," she said.[25]

On March 23, 1938, Warren added to the pressure when he suggested that Eudora compete for the Houghton Mifflin fiction award, given for a first novel. He, Cleanth Brooks, and Katherine Anne Porter would sponsor her. As an afterthought, he asked her for another look at "The Petrified Man." In the fall of that year he bought "A Curtain of Green" and asked yet again to see "The Petrified Man."

Eudora had been so discouraged because "The Petrified Man" had come back so often that she had burned it. After this last request from Warren, she sat down and wrote it again. Since it was a told story, she said, it was easy to remember. "You know, I could sort of play it back like a record in my ear. I couldn't have written an internal story over again, but I wrote that."[26] It appeared in the *Review*'s spring 1939 issue. For years she worried for fear she had done something wrong and the second version was not exactly the story Warren had wanted. When she met him twenty years later, she asked him if what she had done was unethical. "You wrote both of them, didn't you?" he asked.

Following through on Warren's suggestion, she wrote ninety pages of a novel, "The Cheated," for the Houghton Mifflin contest. A girl from Idaho won the competition with a novel about the Mormon migration, and R. N. Linscott sent Eudora's manuscript back with rather severe criticism: she had "apprehended" the situations and characters instead of thinking them out, and the story had "the quality of a dream or fantasy," he said.[27] Eudora threw the manuscript away.[28] (She later said it had been a version of her story "The Key".) Robert Penn Warren made encouraging noises. If "it wasn't that, it will be something else and soon," he said.[29]

Harry Hansen, then the editor of the *O. Henry Prize Stories,* included "The Petrified Man" in the 1939 volume. (Coincidentally, the other Jackson writer, Richard Wright, had a story in the 1938 O. Henry collection, and another in the 1940 collection.) "Speaking of Eudora, did you happen to read in the *New York Times* book review supplement about a story she contributed to last O'Henry collection? Some reviewer picked out her story as being the best and gave it very high praise," John Robinson wrote to Nancy Farley. (It was Robert Van Gelder, one of Eudora's greatest fans, who reviewed the O. Henry collection for the *New York Times* on November 19, 1939.) "I'm going to send you a sketch she sent me some time back," Robinson continued. "She's been writing a good deal recently about circus and carnival folk. She also writes about the rural Oxford people and is going to write a novel about them. I think I told you how much she likes the rural news in the Oxford *Eagle*."[30] That novel, which eventually became *Losing Battles,* published in 1970, had a very long gestation period.

After Eudora became a favorite contributor to *Southern Review,* Katherine Anne Porter wrote her to say that Ford Madox Ford, who had just taken over at the Dial Press, was looking for new authors; Porter had thought first of Eudora and her "admirable short stories" and suggested that she write to Ford and tell him about any book-length collection of stories she might have. (Porter was already famous, having published *Flowering Judas and Other Stories, Hacienda,* and *Noon Wine.*) Porter also said she would be happy to nominate Eudora for a Guggenheim in 1940.

Eudora promptly sent along her stories to Ford, who wrote that she had a very remarkable gift and "should arrive at great things" but he could not be her publisher.[31] She lost this advocate when Ford died unexpectedly in 1939. "I feel that I never thanked him enough," Eudora wrote to Porter. She also told Porter she had written a hundred-page story and would appreciate Porter's advice, but she wanted Porter to do nothing unless it would "leave you untaxed."[32]

Porter invited Eudora to go down to Baton Rouge to see her, but it took Eudora several months to get up the nerve to go. Twice she went as far as Natchez and turned around. She finally made it in July 1939, when Herschel and Norma Brickell, who knew Katherine Anne, went with her. The three of them had dinner at Katherine Anne's house and talked all evening "in the cool old house with all the windows open." Porter was struck by the "quiet, tranquil-looking, modest girl."[33] And Eudora was profoundly impressed by the successful woman writer, stunningly beautiful with her white hair and wide, movie-star eyes. Katherine Anne Porter and Eudora became friends, or rather generous mentor and devoted protégé, and remained friends, though sometimes uneasy ones, until Porter's death. Porter was, Eudora said years later, "the first person I met or knew who very consciously was aware she was an artist and that she was practicing an art and who respected it above all things that anyone could do."[34]

After the visit, Eudora wrote "Miss Porter" a thank-you note. She wanted to send her something for her new house. The best thing would be a mimosa shoot from the garden, but it would be better to wait until fall to send it. She invited Katherine Anne to Jackson. "Maybe we could have a good time—we'd love to see you. I have a little Mozart."[35]

While Eudora was turning out stories, for several months during the summer of 1939 she worked for Bill Hamilton, copying documents and portions of old newspapers in the state archives. Hamilton had written his dissertation at Duke on the Mississippi Territory, and, still at Duke, was working on his book *Anglo-American Law on the Frontier: Thomas Rodney and His Territorial Cases.* She sent carbons of some of the old newspaper stories on the theater to Herschel Brickell, who was writing a book about Natchez. Nash Burger was also working at the archives that summer, doing a history and inventory for Grenada County, and he came in every morning to see that she did not "loll and droop" over the manuscripts.[36] Hamilton paid very poorly; one check on August 9 was for six dollars.

Eudora had to stop working for Hamilton when she got a real job with the Mississippi Advertising Commission. Hamilton congratulated her and hoped she could reform the commission. He had once pointed out half a dozen errors in one of its brochures, but the employee did not seem at all bothered by factual errors.

At the Advertising Commission, Eudora was taken to an office, given a typewriter, a file, and a long list of magazines (ranging from *Town and Country* and *Resort World* to *Farm and Ranch* and the *North American Trapper*), and told to write an anonymous article about Mississippi every day and send it off (without return postage) with suitable photos. It was not like her WPA publicity job—no interviews, no trips, no people; "basement work, like bomb-making." She was supposed to be paid through January but expected to be fired at any moment.[37]

In November 1939, John Woodburn, an editor from Doubleday, traveled through the South looking for new writers, as publishers did in those days. In Baton Rouge, Woodburn heard about Eudora Welty, and he went through Jackson on his way north. Chestina cooked waffles for him, he looked at Eudora's photographs, and he had a fine time. Best of all, he scooped up Eudora's short stories and took them with him. From New York he wrote to thank Eudora for the most impressive and unaffected hospitality he had encountered in the South. He told her that the editors were reading her stories and that he had perjured himself and said she was hard at work on a novel. He also sent her two books, one about Lizzie Borden and one about Ruth Snyder—"two women of great power," as he put it.[38]

In early 1940, however, Woodburn returned the story collection, reporting that he was unable to persuade his colleagues at Doubleday to buy it. Eudora gamely kept sending the manuscript out. Editors at G. P. Putnam's Sons, Harcourt Brace, and Houghton Mifflin rejected the stories and urged her to write a novel, using terms such as "beg" and "beseech." Eudora gave in to the pressure and began "putting down stuff for a novel." She planned to work on it that summer at the Bread Loaf Writers Conference at Middlebury, Vermont. At Herschel Brickell's suggestion, Katherine Anne Porter had recommended her for a fellowship there.[39]

Eudora continued to send individual stories to magazines. "Why I Live at the P.O." was still making the rounds, and she finally sold "Keela, the Outcast Indian Maiden" for nine dollars to James Laughlin of the New Directions Press in Norfolk, Connecticut, to be included in *New Directions in Prose and Poetry.* The story, she said, had been conceived when she was working for the Works Progress Administration and was really about the moral response to the situation of the little black man who was made to eat live chickens in the sideshow.[40]

Chapter 15

Diarmuid Russell

1940

In May, Eudora received a letter from Diarmuid Russell, who offered to be her literary agent. He and Russell Volkening had just opened a new literary agency in New York. Russell was the son of George William Russell, known as A.E., the Irish writer and editor, whose work Eudora had encountered while she was at Wisconsin. Diarmuid came to the United States and worked first in a bookstore and then for several years as an editor at Putnam's. When he was fired for taking the author's part in a dispute over a contract, he and Volkening decided to take the advice of the famed Scribner's editor Maxwell Perkins and open their own agency. Perkins thought there were too few agencies in New York and fewer still that helped their clients with their manuscripts. Russell hoped to fill this need.

When John Woodburn at Doubleday heard that Russell was looking for clients, he suggested Eudora Welty. She received one of Russell's first recruiting letters, a typical soft sell, referring to the "parasitic way an agent works taking 10% of the author's takings." The agent was, Russell said, "rather a benevolent parasite because authors as a rule make more when they have an agent than they do without one."[1]

Eudora had never heard of a literary agent and was not clear about what one was. Nevertheless, she replied immediately: "Dear Mr. Russell,

Thanks for your letter. Yes—be my agent." She also told him that *Southern Review* had been publishing her stories and perhaps the story she enclosed, "Clytie," would sell there. Or would this make his job too easy? she asked.[2]

Russell, surprised and pleased with the promptness of her reply, wrote back immediately to say that he would not dream of sending "Clytie" to the *Southern Review*. Agents took ten percent, he wrote, but he wouldn't take ten percent for sending a story somewhere she could send it herself. He asked her to send him a few more stories. He would keep this first one, which he said he found somewhat obscure, until the others arrived. Sometimes, he said, it was better to offer editors a selection.

"Clytie" is the story of an old maid who is berated by her sister, Octavia. The two of them live with their brother and their half-dead father in a decaying house at Farr's Gin, a crumbling little town where the residents treat the family as ghosts. In despair and confusion, Clytie drowns herself in the rain barrel one morning. Eudora tried to explain to Russell why he found "Clytie" unclear. Clytie could not concentrate, she said, and therefore the face she sought in the barrel was indefinite.[3] It would take a long time for Clytie's story to find a home.

"That was my break, when Diarmuid wrote to me," said Eudora, who was Russell's first client, forty years later. "If it hadn't been for him, I don't know if I'd have ever been published. I really mean it, because he worked like everything just because he believed in the stories . . . When he did think you were good he was tireless . . . Everybody trusted him implicitly. Gee, was I ever lucky."[4]

In her second letter, Eudora told Russell about her short story collection, "by an unknown writer who doesn't ever want to write a novel first."[5] She could not even name all the editors who had seen the stories. Ford Madox Ford had sent them to some editors, and she had sent them to others, and all of them had said they could not publish a short story collection by an unknown writer. She did not want to stop writing short stories.

She wouldn't have to, Russell told her, and he sent the collection out again. (Eudora apparently abandoned "putting down stuff" for a novel.) Maxwell Perkins said Eudora was a good writer, but he would never start off any author with a short story collection. Duell, Sloan & Pierce rejected it, as did Reynal and Hitchcock and Viking Press.[6]

Meanwhile, Eudora sent Russell more stories, all of which had also been rejected by several magazines. Before June was over she sent him a new, very long, romantic story about bandits and a fair maiden at Rodney's Landing, near Natchez. Eudora later said she had dreamed parts of this story and had written down the dreams when she woke up. This story would eventually become *The Robber Bridegroom,* but for some time she and Russell referred to it only as "the fantasy."

Then she sent him "Powerhouse," which she had written after she and other jazz fans in her crowd in Jackson attended a Fats Waller concert. She came home from the concert and in one sitting wrote this powerful short story about a black musician on the road. She explained later that she tried to turn the frantic beat of jazz musicians into an exchange of words to capture the assault of the performance. She said she was not musically qualified to write it, but she was "writing about a demon."[7] She was just "one of the people hanging around listening," she told an interviewer. She was trying to express something about the music in the story, "what I thought of as an improvisation, which I was watching them do, but making him improvise this crazy story, which I just made up as I went . . . I didn't hear anything like that."[8]

Russell was convinced of the high quality of her stories and impressed by their broad range of themes and subjects. He sent them out over and over again. At times he feared his new client would lose confidence in him, as he seemed to be unable to convince editors how good her stories were. Eudora reassured him that she would not be "bitter" if he never sold the stories, just impressed if he did.[9]

Chapter 16

Bread Loaf

1940

On her way to Bread Loaf in the late summer, Eudora met Diarmuid Russell in person in New York City. When Russell took her out to his house at Katonah, New York, and she met his family, it was the beginning of a long and warm friendship.

Then it was off to Bread Loaf. A philanthropist named Joseph Batell had left Vermont's Middlebury College thirty thousand acres of Green Mountain forest and a dozen buildings in what used to be the little town of Ripton. The college used these buildings, including the Bread Loaf Inn, to house two new summer programs. The Bread Loaf School of English lasted six weeks, and the writers' conference, the first of its kind in the United States, was scheduled to fill a blank in the inn's schedule after the School of English. Theodore Morrison, who had been on the staff of the *Atlantic Monthly* but now taught at Harvard, was director that year.

The staff included Eudora's old friend Herschel Brickell, who had left Henry Holt and was back at the *New York Post* as a reviewer. Other staffers were serious writers John Gassner, John Marquand, and Wallace Stegner, and the pulp writer Fletcher Pratt. Visiting speakers were Katherine Anne Porter, W. H. Auden, and the Louisville journalist and author Herbert

Agar. Robert Frost, who lived nearby, and Louis Untermeyer were consultants in poetry.

The fellows, the elite students, got free tuition and room and board. Besides Eudora, the 1940 fellows were Carson McCullers, a twenty-three-year-old Georgia novelist; John Ciardi, a twenty-four-year-old poet; Brainard "Lon" Cheney, a Nashville newspaperman who had published a novel, *Lightwood,* in 1939 and was working on a second; Marion Sims; and Edna Frederikson, a fledgling writer from Harrisonburg, Virginia. Richard Ellmann, who was to become famous as the biographer of James Joyce, was not a fellow but a student working off his tuition in the dining room and on the grounds crew.

McCullers had been born Lula Carson Smith in Columbus, Georgia. She went to New York to study music in 1935, but after she lost her tuition money on the subway, she enrolled in night writing classes at Columbia instead. Whit Burnett of *Story,* one of her teachers, published her first short story. She had won a Houghton Mifflin fellowship to finish *The Heart Is a Lonely Hunter,* which had just been published. *Reflections in a Golden Eye,* which she wrote in two months, was about to be published. People at Bread Loaf that summer described her as "skinny, puckish, androgynous,"[1] "a pug-nosed little girl with black bangs," and a "gangly, skinny girl who wore boys' white shirts and changed them three times a day."[2] Fannie Cheney, Lon Cheney's wife, was less charitable. "She looked just like a Spitz dog," said Fannie. "Her tongue and mouth were black. Untermeyer had a mad crush on Carson; he served cocktails every afternoon made out of the worst gin, and Carson would tell us how Negro spirituals were such a pure art form. She stayed in a state of invincible ignorance. Eudora did not care for her."[3] Eudora, in fact, detested Carson McCullers for her pretensions and poses.

Someone described Eudora that summer as "tall and blonde and thirty-one, with an easy smile and dreamy, quickly averting gaze."[4] She was older than Ciardi but younger than Cheney, who was forty. People who met her for the first time noticed her looks—she was stooped, and her face was not pretty—but they immediately warmed to her freshness and innocence. Those who knew her work, with its revelation of madness, anger, loneliness, and violence, marveled at how she still seemed shy and untouched. Her genuine modesty always surprised people, and her humor and gusto for the droll and absurd delighted everyone who met her. The Cheneys liked her immensely, and Eudora, in her long white nightgown, went to their room every night to talk over the day's events.

Life at Bread Loaf was full of activities: lectures, seminars, plenty of recreation—square dancing in the barn, hikes on the foot trails, baseball games (Robert Frost was the captain of a softball team), swimming, croquet, volleyball, and tennis—and cocktails for the staff and fellows every evening in Treman Cottage, where the seedy living room was filled with ancient wicker furniture. Wallace Stegner described the Treman parlor as a "combination of Plato's Academy and Walpurgisnacht."[5] Kenneth McCormick, an editor at Doubleday who was there that summer, remembered afterward that Eudora "played the piano and sang fabulous ballads."[6]

On the whole, Eudora detested Bread Loaf. She did not find the workshops helpful. The opinion in one workshop, where students and fellows read their work aloud for criticism, was unanimous, for instance, that no one would ever buy her story "Powerhouse." She was appalled at the "poor ladies taking longhand notes," but supposed they would come back next year.[7]

Katherine Anne Porter went to Bread Loaf to read her work and lecture on the techniques of fiction, and spent a great deal of time with Eudora, who always deferred to her. The relationship between the established writer, an older woman who had had many lovers and several husbands, and the newcomer, a still innocent young woman, became more intense. David Laskin, in his book about four literary friendships, *A Common Life,* points out that part of Eudora's charm for Porter was her lack of threat as a competitor for sexual trophies. A few years later, Eudora confided to Caroline Gordon, the novelist and wife of the poet and critic Allen Tate, that she had told Porter she was still a virgin. "And you always will be," Porter had replied.[8]

After Porter finished her lecture at Bread Loaf, she asked if there were questions from the audience. There were many questions, mostly from Eudora. After the meeting, staff and fellows drifted off toward Treman Cottage, Eudora and Porter still talking, oblivious of everyone else. Wallace Stegner recalled watching them at Treman Cottage, "Porter enthroned in an armchair, holding forth in her soft Texas accent, with Eudora sitting worshipfully at her feet."[9]

Three nights later, W. H. Auden, then only thirty-three, read his poetry. He was very shy and self-conscious until he went to the lectern, and then he came alive. This time it was Carson McCullers's turn to monopolize the star of the evening; she and Auden appropriated Wallace Stegner's bottle of bourbon and drank it, talking only to each other.

When she left Bread Loaf, Eudora wanted to go home by way of Saratoga Springs, New York, to see Porter, who had invited her for a visit. Porter had separated from her husband, Albert Erskine, and was living near Yaddo, a writer's colony at Saratoga Springs. Edna Frederikson had offered to drive Eudora, but Eudora hesitated, afraid that the dreaded Carson McCullers might tag along. When McCullers decided to go off to Boston, Eudora thought it would be safe to go to Saratoga with Edna.[10]

Porter was waiting at the gate to the farmhouse where she was staying when Edna and Eudora drove up. She introduced Eudora to James Laughlin, the founder and publisher of the avant-garde New Directions Press, who had bought "Keela, the Outcast Indian Maiden." Porter hoped Laughlin might publish Eudora's story collection.[11]

Eudora described Yaddo as "weird . . . very solemn, cathedral-like, everything done in a hushed way, priceless gems and relics standing in the marble halls, fountains tinkling, chapel-like, tiptoeing, etc."[12] Porter served dinner to Eudora, Edna, and James Still, a young southern writer who had published a novel, *River of Earth,* and a book of poems, *Hounds on the Mountains.* After the dinner party, Still took the two younger women to one of Saratoga's late-night bars where the racetrack people congregated.

Back home in Jackson, Eudora encouraged her friends to try calypso music, which she and the Cheneys had enjoyed at Bread Loaf. Eudora performed on gourds, and other people got combs and put tissue paper on them, and someone used her brother's guitar, and these very serious, intense performers invented calypso songs about local events, including one called "Eudora She Went Up to Bread Loaf."

Chapter 17

The Natchez Trace

1940

*"And at the foot of this ravine ran the Old Natchez Trace,
that old buffalo trail where travelers passed along and were
set upon by bandits and the Indians and torn apart by the
wild animals."*
The Robber Bridegroom

On the long train trip from New York to Jackson, Eudora had begun
to think about her next book. Diarmuid Russell had suggested that she write
about Mississippi history, and she had sent him a long letter telling him how
appealing the suggestion was. There were things about Mississippi, she said,
that only a long-time resident could know—old and new stories about violent events, songs, and Indian legends. She mentioned the sun-worshipping
Natchez Indians, who tortured their victims and had been wiped out on the
site of Natchez; Aaron Burr, who had wanted to start a new empire in the
old southwest, and his friend and ally, Harman Blennerhassett; John James
Audubon, who painted birds; the brigands Murrell and the Harpe brothers;
Jefferson Davis; Lafayette and the pirate Lafitte; and the miraculous occur-

rences of the winter of 1811, when the Mississippi Valley endured an earthquake, a comet arrived, and the river froze.[1]

She decided that the Old Natchez Trace, once an important highway, could be the unifying element for a group of stories. The trace and its history had always fascinated her. "When Eudora Welty talks about the trace, she has the rosy cheeks and the excited look of a little girl," a French reporter said much later. "She begins to resemble a brigand, or the captain of a river boat, a pioneer."[2]

When Eudora got back to Jackson, she drove down to the Trace and walked along part of it. Now abandoned, the roadbed had sunk deep into the ground with wear and erosion, and the banks on either side were thick with wild growth. Once the most important highway in the old southwest, the Trace had been 450 miles long, connecting Nashville to Natchez when Natchez was on the nation's western frontier. Buffalo had pounded out the trail first, then Indians had used it, then missionaries, naturalists, traders, settlers, and highwaymen. Jackson owed its existence to the Trace—the first settlement in the area had been a French trading post established in 1782 on a bluff over the Pearl River, because it was not far from the Trace. Not until a treaty with the Indians opened the territory to serious white settlement in 1820 did LeFleur's Bluff become Jackson, a rough frontier town with dirt streets and wooden sidewalks and a state capitol.

Russell and Eudora had both read Robert Coates's *The Outlaw Years: The History of the Land Pirates of the Natchez Trace,* which recounts in lively fashion the lives and deaths of several bandits and highwaymen, including Micajah and Wiley Harpe, known as Big Harpe and Little Harpe, who were obviously deranged. Another outlaw, John Murrell, was a dandy who had his suits tailored in New Orleans, got his hats from Philadelphia, and rode the finest horses. He was also quite merciless and invariably killed anyone he robbed so he could not be identified.

Eudora approached these tales of the trace with a firm grounding in folklore and fairy tales. After her parents gave her the ten-volume set of *Our Wonder World* on her tenth birthday, her favorite volume became number 5, *Every Child's Story Book,* which was full of fairy tales by Hans Christian Andersen and the Brothers Grimm, Greek and Norse myths, the fables of Aesop, and stories of Robin Hood and Saint George and the Dragon. She loved them, stored them deep in her memory, and retrieved them whenever she needed them throughout her writing life. The stories about the Natchez Trace reminded her of Grimms' fairy tales. Bandits lived in the woods along the Trace, sometimes in caves, carried off maidens, and robbed people of their gold and killed them and threw them in the river. It was all very Grimm.

She began rewriting the "wild and gay and scarey" story about Rodney's Landing, "the fantasy," following Russell's suggestion that she eliminate everything modern about it. While the Grimms' tales, as she pointed out, used elements that were familiar to the hearers at the time—forest, woodcutter, castle, robber baron, serf, brigand, duke, swineherd, meadow, and toll bridge—she saw the possibilities in components that meant more to Americans, especially southerners—the Trace itself, the river country, swamp, the Delta, Indian relics, cabins, old houses, landings, and plantations. She threw in timeless devices of folktales: a wicked stepmother, a talking bird, and disappearance into the forest. Eudora said she wrote "like a demon" until she finished rewriting it, at 102 pages.[3]

The tale, which she eventually called *The Robber Bridegroom,* involves the beautiful blond Rosamond, who has a gentle, rich father and an awful stepmother; a handsome bandit named Jamie Lockhart; and a Fool named Goat. Little Harpe figures in it, as does Mike Fink, the legendary Mississippi boatman. Jamie Lockhart first robs Rosamond of all her clothes and leaves her to make her way home naked; the next day he encounters her again and lays her "on the ground, where, straight below, the river flowed as slow as sand, and robbed her of that which he had left her the night before." He takes her to his hideaway, but his face is always stained with berry juice, so she has no idea what he really looks like. He makes love to her every night and goes out to rob people every day.

It is a violent story—Little Harpe rapes an Indian maiden on a table while a band of robbers look on; several villains, including Little Harpe, the robbers (all but Jamie), and the wicked stepmother are killed. Eudora later defended the violence in the novel by pointing out that history "tells us worse things than fairy tales do. People were scalped. Babies had their brains dashed out against tree trunks or were thrown into boiling oil when the Indians made their capture . . . The Natchez Trace outlaws eviscerated their victims and rolled their bodies downhill, filled with stones, into the Mississippi River."[4]

It was a "wild tale," she told Herschel Brickell, but not historical—in fact, quite inaccurate.[5] "I wrote in a swashbuckling kind of way. I just let go," she said.[6] She never looked anything up while she was writing it, and it was in no sense a historical novel, she told the Mississippi Historical Society in 1975. She used elements from the history books but did not try to keep it historically accurate. For instance, the house that Salome Musgrove, the evil stepmother, wants to build in 1798—"at least five stories high, with an observatory of the river on top of that, with twenty-two Corinthian columns to hold up the roof"—was based on Windsor Castle, near Port Gibson, which had not been built until 1861.[7] Rosamond, the heroine, Eudora said, was based on the "Rodney heiresses" of the period. It was historical fact that Little Harpe kept his brother's head in a trunk; the head was like money in the bank, since he could always turn it in and claim the reward. The mail rider who rescues Rosamond and takes her to New Orleans was based on John L. Swaney, a real mail rider, who was known to have picked up the wife and baby of a bandit and helped them along their way. Eudora's mail rider turns out to be Mike Fink, cowed and disgraced, but as she points out, "Instead of burying itself deep in historical fact, [the book] flew up like a cuckoo and alighted in a borrowed nest of fantasy."[8]

Nash Burger read the tale in manuscript. "I can't go for most of her stories," he wrote to Bill Hamilton, but this was "as original as Irwin Russell's negro dialect verse. . . . She has written a story of the very early Natchez country around Rodney (Mason and Harpe days) in the extremely arch, simple style of the early ballads." It was prose, Burger went on, but it used the impossible, the supernatural, the violence of ballads. "It's as exciting to me as a newly discovered play by Shakespeare. Of course, Eudora . . . always acts as bewildered when you try to discuss literary matters as if she never read a line, much less wrote one."[9]

While she surely wrote this tale out of a passion for the romance of the Natchez Trace, drawing on her knowledge of Mississippi history and tapping her memory of fairy tales and folktales, the story must also have embodied her own personal fantasy. She was a single woman, thirty-one years old, a virgin, at a time and in a place where all women were supposed to be spoken for long before they reached that age. She had seen a lot of handsome, literary John Robinson, who had left Jackson. Did she not long to be ravished, just as Rosamond Musgrove was agreeably ravished by the handsome, berry-stained Jamie Lockhart?

She finished the story by October 1, 1940, and sent it to Russell, who liked it but doubted its commercial value. He sent it on to John Woodburn, who tried to sell it to his superiors at Doubleday. It was "a very savory dish," Woodburn wrote her, but he thought it should be the hors d'oeuvre preceding an entrée, which should be a whole book of stories about Mississippi, some fantastic, some realistic. "Why not go to the window, squash your nose against the window-pane, stare out at the Jackson-vista and dream of a book?" he wrote.[10]

Eudora did just that.

Russell wrote that he was sorry and embarrassed that he hadn't been able to sell the other stories for her. (Although Russell had not sold a single story for Eudora in the six months she had been his client, she had recommended him to Katherine Anne Porter, Peter Taylor, Lon Cheney, and Hubert Creekmore. She wanted all the southern writers to be in Russell's care, she said.)[11] As for writing a novel, Russell said, she must do what she felt like doing. The only real value he could see in writing one, he said, was that a novel was an arduous piece of work that demanded concentration and hard work and "this is good for everybody."[12]

Russell wrote constantly to Eudora, always encouraging her, promising her that editors would someday wake up and recognize the quality of her fiction. He quoted Katherine Anne Porter, who had told him "there was nothing to be done but keep [Eudora] writing, and in the course of time everything would be all right." He agreed heartily.[13]

Chapter 18

The *Atlantic Monthly*

1940–1941

One day Eudora went on a sketching trip with her artist friend Helen Lotterhos to the Old Canton Road, "when the Old Canton Road was in the country." She sat there and read while Lotterhos painted. At one point she looked up from her book and saw the tiny distant figure of a woman come out of the woods and move across a clearing until she disappeared into the woods on the other side. "I knew that she was going somewhere," Eudora said. "I knew that she was bent on an errand, even at that distance. It was not anything casual."[1]

That brief vision lit the fuse for one of her best stories, "A Worn Path." In it, Phoenix Jackson, regular as clockwork, takes the long walk from the Old Natchez Trace to the clinic in town to get medicine for her grandchild, who swallowed lye years ago. Is Phoenix Jackson's grandchild dead? Students write to ask Eudora this question, and people who hear her read "A Worn Path" make the same query. The story would mean less, she tells them, if the child were dead. "While it may certainly suggest that the old lady would probably keep going on her path to the end of her days if the child died before her, for the duration of the story the child is alive and needs help and the old lady is going to get it for him, and the path is worn," she once wrote.[2]

This was actually the first of Eudora's stories that mentioned the Natchez Trace, but it was collected along with her other early stories in her first book in 1941, while the other trace stories appeared later, in *The Wide Net,* published in 1942. She sent "The Worn Path" to Russell, along with "Powerhouse," the story she wrote the night after she went to the Fats Waller concert, which had just come back from *Southern Review.*

She took time to write to Fannie Cheney, commenting on Carson McCullers's story in *Harper's Bazaar,* where to her horror McCullers was identified as "a writer's writer." Since she knew Lon Cheney would never read the story through, she copied out a sentence for him: "Clinging crabwise to the runaway horse there was a grin of rapture on his bloody mouth." Eudora added that "Even nobody's writer couldn't have written that, I say."[3]

Meanwhile, Richard Wright, Eudora's Jackson contemporary, had become famous. He had gone to Chicago, joined the Communist party, moved to New York, and sold some stories to *Story* magazine. In 1940, his novel *Native Son* appeared and became an immediate best-seller.

Eudora's luck also turned. On December 3, 1940, Edward A. Weeks, the editor of the *Atlantic Monthly,* bought both "Powerhouse" and "A Worn Path." It was an astonishing turn of events. "Thank heaven for some perspicuity somewhere," Russell wrote to Eudora.[4]

Eudora was delighted that a magazine as lofty as the *Atlantic* would buy not just one story but two. She had a special feeling for this magazine, since she was distantly related to Walter Hines Page, who had once been the editor. (Like all southerners, she liked to strike up a kinship whenever possible.) And it was delightful that they had bought "Powerhouse," in spite of the unanimous opinion at Bread Loaf that it would never be published.

It was, however, mildly annoying that the *Atlantic* censored "Powerhouse." The editors said they could not publish the lyrics of "Hold Tight, I Want Some Seafood, Mama," the song she had chosen to end it with, with its great line "fooly racky sacky, want some seafood, Mama." She was forced to substitute "Somebody Loves Me, I Wonder Who."[5]

The *Atlantic* paid $200 for each story, less than the *Saturday Evening Post* but more than the *Southern Review,* and the prestige was enormous. She wrote about her good fortune to Robert Daniel, telling him, "An agent did it."[6] John Woodburn said he was as thrilled that the *Atlantic* was taking the stories as if he had written them himself.

In February the *Atlantic* bought a third story, "Why I Live at the P.O.," which had been turned down by *The New Yorker, Collier's, Harper's Bazaar, Good Housekeeping, Mademoiselle,* and *Harper's.* "Why I Live at the P.O." may be Eudora's most popular, best-known story. Years later it prompted Steve Dorner to name the e-mail software program he invented "Eudora." "Working on e-mail day and night, I felt like I lived at the post office," he said. He transposed the title into the slogan "Bringing the P.O. Where You Live."[7]

Eudora has probably read "Why I Live at the P.O." to groups more often than she has read any other story. "I was trying to show how in these tiny little places, the only entertainment people have is dramatizing the family situation, which they do fully knowing what they are doing," she once said. "They're having a good time. There is certainly the undertone, which is one of wishing for change. Even though Sister goes and lives at the post office, she'll probably be home by weekend and it could happen all over again. They just go through it."[8]

Eudora loved a letter she got from a sixteen-year-old girl named Christine in Georgia, who said the story was "so true to life. My brother and sister are always trying to get me in trouble," and who then asked whether the narrator would go back home and whether her parents would take her in if she did. "Christine doesn't know it yet," Eudora told an interviewer, "but she's fixing to leave."[9]

With the first money from the *Atlantic,* Eudora bought a Fats Waller record, "a million" seeds, and a "sweet little" telescope from Sears, Roebuck.[10] The sky seemed to be cloudy all the time after she bought it, but she looked in the neighbors' flower gardens for buds or pests. The Cheneys and Eudora exchanged news of the hated Carson McCullers. Eudora referred to McCullers's new book, *Reflections in a Golden Eye,* as "Reflections in a Golden I" and told the Cheneys she had been singing, "Arson, carson, you've been thinking . . ." To the Brickells, she wrote that McCullers's new book was a little too much for her, and she expressed outrage to Katherine Anne Porter that the reviewer for *Time* had said the work of "that little wretch Carson" was the climax of southern writing.[11]

But things were looking up, all right. William Maxwell, a *New Yorker* editor, whom she had met the last time she was in New York, wrote to ask her if she had a story he could see. She lost the letter temporarily but found it in the unabridged dictionary and replied that she was "fresh out," to use the Mississippi expression, although she would tell Russell to look out for something Maxwell might like. For a Christmas present to herself, she had bought a book by the *New Yorker* cartoonist George Price, she told him. "A little dog is going to carry it to me in my bed on Christmas morning and I am going to have something for him."[12]

Chapter 19

A Curtain of Green

1941

When the new year, 1941, began, Eudora's short story collection was once more at Doubleday. Spurred by the *Atlantic*'s purchase of the two stories, John Woodburn and Ken McCormick had asked for another look.

Diarmuid Russell was not optimistic, and he rejected Woodburn's offer to publish the collection in a limited, autographed edition of a thousand copies. Woodburn then offered a real contract, a $250 advance and a 10 percent royalty. Russell accepted and wrote to Eudora expressing his "pleasure and delight."[1]

Eudora was equally pleased, and wrote to Katherine Anne Porter that she felt "in the most concentrated favor of the gods just now." It was "unbelievable," she wrote Herschel and Norma Brickell. "I have such good news," she told Robert Penn Warren when she wrote for his permission to reprint the stories that had appeared in the *Southern Review*. She owed it all to the *Southern Review*, she told him. Still, she worried that no one would buy the book.[2]

Eudora began revising the stories for publication in book form and typing them up, and Russell worked furiously to place the unsold stories so they could appear in magazines before the book came out. News of the book sale helped influence magazine editors in Eudora's favor. Russell had sent

"Clytie" to the *Atlantic, Story, Mademoiselle, Yale Review, Harper's,* and *American Mercury,* only to see it come back each time. He sent it on Valentine's Day 1941 to *Harper's Bazaar,* and the fiction editor, Mary Lou Aswell, bought it the same day. Where everyone else had seen "obscurity," Aswell saw coherence.[3] (Actually, *Harper's Bazaar* did not run "Clytie" after all. A few weeks later Aswell liked "The Key" so much that Russell took "Clytie" back and let her have "The Key" instead. Russell finally placed "Clytie" with *Southern Review,* which ran it in summer 1941, just before the magazine folded.)

"The Key" was the first of Eudora's many stories to appear in *Harper's Bazaar.* It was the beginning of a long and fruitful association between Eudora and Mary Lou Aswell, who not only was a perceptive reader and editor but became a close friend. Born Mary Louise White in 1902 in Philadelphia, she had attended Quaker schools and Bryn Mawr, done graduate work at Yale and Harvard, and spent time in Paris, where she met Gertrude Stein and other literary American expatriates. Back in this country, she went to work for the *Atlantic Monthly* and married another editor, Edward C. Aswell, in 1935 (Edward became Thomas Wolfe's editor after Wolfe left Maxwell Perkins at Scribner's). The marriage caused their boss to fire them both. Mary Lou went to work for *Reader's Digest* and, in 1941, *Harper's Bazaar.* The mother of two children, she eventually wrote two novels and edited two anthologies.

All Eudora's stories were placed in periodicals after *Decision* bought "A Visit of Charity" for thirty dollars, after thirteen magazines had rejected it. "A Visit of Charity" is about a little girl's visit to the old ladies' home, sometimes seen as a journey to the underworld by a Persephone figure. Eudora has been horrified by letters that ask if the apple the little girl eats after the visit is from the Garden of Eden. "The things some people teach!" she said. "She was just eating that the way you would a Hershey bar—or anything else you'd saved for a reward after an ordeal. I used to visit the old ladies. They scared me. I couldn't wait to leave."[4]

Many letters about which stories would go into the collection flew back and forth between Russell and Eudora and between Woodburn and Eudora. The men wanted to save *The Robber Bridegroom* for the future book about the Natchez Trace, but Eudora wanted to include it. As usual, she deferred to Russell. She wrote Katherine Anne Porter that she didn't know a thing about publishing, but "they are all so good to me." She thought Diarmuid was "in league with the powers," which made her "completely obedient."[5]

In many ways Russell deserved Eudora's reverence and obedience. He was a model agent, answering every letter promptly and reading every manuscript and commenting on it equally promptly. He took her work seriously and could discuss it endlessly. He was completely loyal to her, and never tried to use her to further his own ends with the editors. His hard work and sound literary judgment helped Eudora, an unknown regional writer with a few stories published in literary quarterlies, to become a successful author, with stories in major magazines and a book contract with Doubleday—all in less than a year.

Both Russell and Eudora wanted "The Key and Other Stories," for a title, but Doubleday vetoed it. While the interminable discussions went on, Eudora wrote to a friend in North Carolina to suggest that at the next party everybody should think of a title and send them to her, and she would pull one out of a hat. John Robinson, who was in Jackson one weekend, suggested "Last Night I Heard the Mockingbird Singing," and someone else offered "Magnolias and Magnolia Fisscattas." Eudora's little brother weighed in with "Darkie Victory," while her own favorite was "Gitanjali and Fruit Gathering," but that had already been used.[6]

In the end, "out of pure weariness," Doubleday went with the salesmen's choice of a title, *A Curtain of Green and Other Stories.*[7] John Woodburn pointed out that it could be the first of a series, to be followed by *A Curtain of Blue, A Curtain of Red,* and so forth. "And your last book could just be called *Curtains,"* he said.[8]

The early stories in *A Curtain of Green*—"A Worn Path," "Why I Live at the P.O.," "The Petrified Man," "Death of a Traveling Salesman," "The Key," "Keela, the Outcast Indian Maiden," "Lily Daw and the Three Ladies," and all the others—are among the best Eudora ever wrote. They are not beloved by those Welty scholars who like to analyze and reanalyze the later stories, with their abundant symbols and mythical allusions, but they still vibrate with life and energy. They are dramatic, theatrical enough to have stood the test of time, as Eudora has read them out loud to thousands of audiences over the years.

Russell suggested that Katherine Anne Porter should write an introduction for the book, and John Woodburn went up to Saratoga Springs to ask her in person. She agreed, and they celebrated at the United States Hotel in downtown Saratoga. Eudora was in transports of happiness, overwhelmed that Porter would agree to do such a thing. Maybe she should wait until she saw the collection, with its "poor relations" included, Eudora said. Then if she still wanted to feel responsible for a little introduction, Eudora would be "so very delighted."[9]

While she was retyping the short stories for *A Curtain of Green,* Eudora also managed to write her first Natchez Trace story since *The Robber Bridegroom.* It was "First Love," about a deaf-mute boy who watches Aaron Burr and Harmon Blennerhassett talking in a Natchez tavern. When Russell thought it unsatisfactory, Eudora replied that she was glad he wasn't pleased with it and was sorry she had sent it off so quickly. She still thought, and hoped he agreed, that there was the germ of a good story there. But "don't think I have delusions of grandeur about my little stories."[10] She wrote it over. To her astonishment, Russell sold "First Love" to Mary Lou Aswell. She had been sure no one would ever buy it.

Eudora said later that she wrote "First Love" from the point of view of a deaf-and-dumb boy because she did not want to make up things for a real historical person to say. "I never could understand how people could write historical novels with real people speaking," she said.[11] By using the deaf boy, she could simply say what he thought they said. Oddly, the boy in "First Love" had a factual counterpart; when Aaron Burr was tried under the oaks at Washington, Mississippi, a twelve-year-old deaf boy named Joel Mayes was present.[12]

By the end of February, Eudora had finished retyping all the *Curtain of Green* stories. It gave her a crick in the back, she said, and she dispatched them to Russell so he could send them on to Katherine Anne Porter at Yaddo.[13] Porter had asked about a deadline, and Eudora replied that she did not know the deadline herself but thought it could not be before Porter was ready to do it, some time in the fall. She did not want it to hang over her friend's head. In the end, it was a very hard job getting the introduction out of Porter.

Meanwhile, Eudora wrote a story set in New Orleans, "The Purple Hat." "When I wrote 'The Purple Hat,' I was trying to show off having been to a gambling hall," she said.[14] When it ran in *Harper's Bazaar,* it was illustrated by George Grosz, but it mystified readers. "I wish I hadn't written that story," Eudora said later. "It was just an odd story I wrote in an odd moment, about something I don't know much about: gambling. I really meant it to be no more than a playful ghost story."[15]

Eudora wrote and revised a story called "The Winds," which reflects some of her childhood experiences, including the Redpath Chautauqua and a tornado, in the Congress Street neighborhood in Jackson. It was collected with the Trace stories. Five magazines turned it down before Mary Lou Aswell accepted it for *Harper's Bazaar*. Aswell thought "The Winds" might be the best story Eudora had ever written.[16] It was a girls' story, Eudora and Mary Lou agreed. After it was published, Eudora noted that without exception, men said it was not good and women said it was.[17] Some critics have seen "The Winds," in which a little girl, Josie, has a crush on the older, blond Cornelia across the street, as wildly homoerotic. It is interesting that Aswell, who liked it so much, eventually renounced her heterosexual life, became openly lesbian, and went to Santa Fe to live with the painter Agnes Sims.

Eudora continued to work on her Mississippi stories. She was in "a misery," she wrote to Diarmuid Russell in May, because she could not "make a story do something it cannot do." It laid a "heavy burden" on her and "weighted down my heart and I couldn't do anything." She wanted to write these perfect stories that she could envision. It was like understanding how to juggle, just not being able to do it.[18] This anguish was probably over "A Still Moment," one of the Natchez Trace stories.

She wrote to Porter to tell her that every rose in her garden was in bloom, "and oh, the chinaberry trees in niggertown!" She and her friends went down there and parked every night and sat under them and breathed.[19]

She did not mention the introduction that Porter was supposed to be writing.

Chapter 20

Henry Miller

1941

    Doubleday had commissioned the lubricious author Henry Miller, just back from an expatriate's life in Europe, to travel around the United States and write a book about what he saw in his native land. Woodburn routed him through Jackson and asked Eudora to show him around.

Miller's sexual candor in *Tropic of Cancer* and *Tropic of Capricorn* had shocked Americans. Trying to be helpful to a new writer, Miller wrote Eudora a letter offering to put Eudora in touch with "an unfailing pornographic market" that she could write for if she needed money. Eudora made the mistake of showing the letter to her mother, who refused to have Miller in her house.[1]

When Miller went to Jackson, Eudora did her best to entertain him under difficult circumstances. Doubleday had talked of providing him with a glass automobile so that he could see the country as he traveled, but he arrived with no automobile at all, and Eudora had to drive him everywhere in her mother's car. She persuaded Hubert Creekmore and Nash Burger to go with them. Miller was "infinitely bored," she said. When Burger spoke movingly on local history, Miller would not even look out the car window. Creekmore was familiar with all his works, but Miller did not want to talk about them.

They drove him to Natchez; to the ruins of Windsor, the antebellum mansion outside Port Gibson; to the Civil War battleground at Vicksburg; and to the lost town of Rodney. Miller wore his hat all day, even on picnics, and said nothing. He was not at all like the dashing author of *Tropic of Capricorn* they had expected, but like "the most boring businessman you can imagine."[2]

Desperate, Eudora offered to take him to watch the patients moving out of the old insane asylum building on North State Street to a bigger, new hospital across the river in Rankin County. The patients were supposed to help move themselves, and Eudora thought it would amuse Miller to go watch "those poor old crazy people" carry their beds out and put them in a truck—especially, she said sixty years later, since the superintendent was named Love.[3] Miller declined.

Every night for the three nights he was there, Eudora and her friends took Miller out to dinner at the Rotisserie, Jackson's only good restaurant. The Rotisserie had three entrances. Once they went to the drive-in entrance, once to the basement steakhouse, and the third night to the upstairs room with its band and dance floor. Miller marveled that a town the size of Jackson had "three good restaurants."[4]

In the book he wrote about his trip, *The Air-Conditioned Nightmare,* Miller does not mention Jackson, but he does talk about the South; in a description of the South's battlefields, he lists Vicksburg, among others. (The defeat in the Civil War, he says, was "only a military defeat.") The live oaks in Biloxi got a passing nod, but he seems most moved by the ruins of Windsor, where "nothing now remains of this great house but the high, vine-covered Grecian columns."[5]

It was about this time that Eudora wrote "Asphodel," one of the Natchez Trace stories. She said she got the idea for the story on a picnic at the ruins of Windsor, and perhaps it was the picnic with Henry Miller in his hat that started her on the story. It takes place in the ruins of Asphodel, "six Doric columns, with the entablature unbroken over the first two," which resemble the ruins of Windsor. Three old maids come bearing their lunch in wicker baskets—"ham and chicken, spices and jellies, fresh breads and a cake, peaches, bananas, figs, pomegranates, grapes, and a thin dark bottle of blackberry cordial." As they talk about the past, a bearded man emerges from a little glade. "He was as rude and golden as a lion . . . He was naked." Or he may be a figment of their imagination. As they flee, leaving their shoes behind them, they look back and see a flock of goats coming toward them from the ruin.

When someone asked Eudora years later if she had read the stories in the newspapers in 1932 about Dick Dana and Octavia Dockery, who lived in the ruins of what came to be known as Goat Castle near Natchez, she said she had indeed, but had not had them in mind when she wrote "Asphodel."[6] She sent the story to Russell, who said that a dozen that good would make an elegant book.[7]

Chapter 21

Yaddo

1941

Eudora spent June and July 1941 at Yaddo, the writer's colony outside Saratoga Springs, New York. Katherine Anne Porter, who was there for the summer, had recommended her protégé, giving Eudora another reason for gratitude.

She went to Yaddo with some misgivings. She had heard, she told the Cheneys, that they locked writers in their rooms and shoved food—"good food"—through a slot. Eudora was sure she would write nothing at all under conditions like this, but she might take an old story and push a page through the slot every day—after she got her food.[1]

On the way to Yaddo she stopped in New York, where she went to the top of Radio City to look out over the city at sunset, admiring the river shining before the purple mountains in the distance. Once more she went out to Katonah with Diarmuid Russell. It was almost a year since Russell had written to her the first time, and she told him she had "a tender place" in her heart when the date came around again.[2]

The writers' community at Yaddo occupied a fifty-five-room graystone mansion that Spencer and Katrina Trask had built two miles east of Saratoga Springs, four hours by bus from New York City. The grounds comprised five hundred acres and included four lakes and a rose garden with marble statues.

To Eudora's horror, Carson McCullers was in residence, and not only present but openly, loudly, maniacally in love with Katherine Anne Porter. Dressed in dungarees and a man's white shirt, she followed Katherine Anne around and once threw herself across the doorsill of Katherine Anne's room. Porter, who had a deathly fear of lesbians, was repelled by McCuller's adoration and clung more closely than ever to Eudora, who she said was "150 percent female."

Like a weed, Eudora said, McCullers would come back no matter what you did to her, "but one day she will simply poison herself." That was a mixed metaphor, she said, but she mixed it with her own hand because she meant it for a potion.[3]

Katherine Anne persuaded Elizabeth Ames, Yaddo's director, to let her and Eudora live at North Farm, a few hundred yards down the drive from the main house. An etcher, Karnig Nalbandian, and a composer, Colin McPhee, shared the farmhouse with them. Katherine Anne's combined bedroom and studio was upstairs, and Eudora's bedroom was across the hall. Her studio was in the farmhouse kitchen and had a sign on it: SILENCE: WRITER AT WORK WITHIN.

At the end of each long summer's day, Eudora and Katherine Anne walked single file on the path through the woods to the mansion for dinner. To Eudora, the great room they entered seemed like the stage for a grand opera on which the curtain would go up any minute. The first night she was nervous, thinking that the assembled writers and musicians and artists, together for the first time that day, were "all expected to *perform,* that the assigned soloists and the combined chorus were *us,*" She noticed that the great hall was furnished with throne chairs, divans, velvet stools, even a sleigh, and the tables were set with candelabra, wineglasses, wine.[4] The evening was operatic, Eudora said, but about politics, not the arts, and Katherine Anne's voice could be heard punctuating the discussion, crying *"Au contraire!"* Katherine Anne was worried about the war in Europe and saw fascism in everything she didn't like. Eudora regretted this reaction and felt that people "talk so bloodthirsty."[5]

At night the windows at one end of the great room were open onto the garden, and that first night Eudora watched as the moon climbed higher, above the statues that rose from the flowerbeds stretching out below the balustrade. The fragrance of the summer stock and the nicotiana, even though she could not see them, made her think of home.

During the day Eudora was supposed to spend her time alone in her studio with the sign on the door. She was so self-conscious, she said years later, that she couldn't write anything.[6] "Everything was so tense, so exalted," she said another time.[7] She did work on revisions to "A Still Moment" and managed to read the proofs of *A Curtain of Green* when they arrived.

She enjoyed one of the visiting artists, José de Creeft, a Spanish-born, French-trained sculptor, who had lived in the same studio building in Paris that housed Picasso and Juan Gris. Wearing short shorts and a cap on backward, he would jump on a bicycle and race off to look at stones that were too big for him to haul back. Although he actually did no sculpture at Yaddo that year, he did produce some red and yellow watercolors. When de Creeft needed a piece about himself for the *Magazine of Art* in 1944, he asked Eudora to write it.

It finally dawned on Eudora that not everybody stayed holed up in a studio working all day, and she began walking into Saratoga Springs, where big red-brick hotels with black iron columns lined the main street. Banners and flags hung over the street, flapping above crowds of strollers, which included invalids in town to take the waters, racing aficionados, and tourists. Eudora went to the racetrack when the horses were working out, and to the public halls where people took the waters. She often stopped at the grocery store to buy onions, a soup bone, celery, or carrots for Katherine Anne, who liked to keep a soup pot simmering on the stove. Saratoga, she said, was "mad as anything," with its "assortment of race track gamblers, writers, refugees and, last week, drunk V.F.W.'s."[8]

Herschel Brickell had chosen "A Worn Path" for the 1941 book of O. Henry Prize stories. Eudora wanted him to use "Powerhouse," which she thought was a better story, "if the author had any say-so." "A Worn Path" later won second prize among the stories in this collection.

Katherine Anne, who could not drive, had bought a brand-new Studebaker, and nearly every day Eudora drove her out to the old, rundown clapboard farmhouse, South Hill, that she was having restored. Workmen found bees' nests in the upstairs walls of the house, and tiny lady's slippers that Katherine Anne thought must be a hundred years old. Katherine Anne and Eudora took picnic lunches and listened to the birds and to the workmen and lay in the shady meadow grass and smoked cigarettes. Sometimes Eudora drove Katherine Anne to Albany, where they looked for—and found—antiques and carpets for South Hill.

John Robinson thought Eudora was homesick that summer at Yaddo. "That horrid little McCullers (according to E.) is there," he wrote to Nancy Farley.[9] Eudora was, she wrote to Russell, "depressed and ready to go." She no longer delighted in Saratoga but found the streets held a long procession that was "sometimes Daumier, sometimes Hieronymous Bosch, or Goya nightmare creatures all swathed and draped."[10]

Adding to the tension was the need for Katherine Anne to write the introduction to *A Curtain of Green*. Eudora continued to play the role of worshipful sycophant throughout the summer and never once mentioned the piece, but Woodburn and Russell agonized, and Katherine Anne continued to delay. Although Woodburn was desperate to get his hands on the introduction, he did not have the courage to ask Katherine Anne himself. Instead, he hounded Eudora to ask her. He wrote nearly every day, begging Eudora to speak to her and "as gently, as sweetly, but as insistently as you can, keep her working on that Introduction."

Eudora was with Katherine Anne constantly, but she never did mention it; she did not want to interfere with Katherine Anne's novel writing. Eudora even felt that it was perhaps her fault that Katherine Anne was not coming through. Perhaps she was putting Katherine Anne on the spot; it must be hard to write something about somebody who is staying in the house and waiting for you to write it.[11]

Chapter 22

Publication Party
1941

The situation was desperate, Woodburn wired to Eudora, now back in Jackson. The publication of her book would have to be delayed because Katherine Anne Porter's introduction was not in hand, and if it didn't arrive within the next few days, publication would have to be postponed indefinitely.[1] But Eudora, taking quinine for fever, urged Katherine Anne not to work too hard on it, since she, Eudora, did not want to be "part of the pressure."

At last, on August 31, Katherine Anne wrote to Eudora that she had finally turned out the introduction with no trouble in two evenings' work and mailed it special delivery. In turn, she said, she had received "some very kind and pleasant words from John Broadside."[2] Calling Woodburn Broadside was her little joke.

For the introduction, Porter drew heavily on some brief biographical information that Eudora had sent her at Diarmuid Russell's suggestion. She used a phrase from Eudora's letter, saying that Eudora was "underfoot locally." Welty scholars have debated her meaning in learned journals, not realizing that this is simply a colloquialism that means that Eudora was busy and absorbed in Jackson life and civic work. Porter also repeated Eudora's story about the time one of her stories appeared in the *Atlantic* and her friends asked her, "Eudora, when did you write it?" Not how, or even why, Eudora said, but just when.[3]

Porter commented that the narrator of "Why I Live at the P.O." is suffering from dementia praecox. Eudora disagreed and later said that she had not meant the story to be pathological at all. "I thought it was cheerful on the whole," she said.[4] But at the time, she only gushed gratefully to her mentor when she saw the proofs of the introduction, which Katherine Anne had dated August 19, 1941. She commented on its length, "xxiii" pages, "so long!" Oh, yes, said Eudora, one small thing: could Katherine Anne leave out the line about Bread Loaf and "my quiet horror"? She was indeed horrified at some of the things Bread Loaf professed to do, but she had been invited and had gone for free and had a nice vacation.[5] She clearly thought it a breach of the law of hospitality to say anything uncomplimentary about it—in public.

Publication of *A Curtain of Green* had been delayed until November 7, and Eudora begged Katherine Anne to go to the publication party. When Katherine Anne wrote that she was having trouble with her shoulder, Eudora offered to type anything for her that needed typing. And she asked Katherine Anne, Herschel Brickell, and Cleanth Brooks of the *Southern Review* to recommend her for a Guggenheim so she could work on the stories about the Natchez Trace she had been discussing with Russell.

She wrote a realistic, contemporary Trace story, "The Wide Net." John Robinson had told her about a young wife in the Delta who had disappeared. When her husband and his neighbors dragged the river for her body, they had so much fun they forgot their grim purpose. Eudora used the anecdote as a springboard for "The Wide Net," which she wrote in late summer 1941 and dedicated to John Fraiser Robinson. One of Eudora's most joyous short stories, uncluttered with symbolism and fairy-tale motifs, it was the first story she sold to *Harper's*. Frederick Lewis Allen, the editor who bought it in early 1942, considered it "a work of genius and one of the funniest stories" the magazine had ever had.[6]

Eudora worked in the yard, planting bulbs, sowing winter grass, and watering everything. A woman who grew up in a house whose back yard adjoined the Weltys' yard said that the only thing she remembered about

Eudora was the frequency and fidelity with which both she and her mother worked outdoors. Eudora nearly always mentioned gardening in her letters. In winter she invariably talked about the camellias, and as spring came on she wrote of the flowering quince, yellow jessamine, azaleas, daffodils, and later the roses, irises, and finally the summer flowers. She gave Katherine Anne a lot of advice on growing roses, transplanting irises, and digging up clumps of jonquils to divide them. Before she left Jackson for New York and the publication of her book in November, she made covers for all the camellias from an old tent, so she could sleep in peace if it froze in Jackson.

Eudora kept hoping that Katherine Anne would come to the publication party. She wrote that she would be at the Bristol Hotel, which had "Broadway bad manners" but was "cheap and cashed checks."[7] Porter did not come.

John Woodburn was on jury duty while Eudora was in New York, so she saw him only twice—for the party itself and when he put her on the train for home. The party lasted from five until one-thirty A.M. somewhere in the Village. José de Creeft, the sculptor, and Karnig Nalbandian, the etcher, whom she had met at Yaddo, showed up. Nalbandian appeared at her hotel the day of the party, knocked on her door, hugged her, saw the bed unmade, and said, "Let's go to bed." Wouldn't he rather eat? Eudora asked him. "Ah, sure," he said, but what was that nice smell? It was soap, Eudora told him; would he like a cake? He would. "A little Armenian Pan if I ever saw one," she described him. She was touched that de Creeft would show up for a literary brawl, she told Katherine Anne, but he was the "best one there."[8]

Frank Lyell, her Jackson playmate, came up from North Carolina, and Hubert Creekmore, now working for New Directions Press, was there too.

At the party, an actress congratulated her on writing the book and said, "I expect you'll make a lot of money out of it." Eudora thanked her and said she didn't expect to make much because short stories did not sell well. "My dear, I wouldn't say that," trilled the actress. "I believe de Maupassant sold terribly well."[9]

In fact, the publication of *A Curtain of Green* did attract a great deal of interest. *Publishers Weekly* noted that the press saw it as the work of a "new and important American writer," although the publishers "naturally do not see it as a runaway best seller." People who met the author in New York, said *PW*, were "impressed with the sincerity of her intentions as a writer, her interest in people and her capacity for remembering practically everything she has heard." The article pointed out that she was a watercolorist and a photographer, and "as for music, Miss Welty claims that every southern girl can play one Chopin waltz."[10]

Reviews were good. "Few contemporary books have ever impressed me quite as deeply as this book," wrote Marianne Hauser in the *New York Times Book Review.*[11] In the *Nation,* the poet Louise Bogan compared Eudora to Gogol.[12] However, *Time* commented on her "strong taste for melodrama" and her preoccupation with the "demented, the deformed, the queer, the highly spiced."

Eudora filled her time in New York with art shows, the ballet, and concerts. She went to de Creeft's exhibition and marveled at his virtuosity; he worked in wood, metal, and marble. (A photograph she had taken of de Creeft at Yaddo appeared in the catalogue.) And she visited bookstores to ask if they had a copy of *A Curtain of Green.* They never did, and she asked them to order it for her, thinking this was good for business. (In 1971, after thirty years and two editions, *Curtain* had sold only 6,700 copies.)

She had no copies of *Curtain* herself, and when she got back to Jackson she had to buy one to send to Katherine Anne. She also sent a copy to Dale Mullen at his family's newspaper, the *Eagle,* in Oxford, apologizing that "Retreat," the story that had appeared in *River,* his short-lived literary magazine, had not been used. "Flowers for Marjorie" was more or less the same story, she said, told in a different way.

In the obligatory home-town newspaper interview to mark publication of her book, Eudora said that she knew she was expected to write a novel. "I do not feel drawn to writing a novel now," she said. "They tell me I will later. Perhaps. But right now I want to live here and keep on writing short stories." Then she stated her credo for the world to read: "I do not need New York. I like my part of the country." If she ever wrote a novel, she said, the Mississippi River or a river town would be a part of it.

The reporter said firmly that Eudora was "the same sort of person you went to school with at whose ready wit you giggled" and remarked that the striking thing about *Curtain* was "the absence of any mention of world strife and the centering of interest on the . . . world about you, the beauty parlor, the village idiot, the devotion of the small farmer to his hard living, the faithfulness of the negro."[13]

. . .

The *Robber* manuscript was still circulating, and Russell did not send Eudora the uncomplimentary remarks editors made. Someone at *Story* magazine, for example, called it "a 'fairy tale' with no redeeming qualities such as local color or historical background . . . the flavor of a poorly copied Canterbury Tale."[14]

John Robinson, Eudora's good friend, was following the publication of her short stories with great interest. He thought her "stuff" had a "rare spiritual quality" that he had seen nowhere else. "Sometimes I think it is too tremulous—but I wonder if there are many who do just what she is doing," he said.[15]

In March 1941, Robinson went home to Jackson for a round of farewell parties before he went in the army. He was to go first to Camp Shelby, Mississippi, and hoped to get into the Washington Artillery, an old New Orleans regiment with a distinguished history, renamed the 141st Field Artillery. "It's something so different I can't even guess what it will be like," he said.[16] It was the first time the brush of the war to come touched Eudora's friends.

That fall Eudora went to see Robinson when he had a short leave in New Orleans. She reported to Katherine Anne on the blooming tree dahlias and sweet olives in New Orleans but said nothing about the time she spent with her friend.

Chapter 23

War Comes

1941

The war in Europe was coming closer to Jackson. Dutch and Javanese cadets came for training at the Royal Netherlands Military Flying School at Hawkins Field, and at night their planes flew over so low that Eudora thought they were headed under her bed. (One did fly under the Mississippi River bridge in Vicksburg.) The Dutch were popular, but Jacksonians objected when the dark-skinned Javanese took democracy seriously and turned up at local dances. The army hustled them off to Kansas.

December 7, 1941—Pearl Harbor Day—came. Eudora always remembered that the day before she had been dressed in her Sunday best, sipping champagne at the wedding of John Robinson's sister, Anna Belle, and Paul Davis. "The news didn't penetrate right away," she said in 1991. "No one could believe it. It still doesn't seem real." Not long after the wedding, the groom, the best man, and most of the other men who had been there were in the military. John Robinson was already in the army. Hubert Creekmore was drafted, and Nash Burger left his job at the state archives to go to Pascagoula to work for Ingalls Shipbuilding, which was making aircraft carriers for England and the United States. Americans took over Hawkins Field, and debutantes served punch at parties to Yankee soldiers.

Eudora did publicity for the Victory Book Campaign, the Red Cross, and the War Savings Committee. She tried to persuade people to donate better books to the Victory Book Campaign, which provided material for soldiers to read, but every time she looked in a book box downtown, she saw the same kinds of titles—*Bunny Brown and His Sister Sue at Grandma's Farm, How to Embroider and Tat,* and the complete works of Bulwer-Lytton.[1]

That winter Eudora went down to New Orleans again to see John Robinson, and she reported to Katherine Anne that every time he came to pick her up he brought a handful of camellias—all the bushes were covered with them. Her comment seems to show more interest in the fact that the camellias were blooming luxuriously than in the possibility that John Robinson was making a romantic gesture in bringing them to her. What their feelings were for each other at this point is anybody's guess, but it looked as though Eudora, like most single girls in America, had a beau in the military.

From New Orleans she went over to the little town of Pass Christian on the Mississippi Gulf coast, where the wife of the new owner of the Hotel Grey Castle had offered her a free room. All she had to do was pay for her meals, which were very good but expensive. Robinson and other people came over from New Orleans for the weekend, but during the week Eudora was completely alone. She ate, slept, and walked five or ten miles a day under the live oaks. She had brought her telescope and looked at the oyster schooners with their big sails out on the water. Spring was slow in coming, and the weather was still cold. She did very little writing, but rested. She had written steadily and produced a great many stories for a long period, and now she was tired and might not write any more for a long time. With so many friends going to war, it was almost too much "to pipe up in a small voice and tell a little story."[2]

Nevertheless, she finished revising "A Still Moment," one of the Natchez Trace stories. She said that it was the only time her writing was based on facts she had read instead of living people she had observed.[3] Particularly useful were the journals of the bandit John A. Murrell (1804–1844) and the sermons of the evangelist Lorenzo Dow (1777–1834), who sometimes preached on horseback. Murrell, she told an interviewer from a French paper, "had a white horse that he took for the reincarnation of Jesus Christ. He passed his time killing people. One day he met Lorenzo Dow, who wanted to save souls and kept repeating, like a crazy man, 'I came for souls, and souls I must have.' "

For "A Still Moment," Eudora added another figure to the chance encounter between Dow and Murrell on the Trace: John James Audubon, the naturalist and painter, who painted every species of North American bird known in the nineteenth century and traveled up the Trace after he left New Orleans. She read Audubon's journals too.

"A Still Moment" was not "symbolical," Eudora told Russell; she had been stating literal facts. She admitted that the terms she used sounded as if they were symbols. "These real men with these real convictions and beliefs were all traveling the Trace at the same time, and . . . visual sights were taken directly as personal signs . . . I wanted to show that they were all using the same thing, and that this thing, whose spirit was the little white heron here, has its own life. In this case the literal seemed to me more wonderful than the symbolic."[4]

"A Still Moment" proved hard to sell. Eudora eventually asked Russell if it would be all right to let Paul Engle, the editor of *American Prefaces* at Iowa State University, have the story, although he did not pay anything. The magazine must be good, she said, because it had always rejected everything she had sent in the past.[5]

Although it was unsalable, "A Still Moment," that quintessential Trace story, was her favorite among her short stories. "It struck me as having had a very happy fulfillment of what it set out to do," she said upon rereading it. "It seemed better than I had thought." She was also proud of the fact that Robert Penn Warren liked it best.[6] Warren's poem sequence "Audubon: A Vision" may owe something to this story.

When Bill Hamilton sent her a copy of his work on the Natchez theater, for which she had helped with the research, she promptly mentioned one of the plays in a short story, as she needed a play for an actor of 1818. If she wasn't careful, she wrote to Hamilton, she would have to use footnotes with the Trace stories.[7]

In early 1942, Eudora received a phone call from Elizabeth Spencer, a senior from Carrollton, Mississippi, at Belhaven College, across the street from Eudora's house. Spencer had decided to become a writer.

She was president of the college literary society, where the monthly meetings dragged and seemed boring because nobody had a new story to read. "We used to sit there eating fudge squares and complaining about routine, which dulled our inspiration and blighted our native talent," she recalled.[8] The girls were surprised when they read in the paper that a woman who lived across the street had published a book called *A Curtain of Green*. Here was someone whose inspiration had not been dulled by routine. They decided to invite her to speak to the literary society.

Designated to call Miss Welty, Spencer was nervous. Her hands shook as she held the phone. "One of the world's softest voices" answered the phone. When Spencer issued her invitation, Eudora said she would not speak to the group, but she would be happy to meet informally with them.[9]

Eudora looked forward to the visit to the literary society—it was her first chance to give literary advice. She enchanted the girls, and she was glad to meet Elizabeth Spencer, whom she later described as "a graceful young woman with a slender, vivid face, delicate and clearly defined features, dark blue eyes, in which you could read that Elizabeth Spencer was a jump ahead of you . . . She was already a writer. She went with a determined walk that made her hair bounce."[10] Eudora became Spencer's mentor and friend, and Spencer went on to become an accomplished novelist.

In March 1942, Eudora received word that she had won a $1,200 tax-free fellowship from the John Simon Guggenheim Foundation. Guggenheims were usually used for travel abroad, but the war made that impossible. Eudora has always said that she used the money to buy time to immerse herself in local history. She was furious that Carson McCullers had also gotten a Guggenheim, when people she knew who were "really good artists" were applying unsuccessfully. She told Lon Cheney, without comment, that she had seen an interview with McCullers in the *New Orleans Times-Picayune,* in which McCullers had said she was going back to "the old plantation in Georgia, to sit in her old house there, by a wide table . . . Nothing she liked better than long walks in the woods, peace and solitude."[11]

Chapter 24

The Robber Bridegroom
1942

The *Southern Review* closed down in the spring of 1942, after Louisiana State University withdrew its financial support. It was a shame, Eudora said, since the football team's bulldog still got his daily ration of fifteen pounds of steak. And what would happen to *The Robber Bridegroom,* which had been at the *Southern Review* for months?

Russell had worked very hard trying to sell "the fantasy." He had sent it to Reynal & Hitchcock, to Harcourt Brace, to Doubleday three separate times, and to several magazines—and had always gotten it back. Eudora laughed when she heard he had sent it to *Ladies' Home Journal.* She was afraid Jamie, the rascal hero, would eat all the desserts in the food section and rip the clothes off the fashion models, leaving everyone in the magazine looking "mussed and cross."[1]

Russell sent *The Robber Bridegroom* back to Doubleday in May 1942, and the firm did an about-face, bought it as a novella, and scheduled it for fall publication. John Woodburn told Eudora that *Robber* was his favorite, his "best girl," among her stories, and he would rather see it published than win the Irish sweepstakes. If he liked nothing else, "the old cow of Mobile belongs in the brief roster of magnificent allusions," he told her.[2] (In the book, as the clown Goat is trying to find Rosamond, he thinks he sees her dress flying in the sky. "But then he heard a distant moo and it was only the flying cow of Mobile going by.")

Doubleday seemed excited over *Robber.* The dust jacket, Woodburn promised, would be beautiful, and the whole thing would be "dressed up like a southern belle at the Tulane game." In fact, Woodburn turned down a drawing of Eudora by Karnig Nalbandian because it was not good enough.

Eudora wanted Woodburn to add a subtitle so the title would read, *The Robber Bridegroom: A Tale,* but he refused, saying this would sound slight and precious. If Doubleday wanted to sell it as a novel, it could try, Eudora said, but she had written it for a tale. She listed a number of other possible subtitles: *The Robber Bridegroom: A Mask? The R. B.: Tone Poem? The R. B.: An Elegy? The R. B.: An Idyll? Montage? Technicolorama? Pantomime?*[3]

In the spring of 1942 Eudora saw two spectacles that stimulated her to create another Natchez Trace story, "Livvie Is Back," later collected as "Livvie." The first important visual image was bottle trees, trees with orange and green and blue glass bottles fastened on the end of each limb, around the old houses in the country along Highway 49. An old man had the best ones, she said, an enormous avenue lined with sparkling bottle trees; one of them, a little peach tree, had blue Milk of Magnesia bottles.[4] She took its picture, in black and white, of course. In speaking of the relationship of her photography to her writing, she once used this as an example. Her photographs were black and white, but her stories were in color.

She felt the second visual impact on Easter Sunday, when she saw a young black man on Farish Street wearing a zoot suit with full-legged, tight-cuffed pants and a long coat with wide lapels and big shoulder pads, all in pastels. Eudora said later that the zoot suit was real; she couldn't have made it up.

In the story, an old black man, Solomon, has a bottle tree and a new, very young wife, Livvie. Livvie quietly submits to Solomon for years and then falls in love with Ash, a young man who wears a brilliant zoot suit. It is a very simple story, Eudora said, about "young and old, spring and winter, changes."[5]

That summer Eudora finished "At the Landing," the last of the Natchez Trace tales. It is a curious story. The heroine is Jenny Lockhart, who lives with her grandfather in a house with galleries on the hill at Rodney's Landing, the ghost town on the Mississippi River. They are seldom seen in the Landing, where everyone considers the grandfather too good and Jenny too shy to come outside. Jenny seems to wait in suspended animation, like Sleeping Beauty. There is even a wall of thorns surrounding her, in the form of a rosebush that circles the outdoor pavilion where the cook serves her and her grandfather their dinner. The most exciting daily event in Jenny's empty life is watching "the rude wild Billy Floyd," who sleeps all day and fishes all night, as he walks through town carrying a big fish he has caught. One day Floyd appears in the meadow when she goes to the cemetery to visit her mother's grave. They watch each other wordlessly, as two black butterflies circle above the flowers, "always together, like each other's shadows, beautiful each with the other," choreographed for doom.

After Jenny's grandfather dies, the river floods the town. Floyd rescues Jenny in his boat, but they still do not speak. In the woods, Floyd speaks to her for the first time, and then "he violated her and still he was without care or demand." Next he cooks them a meal of wild meat over a fire. Jenny, unable to tell him of her love, murmurs only that she would like to have a little house. When the flood recedes, he takes her back to her grandfather's house, where she sets to work to clean out the mud left by the river.

Eudora introduces three crones, another motif from folklore and fairy tales. Three old women at the Landing who know everything "about all kinds of love" come to see Jenny to "celebrate her ruin" and to say, "Why don't you run after him?" and "Now you won't love him anymore?" Jenny obediently sets out to look for Floyd and waits for him in a shanty-boat fishing camp, while the fishermen throw knives at a tree. (A WPA historian described the shanty-boat fishermen of the thirties and forties as "retrogrades and riffraff" with unlimited opportunities for dissipation.[6] Eudora photographed this life in the thirties. One of her pictures appeared in the WPA guidebook *Mississippi,* and in a much better reproduction in *Eudora Welty: Photographs.*[7]) The men put Jenny in an abandoned houseboat and "one by one came in to her." About each one, Jenny senses "the smell of trees that had bled to the knives they wore."

While this rape is going on, the men's wives and children are outside. "By the fire, little boys were slapped crossly by their mothers—as if they knew that the original smile now crossed Jenny's face, and hung there no matter what was done to her, like a bit of color that kindles in the sky after the light has gone."

Eudora describes both Floyd's rape of Jenny and the shanty-boat gang rape in an almost offhand way, as if she is saying, "Floyd violates. See Floyd violate." She is fascinated not by action but by *place,* and brings to vivid life the ghost town of Rodney's Landing and its grotesque inhabitants—wild man and crones. She is also concerned, as she often is in her fiction, with the isolation of a human being, Jenny. When she writes about love and violent sex, it seems as if she is fantasizing out of her own need for or fear of sexual fulfillment.

Eudora admitted that "At the Landing" had "lots of faults." "It was obscure. I was really trying to express something I had felt in that place," she said. "It used to be really lost down there. A ghost river town. It was magical to me and I was trying to express some of that lostness and the feeling of enchantment. Maybe I got too carried away with my own words."[8]

Mary Lou Aswell at *Harper's Bazaar* turned down "At the Landing." When she said that it seemed like a condensation of a longer work, Eudora remembered that she had thrown away large chunks of the story, but it was too late to rewrite them.[9] Even though Aswell did not like the story, she was intrigued by the setting and asked Eudora to do a nonfiction piece about the ghost town of Rodney, all that was left of Rodney's Landing.

David Cohn, the guest editor of a special Deep South issue of *Saturday Review of Literature* for September 1942, asked Eudora to review Marguerite Steedman's *But You'll Be Back.* In her review, the first she published, Eudora said it was mostly a novel about things—"wanting things, getting things, losing things, stealing and selling things, and getting better things"—and it did not inquire very deeply into human emotions.[10]

In September, Charles Shattuck, the editor of *Accent,* published "Ida M'Toy," Eudora's nonfiction profile of a tall black woman who had been a midwife in Jackson for years and now ran a secondhand clothing store in her home. Eudora took M'Toy a copy of *Accent* with the article in it, and M'Toy called it "The Book of Ida" and wanted to know why she just got one copy—she needed two hundred to distribute. Eudora told her that they cost thirty cents apiece, and M'Toy said, "My God, there are people who would pay thirty dollars cash on the barrel head to have a copy right at their hand of Ida's life."[11]

Eudora sent the manuscript of an essay for *Harper's Bazaar,* "Some Notes on River Country," to John Robinson, who knew the places she wrote about so well, and told him in a handwritten note that the corn in Mississippi was tasseling and it was a wonderful day for a picnic. She also sent the *Robber* book jacket to Robinson, who was now in the Army Air Corps and stationed in St. Petersburg. *The Robber Bridegroom* was a fairy story, or "rather in the realm of demonology, about early Natchez and the Trace," he told Nancy Farley. "Most imaginative and unreal in a way. So different from her other things . . . I'm very fond of all her Natchez Trace things—most of which are unpublished. She has made her own world there—and with what beauty and feeling—woods mostly, the birds."[12]

The Robber Bridegroom appeared on October 24, 1942, and again Eudora went to New York for publication, although she cut her trip short because one of her brothers left for the army just before she went to New York and the other left just after she returned. In a friend's apartment, she gave a little party for Diarmuid, Henry Volkening, John Woodburn, Michael Seide (a writer friend of Katherine Anne's whom Eudora had met at Yaddo), and Pamela Travers, the creator of Mary Poppins. She served drinks and toasted pecans and some cheese spread—just like a Jackson party, she said.[13]

While she was in New York, Eudora happily spent the $300 in prize money for "The Wide Net" from the *O. Henry Prize Stories of 1941* on a record player, an Ashley Dynaphone, and records at the Gramophone Shop. In the introduction to the O. Henry collection, Herschel Brickell denied having a regional bias and said that in fact he had not voted for the story. The Literary Guild made a bonus book out of the short stories, so Eudora earned still more money.[14]

She spent most of the rest of her time in New York at Katonah with the Russells, where, because her suitcase had been lost, she dressed for dinner by putting on one of Rose Russell's dresses and Diarmuid's shoes, which were turquoise and beaded, from India. During the day she and Diarmuid both painted watercolors, for which activity she wore his dungarees.

Eudora took the long way home and went to see John Robinson in St. Petersburg, where she spent two days swimming in the Gulf and relaxing with him. Robinson liked what he was doing in the Army Air Corps but could not decide whether to stay where he was or apply for Officers Candidate School. He really liked enlisted men better than officers, except for his immediate superior, a second lieutenant, who was a lawyer and a member of the legislature who had been working on a Ph.D. at the University of Texas when he joined the army. But the enlisted men—a Serb with whom he argued constantly and "a little Jewish boy from Philadelphia" who knew everything and spoke Chinese and Portuguese—were "mad." "I'm the only normal person in the crowd, including a technical sergeant who is a crooner on the radio and a jitterbug," Robinson said.[15] In the end he went to OCS.

Eudora had been worried about how reviewers would react to *The Robber Bridegroom,* and to some extent her fears were justified. Most critics were puzzled. A brief review in *The New Yorker* said it was "a bedlam story, or an apparition, or an extravaganza straight out of another world . . . If this *is* a dream, it is one of the gay, soaring kind, without a breath of nightmare and with humor as sly and irresistible as anything in 'Candide,' "[16] But Lionel Trilling in the *Nation* did not like the way Eudora had tried to "translate the elements of European fairy tales into the lore of the American frontier." He complained that its princess was a Mississippi girl who gathered pot herbs at the edge of the indigo field, its mild father-king a planter, its bridegroom, with a secret that must not be pried into, a river bandit, its giant the legendary flatboatsman Mike Fink, its Rumpelstiltskinesque creature of earth a "white-trash boy," its spirits of air Indians. He compared it to the "coy mystifications" of the poet Elinor Wylie and the novelist Virginia Woolf.[17]

The *Philadelphia Inquirer* ran *The Robber Bridegroom* the next year, with illustrations by Ben Dale, as its "Complete Gold Seal Novel," cutting the sections it considered unsuitable, including the sexual intimacies between Rosamond and Jamie Lockhart and the whiskey-selling and drunkenness of the priest Father O'Connell.[18] The note about the author contained a few biographical facts and this last paragraph: "Miss Welty is absorbed in her social occupations and contends, paradoxically, that she has no literary life."

Chapter 25

Leaving Doubleday

1942

When John Woodburn left Doubleday for Harcourt Brace in the late autumn of 1942, he asked Eudora to go with him, promising to publish the Natchez Trace stories in the spring of 1943 on an "impeccable list" that would include Katherine Anne Porter's *No Safe Harbor,* Robert Penn Warren's *At Heaven's Gate,* Ruth McKenney's *Jake Home,* and William Saroyan's *The Human Comedy.* Eudora, who felt loyal to Woodburn, not Doubleday, quickly agreed. Kenneth McCormick of Doubleday protested, saying she was the most promising young writer they had and he felt entitled to her third book.[1] Eudora replied that personal reasons were the relevant ones and the others were irrelevant; her loyalty to Woodburn outweighed her loyalty to Doubleday.[2]

McCormick applied pressure to every point he could, even writing to Herschel Brickell to ask him to intervene. Eudora was surprised that Doubleday voiced any objection. She reported to Brickell that she had heard that Somerset Maugham had told one of the Doubledays that everybody on the Doubleday list was a terrible writer except for Muriel Rukeyser and Eudora Welty; Mr. Doubleday had then asked what these writers were doing and found that Eudora was in the process of leaving. That was when Doubleday started writing to Brickell.[3] She told Katherine Anne Porter that since she had signed with Harcourt Brace for the book of Natchez Trace stories, all of which had been published in magazines, they were now "sorority sisters," since Harcourt was also Porter's publisher.[4]

The title for the eight Trace stories was definitely established: *The Wide Net*. Eudora, still in her early thirties, had turned out these stories with incredible speed in the most productive period of her life. It had taken her six years to write the stories in *A Curtain of Green* and *The Robber Bridegroom*, but she wrote all the Trace stories in a year and a half, from "First Love," in January 1941 to "At the Landing" in the summer of 1942.

But she had written nothing new for many months. She told Katherine Anne that she was thinking of going to New York to stay for several months and write. There she might have privacy. Her brothers were away in the armed services, and she and her mother were living together. At best, she had only semiprivacy at home. Semiprivacy was all right for short pieces, but the longer stories took larger chunks of time.[5]

Christmas 1942 was grim. Eudora had the flu, with all the depression that goes with it, and she missed her brothers and her friends who were off at war.[6] By the time she wrote to Katherine Anne Porter about it, it was a typical January in Jackson, with the temperature in the eighties one day, the twenties the next. The quince was in bloom, and on the warm days the robins started making nests, and butterflies came out as though it were April.

When she made her regular spring trip to New York in 1943, Eudora took only her spring coat, and met icy weather, with snow and sleet. She stayed in Katonah for ten days, and John Robinson, stationed at Harrisburg, Pennsylvania, was able to get there for a picnic one weekend. Whether they were friends or lovers, they cared enough about each other to go to the trouble of getting together all over the map during the war.

While Eudora was in New York, the roses bloomed in Jackson, but she was back in time to see the irises, daylilies, poppies, and larkspurs. She read the galleys of *The Wide Net* and tried to write a story, but the heat was intense, with temperatures in the hundreds. She struggled to keep the garden watered while her mother visited in West Virginia. In the midst of the heat, she got the news that she had again won first prize in the O. Henry contest, this time for "Livvie Is Back." She was the first person in history, Woodburn wrote, to receive two O. Henry firsts in succession. (Wilbur Daniel Steele won two firsts, but they were twelve years apart.) "If this doesn't stop, people will begin to suspect that you write also under the name of Herschel Brick-ell," Woodburn said.[7] Brickell once more had to answer charges that he favored southerners, or even Mississippians, for the O. Henry prizes. He pointed out that "an all-Eastern panel of judges" had made the selection.

This time Eudora spent the prize money at Casey's in New Orleans, on a small, solid mahogany English desk made late in the eighteenth century, with a lid that came down and many pigeonholes. "I never had a desk before so I just *sit* at it," she wrote to Katherine Anne.[8]

John Robinson took part in the invasion of Sicily in July 1943 and to her intense relief came out of it with only a light fever and "bites from sleeping in haystacks." After a week in the hospital, he was sent to North Africa. Eudora resented it when people said how short the conquest of Sicily was proving; it couldn't have seemed a short time to the soldiers involved, she said.[9]

From North Africa, Robinson sent Eudora a note that his French landlady had left for him, written in purple ink: "Madame Brunet requests the officer to please swallow up nothing in the bedroom and bathroom and also not to sit on the bed. Thanks." She was lucky to have all her relatives and best friends in the army still safe, Eudora wrote to Katherine Anne. "John Robinson that I adore so much," she said, was safe in Africa, and writing fiction.

Then Robinson was at Salerno, distinguishing himself as a combat intelligence officer with a night-fighter squadron of the Army Air Force. His superior officer, Sol Katz, who later became a professor of history at the University of Washington, wrote in a recommendation a few years later that "Mr. Robinson performed his duties not merely competently and efficiently, but with great insight and perception."[10]

A nonfiction piece, the elegant, compassionate "Pageant of Birds," which Eudora had written a couple of years before, appeared in the *New Republic* on October 25. She had been walking along Farish Street when she had seen two African American women carrying big paper wings over their arms. She followed them to the Farish Street Baptist Church, which was in the block with the Booker-T moviehouse, the pool hall, the doctor's office, the pawnshop, the "cafe with the fish-sign that says, 'If They Don't Bite We

Catch 'em Anyway,' and the barbershop."[11] Inside the church, she met Maude Thompson, a writer and the director of a playlet called "The Pageant of Birds." It would be presented at seven o'clock that night, and Thompson invited Eudora to return with all her friends. She did return, with one friend, and—because they were white—they were seated on the front row.

The article describes the pageant and tells how the women in the cast were dressed in homemade costumes of bright wings, tails, and crests, "flapping their elbows, dipping their knees." They entered from the front door and proceeded down the center aisle to the front of the church. There was a magnificent eagle, four bluebirds, two robins, four redbirds, two peacocks, goldfinches, canaries, and one blackbird. Eudora thought it was "marvelous . . . original and dramatic."[12]

She had not taken her camera to the performance, but after it was over, she offered to take a group picture of the birds. Four of these photographs appear in *Eudora Welty: Photographs*.

Eudora has said that she and Thompson became friends, probably as much as it was possible for a white woman and a black woman to be friends at that time. "I used to run into her in railroad stations," she told an interviewer much later. "She was a big church worker, and she would go to funerals out of town and maybe do other churchly things, and we always greeted each other and had conversation."[13]

Chapter 26

Trilling vs. Warren

1943

When *The Wide Net* appeared on September 23, 1943, most reviewers found the stories obscure and fanciful. Eudora said that she did not mind being "mysterious," but she did not want to be "obscure." Still, the label would endure. Forty years later, a reviewer writing about *Author and Agent,* a book containing correspondence between Eudora and Diarmuid Russell, said that her letters from the period of *The Wide Net* show her, "just like the stories themselves, on the threshold of giving up daylight logic altogether."[1]

Even Jean Stafford, in the *Partisan Review,* compared *The Wide Net* unfavorably with *A Curtain of Green.* This new book, Stafford said, had "eight stories in a language so vague that not only actual words but syntax itself has the improbable inexactitude of a verbal dream."[2] Stafford and Eudora later became good friends, and Stafford regretted this harsh review. To make amends, she asked to review Eudora's next book.

Diana Trilling, who later made it abundantly plain in her autobiography that she had little use for any literary product that came from outside New York City, said in the *Nation* that "Eudora Welty has developed her technical virtuosity to the point where it outweighs the uses to which it is put, and her vision of horror to the point of nightmare." The stories were so obscure, she said, that she understood only the title story and "Livvie." She added that the book "has tremendous emotional impact, despite its obscurity . . . It is a book of ballets, not of stories; even the title piece is a *pastorale macabre . . .* Miss Welty's prose constantly calls attention to herself and away from the object."[3] (This review makes one appreciate Gore Vidal's observation years later that Diana Trilling's "Book Notes" in the *Nation* went to her head.)

Although Eudora joked about it at the time, Trilling's piece on *The Wide Net* was the only review that ever wounded her. She wrote to Russell that Trilling had said all the things about her that she had said about Carson McCullers.[4] Fifty years later, she could still accurately paraphrase the review. "I remember how sharply that cut," she said.[5]

Robert Penn Warren rose majestically to Eudora's defense and replied to Trilling in an essay, "The Love and the Separateness in Miss Welty," in the *Kenyon Review.* With exquisite courtesy, Warren bowed to Trilling and "her valuable and sobering comments on current fiction" in her "Book Notes." He then set out to counter her criticisms of *The Wide Net.* He said that Trilling had dealt not with Eudora's failures to fulfill the artist's goal but "with the nature of that goal." He considered Trilling's key statement to be that *The Wide Net* had "tremendous emotional impact, despite its obscurity." In essence, Warren asked how Trilling could feel an emotional impact without sensing "some principle of organization, some view, some meaning." Trilling, he said, could not say that Eudora's stories were not fiction but ballets when they had this emotional effect.[6]

Warren was a wonderful champion, and his article was not as self-serving as it might seem. Although he had bought seven of the seventeen stories in *A Curtain of Green* when he was the editor of the *Southern Review,* none of the eight stories in *The Wide Net* had appeared there. He was therefore not defending his own judgment when he took up the cudgels against Mrs. Trilling. He was a figure to be reckoned with, now a professor at the University of Minnesota and the author of two novels, two books of poems, and two textbooks.

Eudora, who still had not met Warren personally, was considerably cheered by his article when she finally saw it, some time after it was published in the spring of 1944.[7] A $1,000 award for *The Wide Net* from the American Academy of Arts and Letters also helped bind the wounds of the book's reviews.

In his article Warren had pointed out that nearly all of the stories in *The Wide Net* were about people who, "in one way or another, are cut off, alienated, isolated, from the world." This aspect of Eudora's fiction strikes many people. It seems logical that these stories of isolation grew from the experiences of her own life, when she was not always but often the outsider—the unpretty toddler, the dateless teenager, the college girl in exile in a single room in a Wisconsin boarding house.

In November 1943, after the book came out, Eudora was killing time, trying Katherine Anne Porter's recipe for potato tart with a "little pastry chimney," although she really preferred Katherine Anne's onion tart—or anything with onions.[8] She went out to do some watercolor painting one afternoon and wrote to Katherine Anne about the wonderful golden light that made cornshocks, haystacks, even cows and the water in a pond look golden. She stayed until after dark and painted the moon rising over a small African American church. A little black dog with a red tongue sat outside, and Eudora said he might have been the devil. She also painted the kitchen furniture; she told Katherine Anne she couldn't stop. She worked in the garden, wrote to John Robinson, and played records.[9]

She was bored, so perhaps she *should* leave Jackson, she said in her letter to Katherine Anne. She was waiting for Pamela Travers, who had called from Santa Fe to say that she would be in Jackson with her little boy, Camillus, but Eudora was sure that Travers had no idea how far it was from Santa Fe to Jackson.

It had been eighteen months since Eudora had sent Russell a story. She often dramatized her attitudes toward her writing for Katherine Anne's benefit, and she wrote to her friend that she had been "feeling frozen and silent" for a whole year but had just finished a thirty-five-page story named "The Delta Cousins." Since Russell was not satisfied with the story, Eudora planned to revise it.[10]

Editors, even Mary Lou Aswell, felt that "Delta Cousins" was too long, especially when they considered wartime paper shortages. Aswell suggested certain cuts and promised to pay $500 for it, the most Eudora had ever gotten, if she would shorten it. Eudora did not want to cut it, and Russell sent it to Edward Weeks, the editor of the *Atlantic,* who kept it but also asked her to cut three or four thousand words. Eudora refused, and the story grew longer.

It was a pity that no one took it, but to use again that old southern circumlocution, it was a blessing. Eudora reported that Russell had said that "Delta Cousins" looked like Chapter Two of a novel and told her to go on with it. "I trusted everything he said, absolutely . . . and 'Delta Cousins' became *Delta Wedding,"* she explained.[11] It was her first full-length novel.

Chapter 27

The *New York Times* Book Review 1944

  "Delta Cousins" was in a kind of limbo when, in early 1944, Eudora decided to spend several months in New York, where she hoped to get some serious writing done. She could share an apartment with Rosa Wells, a friend from Jackson who was working there. Together they moved in at 25 East Tenth Street, the same apartment house where Nancy Farley, John Robinson's good friend from Oxford, lived. Rosa Wells and Hubert Creekmore formed the nucleus of a Jackson-in-New-York group that always looked forward to Eudora's visits.

When Robert Van Gelder, the young maverick who was then editing the *New York Times Book Review,* heard that Eudora was coming to New York, he asked her to work temporarily for the *Book Review* on the copy desk. Eudora accepted. She had already been reviewing books for them, and Van Gelder thought she would be "just the fresh face he needed."

Eudora said she was a complete innocent. "That's what Van Gelder liked," she said. "He liked trying somebody out who had never done this before. The summer before me, he had put a psychiatrist on the job. I liked that. It was refreshing."[1]

Van Gelder, thirty-eight years old, had joined the *Times* in 1928. He had admired Eudora's work ever since he had been a general assignment reporter and book reviewer, and he had interviewed her for the *Times* in 1942, at the time of *The Wide Net*'s publication. He became editor of the *Book Review* in 1943. For his permanent staff he hired Nona Balakian, recommended by John Chamberlin, a daily book reviewer for the *Times,* when she was still Chamberlin's student at the Columbia Graduate School of Journalism.

Van Gelder wanted to educate people through the *Book Review,* and he encouraged his staff to seek out books of high literary quality, translations of foreign writers, and even university press books, which until then had hardly been considered "reviewable." The *Book Review* was dependent on advertising, so Van Gelder could not ignore popular books, but under his leadership, reviews of these books "invariably exposed what was irrelevant or false or blatantly commercial."[2] He was skillful at finding young literary writers who could slash trash with wit and style.

A tyrant named Lester Markel had absolute control over the entire Sunday edition of the *New York Times,* and every new employee at the *Book Review* had to have an interview with him. Eudora's went something like this:

MARKEL: I hear you've applied for a job with our Sunday *Book Review.*

WELTY: No, I was invited to work on it and I'm already working on it. [As she explained later, this was the truth and she could say nothing else.]

MARKEL: It's very irregular.[3]

Eudora settled happily into her job. Van Gelder held no staff meetings, and the galleys and review copies of books poured in each day and were put on shelves in his office. Galleys of the important books went straight out to reviewers. Van Gelder would read reviews when they came in and perhaps pencil a suggestion to the copy editor. The whole staff worked as copy editors, and reviews were distributed "more or less in terms of staffer interest or specialty."[4]

Staff members were free to suggest reviewers to Van Gelder; in fact, they were encouraged to find new reviewers. Eudora suggested her old friends from Jackson: Nash Burger, Bill Hamilton, and Hubert Creekmore.

She also persuaded Katherine Anne Porter to write a review. "Gorgeous of you to do a little James reviewing," she wrote to her friend, and Van Gelder even told Porter that she didn't have to observe the deadline strictly.[5]

Nash Burger recalled later that when his first review (of Joseph Stanley Pennell's *The History of Rome Hanks and Kindred Matters*) appeared on the front page of the *Book Review,* Lester Markel demanded to know who in the hell Nash K. Burger was. Van Gelder told him calmly that "Nash K. Burger is the author of the book review on the front page."[6]

Eudora enjoyed the work on the *Times* and the camaraderie of the office. She once used a pseudonym, Michael Ravenna, for a review of *Artists at War,* by George Biddle, and epic myths have grown up around this.* The job was the only one at which Eudora worked nine to five in an office; at the WPA, she had traveled much of the time, and her job at the radio station had been part-time. The hours did not confine her unduly—she slipped away to see Mae West perform one afternoon. She respected Van Gelder and

---

* Reporters and memoirists have explained that Eudora used "Michael Ravenna" because the hated Lester Markel did not think a southern lady could review wartime novels. Nash Burger recalled that the Ravenna reviews were "frequent and perceptive," that they were often quoted in publishers' advertising, and that "invitations from radio networks for Michael Ravenna to appear" had to be declined.

"That was a mischievous figment of imagination on the part of Nash Burger," Eudora said. "The *Times* did not like to have staffers sign reviews because we were supposed to get other people to do the reviews." Staffers, of course, did sign their names to reviews, but if a staff member happened to have two reviews in one issue, a pseudonym on one of them was in order. "Being a woman had nothing to do with it," Eudora said in 1991. "After all, Van Gelder had hired a woman, hadn't he?" Nash Burger reviewed Franz Hoellering's *Furlough* and Gilbert Gabriel's *I Got a Country* under Ravenna's name. Eudora told an interviewer that she put Ravenna's name on the Burger reviews because she could not think of any other name.

Another staff member maintained that Eudora used the pseudonym as a screen when she reviewed a book by a southern writer whom she knew. It turns out that the staff member was thinking of the fourth occurrence of the Ravenna byline, a review in 1949 of Mississippian Shelby Foote's first novel, *Tournament,* which was written by Nash Burger long after Eudora had left the *Times.* In this review the unsinkable Ravenna actually mentioned other recent southern writers—including Eudora Welty.

The plain facts of the Ravenna byline, clearly established by Pearl McHaney, do not keep the busy Welty scholars from speculating about it. One woman doing research in the Welty manuscripts at the Mississippi State Archives in Jackson announced, "I've cracked the code." Ravenna came, she said, from two sources: "Enna" from the "fair field of Enna," where Persephone was taken, and "Rav" from the verb *to ravish.*

liked her colleagues; Nona Balakian became a lifelong friend. She had many other friends in New York, some from Mississippi, such as Nancy Farley, and others who were writers and editors, including Mary Lou Aswell and Margaret Cousins.

She took reviewing seriously. "I didn't want to give a book a bad review," she recalled years later. "No matter what it is, it's a year out of somebody's life and they did the best they could."[7] She said once that she learned a great deal about writing on the job, but not necessarily about writing fiction. "You wouldn't write a very good review if you kept applying it to what you could learn to write fiction," she said. "You can't mix them."[8]

Eudora took the job at the *Book Review* with the understanding that she would leave at the end of October. When Van Gelder tried to persuade her to stay, she strongly recommended that he hire Nash Burger instead. Burger went up for an interview, was offered the job, turned it down, reconsidered, and later accepted it. He moved with his family to New York and remained at the *Book Review* until he retired.

Chapter 28

How to Make a Novel

1945

When Eudora got back to Jackson, she had to delay work on "Delta Cousins." She took her mother, who had found she had cataracts, to New Orleans to see an eye specialist. Then it was Christmas, and friends who had been away for years were home for the holidays.

"About the same people as usual," John Robinson commented on a party at Eudora's house in January 1945. "Very nice in a way."[1] Before he left Italy, Robinson had sent Eudora a pair of antique Italian china vases; they were "most beautiful," and she was overcome, she said.[2] Hubert Creekmore was home from the navy and on his way to New York, where he had a job as an editor on *Tomorrow* magazine, which had published Eudora's "The Wide Net." He solicited contributions from his Mississippi friends, including George Marion O'Donnell.

When Eudora finally turned to "Delta Cousins," she had at her disposal a mother lode of historical material, thanks to John Robinson. John's great-great-grandmother, Nancy McDougall, began a diary in 1832 when she married Alfred Bassett Robinson, and she kept it up until 1870; by then it filled ten volumes of wide ledger books. John wrote to Eudora about the diaries and told her that the first volume opened with the newlyweds' journey on horseback from Port Gibson to Sidon. Nancy and her new husband rode to Clinton, visited Alfred's older brother, Raymond, and went to Mount Salus to see a Judge Caldwell and his wife. (Eudora used the name Mount Salus in *The Optimist's Daughter*.) The Robinsons traveled incessantly, to buy slaves or to put their sons in college, and took steamboats down the Yazoo to Vicksburg, up the Mississippi to Cincinnati, and down the Ohio River to Virginia. The couple became very rich; when John Robinson checked tax records in Carroll and Tallahatchie counties, he found that when Alfred died in 1858 he left 212 slaves and $600,000 worth of land. During the Civil War, Nancy buried the silver to keep it from the Yankees. The diary was also "a chronicle of illness—yellow fever, cholera, disease of the spleen . . . really malaria though they didn't know it," Robinson wrote to Eudora. And he thought it was very well written.[3]

While Robinson was overseas, Eudora drove up to the Delta to visit his cousins in Clarksdale, who owned the diaries, so she could read them herself. Their contents provided historical background for *Delta Wedding*, with enough left over for another short story, "Kin."

As she wrote, Eudora was vague about what she was working on, "as usual," Nash Burger said, but she did tell him that the piece was longer than what she usually wrote and took place in the mid-1920s. She set the action in 1923 because "nothing happened" that year—no war, no Depression, no Mississippi River flood.[4]

She sent each chapter to John Robinson. "I just made it up as I went; part of it was to entertain him, and part of it was to try to do something Diarmuid thought I could do," Eudora said. "It was the most ill-planned or unplanned of books. I was just writing about what a family is like, trying to put them down in a place where they could just spread themselves."[5]

She also said that she didn't know the Delta well. When she wrote the short story "Delta Cousins," she used just what she had sensed from visits, groping toward the Delta's mood, what the people were like when cotton was everything and the Delta really was a different world. After she visited John's relations, however, she had a better feeling for the Delta's history. "It was the wilderness till just about yesterday," she said. "And I hadn't realized any of this."

It is fascinating to see how she built the novel, braiding three strands of material. Nancy McDougall Robinson's journal provided background; memories of her own experiences added specificity to the action; and her imagination enlarged and enlivened.

The Fairchild family does "spread itself," as Eudora wanted; it dominates *Delta Wedding*. The amplitude of their life at Shellmound, a cotton plantation in the Mississippi Delta, the abundance of coconut cake and ham and turkey and lemonade and guinea eggs, the multiplicity of amusements—horses and automobile rides and boats on the river—their stories of events in the family's romantic past and the equally romantic present, the coming and going of innumerable relations, the activity of countless black servants, the glamour of everybody's favorite, Uncle George: all these dazzling elements showcase Eudora's powers of observation and her gift for the telling detail.

Eudora used great chunks of Nancy Robinson's memoir, including the yellow fever epidemic, for the Fairchilds' history. In the book, a portrait of Mary Shannon Fairchild shows dark circles under her eyes, for it was painted "the year the yellow fever was worst and she had nursed so many of her people, besides her family and neighbors; and two hunters, strangers, had died in her arms."[6] The Grove, the oldest of the three Fairchild houses, is very much like the description of Nancy Robinson's first home in the Delta, "sticks and mud like a dove's nest." In *Delta Wedding* it's "a dove-gray box . . . a cypress house on brick pillars now painted green and latticed over, and its double chimneys at either end."[7] A murder by a Fairchild man was suggested by Nancy's mention of a Robinson who killed a business associate.

Marmion, the grandest Fairchild house, is based on Waverly, the antebellum mansion near Columbus that Eudora and her college friends visited while she was at the W. She simply transplanted Waverly, with its huge boxwood shrubbery, double stairways, octagonal hall, and cupola, to the banks of the Yazoo River and renamed it Marmion. Marmion is also the name of Laura's doll, made by her mother. The name for doll and house comes from Sir Walter Scott's long poem *Marmion: A Tale of Flodden Field*, which contains the song "Lochinvar."

A bee man ferries Laura and her cousin India, both nine years old in 1923, to Marmion, just as a man who raised bees ferried the MSCW students to Waverly. The little girls find a dead goldfinch on the steps, just as Eudora once saw a dead goldfinch on the steps of Waverly. Marmion, grandest of the three Fairchild houses, stands empty, and Dabney and Troy, the bride and groom, will live there after they're married.

Eudora had walked across a railroad trestle when she went to Waverly as a student at Mississippi State College for Women, and she drew on her memory to make a railroad trestle the setting for a key scene in *Delta Wedding*. A near accident on the trestle involving the Yellow Dog, the local train, is described to Laura early in the book and is recounted and referred to over and over again. On the way home from a fishing trip, all the children and Uncle George, plus "ten or twenty Negroes," are walking on the railroad track, singing. On the trestle, Maureen, a cousin, catches her foot in the track. Uncle George kneels down to work it loose as the Yellow Dog comes puffing toward them. Everybody jumps off the trestle out of harm's way except Maureen and George, who cannot get the child's foot loose. The train stops just in time. The incident is clearly going to be part of family legend, and it comes up again and again as each person retells it.

At night Laura and India discuss the movies and books that Eudora had seen and read when she was their age. India tells Laura about the showboat that came when the water in the Yazoo River was high, and the Rabbit's Foot Minstrel; Laura tells India about "Babes in the Wood," Thurston the Magician, Annette Kellerman in "Daughter of the Gods," and Clara Kimball in "Drums of Jeopardy." They both have white dresses, like the dresses Eudora had when she was a child, with blue insertion at the waists and interlocking hoops briar-stitched in the yokes. When she was a child, Eudora was left-handed, just as her grandfather and uncles had been, but her father, who believed the world was organized for right-handed people, "broke her" of left-handedness. In the novel, Battle Fairchild, Laura's uncle, "has broken every child at the table of being left-handed."

Just as most of Eudora's short stories are concerned with an outsider, her first full-length novel broadens to include several outsiders. Eudora has said that she felt she did not know the Delta well enough to write from the viewpoint of a Delta native; thus she used the sensibilities of outsider Laura, a child from Jackson, for a lens. A great deal of the story is told from the viewpoint of the nine-year-old Laura, whose mother has died. Laura has been invited to come to Shellmound to stay with the Fairchilds, her mother's brother's family, for the wedding of Dabney, the second oldest Fairchild daughter. Weddings and funerals are the easiest way to get people together in fiction, Eudora said. "It's a southern mode, but it's more than that. It's a crisis, a climactic moment when everyone is keyed up."[8]

Ellen, the wife of Laura's Uncle Battle, is something of an outsider because she was born and raised in Virginia. Again, the outsider is useful to the author. "It was Ellen showing *me*," Eudora said.[9]

The bridegroom, Troy Flavin, is a real outsider; he is the plantation's overseer and is a product not of the Delta aristocracy but of the hill country's redneck people. Impressive indeed is the way members of the family bite their tongues—most of the time—and rise above class distinctions when talking to him or about him. Uncle George's wife, Robbie Reid, like Troy, comes from a lower-class family. Maureen, though a cousin and blood kin, is not really part of the circle, because she is retarded; her mother dropped her on her head when she was a baby and has not combed her own hair since.

There is no plot in *Delta Wedding,* simply the unfolding of layer upon layer of family relationships, as Laura learns about Maureen and her mother, about George and his wife, about Troy Flavin's antecedents, about the servants. The house servants—Bitsy, Roxie, Little Uncle, Pinchy, Vi'let—are numerous, and so are the field hands. (Aunt Studney, an old black woman in the book, is modeled after an actual person Eudora had heard of during visits to the Delta.) At one point, Pinchy is said to be "coming through." Eudora has said she got more letters about Pinchy than anything else, all asking what "coming through" meant. "It just means you get religion," Eudora said. It was one of many things she said she did not "have the wits to realize would need to be explained."[10]

The cast of characters is huge: Battle Fairchild's two aunts live at Shellmound with the family; two of his sisters live at the Grove, another Fairchild house nearby; another sister comes from Memphis for the wedding, bringing her grandchild, Lady Clare Buchanan, whose name is that of a character in *Marmion.* In fact, Eudora had a hard time keeping track of all the characters. When Edward Weeks was about to serialize *Delta Wedding* in the *Atlantic,* he found that she had miscounted the children; there were ten, not nine. "It was a stern lesson for me," Eudora said. "I knew them all, but I hadn't really said one, two, three, four, five, six . . ."[11] The offspring of Battle and Ellen Fairchild have typical southern names—Shelley, Dabney, Orrin, India, Roy, Little Battle, Ranny, and Bluet (the baby). Maureen is a

Fairchild too, but the daughter of Battle's late brother; Laura McRaven is the daughter of his dead sister, Annie Laurie. When Lady Clare Buchanan arrives, there are eleven children, plus Shelley and Dabney, the two teenage girls.

Before Eudora completely finished *Delta Wedding,* she wrote the short story "The Sketching Trip," which Weeks bought for the *Atlantic Monthly.* Although Weeks told her it had Chekhov's timelessness, she has never included it in a collection. Weeks called her an indispensable contributor and said he was looking forward to publishing all or part of the "enchanting story of the Delta cousins" when she had finished revising it.

Chapter 29

The Other Jackson Writer

1945

Black Boy, the autobiography in which Richard Wright recorded his years of terror and humiliation in Jackson, appeared in 1945. Bill Hamilton, teaching history at Duke, wrote to Eudora's good friend Charlotte Capers, who was acting director of the Mississippi State Archives and acting editor of the *Journal of Mississippi History,* and urged her to get someone to review the book for the journal.

Hamilton felt that Wright was one of the more distinguished products of the public school system of Jackson, and wrote to Capers that his book was "articulate, interesting, honest, and restrained. It deserves neither the type of review you might expect of . . . a Ku-Kluxer, nor one by some incendiary in the Negro press." He suggested a few names as possible reviewers, including Eudora Welty.[1] Capers asked Eudora, but she refused. Finally, Dr. E. Bruce Thompson of Mississippi College reviewed it, calling it a "welcome and convincing refutation of the claims of those Southern whites who boast that they understand the 'nigger' and who naively rationalize that 'niggers' are the happiest and most contented people in the world."[2]

Jackson had no bookstores at that time, and Mrs. Herbert, who ran the Office Supply, the only store in town that sold books, refused to stock *Black Boy.* "I never go in there," Nash Burger said. "She is so narrow and bitter about the 'Negro situation.' " Burger showed the book to his students at Central High and explained that "if they work hard and have as much sense they may be as famous as the Jim Hill School graduate. Their eyes pop to think a Negro could write a book." Burger added, not at all irrelevantly, that he hoped to become a writer and be able to live part of each year "in this lovely state and part of each year *out* of it and away from its boring, illiterate inhabitants."[3]

The attitudes demonstrated by Hamilton and Burger foreshadowed the frustrations that white moderates felt when the "race question" heated up in the fifties and sixties and gripped Mississippi in ten years of turmoil and violence. Eudora's refusal to review Wright's book was consistent with her determined apolitical position as a writer.

Chapter 30

Delta Wedding

1946

Eudora finished *Delta Wedding* in September 1945; Harcourt Brace bought it, and Edward Weeks agreed to serialize it in the *Atlantic* in four parts. It was Eudora's fourth book and her first full-length novel.

When the book appeared in April 1946, the 10,000-copy first printing sold out in less than a month. The *Jackson Daily News* said on May 7 that local bookstores had sold all the copies they had, and estimated "conservatively" that 700 copies had been sold in Mississippi. Harcourt Brace printed another 10,000 in May and 5,000 more soon after. In an ecstasy of local fervor, the *Daily News* reported on May 14 that *Delta Wedding* had moved into thirteenth place on the list of sixteen best-selling novels. (The top three were *This Side of Innocence,* by Taylor Caldwell; *Arch of Triumph,* by Erich Maria Remarque; and *The King's General,* by Daphne du Maurier.)

Eudora's friend Hubert Creekmore also had good news. His novel *Fingers of the Night,* which he had written during the Depression, had finally found a publisher and appeared in May. *Fingers of the Night,* which had begun as a short story called "The Tenant Farmer," repelled and angered Mississippians. The *Daily News* said it belonged in the garbage along with *Sanctuary, Light in August, Tobacco Road,* and "any other nasty drivel purporting to picture life in Mississippi."[1] At his publication party in New York,

Creekmore told Nash Burger and Lehman Engle that he hoped to get a grant so he could live in Mississippi and write another novel.

Nash Burger found *Delta Wedding* hard to read. It was fine "sentence by sentence," but a few pages put him to sleep. He was afraid that the Mississippians who rushed to buy it because it was by a Mississippian and who had not read a book since *So Red the Rose* would be bewildered and "return permanently to the comics and Fred Sullens," editor of the *Daily News*.[2]

Hamilton, who had not read the book, wrote to Eudora that he was beginning to have the impression that she was "always about to step from a white-columned portico into a carriage drawn by horses who have breakfasted on mint juleps." He was going to "commission Hubert Creekmore or Frank Lyell to write the truth for posterity."[3]

John Robinson spent an evening at Eudora's house when the Herschel Brickells, passing through Jackson, were there, and he read aloud to Brickell a review of two nineteenth-century journals that Bill Hamilton had written for the *Times Book Review*. It was the same Sunday that Charles Poore's glowing review of *Delta Wedding* appeared on the cover of the *Book Review*, with a singularly ugly drawing of Eudora by Helen Jay Lotterhos for illustration.

Many reviewers, however, had unkind things to say about *Delta Wedding*. One complained that there were too many names to remember and said the characters seemed as dead as the people whose portraits hung on the wall; another said it was so dull he couldn't get past the first hundred pages, and added—horror of horrors—that Carson McCullers's *Member of the Wedding*, which came out about the same time, was stronger and more clearly drawn. Other reviewers noticed that both books featured girls with male given names and preadolescent attitudes toward brides. Of course, it was the comparison with McCullers's novel that drove Eudora to fury.

Time lambasted Eudora for not criticizing the aristocratic southern way of life, but said that kind of writing was only to be expected from the daughter of an insurance executive and a member of the Junior League.[4] Diana Trilling, unchastened by Robert Penn Warren's magisterial response to her attack on *The Wide Net*, wrote another negative review for the *Nation*. Her main complaint seemed to be that Eudora did not make a moral judgment on the racist society she portrayed.[5]

Eudora was pleased with Herschel Brickell's response to all this. He said he was not surprised at the reviewers' lack of understanding, that the "North simply does not comprehend the South and for that reason will always cherish a kind of fury at it, it doesn't understand our delights and our pleasures or even anything abstract about our ways." He told her she should be happy that the quality of her writing was respected.[6] (Every reviewer did indeed take Eudora seriously as a writer and conceded that she was talented. They just didn't like what she was writing about.)

Years later in an interview, Reynolds Price insisted that *Delta Wedding* was the "single most illuminating book we have about the fantastic complexity of racial relations in the Deep South, how people of enormous culture, kindness, generosity, goodness like the Fairchilds, with great human richness—human in *nature*—were capable of living on a base of virtual slaves. If you want to read an exercise in total silliness, go back to Diana Trilling's review."[7] Eudora did lay bare the old Delta lifestyle as well as anybody ever has. When I started work on a biography of the Greenville newspaper editor and publisher Hodding Carter, liberals and conservatives alike advised me to read *Delta Wedding* to understand the people and their way of life.

Delta Wedding is, however, by no means an exposé of the region's sociological problems. The plight of the Delta Negro was terrible. Richard Wright tells in *Black Boy* how, before he escaped from Mississippi, he discovered while working in the Delta one summer that blacks there were even worse off—exploited more cruelly, discriminated against more thoroughly—than the blacks in Jackson. Critics say that *Delta Wedding* ignores such problems of discrimination and economic bondage. But Eudora by no means ignored them. She showed them to us without editorializing. You can't read *Delta Wedding* without seeing that the black servants and field hands are treated like children, deprived of basic rights, and living in poverty. Eudora, however, directs our gaze elsewhere. She never meant her book to be anything but fiction; she explored relationships, especially in families, and let others write political tracts.

Chapter 31

Portrait Painted

1946

   Feeling rich—the *Atlantic* had paid $1,000 apiece for each of the four installments of *Delta Wedding,* and the book was continuing to do well— Eudora went off to New York and Washington for a long visit in the spring of 1946. Frank Lyell, who was marking time in Washington between military service and graduate school at Princeton, wanted to give a party for her but had no idea where he could have it. He consulted Marcella Comès Winslow, a painter and friend of many writers, who said immediately, "Eudora must stay with me, and the party can be in my garden." Winslow, a war widow and the daughter-in-law of Anne Goodwin Winslow, the Memphis writer, had heard about Eudora from her friend Katherine Anne Porter and wanted to meet her.[1]

Eudora arrived at Winslow's house in Georgetown and was duly feted at a garden party. Among the thirty guests were Alexis Léger, who wrote under the pen name St. John Perse; Grace Guest, assistant director of the Freer Gallery; Margaret D. Landon, who wrote *Anna and the King of Siam;* Mrs. Vernon Kellogg, a poet; and John Carter Vincent and J. Noel Macy, from the State Department. The weather was lovely and everyone seemed happy as they drank rum punch and admired Eudora. Eudora regretted, said Winslow, that she was not a glamorous honoree, and felt in awe of some of the guests, but "she stood out for what she is—the real thing."[2]

Then the visit became hectic. Winslow had rented her house for the summer and had told the tenants they could move in the day after Eudora was to leave. She enjoyed Eudora's visit immensely, and liked her so much that she had an idea. "Don't you think I should paint your portrait?" she asked Eudora. "Yes, I do," replied Eudora.

Winslow had only four hours—two hours in one evening, two hours the next morning—in which to paint it, but the result pleased everyone. That afternoon she piled all her belongings in her car, ready to drive to Vermont. She put the wet portrait, fourteen by ten inches, on top of them and took it to a party at the home of Attorney General and Mrs. Francis Biddle to show it off. "Eudora's portrait has a Delta background," Winslow wrote. "The sky color blends in with her green-blue dress. Miss Guest calls it a minor masterpiece."[3]

Marcella Winslow thought the portrait was the best thing she had ever done. Eudora liked it too and recalled later that to get so much done in a few hours, Winslow had been inspired. The artist hated to part with it, but Eudora wanted to buy it and promised to have a box made so she could ship the portrait back on loan for shows of Winslow's work.

Eudora went from Washington to New York, where she recommended Winslow's portraits of authors to the *New York Times Book Review* staff. In fact, the editors tried (unsuccessfully) to reach Winslow so they could use her portrait of Robert Penn Warren with a review of his new book, *All the King's Men*.

Eudora stayed in Dolly Wells's old room, since Wells had moved in with Jack Wiseman, a young woman from Jackson.[4] Wells gave a party for Eudora and invited Nash Burger, who was by then living in New York, and George Stephenson, another Central High alumnus, who was an Episcopal clergyman in Gulfport holding down a locum for the summer at Trinity Church in New York. Eudora saw Winslow again while she was in New York, this time at dinner at Caroline Gordon's apartment. (Eudora liked Caroline, then separated from Allen Tate, and was impressed that when she lived in Tennessee, Caroline sometimes went out to the car to write to get away from the phone.)

Back home in Jackson, Eudora hung her portrait and thought it looked "too elegant to be me."[5]

Part Three

Stretching Her Wings

Chapter 32

A Literary Magazine?

1946

John Robinson, discharged from the Army Air Corps, headed out west. He wrote a short story about his landlady in Algiers, the one who had written him notes in purple ink, and in August 1946 he sent the badly typed manuscript to Eudora, who was still in New York. It was the first thing he had written since college. Eudora, staying at the Hotel Albert, at University Place and East Tenth, was impressed by the story and sent it to William Maxwell, explaining that she didn't usually meddle, but she thought the piece was so good it should be in *The New Yorker*.[1]

Maxwell replied quickly, saying that the editors liked Robinson's story very much and would send him a check in a week or so. He called Robinson "a natural *New Yorker* writer" and said he was sure this was the first of many pieces they would be taking from him.[2] Robinson was, of course, pleased and told the editors to do any editing they liked and to send his check in care of the Berlitz School of Language in San Francisco, where he was teaching English. The story ran under the title, "Room in Algiers," on October 19, 1946.

Robinson acknowledged that he would never have been bold enough to send a story to *The New Yorker*. He thought, though, that Eudora was too encouraging; he wanted her to tell him what was wrong with his work.[3] (He did not become a regular *New Yorker* contributor; in September and October, Maxwell turned down his pieces "The Folded Leaf" and "This is My Lawful Wedded Wife.")

Meanwhile, Eudora and Robinson conceived the idea of starting a literary magazine that would publish only short stories. Herschel Brickell had told Robinson about Joseph Henry Jackson, the leader of San Francisco's literary set and literary editor of the *San Francisco Chronicle*. Jackson wrote about books in a daily column and talked about them on a radio program on NBC's Pacific network. While Eudora was in New York, Robinson wrote to him about their project. Eudora had been doing most of the groundwork, he said, and was in New York, where a lot of people were enthusiastic and encouraging. He mentioned Allen Tate, Diarmuid Russell, and Lambert Davis, her editor at Harcourt Brace, who had replaced John Woodburn, who had moved on. The whole thing would be scary, he said, "if I didn't know how capable Eudora is—she could really do it alone—I wouldn't have the nerve to attempt it." Eudora had had overtures from "Guggenheims and Rockefellers," and she might get financial backing from the beginning, but if she didn't, she would do it anyway, with her own money. "The main thing we want to be is free and I'm sure Eudora won't accept any sponsorship that breathes down the neck." They might "get chased by the Archbishop or Mr. Hearst," Robinson told Jackson, but he would like to publish the magazine in San Francisco.[4]

In New York, Eudora talked to Russell and Davis about the magazine. Then she went downtown to see Allen Tate for advice. Tate, a poet, critic, and former editor of the *Sewanee Review,* was working as an editor at Holt (where he was shortly replaced by John Woodburn). Tate did not demonstrate the enthusiasm reported by John Robinson. "Don't do it," he told Eudora.

"He surprised me with every word he said," Eudora said. "He gave me caustic information, with stories attached, about the depths I'd be getting into, about how I'd flounder in my ignorance . . . He was ready right then to congratulate me if I would *refrain* from editing a magazine and concentrate . . . on the writing of my own stories . . . He gave me an answer that was not a denial but a deliverance. Thus our long friendship began."[5]

When she got back to Jackson, Eudora sent Diarmuid Russell a completely new short story, "The Whole World Knows," about Randall MacLain of Battle Hill, Mississippi, a man who has just left his wife. He has a domineering mother who says things such as "Now I have two sons who keep things from me." Eudora started work on another new story, about a summer piano recital. She did not yet know that these stories were related.

Chapter 33

San Francisco

1946–1947

Eudora followed John Robinson to San Francisco in November 1946. She intended to stay a few weeks, and she hoped to find out if she could write in a place that was well away from Jackson.

Robinson liked San Francisco, and she liked Robinson and admired him tremendously. He certainly respected her work and her intellect. It is impossible to assess what else they felt about each other. Some of Eudora's friends thought she and Robinson might marry. "They were both tall and slender and literary," a friend said. Bettie Robinson, John's sister-in-law, had a different reaction. "Well, we never thought they'd get married. The families were friends, but there was never a romance," she said.

Eudora's enduring friendship with Robinson appears to be as close as she ever came to romance with a man. During World War II, every unmarried girl *had* to have a man in service whose picture she could have by her bed, a man to whom she could write. Robinson was Eudora's wartime man, someone she could tell Katherine Anne Porter she "adored," someone to visit when he was stationed in Florida, someone to write to when he was in Italy, someone to worry about when a battle was in progress. Her letters to him reveal her warm feelings; sometimes she addresses him as "dearest." Robinson's letters to her and to other people about her mention only his warm admiration for her work; for instance, "She has written some stunning things lately, a couple of stories, one rather long—Mississippi, and perfect as usual," he wrote to Bill Hamilton in November 1946.[1]

From San Francisco, Eudora and John sent a joint Christmas card to the Brickells. They spent Christmas Day with Arthur and Antoinette Foff, two young writers whom Robinson had met. Foff, a twenty-three-year-old native San Franciscan, was a graduate assistant to Alfred Noyes in the Berkeley English Department and wrote an occasional review for Joseph Henry Jackson's book pages in the *Chronicle*. He had sold two short stories, one, "Beautiful Golden-Haired Mamie," to the *Atlantic,* and another, "Sawdust," to *Story,* but neither had been published. He and Antoinette, who was writing mystery stories and would publish two under the name Anton Fereva, were excellent company. While the four of them celebrated New Year's Eve with a meal of spaghetti, they fell to discussing Faulkner's *As I Lay Dying,* and in the excitement of the moment mailed a joint postcard to Diarmuid Russell, who also represented the Foffs.

Eudora stayed in inexpensive hotels such as the Plaza, right on Union Square, where she paid two dollars and fifty cents a day for a room without a bath. It was fine, but it had a five-day limit. She liked the Whitcomb Hotel, on Market Street at the Civic Center; it was convenient to the opera house and to the post office, and actors in traveling shows stayed there. The trouble with hotel rooms, however, was the absence of cooking facilities. She wanted a room where she could have a coffeepot and a skillet and a hot plate. Finally she found a one-room sublet for a month through an advertisement in the *Chronicle*. It was nice and quiet and $14.50 a week. Hotels were warm, but the sublet was cold, with the heat turned off from eight in the morning until eight at night. She sat by the kitchen stove with the oven turned up high and read by the ceiling light and wrote on the kitchen table. "Cheery enough," she said, "but . . . monotonous with crumbs in books and stories getting in the oven."[2]

San Francisco restaurants, she found, were expensive, and she sought out Italian, Chinese, and French places near Fisherman's Wharf, which were cheaper and better. Her favorite bar, La Tosca, had opera scenes painted on the walls and Caruso on the jukebox. At Fisherman's Wharf she bought crabs and had the market man crack them for her, and then she took them home to eat with mayonnaise.

At first she was quite taken with San Francisco and found it hard to stay inside, since the weather was so beautiful. She marveled at the fog and the ocean and rode the streetcar to the beach every day to see the sunset. She saw Danny Kaye perform onstage, bought symphony tickets at a music store on Sutter Street, and went to hear the San Francisco Symphony with Pierre Monteux conducting.

The convenience of the multitude of small grocery stores delighted her. She sometimes bought expensive groceries in the basement of a store called City of Paris, but more often she shopped at the Crystal Market, where endless rows of stalls sold cheese, bread, and fresh honey. George Field, who ran a bookstore near Blum's Candy Store on the corner of Polk and California, would cash checks for her. He also knew books. She scribbled down the names of businesses she saw from the streetcars: Part-Time Antiques and Beaver Hat Works, on Haight Street; Mutual Cleaners, on Clement Street. (She later sent these to *The New Yorker* for "Our Own Business Directory," but they were never used.)

Over time she explored the entire Bay area. Berkeley was drier than San Francisco but full of students, collegiate activities, and elderly retirees. Sausalito was the "drippiest" place she had ever seen. Palo Alto was drier and nicer than San Francisco, but a long bus ride away.

In early 1947, Eudora was still in San Francisco. Her visit, intended to last a few weeks, had stretched into months. She worried about John Robinson, who worked in a factory at night and wrote stories during the day. He was depressed and needed money. Diarmuid Russell, who had taken him on as a client, had not sold a single story.

And she had been writing, sometimes in composition books. In February or March she finished "June Recital," about Cassie Morrison, Virgie Rainey, and Miss Eckhart. "I just *loved* it! I don't know any time in my life I ever felt so embedded and so carried away by the story, I just loved writing it," she said years later.[3] Place, always important in her stories, was doubly important in the origin of this one, for the Welty house was directly across the street from the Music Building at Belhaven College. When Eudora was writing in her room, the windows were open; there was no air conditioning, and she could hear the students practicing the piano. She never saw the students, but she heard the strains of "Warsaw Concerto" and "Country Gardens" over and over again. But "it was 'Fur Elise' that tugged at me," she said. " 'Fur Elise' penetrated into my own life and found me a story to tell. It gave me 'June Recital' and its perpetrator, Virgie Rainey."[4] She created Virgie with immense musical talent, "about which I know nothing."[5]

At the same time, she drew on the memories of her own childhood to picture little girls taking piano lessons, families sacrificing to provide a piano and money for the lessons. Eudora's own piano teacher, like Miss Eckhart, used a fly swatter to slap Eudora's hands when she made a mistake. And when her teacher wrote "Practice" on a page of sheet music, the *p* looked like Miss Eckhart's, "a curly circle with a long tail, as if she might draw a cat." Still, Miss Eckhart was a creature of Eudora's imagination; none of the piano teachers in Jackson were German. When she gave Miss Eckhart the line *Danke schoen,* she had never heard German spoken.

Eudora always felt "oddly in touch" with Miss Eckhart. Miss Eckhart was frightening, eccentric, an outsider, but "she persisted with me," Eudora said. Eudora was not like Miss Eckhart, she maintained; she was not musical, not a teacher, not foreign, not humorless, and she was not "missing out in love."[6] (But wasn't she "missing out in love" as much as Miss Eckhart, in spite of her protest?) At any rate, none of the differences mattered, Eudora wrote, because Miss Eckhart came from her, Eudora. She gave Miss Eckhart her passion for her own "life and work, my own art." That was what they had in common, and it exposed them to risks.

Eudora next wrote a long story set in San Francisco, "Music from Spain," about a little man who slaps his wife, skips work, and spends the day with a Spanish guitarist, wandering around San Francisco from downtown to the Pacific beach. Eudora had walked to Land's End herself one day, and she must have taken the route the little man and the guitarist took in the story. "Music from Spain," the only story in *Golden Apples* set outside Morgana and one of the half-dozen Welty stories set outside Mississippi, shows how well Eudora knew San Francisco. The reader can follow the protagonist on his Joycean odyssey from one end of the city to the other, from the time he leaves his apartment on Jones Street, heads downhill to Sacramento Street and California Street, and goes on to Market Street, past the jewelry shop where he works. Still on Market Street, he sees the Spanish guitarist, whom he heard in concert the night before, and saves him from being hit by an automobile. Their path continues down Market Street to a restaurant on Maiden Lane, where the protagonist buys lunch for the Spaniard, who speaks not a word of English. They walk again until they board a streetcar, at random. They cross Divisadero, passing "steep, fancy-fronted engraved-looking houses with all the paint worn away." When they get off the streetcar, they walk "into the sun and up into the last rim of hills." They reach the embankment "where some of the old graves, still to be ransacked by shovels, stood here and there under the olive trees."[7] On the beach, the little protagonist points up to the cliffs, Land's End. They walk north, climbing up the rocks. When they come down, they go back to the paved streets, and after a cup of coffee together, the protagonist runs off, leaving the Spaniard to catch a streetcar.

The story is obscure. Scholars have disagreed over the meaning of the mysterious events that occur—the hero and the Spaniard see a woman killed by a streetcar, they watch a cat stalking another cat at the beach, and at Land's End the Spaniard picks up the smaller man as though he were going to throw him into the Pacific Ocean. All this is told in a manner heavy with suggestion. But what is it suggesting? Unspoken homosexual longing has been mentioned by one scholar, but this seems very unlike Eudora Welty.

Was Eudora homesick for Jackson? Was that what made her describe the protagonist's memory of the Mississippi winter landscape? "Now when the city opened out so softly . . . it awoke a longing for that careless, patched land of Mississippi winter, trees in their rusty wrappers, slow-grown trees taking their time, the lost shambles of old cane, the winter swamp where his own twin brother, he supposed, still hunted."[8]

Eudora planned to go home in late February, but John Robinson came down with a cold. (He had lived for a while near the beach, and Eudora thought the damp location led to his respiratory troubles.)[9] The cold turned into flu, which threatened to become pneumonia, and Eudora refused to leave town while he was so ill. Although Robinson thought "Music from Spain" was depressing, Eudora mailed it to Diarmuid Russell just before she left San Francisco, in March 1947.

The house her father had built at 741 North Congress Street in Jackson, where Eudora was born in 1909.

From the yearbook, *Meh Lady,* at Mississippi State College for Women, which Eudora attended from 1925 to 1927.

The house on Pinehurst Street where the Weltys moved when Eudora was in high school. It has been her home ever since.

A magnolia, Mississippi's state flower, adorns the crest of the sign at the entrance to MSCW.

Waverly, the antebellum mansion where MSCW students used to go for picnics, later provided a model for Marmion in *Delta Wedding*.

The cast of *Icebound* at MSCW. Eudora is at far right in the back row.

EDITORIAL

Impressions of an Editorial

Cooperation . . . cooperation . . . cooperation . . . what w____
____ . . . Cooperation . . . success in life . . . cooperation
men and women . . . spirit of good fellowship . . . cooperation
____ ____ COOPERATION!

SUBJECT FILE

Eudora did this cartoon for the page that listed staff members of the short-lived *Oh, Lady*, a humor magazine, which was suppressed by the president of MSCW. This is from the issue of May 1927.

Eudora in 1931, when she was writing publicity materials, commercials, and scripts for radio station WJDX in Jackson.

John Robinson's photograph from the University of Mississippi yearbook in 1928.

Eudora with her camera at South Hill Farm near Saratoga Springs, the home of her mentor and benefactor, Katherine Anne Porter, in 1941.

Fellows at the 1940 Bread Loaf Writers' Conference. Left to right, standing, Eudora, John Ciardi, Brainard Cheney, Edna Frederickson, faculty member Louis Untermeyer; seated, Marian Sims, conference director Theodore Morrison, and Eudora's bête noire, Carson McCullers

*For Katherine Anne
with love and gratitude
from Eudora — as of
1941 "A Curtain of Green" (below)
Introduction by KAP
and 1973 now
and the years in between
and to come —*

Eudora liked this photograph of herself and inscribed
a copy to Katherine Anne Porter thus: "For Katherine
Anne with love and gratitude from Eudora—as of
1941 'A Curtain of Green' (below) Introduction by
KAP and 1973 now and the years in between and to
come."

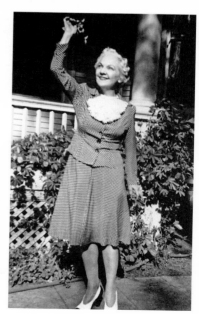

Katherine Anne Porter, who had already
written *Flowering Judas and Other Stories,*
Hacienda, Noon Wine, and *Pale Horse,*
Pale Rider, in the early forties.

Elizabeth Bowen, the Anglo-Irish writer whom Eudora met in 1950.

Eudora with Jeanne Shelley, Una Merkel, and David Wayne from the cast of the dramatic version of *The Ponder Heart,* which played on Broadway in 1956.

The first meeting of the honorary consultants in American letters to the Library of Congress, April 18, 1958. Left to right, seated, Cleanth Brooks, Eudora Welty, John Crowe Ransom, Randall Jarrell; standing, Quincy Mumford, Roy P. Basler, Phyllis Armstrong, R. P. Blackmur.

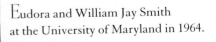

Eudora and William Jay Smith at the University of Maryland in 1964.

Eudora on April 21, 1962.

Eudora at the statewide
celebration in her honor in 1973.

Two towering figures in Southern
literature—Allen Tate and
Eudora Welty—when Eudora received an
honorary degree at the University
of the South in Sewanee.

When Eudora read at the
Pierpont Morgan Library
in 1985, Katharine Hepburn,
left, wanted to meet her. Alice
Tully and Hope Williams are
also in the picture.

Eudora Welty in 1971.

Chapter 34

San Francisco Again

1947

At home, Eudora had John Robinson and his work on her mind; she wrote to Herschel Brickell that his "fine" stories were bound to be published. In the same letter she put in a word for Arthur Foff, telling Brickell that his novel, coming out in the fall, was "good work indeed."

Edward Weeks at the *Atlantic* asked Eudora to cut "June Recital," which was then called "Golden Apples of the Sun," but she refused. Mary Lou Aswell, who bought it tentatively for *Harper's Bazaar,* also wanted it cut. Eudora shortened nothing but the title, cutting it to "Golden Apples," while the text grew from seventy-three to eighty-one pages. Mary Lou took it anyway and paid Eudora $750.

When the story ran in September 1947, it proved, said a paragraph in "The Editor's Guest Book," that you did not have to be a musician to write about music. "Miss Welty tells us she can play only one of the pieces named in her story, 'Playful Kittens,' and she hopes pianists won't tear her to shreds for errors." No credit line identifies the photographer who took the picture of Eudora for "Guest Book," but it seems to be the first of several that *Harper's Bazaar* commissioned by such top photographers as Cecil Beaton, Louise Dahl-Wolfe, and Irving Penn.

To pose for Beaton, Eudora went to his apartment wearing a little black dress, which she thought would be perfect. It was wrong. Beaton was shy and reticent but used a Rolliflex just like Eudora's. Louise Dahl-Wolfe, who was brisk and lively, posed her against a rock in Central Park. She had fun with Irving Penn, who also took her to Central Park and set up some comic poses for pictures in addition to the ones *Bazaar* used. In one she knelt on the ground by a sign that read TO RESTROOMS AND BEAR DEN, and another was rather like the old one of her swathed in a Spanish shawl, sitting in a tree with Frank Lyell at her feet.[1]

When Weeks surprised both agent and author by buying "Hello and Goodbye," a story Eudora had written some time before, she said that he should have taken Robinson's "Rite of Spring" instead.[2] In "Hello and Goodbye," a young Mississippi beauty queen about to leave for New York talks with her predecessor while a photographer poses them at different points on the grounds of the state capitol. (A photograph titled "Hello and Goodbye" and dated "Jackson 1930s" appears in *Photographs,* showing two very dressed-up young women in hats on the steps of the capitol.)

That spring, E. M. Forster wrote Eudora a fan letter, which said that *The Wide Net* was full of "wild and lovely things." It was several minutes before she was able to read the signature, partly because Forster's handwriting was illegible and partly because of her disbelief. "The letter was kindness, undreamed of kindness," she said, and it bore the marks of her tears, she said at a centenary celebration of Forster in 1979. Forster had reinforced her "instinctive belief that mystery in human relationships exists per se," and had strengthened her "recognition of place as a prime source of enlightenment in fiction."[3]

When Robert Van Gelder of the *Times Book Review* asked her to join him in Seattle and lecture at the Northwest Writers' Conference at the University of Washington in August 1947, she agreed. It would be the first speech she had ever made, but the fee of $800 would finance another trip to San Francisco. Lambert Davis, her editor at Harcourt Brace, asked her if she would autograph books at a bookstore while she was there; she refused at first, then agreed.

She worked on her speech that summer in Jackson, writing it in bits and pieces. She planned to talk about Faulkner's "The Bear," D. H. Lawrence's "The Fox," and stories by Katherine Mansfield, Chekhov, Henry James, and Stephen Crane and to draw heavily on Forster's *Aspects of the*

Novel. She decided to tell her listeners to write out of passion, not calculation, to learn sensitivity and perception and not worry.

In Seattle, Eudora joined the other faculty members, including Van Gelder, William Saroyan, and Ned Brown, a Hollywood agent. She worked on the speech until the last minute, and was still throwing out pages when she was on the podium.[4]

The conference hit a new plateau with Eudora's speech, according to a report in the *Seattle Post-Intelligencer.*[5] "Plausibility doesn't matter," she told her audience. "Many times we are most enchanted by the story that is fairy-like." Eudora told Herschel Brickell that she had performed poorly,[6] but Lambert Davis reported that she was a hit at the conference and at the book-signing at the store.[7] While she was autographing, Betty MacDonald, whose *The Egg and I* was a nationwide best-seller, went up and said she had bought several copies of *Delta Wedding* to give to her friends. "And I haven't bought an *egg* yet," Eudora thought.[8]

Back in San Francisco, Eudora settled down in another sublet, rented from a Miss Olson who went back to Moose Jaw, Saskatchewan, for a visit. When the sublet was up, Eudora lived in hotel rooms again, for a while at the Hotel Victoria, near Union Square and Chinatown, paying two dollars a night for a room without a bath and three-fifty for a room with a bath.

After she reworked her lecture on the short story, Edward Weeks bought it for publication in two parts in the *Atlantic* in February and March 1949. When Harcourt Brace wanted to make some use of the speech, Eudora suggested using it as the introduction to a collection of short stories that she and John Robinson would edit.[9] She wanted to lay out examples for people interested in the short story, she wrote to Herschel Brickell.[10] Did he think this was a worthwhile idea? Harcourt said that the authors she had chosen were too expensive, but she could not do anything without Faulkner. Months later, she still thought the idea of an anthology was interesting and asked Brickell if he knew a good reason not to do one. Nothing came of the collection, but Eudora gave the speech on other occasions, and it is published as "Looking at Short Stories" in *The Eye of the Story.*

For a new story, "Moon Lake," Eudora drew again on her memory of childhood. She had gone to Camp McLaurin, across the river in Rankin

County, for two weeks when she was nine years old. "We lived by a lake and slept in tents under the supervision of local young ladies attached . . . to the Jackson YWCA," she has said. "They wore middy blouses and put up their hair in puffs over their ears. One wore an Indian headband, one played a ukelele and they all smelled of citronella."[11]

She had been surprised by the girls from a Jackson orphanage who attended her camp, and she used them in the story. At night she looked out of her tent with the flap pulled back and, like Nina in "Moon Lake," she "saw the whole mysterious night." Except for the lifeguard, Loch Morrison, she made up all the characters, even the formidable orphan Easter. Her brother Edward, who was a Boy Scout, had been a lifeguard and bugler at a girls' camp one summer at an age when he could hardly bear to be around girls. "For Loch at Moon Lake, I didn't change Edward a bit," she said. "But Edward was never called on to perform artificial respiration."[12]

Eudora had probably witnessed artificial respiration when she was at Wisconsin. Just before commencement in 1929, a student drowned in Lake Mendota. He had been swimming from the YMCA pier at the end of Frances Street, right where Eudora lived, to the float about twenty-five yards from shore. As spectators idly watched, he turned over onto his back and then sank. University lifesaving teams could see his body and pulled him up; they took him to shore and, while spectators gathered around, labored for hours, giving him artificial respiration. It is hard not to speculate that young Eudora Welty, who lived so near the Y pier, was in that crowd of onlookers and that the memory surfaced twenty years later. In "Moon Lake," Loch Morrison pulls Easter from the bottom of the lake and then labors for an extremely long time, in front of all the campers, to revive her.

Eudora mailed "Moon Lake" to Russell in September 1947, explaining that it looked " 'like a sector' of a novel (or something)," all about the town Battle Hill, later called Morgana. Loch Morrison was the little boy from "June Recital." Jinny in "Moon Lake" would grow up to be the wife in "The Whole World Knows." It sounded, she said, like "that conglomeration" Russell had talked about.[13] She thought, though, that it would stand by itself as a story.

"I only realized the stories were connected about halfway through the book," Eudora said later. "Some of the people I invented turned out to be not new characters but the same ones come upon at other times in their lives. Quite suddenly I realized I was working on the same people. All their interconnections came to light. That's what I mean by the fascinations of fiction: things that go on in the back of your mind, that gradually emerge. And you say, 'Well, of course; that's what it was all the time.' "[14]

A few weeks later, she wrote a short story, "Shower of Gold," in one day. "Something is probably wrong with it," she told Diarmuid Russell. Typing it, she could see that "Shower of Gold" wanted to make connections with "The Whole World Knows," "June Recital," "Music from Spain," and "Moon Lake." Diarmuid's idea of a "conglomerate," a book of interrelated stories ("but not inter-dependent"), was a good one, she thought. It would be better than trying to make a novel out of the material. She could go on writing the stories as they occurred to her. "Just let the material take its natural course" and perhaps write "a number of additional stories with these characters." She realized she could place the characters far away or go backward or forward in their lives. That way, she said, she could avoid trying to get too much in a single story, because there would be other stories, other chances. And she still would not have the "burden" of a novel, with "all that tying up of threads and preparing for this, that, and the other."[15]

Eudora left San Francisco toward the end of October and went back to Jackson, satisfied that she could write somewhere besides home. But she was apparently depressed that nothing much had come of her relationship with Robinson—no marriage, no real love affair. At what point he came to terms with his homosexuality is not known. (The gay community in San Francisco did not come out of the closet until much later.) It was probably because of the futility of the experience with Robinson that she expressed her distaste for San Francisco in two letters to Katherine Anne Porter. She admitted that the landscape was beautiful, the sunsets magnificent, the moonlight on the sea spectacular. On the other hand, the weather was rainy and cold and she had never been really warm. The fog had made her feel shut in. The streetcar system was slow and tedious, and it was hard waiting on streetcorners in the rain.

She said that it was probably her own fault that she had not been more excited by her surroundings. *"I was troubled a little in my life* [italics added]," she wrote.[16] In another letter she wrote that San Francisco had had a bad effect on her, but all of California lacked substance for her. She liked Arizona, though, when she stopped off on the way home and stayed a while. She was impressed with the great age of the land, the colors, and the Indians. She read geology books and visited the Grand Canyon, admiring the park geologist who gave the afternoon trip lecture for tourists—the history of the Grand Canyon in twenty minutes, with gestures.[17]

Chapter 35

The Levee Press

1948

John Robinson went to Jackson for Christmas and stayed a month or two, but he then went down to the Gulf coast to write. Eudora read Katherine Anne Porter's piece on Gertrude Stein in *Harper's,* which she much admired, and then turned to Euripides and the *Georgics* of Virgil in Cecil Day-Lewis's translation; she went back to Gide's *Journal* and began on Montaigne. She sent off for ship sailing schedules and travel brochures and thought about going somewhere, perhaps to study French.

Jackson got a snowfall in the winter of 1948—in fact, two snowstorms and an ice storm. In late January, everybody in town went sledding, most people on sleds made out of corrugated tin, which they rode down the hills on the Millsaps campus. One Yankee in town "could and did ice skate," Eudora reported. He skated down a street with his hands behind his back while people lined up respectfully on the sidewalk to watch him.[1] Everybody made snowmen; some yards had as many as five. Eudora's snowman had real moss hair and was sitting down in a chair with a drink, a "man of distinction," and the one on the Belhaven campus across the street had a crown of two-foot icicles.

"Music from Spain" had not found a home, and Eudora and Russell decided to let it go to the Levee Press, the publishing company started in

Greenville, Mississippi, by three men: Hodding Carter, publisher of the *Delta Democrat-Times;* Ben Wasson, Faulkner's former literary agent and now the book critic for the *Delta Democrat-Times;* and Kenneth Haxton, who had started a book department in his family's department store in Greenville, Nelms and Blum. *Music from Spain* was the Levee Press's first book; their second would be Faulkner's *Notes on a Horse Thief.* They agreed to publish 775 copies of *Music,* numbered and signed. Twenty-five would go to the author and publishers, and Eudora was to get a 25 percent royalty on the three-dollar retail price.

Eudora wrote to Herschel Brickell and asked if she could dedicate the "little book" to him. She was afraid of offending him because a Spaniard was in it. (Brickell was becoming an expert on Latin America and Spain.)[2] Brickell replied that he would be delighted to have a story about a Spaniard dedicated to him—or one about a Chinese, Hindu, or Eskimo.[3]

Ben Wasson returned the manuscript so Eudora could make some changes, but he wanted it back quickly so they could begin printing the book. While she was retyping "Music from Spain," she practically rewrote it. She also made a startling discovery. The little man who went all over San Francisco with the Spanish guitarist was Eugene MacLain, one of the MacLain twins from Battle Hill. The MacLain twins appear first as children in "Shower of Gold." Eugene's twin brother, Randall, is the married man in "The Whole World Knows." In "Music from Spain," Eugene MacLain is living in San Francisco, married, working in a jewelry store, and occasionally homesick for Mississippi.

Eudora was exultant about the discovery of her protagonist's identity. She said she should have foreseen that the story would be connected to the others, because it worried her that the leading character had no roots. "All there was to do was put two and two together, him and my little group, and I had him by the tail."[4]

After a day of typing on "Music from Spain," she said, a new story, "Sir Rabbit," came as "another dividend from Yeats, by way of 'Leda and the Swan.' "[5] In "Sir Rabbit," King MacLain, Eugene and Randall's father, appears in the woods near Morgana, shoots Junior Holifield, and seduces Junior's wife, Mattie Will, while a black man, Blackstone, watches. (The twins had had Mattie Will in the woods a few years earlier.) It is a brutal story, despite Eudora's clever replication of the poor whites' dialect.

Before Eudora left Jackson in the summer of 1948 for an extended stay in New York, she dealt with details of the business of being a writer. When Harcourt Brace began nudging her for the manuscript of the book of interrelated stories, she warned Diarmuid Russell that it would be misleading to let Lambert Davis think there was anything "novelish" about the book. She was not sure what she would do with the stories, but she would go on "as fancy takes me." She did not need money right then. When she read the galleys of "Music from Spain," she was so depressed about the story she wanted to take back the dedication to Herschel Brickell.[6] She worried a little about the Levee Press; no one there answered her letters or anybody else's, and she heard that it would not allow bookstores a discount of any kind.

John Robinson was in the veterans' hospital with hives; he was taking tests, reading constantly, and swimming in the hospital's pool. William Hamilton visited Jackson briefly. Eudora intended to drive to New York, stopping off at Duke to visit Hamilton, but she got the "malaria fevers" or "something" and decided to take the train instead.

Chapter 36

Musical Comedy

1948

One evening when she was in New York, Eudora was sitting in Schrafft's at Fifth Avenue and Thirteenth Street with Hildegarde Dolson, a client of Russell's whom she had met some time before. Dolson was born in Pennsylvania, attended Allegheny College, and had written a book of humorous essays about her childhood and youth, *We Shook the Family Tree,* which appeared in 1946, and *The Husband Who Ran Away,* a comic novel that would appear in early fall 1948.

The two women agreed that the current Broadway musicals were so bad they could do better, and they decided to spend the summer of 1948 collaborating on their own musical. Eudora sublet an apartment in the Village and spent the weekends with the Russells. When she was lent a house in Bedford Hills, Hildegarde moved out there too so they could continue working.

Writing a musical with a plot was "too much trouble," they decided, so they settled on a series of skits, each to be written by only one of them.[1] Collaboration was not always easy. Eudora found out how inflexible people could be, how unwavering in their feelings about certain subjects. Hildegarde believed what she was told and regarded some things—the leftish newspaper *PM* and psychiatry, for example—as sacred. Eudora regarded nothing as sacred and felt that she had an open mind.[2] Nevertheless, they finished the revue, *What Year Is This?* Hildegarde wrote the opener and four other skits, including one spoofing the size of the *New York Times* (it was so big a small boy emerged from the roll); Eudora wrote "Yes, Dear," about a thinking machine; "What's Happening to Waltzes Like This?"; "Fifty-Seventh Street Rag"; "The Feet-Out Blues"; "Choo-Choo Boat"; and "Bye-Bye, Brevoort."[3] A theatrical agent took it on, and Hildegarde and Eudora talked to composers, including Brown Furlow, who was from Brookhaven, Mississippi, and a music graduate of Louisiana State University. When Lehman Engel read the script, he said, "You'll never get anywhere with it because there's not a blackout in it." Eudora later said that Engel was right. "We never did get anywhere with it, but it was a wonderful excuse to see all the Broadway shows that season."[4]

Eudora's "Bye-Bye, Brevoort," about the razing of the Brevoort Hotel at Eighth Street and Fifth Avenue, a refuge for bohemians and artists since before World War I, was the only one of the skits that had much of a lifespan. It became part of another revue, *Lo and Behold,* mostly written by William Happ. With music by Brown Furlow, *Lo and Behold* was produced in summer repertory in 1949 at the Red Barn Playhouse in Westboro, Massachusetts. According to the playbill, Furlow was "also working on the music for the Eudora Welty–Hildegarde Dolson revue, 'What Year Is This?,' from which the sketch 'Bye-Bye, Brevoort' was borrowed."[5] A review was damning: "Fair enough for a silo tryout, 'Lo and Behold' doesn't have anywhere near the staying power to make a bid for the long stretch . . . [The skit] by Eudora Welty lacks sock . . . Furlow's songs are pleasant but have no distinction."[6]

"Bye-Bye, Brevoort" was also part of *The Littlest Revue,* which opened at the Phoenix Theatre in New York on May 22, 1956. "Eudora Welty's caricature of the old inhabitants of the old Brevoort is wry and enjoyable," wrote one reviewer.[7] The skit was produced again in 1980, by the New Stage Theatre in Jackson, and was anthologized in *Plays in One Act,* edited by Daniel Halpern.

While Eudora was in New York working on the revue, she also spent time on short stories. One came into her head, she said, while she was driving, and "I was writing with one hand and driving with the other."[8] She thought this story might be related to the others, and she was happier about the idea of the book of stories than she had been. By July 1948 she had finished "The Hummingbirds," which brought Virgie Rainey back to town for the funeral of her mother, Katie Rainey, the narrator of "Shower of Gold."

On Sunday, September 19, 1948, Eudora noticed that the *New York Times Book Review* ran five reviews written by graduates of Jackson's Central High School. She herself reviewed *City Limit* ("touching and original"), by Hollis Summers; Hubert Creekmore reviewed *Angel in the Wardrobe,* a novel about contemporary New Orleans, by Robert Tallant; Bill Hamilton reviewed *Dixie Raider: The Saga of the C.S.S. Shenandoah,* about the Confederate raiding boat that burned several United States whaling ships in the Aleutian Islands, by Murray Morgan; and Nash Burger reviewed *The Book of Books,* by Solomon Goldman. Nash's wife, Marjorie Williams Burger, who had also gone to Central High, had a review in that issue too. It was a pretty good record for a Mississippi high school.

Chapter 37

Film Scripts
1948–1949

John Robinson was back on the West Coast, in graduate school at the University of California in Berkeley, when he sold a story, ". . . All This Juice and All This Joy," to Cyril Connolly's *Horizon* in London. The story appeared in November 1948. Eudora told him she was proud of him and said that it spoke well of Mr. Connolly that he had bought the story. The story was good, she told Herschel and Norma Brickell, "but not what he *can* do."[1]

When *Horizon* reached Eudora, she wrote to Robinson that she had read the story again and it still seemed fresh and good. "I wish I could be in *Horizon*," she said.[2] Russell had sent "Sir Rabbit," which was being published in this country in the *Hudson Review*, to *Horizon*, and she had hoped that she and Robinson could be published together.

Eudora and Robinson began working by mail on adapting William Faulkner's *Sanctuary* for a movie; then Eudora veered off on another idea, a movie that would be as "accurate and dramatic as a documentary," based on something she referred to as "Mankind So Far." It would show Asians crossing the Bering Strait and moving south through walls of ice to Arizona and eventually to the tip of South America. The Mesozoic scene would have tree ferns and dinosaurs and "good music to go with it." They could show the development of a species through a series of photographs, the way movie-makers could show the opening of a flower's bloom. Eudora conceded that this movie might be expensive, but what was money to the movies? she asked. The idea of working on a nonfiction project appealed to her, because dangers were inherent in working on fiction—anybody's fiction.[3]

Robinson was enthusiastic about a modern British literature course he took from Mark Schorer, who had by this time published two novels, a volume of short stories, and a scholarly book on William Blake. Schorer had been a classmate of Eudora's at Wisconsin, and she reminded Robinson that he had from time to time "written as snotty a piece of literary criticism as I've ever read."[4] But Mark Schorer thought very highly of Robinson. "As a student . . . he revealed the qualities that I would have expected of a man of his experiences and sensitivity: intelligent critical perception, sound literary judgment, human breadth of interest," Schorer wrote when he recommended Robinson for a grant. "His only flaw (and it is rather part of his attractiveness than a real flaw) is an inclination toward indolence, by which I mean to say that nothing seems to strike him as quite worth a lot of high pressure in the achievement of it. There is a good deal to be said for this attitude, especially in a writer who has no intention of compromising his literary ideals; and I hope that by mentioning it I have not lessened his chances for a grant. He is an admirable and gifted person who knows what he wants and how much he is prepared to pay."[5]

When the end of term neared, Eudora wrote to Robinson about how ridiculous she thought it was for him to have to take exams. She told him he should show Schorer "Juice and Joy" and examine *him*.[6] She agreed with Robinson that Joyce was curiously heavyhanded and non-Celtic, Teutonic even. Yeats could do a chapter's worth in a single line.

Robinson next suggested that they collaborate on a movie script of *The Robber Bridegroom* and said he was making notes. Eudora thought they could do it. It was free, it belonged to her, or "to us," and they could do anything they liked, she said.[7] They conferred by mail on the new project, sending long, single-spaced letters flying back and forth between Berkeley and Jackson, discussing the length and number of scenes, the introduction of characters, possible sites for filming. (Eudora wanted it filmed in Rodney, the ghost town.)

Eudora saw *Sunrise* at Millsaps and knew that that was not their kind of movie, directed by a German with everybody holding very still and moving very slowly. She wanted to keep the fast tempo, and she thought their movie should be more like a Keystone comedy. Harpe, the bandit, should be really scary.

John Robinson sent a twenty-two-page synopsis with eleven pages of notes on the characters and another page about the settings. The "bluff edge is always the verge and brink of discovery," he said. She replied that his definition of the significance of the bluff edge belonged in the Things I Never Knew Till Now Department.[8]

She sent him a list of scenes. (Scene one opened: "A bear looks out of the cave.") She sent two copies of notes on scenes, one for him to mark up and send back to her. She also made a graph of the action. She wrote some of the scenes and asked him about crowd scenes and spectacles. Would they have to show life in the town, the river, and all the dots on the map? she wondered. She asked for help with her dialogue—it was "worse than the forest primeval and murmuring p's and h'locks."[9]

When John sent dialogue, she liked it tremendously and said she wished he could write all of it, because it was hard for her to change what she had written for people to say. On John's recommendation, she saw *Red River,* with Montgomery Clift, and tried to make notes on how many speeches were in a scene or sequence, but she got too interested in the movie. She thought Danny Kaye would be wonderful as Goat.

Eudora found the script of *Things to Come,* by H. G. Wells, in the library, and although the dialogue was so corny she couldn't read it, she was interested that Wells had written prefatory notes for the director and cameramen and that the script was printed in parts one through sixteen.

Real moviemaking, meanwhile, was coming to Mississippi, with Clarence Brown's filming of Faulkner's *Intruder in the Dust* in Oxford. Eudora said she would die to be a Snopes. The local Lowe twins, Edmund and Ephraim, were cast as Vardaman and Bilbo Gowrie.[10]

Eudora and her friends were keenly interested in the presidential election in 1948, between Governor Thomas E. Dewey of New York and the incumbent, Harry Truman, with Henry A. Wallace and Strom Thurmond running as third-party candidates. Bill Hamilton was riding the train from Durham to Jackson on election night and sat up all night listening to the returns. Delighted with the final outcome, he told Eudora it amounted to a left-wing revolution. Eudora listened to Hodding Carter, one of the proprietors of the Levee Press, debate Walter White of the NAACP on national radio and admired the way he defended the racial situation in the South. (Carter had a penchant for criticizing the South and its racial patterns when he was in the South and defending it against what he called northern extremists when he was in the North.) There were other portents of the coming crisis over race in the South. Bill Hamilton told Eudora about Judge Wells, a Jackson notable who was all for states' rights, who commented after reading the Sermon on the Mount to his Sunday school class, "I feel sure that Jesus Christ has been misquoted on some of these statements." Naturally, Judge Wells, although a firm Presbyterian, could not believe that the blessed meek would inherit the earth.

It was late 1948 before the Levee Press finally got *Music from Spain* into print. The small book cost $3.65, whereas *Golden Apples,* which would contain "Music from Spain" and six other stories, would be priced at $3. Joseph Henry Jackson reviewed *Music* in his column in the *San Francisco Chronicle,* saying that it was in "many ways Miss Welty's best book yet" and showed how thoroughly lost Eugene McLain was outside Morgana.[11] Charles Poore, in an otherwise favorable review in the *New York Times,* pointed out that the musical phrases adorning the pages could not be played. Poore's review prompted the actor Maurice Evans to write to Eudora and ask her to delay any "action on adaptation rights" until he had had a chance to read the book. "I have been trying for years to get somebody to write me a 'worm that turns' play and maybe 'Music from Spain' may at last supply the basis," he said.[12] Eudora had always found Maurice Evans boring and stiff on the stage, and she was more excited when the producer Eddie Dowling expressed interest in *Music from Spain.*[13] Dowling, who had produced *Here Come the Clowns, The Glass Menagerie,* and *The Iceman Cometh,* liked *Music from Spain* but saw problems of dramatization. Then he read *The Robber Bridegroom* and loved it, calling it "the most imaginative piece of writing he had read in a long time." It would make a grand operetta, he said, and he was anxious to read what she had written on her scenario. He suggested she try breaking the book down into dramatic form. "Don't worry about the amount of scenes. I can take care of that in production."[14]

Eudora wrote Dowling a long letter about Rodney and enclosed snapshots of the place. She promised to send him the script that she and Robinson were working on.[15]

Chapter 38

The Golden Apples

1 9 4 9

When Eudora finished all the stories about the people in the town of Battle Hill, Harcourt Brace agreed to publish them—but it wanted the manuscript right away. Eudora began to retype the stories, rewriting some of the longer ones, with help from Mittie Welty, her brother Walter's wife, and John Robinson, still in California.

John's help not only saved her time and energy and eyestrain but kept her from further rewriting.[1] He was not, however, to let the typing interfere with his work or their movie, she told him, adding that she only wanted the stories collected because she wanted the money, and maybe they could get money for their movie script. They might even get money for a book of three movie treatments based on folklore—perhaps Paul Bunyan, Johnny Apple-seed, and the Robber, maybe under another name. They could apply next year for a Guggenheim to carry on with the film, she said; she wished they had thought of it before the deadline for applications. She had applied for a Guggenheim grant herself this year, but expected to be turned down because she did not have a specific project and said she just wanted time to think.[2]

As she worked on the short stories, Eudora changed the name of the town from Battle Hill to Morgana. A cousin of John Robinson's had written a book called *Fata Morgana,* a title that had fascinated her when Robinson had told her about it, a decade before.[3] She liked the idea of the *fata morgana,* "the illusory shape, the mirage that comes from the sea," she said.[4] "All the characters were living under dreams or illusions or even possessions."[5] One scholar has noted that Eudora placed her fictional town nineteen miles from Vicksburg, "over the gravel and thirteen little bridges," and east of the Black River, which would place it somewhere close to the real-life towns of Raymond and Utica. This same scholar has pointed out that there are no happy families in Morgana.[6]

The story "June Recital" had been called "Golden Apples," and Eudora wanted to name the collection after it. Editors at Harcourt, however, thought that since it was a book of connected stories, the title should not be the same as that of one of the stories. Eudora thought they were right and admitted that she had always had trouble with titles. She kept *Golden Apples* for the book and renamed the story.[7]

When the Morgana manuscript was finished and had been sent off to New York, Diarmuid Russell telephoned—a very unusual proceeding for him—to say that he thought it was a "very, very good book."[8] Eudora insisted that Harcourt not advertise it as a novel and suggested something like "Variations on a Portfolio"; Harcourt called it a "chronicle" of Morgana.

The Golden Apples got good reviews, and it has fascinated academic critics, who love the allusions to myths and the references to Yeats's poem "The Song of the Wandering Aengus," with its "glimmering girl" who disappears, and its last two lines "The silver apples of the moon/The golden apples of the sun." This poem, which haunts Cassie Morrison, one of the characters, is surely where the title of the book comes from, not from the story of Atalanta and the golden apples, although Eugene MacLain does think of them in San Francisco.

A writer's friends often react oddly to publication of new work. Katherine Anne Porter warned her nephew against "showing off how well [you] can write instead of showing off the people and the meaning of the story . . . Eudora Welty's latest book is a perfect example of what I mean—technical virtuosity gone into a dizzy spin absolutely drunk on language." Porter's biographer attributes her harsh judgment to her anger at not being mentioned in Eudora's two articles on the short story in the *Atlantic* in February and March 1949.

Chapter 39

William Faulkner

1949

Eudora invited Caroline Gordon and Allen Tate, who were back together, to Jackson in the spring of 1949. Any day except Thursday would be fine, she told them, because the Rose Society would be meeting there Friday morning at just about the time they would be wanting breakfast. Eudora laid in some bootleg liquor from the Gulf coast in case the Tates came, but instead she went to Memphis, where the Tates were spending spring vacation with their daughter, Nancy Wood.[1]

Oddly, Eudora had never been to Memphis before, but as she had once said, people in Jackson were divided into two camps, those who went to Memphis and those who went to New Orleans, and she had always gone to New Orleans. Caroline and Allen gave a big cocktail party, where "everybody got drunk."[2] "We had a round of parties in Memphis," Eudora said more moderately years later. "I can't see how we did it."[3]

Eudora wanted to see the Peabody Hotel, with its famous ducks in the lobby. "She was enchanting, adorable," said Nancy Wood. "The first time you saw her, you thought, 'This is the ugliest woman I ever saw.' Then after you got to know her—about fifteen minutes—you thought she was beautiful."[4] Percy Wood, Nancy's husband, who was a medical student, was alarmed by a mole on Eudora's forearm. It was flush with her skin and the same color as a malignant melanoma. Percy called his dermatology professor, who came over to the house and said it was fine. Medical students are easily alarmed.

When Eudora got back from Memphis, she found out she had won a Guggenheim fellowship after all. She felt immensely wealthy when she thought of the $2,500 grant, added to the $5,000 advance for *Golden Apples*. It did not take her long to decide to go to Europe in the fall.

And that summer Eudora finally got a chance to meet William Faulkner. Her admiration for him had always been total and unwavering. She has said that living in Mississippi, in the same state with Faulkner, was "like living near a great mountain, something majestic."[5] She had mentioned him in her one and only lecture, when she said he "was the one ahead of his time—the most astonishingly powered and passionate writer we have." She did not think that enough people appreciated how his work, which showed such "marvelous imaginative power," was also "twice as true as life."

In the spring of 1949 Eudora had spontaneously written to *The New Yorker* to defend Faulkner against what she perceived as an unfriendly review of *Intruder in the Dust*, by Edmund Wilson. The review was "born in New York," she wrote; it had grammatical errors and had lost sight of the book in question. She went on to say that Mr. Faulkner did not need a defender of any sort, "but it's hard to listen to anyone being condescended to, and to a great man being condescended to pretentiously." Wilson was judging a book by pulling out a map, she said.[6]

Before she sent her letter to the magazine, she sent a copy to John Robinson for his approval, and she added some of his comments. (A few years later she would berate Edmund Wilson again for this review, in an unsigned article she wrote for the *Times Literary Supplement* of London. Wilson, she said, "has put himself on record as wondering why on earth Mr. Faulkner doesn't quit all this local stuff and come out of the South to write in civilization." Eudora really had misread Wilson's review. In a letter to the editor of the *TLS*, Wilson said he had never wondered anything of the kind, and quoted several sentences from his review, the most telling of which said, "I do not sympathize with the line of criticism which deplores Faulkner's obstinate persistence in submerging himself in the mentality of the community where he was born."[7]

Eudora freely admitted that she had learned from William Faulkner.

"He showed me that in Yoknapatawpha every single segment of society is represented by place and house and so on. He knew so *much* about all that. He wrote about a much vaster world than anything I ever contemplated for my own work and he made all that so visible and so exactly right."[8] Another time she said she learned from Faulkner how to represent the speech of rural Mississippians. "Reading Faulkner taught me that you can much better suggest the way we speak by cadences and punctuation than by any sort of spelling. Faulkner did it so perfectly!"[9]

And she loved to tell stories about Faulkner, especially the one about the lady writer who was having trouble with a love scene and sent it to "Mr. Faulkner" for advice. When she didn't hear from him, she called him up. "Did you get that love scene I sent you?" she asked. "What did you think of it?" As Eudora told the story, Mr. Faulkner said, "Well, honey, it wasn't the way I would have done it, but you just go right ahead."[10]

In the spring of 1943, Eudora had received a letter from Faulkner—an uncharacteristically admiring letter, according to his biographer, written when he was "in his cups."[11] "Dear Welty," went the letter. "You are doing fine. You are doing all right. I read THE GILDED SIX BITS, a friend loaned me THE ROBBER BRIDEGROOM, I have just bought the collection named GREEN something, haven't read it yet . . . You are doing very fine. Is there any way I can help you? How old are you? . . . Do you mind telling me about your background. My address is below." He signed it in pencil, "Faulkner."[12]

Faulkner was only slightly confused. "The Gilded Six-Bits" was the title of a short story by Zora Neale Hurston, a black writer from Florida who became the first African American admitted to Barnard College. (More than one person has confused her with Eudora, perhaps because "Zora" and "Eudora" sound somewhat alike.)

Eudora folded up the note and sent it off to Nancy Farley, John Robinson's friend, whom she had seen in New York. Farley kept the letter until her death, when her heirs sold it, along with other letters from Eudora, to the Alderman Library at the University of Virginia. Years later, when Eudora heard about this, she called the Alderman Library and said, "Doesn't that belong to me?" The library replied that it belonged to the Commonwealth of Virginia. Eudora wrote indignantly to the library, which then sent her a photocopy.[13]

Now, in the summer of 1949, she was going to meet the writer she admired so much.[14] The chance came through John Robinson, who was back in Mississippi. He had always been a great friend of Robert Farley's, one of Faulkner's good friends, and had in fact lived with Farley and his wife in New Orleans before the war. Now Farley had left Tulane and was following in his father's footsteps as dean of the law school at Ole Miss. An invitation came from Miss Ella Somerville of Oxford for Eudora and John Robinson to come for a visit, saying that she would invite the Farleys and the Faulkners to dinner. The film company was shooting *Intruder in the Dust* in Oxford, and Eudora threatened to drive up to the square in a wagon, wearing a sunbonnet, and wait to be cast as a Snopes.[15]

Ella Somerville was more or less the grande dame of Oxford society and a long-time friend of Faulkner's, who referred to her as Miss Ella. They had both been in the Marionettes, the amateur theatrical society, and she still played golf with him. Her father too had been dean of the Ole Miss law school, and she now ran a place called the Tea Hound, a one-story structure on University Avenue where fraternities held dances and banquets. She was not particularly literary, although she had contributed an article on Stark Young to Dale Mullen's *Oxford* magazine. "Society ladies wrote part of *Oxford*," Mullen explained. "She mentioned *New Republic* in her article, but I'm sure nobody in Oxford subscribed to the *New Republic* at the time."[16]

Ella Somerville served quail to Eudora, John Robinson, the Farleys, and the Faulkners. After dinner they all sang old hymns and a few folksongs around the piano. Faulkner invited Eudora and Robinson to go sailing on his nineteen-foot sloop, the *Ring Dove,* the next day on Lake Sardis. The two of them were late getting to the lake—they got lost and went to Blackjack, Mississippi—and when they arrived, they saw Faulkner in the *Ring Dove* out on the manmade lake. He sailed toward them through dead cypress trees and stumps, lowered the sail, and rowed toward shore, shouting, "You all better take your shoes off and wade out." Eudora was not really dressed for sailing, but she gamely waded out to the boat, ruining the skirt of her good summer dress, and got pulled aboard. She and Robinson also rode in Faulkner's twenty-year-old Ford touring car with holes in the floor and a cupboard latch on the back door.

Neither time that she saw Faulkner did they talk about books or writing. Eudora thought he was wonderful, with "the most profound face," with something heartbreaking in it. She thought he led two lives in Oxford, the visible life and his inner, literary life.[17]

Eudora would have three opportunities to express her admiration for William Faulkner in public. In May 1962 she presented the Gold Medal for Fiction to him at the National Institute of Arts and Letters in New York. Onstage before the presentation, Faulkner kept leaning across to Eudora to ask her when it was going to be over. Her speech was short and graceful. "Mr. Faulkner," she said in closing, "I think this medal, being pure of its kind, the real gold, would go to you of its own accord . . . Safe as a puppy, it would climb into your pocket. But the ceremony is our part of the medal, and to my own lasting pride and pleasure, the institute has given me the honor of presenting it." The microphone had been set for Eudora, who was taller than Faulkner. When Faulkner stepped up to read his acceptance, he failed to lower it, and nobody could hear a word he said. After the ceremony, he wandered off the stage alone.

Faulkner died only two months later. Eudora mourned his death, she said, but mourned more that she did not know a soul within miles to mourn with.[18]

Twenty-five years later, in the keynote speech at the Southern Literary Festival dedicated to the memory of William Faulkner, she said that everyone present was in Faulkner's presence. They could walk to the golf course that used to be the Comptons' pasture, where *The Sound and the Fury* opened, she said, and they must have all been at some time in Courthouse Square, where that book ends. "All around us is the original and concrete thing; but the irrefutable fact is, to begin with, he saw better than we can. And the way to see the reality is to look where we saw it before, in the novels and stories. Faulkner sees with the eyes of the artist and can make us see what is here and at the same time through it to the truth about it, the human truth."[19]

In August 1987, Eudora would speak in Oxford at the official ceremony marking the issue of the William Faulkner postage stamp. She urged her audience to imagine that they were all in the old university post office in the twenties. "We've come up to the stamp window to buy a two-cent stamp, but we see nobody there," she said. "We knock and then we pound, and we pound again and there's not a sound back there. So we holler his name, and at last here he is. William Faulkner. We have interrupted him. Postmaster

Faulkner . . . was in the back writing lyric poems. He was a postmaster who made it hard for you in general to buy a stamp and send a letter or get your hands on any of the mail that may have come for you. Faulkner the postmaster called it quits here in 1924. Faulkner the Poet was able to move on with his pen into his vast prose world of Yoknapatawpha County."[20] Appropriately, she read "Why I Live at the P.O." to the assembled group.

Chapter 40

Abroad

1949–1950

ꙮ Booking passage to Europe was not easy. Cook's did not answer her letters, so Eudora went to a local travel agent and got space on the *Italia,* of the Home Line. It would sail from New York on October 14 and was supposed to reach Genoa two weeks later, stopping at Lisbon, Algiers, Palermo, and Naples on the way. She busied herself getting vaccinations and typhoid shots and had a small cyst taken off her back.

When Eudora boarded the *Italia* in New York, Jean Stafford went down to see her off and presented her with Elizabeth Arden soap, a bottle of scotch, and champagne. Other friends took champagne too, and on Gala Dinner night, Eudora was a heroine, with enough champagne for three tables. She enjoyed her shipmates, many of whom became models for the characters in her story "Sailing to Naples," in which the *Italia* became the *Pomona.* There was the old man from the countryside near Naples with his ten-cent whistle that he blew at random moments, the woman taking her daughter back to Sicily to find her a husband, and a Pole going to Italy to marry an Italian girl he had courted by letter. The voyage was easy and pleasant. Eudora traveled tourist class and liked it; when she was up in first class briefly for a party, it seemed "boring and forced-gay." She found herself one night in a circle doing the shag with an Italian chorus boy from *Annie,*

Get Your Gun, who turned out to be delightful; he had just graduated from Columbia and was on his way to Italy to be in a movie. With this young man, a member of the crew named Reno, and a Spaniard named Antonio, she spent most of the time, talking, reading, or dancing in the front of the ship where the crew went to relax.

The ship neither stopped in Algiers, as the travel agent had promised, nor allowed passengers to get off in Lisbon—Franco was visiting there, and security was strict. When the *Italia* arrived in Sicily, flocks of little boats came out to meet it, just as they do in "Sailing to Naples." Eudora noted one boat in which one man rowed while thirteen other Sicilians waved frantically at the ship. In Naples, where the boat docked briefly, she got along fine, even though she knew no Italian. Leaving the boat in Genoa, though, she found herself bewildered by the language and the bustling, crowded streets. Feeling the need to understand someone, she went to see Danny Kaye in *Wonder Man.* Although his lines were dubbed in Italian, she knew what he was saying and thought he made a fine Italian. She loved it when they turned up the lights in the middle of the picture and sold refreshments. All in all, it took her four whole days to find her way out of Genoa, and another two weeks to book a sleeper to Paris.

Mary Lou Aswell, who had remarried in June and taken a leave of absence from *Harper's Bazaar,* planned to spend the winter in Paris. Friends had cautioned her against her new husband, Fritz Peters, who was manic-depressive with a history of violence, but Mary Lou was determined. Peters, a lanky, blond, handsome, charming young man, had been educated in Paris before the war and had worked as a translator. After his discharge from the army, he had had what was euphemistically called a nervous breakdown and had become a writer. He had just published a novel, *The World Next Door,* based on his experiences in the mental wards of a Veterans Administration hospital. When Eudora reviewed it for *Saturday Review,* she called it "magnificent," "devastatingly moving," and "the best piece of fiction yet produced by a veteran of the recent war."[1] But his marriage to Mary Lou did not last much longer than a year.

Eudora settled down in the Hotel des Saints-Pères on the Left Bank and walked everywhere—to the Louvre, Notre Dame, the Palace of Luxembourg. Paris was cold and dark, but it was beautiful. She loved the violet winter light in the Luxembourg Gardens, with children in caps with rabbit ears playing in the lanes between bare trees. She bought the first of many French berets and wore it that winter.

Eudora's hotel room was blessedly warm—the water pipes ran behind the wall—and when Thomas Cranfill, a professor friend of Frank Lyell's at the University of Texas, and his sister, Betty Cranfill Wright, were in Paris, they stopped by to get warm. Richard Wright, still totally unknown to Eudora, was also in Paris. He had renounced the Communist party and fled the United States because congressional committees wanted to question him about his friends in the party. Guy Davenport, a southern friend of Eudora's, tells an illuminating anecdote about Paris and race in 1949: "I saw Richard Wright at an outdoor table at the Deux Magots. A girl from home was with me, and I said, 'Let me introduce you to Richard Wright' and walked over to him. 'Mr. Wright,' I said, 'this is Dot . . .' And I looked around. 'That girl left,' Wright said. When I told Eudora this story, thinking that she would be as shocked as I was, she said, 'We were like that then.' "[2]

Through Mary Lou Aswell, Eudora met Mary Lawrence Mian, who had written some marvelous pieces for *The New Yorker* about her French in-laws, who lived in the Creuse, in southern France. Mary had grown up in Andover, Massachusetts, and Atlanta, where her father was president of a theological seminary. She had attended Whitman College in Walla Walla, Washington, where her uncle was the president, and Radcliffe, and had done social welfare work in New York. When she met the French sculptor Aristide Mian, she returned to France with him to live. The Mians, now parents of three daughters, lived at Meudon, near Versailles. Eudora saw the Riviera when she, Mary Mian, and Hildegarde Dolson, her collaborator on the musical, went to Nice for Mardi Gras. Then it was back to Italy.

John Robinson had arrived in Florence in January to take up a Fulbright fellowship to study Italian. (When he applied for the Fulbright, he gave as references Eudora; his stepgrandfather, J. K. Vardaman, the ex-governor and ex-senator from Mississippi; and Bob Farley, dean of the law school at Ole Miss, along with Mark Schorer, his teacher at Berkeley, and his Air Corps friend Sol Katz, now a professor at the University of Washington. In her recommendation, Eudora praised him as "genuinely creative . . . [with] a first-rate mind and a natural talent for languages. . . . A warm, good, gracious, independent and highly perceptive personality." In his statement on the application, Robinson pointed out that he had spent two and a half years in Italy during the war and said that he wanted to work for the State Department. His instructor at Berlitz in San Francisco testified to his grasp of spoken and written Italian.)

Robinson had rented the Villa del Beccaro at Mosciano, five miles from Florence, where Dylan Thomas had stayed in 1947 and written the poem "In Country Sleep." The house was, Thomas had said, "among pines and olives, beautifully green and peaceful, a cool, long house with a great garden & a swimming pool. . . . The garden is full of nightingales and orange trees. There are vineyards all around us."[3] At the University of Florence, Robinson met William Jay Smith, an American poet almost ten years younger than he, and Smith's wife, Barbara Howes, also a poet. The Smiths had rented a villa, Il Frosinino, on the other side of Florence, in San Domenico, just below Fiesole. Their house, once the peasant house on Walter Savage Landor's estate, had been refurbished and had a huge loggia in which stood a painted wooden chest and an assortment of wicker chairs and tables, lemon trees, and geraniums. Smith, then thirty-two years old, was the Louisiana-born son of an army officer; he had graduated from Washington University and studied at the University of Poitiers, Columbia University, and as a Rhodes Scholar at Oxford University. He was still a student, this time at the University of Florence. He had published one book of poems and would eventually publish many more. Barbara, then thirty-six, was the daughter of an extremely wealthy New York stockbroker. She had attended Bennington College, published her first book of poems, and edited the literary magazine *Chimera*.

Robinson told the Smiths that his friend Eudora Welty was coming; they knew her stories and were eager to meet her. Actually, when Eudora arrived, the Smiths were in London, but John took her up to Il Fosinino to show her the establishment, and there she met the Smiths' baby, David, who was in the care of his Italian nurse. A few days later the two couples met by chance on the Lung'Arno and immediately began to talk, forming what would become a lifelong friendship.

While Eudora was in Florence, she paid the obligatory call (as all Americans who could get an introduction did) on the connoisseur of Italian Renaissance art Bernard Berenson, at I Tatti, his art-filled villa outside the city. Berenson felt that Eudora had great charm and thought her novels showed talent, but he said that like all Americans, she had found one thing she could do well and kept on doing that. On March 25, when she and

Robinson had dinner at I Tatti, Stephen Spender, the English poet, was there. Spender liked Eudora very much. He found her "tall and dark-eyed, rather craggy, yet soft-looking, a slight rolling of the eyes which went well with her Southern accent." He thought Robinson was "solid but mysterious and subject of much speculation."[4]

Eudora and John spent many evenings with the Smiths, and the four of them took trips around Tuscany, to Siena notably, and finally to Venice. The main piazza made such an impression that Eudora said later that whenever somebody said "San Marco," she did "want to go up on my toes."[5]

Decades later, Barbara Howes captured the essence of the time in Florence in her poem "Interludes with Eudora Welty," which ends:

> *Around this hotel table,*
> *Eudora, the very air*
> *Stirs merle with windfall.*

Chapter 41

England and Ireland
1950

From Italy, Eudora went to London, which she found enchanting in spite of the still-visible war damage. London seemed quiet after Italy. She liked the river, and she admired the swans in Regent's Park. She rode buses and walked around almost at random. She noted that the *Times* reported, "At Kew Gardens there are ample signs that spring, though not unduly hurrying, is with us now in earnest—and not the least is the chiff-chaff calling industriously from the boughs." She checked in with the A. M. Heath literary agency, Diarmuid Russell's British representative, and met Hamish Hamilton, her English publisher. When she saw Ted Weeks, who was on his way to Florence to see the Sitwells, she told him to look up the Smiths and John Robinson and read their work.

John Lehmann, who had published "A Shower of Gold" in his magazine, *Penguin New Writing,* invited her to a party at his house, where she met the historian Veronica Wedgwood, the novelist Rose Macaulay, and Henry Yorke, the novelist who wrote under the name Henry Green. Lehmann recalled that Yorke and Eudora "flung themselves at one another. Henry could not have been more recklessly ebullient, and swept Eudora Welty off her feet." Eudora, who admired his work a great deal, asked him when a new book of his would appear. Yorke replied that that day was the English publication date for *Nothing,* which he said was the first "entirely funny book he had ever tried to write."[1] Eudora remained his fan.

Next was Ireland. "I always wanted to go to Ireland, though I didn't know anyone there," she said years later. She took the ferry to Dun Laoghaire, just outside Dublin, and then "just walked around Dublin, looking at all those places I had read about." As a child, she had liked everything about books, including the way the printed page *looked.* She especially liked the way the illustrator Walter Crane used a big initial at the beginning of each fairy tale in *The Yellow Dwarf,* and she thought of them when she saw the Book of Kells at Trinity College. The guidebooks would have pointed out to her, if she did not know it already, the house at 84 Merrion Square where A.E., Diarmuid Russell's father, had lived, not far from Yeats. It was all "heavenly," she said. A good hiker, she walked out from town and followed country lanes, taking refuge under a hedge when it rained.[2]

In Dublin, she thought of Elizabeth Bowen, the Anglo-Irish novelist who had written *The Last September, The Hotel, The House in Paris,* and *The Death of the Heart.* Bowen had reviewed *Delta Wedding* in the *Tatler and Bystander* when it was published in England, saying "What a beauty!" and predicting that it would be a classic. In Paris, someone had told Eudora that Elizabeth Bowen had said she wished she could meet her. Eudora, who had never in her life looked up anybody she did not know, was tempted. "It was a fantasy almost," she said. "I thought that Bowen's Court [Elizabeth Bowen's ancestral home] was in Dublin; I didn't know it was a long way off."[3]

At any rate, Eudora wrote to Bowen and told her she would like to call on her. Bowen telephoned her at the hotel, told her she was in County Cork, and asked her down for the weekend. Thus began what was one of the most important relationships in Eudora's life.

She took the train to Mallow in County Cork, where Bowen sent a car to meet her. "It was my first sight of the South of Ireland, the real South," Eudora said. "Later on I saw palm trees and fuschia hedges and pink and blue plastered houses that made you think of Savannah or New Orleans. At any rate Elizabeth is a *Southerner.* She said that wherever she went, in the whole world, Southerners were always different from the Northerners. She always felt the congeniality."[4]

At fifty, Elizabeth Bowen was a striking woman. She was tall and large-boned, her copper hair pulled tightly back. Someone described her as "a woman of commanding presence who seemed more quietly masculine than most men and, at the same time, as feminine as our mothers."[5] She had a stammer, but like many Irish people, she liked to talk and did it well. A towering figure in the British literary world, she had an "alive, inevitable, inexhaustible intelligence."[6] The poet May Sarton wrote that Bowen had women lovers, including Sarton; she had a habit, according to her biographer, of beginning intense friendships (with both men and women) and then dropping them ruthlessly. While she had male lovers, among them Seán O'Faoláin, the Irish novelist, and Goronwy Rees, a Welsh journalist and novelist, she was in her way fiercely loyal to her husband, Alan Cameron. Cameron, an educator who was with the BBC's schools service, was stout and red-faced and had a walrus mustache, but none of Bowen's friends was allowed to criticize or discuss him.

Bowen's Court was a square gray Italianate limestone house built in 1776 by Henry Bowen III in the "green rural make-believe of the Irish countryside," as John Lehmann put it. The driveway left the road between Mitchelstown and Mallow and meandered for almost half a mile, passing Farahy Church (where Elizabeth Bowen is now buried) before it reached the house. On the front porch and steps, cushions and deck chairs came out in summer, and there Bowen and her houseguests sat in the long late afternoons, looking out at the vast park, or demesne, as the Irish called it. The lawn under a group of elms nearby was called the lambs' drawing room, because the lambs came down to browse there in the evenings.

Bowen and Cameron had spent the years during World War II in London—the setting for her novel *The Heat of the Day,* which had recently been published—and now that they could once more visit Ireland she was restoring Bowen's Court, room by room, to make it more comfortable. Money from *The Heat of the Day* made it possible for her to add bathrooms and running water for the first time. The rooms were large and handsome, with classical cornices and fireplaces. The long center hall had a fireplace at the end and Pompeiian red damask wallpaper that was fading to apricot. To the right of the hall was the library; to the left, a drawing room and the dining room. On the top floor was the Long Room, designed to be a ballroom but never completed. One visitor said that Bowen's Court was "full of lovely things that seemed barely kept together, and an endearing Irish ramshackleness pervaded it."[7] Bats flew in the attic, and butterflies came in the open windows in the summertime. An old walled garden was full of dahlias and fruit bushes, and the vegetable garden covered three acres.

"You know my passion for her works," Bowen wrote to her friend Charles Ritchie at the time of Eudora's visit. And Bowen took to Eudora personally; she found her very unwriterish and well bred, "quiet, self-contained, easy, outwardly old-fashioned, very funny indeed when she starts talking," but still reserved. "I know little about her life, nor she about mine. I think she's like me in preferring places to people."[8] Another time, Bowen told a visitor who noticed a china chocolate pot that Eudora had sent from America that Eudora was "a perfectly remarkable woman to have come out of that circumstance." A pause. "Mississippi," she added in explanation.[9]

Bowen and Eudora would talk at lunch and spend the afternoon on long walks or riding madly around the neighborhood, with Bowen driving very fast and usually on the wrong side of the road. "Any unexpected sight or view while we are driving about the country makes her start up in the car with a smothered cry as though she had been stung by a wasp," Bowen commented at the time.[10] In the evenings, when neighbors sometimes dropped in, they all drank whisky and played card games, Scrabble, and parlor games.

Oddly, Eudora's old bête noir, Carson McCullers, came to Bowen's Court shortly after she did, but her visit was not the same success. McCullers was, Bowen said, a "handful" and a "destroyer," and she certainly did not build a close friendship with her as she did with Eudora.[11]

After Eudora left Bowen's Court, she went to County Meath to visit Mary Lavin, a great friend of Jean Stafford's and a short story writer admired by Eudora. Lavin lived with her mother, her husband, and her two children in a house near the ruins of Bective Abbey, which in turn was near the Hill of Tara, where the kings of Ireland used to gather for their triennial conference.

From Ireland, Eudora went back to Paris. Just before she left Europe for home, she went down to Meudon for a May Day celebration with Mary and Aristide Mian and their daughters. As she had done throughout her trip, she took pictures of everything and everybody—"a record of happiness," she called it. After the festivities she took the train to the Gare Montparnasse, where she could catch the *métro* to her hotel off the Boulevard St. Germaine, carrying not only her camera but a bunch of lilacs the Mians had given her, some of the leftover food, and presents. As soon as she got on the *métro,* she realized she had left the camera behind at the station. She took the first train back, but the camera was gone. More than the loss of the camera, she regretted the roll of film in it, the pictures of the May Day party. She has said that she felt after that that she didn't deserve to have a camera. "I punished myself," she said. "I was so crushed, and by then cameras were much more expensive."[12]

Rosa Wells, Eudora's Jackson friend who now worked for Harper Brothers in New York, joined her, and together they went back to Italy and caught the *Saturnia* for the homeward voyage. Jack Spalding of Atlanta, a fellow passenger, remembers having a drink with the two women and enjoying Eudora immensely. "She was witty and charming and funny," he said. Her name sounded familiar to Spalding, and he asked her if she had written "A Rose for Miss Emily." "No," Eudora said, "I wish I had."[13] The voyage was peaceful, except for one storm and a breakdown, which the passengers referred to, Thurber-like, as "The Night the Piston Broke."

Chapter 42

The Civil War Redux
1950

As soon as Eudora reached Jackson, the University of Chicago offered her a teaching job. She truly hated the idea of teaching. In 1944, when
the North Carolina College for Women had asked her to come and teach,
she had replied that she was "0 as a teacher—that is 'nought' not 'Oh!' "[1]
Now she said that the offer from Chicago was just the push she needed to
get her back to writing. She also turned down an invitation to teach at a
writers' conference, saying that she didn't have the temperament for it.

She wrote a long story about the Civil War, rewrote it at Russell's
suggestion, and then marveled when Mary Lou Aswell bought it for *Harper's
Bazaar.* "The Burning" was the only story she ever wrote about this subject,
although physical reminders of the Civil War were all around her in Jackson.

LeFleur's Bluff, a settlement on the Natchez Trace, had become Jackson, a rough frontier town with dirt streets and wooden sidewalks and a state
capitol. General Grant's army marched through Jackson on its way to Vicksburg in 1863, but William T. Sherman stayed behind to destroy "railroads,
bridges, factories, workshops, and everything valuable." Jackson was the first
town to undergo Sherman's slash-and-burn program. A year later, the nation
had become used to the idea of burning civilian homes and property, but in
1863 it was a new and horrifying idea. In May 1864, Jackson was the head-

quarters for Confederate forces under General Joseph E. Johnston, who was trying to collect troops to relieve the defenders of besieged Vicksburg. Vicksburg fell on July 4, and it was said that no true Mississippian would ever celebrate the Fourth of July again. Sherman headed back toward Jackson. Fortification Street got its name from the defenses behind which Johnston's Confederates lobbed shells at the Yankees marching in from Port Gibson. To everyone's amazement, Johnston held Sherman off for seven days. During the battle, residents had to flee their homes, which were close to the trenches, and survive as best they could in the swamps. They returned to find their houses burned. What the Yankees did not burn, the retreating Confederates did, trying to destroy General Johnston's supplies before the Federal forces got them. People ruefully called the town Chimneyville, because only the chimneys were left standing. (The name Chimneyville has stuck; there is a Chimneyville Barbecue near the Old Capitol.)

Eudora, the child of nonsouthern parents, has said that she thought that the total destruction was "kind of nice . . . a fresh start." But there had not been a "fresh start." Jackson became a center of political ferment, and ex-slaves seized the large plantations near town and took up arms. White citizens armed themselves and formed the Ku Klux Klan to restore white supremacy.

Bitter memories of Reconstruction shaped the racist attitudes of the parents of Eudora's friends. Eudora never fell for the mystique of the romance of the Lost Cause. She didn't even like to read about the Civil War. "I hate the Civil War," she said once. "I hate it. I have never read *Gone With the Wind*. I'm totally ignorant about the Civil War . . . But I just hate it, all those hideous battles and the terrible loss."[2] Elizabeth Bowen understood her revulsion, she said, because of the visibility of the churches and abbeys that Cromwell had burned in Ireland.

"The Burning," which reflects a familiar theme in stories about the defeat of the South—white aristocrats are unable to cope with what they see as the destruction of their culture, while black people display a tough survivor's spirit—won an O. Henry award. When Shelby Foote, the novelist and Civil War historian, wanted to reprint it in a collection of Civil War stories, however, Eudora told him she hated for him to use it because it was the worst story she ever wrote. He replied that he thought it was a good story and he was the Civil War expert.[3]

When Eudora heard that Mary Lou Aswell and Fritz Peters were separating, she decided to use the money from "The Burning" on a trip to New York in November to see Mary Lou. She would stay at the Grosvenor Hotel instead of with her old friend from Jackson, Dolly Wells, because, as she wrote to a friend, she was feeling tired and depressed. She planned to stay a month or longer, work in the mornings, "play in the evenings."[4]

Why was she depressed? Probably John Robinson was the cause, although she must have known for some time that her relationship with him would be no more than platonic. He had at last faced up to his sexual orientation and had left Italy to travel with a friend, Enzo Rocchigiani, to Mexico through Lisbon, the Madeiras, the Canaries, Venezuela, Curaçao, Haiti, Cuba, New Orleans, and finally Vera Cruz. Robinson would spend the rest of his life—more than forty years—with Rocchigiani, most of it in Europe. When he went back to Mississippi to visit his family, he always saw Eudora. They remained good friends, and Robinson admired Eudora to the last. What Eudora's feelings were toward him remain a mystery, but it is impossible not to believe that when he turned to Rocchigiani, it was a great loss for her.

When the two men went off to Mexico, however, Eudora was as supportive as ever and got Robinson a commission to write a weekly letter from that country. Robinson found it hard to produce a newsy column when he lived like a hermit, he said. He had published his third short story, "The Inspector," in the June 1950 issue of *Harper's,* and dedicated it to Eudora. "A nice feeling," Eudora said.[5] The story was based on Robinson's experiences as an insurance adjuster before World War II.

In New York that fall, Eudora saw William Jay Smith and Barbara Howes, who had also left Florence and were living in Vermont. They went to New York for the publication of Smith's new book, *Celebration at Dark.* The three of them had the chance for good long talks between running around to parties for Bill's new book and going to see Carol Channing and an exhibition of Toulouse-Lautrec paintings.

Elizabeth Bowen

1950

In the spring of 1950, Elizabeth Bowen paid her first visit to the United States in seventeen years, and Eudora hoped to see her while she was in New York. Better than that, Bowen paid Eudora and her mother a visit in Mississippi, the first of several. She gamely ate fried catfish and enchiladas and drank chicory coffee.[1] She liked the Mississippi people she met. They were like the Irish, "warm and gay and friendly," she told Eudora's good friend Charlotte Capers.[2] Eudora rounded up other friends to meet Bowen and took them to Allison's Wells, a favorite restaurant outside Jackson.

Bowen also found a bond with Eudora's mother. When Chestina was a child, she had very long hair. Her parents, who believed that too much hair weakened a person's health, wanted to cut it. Chestina refused. Her parents offered a pair of gold earrings. Chestina refused. When they raised the ante to a full set of the works of Charles Dickens, shipped upriver to Clay from Baltimore, she caved in. Years later, on a trip to visit family in West Virginia, Chestina showed Eudora where she had begun to read Dickens—under the bed, by the light of a candle. She took the set of Dickens with her when she went to Jackson, but Eudora never read it. "When I was little I was so perverse that when my mother said, 'You have to read Dickens—I read Dickens at your age,' I wouldn't read him," she said. This refusal to read

Dickens, when Eudora was always ravenous for new reading material, could not indicate more clearly her ambivalence about her mother and her ideas. But like Chestina Welty, Elizabeth Bowen had read the novels of Dickens when she was a child. Eudora said she guessed she'd have to go on and do it, but the other two said it was too late. "You have to read Dickens when you're very young," said Eudora. "They agreed on that. That's when he's a master."[3]

Eudora took Bowen down to the Gulf coast to see Elizabeth Spencer, the Belhaven girl who had become a published novelist, and to her beloved ghost town of Rodney, where Bowen admired the wildflowers (corydalis, blazing star, lady's slipper, Indian pink, blue loam violet, starry campion, bloodroot). But it was in Natchez that they saw a ghost. They went to see Longwood, the most famous of Natchez's antebellum showplaces. Longwood stood empty, but Eudora knew that Bowen liked old houses and would be fascinated.

The two women got out of the car on Sunday morning and walked up through the woods. They were outside the house when an old man came out of the woods and said, "Would you like to see the house? I can take you over it if you'd like to."

Elizabeth Bowen said they would like very much to see it.

They went inside, and the man offered them a drink. Since it was ten o'clock on Sunday morning, they declined, but they followed the talkative old man around the house.

When Eudora got back to Jackson, she told a friend about seeing Longwood and the caretaker who took them around.

"Oh, he couldn't have," said the friend. "He was killed in an automobile accident three months ago." She insisted there was no one in the house now.

"There *was* somebody at the house," Eudora said later.[4]

Everybody in Natchez assumed that Elizabeth Bowen had come all the way from County Cork to see Natchez, and thought her lucky to get to visit their town.[5]

Bowen's Court

1951

Eudora's brothers were handsome, charming, dark-haired young men with immense talents. "All three of the Welty children could do any-thing—paint, write, or play music," a friend of the family has said. Both Walter and Edward were fine athletes, championship golfers; Walter, espe-cially, competed throughout the state. As children, Eudora and Edward, who was three years younger than she, had made each other laugh. It was with Edward that Eudora honed her wit; a cousin remembers how they clowned together, each egging the other on during summer visits to relatives. Edward later published cartoons in sports magazines. But he had emotional problems, of which Eudora has never spoken publicly, mentioning only "mental prob-lems" occasionally in letters to close friends. Trained at Georgia Tech, he became an architect and won first prize in a national contest for the best house design sponsored by the National Association of Home Builders. In 1950 he had what Eudora called "mental troubles," and after Christmas she went with him to Foundation Hospital in New Orleans. While they were there, a cold spell struck. Pipes burst, the hospital's heat went off, and pa-tients were wrapped in blankets to keep them warm.

Elizabeth Bowen had invited Eudora back to Bowen's Court for a longer visit in April 1951, and Eudora accepted. A $1,250 advance for an untitled book of unwritten short stories from Harcourt Brace would make it possible, and she booked passage on the *Liberté* for March 14, sailing to Plymouth.

She planned to stay in London before she went to Ireland, and to try to work there as she had in San Francisco, "in a new place," where she could "feel the life of a strange city going on around her."[1] Accordingly, she wrote to ask Elizabeth if she knew of a small flat, not too expensive, where she could stay. Back from New Orleans, she was thrilled when she opened a letter from Bowen (read by candlelight, because an ice storm had cut off the electricity) offering her the use of her house near Regent's Park. Eudora accepted and said she would bring some work, bits and pieces she had collected toward a story.

Hubert Creekmore, Mary Lou Aswell, and Jean Stafford saw her off on the *Liberté,* showering her with flowers and Jack Daniel's for the voyage. The ship, to her disappointment, was full of rude Germans, not French people. Lauren Bacall and Humphrey Bogart were on board but several layers above Eudora, who was in tourist class. In London, she stayed briefly at the Montague Hotel and then moved into Elizabeth Bowen's high-ceilinged house in Clarence Terrace. She tried to work, but spent most of the time staring out the drawing room window at Regent's Park and the swans on the lake.

It was lovely being back at Bowen's Court in April. Bowen liked to work at her writing in the morning—she had started a novel—and Eudora worked on a long story that became "The Bride of the Innisfallen." It was about a group of people traveling together by chance on the all-night train from Paddington Station in London to Fishguard and thence by ferry to Cork, the route Eudora had taken. It is a difficult story, with shifting points of view and hazy intention. One critic has said that for the American girl in the story (only a young boy, Victor, is given a name), the journey "is coming into an awareness of death."[2] The bride of the title, incidentally, is a young woman in white who appears very briefly on the ferry, the *Innisfallen,* just as the passengers disembark in Cork.

At Bowen's Court, hostess and guest stopped work each day at about eleven for a glass of sherry, then went back to work until lunchtime. "Eudora Welty is staying in the house—working away at one of her great short stories in another room. This is ideal: I'm so fond of her, and her preoccupation during the day with her own work gives me a freedom unknown when one has an ordinary guest," Bowen wrote to a friend.[3]

In the afternoons, they went on long walks or a drive around the countryside, to Crosshaven, Mallow, Cork, Ferway, Yarhal, Kisale, Limerick, Coshel, Cahir, Mitchellstown, Killarney, Kemmane, Shannon, and, of course, the nearest village, Kildorrery. In the evenings they played games. Eddy Sackville-West, the heir to Knole, in Kent, one of the greatest houses in England, had bought a house nearby and was a frequent visitor. He was the author of a number of books and with his cousin Vita Sackville-West had translated Rainer Maria Rilke's poetry for Leonard Woolf's Hogarth Press. He was a tall man with extremely conservative views. "I *hate* equality," he said, and he did not believe in education for the masses. He loved to play Happy Families, a children's card game very much like Go Fish. "You try to get all the family in your hand by asking, 'May I have?' except that it's done with Victorian decorum," Eudora said. "The cards are designed with Dickens-like illustrations and names like Mr. Bones, the butcher, and Mrs. Bones, the butcher's wife, and Miss Bones, the butcher's daughter, and Master Bones, the butcher's boy, all with huge heads and little bodies . . . You say, 'May I have Mrs. Bones, the butcher's wife?' and I say, '*Sorry,* she isn't at home.' So you've missed your turn. There are more thanks and a lot of politeness. I would get the giggles to see Elizabeth and Eddy being so unfailingly *courteous* to each other."[4]

"Elizabeth Bowen was an 'intaker,' " Eudora said decades later. "She just took everything in. She was curious and fascinated by people she met . . . She would come in and she would know that there may have been two people at odds just about ten minutes before. And she was always in command . . . She had the best time."[5]

Eudora spent her forty-second birthday, April 13, 1951, at Bowen's Court and loved it. Her letters to Bowen later reveal that the whole visit was an unparalleled joy.

She went to Dublin and stayed at the Shelbourne Hotel, because Bowen had just finished writing a popular history of this venerable hotel, which had been facing St. Stephen's Green since 1824. (Thackeray stayed there and wrote about the chambermaid who propped up the window with a broom, and George Moore set his novel *A Drama in Muslin* there in 1886.) It was much grander than the hotels where Eudora usually stayed. Her room, number 415, which faced the green, had a big table in the middle of the floor, an armoire, a marble fireplace, three chairs, and a double bed. She wrote a long thank-you letter to Bowen and addressed the envelope in the writing room, where a woman was combing her Pekingese with a blue baby-comb and a man was counting something mysterious. It made her happy, she said, just to think of Bowen's Court and Elizabeth, and her visit had been the loveliest time she had ever had.

In a later letter from London, she thanked Bowen again. Each day had stretched out to far ends, she said, all "lovely" like the points of a star.[6] There had been many "so nice, delicious, sunny, luxurious, darling, whizzing, comforting, filling, funny, beautiful indelible things." She wondered if she could ever go back, but said that was greedy. "I miss and will miss and have missed you . . . it's so strange, isn't it, the crisscross where and when we are with all we love and must love."[7]

From London, Eudora traveled to the Cotswolds and to Brighton, about which she wrote a short story, never published. In Kent, at Diarmuid Russell's instigation, she went to Dunstall Priory, the country home of the Irish writer Lord Dunsany, whose short stories she had read long ago in the old *Vanity Fair*. Lord Dunsany, whose whole name was Edward John Moreton Drax Plunkett, eighteenth Baron Dunsany, had an obsession about not docking the tails of spaniels. He proudly showed off his dogs, the "only three spaniels with tails in the world." Then it was back to London, while Bowen went to the United States in connection with her service on the Royal Commission on Capital Punishment. Eudora wrote to Bill Smith and Barbara Howes in Vermont, Hubert Creekmore in Yaddo, and Marcella Winslow in Washington, urging them to try to meet her.

Eudora liked London immensely. In 1985, when the *New York Times* asked her what her dream destination was for travel, she said that she wanted nothing more than to go back to England. "I love it there," she said. "I have friends there. I have been thinking about how England looks in the spring, and I want to be there. London, I love that city so. I could live there quite easily."[8]

From London she mailed "The Bride of the Innisfallen" to Diarmuid Russell, who sent it to *The New Yorker*. The editor returned it to him with "annotations." Eudora thought Mary Lou should have it for *Harper's Bazaar,* if she wanted it, but *The New Yorker* would pay well. She would have to see the editor's questions. It was her favorite story and she felt protective toward it. William Maxwell, the *New Yorker* editor who had been her friend for some time, tried to help, but she still had to answer twenty-six questions about such things as which doors were used for entrances and exits and who was speaking, and Harold Ross wanted to know how she knew the bride was a bride. Eudora replied that she had no idea.[9] The story marked her first appearance in *The New Yorker,* except for her letter protesting Edmund Wilson's review of *Intruder in the Dust.*

Elizabeth Bowen went to London to see her off. On the *Ile de France,* bound for home, Eudora put yellow roses from Bowen in her drinking glass on her bedside shelf and carefully stowed the china and a painting she had acquired in Ireland, nicely packed by her and Bowen, as well as hoops for hoop skirts for her nieces. Right away she wrote to Bowen, a letter so warm and grateful, so full of tender recollections of her visit, that she sounds almost incoherent with ecstasy. "You were sweet . . . you did *so much*—but I let you, loved it and took my pleasure, I let you as I love you," the letter reads. "Thank you for all that 'thank you' can be said for—I'll never, never forget any of those days and nights . . . I wish I had known all my life of this visit, and could have known the anticipation—somehow I believe that all *that* happiness came too and when the visit was happening—or it reached back . . . To be happy, gives me a sense of my life." All her experiences were locked up inside her, and she felt "like one of those treasures in fairy tales, one of those golden walnuts that could open and little gold carriages and prancing horses would drive right out, with people inside waving and jewels flashing and tiny carriage dogs jumping and the wheels spinning."[10]

Chapter 45

The Enigma

1951

On her way home from the British Isles that summer, Eudora spent a week in New York. She was ill most of the time, mostly, she said, from regret at being back in the United States.[1] She also worried about John Robinson, who met her at the boat and later put her on the train for Jackson. He looked well; he was still with Enzo Rocchigiani; but he was only working two days a week in a clerical job at the *New York Times* and was not doing any writing. She told friends in letters that he was "at the brink"; if he did not find a better job, she feared that he faced disaster.[2]

When she got home in early August, Jackson was so hot the bedpost felt warmer than her hand; when it rained, it was like water splashing on a hot stove. She wrote to Elizabeth Bowen (while she was drinking coffee from a cup bought in Limerick), urging her to write a story for *The New Yorker* so she could reap some of the wonderful money they paid.[3] Bowen was coming to the United States that fall and was scheduled to lecture in New Orleans. Eudora looked forward to her arrival and a promised visit to Jackson.

Late in August the heat eased a little—the thermometer slid down to the nineties. Eudora wanted to invite Mary Lou Aswell, undecided about her future, to come to Jackson, but she dared not. Her brother Edward's breakdown had lasted a year, and her mother was so worried about him that the house was too gloomy for visitors. Only after Eudora persuaded Chestina to visit her family in West Virginia did she feel free to invite Mary Lou and Jean Stafford.[4] Neither one accepted. Instead, Eudora fled to the air-conditioned Monteleone Hotel in New Orleans.

One day she rode down to Venice, Louisiana, with a young Harvard professor named Carvel Collins. Eudora wrote to Elizabeth Bowen that on the long drive they saw crawfish scuttling across the road. They crossed the Mississippi at Pointe à la Hatche on a ferry loaded with Cajuns who gave each other baskets of shrimp. "Coals to Newcastle!" said Eudora. They saw a cemetery with two rows of elevated graves and went to a roadhouse called the Paradise.[5] All of this went into the short story "No Place for You, My Love."

Originally called "The Gorgon's Head," the story was about an enigmatic woman and a northern man who follow the same route to Venice. In the first version, Eudora said, she wrote subjectively, about "a girl in a claustrophobic predicament . . . the over-familiar, monotonous life of her small town, and immobilized further by a prolonged and hopeless love affair; she could see no way out."[6] This sounds very autobiographical: Eudora was recovering from the long, hopeless relationship with John Robinson, and perhaps she met Carvel Collins at a party and embarked on the automobile trip with him on an impulse, just as the girl in the story did.

Eudora changed the girl to a midwesterner. The story, she said, during this revision "proved itself alive; now it took on new energy. That country— that once-submerged, strange land of 'south from South'—which had so stamped itself upon my imagination put in an unmistakable claim now as the very image of the story's predicament."[7]

While she was in New Orleans, she arranged for the framing of the prints she had bought in Ireland and a sketch of the Shelbourne. It made her think of Elizabeth Bowen, to whom she wrote a letter full of welcome and love, saying that she was counting the weeks until Elizabeth arrived. She wanted her to come to Jackson and stay as long as possible.[8] Another letter was full of anticipatory joy. She was excited that Elizabeth was in the United States, happy and relieved that she had crossed the ocean safely. She hoped the time would stretch when Elizabeth was with her so they could squeeze in more activities.[9]

Bowen at last arrived in Jackson on Thanksgiving night. There was apparently some uneasiness in the house. When Eudora wrote to her after the visit, she vowed that next time Elizabeth came, God willing, she would have a place of her own with space for Elizabeth to stay and write.[10]

Eudora traveled with Bowen to New Orleans for a lecture at Tulane; to Shreveport, where Bowen talked to a women's group (and they both stayed in the home of a woman with a memorable name: Mrs. Peachy Gilman); and to another lecture in Chicago, where they spent five days together. After this Eudora wrote another ecstatic letter to Elizabeth, about the Drake Hotel and "our" restaurant in "sweet, deep-carpeted Chicago!"[11]   .

Bowen's visit was "a dear wish come true," Eudora wrote right after she left.[12] Later, she wrote to say that she wished Elizabeth were still in Jackson, that she missed her terribly.[13] She was still in awe of Elizabeth for having given forty-nine lectures on this trip. She thought southern audiences might be a little better, because at least the women drove eighty miles and listened and loved her. Eudora hated the people who had taken Elizabeth's attention away from her, but nothing could have spoiled their time together.[14]

Elizabeth Bowen and Eudora kept up their friendship as long as Bowen was alive. Eudora visited Elizabeth in London in 1954 and spent two weeks at Bowen's Court that same summer. In the summer of 1959, Elizabeth was forced to sell Bowen's Court, and she spent much of her time in the United States after that, serving as writer-in-residence at many colleges. In January 1960, accompanied by her agent's wife, Catherine Collins, she made a trip to the Deep South for *Holiday* magazine and went to see "my beloved Eudora Welty."[15] Collins had friends in Jackson and did not spend much time with Eudora, but remembers that she "told us how to beat Prohibition, which grocery store to go to, to go in the back entrance, and what to say."[16] Eudora and Elizabeth saw each other briefly at Bryn Mawr in March 1960 and in Washington in 1961. In January 1971, two years before she died, Elizabeth, a visiting writer at Princeton, went down for a week in Jackson, a splendid visit that included a party and automobile rides through the winter landscape. It was always unexpected but wonderful when Elizabeth could come, Eudora said about that visit.[17] There were probably other meetings—

one of Elizabeth Bowen's biographers has said that Eudora was her "favorite American"—but records of them are not available.[18]

Elizabeth Bowen, a lifelong chain smoker, died on February 22, 1973, of lung cancer. Before her death she sold her papers to the University of Texas, including letters that Eudora had written to her in 1951, after her second visit to Bowen's Court and after Bowen's second visit to Jackson in the fall of that same year. No later letters from Eudora are among the papers at Texas. Over the years Eudora occasionally mentioned that she had seen Elizabeth, but she never went into details.

Eudora's letters at Texas are tantalizing—ardent and full of wonder, love, and gratitude. It is not clear exactly what her relationship with Bowen was—or whether it changed over the years—but the letters make it plain that for a time, at least, it was charged with emotion. Eudora adored Elizabeth, and to say she enjoyed the friendship is to understate it; she *reveled* in it. Their relationship invited speculation and gossip. Katherine Anne Porter, jealous of Bowen's influence, said that Eudora had at last fallen into very bad company, that Bowen was a lesbian.[19] Nancy Spain, an English journalist, told Rebecca West "the strangest tale about Elizabeth Bowen and Eudora Welty," according to a 1955 letter of West's.[20] West did not elaborate, and both she and Nancy Spain are dead.

No one knows the truth about Eudora's sexuality. Most of her men friends—John Robinson, Hubert Creekmore, Frank Lyell, Lehman Engel, Reynolds Price—were gay, as were many of her women friends. She has always refused to say anything at all about her private life, despite the many interviews she has given. She once told how someone in an audience had asked during the question period after a reading why she wasn't married. "Are you a lesbian?" he asked. "I am not, but I didn't answer the question," she said. She told a *Manchester Guardian* reporter that she "did not choose" to live alone.[21] And she told another reporter, "Various things caused me to stay single . . . I'm sure I would have been very happy had I married and had children. I'm a natural person in that way. But on the other hand I've had many compensations. Your personal life is something you work out as you can."[22]

Chapter 46

To and Fro

1952–1953

⟡ Eudora met Robert Penn Warren for the first time in February 1952, when he went to Jackson to speak at Millsaps College. She attended his lecture, and he went afterward to her house, where they laughed together for hours. "I had a perfectly wonderful time," he said when he left. "Not a serious word was spoken all evening."[1]

Katherine Anne Porter was scheduled to lecture at Millsaps on March 7 and a week later in another Mississippi town. Eudora urged her to spend the week between the lectures with her. They could drive down to the Gulf coast for a few days, she said; she would have her little Ford with the top down. With the money from a *New Yorker* story, she had bought herself a new car, and one for a niece as well. Porter agreed and went to Jackson, where she stayed in a hotel. Eudora, of course, wanted to invite her to dinner, but told Katherine Anne she had to ask her mother first. Katherine Anne was amazed and outraged that Eudora, a woman of forty-two, had to ask permission from her mother. The truth was that Mrs. Welty had taken a thorough dislike to Katherine Anne Porter—it was almost as bad as her refusal to allow Henry Miller in the house—and Eudora had to do some strenuous arranging.

At any rate, Eudora and Katherine Anne sped off to Pass Christian on the Mississippi coast, which had been a favorite resort for rich southern planters before the Civil War. They stayed in a rather grand hotel that Eudora was fond of, the Miramar. Eudora introduced Katherine Anne to her own protégé, Elizabeth Spencer, who was living on the Gulf coast. Katherine Anne, a native of Texas, was immensely pleased and interested when Eudora drove her along the Gulf into Louisiana. "All of that country meant something to her, which Jackson didn't," Eudora said.[2]

While Porter was in Jackson, Eudora gave a radio talk about her work. She spoke of her with her usual reverence and admiration, and quoted Porter's description of herself as a "precocious, nervous, rebellious, unteachable" girl who "taught herself to write, alone and unassisted in the wilderness."[3] She talked about Porter's stories, citing "Noon Wine" as the finest, and about the centrality of good and evil in Porter's work. The radio speech and her later essay "Katherine Anne Porter: The Eye of the Story" were so laudatory that surely the protégé generously repaid her mentor.

Eudora's next visitor was P. H. Newby, a BBC writer who described himself as a "weekend novelist," though he was the author of twenty novels, including the Booker Prize–winner *Something to Answer For*. When he went through Jackson on a State Department tour, he was so reserved that all Eudora could get out of him was that the South was a lot like Egypt—it had lots of blacks, but more trees. He wanted her to show him crocodiles; she took him to Vicksburg, and he said, "Hello! Fancy seeing Hereford cows this far from their home." Mrs. Welty consistently called him "Mr. Pamby."

In April, Katherine Anne Porter canceled a scheduled appearance at the annual literary festival at Mississippi State College for Women, and Eudora was called upon to take her place. She gave a short speech before an enormous crowd. As soon as she finished, three fifths of the audience stood up and rushed out; teachers had given the girls permission to cut class to hear Eudora, the alumna, speak. The visiting poet, Randall Jarrell, who had to talk to the small remnant of the audience, liked Eudora. She was "one of the three or four nicest writers I've ever met—somewhat homely, but so sympathetic, natural, and generally attractive that you quite forget it, particularly since you feel you've known her always," he reported.[4]

The rest of the festival was dreadful. The college president's wife, "an old fanatic who looked and dressed like Gandhi," according to Jarrell, spoke on the decline of modern literature since the dime novels of E.D.E.N. Southworth, "which had Standards," happy endings and nice uplifting subjects— and Southworth "believed that man was created by God." After Jarrell and Eudora stood in a receiving line for an hour that afternoon, the dean of the graduate school at the University of Mississippi spoke, defending the Forgotten Man—the reader—and ranting about the crimes of Faulkner, Hemingway, Fitzgerald, publishers, and modern poets. Jarrell, who thought the speech was "vicious" and "spiteful," said that Eudora was white with anger. "What would it have been like if we hadn't been here?" she asked Jarrell later.[5]

Eudora was elected to membership in the National Institute of Arts and Letters in April and went to New York for the investiture in May. Installed at the same time were Tennessee Williams, Newton Arvin, Louise Bogan, Jacques Barzun, Henry Steele Commager, Waldo Frank—and Carson McCullers.

In New York Eudora made her first recording for Caedmon Records. Two young women just out of college had had the idea of recording writers reading their own works, and Eudora went to an apartment they had borrowed for her first recording session. She read "Why I Live at the P.O.," "A Memory," and "A Worn Path." "Every time a truck went by, someone would shout, 'Hold it,' " she recalled. "And we'd wait." When they took a break and went to lunch at a restaurant, each person was expected to pay for her own lunch.[6]

In New York, Eudora, John Robinson, Hubert Creekmore, and Dolly Wells had a reunion, and she conferred with William Maxwell at *The New Yorker* about "Kin," a "surprise" short story that had surfaced while she was working on a longer story. Maxwell paid $695 for "Kin." Later he paid $1,610 for "No Place for You, My Love," the story about the trip down to the country south of New Orleans. Maxwell reported to Eudora that William Shawn hoped she would be able and willing to clarify the relationship between the man and the woman during that "timeless trip to the jumping off place."[7] In many ways, Maxwell replaced Mary Lou Aswell as Eudora's mentor-editor.

By September, John Robinson was back in Europe, living with Enzo Rocchigiani and teaching in Frankfurt. In September Eudora made another escape to New York, staying for a while in the apartment that William Jay Smith and Barbara Howes had sublet for the winter, and then in the Hotel Irving on Grammercy Park, for a month in all.

In the presidential election of 1952, Eudora was an ardent supporter of Adlai Stevenson in his losing race against Dwight Eisenhower. When Stevenson lost, she mourned. Diarmuid Russell told her that if a stray bullet were to hit Eisenhower on his post-election trip to Korea, the next president would be not the vice president (Richard Nixon) but the opposing candidate, Adlai Stevenson. When she relayed this to Robert Penn Warren, he suggested that she call the *New York Times* and ask if this were true. He told her to say, "This is Charlotte Corday, C-O-R-D-A-Y, and I want to ask a question."[8]*

---

* Charlotte Corday stabbed Jean-Paul Marat, a leader of the French Revolution, while he was in the bathtub. Jacques-Louis David recorded the event for history in a famous painting, *The Death of Marat*.

Chapter 47

The Ponder Heart

1954

◆ Eudora had almost finished what she called the "Uncle Daniel story," which she expected to include in the collection for which Harcourt had already given her an advance. Russell thought "Uncle Daniel" could stand alone and she should fill the collection with other stories and make more money.

Before "Uncle Daniel" was quite finished, Eudora took it to New York in January 1953 and read it out loud to William Maxwell. It took all day, with time out for lunch. Maxwell laughed so hard that he cried. He thought Eudora as a reader was better than a whole company of actors.[1] She promised Maxwell, who said it was the funniest story ever written, first refusal of the finished product.

When Eudora was a child, Jackson had a town character named Wiley Cooper, who was "happy, somewhat fey, and a friend to all." He loved to climb up on the bandstand in Smith Park and make speeches "on subjects not altogether clear." He often attended evening services at the Baptist Church, where he would sing loudly or even "testify" to his faith in God at great length. He handed out gum or candy or small coins to everyone he met, and he loved to be around people. Nash Burger always felt that Eudora had spruced him up, endowed him with a fortune, and moved him from Jackson to Clay to turn him into Uncle Daniel Ponder.[2]

Back in Jackson, Eudora wrote "Sailing to Naples," a story based on memories of her first trip to Europe, in 1949, and another story, called "Spring." When she finished revisions on the Uncle Daniel story, which was now long enough to be a book called *The Ponder Heart,* Harcourt Brace agreed to a $5,000 advance and set publication for January 1954. *The New Yorker* paid $7,700 for serial rights to the book, and the Book-of-the-Month Club selected it for an alternate and paid $4,000, of which Harcourt got half.

Eudora continued to entertain visitors. Mary Lou Aswell came down for her summer vacation and they went to the Gulf coast and New Orleans, where they heard Lizzie Miles sing "Bill Bailey, Returnez à la Maison." "The whole thing was like a trip to Europe," Aswell told Bill Smith and Barbara Howes.[3]

In September, while Eudora was in New York with her niece Elizabeth Welty, she went over the *New Yorker*'s proofs of *The Ponder Heart.* Maxwell was delighted with her work; he found the changes always funnier than the original, and he liked her firmness about unhelpful suggestions.

The New Yorker printed *The Ponder Heart* late in 1953, and the book came out in January 1954, illustrated with line drawings by Joseph Krush. It is a very funny book. The characters are droll, and the situations so outlandish that even the most resolutely serious reader must chuckle a little. If it had no artistic merit at all, it would still be an extremely valuable document for recording with scrupulous fidelity the speech and folkways of the rural South of the thirties. Eudora can find the telling detail to put her characters in place; for instance, "portulaca in pie pans" on the front porch is a perfect example of what the Peacocks, poor rednecks, would have for houseplants. "And the mirror on the front of the house: I told you," says Edna Earle. "In the yard not a snap of grass—an old auto tire with verbena growing inside it ninety to nothing, all red. And a tin roof you could just imagine the chinaberries falling on—ping!"

The book also reflects with great accuracy the racial mores of the thirties. White lawyers in court address elderly black men as "Uncle" and call black women either by their first names or "Woman." The characters treat black servants with the customary offhand tyranny of real life in Mississippi.

Edna Earle, the narrator, like Sister in "Why I Live at the P.O.," is a consummate storyteller. (She is named for the heroine of the novel *St. Elmo,* by Augusta Jane Evans, which was published in 1867 and was immensely popular in the South. For fifty years, southern mamas who were fans of *St. Elmo* named helpless girl-babies Edna Earle.) Edna Earle is the proprietor of the Beulah Hotel in the small Mississippi town of Clay and the niece of the book's protagonist, Uncle Daniel.

Uncle Daniel was, as his father used to say, "behind the door when brains were given out," but he is utterly selfless, and Edna Earle tells us frequently that he is beloved by all the people in Clay. He gives everything away, from cemetery lots to the change in his pocket. He gave Edna Earle the hotel. His father once committed him to the insane asylum in Jackson, but Uncle Daniel somehow managed to get out, leaving his father in the asylum in his place. This maneuver brought on the death—from the tricky Ponder heart—of old Mr. Ponder. "It's our hearts. We run to sudden ends, all we Ponders," says Edna Earle, although the doctor said he "just popped a blood vessel."

Uncle Daniel falls in love with Bonnie Dee Peacock, who works in the dime store, and marries her. Bonnie Dee, underweight and undernourished, can make change and cut hair and that's about all. She dies during a thunderstorm, perhaps scared to death, perhaps tickled to death by Uncle Daniel, who is tried for murder and, of course, swiftly acquitted by the jury. He then gives all his money away—cash he got from the bank on his way to the trial—in the courtroom.

The hilarity of *The Ponder Heart* and its hundreds of phrases that bring to life a time and a place do not obliterate the dark undercurrent. Katherine Anne Porter saw pathology in "Why I Live at the P.O.," while Eudora said she thought it was "cheerful." Eudora thought Uncle Daniel was completely lovable and the situation was funny, but *The Ponder Heart* is, after all, a story about a retarded man who is responsible for the death of his father and his retarded wife.

Eudora has said often that she does not write about violence; violence is prevalent in the South, she told the *Washington Daily News,* you can see it in the newspapers, "but it just doesn't interest me."[4] Yet her works are full of violence—rape *(The Robber Bridegroom,* "At the Landing," and "Sir Rabbit"), murder ("Sir Rabbit," "Flowers for Marjorie," and arguably *The Ponder Heart),* and suicide ("Clytie" and "The Burning"). Although Eudora describes most violent acts gently, in the matrix of social comedy, she achieves an extremely sinister effect.

She has also objected when anyone calls her characters grotesque. The only real grotesque she has created, she said, was the little " 'freak' in 'Keela, the Outcast Indian Maiden,' and he was only a short-term freak, really a harmless little old man. I think of my characters simply as characters . . . each story being its own world . . . Grotesques would be the opposite of what I strive for," she said.[5]

The Ponder Heart got good reviews. The daily reviewer in the *New York Times* called it a "wonderful tragicomedy of good intentions in a durable sinful world." Faulkner was the South's Wagner and Beethoven, he said, but Miss Welty its Mozart.[6] Eudora was from Mississippi, not far from Faulkner's Yoknapatawpha country, echoed an admiring review in the *Herald-Tribune,* "but the hoot-owls are gentler in her big woods and the sun shines more warmly on her courthouse steps. These Ponders are right nice folks to know."[7] V. S. Pritchett, whose short stories Eudora admired inordinately, wrote a virtual hymn of praise in the *New York Times Book Review,* saying that there was "not a mistake" in the book.[8] Under the headline "Welty Country," the *Book Review* ran several of Eudora's photographs of Mississippi scenes, with captions that related them to *The Ponder Heart.* For a photograph of storefronts in a small southern town, for instance, the caption said, "The office of Judge Tip might be upstairs," and a photograph of the Vicksburg courthouse was labeled "This is a little grand for Clay."

In England, the novelist Kingsley Amis demolished the book in the *Spectator* of October 29, 1954. "Uncle Daniel Ponder is just the *most* adorable old character you-all ever saw in all your sweet life . . . and if that ain't enough to make a *novel,"* then there was the "way the story (if you-all can *call* it that) gets told, just the cosy, friendly way I'm *talking* to you-all right now, hush my mouth. It can be hushed at any time, fortunately, by simply closing the covers, an exercise I found irresistibly attractive."

One thing that pleased Eudora about the book: she received letters from all over Mississippi in which people asked, "How did you know about my uncle?"[9]

Chapter 48

The First
Honorary Degree
1954

English professors at the University of Wisconsin began to think about giving an honorary degree to Eudora Welty in 1952. She was not a unanimous choice at first. In a tepid recommendation, Professor Helen White, who had been in the English Department when Eudora was a student there, said that *Delta Wedding* was "very normal, very warm, very human." She mentioned Eudora's "extraordinary acuteness of sense perception" and her "imaginative delicacy," and pointed out that "rape, lynching, and riots might have never been heard of so far as she is concerned. And while she has an extraordinarily rich and expressive vocabulary . . . there isn't a speech in the whole book that you couldn't read to either your grandmother or a granddaughter."[1] Another faculty member disagreed: "As far as I can gather there is no reason under heaven why Wisconsin should give her an honorary degree," he wrote.

On December 14, 1953, the English professor Ruth Wallerstein wrote an impassioned letter backing Eudora, whom she described as a "very distinguished short story writer and novelist, certainly one of the top handful now writing in the United States. Brilliant from the beginning, she is steadily growing in stature . . . The English department has expressed to me its wish as a whole to support Miss Welty's candidacy . . . Younger men feel that she is almost certain very shortly to begin to be invited to accept a number of degrees. It would be a great pity if her *alma mater* should lose this chance to recognize her early."

At commencement in 1954, twenty-five years after she graduated, Eudora Welty received the honorary degree of doctor of letters from Wisconsin president E. B. Fred. In a few years she would begin to receive these degrees by the handfuls, just as Ruth Wallerstein predicted.

Chapter 49

Cambridge
1954

Eudora truly hated the thought of lectures, and when the Fulbright people invited her to spend six weeks at an American Studies Conference for British secondary school and college teachers at Cambridge University in England, she hesitated. If she went, she would have to give three public lectures and to lead discussion groups on American literature. Her first impulse was to say she had never lectured before (forgetting her Seattle lecture on the short story), that she had no business being on a platform, that she was scared and had no voice. But more than she hated to lecture, she loved to travel. She would agree to almost anything for a trip.

She accepted, and worked off and on during the fall of 1953 and the winter and spring of 1954 on her lectures. In May 1954, the United States Supreme Court made its historic ruling to outlaw segregation in public schools, in *Brown* v. *Board of Education*. Immediately, the first White Citizens Council was organized in Indianola, in the Mississippi Delta, and Mississippi's long and bloody resistance to the ruling began. Before Eudora left for Cambridge, members of the White Citizens Council went from door to door in Jackson to recruit new members and to survey the "expected conduct" of every white resident of the town. Eudora and her friends, among the few moderates in Mississippi, were appalled at these activities. (Hodding

Carter referred to the White Citizens Council scornfully as the "uptown Ku Klux Klan.")

Eudora wrote a long paper that became immortal as her famous essay "Place in Fiction," and used it to make two of her Cambridge lectures. The text of the lectures was much longer than the essay, because she felt that her English listeners needed more examples of American writers' work than American readers would. For the third lecture, she "whacked and adjusted" her old Seattle speech on short stories.[1] Before she went to England, she also had to finish up the collection of short stories *The Bride of the Innisfallen* for Harcourt Brace.

In July she arrived for a brief whirl in London. She was now famous enough for her English publisher, Hamish Hamilton, to arrange for flowers in her hotel room and offer an invitation to lunch. She went to the theater and saw a few old friends before she went on to Cambridge and Peterhouse College, site of the conference. Eudora, the first woman to be invited to a Fulbright conference, and Jack Fischer, the editor of *Harper's*, were the only two nonacademics invited; the others were professors of American history, economics, sociology, or literature.[2]

The beauty and the age of Cambridge impressed Eudora, and so did Peterhouse, on Trumpington Street, the oldest college there, whose original thirteenth-century buildings, the Hall and Buttery, still stand on the south side of the Old Court. With its antipathy to women and its obsession with the contents of its cellars and the quality of its meals, Peterhouse was hilariously lampooned in *Porterhouse Blue*, a 1974 novel by Tom Sharpe, which was made into a television series in 1989. Eudora, with rooms in St. Peter's Terrace, did not live in college, but she was the first woman to cross the threshold of the Hall at Peterhouse. When officials invited her to a special dinner in Hall, they told her that they had debated a long time over whether to ask her. No woman had ever even been there, including Queen Victoria, who *asked* and was refused. Eudora wondered about the correct thing to do. She decided to accept—"to back out would sort of demean the *greatness*, the *momentousness*, of the invitation." Besides, she was curious.[3] Hall at Peterhouse was impressive, with long tables, stained glass, and portraits, and it interested her that the port and cigars were passed to her just as they were to the men.

Each morning tea was brought to her at 7:30, and that gave her the energy to walk to Hall for breakfast at 8:15. After listening to a lecture, she had coffee in the common room and looked at her mail. Another lecture was followed by lunch and afternoon discussion groups. She was free to get her own tea or drinks, and at night there were concerts and plays. It rained every day but two of the thirty-five she was in Cambridge, but Eudora rejoiced at the number of rainbows she saw over Trumpington Street.

David Daiches, a Scot and a fellow at Jesus College, and his wife liked Eudora immediately. "She was outgoing and curious, and we drove her around," Daiches recalled. "At first sight she was not an attractive woman, but the minute she began to talk that did not matter. She was lively and witty and I felt as though I had known her all my life. She was full of curiosity. About architecture, she wanted to know not just about the historic buildings but about cottages and how ordinary people lived. She liked her liquor, preferably bourbon, but drank Scotch in pubs—it was a case of desperation."[4]

Eudora was impressed with the quality of her students. They had read widely and wondered a great deal about America. Friendly, open, and quickly sympathetic, they were full of questions. Regionalism was rampant. She warned novelist Peter Taylor, who was to be the literary representative at the 1955 conference, to be wary of a room full of "Londoners, Scots, Welshmen, Yorkshiremen, and Irishmen," who could be contentious.[5]

At discussion groups in her rooms, Eudora passed out books and stories for reading, and the group talked about them the next time they met. She had expected her students to buy cheap editions of American writers such as Faulkner and Katherine Anne Porter, but none were in print in England, so she had to provide the reading material. Often her group ended up going for a walk, having tea, or visiting a pub. In addition to the lectures and discussion groups, there were garden parties and other social events. Eudora was busy.

E. M. Forster, who was still at King's College, Cambridge, and working on *Marianne Thornton,* invited her to lunch. "The luckiest thing happened," she said. "Our waiter was drunk and he came lurching on like a Shakespearean clown, and that put us both at ease and made our meeting so easy."[6]

Another friend drove her to Rodmell so she could see Monk's House, Virginia Woolf's country home. "We stood there with our backs to the River

Ouse, and before us the flower-covered house, the windows of the room in which she had written during the last years of her life," Eudora said.[7] Virginia Woolf was the one who opened the door, she explained another time. "When I read *To the Lighthouse,* I felt, Heavens, *what is this?* I was so excited by the experience I couldn't eat or sleep."[8]

After the conference, Eudora spent four weeks traveling in Scotland, Wales, and Ireland. While she was in Great Britain she wrote an article, which appeared unsigned in the *Times Literary Supplement* on September 17, 1954. This issue had a number of pieces on writing in the American South. In "Place and Time: The Southern Writer's Inheritance," Eudora had a number of amusing things to say in defense of southern writers. She mentioned, without naming it, a small Mississippi town on the river—it was Greenville—where seventeen authors were being published nationally "and a Pulitzer prize winner [Hodding Carter] edits the paper." Of course, it was true, she conceded, that nobody was *buying* books in that little town. "They are reading the old ones and writing the new ones," she said.

When she was in London on her way home in September, she was invited to a reception at London University for the American Fulbright fellows—professors and students—who just arrived on board the *United States* for a year's residence in Great Britain. A rumor had spread through the group that T. S. Eliot, every graduate student's idol in those days, would be present. Most of the Americans were disappointed indeed to find the author of "Why I Live at the P.O." instead of the man who wrote *The Waste Land.* Only the southerners were delighted. "I remember she was tall and giggly and talked about how much she had enjoyed the musical *The Boyfriend,*" one of those southerners recalls. Another remembers that she was already "humpbacked"; osteoporosis had begun to take its toll. She was only forty-five.

Chapter 50

Reynolds Price

1955

When Duke University invited Eudora to lecture early in the spring term of 1955, she replied that she never lectured. In the end, although North Carolina was not as exotic as Cambridgeshire, she agreed to go. She would use part of her Cambridge lecture and speak on "Place in Fiction."

Her train arrived at Durham late—at two o'clock on a February morning. She had insisted that no one from the university meet her and assured them that she could manage for herself. She was the only person to get off the train, and she could see no lights at the station or in the town. Neither a porter nor a taxi was around. Then she saw a solitary figure, a young man dressed in a white suit, waiting in the shadows. He was very slender and beautiful, she recalled later, and he came, took her bag, and told her that she did not have to say a word, that he would see her safely through the deserted streets to her hotel. "He was a savior dressed in white," she said.[1]

The young man was Reynolds Price, the author, who was then a student at Duke. He knew her work and he liked it; her world seemed closer to his own than Faulkner's did. If she wrote about people like that, he reasoned, then perhaps he could write about the people he knew. He was delighted that she had come to lecture at the Women's College on East Campus, and he knew what her plight would be when she arrived in the middle of the night at the downtown station, right behind the courthouse and the jail. He knew there would be no taxi and no way for her to get to the old Washington Duke Hotel, and he took it upon himself to rescue her. "I just decided I would go down and meet the great writer and take her to her hotel. She seemed pleased and grateful," he recalled. He also said that since the meeting took place in February, he probably would have worn his light gray suit, not a white one.[2]

It was the beginning of a warm and lasting friendship. The meeting started Price on his life's work. He was taking a writing class from William Blackburn, who had taught William Styron a few years earlier. For a class assignment, Price had just written his first short story, "A Chain of Love," about a girl named Rosacoke Mustian. Eudora read this story, said it was professional, and sent it to Diarmuid Russell. It was published in a short story collection and grew into Price's first novel, *A Long and Happy Life.* Eudora's judgment on his story provided young Price with validation. "If someone that good said I was good, then I was right to devote the rest of my life to proving her correct," he said. "She didn't say, 'This is the best story by a college student that I have read in the past five years,' but, 'This is an excellent *story.* Let me see the rest of your stories.' "[3]

At Duke, Eudora urged young would-be writers not to "drift." "One who drifts from place to place is apt to know none of them well, and when he attempts to write, his theme is usually reducible to two words, 'I'm drifting.' " She also said that the fatal limitation of science fiction was that it dealt with "places which we do not know and probably will not know. Science fiction amuses but it cannot move." A student reporter called her lecture "a beautiful evening—one filled with the graces—intellectual and spiritual—of a lady who happens to be, in addition, perhaps the finest short story writer operating in the United States."[4]

Reynolds Price was also the editor of the *Archive,* the undergraduate literary magazine, and he asked if he might publish her lecture, which he admired, in his last issue. Eudora said that William Hamilton, her old friend who was a professor of history at Duke and editor of the *South Atlantic Quarterly,* had also asked for it. Hamilton planned to run the essay in *SAQ* in January 1956 and placed no impediment on the *Archive*'s running it first. Price printed "every word" of the lecture and illustrated it with three Welty photographs of Mississippi.[5]

Price has been singing Eudora's praises ever since, calling her in various interviews "our greatest living comic novelist," "the great custodian of the oral history of the South," and "the living writer that I admire most."[6]

At least a month before she went to Duke in 1955, Eudora had started work on a rough draft of what would become *Losing Battles,* which was not published until 1970. It was already a story of "unpublishable length" about a family reunion where everybody talked all the time, and a baby in it was named Lady May. It was set in poverty-stricken Tishomingo County in the hill country in northeastern Mississippi, where white farmers scratched a meager living from the poor soil. The place had fascinated Eudora since her WPA days, when she had known she would write about it someday. The people were very different from the people she knew in Jackson, but something about them struck a chord with her. The hill country tale was the first story she had worked on in two years, she told Robert Penn Warren, and she was having a good time with it, although she could work on it only sporadically.

The Bride of the Innisfallen, stories she had been writing for five years, was published in April 1955. Eudora later remarked that the critics had always called her parochial because everything that she wrote was about the South. When *The Bride of the Innisfallen* appeared, with most of its stories set in Europe, she said they complained that "she should stick to what she knows best."[7]

Hubert Creekmore, who was now living in Jackson, gave a "teeny party for Eudo" two days after publication to celebrate.[8] Eudora's social life in Jackson had a definite shape now: pleasant parties and picnics with Charlotte Capers, now the permanent director of the state archives, and visits with Hubert Creekmore and Frank Lyell when they were in town, with James Wooldridge, who worked at the archives, and with Seta Alexander Sancton when she was in town. Creekmore, who had been back a short time, was already getting restless. "Mississippi is disgusting and frightening with its segregation fanaticism and I'll be glad to get away from it . . . Furthermore, it was all very dull," he wrote to friends in late 1955.[9]

In May Eudora went to New York to receive the William Dean Howells Medal from the National Academy of Arts and Letters, awarded for *The Ponder Heart* as "the most distinguished work of American fiction published within the last five years." From New York she traveled to Oxford, Ohio, to receive her second honorary degree, this one from Western College for Women, a small college that no longer exists. She had no connection whatsoever to Western College, but she received the degree because the small but excellent English Department wished to honor literary merit.

Reynolds Price graduated from Duke and went to Merton College, Oxford, as a Rhodes Scholar, but he kept in touch with Eudora while he was abroad—and ever after.

Chapter 51

Uncle Daniel on Stage

1956

As soon as *The Ponder Heart* was published, people wanted to put it on the stage. Eudora, an occasional actor and backstage crew member and a passionate theatergoer since childhood, was delighted when producers were interested. In fact, when it looked as though *The Ponder Heart* might become a musical, she wrote to Danny Kaye, telling him how much she admired his work and asking him if he would consider being in it. Kaye told her he would be unable to make a commitment.[1]

Nothing came of the musical, but Joe Fields and Jerry Chodorov, the team who had turned *My Sister Eileen* into *Wonderful Town,* undertook to put "Uncle Daniel" onstage. They wrote Eudora cheerily on December 28, 1954, that they were going to start right away with their adaptation and would send her a first draft. They wanted to meet her, they said, because Lehman Engel had told them about her.

Chodorov and Fields made a trip to Mississippi, as they put it, to "sop up some local color." They wanted to spend a little time in the places she wrote about and to "meet some of your people, or at least listen to them," and because of the finale, the trial scene in the book, they wanted to spend a couple of days in a courtroom.[2] Since northerners never understand how far apart places are in the South, they flew to Atlanta, rented a car, and started driving to Mississippi. As soon as they crossed the state border, they acquired an insight into southern ways. When they parked the car in Meridian and got out, the car immediately rolled forward, crossed the sidewalk, and crashed into the window of a jewelry store. The excitement broke the tedium of the long afternoon and everyone in town enjoyed it immensely. The owner of the store said he would gladly have given them anything in the window; they need not have crashed into it to get what they wanted. The two policemen who investigated marveled to each other about the accuracy of the aim of the car—a bull's-eye, they said.

When Chodorov and Fields visited a courtroom, "the defendant, a real gangster, pleaded guilty in the middle of the trial," Chodorov said. "It was just what we were looking for." They were forever noncommittal about southern food. "We ate some," one of them said, "but it wasn't sowbelly."[3]

Eudora was in New Orleans when they reached Jackson. When she returned, she found a vase of enormous red roses on the table, with a card from Chodorov and Fields that said, "Welcome home, kid, you're gonna like it here." During a brief visit at her house, they read the play to her, but it was several days before she could sit down with the script and read it for herself. She thought it was "a mess, vulgar, feeble, and no characters—just gags," and the playwrights kept wanting to put Uncle Daniel in bed with Bonnie Dee.[4] When she wrote to Chodorov and Fields, however, she was very gentle, saying at first that she admired the skill with which they had made dramatic changes in her story to make it more stageworthy. The expert hand was visible, she said, and she was glad to see they felt the same affection for Uncle Daniel that she did. She brought up three points for them to consider: Uncle Daniel's innocence must be more carefully established and demonstrated. Could they salvage from the first pages of the book and add to someone's speeches the list of what he had given away before? She had put it in to show the local way of life as much as to herald what was to come. They needed to establish a stronger point of view; without Edna Earle as narrator, the play wavered. She did not like the way everyone had an angle. Miss Teacake, she said, would not calculate about her alimony, and Bonnie Dee would not know about maintenance money. It was wrong to have the community out to cut Uncle Daniel down to size—they loved him and enjoyed him. The hotel in a decaying southern mansion was a false note—there was no decadence here. It was a plain frame building, built to be a hotel.[5]

Chodorov and Fields took her suggestions in good part and revised their script several times. Slowly, over the next nine months, the production came together, while Eudora was busy with her mother, who was having trouble with her eye. Robert Douglas was hired to direct, David Wayne to play Uncle Daniel, and Una Merkel to play Edna Earle. Eudora was pleased with the casting of Wayne, who had won two Tonys.

In October Douglas, an Englishman who had never directed a play in the United States, came to Jackson on his way from Hollywood to New York. Eudora thought him "nonchalant" and told him that the current script was terrible and vulgar. Douglas assured her that still another version was waiting for him in New York. She complained that Chodorov and Fields had eliminated the two most dramatic incidents, the ball of fire and Uncle Daniel giving away his money. Douglas asked her if she would "try to fix it up," and she told him she "wouldn't touch it with a ten-foot pole."[6] She said later that she had had no idea that playwrights might turn out as many as twenty versions of the script before a play opened.[7]

While Douglas was in the South, he watched trials in country court-houses and went back vowing that the trial in the play would be the most informal and friendliest trial for murder ever seen on the stage. He based many details of the action on notes he took on his trip. He said he saw even funnier things but couldn't use them because Broadway wouldn't believe them.[8]

As late as November 1955, Eudora was pessimistic about the play. The script was pretty bad, she told Bill Hamilton, and there would be no resemblance left to her "little story."[9] She heard rumors that the title had been changed to *The Prize in the Crackerjack Box* and then to *The Happy Heart.* The music her old friend Lehman Engel had written for it had been dumped so that Joseph Fields's sister Dorothy could write a song "to entice Paramount and Bing Crosby to buy the play."[10]

Her spirits lifted in January, after the play had tried out in New Haven, where Dolly Wells went to see it. It was very funny indeed, Wells said, and would be a hit. Then Lehman Engel went to see the tryout in Philadelphia and warned Eudora that it was clever but even farther away from her book. In Boston, *The Ponder Heart* stirred up a tempest. One reviewer, Eliot Norton in the *Boston Post,* said that "children laugh at cripples; adults don't," and that there was not a likable character in the play, just juvenile caricatures. His article was so vitriolic that he was removed from the pass list for the Schubert theater. The two-week tryout stretched to three.[11] Rose Russell, Diarmuid's wife, went up to Boston and reported that the play was certain to be a hit. If it survived Boston, Eudora told Bill Hamilton, it would open in New York on February 16.

Excitement in Jackson mounted. There was talk of chartering a Ponder Plane to take Eudora's friends to New York for the opening. Norman Shavin of the *State-Times* asked Hubert Creekmore in New York to send a piece for the Sunday paper on his reactions to the play with "tidbits on Eudora, etc."

On opening night at the Music Box Theatre, Eudora wore a black lace dress adorned with a white orchid, and her picture was on the front page of the *State-Times* in Jackson. A host of New York friends were with her— William Maxwell and his wife, Diarmuid and Rose Russell, Rosa Wells, Hubert Creekmore, Nona Balakian of the *Book Review,* Hildegarde Dolson, and Mary Lou Aswell. Lehman Engel was there for a moment before his own show, and gave a party for Eudora afterward. Charlotte Capers was one of several people who traveled from Jackson for the opening. One newspaper report said an "unnamed wag whistled the opening bars of 'Dixie' during intermission and the crowd snapped to attention."[12] "It was one of the scariest evenings of my life," Eudora said. After the play was over, a press agent found her sitting patiently in the almost deserted theater. She wanted to congratulate David Wayne, she said, but she was afraid they wouldn't let her backstage.[13] They did let her backstage, and feeling that they had a hit, the cast fought to hug her. David Wayne kissed her on both cheeks.

This would not be her last play, she told a reporter at the opening night party, when the reviews appeared. She was "coming back to Broadway."[14] It was a "strange, glorious, lucky evening," she said later, and she was grateful to her friends, who stood by her to thank the Lord and celebrate. She called her mother at midnight to report on the evening.[15]

One reporter who interviewed her at the Algonquin found her a "tall, vague, rather angular Southern lady who manages to be imposing and a trifle fluttery all at the same time," and said that she would "soon be Mississippi's wealthiest writer of short story-novels."[16]

"Life on West 45th Street in the Broadway section is more like Mississippi these days than New York," began Hubert Creekmore's article in the *State-Times,* referring to the facts that *The Ponder Heart* was playing next door to Tennessee Williams's *Cat on a Hot Tin Roof* at the Morosco and that Lehman Engel was conducting the music for *Fanny*. People familiar with Eudora's book might be upset by the omissions and changes, especially in the final courtroom scene, Creekmore said. Chodorov and Fields insisted that the book's ending, when Uncle Daniel gives away all his money, worked in the book and would work in a film but would never do on the stage. Creekmore was impressed with the authenticity of the sets, designed by an Alabaman, Ben Edwards. Edwards "showed the monument to the Confederate soldier in the square behind the Beulah Hotel and what you might swear was the courthouse at Raymond," wrote Creekmore. "His courtroom scene was perfect, even to the ceiling fans that didn't run."[17]

David Wayne lived up to Eudora's expectations as Uncle Daniel, a man twenty years older than he was. She felt that Wayne had saved the play.[18] As soon as Chodorov and Fields cut something out of the book, Wayne put it back into the play—it was magic, she wrote to Robert Penn Warren.[19]

Although she was still disappointed in the play and felt that the authors belonged to the "Broadway gag department," she gradually warmed to it. She was at first taken aback by the fact that Edna Earle, her narrator in the book, was "reduced to the background, sort of whimpering on the porch as Uncle Daniel goes through his antics." After she saw the play several times, she began to understand that they couldn't possibly have turned the book into a play without changing it. "The stage is a totally different concept," she said.[20]

She went to the theater to watch *Life* photographers take pictures for a feature on *The Ponder Heart*. They worked onstage and climbed ladders to capture the actors in action. *Life* ran the feature—nine pictures and a short text spread over four pages—on March 5, the same issue in which William Faulkner's "A Letter to the North," about the civil rights struggle, appeared. Eudora preferred photographs taken from the audience's point of view and ordered stills like the ones in the lobby. She framed Uncle Daniel and Bonnie Dee eating ice cream cones and put the picture on her mantel.

Eudora had begun getting weekly royalties after *Ponder Heart* had earned back her advance in Philadelphia. The show had to gross $16,000 a week to survive, and for a while it succeeded, but it was tough going. *Cat on a Hot Tin Roof* was a steady sellout, while the future of *Ponder Heart* was not that bright.

Madora Hall Sharp, the society editor of the *State-Times,* wrote approvingly that Eudora was "as completely untouched by fame as it is humanly— or divinely—possible to be." Eudora was so modest, she reported, that news of an honorary degree from Smith had to be forced out of her. Sharp described her as "the well-heeled, fair-haired lady of the South" who had "never belonged to a literary group. In fact, she isn't a 'joiner,' belonging, chiefly, to the Junior League of Jackson and to Galloway Memorial Church."[21]

After the excitement of the play, Eudora felt let down and restless in Jackson and wanted to spend a month in New York. She wrote to Hubert Creekmore, who had tried several times to return to Jackson to live, about the depression that came over one in Jackson, sure that he would understand. She didn't know what would happen if she didn't get some work done, she told him, and if she could stay in New York for a whole month she might be able to collect her wits. And she wanted to write a play.[22]

She did go to New York, but she took her mother so Chestina could see *The Ponder Heart* and meet her New York friends. They stayed at the Algonquin. Eudora joined the spectators onstage during the courtroom scene. Her unexpected face did not throw David Wayne at all; he ad-libbed, "Can you see all right, Miss Welty?"[23] Mrs. Welty went back home accompanied by Jimmy Wooldridge, who wrote to Hubert Creekmore, "Me and Mrs. Welty made it home fine."[24] Eudora sent silver cups, suitably engraved, to members of the cast. "In case you are not truly aware of it," wrote Una Merkel in her thank-you note, "the entire cast is in love with you, all of us."[25]

For a short time, Eudora's work was in two New York theaters at the same time. *The Littlest Revue,* conceived by Ben Bayley, included the "Bye-Bye, Brevoort" sketch in a collection of skits written mostly by Ogden Nash and Vernon Duke. The revue opened on May 22 at the Phoenix Theater, at Second Avenue and Twelfth Street. Wolcott Gibbs mentioned "Bye-Bye" in his review in *The New Yorker,* calling it a "cockeyed tribute to a lost past," but most reviewers ignored Eudora's contribution. The revue never made it to Broadway, and *The Ponder Heart* closed on June 27.

Back home in June, Eudora worked on dialogue. She had to get a play out of her system before she could do any other work, she said. She told Hubert Creekmore about a party at Allison's where they sat on the upstairs porch in rocking chairs that were coming apart and "drank whisky and came apart" themselves.[26] There always seemed to be more parties in the summer, when Frank Lyell was at home. He gave a party when Robert Daniel came to visit him, as he had twenty years before. Now in their late forties, Eudora and Frank and Hubert were still as companionable as they had been twenty years earlier. Hubert, who had once been a kind of mentor to Eudora, was barely supporting himself as a writer, and Frank had written nothing since his dissertation, while Eudora was a published writer with an international reputation and famous friends.

In early September, Eudora decided to take her nieces, Elizabeth and Mary Alice, who were about nine and ten years old, to New York for a week. They could not get there before *Ponder Heart* closed, but she took them to the Wednesday matinee of *Damn Yankees* and to *No Time for Sergeants,* to the Empire State Building, and to the Museum of Natural History to view the new *Tyrannosaurus rex*. Hubert Creekmore played the role of uncle to perfection and showed them his apartment, took them out to eat, shepherded them about town, and saw them off on the train.

Then in October the Jackson Little Theater opened its season with a production of *The Ponder Heart,* with Charlotte Capers playing Edna Earle. Eudora, attending some of the rehearsals to answer questions, was amused to find the cast "dear-hearting" each other all over the place.

On opening night she reserved a row for her mother, Walter, Walter's wife Mittie, the girls, Mittie's mother, Mrs. Creekmore, as well as for her friends Jimmy Wooldridge and Major White. Mrs. Creekmore reported to Hubert that the play was "a scream" from first to last, that Eudora wore a corsage and looked "real nice," and that "Eudo, Major, and Jimmy" said the storm onstage was better in Jackson than it had been in New York. "Did you catch the taxi driver, 'Old Man Creekmore'?" she asked Hubert.[27]

This was the first of many occasions when Eudora was recognized as the local celebrity.

Part Four

The
Last Years

Chapter 52

Dark Days Begin

1956

Family problems consumed Eudora during the bleak years from 1956 to 1966. She was concerned about both her brothers. In 1955, when his emotional problems surfaced again, Edward left the Jackson architectural firm of R. W. Naef, where he had been working for sixteen years, and went out on his own. As Edward's mental health deteriorated, the physical health of Walter, Eudora's youngest brother, also began to fail. Walter, who was only forty-one in 1956, suffered cruelly from arthritis. Like his father, he was in the insurance business, but he worked for Standard Life, another Jackson company, instead of his father's old firm, Lamar Life.

While the health of her brothers was a continuing worry, Eudora's mother became her principal care and burden, sapping her energy for nearly eleven years. Chestina's eyesight had gradually worsened until she could no longer read. In 1955, doctors advised an operation for a cataract. She decided to have the surgery done in New Orleans, just as Laurel's father does in *The Optimist's Daughter* (which Eudora began writing immediately after her mother's death), and of course Eudora went with her. The operation did not go well, and Chestina had to have another. Eudora's attention to her mother never faltered, although the kindest and most generous of family friends admit that Mrs. Welty could be difficult.

Robert Drake, an English professor and a friend of Frank Lyell's, stopped off in Jackson to meet Eudora on a train trip from New Orleans to North Carolina shortly after the surgery. On the way from the train station, Eudora apologized profusely for not asking him to lunch. At the house Mrs. Welty kept coming into the room where he and Eudora were visiting. "Eudora couldn't talk frankly," Drake recalled. "She said, 'You see how it is. I can't leave home whenever I like.' "[1]

Once when Eudora was going over the household accounts, Chestina said, "Now with all your figuring, do you know how you're going to send my body back to West Virginia?" Another time, when Eudora was leaving for the grocery store, saying, "I'll be right back," Mrs. Welty said, "When you die, those words ought to be engraved on your lips—'I'll be right back.' " But Drake said that Mrs. Welty was very pleasant while he was there and displayed pride in Eudora's achievements, especially her lectures at Cambridge. Sometimes Mrs. Welty was genuinely awed by Eudora's accomplishments. When *The New Yorker* published a poem, "A Flock of Guinea Hens Seen from a Car," which Eudora had scrawled on a Christmas card while she was in the car—and paid her eighty dollars—Mrs. Welty could only gasp, "Eudora Alice Welty!"

Walter's health deteriorated rapidly. He had already been to the famed Oschner Clinic in New Orleans, where doctors examined him and sent him home with orders to do exercises and take hot baths, aspirin, and ACTH.

Whenever Walter was in the hospital, Eudora took over much of the care of her nieces, so that Mittie could be with him. All this left Eudora with very little time to write—and not being able to work lowered her spirits, she told friends.

After this trip to the clinic, he was able to work about four hours a day. Then shingles set him back. Cortisone seemed to help. Then he had to have surgery for impacted wisdom teeth. Eudora admired the good front that he and Mittie put up, but she learned that Walter did not like to be asked how he was. As everyone said, the Weltys all kept themselves to themselves.

Mrs. Welty had to have antibiotics for an infection in her eyes. Walter was hospitalized again, and even Mittie got sick.

When everyone finally got better, in April 1956, Eudora managed to get away to New York. Hubert Creekmore, who was working in the textbook division at Houghton Mifflin, gave a party for her, and she went to another at Martha Graham's. She traveled by way of Washington, where she read "Place in Fiction" at the Institute of Contemporary Arts, part of the Corcoran Gallery. "Place in Fiction" served Eudora well for years; whenever she needed a lecture, out it came. And now Mrs. Henry Louis Cohn of the House of Books in New York wanted to reprint it in a special edition as part of the Crown Octavo Series.

When Eudora returned to Jackson, her mother's eye seemed better; she was taking allergy shots to protect her from the pollens that caused it to act up. And when Eudora could find household help, she was finally able to get some work done. With someone looking after her mother, she took off one day in August and treated her nieces to a trip to New Orleans for the day.

Frank Lyell was in town that summer, and Seta Alexander Sancton and her husband, Tom, were living in Jackson again, so "the gang's" social life picked up. Eudora gave a party for Elizabeth Spencer and her husband, John Rusher, when they went through Jackson on their way from New Orleans to Carrollton, Spencer's home town.

In the fall of 1957, Walter was back in the hospital; the doctor said the problem was his heart and told Mrs. Welty he would not live more than two years. "No one knows it's his heart, except the family," Mrs. Creekmore wrote to Hubert. If the insurance company knew it, they would retire him, she said.[2] Walter did not improve. At Christmas 1957, Eudora still had full-time household help and was able to have a party for Dolly Wells and Frank Lyell, who were home to visit families. The family was terrified in January 1958, when Walter had to go back in the hospital with chest pains. Eudora and Mrs. Welty kept the girls, and Eudora drove them to school and picked them up. Things could only get worse, the doctor told the women. Mittie and Eudora conferred and decided to take Walter to the Veterans Hospital in Hot Springs, Arkansas. "But don't mention this," Mrs. Creekmore warned Hubert. "You know how close-mouthed the Weltys are."[3]

Instead they took Walter to Foundation Hospital in New Orleans, where "a lady doctor" tried hot paraffin baths for his arthritic hands, infrared lamps on his back, and hot sandbags on his knees. Then a heart specialist weighed in with a more cheering forecast. He drew a pint and a half of fluid from the heart sac, which had been pressing against the muscle. This doctor thought that the heart itself might not be affected and that only the sac's membrane might be inflamed. He said that Walter's case was rare and a recurrence still rarer. While Walter was in the hospital, Mittie stayed with him, and once more Eudora and Mrs. Welty kept the girls.

In February, Eudora thought Walter looked better than he had in a year; he was able to get up for meals and to walk around. But in the spring he was worse, and he went back to the New Orleans hospital, where the doctors ended up prescribing fifty-nine pills a day. Because Eudora and Mrs. Welty kept the girls while Walter and Mittie went to New Orleans, Eudora had to miss a meeting at Yaddo. In April, although Walter was still in bed most of the time, he had improved enough for Eudora to make a quick trip to New York.

That spring of 1958, John Robinson was home for several weeks from Bad Hamburg, Germany, where he and Enzo Rocchigiani lived. He worked in Giessen, where he spent three nights a week. He and Eudora were still friends, and he was concerned about the strain under which she lived. He tried to get her to go to Oxford with him to visit the Farleys and Ella Somerville. He said, in fact, that he thought it would be good for both her and her mother if Eudora went away for a while.[4]

In May, Walter could not focus his eyes or stand upright. The cardiologist decreed that he was taking too many pills, and when they cut down on the pills, he did seem to improve. Then he had an attack of dysentery and was back in the hospital in August for a few days. The doctors did not remove a lump under his arm, but ran tests and x-rays and gave him a brace for his hand and liver shots. He was "no worse" on August 16, according to Hubert Creekmore's mother.[5]

In June, Jimmy Wooldridge reported to Hubert Creekmore that "Eudora had us (the poor pitiful remnants of the basic) over for dinner last Saturday night. Both she and Mrs. Welty seem to be doing fairly well now."[6] In July, Eudora found time to talk with the Summer Players at the Jackson Little Theater, answering questions from the actors and crew who were taking part in a production of "Bye-Bye, Brevoort." Frank Hains, the *Daily*

News columnist, said that while he listened to the session, he could not help thinking "how remarkably fortunate and blessed" they all were to be able to sit in the same room with "the greatest living exponent of the short story in the English language." It was sad, he said, that Jackson never seemed to be aware "of this great artist."[7] That situation was about to change.

Chapter 53

A Glimpse
of the World
1958–1959

As family illnesses kept Eudora from writing, she began, at forty-nine, to doubt her own existence. As if her self-doubts weren't enough, she heard that someone on the *Last Word* radio program had asked if she were still living. Fortunately, an invitation came along, she told Hubert Creekmore, that made her sure she wasn't dead yet.

President Katharine E. McBride of Bryn Mawr College invited Eudora to be the Lucy Martin Donnelly Fellow at the college in 1958–1959. Donnelly fellows received a stipend of $3,000 for the academic year and had absolutely no duties—they were free to use the time solely for writing or research. The only requirement was that they be in residence "some time during the academic year." The award was offered only every other year; Elizabeth Bowen had been a previous fellow, in 1956–1957.

Eudora accepted with alacrity. An award like the Donnelly fellowship, which "meant you didn't have to teach a class or give lectures or something," bought Eudora time, she said. "And anything that buys you time is God-given, God-sent."[1] It was the nicest thing that had ever happened to her, she wrote to Bettina Linn, a friend of Mary Lou Aswell's who chaired Bryn

Mawr's English Department. (Miss Linn's friends called her "Benjie.") Eager to please, Eudora offered to keep "informal office hours" so she could read students' stories and talk to the authors about them. Since her family's health was so precarious, she said, it would be better if she came for two short visits rather than one long one.

She was at Bryn Mawr for two weeks beginning November 4, 1958, staying in the Deanery in a room that had a brass bed from India and an inlaid French desk. Benjie Linn and Laurance Stapleton of the English Department lavished hospitality upon her and became her lifelong friends. Dr. Samuel Chew, also of the English Department, drove her to Valley Forge and told her he knew how to drive to the Pacific Ocean without encountering a traffic light. She heard Lily Taylor of the Classics Department happily describe her visit to London for the coronation of Queen Elizabeth, which she was able to follow in Latin.

When Eudora was asked to serve as an unpaid honorary consultant in American letters at the Library of Congress, she accepted. (Faulkner and James Gould Cozzens turned it down.) She went to her first meeting of the consultants in April 1958. She already knew two of the others, Cleanth Brooks and Maxwell Anderson, but she met the poet and critic John Crowe Ransom and the critic R. P. Blackmur for the first time. She found Ransom "a dear man," but disliked Blackmur, who requested the others not to call Robert Frost a poet but to refer to him as "a person." Randall Jarrell, the poet in residence at the library, was on his best behavior when he met with the consultants. At the Jarrells' house for lunch, Eudora was fascinated when Jarrell kissed his wife's arms as she handed him a cocktail.

While Eudora was in the East for the Bryn Mawr visit in the fall of 1958, she again went to Washington, where she had agreed to lunch with some of the Library of Congress staff, meet with the press, and read her work on the night of November 3. (She refused a request to record her views on current literature for the library's archives, saying that she was not in the lecture business.) An eager crowd heard her read "Lily Daw," "A Worn Path," and "Ladies in Spring." Three Washington newspapers ran stories on her on November 4. They all gushed. "Miss Eudora Welty, as shy and southern as a mocking bird, was in Our Town yesterday, whistling Dixie in a new and gentle way," wrote Tom Kelly in the *Daily News,* where he described her as a "tall, slim, self-effacing gentlewoman from Mississippi." She told him she never wrote around the clock; "I always stop so I can go visiting in the evening."[2] She told the *Washington Post* that she might have to do a sequel to *The Ponder Heart,* " 'Uncle Daniel in Alaska.' "[3]

Chapter 54

Walter Dies

1959–1961

Eudora was on another trip to the East when her mother called to tell her to come home. Walter's condition was worse. He was in fact dying. Hubert Creekmore, who was in Jackson shortly before Walter's death on January 9, 1959, said he "looked like a corpse then, poor thing, and was so drawn in his face, so wracked and gnarled with arthritis all over, that it's really a blessing."[1]

Walter was only forty-three. His obituary spoke of his prowess at golf—he had won both the Jackson city-wide championship and the Colonial Country Club championship—and his work as an officer of the Standard Life Insurance Company. "He was one of the sweetest people," John Robinson wrote. Everyone had been hoping that some cure could be found, "but they could never get at just what it was . . . Mittie is a remarkable girl and the two children are sweet as can be—good they have Eudora and Mrs. Welty who are crazy about them."[2]

"Eudora and Mittie and the children and Mrs. Welty all bore up very stoically," said Hubert Creekmore.[3] "Stoic" is the right word. Eudora, schooled by her mother to be "close-mouthed," to reveal nothing to outsiders, "bore up." Three months later she was off to Bryn Mawr for another two-week stint as a Donnelly fellow, but her visit was cut short after a few days, when her mother fell in the living room and cut her cheek "to the bone." Mrs. Welty had been dizzy from high blood pressure, Mrs. Creekmore wrote to Hubert, and did not have a stroke or break a bone. "They did not tell Eudo to come—left it up to her," Mrs. Creekmore said. Of course Eudora went. She was met in Meridian by Jimmy Wooldridge. Mrs. Welty was in the hospital for more than a week, and then went home and began to try to walk. Eudora vowed not to leave home before fall, and by June Mrs. Welty was well enough to be taken for a ride in the automobile. Then she was back in the hospital in August with a high fever from a kidney infection.[4]

At home, Chestina suffered from blackouts, for which her doctors could find no cause. Diarmuid Russell steamed and fussed that the illness was "an undue, unfair burden on Eudora . . . Eudora was assuming too much responsibility."[5] He was well aware that the financial burden had become heavier. No book money was coming in, and the women virtually lived off the income from Eudora's book reviews in the *New York Times* and from the money she got for college visits.

Eudora would scarcely leave her mother, who was seventy-six years old. By October 1, Mrs. Welty could walk around the yard if supported by Eudora, but she could not be left alone. Although they found practical nurses for night and day, Eudora was still tied down. She did go out one night, when Jimmy Wooldridge cooked a ham casserole for the "basic." "Eudora hovers and I know Mrs. Welty would much rather be left alone," Wooldridge said. Eudora was looking much better, but Wooldridge was afraid she would collapse.[6]

Nurses were hard to find but necessary, since it took two people to lift Mrs. Welty. When Eudora found nursing help, the women often presented difficulties. "There's some kind of cruelty in some forms of nursing," Eudora said. "They would advertise, 'Settled white Christian lady with no home ties will come and stay with you and nurse your . . .' And that's what we needed, but it depended on the person. Some of them were horrors and some were as kind as could be. They were old ladies without anything to do, and they would say: 'I am glad to get this job because it's getting cold weather.' You know—time to come in."[7] (Eudora used some of the "horrors" in the character of Lexie in *Losing Battles*.)

When nurses could be found, Mrs. Welty could be extremely difficult. "She fired one nurse because . . . she mispronounced the word 'gesture' when she was reading out loud to her," Eudora said. Her mother did not like for the nurses to read to her; she wanted Eudora to read the Bible to her, especially the Book of Esther in the King James version.

All Eudora's friends worried about her endlessly. Hubert Creekmore referred to her "arid attitude of doing nothing" about work. Dolly Wells told him she thought it was Eudora's empathy with anyone's ills. "But you can't just go on day after day for years doing this without some adjustment," Hubert said.[8]

However, Eudora continued faithfully to look after her mother and never, over the course of all those years, displayed the slightest bitterness, regret, or self-pity. She might complain of being depressed or lament that she had no time to write, but these remarks were made almost in passing. She never complained about her mother.

In March 1960, Eudora, refusing to leave Chestina, turned down a $7,500 grant from the Ford Foundation that would have paid her to observe and study playwriting at the Phoenix Theater and the Actors Studio in New York. Diarmuid Russell was in despair over her situation, financial and emotional. He urged her to send him a chunk of the story she was working on, the "reunion novel"—he could get a "drop of money (a large drop)" for it.[9]

That spring Mrs. Welty was up and down, in bed, out of bed, wearing new glasses that helped a lot, suffering a "silent stroke," and totally irrational from time to time. Eudora had trouble finding help during the week and never had any on weekends. Chestina was unpredictable. Sometimes she would not talk to Mittie or her granddaughters when they went to see her. In May, Mrs. Creekmore reported to her son that "Mrs. Welty acted up terribly and didn't want Eudo to talk at Millsaps," where she was scheduled to participate in a symposium on "The Artist and the Critic." Eudora went anyway. "Then the next day she was so sorry she did that way," said Mrs. Creekmore. "It is her mind."[10]

When Mrs. Welty had to go back in the hospital, she accused Eudora of putting her in an institution. When she got home, she was still furious. The doctor told Eudora she would have to put her mother in a nursing home, but

Eudora refused. The doctor said Eudora would crack up if she didn't, and Eudora promised to try to get out more.[11]

In October, Eudora did take Mrs. Welty to a nursing home, but she stayed only one day. Eudora found help for a while and then put her mother back in the nursing home, where she stayed briefly, but only long enough for Eudora to get a little rest. Jimmy Wooldridge took her to the opera, and she went to a small dinner party at Charlotte Capers's house, but such outings were rare. She could not accept the invitation to be one of the distinguished American artists and writers at John F. Kennedy's inauguration, in January 1961.

Her mother was well enough for Eudora to have Mittie and the girls for dinner, but then she got worse, and "had one of her spells and talked awful to Eudo right in front of the nurse. It nearly kills Eudo," said Mrs. Creekmore.[12] Three weeks later, Eudora assembled a cadre of practical nurses so she could leave for a visit with friends at Bryn Mawr and New York and attend an international symposium at Vassar. At Vassar, she found to her horror that the symposium met from breakfast until midnight every single day. Still, it was an interesting group of women, and "after they thought they'd said what they ought, they said what they wanted to, and then it was real and exciting," she said.[13] On this, her first trip away from Jackson and her mother in more than a year, she realized how dreary and confining her life at home was and vowed to get away more often.[14]

Jimmy Wooldridge thought Eudora "seemed better for her little trip. Mrs. Welty does all right when Eudora is gone but when she returns all the turmoil begins. Don't see why Eudora doesn't just go to New Orleans or some other nearby place and settle down to work and come in from time to time to check on her mother. She will never do this."[15] He was right.

Always a good citizen, Eudora took time to write a piece marking National Library Week, in which she lamented the empty bookshelves in the Mississippi state prisons at Whitfield, Parchman, and Ellisville. In September she went to Chicago and from there to New York, where she gave William Maxwell a portion of the story about hill country people she was working on. The basic plot of what would become *Losing Battles* was already in place in 1962, for Maxwell said he found it difficult "not knowing how they got the car down in time for the funeral and what part Footsie Kilgore played in the operation."[16] She returned to Jackson by way of Washington, where she saw Katherine Anne Porter and was able to spend time with other friends. It is impossible to overestimate how much good friends meant to Eudora. All her life she cultivated friendships as she did her camellias, and the friends reciprocated with unstinting approval and support.

Chapter 55

Writing in Dark Days

1962–1964

Lecturing was no more attractive to Eudora than it had been, but it brought in money. She agreed to be the William Allen Neilson Professor at Smith College in Northampton, Massachusetts, for the spring semester of 1962. Since the professorship required her to give three public lectures, she dusted off "Place in Fiction" from Cambridge and "Short Stories" from Seattle, and produced a new one, "Words into Fiction," which was not published until 1965. Previous Neilson professors had been physicists, musicians, and political economists. T. C. Mendenhall, the president of Smith, said that since this was the first time they had had "a creative writer (as they are sometimes called)," it was most proper that she speak so directly about writing.

After a pleasant stay at Smith—she had a nice, warm apartment and time to write—Eudora went home during spring vacation and was pleased to find that Mrs. Welty had done well during her absence and seemed better. Before she went back to Smith, Eudora used "Place in Fiction" as the keynote speech at the Southern Literary Conference at Converse College in Spartanburg, South Carolina. This was the only time that she met Flannery O'Connor, who spoke the next day. "I really liked Eudora Welty—no presence whatsoever, just a real nice woman. She read a paper on 'Place in

Fiction.' It was beautifully written but a little hard to listen to as is anything that is meant to be read," O'Connor said.[1] Years later, a Vassar student asked Eudora about her relationship as a writer to Flannery O'Connor. "Well, you know, Flannery talks about hell and damnation," Eudora replied, "and all I know about hell and damnation I learned from Flannery O'Connor."[2]

When she returned to Jackson, Eudora took a group of her best friends to the Rotisserie (that restaurant where long ago she and Nash Burger and Hubert Creekmore had taken Henry Miller) for dinner. They all thought she looked splendid after a semester away, and were glad to hear that she planned to go away again in the fall. Mrs. Welty, blessedly, continued to improve. She could walk with Eudora's help and play bridge whenever Eudora could gather a foursome for her. Then, in August, disaster struck the household again. Mrs. Welty fell off the bed and broke her hip. An ambulance took her to St. Dominic's for surgery; Eudora heard the news that she would spend six months in a wheelchair. Eudora's friends, in letters to each other, blamed the nurse's negligence for the fall.

Eudora, now fifty-three, was trapped again, while everyone around her boiled in indignation at the forced integration of the University of Mississippi. The generations were split. Mrs. Creekmore, for instance, heartily supported Governor Ross Barnett and his defiance of the courts at Ole Miss, while her son and his friends, including Eudora, were appalled.

Eudora escaped to Yaddo, where she planned to write for three weeks, but once more she was summoned home when her mother took a turn for the worse. She had to assume her mother's full care with no nursing help at all until November, when she did get to New York.

At last she yielded to the doctor's urgings and moved Chestina to a new nursing home, the Martha Coker Nursing Home in Yazoo City. "I never thought I would put her in any nursing home," Eudora said thirty-some years later, still racked with guilt. "I felt like I crumbled when I took my mother to that nursing home. I could drive there every day, but it was not the same . . . and she felt betrayed."[3]

In early April 1963, just after publication of her *Selected Stories,* she went to Davidson College at the invitation of a fellow Mississippian, Bill Ferris from Vicksburg, the student chairman of the Book-of-the-Year program. The entire student body heard her read her work and discussed it with her. On that trip she also went to the University of Arkansas, Duke,

Vanderbilt, Yale, and the University of Texas. When she went back to Jackson, she took her mother home from Yazoo City and found two nurses to help with her care.

Two months later, in June, Medgar Evers, the NAACP's civil rights leader in Jackson, was shot by an unidentified killer. In one sitting, Eudora wrote the short story "Where Is the Voice Coming From?," a first-person soliloquy that is a reconstruction of what Eudora thought ran through the mind of the man who shot Evers in the back late one night as he entered his house. Other people's stories written about the South at the time of the civil rights struggle seemed synthetic and made her uneasy. As soon as she heard about the murder, she was sure she knew what was in the killer's mind. She had lived all her life where it happened and had been "writing about that world of hate" in which she had grown up, and she felt she could speak with authority. "I didn't think anything else written about things like that were anything . . . but . . . tracts."[4] "Where Is the Voice Coming From?" is one of her most remarkable stories, and the circumstances under which she wrote it—in one sitting, while her mother was ill—make it seem even more of an accomplishment.

William Maxwell loved the story and tore apart the forthcoming June 26 issue of *The New Yorker* to get it in. After Maxwell bought it, Bryon de la ("Delay") Beckwith was arrested for the murder of Medgar Evers. Beckwith was not a poor white, as the killer in Eudora's story had been; he was a member of an elite Delta family. A friend who said, "You thought he was a Snopes, but he was a Compson" was right. Eudora's assumption that the killer was a poor redneck "represented wishful thinking by a member of Mississippi's tiny enlightened class," said Adam Nossiter in a book about the case.[5] Eudora may have erred on Beckwith's social standing, but she had gotten so many details right that after the arrest she had to spend hours on the phone with *New Yorker* editors and checkers, changing times and makes of cars and other details to avoid a possible libel suit.

When someone called from New York to ask if there had been any repercussions from the story—any crosses burned on her lawn—she said of course not. "People who burn crosses don't read the *New Yorker*. Don't people know the first thing about the South?"[6]

When Beckwith was finally convicted of the murder in a third trial in 1994, Eudora said she was "glad of the verdict" and added, "Just be glad

[Mississippi] does also produce a Medgar Evers to counter the Beckwiths of this world."[7]

Eudora wrote a children's book, *The Shoe Bird,* in 1963 in order to put a new roof on the house. Harcourt Brace held an option on her next work, and Russell was glad to let them exercise it on a children's book. He felt the "reunion novel" would be a big, important book, and he wanted to be able to place it elsewhere if the new management at Harcourt did not appreciate Eudora properly.

The Shoe Bird is in the admirable tradition of E. B. White's children's books—creatures talk and act out a fantasy—but it lacks the underlying *gravitas* of White's work. The hero is Arturo, a parrot who lives at the Friendly Shoe Store. Arturo repeats whatever he hears, and when he repeats, "Shoes are for the birds," all the birds in the world gather at the shoe store one night to be fitted for shoes. It is pleasant comedy, with much wordplay, but Eudora, like so many successful writers for adults, lowered her standards when she wrote for children. For instance, the author who has insisted more than any other person in the world on the importance of place did not set *The Shoe Bird* in a definite place. It's in some vague Friendly Shoe Store. Where? Mississippi? Michigan? It could be anywhere.

While adult fans of Eudora's work approved *(The New Yorker* compared *The Shoe Bird* to Chaucer's *Parliament of Fowls,* and the ever-faithful *New York Times* said that children would "be sure to love the words and the birds"), the powers that be in the children's book world found it lacking. The prestigious and influential *Horn Book* did not even review it. *Library Journal* profoundly disapproved of the "mélange of stereotyped characterizations of birds based on their names (Mockingbird mocks and Pigeon wants to pigeonhole information) and the heavy-handed moral."[8]

In April 1968, the Jackson Ballet Guild held the world premiere of a ballet based on *The Shoe Bird,* with music composed by Lehman Engel. Engel conducted the orchestra on opening night—and that was the last heard of *The Shoe Bird.*

Chapter 56

The College Visitor

1960—1980

~~ During the sixties, Eudora began to refine the college visit into an art form, she found out that colleges were as happy to have her read her short stories as they were to have her lecture. Writing a new lecture was hell, but reading an old short story was easy—and she did it very well.

She needed the money that came from college visits, but they created a vicious circle: because she had no time to write, her income fell, so she traveled more to college campuses and had even less time to write. The travel was hard, especially for Eudora, who would not fly. Still, college visits offered compensations besides the financial rewards. They served as a blessed diversion from her unending duties at home and offered badly needed gratifications. Faculty members were deferential, if not obsequious, and the students were awestruck and respectful. The visits surely boosted her spirits and strengthened her ego, no matter what inconveniences she had to endure. In a sense, these visits provided her with an emotional life of some kind in the absence of husband, children, or lover. The constant motion must have helped to camouflage the essential emptiness of her life.

Eudora told the novelist Anne Tyler that colleges kept inviting her because she was so well behaved, always on time, and "I don't get drunk or hole up in a motel with my lover."[1] She never made passes at students, as some male writers did, and never made outrageous demands about money or housing or anything else. She was always courteous and invariably kind to students, in whom she seemed genuinely interested. She had the stamina to endure enough hours of readings, discussion groups, autographings and social events to satisfy the most insatiable of English faculties. And when she left, she sat down and immediately dispatched handwritten thank-you notes to the people who had invited her. After a visit to Bryn Mawr, the college sent her a check for $150.49 for her train fare to Philadelphia. She replied that the trip cost her only $105.61 and enclosed a check for the difference.

In April 1964 she went by bus from Memphis to the Tennessee Library Association convention in Gatlinburg, where she was to read the essay she had written some time before on the pleasures of reading in the library as a child. She refused to take money for her transportation from the librarians; she said the bus from Memphis cost very little and the fee for the lecture would be quite enough.[2]

"She came to my class in creative writing at Vassar and we sat for two hours in my living room and it was marvelous," said Professor William Gifford. "She was so gentle, the kindest person. She talked about her experiences in writing and asked the students about their experiences."[3] *The Vassar Chronicle* commented on her "soft, melodious voice, her deep southern accent," and how "her own vital, personalized idiom charmed and delighted her audience. We shall not forget the way she described the story with a little baby moral in her arms, trying to skate across the thin ice of believability."[4]

Another time at Vassar the weather was so fine that she met with some classes outside. Helen Lockwood, chair of the English Department, visiting one of the classes, asked Eudora if she didn't think there was a place for the old-fashioned story with a clear plot, like the tale of Saint George and the dragon. "Yes," said Eudora politely, adding, after a moment's reflection, a wry, Weltyesque remark. "But the second dragon had better be funny."[5]

At every college she ever visited, someone has a favorite anecdote about her. A. Walton Litz, who invited her to Princeton when he was chairman of the Humanities Council, took her over to the campus art museum. "She fell in love with a small Boudin—people on the beach with umbrellas," Litz recalled. "It was a tiny painting, but she said it had several human dramas going on."[6]

At the University of North Dakota, she was on a noontime panel with the writers Tillie Olsen and Ring Lardner, Jr. The audience included very young high school students with bag lunches. After each of the panelists spoke, a microphone was opened for questions. Joanna Maclay, who moderated the panel, recalls with awe two answers Eudora gave to questions.

One student directed a question to Eudora. "Mrs. Welty, we read your story 'Why I Live at the P.O.,' and what I want to know, did you or somebody you know live at the post office?"

"If you're asking did I or anyone I know actually live at the post office, the answer is no," she said. "If the question is, is the story true, the answer is yes."

Then a big man with a beard asked belligerently of the panel at large, "How can you tell the difference between literature and propaganda?" No one on the panel spoke. Then Eudora took the microphone and said, "I should think instantaneously."[7]

She herself told the story about the time she stood at the podium at one college to read and realized she had forgotten her glasses. She was able to tell the story from memory, while pretending to read, she said.[8]

Another time she forgot to take a copy of her book with her when she went to the University of Houston. Jo Woestendiek, who had just been named book review editor of the *Houston Chronicle,* went down to the Shamrock Hotel to interview her, but she found her a difficult interview. "I didn't have a story and I got up to leave," Woestendiek recalled, "and she said, 'You know, I came here to read but I left my book at home. Could you drive me downtown to get another one?' " Woestendiek drove her downtown, and "everything she said was worth a quote. There was a new skyscraper in the skyline, tall black glass. She said it looked like a shroud. We went to a bookstore on Main Street and she said, 'Don't tell them who I am.' We went in and she bought the book. I got a good story after all."[9]

Eudora was the first visiting celebrity at the Centennial Humanities Seminars at the University of Kentucky in 1965. Guy Davenport, chairman of the English Department, was given "unlimited funds" to pay any speakers for the seminars he wanted. Although he had not met Eudora Welty, he loved her work. She came for a week's visit. "One day she noticed that the Beatles movie *A Hard Day's Night* was on, and she asked if we couldn't skip class and go to the movie," Davenport recalled. "We did. She loved it."[10]

In Asheville, at a question-and-answer section after a reading, someone asked an interminable question that boiled down to "How can we preserve the oral tradition in the South?" She replied, "Talk."[11]

From the early sixties on, she went to Agnes Scott College, in Atlanta, every year. "She could draw more people than a rock star," said Jane Pepperdene, a former English teacher. "We once turned away two thousand people who wanted to hear her read—*turned away* two thousand people. We brought her back over and over. She had an exquisite sense of self, like 'proper love of self is the beginning of all the rest,' in the *Convivia.*"[12]

"We had a lovely visit at Agnes Scott one time," recalled Guy Davenport. "They met me and Eudora at the airport when our planes arrived at the same time from different directions. The lady teachers of English already had Eudora. She saw me and ran over and hugged me. It was the making of me. They had lots of student work for her to read. She was kindness itself. The most hopeless story, she would find something good to say about it."[13] Davenport once rescued Eudora from a long book signing and terrible cocktail party, where the noise level was like that of a battlefield.

Indefatigable, she could survive a week-long schedule like one she had at the University of Mississippi in March 1964. On Monday she conducted a seminar on American literature, which included questions and answers about her own work and that of her contemporaries; on Tuesday she led a seminar on creative writing, discussing technical problems in writing short fiction; on Wednesday she presided at an informal coffee hour with the university scholars; on Thursday she led a seminar on the use of myth, folklore, and ritual in fiction, with special attention to *The Golden Apples,* and on Thursday night she gave her lecture, "Words into Fiction."

At Purdue University, Caroline Gordon, divorced from Allen Tate and teaching that year, had her to breakfast on Ascension Day. Eudora admired her needlepoint work titled "I Cannot See the Flowers Beneath My Feet" and her paintings of saints, which were stored in stacks on the floor. The fragrance of lilacs drifted through the window, and the food was delicious. Eudora marveled at Caroline and her energy in teaching and commenting on so much student writing.[14]

When Eudora, then seventy-two, stepped to the podium at Converse College in 1982, a thunderous standing ovation greeted her, a newspaper reported.[15] Her voice as she read recalled "soft, white curtains blowing somewhere at the back of the house, was melodious, rich, sure."[16] The audience of 3,500 sat transfixed for a full hour before erupting into another standing ovation. A professor remembers Eudora at a reception at the home of the president. When he asked her if she would have some sherry, she surprised and delighted him by asking if she could have some bourbon instead.

A young professor at the Citadel, Tony Redd, was struck by "how very much she enjoyed 'performing' before an audience and by how excellent a 'performer' she was."[17] Eudora was a guest of honor at the Citadel's Friday afternoon parade, and Redd noticed that she stood (as did everyone else) not only for "The Star-Spangled Banner" but for "Dixie." When Redd drove her through Lesesne Gate onto the campus, she commented that the buildings looked like Windsor Castle as John Piper had painted it.

Eudora was finally invited to Randolph-Macon Woman's College in Lynchburg, fifty years after she had gone there to enroll in 1927 and had left "weeping across the James," on the train to Wisconsin. This time, when she walked into the jammed auditorium, the audience rose to its feet. At a small party, she saw a Randolph-Macon chair and said, "A friend of mine in Jackson has a Randolph-Macon chair, and every time I go to her house I sit in it." She explained how her MSCW credits had been refused. After she left, the faculty voted unanimously to award her one of Randolph-Macon's rare and highly prized honorary degrees. "This was a big deal," said Professor Carolyn Bell. "Randolph-Macon gives almost no honorary degrees, has given only a handful in its hundred-year history. We don't do it."[18] But they gave one to Eudora Welty, and she went back for commencement in 1981 and accepted it.

Chapter 57

Millsaps

1964

The need for money drove Eudora, who had always stubbornly refused to become a teacher, to ask Millsaps College about the possibility of her teaching there. Millsaps immediately created the position of writer-in-residence for her for the fall term and asked her to conduct a twice-a-week seminar on the art of fiction. She knew writing could not be taught, but she thought it might be helpful to read stories aloud in a class and talk about them.[1]

Meeting her first class that fall, she told the students that this was her first attempt at teaching a group for any length of time and the prospect frightened her. When the students confided that they were equally scared, "the cooperative relationship of the class was established," reported a student. "From then on Miss Welty's viewpoint was always as one writer speaking with other writers about common problems."[2]

Eudora enjoyed the Millsaps connection. Several members of the faculty, who were among the few liberals in town during the sixties, when racial tension pervaded life in Jackson, became her friends. She liked her students, eighteen boys and girls, all bright, who met with her from 3:30 to 5:30 P.M. on Tuesdays and Thursdays. Not all of them were English majors, she noted with pleasure; in fact, two were French majors who had been in

Algiers, and they contributed very useful information when the class discussed Camus. For a textbook, Eudora used a paperback edition of short stories edited by Seán O'Faoláin. She told the students they could write short stories themselves, but she set no deadlines. She was pleased with the first stories that came in.

After a while, she too began reading her new work in class. "I'd read finished work before," she said, "but it was only when I read work in progress out loud that I saw for the first time all its weaknesses, and I could objectively judge it. I learned so much in that class."[3] The students, in turn, were fascinated to hear her comment on a rough spot in a student's story and then explain how she had dealt with a similar problem in one of her own stories.

The local newspaper, which was beginning to record Eudora's every move, reported that no auditors were permitted in her class. "In her soft voice and unassuming manner, Miss Welty discussed the stories with the class rather than lecturing to them," one newspaper account said. "Particularly enriching for the students are her personality sketches of the authors she has met and known in Europe as well as in this country."[4]

The climax of this semester as writer-in-residence came on December 2, when Eudora gave a public lecture on "The Southern Writer Today." The *Clarion-Ledger* announced that she had written the paper especially for the lecture. She chose that topic, she said, because she was asked so often what southern writers were going to do in the face of the racial situation. She tried to answer the question as best she could. The lecture was published in the *Atlantic* in June as "Must the Novelist Crusade?" It was her resounding answer to critics who demanded to know why she wasn't *doing* something about the civil rights movement.

Eudora felt strongly that writers should not write to achieve social ends and that the problems facing southern novelists were the same problems novelists anywhere had always faced. "No writer writes without a moral point of view and without wanting to express what he feels about justice and injustice and all," she said. "But a fiction writer should let writing speak for itself. His function is not to lecture the public. He must, in fact, scrupulously keep preaching out of his writing. Chekhov once wrote in a letter, 'It's not up to me to say that it's bad to steal horses. Everybody knows it already.' That's what I feel to the bone about fiction writers."[5] Another time she said that there are always "human threats to people. That's the life of which you are writing and of which you are taking part. As long as you are writing an honest story about human beings you're writing about the same thing."[6]

Eudora continued to teach at Millsaps for several semesters, and among her students was Ellen Gilchrist, a native of Vicksburg and a graduate of Millsaps. By the time she took the class, Gilchrist was in her thirties, on her way to becoming a well-known short story writer, novelist, and radio commentator on PBS.

At one point, so the story goes, some of the young men in Eudora's class decided to tease her. Their short stories got rowdy, then rowdier and sexier. She never turned a hair but calmly discussed the use of point of view and other matters of technique in the stories. She never said, "Now, that's enough." The young men, awed at her composure, gave up.[7]

Chapter 58

The Last Short Story

1964—1966

᠍᠍᠍ The long hot summer of 1964 seemed to last forever in Mississippi, as young civil rights workers from all over the country converged to lead demonstrations and protests for the right to vote. White Mississippians resisted to the bitter end, even killing three CORE workers in Philadelphia, Mississippi—Michael Schwerner, James Chaney, and Andrew Goodman. The summer's activity led to passage of the landmark Voting Rights Act of 1965 and left a residue of bitterness among both blacks and whites in the state.

The unceasing racial turmoil began to take its toll on Eudora by the summer of 1965. The whole struggle was so wearying that she did not want to think about it, she said. She was either "tired or a coward," she added.[1] Nevertheless, she wrote "The Demonstrators," her second short story about the civil rights movement. *The New Yorker* bought it, and although it was not published until a year later, it won the O. Henry prize for 1967.

"The Demonstrators" is the story of one night in the life of Dr. Strickland, a general practitioner in the town of Holden, Mississippi, on the edge of the Delta. He has lived all his life in Holden, where his father also practiced medicine. On the night of the story, he is called to attend Ruby Gaddy, a young black woman who has been stabbed with an ice pick on the steps of the Holy Gospel Tabernacle, a black church. The electricity is off in the black neighborhood, and it is some time before Dr. Strickland recognizes Ruby as the maid who cleans his office every day. (For the doctor's call at Ruby's house, Eudora summoned memories of her own Depression-era visits to black homes in Jackson.)[2] The doctor ascertains that Ruby's assailant was a man named Dove Collins, and he later stumbles on Dove, mortally wounded and lying in the street downtown. It turns out that Dove stabbed Ruby and she stabbed him back. He crawled off and fell down a bank; the men who had seen the stabbing assumed he was dead.

The irony in the story is the coverage of the double killing by the local newspaper, which emphasizes that there was no racial element in the crime. "That's one they can't pin the blame on us for," the paper quotes the exultant sheriff as saying, and the pastor of the white Baptist church remarks on the behavior of blacks and adds, "And yet they expect to be seated in our churches." (The paper spelled Dove as "Dave.")

Eudora said that "The Demonstrators" was meant to be "an observation of the way a small-town society in the South is often in the control or the grip, whether benevolent or malevolent, of the solid, powerful family. It makes it all the harder for any change to penetrate a town like that."

While Eudora was in Oxford in 1965 for a meeting, John Robinson, home from Italy to visit his family, went up and took her to a dinner party at Nancy Farley's house. They drove back by way of Yazoo City to visit Mrs. Welty in the nursing home. The nursing home was not completely satisfactory: it was modern and well run, but it was expensive, and Mrs. Welty often railed against it.

Instead of giving another lecture at Millsaps, where she had willingly agreed to serve a second year as writer-in-residence, Eudora read from work in progress, the "reunion novel." A reporter described in detail the excerpt she read: "Miss Welty asked her audience to imagine a family reunion in the red clay hills of Mississippi during the depression . . . Miss Welty read only a portion of her novel; yet the audience was caught up in the lives of the characters. She successfully wraps the serious business of life in a cloth of humor, about which Seán O'Faoláin has said, 'Behind the joke there lurks the groan; but it is a long way behind.' "[3]

Diarmuid Russell had seen part of the "reunion novel" and thought it was ready to send out to publishers. Eudora hesitated, fearing that anybody who read it would find it "inconsequential" because she ignored the civil rights struggle. On July 7, 1965, Bennett Cerf, the iconoclastic publisher at Random House, who had heard rumors about the novel, offered an advance of $35,000 sight unseen. That was a large advance for the time. Russell regarded Random House and Cerf as a wonderful fallback possibility.[4] It must have been heavenly for Eudora to think, if only briefly, of a new book instead of family problems and illness.

Chapter 59

Death and Bereavement
1966

In the fall of 1965, Eudora's brother Edward broke his neck and had to spend six weeks in traction, followed by a protracted stay in the veterans' hospital in a cast. On Thanksgiving Day, Mrs. Welty had a stroke that left her comatose. She no longer spoke or recognized Eudora when she came, "though Eudora thought she did once or twice."[1] In spite of the family illnesses, the teaching, and the trips to college campuses, Eudora still worked on her novel.

In fact, she has told how when she drove to Yazoo City, she would not try to think of the novel, but "something would start flowing through my head about the story and I would think, 'This is the word I was trying to think about yesterday!'" She would write it down in a shorthand notebook with a heavy cardboard cover, so she could write with one hand and keep the other hand on the wheel and her eyes on the road. She had to decode the scrawls as soon as she got home or she would never be able to read the notes. "It was just like your mind was saying, 'All right, I've got you now, and I'm going to fill in these things that you missed yesterday,'" she said.[2]

At Christmas, Hubert Creekmore was home for the holidays and found Eudora "worn out from her daily trips to Yazoo City."[3] Edward was still in the hospital—his broken neck would not heal—and Eudora shuttled between hospital and nursing home. "Why ever does Eudora go over there every day when there is nothing at all she can do?" wondered William Jay Smith, whose sentiment was echoed by all her friends.[4] Regretfully, she turned down an invitation to Katherine Anne Porter's Twelfth Night party in Washington, where many of her favorite people were going to be, Smith and Robert Penn Warren among them. She would have loved, she said, to catch the overnight train and appear on Katherine Anne's doorstep and burn the wreaths, hug and be hugged, and drink champagne.

On Thursday, January 20, 1966, Chestina Welty died—peacefully, according to the paper, but others have said that she died railing at her daughter, just as Becky McKelva did in *The Optimist's Daughter,* "old, blind, raving and reciting passages from McGuffey's Reader."[5] Whatever the case, her death was a blessing all round, Hubert Creekmore said.[6] It lifted an enormous burden from Eudora, but left her, as the deaths of close family members do, to deal with her own conflicted feelings of grief and guilt.

Chestina Welty left Eudora the house on Pinehurst and all the furniture and personal property except for stocks and bonds. She left to Edward a duplex apartment next door, and to Mittie Welty and her two daughters stocks equal to the value of the apartment (about $15,000, according to documents filed in chancery court), along with $5,000 for each of the girls to help finish their education. The remaining stocks were to be divided in three parts, with equal shares going to Edward, Mittie and her daughters, and Eudora. After all the bills were settled, Eudora got $11,000 in addition to the house.

Four days after Chestina's death, Edward also died. The deaths, so close together, of a strong mother and a beloved brother must have meant a bereavement beyond endurance. Even though in a sense each death was a release—Chestina's from the agony of her existence, Edward's from the mysterious problems that had plagued him and his family—grief was inevitable. But Eudora was indomitable. Sympathetic friends rallied—flowers and food filled the house on Pinehurst—and within a month she was back on the lecture trail, fulfilling commitments made some time before and grateful, she said, for the work.[7]

Grief and loss were not over for the fifty-seven-year-old Eudora in that dreadful year. In June, Hubert Creekmore, her old friend and her sister-in-law Mittie's brother, died in New York in a taxi, on the way to the airport to catch a plane for Spain. Eudora and Mittie could find out very little about his death. Mittie wanted to fly up and Eudora offered to go with her, but Mittie's other brothers persuaded her against it. For a long time, Hubert's luggage remained at the air terminal and his apartment stayed locked. Finally a funeral was arranged in Jackson. It was almost a year before John Schaffner set up a memorial service in New York. When he finally did, Eudora sent a message to be read at the service. Hubert, she said, was "my loved friend and counselor and good critic, part of my Jackson and my home, the most familiar part of Christmas and the holidays at home, the first friend I called when I was in New York."

Chapter 60

Grief into Fiction

1966

Not long after Chestina's death, Eudora was on the road, reading her stories and apologizing because she had not been able to write a new lecture. No clue to the grief she must have felt, the sense of loss and desolation at the deaths of a mother and brother, appears in available letters that she wrote at this time. As always, she was a private person, guarding her deepest feelings from other people.

What she did do, however, was to lay aside the "reunion novel" to work on another piece of fiction, the most autobiographical and subtlest of her novels, *The Optimist's Daughter*. Soon after it was published, Eudora both conceded and denied that it was autobiographical. "The book wasn't about me," she told *Women's Wear Daily,* "but about emotions close to me."[1]

She wanted to show, she said much later, "in a quiet way . . . more of life than I had been able to do with some of the others." The novel has a smaller cast and a "direr situation," but she wrote it, she said, when she was feeling dire, after the deaths of her mother and brother.[2]

Working on the novel must have helped her come to terms with her mother's life and death, for she turned back to her own childhood and to the stories her mother had told her about life in the West Virginia hills. She created the character of Becky McKelva, who had a childhood very like Chestina Welty's. Chestina had lived on top of a mountain near Clay, or Clay Courthouse, as the little county seat of Clay County was sometimes called, with her widowed mother and five younger brothers, all left-handed and all banjo players. Chestina's father had been a colorful country lawyer, Edward Raboteau Andrews, who had grown up in Benevolence, Georgia, the son of C. C. Andrews, president of a college in North Carolina.[3] Ned went to the University of Georgia. His sister, Stella Andrews Upshur, was a newspaper-woman in Norfolk, Virginia, and the author of a book, *Private Lives of the Lovelorn.* A cousin, Walter Hines Page, from North Carolina, wrote one novel, *The Southerner,* and edited the *Atlantic Monthly.* When Ned's parents moved to Virginia, restless Ned struck out for West Virginia, where he married Eudora Carden, for whom Eudora, of course, was named.

Ned Andrews practiced law in Clay Courthouse, performing legendary legal feats that were written down in the local history books. A fellow lawyer said that Andrews "could prepare any sort of a court paper, whether a bill in equity, a declaration, a decree, or other order," faster and more easily than any other lawyer he knew. "If he had only been blessed with [a] knack of unremitting zeal and constant application, he would have been a wonderful lawyer. But Ed didn't love work . . . Ed did like to fish, and he was as hard to match with a gig as he was before a jury."[4]

Andrews died young. In March 1899, when he was only thirty-seven, he apparently suffered a ruptured appendix. He needed to get to a hospital, but the mountain roads were impassable because of ice and snow, and slides had blocked the local traintracks. A neighbor carried Andrews and Chestina, his eldest child, then fifteen years old, on a skiff down the Elk River to Charleston, West Virginia.[5] From Charleston, Chestina took her father on the train to Johns Hopkins in Baltimore, where he died on Saturday, March 25, 1899. Chestina then took his body home. It was this epic tale of her mother's ghastly journey that Eudora recounted as fiction in *The Optimist's Daughter.*

After her father's death, Chestina rode horseback to teach in a country schoolhouse, where she showed that she was tough enough to whip her pupils if they did not behave. When school closed for the summer, she took classes at Marshall College. Her five younger brothers did what they could to help the family financially. They grew up and prospered; Carl Andrews became a banker, mayor of Charleston, sheriff of Kanawha County, and a candidate for governor of West Virginia in 1940.

Becky McKelva is plainly based on Chestina Welty; she has the same West Virginia childhood and the younger brothers. Just as Chestina did, Becky McKelva rides horseback to her schoolteaching job after her father dies. Becky marries a lawyer and moves to Mississippi, where she forever misses the mountains.

In real life, while Eudora was still the only child, Chestina took her on the train to West Virginia to visit her family. Eudora remembered getting off the train on the banks of the Elk River; her mother tugged the rope of an iron bell, and in response a boat appeared suddenly with all five of Eudora's uncles in it. They went up to the top of Blue Knob, to a weathered gray wooden house with a center hall and "the light of day at each end." Her uncles' banjos hung on pegs in that hall.

In the novel, Eudora gave to Becky's daughter, Laurel McKelva Hand, her own memories of her mother and her grandmother and of visiting West Virginia at the age of about three. She put in everything that she remembered—the shoals in the Elk River, the mountains, the white strawberries, the way her uncles looked coming home at night "through the far-off fields, just white shirts showing down the mountain. All the physical sensations were memories of about age three, when you really have sharp sensory perceptions," she said.[6] "I was there many other times, but I used those sharp memories you have when you first begin to notice things." It was the first time, she said, that she had used personal memory without translating it entirely into fictional characters.[7]

Eudora's uncles were all great storytellers, and she listened to them with delight on the summertime visits to West Virginia, which became family reunions. Everybody knew their stories, but the boys loved to tell them and everybody loved to hear them over again. They all broke into gales of laughter at the mention of any name.[8] The brothers could also play musical instruments by ear, and Eudora listened, enchanted, to old songs and ballads that they played in unison.

In the novel, Laurel McKelva Hand is a young widow who lives in Chicago. Her mother is dead. Laurel is in New Orleans to be with her father, Judge McKelva, as he prepares for surgery for a detached retina. Eudora drew on memories of the trips with her mother to New Orleans for eye surgery, the sandbags placed so Mrs. Welty could not move her head, even though she had cataracts instead of a detached retina. Only someone familiar with southern hospital waiting rooms could have described Archie Lee and his family, who wait for their father's death while Fay and Laurel wait for the judge's.

Fay, the judge's second wife, forty years old—younger than Laurel—is "bony and blue-veined," towheaded, with "round, country-blue eyes and a little feist jaw"; she is an older, meaner version of Bonnie Dee Peacock in *The Ponder Heart.* Fay is self-centered and grasping, completely insensitive to other people. Eudora has maintained that no one in her family was like Fay. "Not in my family, but I've seen a many, a many," she said. Eudora's brother Edward married a woman from a lower social stratum, and she was certainly never part of Eudora's circle as was Walter's wife, Mittie. Fay is lower-class, pushy, selfish, and above all ignorant of tradition and of the mores of the McKelvas and their friends. She has no feeling for the past, no understanding of what has happened before. Eudora insists that Fay's character has nothing to do with class.[9]

During Judge McKelva's long convalescence after surgery, Fay, fretting that it's Mardi Gras time in New Orleans and she's missing the fun, shakes the judge, who is supposed to lie perfectly still, and cries, "Enough is enough!" "She was abusing him," says a nurse in horror. When Judge McKelva dies, the description in an early version (eliminated in the book) reads, "His whole pillowless head went dusky, as if he laid it under the surface of dark pouring water and held it there." This brings immediately to mind Eudora's account of her own father's face as he died while receiving a blood transfusion from his wife. "All at once his face turned dusky red all over," she wrote in *One Writer's Beginnings.*

When Laurel and Fay take the judge's body back to Mount Salus, the women who had been bridesmaids at Laurel's wedding rally around. In the South, a woman's bridesmaids were important friends throughout her life. In her memoir of growing up in Jackson, Seta Alexander Sancton tells how she played "The Rabbit" at her first piano recital—the song lasted thirty seconds—and received fifteen baskets of flowers from her aunts, her grandmother, and her mother's bridesmaids. Eudora had no relatives or maternal bridesmaids in Mississippi, and she told one interviewer that it was in the homes of her friends who grew up with large extended families that she realized that "interesting situations can, and notably do, take place at home."[10]

Before the funeral, Fay's family shows up from Texas, although Fay has told Laurel that they are all dead. Eudora's detailed description of Fay and her family, looked down upon by the elite of Mount Salus, lacks the compassion and sympathy for poor whites that she usually showed in her fiction. "I really did hate Fay," Eudora said. "I tried to be fair by bringing in her family. I really did! I thought they would explain her!"[11]

The morning after the funeral, Laurel confronts the past, her mother's life and death, and her own brief marriage, remembered as perfect until her husband, Philip Hand, was killed in the Pacific during World War II. Like Eudora's mother's last years, Laurel's mother's were miserable, full of suffering, blindness, anger, immobility, and finally unconsciousness. "Your mother died a crazy!" taunts Fay on that last morning.

Laurel clashes with Fay over a breadboard that her husband Philip made for her mother. Fay has used the breadboard for cracking nuts and scarred and soiled it. Laurel, aware of Fay's role in her father's death and unable to share this knowledge with anyone, not even her bridesmaids, almost hits Fay with the board. She stops short of violence, but recognizes her anger and puts the board down, relinquishing it to Fay. Fay merely thinks she's crazy.

Eudora said that she hated what Fay stood for. "She's the one who doesn't understand what experience means and doesn't learn anything," she said. "And to me, that is horrifying and even evil, almost sinful. And I may have gone overboard in that case. I have been accused of it."[12] She noted with some amusement that French reviewers said that Fay was the only sympathetic character in *The Optimist's Daughter*.[13] And the truth is, it is possible to find some sympathy for Fay, who is snubbed and ignored by everyone in Mount Salus, a town that must have been very dull indeed.

Shaken after the scene with the breadboard, Laurel realizes that she must also relinquish the past. She rushes out of the kitchen and gets in the car to go to the airport and return to Chicago and her life there. There is nothing left for her in Mount Salus. And she must live in the present, make a life for herself without parent, sibling, husband—a life presumably filled with creating art.

Eudora explained some of the sources for components of *The Optimist's Daughter*. Philip Hand, Laurel's husband, was an amalgamation of several young men Eudora had known, with elements from her brothers' personalities worked in. Without mentioning John Robinson's name, she referred to him, saying that she had a friend who had fought in the Italian campaign. She went on to say, "My friend in World War II married into—well, when someone was lost like Phil, I—I knew what that feeling was like. How could I not have? . . . It was a bad war." Certainly John Robinson, living with Enzo, could be said to be "married into—well, . . . lost." The kamikaze incident in the novel had happened to Eudora's brother Walter. "He was in the Navy at Okinawa, and later he was asked, 'How close have you come to a kamikaze?' And he said, 'Close enough to shake hands with.' So I put that in the story. Who could ever make up a thing like that?"[14] Edward had made a breadboard for their mother, but "Philip Hand did not have his character," she said.[15]

Eudora had personally seen the Mardi Gras costumes that she describes in the book—the couple dressed as skeletons and the man clothed in Spanish moss. In fact, she went back to old photographs she had taken in New Orleans and looked at costumes. "You can't *make up* something fantastic," she said. "I used the photographs as I might use notes."[16]

One scholar has seen *The Optimist's Daughter* as a classical elegy, pointing out that it has all the elements except the invocation to the Muses: a pastoral setting with rustic and rural folk, youth cast off, a catalogue of flowers in Becky's garden, grieving, negligence of responsible people, and the decay of institutions, as in the plastic poinsettias. There are consolations, one being that memory expresses the continuity of love—"To the memory, nothing is ever lost," realizes Laurel—and another being the satisfactions of art and doing things with your hands. Turning to new fields is represented by the children's hands reaching out.[17]

To see the novel as an elegy for Eudora's life may be entirely appropriate. In the book, Laurel sets free a chimney swift that has flown into the house. Eudora has said that the bird represents the past; perhaps she was freed by the death of her mother just as the bird was set free. Even so, it is not a joyous story, and to read it as a reflection of Eudora's life is to be moved to despair. Eudora, unmarried, childless, now totally unencumbered, could only return to *her* life in the arts, a life that is in many ways arid of intimate human relations, in spite of its richness in creativity and intellectual experience.

Losing Battles

1970

＿ For twelve years, while her brothers and her mother were ill and dying, while she wrote book reviews and a children's book and traveled to colleges all over the country and taught a class at Millsaps, and while she worked on *The Optimist's Daughter,* Eudora had written bits and pieces of her "reunion novel" whenever she could find the time. She stuck the pages in boxes. When she finally gave her full attention to the project, she found many different versions of each episode. She spread them all on her bed, cut pages apart, and put pieces of pages together with pins. She made a happy discovery: the story had vitality—it was alive.

The novel, titled *Losing Battles,* is set in northeast Mississippi, the poorest section of the poorest state, where the people have nothing, except maybe a scrap of eroded land. They are uneducated but for what they have learned from country schoolteachers. "Life there was so whittled down to the bare bones of existence," Eudora said.[1]

When she first visited Tishomingo County in the thirties, working for the WPA, Eudora knew she was going to be a writer and spoke to friends about writing a novel about these people. When she began work on *Losing Battles,* a great deal of what she had learned in her WPA days came back to her. The hill country was very different from Jackson, the Delta, or coastal

Mississippi. She was struck by the absence of any history except the daily struggle to keep the family alive. And what, she asked herself, was more important than the family? She knew she wanted a chorus of voices, "everybody talking and carrying on at once, something vocal and dramatized," she said.[2]

There are no black people in *Losing Battles,* because northeast Mississippi had no plantations and not many blacks, just poverty-stricken white hill farmers. Eudora set the story during the Depression, when times were hardest. The people were poor, but she did not want it to be a novel of despair. She wanted to show indomitability. "It's a novel of admiration for the human being who can cope with any condition, even ignorance, and keep a courage, a joy of life, that's unquenchable," she said.[3]

The ability to maintain a joy in life no matter what happens is one of Eudora's own skills, but not much else in the novel is autobiographical. The schoolteacher, Miss Julia Mortimer, is based on Miss Lorena Duling, the principal of Davis School. When Eudora was five and already knew how to read, her mother took her across the street to this school. Miss Duling, who ran a tight ship, told Mrs. Welty that Eudora might as well start first grade in January 1914.

Miss Duling was one of those teachers who were "like missionaries," determined to teach the heathen.[4] "You couldn't even leave the classroom without a written excuse from home, and then you'd have to get past Miss Duling in the principal's office. You couldn't. [She] could freeze you, maybe kill you, with the look of her eyes."[5] Everyone was terrified of her. It was rumored that she kept a whipping machine in her office. Eudora years later maintained that there had been *something* covered up in there, perhaps an adding machine or even a dress model.[6]

Children who didn't even go to Davis School were in awe of Miss Duling. Seta Sancton recalled in her memoir that her grandmother always invited Miss Duling to holiday dinners because Miss Duling had taught all her sons at Davis School. Seta's uncles, who had cowered before Miss Duling when they were in school, laughed and joked with her when they were grown. "Her eyes twinkled at parties but not at school," said Seta, who went to Power School.[7] Incidentally, when Eudora was in the fourth grade, Miss Duling arranged for a spelling match between her class and the members of the state legislature. The fourth grade won.

At first, as she always did, Eudora thought *Losing Battles* would be a short story; it would end when the hero, Jack Renfro, got home from Parchman Prison. (As Eudora wrote version after version, Jack's name changed from Joe Quick Bunting to Buford Bunting to Jack Renfro.) As she attempted to show the difference between how people thought of him and what he was, she realized that she was working on a novel, not a short story. "I was hooked," she said. "As soon as he appeared, I was just crazy about him and I had to go and have him in the scene. So I kept doing it."[8] She wanted all the action to occur in one day, but the reunion was on Sunday and she had to have a Monday, so she began putting things in a folder marked "Next A.M."[9]

To be sure characters moved around without running into each other, she made a diagram of the house.[10] She wanted an open stage where she could present this family, show them living without props, only that unbreakable will to live.[11] The writing of the book—all dialogue or action, with no excursions into the minds of the characters—was difficult, but she wanted the characters to reveal themselves and each other through action and talk.[12]

Eudora liked writing dialogue. It was easy, she said, when you have a good ear, and she thought she had one. As the book went on, it got harder, since the dialogue had to do so many things at once—"reveal what the character said but also what he thought he said, what he hid, what others were going to think he meant, and what they misunderstood, and so forth, all in this single speech." Like P. G. Wodehouse, she sometimes laughed out loud while she was writing dialogue. She would even imagine things that her characters might say and write out a scene for her own amusement, knowing that she could not use it. "Dialogue comes from memory," she said. "You don't know you've remembered but you have. And you listen for the right word in the present and you hear it. Once you're into a story, everything seems to apply—what you hear in a city bus is exactly what your character would say on the page you're writing."[13]

Eudora said she threw away as much as she kept in the book and had great piles of pages fastened together with paper clips, pages that remained unnumbered until they went off to the printer.

When she finished *Losing Battles* in 1969, Russell sent it to Harcourt Brace, where it was received with a shocking lack of enthusiasm. The editors wanted revisions, and they had the temerity to suggest that she "collaborate" with someone on cuts and changes. Furthermore, they wanted to publish *The Optimist's Daughter,* which had appeared in *The New Yorker,* in a book with other, older stories. Russell and Eudora agreed that he must withdraw both manuscripts.[14] William Jovanovich, head of Harcourt Brace, sent roses and tried to get Eudora to change her mind. She was firm, however, and Russell set out to find a more enthusiastic publisher and more money. Eudora wanted $50,000, according to one publisher, who was under the impression that she needed the money to pay her brother's debts.

Fifty thousand dollars was a big advance at that time, and in the end it was Albert Erskine at Random House, the man who in the thirties had discovered Eudora's short stories at the *Southern Review,* who came up with it. The book more than earned back its advance and has been in print ever since it was published in 1970.

Losing Battles became a best-seller almost as soon as it appeared. It was a fluke, Eudora said, but she was happy and relieved at the reviewers' reception. She had been afraid that critics would ask why she didn't deal with racial problems and all the "relevant" issues. Instead, publication of *Losing Battles* on her sixty-first birthday, April 13, 1970, was the occasion for critics not so much to review an important new novel but to celebrate the life and work of Eudora Welty. On the front page of the *New York Times Book Review,* James Boatwright, the editor of *Shenandoah,* which had the year before published an entire issue called "A Tribute to Eudora Welty," said her career was "instructive" and the new book was a "joyous, rich, uproarious comic spectacle, teeming with brilliant characters."[15] An interview conducted by Walter Clemons accompanied the review.

"The Lesson of the Master" was the headline on *Newsweek's* review, by Jack Kroll. In the *Washington Post,* Eudora's friend and disciple Reynolds Price compared the book to *The Tempest, A Winter's Tale, War and Peace,* and *Huckleberry Finn.*[16] *The New Yorker* said it was "as if Mark Twain and the Shakespeare of 'A Midsummer Night's Dream' had collaborated in celebrating three basic human rituals: a birthday, a wedding, and a funeral."[17]

A few found fault. The daily *New York Times* spoke of "endless talk" and "pointless activity." The *Washington Post Book World* said that because of the absence of internal monologues, the characters seemed mythological and were all-knowing.[18]

When *Losing Battles* appeared in England twelve years later, its reception was less than enthusiastic. "I hated it," said Selina Hastings in the *Daily Telegraph,* calling it "436 dire pages in which a group of semi-literate farmers and their wives and their cousins and their aunts, gathered together for a family reunion, sit and holler at each other until the reader grows sick and faint with boredom."[19]

Reviewers did not mention the presence of real evil in the book. Aunt Lexie is obviously based on some of those "good Christian women" who helped nurse Chestina Welty. Lexie has been taking care of the respected schoolteacher, Miss Julia Mortimer, who has just died, and has by her own account mistreated, imprisoned, and starved her patient. "Without a trace of sentimentality Welty makes it clear that not all manifestations of evil can be justified or explained away . . . her vision of the world admits the existence of unadulterated evil," a Danish scholar wrote twenty years after the publication of the book.[20] This same scholar caught one tiny error in *Losing Battles:* Granny Vaughan can't be a hundred, as she claims, or ninety, as she's supposed to be. She was a little girl when she faced down General Grant, so she can't be more than seventy in 1930.

Reviewers also did not comment on one of the more puzzling aspects of the book. The reunion celebrates the birthday of Granny, Elvira Jordan Vaughan. Granny and her husband raised her daughter's children, the Beechams, after Mr. and Mrs. Beecham left in a buggy in the dark of night without a word to anyone, went off Banner Bridge, and were killed. Where were they going? Why did they abandon their children?

To celebrate the publication of *Losing Battles,* Eudora's friends in Jackson threw a party. They had a gold pin with "Losing Battles" engraved on it and a banner inscribed with the words "I call this a reunion to remember, all!" The food duplicated the dinner at Granny's reunion. A poem was read; in part it said

> *All our love to The Eudora*
> *Now, as always, we adore her.*
> *The light of fame Eudo reflects*
> *Set us to cooking chicken necks.*[21]

Time magazine listed *Losing Battles* as one of the top ten novels of 1970. It was one of ten nominees for the National Book Award, which was won by

Saul Bellow's *Mr. Sammler's Planet,* and one of three finalists for the Pulitzer, along with *Mr. Sammler's Planet* and Joyce Carol Oates's *The Wheel of Love.* The Pulitzer board seriously considered recognizing Eudora Welty for her lifetime achievements but refrained because of the jury's opinion that *Losing Battles* lacked "the freshness of some of her earlier work."[22] No award at all was made for fiction that year.

Chapter 62

Another Book,
More Honors
1971

Somebody described Eudora about this time as "a tall, gray-haired lady with bright blue eyes and a droll, shy smile."[1] She was a celebrity in her home town and winning more and more national recognition. She swept off in triumph to Peterborough, New Hampshire, to receive the Edward Mac-Dowell Medal on August 23, 1970. She would return to Jackson, she said there, and add "another story or two" to a "collection soon to be published."[2]

She had a lot of work that was newer than *Losing Battles,* she told William Thomas of the *Memphis Commercial Appeal* two months later, in October. It was mostly short stories, she said, and "when I've written a couple more I'll have enough for a book."[3] Thomas marveled that when she wrote, mostly in the morning, in her bedroom, she still used an upright Royal typewriter.

Eudora spent 1971 very quietly. Most days she joined friends for drinks or lunch or supper, at her home or theirs. When they came to Eudora's house, she said she served either ham or oysters. "Two dishes—I don't see how anybody can complain," she said.[4] About this time she had the unusual experience of being thrown out of a Jackson restaurant because she was with two young men with "Jesus haircuts." The waitress had told them not to feel bad, since the restaurant threw people out all the time for having long hair.

Eudora wrote a letter to the *Clarion-Ledger* protesting that her friends were not drunk or disorderly but "sitting there like shorn lambs hoping for a shrimp cocktail."[5]

She vowed she would make no more speeches, even in Jackson, but she did write a charming foreword, "The Flavor of Jackson," for the *Jackson Cookbook,* which was published to raise money for the local symphony orchestra. As always, with a few well-chosen words she could bring to life the vanished city of her childhood. Jackson, she admitted tactfully, was not a town of gourmet restaurants. "One Mexican at his hot tamale stand on the corner of North West and Hamilton during the cold months couldn't make us cosmopolitan . . . The word for the Jackson flavor is 'home.' " She recalled dishes famous in Jackson, such as bridesmaids' salad, which was all white, down to white grapes, or pressed chicken, because it was so much trouble to make. All "refreshments" for parties, she said, were "rich—thunderously rich." She mentioned the two bachelors who were said to have "brought mayonnaise" to Jackson, and recalled that everything was made from scratch, with a barrel of flour in every kitchen and coconuts cracked open and grated fresh for Christmas. She even singled out a few famous Jackson recipes that she used herself—Mrs. Cabell's pecans, Mrs. Wright's cocoons, and Mrs. Lyell's lemon dessert. (All are in the "Heirloom Recipe" chapter of the cookbook.)[6]

Incredibly generous about writing prefaces for the books of her friends, Eudora wrote another cookbook preface when her old friend Winifred Green Cheney published *The Southern Hospitality Cookbook* a few years later. Cheney had often appeared with "something on a tray" when Eudora was working to meet a deadline and had also been one of the people who provided support after the death of her mother. The section in Cheney's book called "Eudora's Niche" is another marvelous commentary on Jackson's ideas about good food. The "niche" includes Chestina Welty's recipe for green tomato mincemeat, Eudora's fig preserves, and four dishes that Cheney created for special occasions involving Eudora—apples Eudora, a seafood casserole, raspberry rapture, and squash Eudora, which combines yellow squash and chicken livers in a casserole. Cheney advises readers to serve the last at lunch with a "chilled garden tomato, peeled and stuffed with cottage cheese mixed with well-seasoned mayonnaise; Kentucky Wonder pole beans cooked with ham nubbins; a pickled peach; hot buttered biscuits; and your own blackberry jelly."

Ever eager to boost Eudora's income, Diarmuid Russell had suggested several years before that she select some of her old photographs for a book and write an introduction for it. In November 1971, Random House published *One Time, One Place: Mississippi in the Depression, A Snapshot Album,* complete with a foreword, by Eudora Welty. It contained a hundred photographs, a fraction of those she took while she was working for the WPA. Most of the pictures had been taken with her first camera, a Kodak she described as "one step more advanced than the Brownie."

The remarks of two critics seem in this case to be remarkably apt. Paul Marx, an English professor at Yale, who reviewed *One Time, One Place* for the *Nation,* understood exactly what Eudora had done. He pointed out that her pictures showed rural and small-town Mississippi black society in the 1930s, which had a now-lost "wholeness and a cohesiveness" and showed contentment amid stark poverty. "Her one time and one place is that of the individual subject at the moment the shutter snapped," he wrote. "She has no interest in proving or disproving anything . . . Miss Welty took her pictures . . . without condescension. More than by the vanished years, she says, her pictures of blacks are dated now by the trust that is so plain to see in her subjects."[7] The pictures were uneven in technical quality, said Madison Jones in the *New York Times Book Review,* but their merit lay in their subject matter. As a photographer, Welty was no more like the makers of documentaries than as a writer she was like the social realists, he said.[8]

In 1972, President Nixon appointed Eudora to a six-year term on the National Council of the Arts. Council members were paid a hundred dollars a day, or whatever the going fee was for government consultants, plus their expenses to go to meetings.

Michael Straight, deputy director of the National Endowment for the Arts, had a hard time finding a voice for literature for the National Council of the Arts, which advised the endowment on its grants to support cultural endeavors. "Writers are loners; they do not think in terms of government," Straight said. "They do not think in terms of their fellow writers. They think in terms of the page in front of them . . . It was very difficult to come up with a first-class writer who was able to think deeply and clearly about the ways in which the federal government could relate to the artist in America."[9] Straight, who revered Eudora's work and regarded *Losing Battles* as one of the greatest American novels of the century, decided to recommend her. President Nixon, who owed Senator Eastland of Mississippi a favor, was enthusiastic.

The White House put through a call to Eudora. She was not at home, but a painter who was working in the house answered the phone. "This is the White House calling," said the operator. "There ain't no White House in Jackson," said the painter. When the operator finally made it plain that the president of the United States was calling, the painter, thinking that Miss Welty was in trouble with the law, panicked. "She done took off," he said. When Eudora got home, the painter told her some fool had called and said it was the White House. "But I told him you took off and wouldn't be back." Fortunately, the White House called again and got Eudora herself. She explained it all to the painter, who was impressed enough to put three extra coats on the back staircase because he wanted the president of the United States to think it was a good job.

Straight said that no one who served on the council was ever more revered than Eudora Welty.[10] To Eudora, however, the council seemed a strange outfit.[11] She rather enjoyed its work of granting funds to small presses and quarterly magazines and placing poets and fiction writers in elementary and secondary classrooms, but she would much rather serve on the panel that awarded grants to writers, she said.[12]

Chapter 63

Glory, Laud, and Honor
1972–1974

In Eudora's life, visits to and from old friends were extremely important. In February 1972, she went to San Antonio for a week for the opening of an exhibition, "Man and Magic, Work of Agnes Sims," that celebrated the dedication of a new wing at the Marion Koogler McNay Museum. Agnes Sims was the painter with whom Mary Lou Aswell lived in Santa Fe. John Leeper, the director of the McNay, and his wife, old friends of Sims's, gave a dinner party after the exhibition's opening, and Aswell, Sims, and Eudora, along with Frank Lyell, down from the University of Texas, and other local guests, attended. Eudora was the hit of the evening, "like your favorite aunt, immediately," Leeper said.[1]

The next month Eudora was in Washington and spent an afternoon with Katherine Anne Porter. It was, on the surface, like old times. Katherine Anne served fresh asparagus drenched in butter, catfish, cornsticks, strawberry compote, and gallons of champagne. The two women, one eighty-two, the other sixty-three, friends since 1938, talked for hours. At least, Katherine Anne talked, until Eudora's head throbbed. Although Eudora wrote her friend a fond, effusive note, she told other people that she was worried about Katherine Anne's state of mind and felt that her fantasies had a "sad and desperate" quality. But she added, perhaps the talking and the fantasies were how Katherine Anne hung on to life.

Eudora returned to New York that month to receive the Gold Medal for the Novel from the National Institute of Arts and Letters. The medal, awarded only once every ten years, had gone to William Faulkner in 1962, and Eudora had presented it to him. On the train to New York, she went into the dining car early one morning for coffee and ran into Bunt Percy, Walker Percy's wife. Percy was on his way to be inducted into the institute. Eudora told Bunt that she would love to meet him, and Bunt duly reported this to her husband. Assured that Bunt wasn't kidding, he went and knocked on Eudora's roomette door, and they sat "knee to knee" and rejoiced that they were heading to the same event.[2]

Eudora and Percy were interviewed together when William F. Buckley, Jr., went to Jackson to tape his television program, *Firing Line,* in December 1972. Buckley told them he was going to ask questions about things like the Agrarians and southern literature, but Eudora felt that he baited them and that while Percy was able to match wits with Buckley, she wasn't.

Buckley asked how, from a moral point of view, writers could stay in the South. Percy tried to explain that from a novelist's point of view, "human relations are much more complex than saying that the white racist is wrong and the black protester is right." Buckley, continuing, said that many people who were not being persecuted themselves had left Germany during the thirties. Percy said that he was sure some southern writers did leave—all the Agrarian writers "who were defending the values of the old South seem to have ended up in northern universities," he said.[3] Eudora made the point she had made often enough before: writers served the world if they wrote honest stories about human beings. They did not need to take up causes and write tracts. She was annoyed when the *Mississippi Quarterly* reprinted the interview in full.[4]

The Optimist's Daughter won the Pulitzer Prize for fiction in 1972. "I was on the committee, and I insisted that it win because *Losing Battles* had been passed over," said Guy Davenport.[5] The other two judges, Herman Kogan of the *Chicago Sun-Times Books* and Edmund Fuller of the *Wall Street*

Journal, agreed with Davenport. It was one time that there was no quibbling from the Pulitzer organization or from critics, said John Hohenberg in his book about the Pulitzers.[6] Eudora found out about the Pulitzer when Frank Hains at the *Daily News* called her up and said, "How does it feel?" and she looked out the window and saw two strangers with cameras coming up the front walk.[7]

The announcement of the Pulitzer came during Mississippi Arts Festival Week, May 1–6, 1973, which was a Eudora Welty Celebration, planned and carried out by a statewide committee of a thousand members. Wednesday, May 2, was officially declared Eudora Welty Day by Governor William Waller. This was an enormous honor. Members of the committee tried to do everything they could to make it a memorable occasion, including asking Eudora for a list of out-of-town friends to invite. Eudora gave them the list and wrote to each person on it herself, explaining diffidently that she knew they were too busy to come, but the committee had asked her for names, so she had furnished them, but they were not to feel that they had to inconvenience themselves. A great many of those invited did come. On May 1, Eudora had her out-of-town friends for drinks and a buffet dinner at her house, which was awash in flowers and casseroles and messages from friends and neighbors.

After a week of steady rain, the sun broke out on May 2, in time for ceremonies honoring Eudora in the House of Representatives chamber in the Old Capitol. Standees lined the walls of the chamber, and others sat and squatted on the floor. More people listened to the program through a sound system set up in the halls and rotunda. Eudora received three standing ovations, the first when she came in, wearing a pink-and-white silk dress. Governor Waller read his Eudora Welty Day proclamation and presented her with the Governor's Outstanding Mississippian Award. Eudora then read several scenes from *Losing Battles,* saying at one point, "I think I'll just quit here," but changing her mind and reading more. "The house was hot, but nobody seemed to mind," said the *Clarion-Ledger.*

Eudora then spent hours greeting the people who came to pay her homage at a reception in the Archives and History Building. The festivities went on all day, ending with a performance of *The Ponder Heart* at the New Stage Theatre (the successor to the Little Theater) and a black-tie after-theater supper. Among the out-of-town guests were Reynolds Price, Ross Macdonald, William Jay Smith, Nona Balakian, Mary Louise Aswell, and Agnes Sims. Diarmuid Russell, still convalescing from an operation and cobalt treatments for lung cancer, made his first trip to Jackson for the event, and he and his wife, Rose, stayed with Eudora for a week. "His mind and spark are as ever," Eudora told William Jay Smith.[8] Sadly absent was Eudora's favorite, Elizabeth Bowen, who had died just months before. Katherine Anne Porter had talked of going but was unable to manage it, to the relief of a great many people. (Katherine Anne could not endure two of Eudora's friends, and when it looked as though she might appear, Eudora had to put them in separate hotels and ask Smith to keep a steady eye on Katherine Anne to prevent fireworks.)

Throughout Festival Week, the Old Capitol Museum featured an exhibition of Welty manuscripts, published books, letters, scrapbooks, and photographs. The New Stage Theatre presented *The Ponder Heart* all week, and the Film Celebration included three Welty films—*Season of Dreams,* made from several short stories; *One Time, One Place,* a film about the book of the same title; and *A Conversation with Eudora Welty,* an interview with Frank Hains, the local arts columnist. On Thursday night, *The Robber Bridegroom* was presented at Jackson Municipal Auditorium.

"For the visitor from the East, the celebration had a fairy-tale quality," wrote Nona Balakian in the *New York Times Book Review.* "Writers in America are not supposed to be famous and happy at the same time . . . Yet here was a writer perfectly attuned to her milieu."[9] No Mississippi writer, not even William Faulkner—especially not William Faulkner—had ever received such a tribute from the citizens of the state.

Honors followed honors. With each new one, Eudora was "genuinely surprised, genuinely pleased, genuinely grateful." Charlotte Capers told a newspaper reporter that Eudora was "almost beatified in Jackson . . . Jacksonians, along with Mississippians, have a terrible inferiority complex—they feel that everything in the world people say about them is bad and they have the feeling that everything she's saying about Mississippi is good and funny and true." Mississippians felt that Faulkner had cared nothing for the state and had given it a bad name. Besides, he was hard to read. On the other hand, Eudora was personally popular and everybody felt that she represented the state and its people fairly. "We need this and we're grateful for it," Capers said.[10]

More and more reporters made the trip to Jackson and located the house on Pinehurst, "the only two-story house on the block." They wrote down the details of the house—the bottom story was brown, the top was speckled and half-timbered. Inside, Eudora offered them coffee and biscuits and jelly and talked about her childhood and the way she wrote. She told one reporter from New Orleans that she would like to write an original screenplay, because she felt there was a close kinship between movies and short stories.

In October 1973, Eudora was the only novelist invited to participate in an international seminar at the University of Nebraska honoring Willa Cather on the hundredth anniversary of her birth. That trip gave her a chance to ride the Burlington Zephyr from Lincoln, Nebraska, to Chicago, where she lectured at the University of Chicago.

From there she went on to New York, where she spoke at the Museum of Modern Art about her Depression photographs. John Szarkowski, curator of photographs at the museum, introduced her by reading a paragraph from the story "A Memory," in which the narrator describes watching everything: "All through this summer I had lain on the sand beside the small lake, with my hands squared over my eyes, fingertips touching, looking out by this device to see everything: which appeared as a kind of projection." "Only a great photographer," said Szarkowski, "could write like that!"

Eudora assured her audience that she was not there under false pretenses, because she was not under any pretenses. "I took pictures because I loved the use of the camera, just as I write stories because I love the use of words."[11] She read from the introduction to *One Time, One Place* and talked briefly about some of the pictures she had taken. When she finished, the applause was deafening.

In February 1974, Eudora went to an Arts Council meeting in Washington and to Bryn Mawr for a few days, and then rode the Trailways bus to Hollins College for another "Celebration for Eudora Welty." She was almost sixty-five years old, moving more slowly but still full of enormous stamina for festivities of this kind. During her two days at Hollins, she heard five papers read in her honor, listened to a panel talk about her work, attended two banquets and a late-evening cocktail party, and read from *Losing Battles* in the icy college chapel. Younger people complained that they were exhausted while she was still going strong. William Jay Smith, who was on the faculty and had arranged the celebration, had told her that she did not have to be there to hear people read papers about her work and talk about it on a panel, but she sat through it all.

Chapter 64

The Robber Sings

1974–1976

From the time it was published in 1942, *The Robber Bridegroom* had appealed to people who wanted to turn it into a musical comedy, but nothing happened until 1974. That year Gerald Freedman, who had directed the original production of *Hair,* staged a workshop production of a musical version of *Robber* with book and lyrics by Alfred Uhry and music by Robert Waldman, at the Musical Theater Lab at St. Clement's Church in New York City. Uhry, who taught film and theater at the Calhoun School, a New York prep school, was a Georgian who "grew up on Eudora Welty, Carson Mc-Cullers, Thomas Wolfe, and loved it." He later wrote *Driving Miss Daisy.* When Uhry and Waldman were in college, everybody else at Brown wanted to be a dentist or to work for IBM, but the two of them wanted to write musicals. They both learned "valuable lessons in advanced songwriting" when they worked for Frank Loesser's music publishing firm. When their musical version of *East of Eden* flopped, they looked for a "small, very American musical theater piece that could travel." They seized on *The Robber Bridegroom* after Uhry found a copy in a secondhand bookstore.[1]

With Rhonda Coullet as Rosamond and Raoul Julia as Jamie, their version of *The Robber Bridegroom* ran for only a week, but John Houseman, director of the Acting Company, a national repertory group connected with the Juilliard School, saw it and decided to bring it to the Harkness Theater in the fall of 1975. Houseman installed two Juilliard graduates who were members of the Actors Company as stars—Patti LuPone as Rosamond and Kevin Kline as Jamie—and sent it on a long nationwide tour. When the touring company got to the Municipal Auditorium in Jackson, Mayor Dale Danks declared October 24, 1974, to be Eudora Welty Day. Eudora wondered what you did on your day. A reporter suggested that she could take a walk down Capitol Street. "And wave at people," Eudora said. She had seen the workshop production in New York and thought it was "full of high spirits and young people having an awfully good time." She was "enormously delighted . . . It is not exactly like my book, but it did what any play should; it took some things and expanded them and left others out."[2]

When *The Robber Bridegroom* opened at the Harkness, it was a great time for a musical in New York; a musicians' strike had stilled the orchestras in Broadway theaters, but the Harkness, on upper Broadway, was unaffected. There were some decidedly un-Welty-like touches, including four-letter words, nudity, simulated copulation, and changes in tone. For example, in the book, Salome, Rosamond's stepmother, says to her, "If you come back without the herbs, I'll break your neck." Onstage, Salome says, "If you come back without them herbs, I'll kick your butt up between your shoulder blades."

Eudora, in town for the opening, gamely praised the play. In an interview that appeared the day of the opening, she said she was pleased with the way the musical "captured the feeling of the frontier." When she had written *Robber,* she had combined fairy tales and history without looking anything up. "Youthful exuberance," she said. While the production was very different from her book, that was the way it should be. "I love the theater," she said, "and I'm absolutely thrilled if someone uses my work." Plus, she had admired John Houseman since she had been in school at Columbia, she said.[3]

The reporter, like all reporters who met Eudora, was completely captivated and praised her gentle manner, her soft drawl, and even her yellow dress, which seemed to speak of southern specialties like "sunshine, lemonade, and buttercups." Eudora told her, incidentally, that she would go back to Jackson and pick up a short story she had been working on. She was "getting together a collection . . . I'm always working on something . . . why, I wouldn't think life as worth living without my work."[4]

The Robber Bridegroom was scheduled to open at the Biltmore on Broadway, with a new cast—Barry Bostwick as Jamie and Rhonda Coullet back as Rosamond—on October 6, 1976. Bostwick, a California-bred actor, saw Jamie as a "manchild, a playful person who has the power to charm everybody and who can be what anybody wants him to be. His nemesis is that he falls in love . . . and that unmasks him . . . You know, it's really a sad story."[5]

Opening night had to be delayed from October 6 until October 12 because Bostwick fractured his left elbow when he fell twelve feet to the stage floor after the rope he used to swing onstage broke during the final dress rehearsal. He played Jamie with his arm in a cast, which bothered some critics but was regarded as an asset by others.

At the opening night party, the *New York Times* reported, the cast and Eudora made a fuss over each other. "I admire you all tremendously," Eudora told them over and over. "Such youth and high spirits. Why, it all fit my book perfectly." "No matter what violence is committed to her novella," said John Houseman, "she still looks happy."[6]

Reviewers liked the exuberance of the show but faulted the music, which some deemed machine-made and unmemorable. Walter Kerr praised the ingenuity of the staging. When a paddle-wheel steamer was needed, two men stood in front of a cutout shaped like a riverboat and picked up two sawhorses and spun them in their arms. "Do you know what?" asked Kerr. "It looks more like a churning packet getting up steam than anything old Mark Twain ever piloted."[7]

The production did not last long and lost a total of $363,000 for its backers, according to *Variety*.

Chapter 65

The Image

1975–1977

Mayor Dale Danks of Jackson proclaimed October 27, 1977,
Miss Eudora Welty Day. "Always the 'Miss' in honor of her
Southern gentility," commented the Jackson Daily News.

Proceeding triumphantly from college campus to college campus, from dais to dais, Eudora became an immensely popular entertainer. She traveled and spoke and read to large, enthusiastic audiences and gave interviews constantly, but she still managed to rule out questions about her personal life. No one else in public life has managed quite so well to avoid giving out biographical information.

When a reporter from a Boston newspaper asked her a question about her unmarried state, she said, "I wonder what my parents would think if they could hear that question. I wonder what your parents would think." She was never rude. Instead, she managed to project an enduring image by being always nice—sometimes funny and amusing, but always polite and patient. In the late seventies, a reporter who covered her on one of her many college visits clearly perceived her the way she wanted to be seen. Eudora Welty looked, she wrote, "as though she should be at home under the light of a Tiffany lampshade, painting violets on china plates." She was "a lady's lady" in polished cotton, a self belt, black patent shoes, and hands that looked more at home in gloves than on a typewriter keyboard, but nevertheless, there she was, "on stage in her long teal blue gabardine dress, reading aloud from work she has created in solitude."[1]

There is no doubt that Eudora believed this image armored her from the slings and arrows of outrageous biographers, of whom she had a poor opinion. She felt that Arthur Mizener's biography of Ford Madox Ford, *The Saddest Story,* "falls short," as she put it in a review, and she regarded Joan Givner's biography of her friend Katherine Anne Porter as intrusive, sensational, and inaccurate—quite beyond the pale. She was, however, unfailingly courteous to Joan Givner when she saw her.

Mary Aswell Doll, Mary Lou Aswell's daughter, wrote a memoir of her mother and sent the manuscript to Eudora. "I thought she would appreciate it," Doll said. "And I thought she might help me get it published. Instead, she sent the manuscript back to me with a letter that said she stopped reading it at the point when I described my mother's lesbian experiences and refused to read any more. She said, 'I was not one of your mother's lesbian friends.' "[2]

Eudora obviously regarded these biographical works as unspeakable intrusions into the lives of her friends. And when people began making tentative efforts to write her biography, she became almost irrational. Floyd Watkins, a professor of English at Emory University, began a book that would examine her background and its effect on her work, just as he had explained how details from Robert Penn Warren's childhood and youth had shown up in his work in *Then and Now.* Eudora became furious with Watkins; she described the quite ordinary biographer's questions he asked her and her relatives as "impertinent." Out of respect for a woman he admired tremendously, Watkins abandoned his project. Albert Devlin, a professor of English at the University of Missouri and the author of two books of Welty criticism, was fiercely warned off when he began biographical research. Later, David Laskin finished *A Common Life,* his delightful book about four literary friendships—Hawthorne and Melville, Robert Lowell and Elizabeth Bishop, Henry James and Edith Wharton, and Katherine Anne Porter and Eudora Welty. Eudora refused him permission to use any of her unpublished photographs or to quote from her letters. "She was polite," Laskin said, "but cool, uncooperative, and needlessly defensive."[3]

Did she fear that biography would somehow tarnish the image she had so carefully cultivated? She had sought fame and enjoyed celebrity, but she found the new fashion for revealing everything about an artist's life threatening.

Even though she was concerned about appearances, Eudora did not hesitate to speak out after an old friend was murdered. Frank Hains, the arts editor of the *Jackson Daily News* and one of Eudora's most faithful cheerleaders, was killed at his home on Webster Street in July 1975. A teenager who was living temporarily with Hains discovered his nude body—face down, with wounds from a blunt object on his head, his hands and feet bound with neckties, and his mouth gagged with a necktie—early in the morning of July 14.

Hains and Eudora had been friends for years; like her, he had been one of the cofounders of the New Stage Theatre. Since 1956 he had written a daily column in which he had untiringly chronicled Eudora's achievements and honors. After a man with a record of arrests for sodomy, rape, and murder was charged with Hains's murder, gossip in Jackson about Hains's lifestyle became hysterical and malevolent. To salvage Hains's reputation and dampen the gossip, Eudora wrote a letter that was printed under the logotype of Hains's old column but bore the subhead "In Memorium" (there was a poor speller on the copy desk) and her name in boldface capital letters. She paid tribute to Hains's mind, "first-rate—informed, uncommonly quick and sensitive, keenly responsive." She praised his work for the arts, his lifelong enchantment with the world of art, and his unusual gift for communicating his pleasure in it. Her words had a powerful calming effect on the people of Jackson.[4]

Eudora's circle of friends was narrowing. Her old friend Frank Lyell came home from a trip to Europe in 1977 feeling terrible. He went straight to the hospital, where doctors diagnosed congestive heart failure and put him in intensive care. Eudora visited him briefly three or four times before he died after a week in the hospital. Eudora deeply mourned his death; she and Frank had been "close for forty-six years," since she had gone back to Jackson in 1931, she wrote to a friend.[5]

Chapter 66

Still Reading

1977

During the winter of 1977, Eudora finally read *Middlemarch* for the first time. Dark memories of *Silas Marner* from high school had made her avoid George Eliot until Shelby Foote found out she had never read *Middlemarch* and sent her a copy. It was "heavenly," she said, "like fresh air for my soul."[1]

All her life, of course, Eudora had devoured books. Chestina read out loud to her children, and long after Eudora was grown, when she read, she still heard a voice.[2] When Eudora began to read herself, she said she was an ideal reader, never disappointed in a book, but "feeling every pain and pleasure suffered by all the characters. Oh, but I identified! Or tried to." When she was reading *The Five Little Peppers,* Eudora decided that she wanted to be poor. "I hoped and prayed we were, just so I could do like Polly Pepper and bake a cake in a stove with a hole in it," she said. She asked her mother if they were rich or poor; her mother wisely did not answer.[3]

At one point in her childhood, Eudora was put to bed for several months for what the doctor called "a fast-beating heart"—and she loved it. She spent the day in her parents' bed in the upstairs front bedroom, where she could watch Davis School across the street, and she seized the opportunity to read.[4] The bed was piled with books; Robert Louis Stevenson's "In the Land of Counterpane" seemed eminently apt. Or she could look out the window as much as she wanted. "Anything that leads to uninterrupted meditation, or . . . Imagination" was a good thing, she realized later.

Eudora was a fast reader—too fast, she said. She finished books so quickly that finding enough to read became a problem. When she was nine, her mother introduced her to the public library. She assumed when she saw the library shelves full of books that she could read as fast as she pleased; there would always be more. But Miss Annie Parker, the librarian, had a rule that no one could take more than two books at one time and no borrower could return them the same day. "What do you *mean* coming here the same day?" she would ask the rapid reader who dared to try.[5] When the librarian refused to let Eudora take out an adult book, independent-minded Chestina went back with her to tell Miss Parker that her little girl could check out any book she wanted except books by Elsie Dinsmore. (Miss Parker also often said to little girls, "What do you *mean* coming here without a slip on? I can see right through you.")

At the library, Eudora discovered series of books—*Oz, The Little Colonel, The Green Fairy Book* (and the *Red, Blue,* etc. *Fairy Books*). When her grandfather in Ohio sent her a dollar for Christmas, she went to Kress's and bought ten volumes in the Campfire Girls series. She was disappointed in them, and eventually in all series (although she did say once that *Automobile Girls Along the Hudson* was her favorite book). Then she discovered Mark Twain on the shelves at home—twenty-four volumes and "good all the way through."[6] (It is *very* odd that she did not turn to her mother's volumes of Dickens.)

When she was grown, she continued to read voraciously, everything from the Irish poets to mystery stories. She would obligingly write a blurb or even a preface for almost any book if a friend requested it, and that required reading the books. She seemed to read everything, but she did make some exceptions. In 1949, she could not finish Mary McCarthy's utopian novel, *The Oasis.* One thing that turned her off was obscenity. When she had to read stacks of novels by authors up for grants from the Institute of Arts and Letters, she complained that there were so many four-letter words in them that it was hard to tell one novel from another.[7]

Her interest in mysteries never flagged; she wrote countless blurbs for the mystery stories that her friend Joan Kahn published at Harper & Row.

Mentioning her devotion to the genre to an interviewer from the *New York Times Book Review,* she admitted that she once wrote Ross Macdonald a fan letter but never mailed it. "I was afraid he'd think it . . . icky," she said. When Macdonald read the interview, he wrote Eudora a fan letter because he had been reading her books. They struck up quite a correspondence. John Leonard, then the editor of the *Book Review,* asked Eudora to review Macdonald's *The Underground Man* in 1971. She called it a "stunning achievement" in a four-thousand-word review, which the copy editor "reluctantly whittled down to a manageable twenty-five hundred."

When Leonard learned later that Eudora and Macdonald just happened to be in New York and staying at the Algonquin, he made sure the two writers met.[8] Macdonald dedicated *The Sleeping Beauty* to Eudora in 1973, and she returned the favor in 1978, dedicating her book of essays *The Eye of the Story* to Kenneth Millar (Macdonald's real name).

The work of William Faulkner obviously meant a lot to Eudora, as did the books of Anton Chekhov, Jane Austen, Henry Green, Willa Cather, E. M. Forster, Nathaniel Hawthorne, V. S. Pritchett, and Virginia Woolf. When she reviewed a book, she nearly always found something good to say about it. She liked books in a wholehearted, old-fashioned way, and her reviews and critical articles vibrate with her admiration and enjoyment of the work she is writing about. Not for her the tedious academic analysis meant to impress. She offers joyous appreciation and communicates her enthusiasm with specific examples. Here she is on Jane Austen: ". . . the noise! What a commotion comes out of their pages! Jane Austen loved high spirits, she had them herself, and she always rejoiced in the young. The exuberance of her youthful characters is one of the unaging delights in her work."[9]

In the spring of 1977, Eudora went to Cornell University to talk about Chekhov. In preparation, she reread the works she knew and read others for the first time. It was "just like the angels singing" to her.[10] James McConkey, a professor at Cornell, had organized a year-long celebration of Chekhov, with contemporary writers coming in one at a time to talk about him. "I reasoned this way," he said. "I like Chekhov. And these are writers that I like. Therefore, they must like Chekhov." His logic was sound. Eudora had always admired Chekhov. She once told a group of students at Agnes Scott that she had learned the most from Chekhov. Read all of Chekhov, she told them.[11] She felt that Chekhov was "kindred," and agreed with Stark Young that Chekhov was very close to the South in the way he took for granted a sense of family. Russian humor was like southern humor, she said. In *Uncle Vanya* and *The Cherry Orchard*, people were always gathered together and talking and talking, but no one was really listening.[12]

Rereading Nathaniel Hawthorne's *Tales and Sketches* in 1980 was wonderful, Eudora said, "one masterpiece after the other."[13] When she was one of four readers chosen to celebrate the publication of the first four volumes of the Library of America at the Pierpont Morgan Library, Eudora chose "The Birth-mark," Hawthorne's tale of a beautiful young wife with a mark on her cheek and her husband's fatal decision to remove it.

Chapter 67

O x f o r d

1 9 7 9

Eudora was back in England for most of the summer of 1979, artist-in-residence at the British Studies Program sponsored by several small southern colleges at University College, Oxford. The dean of the program, English professor Yerger Clifton of Rhodes College, then Southwestern, had asked her to "share her sensibilities and critical abilities."[1]

Clifton was from Jackson but had been educated at Oxford and at Trinity College, Dublin. He had spent so much time in the British Isles that he had an accent that was half English, half southern. One day one of the students asked Eudora where she was from.

"Jackson," said Eudora.

"Dr. Clifton is from Jackson, but you don't talk like him," the student replied.

"Oh, yes," said Eudora, "everybody in Mississippi talks like Dr. Clifton."[2]

Eudora was very visible—she ate meals in hall and attended the morning lectures by British scholars. She particularly enjoyed Stanley Bindoff's lecture about the princes in the Tower, because he discussed Josephine Tey's *Daughter of Time,* one of her favorite mystery novels, which concerned the princes' death.

"She was lionized at Oxford," said William P. Cocke, a Sewanee professor who taught there that summer. "Lord Goodman, the master of University College, Isaiah Berlin, A. L. Rowse, John Bayley—they all wanted to meet her."[3]

A. L. Rowse had long admired Eudora's work. In 1956, when Rowse visited Duke, he told William Hamilton that he was "madly jealous" of him because he was a friend of Eudora's. Rowse had read all her books he could get his hands on and had talked about her with Elizabeth Bowen and longed to meet her.[4]

"Eudora fitted in at Oxford," Rowse said. "Those wonderful large intelligent eyes, responding to everything. She didn't talk much—like a true novelist, she was observing and taking in everything. She said she was awed by all the historic beauty of Oxford, but otherwise she gave the impression of being one of the girl students. That was her youth of spirit, her sweetness, and her modesty. It is a mistake to be too modest. Eudora was so set on keeping her life private that people overlooked her great distinction. They need to be *told* what is what. But Eudora held back."[5]

Like other staff members, Eudora had groups of students in her rooms for tea a couple of afternoons a week. "Everybody got to go to at least one tea with her," said Katherine Merrill, a Birmingham-Southern student. "You got the invitation in the mail the day before and you had to dress up and go, but everybody wanted to go. I had the immense pleasure of walking around Oxford with Eudora Welty and A. L. Rowse one day. He was there for several days, and they were always talking or out walking. They had a mutual admiration society. I asked her one time if she was working on a new book, and she said she was working on a story about a woman named Terri. She was using the contemporary name, she said, because she was writing about a strong, independent woman."[6]

The students enjoyed Eudora immensely. "She was eager to interact," recalled John Blincow, a Sewanee student. "She wanted to mix, and she went on sightseeing trips that the session sponsored. She was a great storyteller—her recollections of the thirties and forties were striking."[7] To another student, she seemed frail on first meeting, but a "certain intensity came out when she read or lectured."[8] The same experience was reported by another student, who said, "What I found most interesting was the way this quiet, grandmotherly person was transformed into an actress and entertainer when she read some of her short stories . . . It was as if Eudora Welty lived *through* this character in 'Why I Live at the P.O.' "[9]

After tea with the students, Eudora joined faculty members and their wives for drinks in the senior common room. (The Americans had bought bourbon on the plane and brought it down to Oxford.) She joined teachers too for trips to theaters and concerts. With the Cockes, she went for lunch at a tavern on the river outside Oxford where peacocks strutted and also to an outdoor performance of *A Midsummer Night's Dream*. She saw *The Importance of Being Earnest* with Joseph and Mary Sue Cushman.

One morning she told Cocke she needed help to get her hair done.

"Eudora, I never have done anybody's hair," Cocke said.

Eudora explained that she didn't know where to go. Cocke made a few inquiries and went back to suggest Selfridge's. The next day he asked her, "Well, how did it go?"

"Not very well," Eudora said.

"Why?" said Cocke. "Your hair looks nice."

"I didn't hear any gossip," Eudora said. "I don't go to get my hair done. I go to hear gossip."[10]

This is indeed an appropriate comment from the author of "The Petrified Man," a story that is a monologue by a beauty parlor operator.

Chapter 68

"Mississippi
Joins the World"
1980

William Winter, young and progressive, was elected governor of Mississippi in 1979. Moderates rejoiced at this signal that the state's long war against civil rights and modern times was over. Winter underlined the change in the atmosphere when he invited both Eudora Welty and Margaret Walker, an African American writer from Jackson, to read at festivities celebrating his inauguration in 1980. Eudora raised her voice in a paean of thanksgiving. "Mississippi is no island," she said in her speech. "We have . . . consciously and voluntarily joined the world."

"No one thought he could be elected," she said of Winter to a friend, "except that he was defeated before by a scoundrel, so when he ran again, for the third time, I think everybody thought, well, look what we got when we didn't vote for him."[1]

In early June, Eudora received the Presidential Medal of Freedom from President Jimmy Carter on the South Lawn of the White House. "Oh, you're famous now, Eudora, sure enough," said a southerner at the ceremonies. "Did they give you a lot of money, too?" "No," Eudora said, "and I don't need any with what I got." She was as pleased with the award "as a dog with two tails," according to Henry Mitchell of the *Washington Post*.[2] The medal was gold and red enamel with five eagles forming a circle on the outside.

The whole thing hung from a blue-and-white ribbon. Eudora told reporters that she was working on a story in her head. "It doesn't seem to fit as a short story, but it's not at all something I want to make a novel of," she said.

Eudora was putting up a good front for the friend who asked her about money. The only reason she continued to travel to colleges and read, she said, was because she needed the money. Friends conspired to do something about this. Walker Percy knew that Robert Coles was on the board of the Lyndhurst Foundation in Chattanooga, which gives grants of substantial support for three years to "individuals of promise or distinction." Percy mentioned to Coles that Eudora was "near the edge" financially, and Coles mentioned it to his fellow trustees, who were, according to Coles, "pleased, *honored,* to extend to Miss Welty the Lyndhurst Prize."[3] It carried a substantial cash benefit.

Later that year she received more cash awards—the 1979 Medal for Literature from the American Book Awards was accompanied by a $15,000 cash prize. In 1989 the National Endowment for the Arts gave her an award of $40,000, no strings attached. In 1991 she received the $20,000 Peggy V. Helmerich Distinguished Author Award, the National Book Foundation's Medal for Distinguished Contribution to American Letters (with a $10,000 prize), and the Rea Award for the Short Story (with a $25,000 prize).

Collected Stories, published in 1980, brought together all Eudora's stories from the four previous collections and added the two civil rights stories, "Where Is the Voice Coming From?" and "The Demonstrators." Rereading all her own stories was "like watching a negative develop, slowly coming clear before your eyes. It was like recovering a memory," she said.[4] In December, *People* magazine named Eudora one of the "25 Most Intriguing People of 1980." The publication of the *Collected Stories* showed, the magazine said, that she had "no living rival in the fine Southern art of storytelling. The vast blue eyes of Eudora Welty take in everything. From shrewd observation of the human comedy in her lifelong home of Jackson, Miss., Welty has constructed a body of fiction that invests the grotesque with meaning and the ordinary with beauty."[5]

By this time local papers had begun to refer to Eudora routinely as "Mississippi's greatest living writer" and "national treasure" when they printed the news of her activities: reading at the Millsaps Friday Forum; being honored by the Friends of Belhaven College Library; being the subject, with Walker Evans, of a book of photographs; appearing on three segments of the series *The Originals: The Writer in America,* on PBS.

When Eudora traded in her old typewriter for an electric model in April 1981, it made headlines in the *Jackson Daily News.* She was very pleased that Royal Typewriter gave her a fifty-dollar trade-in toward a new electric. "Go back and get that typewriter," someone said. "They'll sell it for a souvenir." The newspapers commented on her modesty in not selling it herself as a souvenir.

The April 3, 1981, issue of *Publishers Weekly* ran a photograph of the Raiders, the football team of the Archbishop Rummel High School in Metairie, Louisiana, wearing T-shirts with the legend "I Love Eudora Welty." The boys were the founding fathers of the Eudora Welty Adoration Society, *PW* reported, and claimed they had won the district championship because they were on a literary high.

In late 1981, Greenville businessman LeRoy Percy suggested at a meeting of the Millsaps College board of trustees that Millsaps establish a chair in southern studies, to be held by a visiting scholar each year. Percy said that the First Mississippi Corporation, of which he was chairman, would contribute $250,000 to the endowment. (LeRoy Percy was Walker Percy's brother and had a son on the English faculty at Millsaps.) Welty, also a member of the board of trustees at Millsaps, thought it would be a wonderful thing. "I was nodding my head at everything he said," she said. "I was ready to second the motion." Then Percy proposed that the chair be named the Eudora Welty Chair of Southern Studies. "In my honor! Nothing could have pleased me more," said Eudora.[6]

Walker Percy was Eudora's first choice to be the first occupant of the chair, but he refused; Cleanth Brooks took it instead, in the spring of 1983. But Walker Percy did speak at the ceremonies marking the inauguration of the chair, choosing as his topic "Novel Writing in an Apocalyptic Time."

Chapter 69

Uncle Daniel Sings

1982

In 1979, Alice Parker, a Boston-born, Juilliard-educated composer who had worked as an arranger for the Robert Shaw Chorale for twenty years, paid sixty cents in a secondhand book store for a copy of *The Ponder Heart*. She loved it and decided to turn it into an opera. She did not see a single operatic stereotype in the whole thing. "It was totally believable. I couldn't get it out of my head," she said.[1] After receiving permission to base an opera on the book, Parker wrote a libretto and composed music that "grew out of the cadences of Southern speech and included blues and rags, spirituals and barbershop quartets."[2]

When Parker brought her book and music to Jackson, Eudora invited people from New Stage, where she was a board member, to come and listen as Parker played and sang the whole thing. Everyone liked it. When no other theater would produce it, New Stage decided to do it themselves. They put on a two-week workshop session while they worked to raise the money for a full production in Jackson. A grant of $48,000 from the Mississippi Department of Economic Development stimulated private and corporate donors to bankroll the $138,000 production.

William Partland, New Stage's professional director, cast all but six of the parts locally and chose the musicians from the Jackson Symphony. Two nights of previews and two nights of performances were set in September. Rehearsals, with Eudora and Parker both in attendance, began on August 1, 1982. Although Eudora was not officially involved with the opera production, she admitted that she was totally caught up in it. "I wouldn't dream of saying, 'I think it ought to be done this way.' I was just there to be a kind of resource," she said.[3] Partland, however, said she was invaluable. "She cured one scene by saying, 'Well, what we don't want to do here is *dither,*'" he said.[4]

Newspapers from all over the country sent reporters and music critics to opening night. CBS-TV's *Morning News* interviewed Eudora in her back yard. Townspeople joined in the excitement—the theater's cleaning lady had tickets, and so did the proprietors of Fannye Mae's Beauty Parlor, where Eudora got her hair done every Wednesday at one-thirty. Eudora drove her old red Oldsmobile to the airport six times to meet friends from out of town, Reynolds Price from Durham and Joan Kahn from New York among them.

Opening night was another one of those gala, celebratory events with which Jackson showed its affection and respect for Eudora. Lamar Life Insurance Company bought an advertisement for the back cover of the program that proclaimed, "The genius of authoress Eudora Welty is a reflection of her father: Christian Webb Welty, who also became a legend in his own time." A black-tie party at the governor's mansion preceded the opening, and after the show, a Jackson woman entertained 350 people for dinner. "The people [Eudora] knew—and she seemed to know most people at both parties—would approach her, grasp her long, slender hands and lean forward to hear her soft voice. Then they'd smile and laugh at something funny she'd said."[5]

Critics spoke well of the book but found fault with the music, although *Opera News* praised the barbershop quartet version of the newspaper ad in which Uncle Daniel asks Bonnie Dee to return home.

The opera production made Eudora think more about Uncle Daniel. A young woman working at the theater had asked her, "What is it with Uncle Daniel? Is he spacy or something?"

"Not to me," said Eudora.

"Is he naive?" asked the young woman.

"He's *innocent,*" said Eudora.

It made her wonder, she said, whether a certain kind of southern bachelor who lived with his parents and remained good and simple and unchanged by experience had died out.

New Stage turned a profit of $50,000 on the opera and established an endowment to produce one new play each year in a series that they named for Eudora. It was perfectly fitting, said Jane Reid Petty, New Stage's director, since Eudora had been a board member for years, always supportive and generous. "She would never accept any royalties from New Stage," Petty said.

Reynolds Price's *Private Contentment,* a play originally written for television, was chosen to be the first production in the series. The whole thing, said Eudora, "just stops me in joy . . . in my tracks."[6]

Chapter 70

Harvard and Stanford

1983

David Herbert Donald, chairman of the program in the history of American civilization at Harvard, was in charge of a new lecture series at the university. A native of Mississippi and a graduate of Millsaps, Donald thought it would be nice to have a southerner as the first Massey Lecturer. He and Daniel Aaron, another professor in the program, chose Eudora Welty.

At first Eudora said she could not possibly lecture to graduate students at Harvard. "I'm not an academic," she said. "I don't know anything they don't know better."

"You know one thing," Aaron said. "That's what in your life made you become a writer."

Eudora began to think about it, "and it rather interested me," she said.[1] In the course of a year, she wrote three lectures: "Listening," which described how her literary sensibility awakened through hearing gossip; "Learning to See," which told how she began to see things and try to capture them; and "Finding a Voice," in which she read from several of her short stories and talked about each one.

The lectures were scheduled for the last week in April 1983, in Longfellow Hall at the Graduate School of Education. When David Donald introduced her, he announced that she had just won the American Book Award for paperback fiction for her *Collected Stories.* Then he quoted from Eudora's essay "The Radiance of Jane Austen" and introduced her as "our own Jane Austen."

Eudora was nervous about the lectures. As she began, she explained that it was hard to speak about herself, but the audience was so receptive at the first lecture that she relaxed. The *Harvard Crimson* reported that crowds of more than 450 "swarmed" the auditorium to hear all three talks and that overflow crowds watched it on closed-circuit television in another room.

Eudora pointed out in her first lecture that "I never do get very old in these lectures," and indeed she talked about her development as a writer from childhood only until the time she began to publish short stories. She received an extended standing ovation at the end of the third lecture, and afterward "listeners, bringing flowers, waited in long lines for the privilege of speaking to her. Not bunches of flowers. Just one flower."[2]

"Everyone liked the lectures," Daniel Aaron said, but one senior said later, "To me there was something wrong about that small, honest figure at the center of primed, anticipatory, well-read lit crit groupies. It was almost like seeing a Delta bluesman before a respectful, befurred audience at Carnegie Hall—it's the right kind of art in the wrong sort of venue."[3]

A few months later, the creative writing program at Stanford University invited Eudora to Palo Alto to read. Her short stories were taught in Stanford's survey courses and one of her novels would be included when a professor organized a course in southern literature, but John L'Heureux, the program director, did not think that she would be as big a draw as Grace Paley or Donald Barthelme or E. L. Doctorow, for instance, had been.

Andrew Hudgins, the Alabama-born Wallace Stegner Fellow in Poetry at Stanford that year, was called on to be her driver because, he says, he had a southern accent. As he drove Eudora and L'Heureux toward Kresge Auditorium for the reading, Eudora said to L'Heureux, "I hope you won't be too disappointed if only a few people turn up." L'Heureux reassured her routinely.

They were greeted by an overflowing house, which astonished both Eudora and her escorts. Thirteen hundred people were packed into the auditorium, which had a capacity of six hundred. Fans sat in the aisles and on the steps to the stage, and even perched cross-legged on the stage itself.

Hudgins, with Eudora in tow, had to push a way through the crowd as he shouted, "Coming through, please. Please let Miss Welty through."[4]

The reading began, but when an "elderly gentleman" fainted in the back of the packed auditorium, campus police insisted that Eudora stop reading so they could clear the hall. It was unsafe, they said. Everyone who did not have a seat had to go outside, and the reading was not to resume until a large video screen and speakers could be set up outdoors. Eudora sat on the stage, signing autographs for people who brought books up to her, while outside the ejected crowd grew restless and resentful. Hudgins pondered with some delight the prospect of a Eudora Welty riot at Stanford University. "Welty was overwhelmed by the size of the audience, but she appeared calm, gracious, and eager to please," L'Heureux said later.[5]

Eventually, Hudgins, who stood outside, heard "Why I Live at the P.O." and "Powerhouse" "roll out of the speakers. It was one of the two or three best readings I've ever heard," he said. "And for the first time I 'got' 'Powerhouse' on a level other than the intellectual."[6]

"We failed to consider how phenomenally attractive she is to millions," L'Heureux told the student newspaper. "And here they are."[7] Years later, he recalled Eudora as the "most giving and accessible of our readers."[8]

One Writer's Beginnings

1 9 8 4

In February 1984 the Harvard University Press published Eudora's Harvard lectures as *One Writer's Beginings,* a memoir that promptly garnered lavish reviews, became a raging best-seller, and stayed on the *New York Times* best-seller list for almost a year. It was the first best-seller the Harvard Press had ever had, and it is worth noting that it was written by a woman, and a *southern* woman at that. When Eudora autographed the book at Lemuria Bookshop in Jackson on Valentine's Day, the store sold 650 copies in one day.

The whole thing was unbelievable, and she was thrilled, she told the *New York Times.* "I knew the lectures would turn into a book, but it never occurred to me that it would be of interest outside Boston."[1] She wanted to get back to work on the short stories she had interrupted to write the memoir, she added.

One Writer's Beginnings is warm, appealing, beautifully written, and full of information about Eudora's childhood and the forces that drove her to become a writer. But there were those who found it too good to be true. "No memoir has been more admired and loved in recent years," wrote Carolyn G. Heilbrun some time later. "I do not believe in the bittersweet quality of *One Writer's Beginnings,* nor do I suppose that the Eudora Welty there evoked could have written the stories and novels we have learned to celebrate . . . She wishes to keep meddling hands off the life. To her, this is the only proper behavior for the Mississippi lady she so proudly is . . . There can be no question that to have written a truthful autobiography would have defied every one of her instincts for loyalty and privacy." Heilbrun conceded that Welty was the "kindest, gentlest person imaginable" and speculated that life might be better "if we were all like Eudora Welty," but she went on to decry the "nostalgia" in *One Writer's Beginnings,* which "must mask the unrecognized anger from her childhood."[2]

An astonishing number of people agreed with Heilbrun, finding something fishy about *One Writer's Beginnings* and calling the whole thing "too happy to be credible." In an unusual show of spirit, Eudora denounced literary critics in general and feminist critics in particular. "There's a whole gang of them," she said. "I cannot follow anything these writers say . . . It's terribly boring." She singled out "one feminist" who she said took her to task for not telling the truth about herself in her autobiography. "I'm glad I had a nice childhood; I learned a lot from my childhood," she said.[3]

Partial confirmation of Eudora's rendering of a happy, sheltered, and carefree life for well-off white children in Jackson comes from *The World from Gillespie Place,* by Seta Alexander Sancton, who grew up in Jackson at the same time and recalls the same cozy world of comfortable home, affluent family, and kindly community. A feminist critic might point out that Seta and Eudora are both southern ladies, conditioned to paint a rosy picture of home and family. But this carries regional stereotyping to a comic extreme. Southern ladies have been known to complain about their childhoods.

"An autobiography is the truest of all books," Mark Twain wrote to William Dean Howells, "for while it inevitably consists mainly of extinctions of the truth, shirkings of the truth, partial revealments of the truth, with hardly an instance of plain straight truth, the remorseless truth is there, between the lines."

Even though all memoirs are false to some extent, *One Writer's Beginnings* may be less false than tell-all, let-it-all-hang-out autobiographies, which are often extremely unfair to other members of the writer's families. As someone has wisely pointed out, memoirs tell more about the person at the time they were written than they do about the time written about. In decrying the "accuracy" of *One Writer's Beginnings,* critics overlook what it reveals about Eudora's character in her mature years. Of course there were dark moments in her childhood and adolescence. No girl could go through high school without a real date and not know the nature of true suffering. A little girl with a mother like Chestina, who set high standards for her daughter, is bound to feel some resentment and rebellion. A woman with a brother who had a "nervous breakdown" must have felt from time to time that her family was dysfunctional.

But the secret of true happiness is often the ability to recall a childhood as happy, to have worked through all the horrors and terrors and put them behind, and, freed of them, to describe the early years in a family with humor and grace.

Eudora makes her childhood look happy, ignoring a difficult mother and a troubled brother, and in doing so she tells us a lot about her own inner strength, her own secure evaluation of herself, and her success at coming to terms with life as it is. The grownup who can understand that her parents did the best they could is the rich and happy person. By many standards, Eudora Welty's life has been a long ordeal of personal loss, grief, hard work, and loneliness. The fact that she does not see it that way adds to her glory.

Eudora certainly reveals no intimate details of her love life or sex life in her memoir—she makes a point of stopping while she was still quite young. She once told an interviewer that she was a private person and was puzzled that people would want to know about her private life. "People ask anything personal," she said. "People will raise their hands and ask about my sex life. I say, 'Isn't that a private matter?' I'm amazed people are interested in such things. I think it's funny. I'm not outraged. I'm just a private person, but I tell my innermost secrets through my fiction. It's all there. I'm just trying to make a point in fiction."[4]

But what can we learn about Eudora's innermost life from her fiction? Of all her fictional characters, she has said she has most in common with Miss Eckhart in "June Recital," the old maid music teacher whose art is of paramount importance, a woman of hidden passion who tries to throw herself into the grave of the one man who might have been her suitor. Eudora has also said that *The Optimist's Daughter,* in which the heroine, Laurel, is widowed young after a brief marriage and is haunted by her family's past, is autobiographical. Other bits and pieces of real life are scattered about in her work, but if she has told her "innermost secrets" in her fiction, she has told them in code.

I think there are two conclusions we can draw about her private life. First, there are simply some things that we do not know and may never know about Eudora Welty, such as the real nature of her relationship with Elizabeth Bowen. Second, and at the same time, I suspect there is not an awful lot more to know. Like Miss Eckhart, she has found adventure and passion in her work. Unlike Miss Eckhart, she has found joy in a wide circle of loving friends. She has come to terms with her own past and with her family.

USA Today named *One Writer's Beginnings* one of the ten best books of 1984, and its design won it a place in the 1984 Book Show sponsored by the American Institute of Graphic Arts, which listed its author as Eudora Welty and its photographer as Christian Welty.

While *One Writer's Beginnings* was rocketing into the stratosphere, Eudora celebrated her seventy-fifth birthday. She marked the occasion by presenting five hundred negatives of photographs taken by her father to the Mississippi Department of Archives. The gift was "doing honor to my roots," she said.[5] And the archives in turn mounted an exhibition of Welty family photographs at the Old Capitol Museum to celebrate her birthday. Patti Carr Black, the director of the museum, used the photographs in a catalogue of the exhibition, and Eudora furnished captions orally as she identified the pictures for Black.

Jackson went all out to celebrate Eudora's birthday, which came in the middle of the Southern Literary Festival at Millsaps on April 12–14. The festival had as its theme "Honoring the Seventy-Fifth Birthday of Eudora Welty." Eudora's eyesight was still good, though her hearing had diminished somewhat. She was still writing, she insisted. She was charitable toward the scholars who were doggedly analyzing her work at the Southern Literary Festival. "I think that whatever makes people feel in touch with a [she paused to think this through] . . . with a work of art—let's call it what it is, or what we all hope it is—is helpful," she said.[6]

Eudora herself read a short story she had written at sixteen, which had just been returned to her by Ralph Hilton, who had kept it for sixty years.

"Most of it is pretty bad," she said before she began. "A lot of it sounds like a prissy little girl saying, 'See how smart I am?' " One reporter mentioned that she described some sound as "like fat people falling downstairs."[7]

Eudora, wearing an orchid corsage "as big as a catcher's mitt," attended the whole symposium. "I just feel like it's all for me and it would be rude to miss one of the speakers," she said. "I can just hear my mother saying, 'Girl, you're getting a little too much attention.' " She had, she said, gotten so much attention that she began to think she "had no use here on earth."[8]

On her actual birthday, in the middle of the festival, the University of Mississippi Center for the Study of Southern Culture entertained at a champagne supper in her honor at the home of Mrs. Warren D. Reimers. Stephen Spender and Ellen Gilchrist were among the guests, as were the celebrities speaking at the festival. Out-of-town reporters wrote enthusiastically about Mrs. Reimers's white-columned mansion and the refreshments, which were very southern and mostly white—cayenne-spiced cheese straws shaped like the state of Mississippi, chicken biscuit sandwiches, fresh strawberries, and cakes. Eudora, clad in shimmering pearl gray, sat in a big chair and sipped champagne while the guests went over one by one and knelt at her side to converse.

The best time for Eudora was after the festival, when she and a few of her best friends went to Bill's Burger House, her favorite Jackson restaurant since the Rotisserie had closed. Bill did not have a liquor license, but he always brought out a bottle of bourbon from the back for Eudora.[9]

Bill's was really a burger house by day, but at night it became a Greek restaurant where Bill cooked for his special patrons. He had invited Eudora for a birthday party, and his two little girls made decorations out of tissue paper and blew up balloons. Bill made a cake in the shape of a book, with a bookmark inscribed in icing "God Bless America and Eudora on her 75th birthday." Greek music played through speakers, Bill poured Greek wine, and in came a belly dancer. After every whirl, the belly dancer would stop and stare at Eudora and say, "Happy birthday." She even had "Happy Birthday" written on her belly.[10]

There were other high notes. *People* named Eudora one of "Ten Great Faces" in its cover story on April 30, 1984, along with pop celebrities such as Princess Diana, Meryl Streep, and Mick Jagger. To choose the ten, the magazine had consulted modeling-agency head Eileen Ford, writers Truman Capote and Gloria Steinem, photographer Yosuf Karsh, film producer Robert Evans, and artist Andy Warhol. Steinem said that Eudora was an ordinary woman, "yet in those eyes is the whole world." Capote said that you would never forget her face. And in January 1985, *W,* the diary, if not the Bible, of the fashion industry, listed Eudora as someone who had style. She was in motley company this time, with Ronald Reagan, Prince Edward, Leontyne Price, the concierges at the Ritz Hotel in Madrid, Calvin Klein, Annie Dillard, and Ross Perot.

The girl who was remembered for being so ugly had reached a pinnacle where her looks and style clearly eclipsed those of the Jackson belles who had been invited to dances in the Delta. She had achieved a great deal, by persistence and hard work at her art, by never faltering as a dutiful daughter, and by cultivating the quiet modesty that struck everyone she met.

Chapter 72

The Last Chapter

A storm coated Jackson in thick ice in the winter of 1985. Many people were without light and heat for several days. Eudora's electricity stayed on and her telephone continued to function, but she was housebound for nearly a week. Most dogs refused to go outdoors, but Charlotte Capers's dog did venture out and returned with a frozen mouse. Eudora said she was able to get some writing done while she was isolated.[1]

After the storm, in May, Eudora went to New York to read at the Pierpont Morgan Library. The director, Charles Ryskamp, invited her to read for the annual meeting of the Association of Fellows of the library, but so many people wanted to hear her that he had to schedule two readings, one for the fellows and one the night before for other people.

Local honors multiplied. The Mississippi Department of Archives and History began a year-long program, funded partly by the Mississippi Committee for the Humanities, to encourage the appreciation and understanding of Eudora's work all over the state. Suzanne Marrs, a professor at the State University of New York in Oswego, was appointed scholar-in-residence to implement the program. During her first six months, Marrs compiled her elegant catalogue of the Welty papers in the archives; then she crisscrossed the state, talking about Eudora's works at seminars for English teachers, on radio programs, in libraries, and in classrooms.[2] In Pascagoula, for example, Marrs drew a standing-room-only crowd composed of lawyers, senior citizens, teachers, high school students, librarians, businessmen, and aspiring writers. All programs were free and open to the public. Not many times has a state paid someone to promote the work of one of its authors.

When the Jackson public library moved to new quarters in the remodeled Sears, Roebuck building on North State Street in early 1986, the city council voted unanimously to name it the Eudora Welty Library. The library opened with yet another hometown celebration of Eudora Welty, this one called "A Toast to Eudora." The Friends of the Library invited everyone in town to come, eat, listen to the Chimneyville Jazz Band, and view the new facility.

Not long after the library opened, Eudora deeded her home to the Mississippi Department of Archives and History. This enabled her to occupy it as long as she lived without paying taxes. In 1995 the Mississippi legislature appropriated funds to buy Eudora's birthplace at 714 North Congress Street and turn it into a writers' center, so both the Welty homes in Jackson would be preserved. To get money to maintain the house on Pinehurst, the Mississippi Department of Archives and History in 1992 sponsored the production of sixty portfolios of her photographs and put them up for sale at $7,500 apiece. Each portfolio contained sixteen-by-twenty-inch prints. Eudora, who retained the copyright, got five portfolios but no money. She was anxious that everyone understand that she was not "even indirectly receiving any benefit" from the project. The first portfolio was auctioned, while the other fifty-four were sold through the Old Capitol Museum. Profits were split sixty-forty between the archives and the printing company, and the archives intended to place two thirds of its share, about $80,000, in a trust fund for the management of Eudora's residence after her death.[3]

Eudora's willingness to perform civic good deeds was stretched almost to the ridiculous that same month. The renovated Jitney Jungle #14, where Eudora and her mother had shopped for groceries since 1929, opened at the corner of Fortification and North Jefferson streets. It had been the first self-service grocery store in Jackson. Eudora wrote a testimonial that appeared in the full-page newspaper advertisement announcing the reopening. "The store was just a novelty," she said, "the very conception of it something totally new. This was the first store where you actually go behind the counter to get what you needed . . . I feel the same way about Jitney #14 as I do about story writing . . . you can't live in the past and you must be aware of reality. You need to reflect change and progress with the times."[4]

"I still have stories to write," Eudora announced in 1988. "I need six weeks without distraction to work on a couple of stories in my mind." Since the arthritis in her hands prevented her from typing, she wrote in longhand, trying to get used to working with a typist.[5] She described an ideal work day as being uninterrupted by telephone or doorbell, stopping for a drink—bourbon and water—and watching the *MacNeil-Lehrer NewsHour.* Then she would like to do something different, see a friend and go out for dinner. "Even if I found out the next day that what I had done was really not very good, I would know it was important, because it was a bridge to something. I would know where to go from there. I don't think any writing is ever really lost, because it all teaches you something. Even the bad teaches you something."[6]

On Eudora's eightieth birthday, in 1989, Roger Mudd served as master of ceremonies when the Jackson Symphony Orchestra performed two new works dedicated to Eudora by Mississippi composers. Both rated standing ovations. At the concert's close, the audience sang "Happy Birthday" and gave Eudora a standing ovation.

Later, in October, the Friends of the Eudora Welty Library staged a fund-raising art sale called "Homage to Eudora Welty." Twenty-five artists had based work on a line or a theme from a Welty story. The most remarkable was a recreation of the table that Mrs. Morrison described to her son, Loch, after the rook party in "June Recital": "an orange scooped out and filled with orange juice, with the top put back on and decorated with icing leaves, a straw stuck in. A slice of pineapple and a heap of candied sweet potatoes on it, and a little handle of pastry. A cup made out of toast, filled with creamed chicken, fairly warm. A sweet peach pickle with flower petals around it of different-colored cream cheese. A swan made of a cream puff. He had whipped cream feathers, a pastry neck, green icing eyes. A pastry biscuit the size of a marble with a little date filling."

In November, *Photographs,* a collection of photographs taken by Eudora from the 1920s to 1950, was published by the University Press of Mississippi. Eudora wrote nothing new for the book, but talked at length for an interview, which served as an introduction.

Eudora told a reporter in October 1990 that she woke up early every morning, made coffee, and went into the lounge to write. She said she hesitated to begin a story unless she felt she would have time to give to it at the right moment, but that she liked to work on a story when she was "in the grip of a powerful idea."[7] Another interviewer that year found her "haggard," and the house shabby with an "antique television on a rickety stand with rabbit ears for antenna . . . And a sofa completely inundated with books."

That same year Eudora was injured in an airport. Arthritis coupled with osteoporosis made it difficult for her to go up and down stairs. When the airport elevator was broken, airline employees carried her up a flight of stairs—and dropped her. She was in the hospital for a month. When she went home, her nieces established her downstairs for good.[8] A nurse came in every morning to help care for her and to drive her anywhere she wanted to go, including the beauty parlor.

The accident was a turning point. Until this time, Eudora had always stoutly maintained that she was still writing, but now she admitted that her writing days were over. Arthritis prevented even the use of longhand, she said, and she could not get used to dictating.[9] And her poor hearing depressed her. "I do love to hear gossip," she said.[10]

She did collaborate on an editing job. After five years of work, the *Norton Book of Friendship,* on which Eudora and Ronald A. Sharp, a professor of English at Kenyon College, had collaborated, appeared in 1992. Sharp, who had taught a course at Kenyon on the literature of friendship, had won the assignment to do the book and then asked Eudora to be a coeditor. She hesitated: she had never been a collaborator, and she was afraid she didn't know enough about the subject. After a forty-minute conversation, she agreed. Sharp, who brought a scholar's point of view, was delighted at Eudora's creative ideas. At the last stage, when they had assembled all the pieces they wanted to include, they rented the room the Rotary Club used at the Sheraton Hotel in Jackson in which to do the final sorting and arranging. Each contributed an introduction. "It was so much fun to do," Eudora said, "we should have made another book with all the things we had to leave out."[11]

. . .

By this time Eudora had been sanctified, canonized, apotheosized in Jackson, the town where she had ridden her bicycle around the rotunda of the state capitol, where she had made friends, if not conquests, in high school, where she had first begun to write, and where she had written nearly all of her work. The town had nurtured her and now it rewarded her. Her portrait hangs in the Eudora Welty Public Library, where the staff tells visitors that "Miss Welty should win the Nobel prize." Another portrait hangs in the library of the Mississippi Department of Archives and History, where her papers are kept. Still another portrait hangs at Millsaps College, where she taught writing and served on the board of trustees. A photograph of her and a selection of large prints of her early photographs adorn the walls of the café at the State Art Museum. Everyone speaks reverently of "Miss Welty."

Eudora told a reporter that she was still waiting for the expected moment of adulthood, when a transformation would come over her. "I keep looking forward to it," she told an interviewer when she was in her eighties. "Maybe it happened years ago and I didn't know it."[12]

Her life had apparently been quite satisfactory. She had traveled and seen the world, but she had always come home to Jackson. "I've stayed in one place . . . It's become a source of all the information that stirs my imagination," she said.[13]

Acknowledgments

I AM GRATEFUL to many people for the information and advice they gave me, especially Daniel Aaron, Tammy Allen, Yogi Anderson, Milton Babbitt, Hans Beacham, Carolyn Bell, John Blincow, Frances Boeckman, Bill and Raymona Bomar, R. Britt Brantley, Mildred H. Bray, Mr. and Mrs. Carroll Brinson, Clarence Brown, Robert Bullard, Peter Bunnell, Nash Burger, Alfred Bush, Ken Byerly, William Cain, Richard Calhoun, Julia Cass, Pauline Chakeris, Fannie Cheney, Flagg Chittenden, Blair Clark, William P. Cocke, William Coffey, Robert Coles, Catherine Collins, Lester Connell, Barnaby Conrad, C. W. W. Cook, George Cress, Marcie Crimmins, Mary Sue and Joe Cushman, David Daiches, Dorothea Daniel, Guy Davenport, Jack P. Dean, Jessica Delahoy, Albert Devlin, Marc Dolan, Mary Aswell Doll, Lenthiel Downs, Robert Drake, Elaine Eff, T. W. Eva, Elizabeth Evans, John Fairhall, Pic Firmin, Fannie Flagg, George Garrett, Mary Garstang, Anna Geske, William Gifford, Robert S. Gingher, Joan Givner, Gerhard von Glahn, Mary Ann Glazer, Vesta Gordon, Herschel Gower, Naomi Rabe Graham, Paola and Howard Greenfeld, Jan Nordby Gretlund, Justin Harmon, James A. Haught, Ann Hewitt, Liz and Samuel Hynes, Philip Hoare, Florence Hoffman, Helen Perry Hopkins, Andrew Hudgins, David C. Humphrey, Sally Jacobs, William Johnson, George Kennan, Stuart Kidd, John M. Kilgore, Carole Klein, Margaret Knox, Michael Kreyling, David Laskin, Nancy Lewis, John L'Heureux, W. H. Luehlfing, Joanna Maclay, Willana Buck Mallett, Rebecca Mark, James McConkey, Patsy McDaniel, Glen E. McGinnis, Paula and William McGuire, Norman McMillan, Marion Meade, Joan Mellen, Alice Merchant, Dr. Katherine Merrill, Paul Miles, Michael Milligan, Frederick Morgan, Barry Moser, Dale Mullen, Luther Munford, Carol Newell, John T. Oliver, Lisa Paddock, Jane Pepperdene, Professor Victor Perella, Mrs. Louis Pettit, Noel Polk, Tony Redd, Marion

Reel, Byron Riggan, Marshall Riggan, François Rigolot, Erling Riis II, Suzy Rivitz, Enzo Rocchigiani, Carl Rollyson, A. L. Rowse, Charles Ryskamp, Father Patrick Samway, Seta Sancton, Viola Sanders, Frances Wright Saunders, Doris Shapiro, Jerry Showalter, F. Alvin Smith, Frank Smith, Gregory Smith, Kathleen E. Smith, Robert Snow, Jack Spalding, Elinor Hegland Spring, John W. Stevenson, Charles A. Stewart III, Michael Straight, Roger Straus, Erika Foff Teahan, Stella Trafford, Jeremy Treglown, Tom Underwood, Grace Van Antwerp, Judy Waldron, Aimee Shands Walsh, William W. Ward, Scott Ware, Floyd Watkins, Howard Weinbrot, Robert Welker, Erskine Wells, Bill Whittington, Larry Williams, Joel Williamson, Jo Woestendiek, Nancy Tate Wood, and Margaret Woolover.

I owe a great deal to Welty scholars and a special debt to certain published works, without which I could scarcely have undertaken the biography: Noel Polk's *Eudora Welty: A Bibliography of Her Work;* Suzanne Marrs's *The Welty Collection;* Michael Kreyling's *Author and Agent: Eudora Welty and Diarmuid Russell;* and Peggy Prenshaw's *Conversations with Eudora Welty.*

I would also like to thank the many men and women in libraries and archives around the world who provided assistance and information: Frieda Davidson, Mississippi University for Women; Henry Holmes, Jan May, Anne L. Webster, Nancy Bounds, Victor Bailey, Joyce Smith, Joyce Dixon, Betty Robinson, Sara Clark, Marie Hays, and Forrest Galey, Mississippi Department of Archives and History; Lynne Mueller and Mattie Sink, Mississippi State University Library; Helene Whitson, Special Collections, San Francisco State University; William Roberts, Bancroft Library, University of California at Berkeley; Mary Ann Quiring, Public Library, Lewiston, Montana; Cathy Jacob, Steve Masar, Bernie Schermetzler, and Frank Cook, University of Wisconsin Archives; Margaret Goostray, Mugar Library, Boston University; Barbara Volz, Special Collections, Princeton University; Soowon Kim, Gest Oriental Library, Princeton University; Mary George, reference librarian, Princeton University; Annie Armour-Jones, University of the South Archives; Cathy Henderson, Humanities Research Center, University of Texas; Lorett Treese, Bryn Mawr College Archives; Marda Goodwin, Smith College Archives; Jacqueline Cox, Kings College Library, Cambridge University; Maris Wolfe and Michael Sims, Vanderbilt University; Kevin Ray, Washington University Library; Michael Bott, University of Reading Library; John M. Kilgore and Bernard Crystal, Special Collections, Columbia University; Joan Tafoya, Museum of Fine Arts, Santa Fe; Judy Sellers, Museum of International Folklore, Santa Fe; Elaine Felsher, Time, Inc. Archives; Alice Birney, Frederick Bauman, Ernie Emrich, Jeffrey M. Flannery, Michael Klein, Kathleen McDonough, and Mary Wolfskill, Manuscript Reference, Library of Congress; Therese Mullingan, International Museum of Photography, Rochester, New York; Susan Marcotte, Archives of American Art, Washington; Beth Alvarez, curator of literary manuscripts, University of Maryland; Carol Walter, Duke University Archives; Maurice S. Toler, university archivist, North Carolina State University; Betty Carter, archivist, University of North Carolina at Greensboro; Cecilia Steinfeldt, Witte Museum, San Antonio; Susan McAuliffe, San Antonio Museum of Art; John Leeper, Ann Jones, and Heather Lammer, McNay Museum, San Antonio; staff, Westminster Central Reference Library, London; Lynn Beideck-Porn, University of Nebraska Archives; Frank E. Stanger, Special Collections, University of Kentucky; Florence W. Hoffman, archivist,

Denison University; Kathryn L. Beam, University of Michigan Library; Lori N. Curtis, Special Collections, University of Tulsa; Dulcie Schackman, Institute of International Education; Bettie Austin, archivist, University of Arkansas; Michelle Cale, Royal Commission on Historical Manuscripts, London; Lorna Knight, Literary Manuscript Collection, National Library of Canada; Susan Thach Dean, Special Collections, University of Colorado; Christine Weideman, archivist, Beinecke Library, Yale University; Elaine Engst, curator of manuscripts, Cornell University; Stephen Ennis, manuscripts curator, Emory University; Judith Segal, library director, Hollins College; Robert T. Chapel, Library, University of Illinois at Urbana-Champaign; M. N. Brown, curator of manuscripts, Brown University.

And I appreciate the hospitality of the many who provided food and shelter when I was on research trips: Lynn Cooksey, Clovis and Maryann Heimsath, Peggy and Maurice Duvic, Abigail Trafford, Pearl and Tom McHaney, Suzy Rivitz and Tom Underwood, Peter and Catherine Waldron, and Roxane and Martin Waldron.

And a special thank-you to Celia and the late John Emmerich and to Diddle and Jackie Enochs, who first encouraged me to take on this project.

The people who read all or part of the manuscript deserve enormous thanks: Martha Lou Stohlman, Robert Sherrill, Lolly O'Brien, Ashley Brown, David Laskin, Abigail Trafford, and Nancylee Jonza.

A tip of the hat to the monthly biography seminar at New York University, where I have learned much and soaked up much encouragement, and to my various editors at Doubleday: the late Jacqueline Onassis, Deb Futter, Bruce Tracy, and the one who ended up with all the work, Betsy Lerner; and to copy editor Liz Duvall, art director Mario Pulice, and designer Maria Carella. Above all, I'm indebted to my agent, Elizabeth Frost-Knappman of New England Publishing Associates.

A Note on Sources

For information on Eudora Welty I have mined many collections of papers in various libraries. The following abbreviations are used to designate those concerned. Unless otherwise noted, a cited document can be found among the recipient's papers, as noted below:

EW.   Eudora Welty, whose papers are at the Mississippi State Department of Archives and History (MDAH), Jackson, Mississippi.

BC and FC.   Brainerd and Fannie Cheney Papers, Special Collections, Heard Library, Vanderbilt University, Nashville, Tennessee.

DR.   Diarmuid Russell.

EB.   Elizabeth Bowen, Elizabeth Bowen Papers, Harry Ransom Humanities Research Center, University of Texas, Austin.

HB and NB.   Herschel and Norma Brickell, Brickell Papers, Special Collections, University of Mississippi, Oxford.

HC.   Hubert Creekmore, Creekmore Papers, Special Collections, Mugar Library, Boston University.

JR.   John Robinson, MDAH.

JS.   Jean Stafford, Jean Stafford Papers, Rare Books Room, University Libraries, University of Colorado, Boulder.

KAP.   Katherine Anne Porter, Archives and Manuscripts, McKeldin Library, University of Maryland, College Park.

LH.   Lodwick Hartley, Southern Historical Collection, Wilson Library, University of North Carolina, Chapel Hill.

NF.   Nancy Farley, William Faulkner Collection, Alderman Library, University of Virginia, Charlottesville.

RPW.   Robert Penn Warren, *Southern Review Collection,* Beinecke Library, Yale University.

WJS.   William Jay Smith, Modern Literature Collection, Olin Library, Washington University, St. Louis, Missouri.

WH.   William Hamilton, Hamilton Papers, Perkins Library, Duke University, Durham, North Carolina.

Letters to other addressees can be found:

Cleanth Brooks, Cleanth Brooks Papers, Beinecke Library, Yale University.

Robert Daniel, Daniel Papers, Archives and Special Collections, Jessie Ball duPont Library, The University of the South, Sewanee, Tennessee.

Ford Madox Ford, Rare Books and Manuscript Collection, Carl A. Kroch Library, Cornell University, Ithaca, New York.

Joseph Henry Jackson, Bancroft Library, University of California, Berkeley.

William Van O'Connor, George Arents Research Library, University of Syracuse, Syracuse, New York.

George Marion O'Donnell, Modern Literature Collection, Olin Library, Washington University, St. Louis, Missouri.

Floyd Watkins, Robert W. Woodruff Library, Emory University, Atlanta, Georgia.

Books by Eudora Welty are identified in the notes by abbreviations:

CG.   *A Curtain of Green and Other Stories,* Doubleday, 1941.

RB.   *The Robber Bridegroom,* Doubleday, 1942.

WN.   *The Wide Net and Other Stories,* Harcourt Brace, 1943.

DW.   *Delta Wedding,* Harcourt Brace, 1946.

GA.   *The Golden Apples,* Harcourt Brace, 1949.

PH.   *The Ponder Heart,* Harcourt Brace, 1954.

BI.   *The Bride of the Innisfallen and Other Stories,* Harcourt Brace, 1955.

SB.   *The Shoe Bird,* Harcourt Brace, 1964.

LB.   *Losing Battles,* Random House, 1970.

OTOP.   *One Time, One Place,* Random House, 1971.

OD.   *The Optimist's Daughter,* Random House, 1972.

Eye.   *The Eye of the Story: Selected Essays and Reviews,* Random House, 1978.

CS.   *The Collected Stories,* Harcourt Brace, 1980.

OWB.   *One Writer's Beginnings,* Harvard University Press, 1984.

Morgana, Morgana: Two Stories from "The Golden Apples," University Press of Mississippi, 1988.

Photographs. Photographs, University Press of Mississippi, 1989.

WE.   *A Writer's Eye, Collected Book Reviews,* University Press of Mississippi, 1994.

FR.   *The Norton Book of Friendship,* editor, with Ronald Sharp, Norton, 1991.

Notes

Chapter 1:
The Teenager

1. Interview, Milton Babbitt, Feb. 18, 1994.

2. Interview, Stella Mallett Trafford, July 21, 1994.

3. Interview, Robert Bullard, June 21, 1994.

4. Interview, Sarah Gordon Hicks, July 30, 1994.

5. Interview, Willana Buck Mallett, Jan. 28, 1996.

6. Peggy Whitman Prenshaw, *Conversations with Eudora Welty* (Jackson: University of Mississippi Press, 1984), p. 33.

7. Louis Rubin, ed., *American South: Portrait of a Culture* (Baton Rouge: LSU Press, 1980), p. 76.

8. Mallett interview.

9. Edwin McDowell, "Publishing: Lost Papers of Eudora Welty Found," *New York Times,* June 19, 1981, p. C4.

10. Nash K. Burger, "Eudora Welty's Monsieur Boule and Other Friends: A Memoir of Good Times," *Southern Quarterly* 32, no. 1 (Fall 1993), p. 11.

11. Ibid.

12. Prenshaw, *Conversations,* p. 206.

13. Seta Alexander Sancton, *The World from Gillespie Place* (privately printed), p. 103, MDAH.

14. "Miss Comly's 'Slumber Party,'" *Jackson Daily News,* Apr. 26, 1925. MDAH.

Chapter 2:
Richard Wright, 1923–1925

1. Lehman Engel, *This Bright Day: An Autobiography* (New York: Macmillan, 1974), pp. 21–22.
2. Prenshaw, *Conversations,* p. 176.
3. Jeanne Rolfe Nostrandt, "Fiction as Event: An Interview with Eudora Welty," *New Orleans Review* 7, no. 1 (1979), pp. 26–34.
4. Michel Fabre, *The Unfinished Quest of Richard Wright,* trans. Isabel Barzun (New York: Morrow, 1973), p. 57.
5. Ibid., p. 52.
6. Rubin, *American South,* p. 72.
7. Miriam Horn, "Imagining others' lives," *U.S. News and World Report,* Feb. 15, 1993.

Chapter 3:
Role Models

1. "La Sereine du Mississippi," *L'Observateur/Livres,* 31 jan.–6 fev., 1987. Welty Papers, MDAH.
2. *OWB,* p. 17.
3. Connie Shearer, "Eudora Welty Writes of Drama of Life," *Charleston Gazette,* Oct. 23, 1987.
4. Prenshaw, *Conversations,* p. 205.
5. Ibid., p. 164.
6. Ibid., p. 202.
7. Reprinted in *The Firing Line,* magazine of the Lamar Life Insurance Company, January 1981.
8. Ibid.
9. "Courtesy of the Garden Lovers Club," *Clarion-Ledger,* Oct. 14, 1928, n.p. Welty subject files, MDAH.
10. Sancton, *The World,* p. 95.
11. Suzanne Marrs, with Michael Kreyling, "Two Writers' Beginnings: Eudora Welty and Richard Wright." Unpublished paper.

Chapter 4:
The W, 1925–1927

1. Ruth McCoy Harris to Helen Perry Hopkins, Oct. 23, 1983, courtesy of Stephen Pieschel.
2. *LB,* p. 246.

3. *OWB,* p. 77.

4. *LB,* p. 246.

5. Lillian MacLaughlin to Helen Perry Hopkins, June 17, 1983, courtesy of Stephen Pieschel.

6. *LB,* p. 248.

7. Mrs. John D. Johnston to Helen Perry Hopkins, June 20, 1983, courtesy of Stephen Pieschel.

8. Helen Michel Pfeifer to Helen Perry Hopkins, July 13, 1983, courtesy of Stephen Pieschel.

9. *Spectator,* Oct. 27, 1925, p. 1.

10. *Spectator,* Nov. 14, 1925, p. 2.

11. *Spectator,* Dec. 11, 1926, p. 4.

12. Burger, "Eudora Welty's Monsieur Boule."

13. *Spectator,* Nov. 14, 1925, p. 4.

14. *OWB,* p. 79.

15. *Spectator,* Nov. 28, 1925, p. 7.

16. *OWB,* p. 79.

17. *Spectator,* Nov. 27, 1926, p. 8.

18. *Spectator,* Apr. 1, 1927, p. 3.

19. Richard Ford, "Bonhomie for a Southern Belletrist," *The New Yorker,* Feb. 19, 1996, p. 36.

20. *LB,* p. 246.

21. Mrs. D. N. Magruder to Helen Perry Hopkins, July 5, 1983, courtesy of Stephen Pieschel.

22. Katie Davidson Guion to Helen Perry Hopkins, n.d. [1983], courtesy of Stephen Pieschel.

23. Mrs. Graham Herndon Hicks to Helen Perry Hopkins, July 12, 1983, courtesy of Stephen Pieschel.

24. Kathleen Yerger Johnson to Helen Perry Hopkins, June 24, 1983, courtesy of Stephen Pieschel.

25. Ruth McCoy Harris to Helen Perry Hopkins, Oct. 23, 1983, courtesy of Stephen Pieschel.

26. Ibid.

27. Nash K. Burger, "Eudora Welty's Jackson," *Shenandoah* 20, no. 3 (Spring 1969), p. 12.

Chapter 5:
On, Wisconsin, 1927–1929

1. Michael Kreyling, *Author and Agent: Eudora Welty and Diarmuid Russell* (New York: Farrar, Straus, 1991), p. 10.

2. Interview, Carolyn Bell, Apr. 6, 1994.

3. Allan G. Bogue and Robert Taylor, eds., *The University of Wisconsin: One Hundred and Twenty-Five Years* (Madison: University of Wisconsin Press, 1979), p. 63.

4. *Daily Cardinal,* Sept. 21, 1927, p. 1.

5. Bogue and Taylor, *University,* p. 46.

6. Interview, Mary F. Garstang, Feb. 18, 1995.

7. Interview, Marion B. Gallinger Reel, Feb. 16, 1995.

8. Ibid.

9. Garstang interview.

10. Elinor Hegland Spring to AW, Mar. 6, 1995.

11. Kreyling, *Author and Agent,* p. 10.

12. Jonathan Yardley, "A Quiet Lady in the Limelight," *Miami Herald,* Feb. 17, 1974, p. 1L.

13. *Daily Cardinal,* Oct. 26, 1927, p. 1.

14. Kreyling, *Author and Agent,* p. 10.

15. Interview, Lester Connor, Mar. 9, 1995.

16. Kreyling, *Author and Agent,* p. 10.

17. *Wisconsin Literary Magazine,* Apr. 1928, p. 34.

18. Naomi Rabe Graham to AW, Nov. 5, 1994.

19. EW to JR, n.d. John Robinson Papers, MDAH.

20. *Daily Cardinal,* Feb. 17, 1929, p. 1.

21. Nostrandt, "Action as Event," p. 28.

22. Jan Nordby Gretlund, *Eudora Welty's Aesthetics of Place* (Cranbury, N.J.: University of Delaware Press, 1994), p. 403.

23. Nostrandt, "Fiction as Event," p. 29.

24. Gretlund, *Aesthetics,* p. 401.

25. Nostrandt, "Fiction as Event," p. 28.

26. Yardley, "A Quiet Lady."

Chapter 6:
Columbia, 1929–1931

1. Maxwell Perkins to EW, Sept. 5, 1929. Scribner Archive, Special Collections, Firestone Library, Princeton University.

2. Mary Chamberlain, ed., *Writing Lives: Conversations Between Women Writers* (London: Virago, 1988), p. 252.

3. EW, "Weekly Baby Clinic Is Becoming Popular Here," *Jackson Daily News,* May 25, 1930, p. 1A.

4. EW, "Vacations Lure Jacksonians; Large One Underway Soon," *Jackson Daily News,* June 15, 1930, p. 1.

5. *Clarion-Ledger,* June 22, 1930. Welty Papers, MDAH.

6. Sally Jacobs, "One Writer's Vision," *Boston Globe,* Nov. 29, 1992. BGM, p. 15.

7. Interview, Aimee Shands Walsh, June 11, 1994.

8. Prenshaw, *Conversations,* p. 247.

9. Ibid., p. 217.

10. Danny Heitman, "Eudora Welty," *Baton Rouge Advocate,* July 17, 1994, "Magazine," p. 16.

Chapter 7:
Home Again, 1931

1. Heitman, "Eudora Welty," p. 16.

2. The draft of Christian Welty's speech is in the Lamar Life Insurance Archive, MDAH.

3. *Clarion-Ledger,* Sept. 26, 1931.

4. Yardley, "A Quiet Lady."

5. Prenshaw, *Conversations,* p. 3.

6. Lamar Life Insurance Company 50th Anniversary Booklet, MDAH.

7. Ibid.

8. *Lamar Radio News* 2, no. 2. MDAH.

9. EW to *The New Yorker,* Mar. 15, 1933. *The New Yorker* Archive, New York Public Library.

10. Charlotte Capers, "The Narrow Escape of 'The Petrified Man': Early Eudora Welty Stories," *Journal of Mississippi History* 41, no. 1 (February 1979), p. 36.

11. Interview, Milton Babbitt, Feb. 18, 1994.

12. Capers, "The Narrow Escape," p. 26–27.

Chapter 8:
Local Literati, 1931–1935

1. Albert J. Devlin, "Jackson's Welty," *Southern Quarterly* 20, no. 4 (Summer 1992), p. 72.

2. Prenshaw, *Conversations,* p. 245.

3. EW to WH, Mar. 25, 1968.

4. Drafts are in the Hubert Creekmore Papers, Special Collections, Mugar Library, Boston University.

5. Interview, Milton Babbitt, Feb. 18, 1994.

6. Interview, Seta Alexander Sancton, June 20, 1994.

7. Prenshaw, *Conversations,* p. 201.

8. EW to Robert Daniel, Dec. 23, 1935. Robert Daniel Papers, Archives and Special Collections, Jessie Ball duPont Library, University of the South, Sewanee.

9. Engel, *This Bright Day,* p. 39.

10. *Photographs,* p. xxi.

11. Interview, Nash Burger, Apr. 19, 1994.

12. Clarence Brown, "Eudora Welty at Home." Manuscript prepared for *Bostonian Magazine,* p. 5. Courtesy of Clarence Brown.

13. Nash Burger to WH, Oct. 21, 1935.

14. Brown, "Eudora Welty at Home."

15. Gretlund, *Aesthetics,* p. 409.

16. Marrs, "Two Writers' Beginnings."

17. Seta Sancton to AW, June 8, 1994.

18. EW, "A Note about New Stage." *Standing Room Only: A Cookbook for Enter-taining* (New Stage Theatre, 1983) n.p.

Chapter 9:
The Journalist, 1933–1935

1. Prenshaw, *Conversations,* p. 204.

2. Margaret Conklin to HC, Aug. 1, 1933.

3. Ken Toler and Hodding Carter, who were working together for the Associated Press covering the special session of the Legislature called by Gov. Theodore Bilbo in 1932, were both fired. Carter went back to his home town of Hammond, Louisiana, and started his own paper; Toler went to work for *The Commercial Appeal.*

4. Charles Ealy, "First Lady of Literature," *Dallas Morning News,* Oct. 11, 1992, p. C1.

5. Elizabeth Bennett, "At Home with Eudora Welty," *Houston Post,* Dec. 1, 1991, p. E1.

6. Robert H. Coates, "Onward and Upward with the Arts: Life of the Party," *The New Yorker,* Jan. 12, 1935, pp. 44–49.

7. EW to *The New Yorker,* Jan. 16, 1935. *The New Yorker* Archive, New York Public Library.

8. Wolcott Gibbs to EW, Jan. 28, 1935. *The New Yorker* Archive, New York Public Library.

Chapter 10:
The WPA, 1935–1936

1. *Photographs,* p. xxv.

2. Jacobs, "One Writer's Vision," p. 28.

3. Prenshaw, *Conversations,* p. 178.

4. Chris Waddington, "Welty on Life Through the Lens," *New Orleans Times-Picayune,* Dec. 18, 1992, "Lagniappe," p. 24.

5. Prenshaw, *Conversations,* p. 157; *Photographs,* p. xix; Prenshaw, p. 3.

Chapter 11:

Photography, 1935–1937

1. *Photographs,* p. xiii.

2. Prenshaw, *Conversations,* p. 156.

3. Ibid.

4. *Photographs,* p. xxvi.

5. Rubin, *American South,* p. 81.

6. *Photographs,* p. 81.

7. Federal Writers Project of the Works Progress Administration, *Mississippi: A Guide to the Magnolia State* (New York: Hastings House, 1938), pp. 9, 16, and 449.

8. M. Lincoln Schuster, ed., *Eyes on the World: A Photographic Record of History-in-the-Making* (New York: Simon & Schuster, 1935), p. 261.

9. *Photographs,* p. xxii.

10. Waddington, "Welty on Life," p. 24.

11. *Photographs,* p. xvi.

12. Ibid., p. xxvii.

13. Ibid., p. xvi.

14. Waddington, "Welty on Life," p. 24.

15. *Photographs,* p. xvi.

16. Waddington, "Welty on Life," p. 24.

17. *Photographs,* p. xxi.

18. Stuart Kidd, "Eudora Welty's Unsuccessful Application to Become a Resettlement Administration Photographer," *Eudora Welty Newsletter* 14, no. 2 (Summer 1992), pp. 6–8.

19. Whit Burnett to EW, Feb. 24, 1938.

20. Harrison Smith to EW, Apr. 2, 1935.

21. Capers, "The Narrow Escape," p. 27.

22. EW to Robert Daniel, July 29, 1935.

23. *Manuscript* 3, no. 3 (June 1936), p. 2.

24. EW, lecture at Museum of Modern Art, Nov. 14, 1973. Tape courtesy of Peter Bunnell.

25. Samuel A. Robbins to EW, July 18, 1936, and Nov. 21, 1936.

26. *Photographs,* p. xiii.

27. MOMA lecture.

28. Samuel A. Robbins to EW, Dec. 14, 1936.

29. Frank Hall Fraysur to EW, Jan. 29, 1937.

30. "Life on the American Newsfront," *Life,* Nov. 8, 1937, p. 33.

Chapter 12:

The First Stories, 1931–1936

1. Capers, "Narrow Escape," p. 27.

2. *St. Nicholas* 51 (Nov. 1923), p. 108.

3. J.H.W., secretary-treasurer, to EW, Aug. 29, 1921. MDAH.

4. EW., "That Bright Face Is Laughing," *Kenyon Review* 5, no. 2 (Spring 1983), pp. 120–21.

5. Manuscript copy, "Lilies That Fester," courtesy Mrs. Robert Daniel.

6. Sally Wolff, "The Domestic Thread of Revelation: An Interview with Eudora Welty," *Southern Literary Journal* 25, no. 1 (Fall 1992), p. 23.

7. *OWB,* p. 38.

8. Ibid., p. 18.

9. First draft, Massie lectures. Welty Papers, MDAH.

10. Horn, "Imagining."

11. Gretlund, *Aesthetics,* p. 373.

12. Elizabeth Evans, "Eudora Welty and the Dutiful Daughter," *Eudora Welty: Eye of the Storyteller,* ed. Dawn Trouard (Kent, Ohio: Kent State University Press, 1989), p. 60.

13. Both unpublished stories in Box 1, Welty Papers, MDAH.

14. Prenshaw, *Conversations,* pp. 36–37.

Chapter 13:

Getting Published, 1936–1940

1. John Rood to EW, Mar. 19, 1936.

2. Heitman, "Eudora Welty," p. 16; Prenshaw, *Conversations,* p. 208.

3. Ibid., p. 318; EW, "Looking Back at the First Story," *The Georgia Review* 33, no. 4 (Winter 1979), p. 752.

4. EW, "Looking Back," p. 755.

5. Ibid.

6. Prenshaw, *Conversations,* p. 188.

7. Nostrandt, "Fiction as Event," p. 30.

8. Frank E. Smith, "Dale Mullen and Modern Mississippi Literature," *Journal of Mississippi History* 48, no. 4 (November 1986), pp. 257–70.

9. EW to Robert Daniel, Oct. 13, 1936.

10. Sally Wolff, "The Domestic Thread," p. 21.

11. Dale Mullen to HC, Apr. 17, 1934.

Chapter 14:
More Stories, 1936–1940

1. EW, "There," *The Bozart-Westminster,* Autumn 1936 (published by Oglethorpe University Press, Atlanta, Georgia), p. 10.

2. RPW to EW, Jan. 13, 1937.

3. RPW to EW, Feb. 4, 1937.

4. Nostrandt, "Fiction as Event," p. 34.

5. Arnold Gingrich to EW.

6. Donald E. Stanford, "Eudora Welty and the Pulitzer Prize." *Southern Review* 9, no. 4 (Autumn 1973), p. xx.

7. Prenshaw, *Conversations,* p. 347.

8. Nostrandt, "Fiction as Event," p. 31.

9. JR to WH, May 6, 1937.

10. Interview, Willana Buck Mallett, Jan. 28, 1996.

11. EW to George Marion O'Donnell, July 27, 1937. O'Donnell Papers, Modern Literature Collection, Olin Library, Washington University, St. Louis.

12. Robert Farley to WH, Oct. 21, 1937.

13. Shearer, "Eudora Welty Writes."

14. EW to George Marion O'Donnell, July 27, 1937.

15. *OWB,* p. 89.

16. RPW to EW, Feb. 22, 1938.

17. Nostrandt, "Fiction as Event," p. 32.

18. EW to Diarmuid Russell, Nov. 5, 1940, quoted in Kreyling, *Author and Agent,* p. 49.

19. JR to Nancy Farley, Jan. 21, 1938. Faulkner Collection, Alderman Library, University of Virginia, Charlottesville.

20. Nostrandt, "Fiction as Event," p. 30.

21. Harold Strauss to EW, May 13, 1936 and May 27, 1936.

22. Harold Strauss to EW, Nov. 1, 1937.

23. Harriet Colby to EW, Feb. 16, 1938, and Apr. 27, 1938.

24. Harriet Colby to EW, May 28, 1938.

25. Whit Burnett to EW, July 14, 1938 and HC to EW, July 19, 1938.

26. Capers, "Narrow Escape," pp. 25–36.

27. R. N. Linscott to EW, Sept. 17, 1938.

28. Kreyling, *Author and Agent,* p. 20.

29. RPW to EW, Sept. 28, 1938.

30. JR to Nancy Farley, Jan. 19, 1940.

31. Ford Madox Ford to EW, Jan. 7, 1939.

32. EW to KAP, July 17, 1939.

33. KAP, "Introduction," *CG,* p. xi.

34. David Laskin, *A Common Life* (New York: Simon & Schuster, 1994), p. 199.

35. EW to KAP, n.d.

36. EW to WH, n.d.

37. EW to KAP, n.d.

38. John M. Woodburn to EW.

39. EW to KAP, Mar. 2, 1940.

40. Prenshaw, *Conversations,* p. 179.

Chapter 15:

Diarmuid Russell, 1940

1. Kreyling, *Author and Agent,* p. 9.

2. Ibid., p. 23.

3. Ibid., p. 24.

4. Nostrandt, "Fiction as Event," p. 27.

5. Kreyling, *Author and Agent,* p. 24.

6. Diarmuid Russell, "First Work," *Shenandoah* 20, no. 3 (Spring 1969), p. 17.

7. Draft of Massie lectures. Welty Papers, MDAH.

8. Prenshaw, *Conversations,* p. 327.

9. Kreyling, *Author and Agent,* pp. 41, 27.

Chapter 16:

Bread Loaf, 1940

1. David Howard Bain, *Whose Woods These Are* (Hopewell, N.J.: Ecco Press, 1993), p. 46.

2. Virginia Spencer Carr, *The Lonely Hunter: A Biography of Carson McCullers* (Garden City, N.Y.: Doubleday, 1975), p. 111.

3. Interview, Fannie Cheney, Apr. 10, 1994.

4. Bain, *Whose Woods,* p. 45.

5. Theodore Morrison, *Bread Loaf Writers' Conference: The First Thirty Years (1926–1955)* (Middlebury, Vt.: Middlebury College Press, 1976), p. 38.

6. Ken McCormick to EW, Mar. 28, 1946. Doubleday Archive, Library of Congress, Washington, D.C.

7. EW to Brainerd and Fannie Cheney, Jan. 22, 1941. Cheney Papers, Special Collections, Heard Library, Vanderbilt University, Nashville, Tennessee.

8. Nancy Tate Wood to AW, Oct. 26, 1994.

9. Bain, *Whose Woods,* p. 47.

10. EW to KAP, n.d.

11. Kreyling, *Author and Agent,* p. 40.

12. EW to Brainerd and Fannie Cheney, n.d. [October 1941].

Chapter 17:

The Natchez Trace, 1940

1. Kreyling, *Author and Agent,* p. 43.
2. "La Sereine du Mississippi." Welty Papers, MDAH.
3. EW to Diarmuid Russell, quoted in Kreyling, *Author and Agent,* p. 45.
4. EW, "Fairy Tale of the Natchez Trace: A Paper Read to the Annual Dinner Meeting of the Mississippi Historical Society, Jackson, Mississippi," Mar. 7, 1975 (Jackson: Mississippi Historical Society, 1975), p. 18.
5. EW to HB, Oct. 4, 1940.
6. Kate Tyndall, "Eudora Welty Tells Stories of Life's Dramas," *Charleston Gazette,* Oct. 23, 1987.
7. EW "Fairy Tale," p. 13.
8. Ibid., p. 20.
9. Nash Burger to WH, n.d.
10. John Woodburn to EW, Nov. 26, 1940.
11. EW to Fannie and Brainerd Cheney, n.d. [October 1941].
12. Diarmuid Russell to EW, Nov. 7, 1940, quoted in Kreyling, *Author and Agent,* p. 50.
13. Diarmuid Russell to EW, Oct. 29, 1940, quoted in Kreyling, *Author and Agent,* p. 48.

Chapter 18:

The *Atlantic Monthly,* 1940–1941

1. Prenshaw, *Conversations,* p. 167.
2. Written, not used, for *This Is My Best,* ms. in Welty Papers, MDAH.
3. EW to Fannie and Brainerd Cheney, n.d. [October 1941].
4. Diarmuid Russell to EW, Dec. 4, 1940, quoted in Kreyling, *Author and Agent,* p. 53.
5. Prenshaw, *Conversations,* p. 209.
6. EW to Robert Daniel, Christmas card, 1940, n.d.
7. Jo Thomas, "Satisfaction in Job Well Done Is Only Reward for E-Mail Software Inventor," *New York Times,* Jan. 21, 1997.
8. Charles Ruas, *Conversations with American Writers* (New York: Knopf, 1984), p. 10.
9. Barbara Lazear Archer, "The Color of the Air," *Saturday Review,* Dec. 1984, p. 34.
10. EW to Brainerd and Fannie Cheney, Jan. 22, 1941.
11. EW to HB and NB, Feb. 13, 1941; EW to KAP, Feb. 22, 1941.
12. EW to William Maxwell, Dec. 22, 1940. *The New Yorker* Archive, New York Public Library.

Chapter 19:
A Curtain of Green, 1941

1. Diarmuid Russell to EW, Jan. 21, 1940, quoted in Kreyling, *Author and Agent,* p. 51.

2. EW to KAP, Feb. 13, 1941; EW to HB and NB, Feb. 13, 1941; EW to RPW, Jan. 24, 1941; EW to John Woodburn, Jan. 29, 1941.

3. Kreyling, *Author and Agent,* p. 64.

4. Archer, "Color of the Air," p. 34.

5. EW to KAP, Feb. 15, 1941.

6. EW to Lodwick Hartley, Feb. 25, 1941. Hartley Papers, Southern Historical Collection, Wilson Library, University of North Carolina, Chapel Hill.

7. Diarmuid Russell to HC, June 16, 1941.

8. Robert Wilson, "The Journey to a Writer's Golden Hour," *USA Today,* Nov. 21, 1991, p. D1.

9. EW to KAP, Feb. 15, 1941.

10. EW to Diarmuid Russell, Jan. 18, 1941, quoted in Kreyling, *Author and Agent,* p. 58.

11. Albert J. Devlin and Peggy Whitman Prenshaw, eds., *Welty: A Life in Literature* (Jackson: University Press of Mississippi, 1988), p. 19.

12. Gretlund, *Aesthetics,* p. 337.

13. EW to Lodwick Hartley, Feb. 25, 1941.

14. Gretlund, *Aesthetics,* p. 408.

15. Prenshaw, *Conversations,* p. 63.

16. Kreyling, *Author and Agent,* p. 84.

17. EW to Diarmuid Russell, Jan. 9, 1943, quoted in ibid., p. 85.

18. EW to Diarmuid Russell, quoted in ibid., p. 73.

19. EW to KAP, May 1, 1941.

Chapter 20:
Henry Miller, 1941

1. Bennett, "At Home with Eudora Welty," p. E1; *Photographs,* p. xxii.

2. Prenshaw, *Conversations,* p. 201.

3. George Plimpton, "Eudora Welty: Two Encounters," *Paris Review* 134 (Spring 1995), p. 259.

4. *Photographs,* p. xxii.

5. Henry Miller, *The Air-Conditioned Nightmare* (New York: New Directions, 1945), p. 286.

6. Charles East, "The Search for Eudora Welty," *Mississippi Quarterly* (Fall 1973), p. 481.

7. Kreyling, *Author and Agent,* p. 72.

Chapter 21:

Yaddo, 1941

1. EW to Brainerd and Fannie Cheney, May 1941.
2. EW to Diarmuid Russell, quoted in Kreyling, *Author and Agent,* p. 74.
3. EW to KAP, n.d.
4. EW, "My Introduction to Katherine Anne Porter," *Georgia Review* 44, nos. 1, 2 (Spring/Summer 1990), p. 19.
5. Kreyling, *Author and Agent,* p. 75.
6. Prenshaw, *Conversations,* p. 318.
7. *Photographs,* p. xxi.
8. EW to HB, June 8, 1941.
9. JR to Nancy Farley, June 30, 1941.
10. EW to Diarmuid Russell, July 1941, quoted in Kreyling, *Author and Agent,* p. 77.
11. EW, "My Introduction," p. 21.

Chapter 22:

Publication Party, 1941

1. John Woodburn to EW, July 31, 1941.
2. KAP to EW, Aug. 27, 1941, quoted in EW, "My Introduction," p. 24.
3. EW to KAP, Mar. 16, 1941.
4. Interview with Eudora Welty, *Comment,* Oct. 16, 1965. Welty Papers, MDAH.
5. EW to KAP, n.d.
6. Kreyling, *Author and Agent,* p. 87.
7. EW to KAP, n.d.
8. EW to KAP, n.d.
9. Untitled clipping from *Publishers Weekly,* Dec. 6, 1941. Welty Papers, MDAH.
10. Ibid.
11. Marianne Hauser, "A Curtain of Green," *New York Times Book Review,* Nov. 16, 1941.
12. Louise Bogan, "The Gothic South," *Nation,* Dec. 6, 1941, p. 572.
13. Bette Barber, "Novel Can Wait, Says Jackson Author," *Jackson Daily News,* Dec. 1, 1941, p. 3.
14. Reader's report, signed D.L., Sept. 12, 1941. *Story* Magazine Archive, Special Collections, Firestone Library, Princeton University.
15. JR to Nancy Farley, Mar. 11, 1941.
16. Ibid.

Chapter 23:
War Comes, 1941

1. EW to KAP, n.d.
2. EW to KAP, n.d.
3. Gretlund, *Aesthetics,* p. 412.
4. EW to Diarmuid Russell, Jan. 16, 1942, quoted in Kreyling, *Author and Agent,* p. 86.
5. Ibid., 87.
6. Gretlund, *Aesthetics,* p. 412.
7. EW to WH, Mar. 1941.
8. Elizabeth Spencer, "Eudora Welty: An Introduction," *Eudora Welty Newsletter* 3, 1-B (April 1929), p. 2.
9. Prenshaw, *Conversations,* p. 7.
10. EW, "Foreword" in *The Stories of Elizabeth Spencer* (Garden City, N.Y.: Doubleday, 1981).
11. EW to Brainerd Cheney, Apr. 18, 1942.

Chapter 24:
The Robber Bridegroom, 1942

1. EW to Diarmuid Russell, Feb. 26, 1941, quoted in Kreyling, *Author and Agent,* p. 66.
2. John Woodburn to EW, June 4, 1942.
3. EW to John Woodburn, July 26, 1942. Doubleday Archive, Library of Congress.
4. Gayle Graham Yates, *Mississippi Mind: A Personal Cultural History of an American State* (Knoxville: University of Tennessee Press, 1990), p. 150.
5. Ibid.
6. Mary Hughes Brookhart and Suzanne Marrs, "More Notes on River Country," *Mississippi Quarterly* 39 (Fall 1986), p. 509.
7. "Shantyboat Life," Federal Writers Project, *Mississippi* (New York: Hastings House, 1938), p. 16; *Photographs,* p. 109.
8. Prenshaw, *Conversations,* p. 190.
9. Kreyling, *Author and Agent,* p. 92.
10. *WE,* p. 3.
11. EW to Charles Shattuck, Sept. 1, 1942. Shattuck Papers, Library, University of Illinois, Urbana.
12. JR to Nancy Farley, Sept. 21, 1942.
13. EW to KAP, n.d.
14. EW to KAP, n.d. [October 1943].
15. JR to Nancy Farley, Sept. 21, 1941.
16. *The New Yorker,* Oct. 24, 1942.
17. Lionel Trilling, "American Fairy Tale," *Nation,* Dec. 19, 1942, p. 686.

18. W. U. McDonald, "Miss Eudora's 'Dirty' Book: Bowdlerizing *The Robber Bridegroom." Eudora Welty Newsletter* 11, no. 2 (Summer 1987), p. 4.

Chapter 25:
Leaving Doubleday, 1942

1. Ken McCormick to EW, Dec. 2, 1942, MDAH.

2. EW to Ken McCormick, Dec. 11, 1942.

3. EW to HB, Jan. 25, 1943.

4. EW to KAP, n.d.

5. EW to KAP, n.d.

6. EW to KAP, n.d.

7. John Woodburn to EW, Aug. 23, 1943.

8. EW to KAP, n.d. [November 1943].

9. EW to KAP, n.d. [October 1943].

10. Recommendations, Fulbright Fellowship application, 1949. Institute of International Education, New York.

11. *Eye,* p. 315.

12. *Photographs,* p. xxvi.

13. Ibid., xxvii.

Chapter 26:
Trilling vs. Warren, 1943

1. Michael Upchurch, " 'Golden' Nuggets of Eudora Welty," *Atlanta Journal-Constitution,* Apr. 14, 1991, p. N8.

2. Charlotte Margolis Goodman, *Jean Stafford: The Savage Heart* (Austin: University of Texas Press, 1990), p. 146.

3. Diana Trilling, "Fiction in Review," *Nation,* Oct. 2, 1943, pp. 386–87.

4. EW to Diarmuid Russell, Oct. 18, 1943, quoted in Kreyling, *Author and Agent,* p. 101.

5. Heitman, "Eudora Welty," p. 16.

6. Robert Penn Warren, "The Love and Separateness in Miss Welty," *Kenyon Review* 6, no. 2 (Spring 1944), pp. 246–59.

7. EW to Lodwick Hartley, n.d. [1944].

8. EW to KAP, n.d. [Fall 1943].

9. EW to KAP, n.d. [October 1943].

10. EW to KAP, n.d. [Fall 1943].

11. Prenshaw, *Conversations,* p. 180.

Chapter 27:
The *New York Times Book Review,* 1944

1. Heitman, "Eudora Welty," p. 16.

2. Nona Balakian, *Critical Encounters: Literary Views and Reviews, 1953–1977* (Indianapolis: Bobbs-Merrill, 1978), p. 15.

3. *We,* p. xviii.

4. Pearl Amelia McHaney, *The Monster Upon the Bank: Eudora Welty's Book Reviews and Major Essays.* Ph.D. dissertation, College of Arts and Sciences, Georgia State University, p. 28.

5. EW to KAP, n.d.

6. *We,* p. xix.

7. Bennett, "At Home," p. E1.

8. *We,* p. xix.

Chapter 28:
How to Make a Novel, 1945

1. JR to WH, Jan. 29, 1945.

2. EW to Nancy Farley, June 16, 1945.

3. JR to WH, Jan. 29, 1945.

4. Nash Burger to WH, Apr. 1945.

5. Albert J. Devlin, *Welty: A Life in Literature* (Jackson: University Press of Mississippi, 1987), p. 9.

6. *DW,* p. 41.

7. *DW,* p. 37.

8. "Weddings and Funerals: Eudora Welty Speaks to Young Writers," *Silhouette, Silhouette: Virginia Tech Student Literary Magazine* 2 (Spring 1979), pp. 1–5.

9. Devlin, *Welty,* p. 10.

10. Gretlund, *Aesthetics,* p. 413.

11. Prenshaw, *Conversations,* 175.

Chapter 29:
The Other Jackson Writer, 1945

1. WH to Charlotte Capers, Mar. 29, 1945. Hamilton Papers.

2. E. Bruce Thompson, "Black Boy: A Record of Childhood and Youth," *Journal of Mississippi History* 7, no. 3 (July 1945): pp. 178–80.

3. Nash Burger to WH, Apr. 1945.

Chapter 30:
Delta Wedding, 1946

1. *Jackson Daily News,* May 23, 1946.
2. Nash Burger to WH, n.d. [1946].
3. WH to EW, May 23, 1946, Hamilton Papers, Duke.
4. Prenshaw, *Conversations,* p. 182.
5. Diana Trilling, "Fiction in Review," *Nation,* May 11, 1946, p. 578.
6. Kreyling, *Author and Agent,* p. 113.
7. Jefferson Humphries, ed., *Conversations with Reynolds Price* (Jackson: University Press of Mississippi, 1991), p. 47.

Chapter 31:
Portrait Painted, 1946

1. Marcella Comès Winslow, *Brushes with the Literary: Letters of a Washington Artist, 1943–1959* (Baton Rouge: Louisiana State University Press, 1993), p. 171.
2. Ibid., p. 174.
3. Ibid., p. 175, clipping from *Washington Post,* Apr. 17, 1952. Marcella Comès Winslow papers, Archives of American Art, Washington, D.C.
4. Nash Burger to WH, July 25 [1946].
5. Winslow, *Brushes,* p. 185.

Chapter 32:
A Literary Magazine? 1946

1. EW to William Maxwell, Aug. 9, 1946. *The New Yorker* Archive, New York Public Library, New York.
2. William Maxwell to EW, Aug. 19, 1946. Hamilton Papers, Duke.
3. JR to WH, Nov. 5, 1946.
4. JR to Joseph Henry Jackson, Nov. 25, 1946. Joseph Henry Jackson Papers, Bancroft Library, University of California, Berkeley.
5. EW, "For Allen Tate," *The Quarterly Journal of the Library of Congress* 36 (Fall 1979), p. 354.

Chapter 33:
San Francisco, 1946–1947

1. JR to WH, Nov. 5, 1946.
2. EW to KAP, Jan. 27 [n.d.].

3. Yates, *Mississippi Mind,* p. 153.

4. *Morgana,* p. 147.

5. Prenshaw, *Conversations,* p. 333.

6. *OWB,* pp. 100–101.

7. *CS,* p. 412.

8. Ibid., p. 399.

9. EW to KAP, n.d.

Chapter 34:

San Francisco Again, 1947

1. *Photographs,* pp. xix–xx.

2. Kreyling, *Author and Agent,* p. 126.

3. Judith Scherer Herz and Robert K. Martin, eds., *E. M. Forster: Centenary Evaluations* (Buffalo: University of Toronto Press, 1982), p. 298.

4. Kreyling, *Author and Agent,* p. 128.

5. *We,* p. xxvii.

6. EW to HB, Feb. 15, 1948.

7. Lambert Davis to EW, Aug. 28, 1947.

8. Unidentified clipping, n.d., MDAH.

9. Kreyling, *Author and Agent,* 140.

10. EW to HB, Feb. 28, 1948.

11. *Morgana,* p. 149.

12. Ibid., pp. 150, 151.

13. Kreyling, *Author and Agent,* p. 134.

14. Prenshaw, *Conversations,* p. 42.

15. Kreyling, *Author and Agent,* 136.

16. EW to KAP, Jan. 27 [1948].

17. EW to KAP, Jan. 25 [1948].

Chapter 35:

The Levee Press, 1948

1. EW to KAP, Jan. 25 [1948].

2. EW to HB, Feb. 15, 1948.

3. HB to EW, Feb. 21, 1948.

4. Kreyling, *Author and Agent,* p. 141.

5. Ibid.

6. EW to NB and HB, n.d.

Chapter 36:

Musical Comedy, 1948

1. Rhea Talley, "Eudora Welty Joins Hegira of Mississippians to Europe," *Memphis Commercial Appeal,* July 17, 1949, p. V4.

2. EW to JR, n.d. [1948].

3. Typescript in Box 85, Welty Papers, MDAH.

4. Prenshaw, *Conversations,* p. 207.

5. Peggy Whitman Prenshaw, "Sex and Wreckage in the Parlor: Welty's 'Bye-Bye Brevoort.' " *Southern Quarterly* 33, nos. 2–3 (Winter-Spring 1995), p. 108.

6. Unidentified clipping, *Lo and Behold* file. New York Public Library for the Performing Arts, Lincoln Center.

7. Prenshaw, "Sex and Wreckage," p. 108.

8. Kreyling, *Author and Agent,* p. 143.

Chapter 37:

Film Scripts, 1948–1949

1. EW to HB and NB, n.d. [New Year's Eve, 1948].

2. EW to JR, n.d. [Dec. 1948]; EW to JR, Friday, n.d. [November 1948]. Welty Papers, MDAH.

3. EW to JR, [1948]. Welty Papers, MDAH.

4. EW to JR, Friday, n.d. [November, 1948]. Welty Papers, MDAH.

5. Recommendation, Fulbright Fellowship application, 1949. Institute of International Education, New York.

6. EW to JR, n.d.

7. EW to JR, Friday, n.d. [November 1948].

8. JR to EW, n.d.; EW to JR, n.d. [Wednesday AM].

9. EW to JR, Thursday, n.d.

10. EW to JR, n.d.; EW to Alice Farley O'Brien, Feb. 21, 1949. Nancy Farley papers, Faulkner collection, Alderman Library, University of Virginia, Charlottesville.

11. Joseph Henry Jackson, "Bookman's Notebook," *San Francisco Chronicle,* Sept. 12, 1949, p. 14.

12. Maurice Evans to EW, Jan. 3, 1949.

13. Kreyling, *Author and Agent,* p. 145.

14. Eddie Dowling to EW, Feb. 5, 1949.

15. EW to Eddie Dowling, Feb. 14, 1949. Welty Papers, MDAH.

Chapter 38:
The Golden Apples, 1949

1. EW to JR, n.d. [Jan. 27–29, 1949].
2. EW to JR, n.d. [Jan. 27–29, 1949].
3. JR to EW, May 1937. Welty Papers, MDAH.
4. Prenshaw, *Conversations,* p. 88.
5. Yates, *Mississippi Mind,* p. 153.
6. Gretlund, *Aesthetics,* p. 190, 186.
7. Nostrandt, "Fiction as Event," p. 28.
8. Prenshaw, *Conversations,* p. 192.

Chapter 39:
William Faulkner, 1949

1. EW to Caroline Gordon, n.d. [1949]. Caroline Gordon Papers, Special Collections, Firestone Library, Princeton University.
2. Interview, Nancy Tate Wood, Oct. 26, 1994.
3. Interview, EW, Feb. 16, 1989.
4. Wood interview.
5. Prenshaw, *Conversations,* 79.
6. "Department of Amplification," *The New Yorker,* Jan. 1, 1949, p. 50.
7. "American Writing Today," *Times Literary Supplement,* Oct. 8, 1954, p. 641.
8. Prenshaw, *Conversations,* p. 220.
9. Ibid., p. 208.
10. Ibid., p. 79.
11. Joseph Blotner, *Faulkner: A Biography,* One-Volume Edition (New York: Random House, 1984), p. 450.
12. Quoted in Joan St. C. Crane, "William Faulkner to Eudora Welty: A Letter," *Mississippi Quarterly* 42, no. 3 (Summer 1989), p. 223.
13. Prenshaw, *Conversations,* p. 322.
14. There is some confusion about the date that Faulkner and Welty met. Kreyling places the meeting in 1948, but a letter from Welty to Jean Stafford, although undated, places it in 1949 because Welty recounts the recent meeting, then talks about booking passage for Europe on the *Italia* in Oct.—the trip she began in 1949.
15. EW to Caroline Gordon, n.d. [1949].
16. Interview, Dale Mullins, Sept. 29, 1994.
17. EW to JS, n.d. [1949].
18. EW to WH, July 8, 1962.
19. Frank Hains, "Welty Delivers Key Tribute to Faulkner," *Jackson Daily News,* Apr. 25, 1965, p. 8F.
20. Doreen Fowler, ed., *Faulkner and the Craft of Fiction* (Jackson: University Press of Mississippi, 1989), pp. 215–16.

Chapter 40:
Abroad, 1949–1950

1. "The Mind in Torment," *Saturday Review,* Sept. 17, 1949, p. 11.
2. Interview, Guy Davenport, Apr. 11, 1994.
3. Paul Ferris, ed., *The Collected Letters of Dylan Thomas* (London: J. M. Dent & Sons, 1985), p. 629.
4. Stephen Spender, "Notebook-X," *London Magazine,* June-July 1976, pp. 9–10.
5. EW to WJS and BH, n.d. William Jay Smith Papers, Olin Library, Washington University, St. Louis, Missouri.

Chapter 41:
England and Ireland, 1950

1. John Lehmann, *The Ample Proportion: Autobiography III* (London: Eyre and Spottiswoode, 1966), p. 108.
2. Devlin, *Welty,* p. 5.
3. Ibid.
4. Ibid.
5. John Malcolm Brinnin, *Sextet* (New York: Delacorte, 1981), pp. 165–66.
6. Harvey Breit, "Talk with Miss Bowen," *New York Times Book Review,* Mar. 26, 1950, p. 27.
7. Frances Partridge, *Everything to Lose* (London: Victor Gollancz, 1985), p. 259.
8. Victoria Glendinning, *Elizabeth Bowen* (London: Weidenfeld and Nicolson, 1977), p. 209.
9. Brinnin, *Sextet,* p. 174.
10. Glendinning, *Bowen,* p. 209.
11. Carr, *Lonely Hunter,* p. 356.
12. *Photographs,* xviii.
13. Interview, Jack Spalding, May 22, 1994.

Chapter 42:
The Civil War Redux, 1950

1. EW to Lodwick Hartley, Mar. 17, 1944. Lodwick Hartley Papers, Southern Historical Collection, Wilson Library, University of North Carolina, Chapel Hill.
2. Devlin, *Welty,* p. 20.
3. Prenshaw, *Conversations,* p. 221.
4. EW to WJS and BH, n.d.
5. EW to WJS and BH, n.d.

Chapter 43:
Elizabeth Bowen, 1950

1. EW to KAP, n.d.; EW to WJS, n.d.
2. Prenshaw, *Conversations,* p. 8.
3. Devlin, *Welty,* p. 14.
4. Ibid.
5. EW to WJS, n.d.

Chapter 44:
Bowen's Court, 1951

1. EW to EB, Jan. 19, n.d.
2. Don Harrell, "Death in Eudora Welty's 'The Bride of the Innisfallen,'" *Notes on Contemporary Literature* 3, no. 4 (September 1973), p. 2.
3. Glendinning, *Bowen,* p. 210.
4. Devlin, *Welty,* pp. 6–7.
5. Ibid., p. 13.
6. EW to EB, n.d.
7. W to EB, n.d.
8. Fred Ferretti, "A Year's Worth of Travel," *New York Times,* Dec. 29, 1985, section 10, p. 1.
9. EW to EB, Aug. 6, 1951.
10. EW to EB, n.d. [July 13, 1951].

Chapter 45:
The Enigma, 1951

1. EW to WJS, n.d.
2. EW to WJS, n.d.; EW to EB, n.d.
3. EW to EB, Aug. 6, 1951.
4. EW to JS, n.d.
5. EW to EB, Aug. 17 [1951].
6. *Eye,* p. 111.
7. Ibid.
8. EW to EB, Sept. 16 [1951].
9. EW to EB, n.d.
10. EW to EB, Dec. 6 [n.d.].
11. Ibid.
12. EW to EB, Nov. 29 [n.d.].
13. EW to EB, Dec. 6 [n.d.].

14. Ibid.

15. Glendinning, *Bowen,* p. 209.

16. Interview, Mrs. Alun Collins, Nov. 19, 1994.

17. EW to WJS, Mar. 14, 1973.

18. John Halperin, *Eminent Georgians* (New York: St. Martin's Press, 1995), p. 122.

19. Joan Givner, *Katherine Anne Porter* (New York: Touchstone/Simon & Schuster, 1982), p. 371.

20. Rebecca West to Emanie Arling, July 12, 1955. Rebecca West Papers, Beinecke Library, Yale University.

21. Josyanne Savigneau, "French About to Discover the Little Old Lady from Jackson," *Manchester Guardian Weekly,* Dec. 13, 1987, p. 16.

22. Michael Skube, "A Conversation with Eudora Welty: A Worn Path," *Atlanta Constitution,* Mar. 17, 1996, p. L12.

Chapter 46:
To and Fro, 1952–1953

1. Prenshaw, *Conversations,* p. 165.

2. Gretlund, *Aesthetics,* p. 377.

3. Laskin, *Common Life,* p. 255.

4. Mary Jarrell, ed., *Randall Jarrell's Letters* (Boston: Houghton Mifflin, 1985), p. 341.

5. Ibid., p. 343.

6. Anne Hobson Freeman, "Eudora Welty Celebrates the Spring," *Bryn Mawr Alumnae Bulletin,* Spring 1980, p. 7.

7. William Maxwell to EW, Aug. 7, 1952.

8. EW to JS, n.d.

Chapter 47:
The Ponder Heart, 1954

1. Kreyling, *Author and Agent,* p. 163.

2. Nash K. Burger, *The Road to West 43rd Street* (Jackson: University Press of Mississippi, 1995), p. 38.

3. Postcard, Mary Lou Aswell to Mr. and Mrs. William Jay Smith, May 1953.

4. Quoted in *Jackson Daily News,* Nov. 9, 1956. Welty subject files, 1957–60, MDAH.

5. EW to William Van O'Connor, Jan. 18, 1957, William Van O'Connor Papers, George Arents Research Library, Syracuse University.

6. Charles Poore, "Books of the Times," *New York Times,* Jan. 7, 1954, p. 29.

7. Lewis Gannett, "Book Review," *New York Herald-Tribune,* Jan. 1, 1954.

8. V. S. Pritchett, "Bossy Edna Earle Had a Word for Everything," *New York Times Book Review,* Jan. 10, 1954, p. 5.

9. Quoted in *Jackson Daily News,* Nov. 9, 1956. Welty subject files, 1957–60, MDAH.

Chapter 48:
The First Honorary Degree, 1954

1. Letter of recommendation to Andrew Weaver. Honorary degree files, University of Wisconsin Archives, Madison.

Chapter 49:
Cambridge, 1954

1. EW to Peter Taylor, n.d. Peter Taylor Papers, Heard Library, Vanderbilt University, Nashville, Tennessee.

2. Final Report, The American Studies Conferences in the United Kingdom, 1952–1955. Special Collections, University of Arkansas Libraries, Fayetteville.

3. Devlin, *Welty,* p. 12.

4. Interview, David Daiches, Aug. 23, 1994.

5. EW to Peter Taylor, n.d.

6. Walter Clemons, *New York Times Book Review,* Apr. 12, 1970.

7. *Photographs,* p. xxiii.

8. Prenshaw, *Conversations,* p. 75.

Chapter 50:
Reynolds Price, 1955

1. Dannye Romine Powell, *Parting the Curtains: Interviews with Southern Writers* (Winston Salem, N.C.: John F. Blair, 1994), p. 340.

2. Humphries, *Conversations with Price,* p. 169.

3. Ibid., pp. 11, 170.

4. Miki Southern, "Eudora Welty Notes Importance of Place in Fictional Writing," *The Duke Chronicle,* Feb. 26, 1955, p. 8

5. Reynolds Price, "The First Printing of 'Place in Fiction,'" *Eudora Welty Newsletter* 3B (April 1979), p. 6.

6. Humphries, *Conversations with Price,* pp. 73, 64, 43, 242, 230.

7. Prenshaw, *Conversations,* p. 312.

8. HC to WJS, Apr. 8, 1955.

9. HC to WJS, Dec. 17, 1955.

Chapter 51:

Uncle Daniel on Stage, 1956

1. Danny Kaye to EW, Oct. 8, 1954.

2. Chodorov and Fields to EW, Feb. 19, 1955.

3. Unidentified clipping in Box 113, Welty Papers, MDAH.

4. EW to RPW, Oct. 30, 1955.

5. EW to Chodorov and Fields, Mar. 28, 1955. Welty Papers, MDAH.

6. Kreyling, *Author and Agent,* pp. 177–78.

7. EW, "Chodorov and Fields in Mississippi," *Eudora Welty Newsletter* 3 no. 1B (April 1979).

8. Clipping from *New York Herald Tribune,* Apr. 1, 1956, in Box 113, Welty Papers, MDAH.

9. EW to WH, July 13, 1955.

10. Kreyling, *Author and Agent,* p. 181.

11. Harold L. Carl, "Two on the Aisle," Portland, Maine *Sunday Express,* Feb. 8, 1956.

12. Unidentified clipping in Welty subject files, MDAH.

13. Ibid.

14. Mark Baron, "Eudora Welty at Premiere; 'Ponder Heart' Appears Hit," *Jackson State-Times,* Feb. 17, 1956.

15. Mrs. H. H. Creekmore to HC, Feb. 18, 1956.

16. Unidentified clipping in Welty subject files, MDAH.

17. HC, "Behind Scenes After 'The Ponder Heart,' " *Jackson State-Times,* Feb. 18, 1956.

18. EW to Anna Riddick, n.d. Papers of Lodwick Hartley, Southern Historical Collection, University of North Carolina, Chapel Hill.

19. EW to RPW, n.d.

20. Don Lee Keith, "Eudora Welty: 'I Worry Over My Stories,' " *New Orleans Times-Picayune.* Undated clipping in Welty Papers, MDAH.

21. Madora Hall Sharp, "This Week's Salute," *Jackson State-Times,* July 1, 1956, p. B8.

22. EW to HC, Mar. 21, 1956.

23. Unidentified clipping in Welty subject files, MDAH.

24. James Wooldridge to HC, May 16, 1956.

25. Una Merkel to EW, June 9, 1956.

26. EW to HC, June 21, 1956.

27. Mrs. H. H. Creekmore to HC, Oct. 18, 1956.

Chapter 52:
Dark Days Begin, 1956

1. Interview, Robert Drake, Sept. 21, 1994.
2. Mrs. H. H. Creekmore to HC, Oct. 27, 1957.
3. Mrs. H. H. Creekmore to HC, Jan. 17, 1958.
4. JR to Nancy Farley, Dec. 9 [1958]. University of Virginia.
5. Mrs. H. H. Creekmore to HC, Aug. 7, 1958.
6. James Wooldridge to HC, June 3, 1958.
7. Frank Hains, "On Stage," *Jackson Daily News,* July 21, 1958.

Chapter 53:
A Glimpse of the World, 1958–1959

1. Prenshaw, *Conversations,* p. 139.
2. Tom Kelly, "The Violent South 'Just Doesn't Interest Me'—Miss Welty's Picture in Coziness," *Washington Daily News,* Nov. 4, 1958.
3. Paul Sampson, "Author Welty Plans Story on Hill Folk," *Washington Post,* Nov. 4, 1958.

Chapter 54:
Walter Dies, 1959–1961

1. HC to WJS, Feb. 1, 1959.
2. JR to Nancy Farley, Jan. 29, [1959].
3. HC to WJS, Feb. 1, 1959.
4. Mrs. H. H. Creekmore to HC, Apr. 23, 1959, Apr. 30, 1959, May 8, 1959, June 18, 1959, and Aug. 8, 1959.
5. Kreyling, *Author and Agent,* p. 192.
6. Jimmy Wooldridge to HC, Oct. 5, 1959.
7. Gretlund, *Aesthetics,* p. 418.
8. HC to WJS, Dec. 20, 1959.
9. Kreyling, *Author and Agent,* p. 199.
10. Mrs. H. H. Creekmore to HC, May 16, 1960.
11. Mrs. H. H. Creekmore to HC, Sept. 3, 1960.
12. Mrs. H. H. Creekmore to HC, Feb. 2, 1961.
13. EW to WJS, Mar. 25, [1961].
14. Postcard, EW to WJS, date illegible.
15. Jimmy Wooldridge to HC, n.d., 1960.
16. William Maxwell to EW, Oct. 4, 1961.

Chapter 55:
Writing in Dark Days, 1962–1964

1. Sally Fitzgerald, ed., *The Habit of Being: Letters of Flannery O'Connor* (New York: Vintage Books, 1979), p. 471.

2. Interview, William Gifford, Feb. 5, 1995.

3. Willie Morris, "Miss Eudora," *Southern Living,* Oct. 1995, p. 106.

4. Prenshaw, *Conversations,* p. 107.

5. Adam Nossiter, *Of Long Memory: Mississippi and the Murder of Medgar Evers* (New York: Addison Wesley, 1994), p. 108.

6. Prenshaw, *Conversations,* p. 31.

7. Jerry Mitchell, Associated Press file from Jackson, Feb. 25, 1994.

8. Jeanne B. Hardendorff, "Junior Books," *Library Journal* 89 (December 1964), p. 5012.

Chapter 56:
The College Visitor, 1960–1980

1. Anne Tyler, "A Visit with Eudora Welty," *New York Times Book Review,* Nov. 2, 1980, p. 30.

2. EW to Dorothy E. Ryan, Apr. 24, 1964. Courtesy Miss Ryan.

3. Interview, William Gifford, Feb. 5, 1995.

4. Sue Smith, "Eudora Welty Has Own Special Idiom," *Vassar Chronicle,* May 12, 1956, p. 1.

5. Gifford interview.

6. Interview, A. Walton Litz, Apr. 21, 1994.

7. Interview, Joanna Maclay, Sept. 14, 1994.

8. Joseph Dumas, "An Afternoon with Miss Welty," *Mississippi* 12, no. 5 (May/June 1994).

9. Interview, Jo Woestendiek, Feb. 25, 1995.

10. Interview, Guy Davenport, Apr. 11, 1994.

11. Interview, Carole Klein, Mar. 19, 1994.

12. Interview, Jane Pepperdene, Apr. 9, 1994.

13. Davenport interview.

14. EW to Caroline Gordon, May 24, 1964.

15. Unidentified clipping, Converse College Archives, Spartanburg, South Carolina.

16. Fragment of clipping from *Charlotte Observer,* Apr. 11, 1982, p. 9F. Welty subject files, MDAH.

17. Tony Redd to AW, Apr. 4, 1995.

18. Interview, Carolyn Bell, Apr. 6, 1994.

Chapter 57:
Millsaps, 1964

1. Prenshaw, *Conversations,* p. 44.
2. Sara Ann Wier, "Eudora Welty Conducts Short Story Workshop; Offers Advice, Example for Aspiring Writers," *Purple and White,* Nov. 21, 1964, p. 4.
3. Powell, *Parting the Curtains,* p. 330.
4. "Miss Welty's Lecture Set for December 2," *Clarion-Ledger,* Nov. 29, 1964.
5. "Welty: On South and Criticism," *The Carolinian,* Mar. 25, 1966, n.p. Courtesy of Betty Carter, Archives, University of North Carolina, Greensboro.
6. Prenshaw, *Conversations,* p. 108.
7. Interview, George Garrett, Oct. 5, 1995.

Chapter 58:
The Last Short Story, 1964–1966

1. EW to RPW, Aug. 22, 1965.
2. Marrs, " 'The Treasure Most Dearly Regarded,' " p. 81.
3. Norma Craig, "Eudora Welty Gives 'A Part of Me' to Millsaps, Jackson," *Clarion-Ledger,* May 23, 1965.
4. Kreyling, *Author and Agent,* p. 203.

Chapter 59:
Death and Bereavement, 1966

1. HC to WJS, Jan. 25, 1966.
2. Powell, *Parting the Curtains,* p. 333.
3. HC to WJS, Jan. 25, 1966.
4. WJS to HC, Jan. 15, 1966.
5. Louise Westling, *Sacred Gardens and Ravaged Gardens: The Fiction of Eudora Welty, Carson McCullers, and Flannery O'Connor* (Athens: University of Georgia Press, 1985), p. 46.
6. HC to WJS, Jan. 25, 1966.
7. EW to Peter Taylor, Mar. 17, 1966.

Chapter 60:
Grief into Fiction, 1966

1. Francoise Sciaky, "Eye View," *Women's Wear Daily,* June 19, 1972.
2. Yates, *Mississippi Mind,* p. 155.

3. Eudora Welty always says her grandfather came from Virginia and attended Trinity (now Duke). But his obituary in the *Clay County Star,* Mar. 30, 1899 (vol. 3, no. 3), said he was born in Georgia and attended the University of Georgia. A cousin confirmed these facts. Researchers have not been able to find traces of him at Trinity or at the University of Virginia. In fact, Eudora Welty once asked William Hamilton, who taught at Duke, to check to verify her mother's story that Ned Andrews had been a founder of the Columbian Literary Society. The friend could not find his name. According to Eudora's cousin, it was Ned's father, C. C. Andrews, who went to Trinity. EW to WH, Mar. 12, 1952, WH to EW, Apr. 9, 1952.

4. Barbara Wilkie Tedord, "West Virginia Touches in Eudora Welty's Fiction," *Southern Literary Journal* 18, (Spring 1986), p. 48.

5. Clipping from *Clay County Star,* Mar. 30, 1899, vol. 3, no. 3, in Floyd Watkins Papers, Woodruff Library, Emory University. In *One Writer's Beginnings,* Eudora Welty says that a neighbor poled them across the Elk on a raft with a fire on it to keep her father warm. On the other side, they got to a railroad and flagged the train down.

6. Prenshaw, *Conversations,* p. 213.

7. Nostrandt, "Fiction as Event," p. 27.

8. Ibid.; Prenshaw, *Conversations,* p. 212.

9. Gretlund, *Aesthetics,* p. 413.

10. Prenshaw, *Conversations,* p. 212.

11. Yates, *Mississippi Mind,* p. 155.

12. Ibid.

13. Prenshaw, *Conversations,* p. 216.

14. Sally Wolff, " 'Among Those Missing': Phil Hand's Disappearance from *The Optimist's Daughter,*" *Southern Literary Journal* 25, no. 1 (Fall 1992), pp. 77, 82.

15. Sally Wolff, "Some Talk about Autobiography: An Interview with Eudora Welty," *Southern Review* 26, no. 1 (Jan. 1990), p. 85.

16. *Photographs,* p. xvi.

17. Interview, Carolyn Bell, Apr. 6, 1994.

Chapter 61:
Losing Battles, 1970

1. *Photographs,* p. xv.

2. Prenshaw, *Conversations,* p. 31.

3. Ibid., p. 48.

4. Nostrandt, "Fiction as Event," p. 29.

5. Prenshaw, *Conversations,* p. 205.

6. Ibid., p. 291.

7. Sancton, *The World,* p. 188.

8. Suzanne Marrs, "The Making of Losing Battles: Jack Renfro's Evolution," *Mississippi Quarterly* 37 (Fall 1984), p. 469; Prenshaw, *Conversations,* pp. 46, 181, and 309.

9. Prenshaw, *Conversations,* p. 46.

10. Interview, William Gifford, Feb. 5, 1995.

11. Prenshaw, *Conversations,* p. 50.

12. *Photographs,* p. xv.

13. Prenshaw, *Conversations,* p. 77.

14. Kreyling, *Author and Agent,* pp. 206–7.

15. James Boatwright, "I Call This a Reunion to Remember, All!" *New York Times Book Review,* Apr. 15, 1970, p. 1.

16. Reynolds Price, "Frightening Gift," *Washington Post,* n.d. Welty subject files, MDAH.

17. Howard Moss, "The Lonesomeness and Hilarity of Survival," *The New Yorker,* July 4, 1970, p. 76.

18. Richard Rhodes, "The Family Way," *Washington Post Book World,* n.d. Welty subject files, MDAH.

19. Selena Hastings, "Recent Fiction," *The Daily Telegraph,* July 1, 1982, p. 12.

20. Gretlund, *Aesthetics,* p. 280.

21. Charlotte Capers, "Eudora Welty: A Friend's View," *Eudora Welty: A Form of Thanks,* eds. Louis Dollarhide and Ann J. Abadie (Jackson: University Press of Mississippi, 1979), p. 131.

22. John Hohenberg, *The Pulitzer Prizes: A History of the Awards in Books, Drama, Music, and Journalism, Based on the Private Files Over Six Decades* (New York: Columbia University Press, 1974), p. 321.

Chapter 62:
Another Book, More Honors, 1971

1. Prenshaw, *Conversations,* p. 30.

2. Bill Kovach, "Eudora Welty Receives MacDowell Medal, N.H.," *Clarion-Ledger,* Aug. 30, 1970, p. 22.

3. William Thomas, "Eudora Welty," *The Commercial Appeal,* Oct. 25, 1970, "Mid-South Magazine," p. 1.

4. Dannye Romine, "Lady Fingers on the Pulse of the South," *Charlotte Observer,* Apr. 17, 1977.

5. Frank Hains, "On Stage," *Jackson Daily News,* Aug. 17, 1972.

6. Eudora Welty, "The Flavor of Jackson," *Jackson Cookbook* (Jackson: Symphony League of Jackson, 1971), n.p.

7. Paul Marx, "The Moment the Shutter Snaps," *Nation,* Jan. 17, 1972, p. 92.

8. Madison Jones, "One Time, One Place," *New York Times Book Review,* Nov. 21, 1971, p. 60.

9. Oral history interview with Michael Straight, Columbia University.

10. Ibid.

11. EW to Allen Tate, Jan. 21, 1973. Allen Tate Papers, Special Collections, Firestone Library, Princeton University.

12. EW to JS, June 7, 1974.

Chapter 63:

Glory, Laud, and Honor, 1972–1974

1. Interview, John Leeper, Oct. 2, 1995.

2. Jay Tolson, *Pilgrim in the Ruins: A Life of Walker Percy* (New York: Simon & Schuster, 1992), p. 375.

3. Prenshaw, *Conversations,* p. 99.

4. EW to Cleanth Brooks, Jan. 19, 1974. Cleanth Brooks Papers, Beinecke Library, Yale University.

5. Interview, Guy Davenport, Apr. 11, 1994.

6. Hohenberg, *Pulitzer Prizes,* p. 323.

7. Prenshaw, *Conversations,* p. 191.

8. EW to WJS, Mar. 14, 1973.

9. Nona Balakian "A Day of One's Own," *New York Times Book Review,* May 27, 1973, p. 23.

10. Yardley, "A Quiet Lady," *Miami Herald,* Feb. 17, 1974, p. 1L.

11. Tape of Welty lecture, MOMA, Nov. 14, 1973. MOMA, courtesy of Peter Bunnell.

Chapter 64:

The Robber Sings, 1974–1976

1. "How 'The Robber Bridegroom' Eloped from Long Island to Broadway," *New York Post,* Nov. 9, 1976, p. 20.

2. "Miss Welty," *Jackson Daily News,* Jan. 25, 1978, p. 1S.

3. Sylvane Gold, "Eudora Welty Says Staged 'Robber' in Right Hands," unidentified clipping in *Robber Bridegroom* file, New York Public Library for the Performing Arts, Lincoln Center, New York.

4. Ibid.

5. "It's Barry Bostwick, the Mystical Bridegroom," *New York Times,* Nov. 2, 1976. *Robber Bridegroom* file, New York Public Library for the Performing Arts, Lincoln Center, New York.

6. Untitled clipping, *New York Times,* Oct. 15, 1976. *Robber Bridegroom* file, New York Public Library for the Performing Arts, Lincoln Center, New York.

7. Walter Kerr, "The Mysterious Power of Props: Author's Friend, Actor's Enemy," unidentified clipping in Welty Papers, MDAH.

Chapter 65:
The Image, 1975–1977

1. Dannye Romine, "Lady Fingers On The Pulse Of The South," Charlotte Observer, Apr. 17, 1977.

2. Interview, Mary Aswell Doll, Nov. 30, 1995.

3. Interview, David Laskin, Apr. 17, 1996.

4. EW, "On stage," Clarion-Ledger-Jackson Daily News, July 27, 1975, p. H16.

5. EW to John Lehmann, July 30, 1977. John Lehmann Papers, Special Collections, Firestone Library, Princeton University.

Chapter 66:
Still Reading, 1977

1. EW to Jean Stafford, Feb. 10, 1976.

2. OWB, p. 11.

3. Prenshaw, Conversations, p. 143.

4. Ann Cresswell, "The Individual, Not the Trend, Is Important to Writer, Jackson Author of Delta Wedding Believes," Clarion-Ledger Magazine, Jan. 18, 1948, p. 4.

5. Prenshaw, Conversations, p. 209.

6. Eye, p. 285.

7. EW to RPW, Nov. 16, 1970.

8. John Leonard, "I Care Who Killed Roger Ackroyd," Esquire, August 1975, pp. 60, 61.

9. Eye, p. 3.

10. Prenshaw, Conversations, p. 195.

11. Emma Edmunds, "The Essential Eudora Welty," Atlanta Journal and Constitution, Nov. 23, 1978, p. H25.

12. Prenshaw, Conversations, p. 74.

13. Untitled clipping, New York Times Book Review, Dec. 5, 1982, p. 9.

Chapter 67:
Oxford, 1979

1. "Eudora Welty Named Oxford 'Artist in Residence,'" Memphis Press-Scimitar, Apr. 5, 1979. Welty subject files, MDAH.

2. Interview, Joseph Cushman, Feb. 15, 1995.

3. Interview, William P. Cocke, Feb. 16, 1995.

4. WH to EW, Jan. 9, 1956.

5. A. L. Rowse to AW, Mar. 18, 1995.

6. Interview, Katherine Merrill, Feb. 28, 1995.

7. Interview, John K. Blincow, Jr., Feb. 14, 1995.
8. John T. Oliver to AW, n.d., [1995].
9. Larry Williams to AW, Jan. 4, 1995.
10. Interview, William P. Cocke, Feb. 15, 1995.

Chapter 68:
"Mississippi Joins the World," 1980

1. Ruas, *Conversations with Writers,* p. 15.
2. "Heroes of Peace, Champions of Beauty, Eudora Welty's Garden of Triumphant Simplicities," *Washington Post,* June 10, 1980, pp. B1, B11.
3. Robert Coles to AW, Oct. 19, 1995.
4. Tyler, "A Visit," p. 32.
5. "The Nation's Critics Bow Before the Small-Town Tales of a Masterly Southern Writer," *People,* Jan. 5, 1980.
6. Lillian Mirando, "Lasting Tribute to Eudora Welty: Millsaps College Literary Chair," *Clarion-Ledger,* May 9, 1982, p. H1.

Chapter 69:
Uncle Daniel Sings, 1982

1. Bill Nichols, "Singing Praises of 'Ponder Heart,' " *Clarion-Ledger,* Mar. 23, 1982.
2. "Welty Story Now Opera," *New York Times,* Aug. 2, 1982, p. 15.
3. Julia Cass, "Southern Writer with Heart," *Philadelphia Inquirer,* Sept. 13, 1982, p. D1.
4. Ibid., p. D6.
5. Ibid., p. D1.
6. Leslie R. Myers, "Welty, New Stage Mesh Talents for Playwright Series," *Clarion-Ledger,* Apr. 11, 1984.

Chapter 70:
Harvard and Stanford, 1983

1. Prenshaw, *Conversations,* p. 24.
2. William Maxwell, "The Charged Imagination," *The New Yorker,* Feb. 20, 1984, p. 135.
3. Marc Dolan to AW, Dec. 15, 1994.
4. Andrew Hudgins to AW, Nov. 13, 1995.
5. John L'Heureux to AW, Nov. 21, 1995.
6. Andrew Hudgins to AW, Nov. 13, 1995.

7. Lisa Lynch, "Overflow Crowd Attends Reading by Author Welty," *Stanford Daily,* Nov. 15, 1983. Clipping courtesy of Stanford Archives.

8. John L'Heureux to AW, Nov. 21, 1995.

Chapter 71:
One Writer's Beginnings, 1984

1. Edwin McDowell, "The Beginnings of Best-seller Status," *New Orleans Times-Picayune,* Mar. 18, 1984.

2. Carolyn G. Heilbrun, *Writing a Woman's Life* (New York: Norton, 1988), pp. 13–15.

3. Graeme Tytler, "Eudora Welty," *Baton Rouge Advocate Magazine,* Oct. 28, 1990. Welty subject files, MDAH.

4. Susan Phillips, "Giving Pleasure Pleases Writer," *News and Daily Advance,* Apr. 17, 1986, p. D1.

5. "Mississippi Writer Honors Roots," *Knoxville News Sentinel,* Apr. 15, 1984. Welty subject file, MDAH.

6. Gregory Jaynes, "In Mississippi: A Diamond Jubilee," *Time,* May 7, 1984, p. 17.

7. Beverly Lowry, "Eudora, So Do We," *Vanity Fair,* July 1984.

8. Jaynes, "Diamond Jubilee," p. 13.

9. Fay S. Joyce, "Eudora Welty Honored On Her 75th Birthday," *New York Times,* Apr. 16, 1984, p. 21.

10. EW to RPW, May 3, 1984.

Chapter 72:
The Last Chapter

1. "Jackson Communiqué," *The New Yorker,* Feb. 18, 1985.

2. "Grant Funds Statewide Study of Welty Works," *Hattiesburg American,* Apr. 28, 1985. Welty subject files, MDAH.

3. "Eudora Welty Overseeing Publication of Her Popular Photos," unidentified clipping of Associated Press story. Welty subject files, MDAH.

4. Clipping in Welty subject files, MDAH.

5. Jerry Kinser, "Time of Essence to Eudora Welty," *Biloxi Sun-Herald,* Oct. 9, 1988. Welty subject files, MDAH.

6. Powell, *Parting the Curtains,* p. 33.

7. Tytler, "Eudora Welty."

8. Elizabeth Bennett, "At Home with Eudora Welty," *Houston Post,* Dec. 1, 1991, p. E1.

9. David Streitfeld, "Eudora Welty in Her Own Words," *Washington Post,* Dec. 4, 1992, p. D1.

10. Charles Ealy, "First Lady of Literature," *Dallas Morning News,* Oct. 11, 1992, p. C1.

11. Robert Wilson, "The Journey to a Writer's Golden Hour," *USA Today,* Nov. 21, 1991, p. D1.

12. Ealy, "First Lady," p. C1.

13. Michiko Kakutani, "South Is Wherever Eudora Welty Is," *New York Times,* June 27, 1980. Library of Congress files, Library of Congress.

Photo Credits

Welty birthplace photo, cartoon from *Oh, Lady,* Eudora at WJDX, and Eudora in 1971, from the Mississippi Department of Archives and History.

Pinehurst Street house, courtesy of the Jackson *Clarion-Ledger.*

Eudora's yearbook picture and photograph of cast of *Icebound,* courtesy of Wesley Ellis.

John Robinson's yearbook picture, courtesy of Robert Jordan, University of Mississippi Imaging Services.

Bread Loaf Fellows photo, courtesy of Bread Loaf Writers' Conference, Middlebury, Vermont.

Eudora with camera, inscribed photo of Eudora, photo of Katherine Anne Porter, and picture of Eudora and William Jay Smith, courtesy of McKeldin Library, University of Maryland.

Photo of Elizabeth Bowen, courtesy of Humanities Research Center, University of Texas.

Eudora with *Ponder Heart* cast, consultants to Library of Congress, and Eudora in 1962, from Library of Congress.

Allen Tate and Eudora Welty, courtesy of University of the South archives.

Eudora at statewide celebration, courtesy of Mary Aswell Doll.

Eudora at Morgan Library, photo by David A. Loggie, courtesy of Pierpont Morgan Library.

Index

Ann Waldron is the author of two critically acclaimed southern biographies, *Close Connections: Caroline Gordon and the Southern Renaissance* and *Hodding Carter: The Reconstruction of a Racist*. She has been a reporter and columnist for the *Miami Herald* and the *St. Petersburg Times*. An editor and writer at Princeton University, she is also the author of seven books for children.

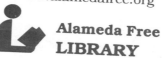